Willa Cather

O Pioneers!

The Song of the Lark

Alexander's Bridge

and Selected Stories

BARNES
&NOBLE
BOOKS
NEW YORK

This edition published by Barnes & Noble, Inc.

1993 Barnes & Noble Books

ISBN 1-56619-108-4

Book design by Stephen Morse

Printed and bound in the United States of America

M 9 8 7 6 5 4 3 2

Contents

Introduction

*W*illa Cather's life coincided with a huge sociological and spiritual change in American society—a shift from predominantly rural to urban, agricultural to industrial, traditional to modern—and by focusing on the earlier way of life, she brilliantly chronicled what America was, and what it would become. Her wonderful evocations of life on the prairies and the closing of the frontier have made her one of the most highly praised and enduring of American writers.

Though she is most often associated with the midwestern prairies, Willa Cather was actually born on Dec 7, 1873, in the backwoods town of Gore, in Virginia's Shenandoah valley, where her family had lived since colonial times. Her grandfather, William Cather, did not believe in slavery and favored the Union in the Civil War, creating a rift in a family of Confederate sympathizers. Her maternal grandfather, William Boak, was an ardent secessionist, and had served three terms in the Virginia House of Delegates. Her only work of fiction to deal with this society and the issues it faced was her last novel, *Sapphira and the Slave Girl*.

Figuring prominently in both that novel and the family life was Cather's maternal grandmother, Rachel Seibert Boak, one of the most important figures in Cather's life and fiction. Strong-willed, courageous, and enduring, she represented the rugged pioneer individualism so crucial to her granddaughter's art. She lived with the family from the time her husband died until her own death, and taught Willa to read and write.

In 1883, when Cather—nicknamed Willie by her family—was nine years old, her father sold their Virginia holdings and moved the family to Webster County, Nebraska. She later remembered vividly the trauma of leaving a wooded valley for the flat, empty land that seemed "as bare as a piece of sheet iron." The most significant event of her young life, the move was certainly a shock to the girl, but it was also the beginning of a fierce love for both the new land and its people.

Her father, Charles, tried farming for about eighteen months, but soon gave that up and moved the family to the small town of Red Cloud, where he went into the insurance business.

Red Cloud was a local market town of about 2,500 people. While it had the raw harshness and often the violence of frontier life, there was, in fact, a good deal of intellectual stimulation available to Willa, due to the large number of European immigrants who settled there. Many of Cather's neighbors had impressive libraries, gave music lessons, put on amateur theatricals, and attended performances of road companies that played in Red Cloud's opera house.

Cather always had a special affection for her father, an easygoing, gentle, quiet man who had no great success in business but still managed to provide adequately for his growing family. Her mother, Mary, was unlike her husband: energetic and driving, a hard disciplinarian, but generous and with a love of life inherited from her own extraordinary mother. A good many scenes and people from her years on the farm and in Red Cloud appear in Cather's fiction. *The Song of the Lark,* though its central character is a musician, recounts some of Cather's own struggles to develop her talent amid the strictures of small town life.

Willa entered the University of Nebraska, at Lincoln, in the fall of 1891, initially determined to study medicine. But when a Lincoln newspaper published a freshman paper she wrote she became immediately hooked on writing. While at the university she was active in literary circles, serving as editor of two student magazines. By her junior year she was supporting herself as a journalist, beginning as a reviewer and columnist for the *Nebraska State Journal*. Around the time of her graduation she began writing stories, and her first works were published in the *Overland Monthly,* a national magazine. In 1896, a year after she graduated, she left to take a position with the *Home Monthly,* a small magazine in Pittsburgh. She would never live in Nebraska again.

She stayed in Pittsburgh for ten years, first with *Home Monthly,* then with the *Pittsburgh Daily Leader* as editor and writer. She quit journalism and for five years taught high school Latin and English, using the summers to write short fiction.

A young woman on her own, Cather pursued an active social life in Pittsburgh. It was at this time that she met Isabelle McClung, who was to become her dearest friend, as well as her alleged lover, for over fifteen years. Isabelle was the daughter of a prominent judge, who had gained a notoriety for having tried the case of Alexander Berkman, the anarchist who tried to assassinate steel tycoon Henry Clay Frick. Willa moved in with the McClung family in 1899 and shared a bedroom with Isabelle.

Early biographies of Willa Cather do of course speak of her great friendship with Isabelle McClung, but not of their love. Only relatively recent works have examined Cather's lesbian relationships; it has become almost fashionable to do so. The fact itself, however, is worth little more than a mention in any look at her life, primarily because Cather herself did not consider it particularly important to her. Such things were not spoken of in her time; she herself never talked or wrote of her sexuality; and it is not reflected in her work. It is only important to know that Isabelle was a great influence in Willa's life—*The Song of the Lark* is dedicated to her—and that they had a long, intimate, and emotional relationship that lasted until Isabelle's marriage in 1916. This was a painful event in Cather's life, though the women remained close friends until her death.

In 1905 her first story collection, *The Troll Garden,* was published to critical acclaim. These stories hold up wonderfully today, particularly in their examination of the creation of art, and the artist's role in American society. The three stories reprinted here from *The Troll Garden* all deal perceptively with the subject: *Flavia and her Artists* is about a woman who collects artists; *The Garden Lodge* about a woman who gave up a concert career for marriage; and *The Marriage of Phaedra* about a British painter.

The year after *The Troll Garden* was published, S. S. McClure hired Cather to write for and help edit his magazine, *McClure's.* She settled in New York, and lived there for the rest of her life, except for trips back to Nebraska to visit, and to the southwest and Europe. *McClure's* was one of the leading muckraking magazines of its day, and though Cather was more interested in its literary aspects, she became managing editor in 1909. In this capacity she published the fiction of Theodore Dreiser, O. Henry, and Jack London, among other notable writers. She became one of the most successful editors of her time, when journalism was almost wholly dominated by men.

Despite this success, the six years at *McClure's* were frustrating for Cather who, with the encouraging notices on *The Troll Garden,* was determined to write fiction full time. In 1912, after finishing her first novel, *Alexander's Bridge,* she finally made her break.

After fifteen years in the east, Cather began looking back at her childhood on the prairie, at a way of life that had suddenly disappeared with the coming of the twentieth century. She found that she had distanced herself enough from Nebraska at this time to turn her memories into art. It is this long perspective on her experience that gives Cather's best work about Nebraska a rich aura of nostalgia and converts it into drama. And in doing so, she created a major and enduring work of American art.

For *O Pioneers!* is nothing if not a quintessentially American story, from its rugged setting to its nostalgia for the past and its fiercely independent characters. At the center is Alexandra Bergson, the oldest child of a Swedish immigrant who dies in the struggle to tame a wild land. Alexandra holds the family together with her industry and vision, and pushes her brothers to make something of themselves. They turn mean-spirited, but Alexandra endures, the novel ending with a note of hope: "Fortunate country, that is one day to receive hearts like Alexandra's into its bosom, to give them out again in the yellow wheat, in the rustling corn, in the shining eyes of youth." Cather had witnessed the closing of the frontier, the transformation of America from a rural to an urban society, and in this novel turned skillfully to the past to show how much had changed in a single generation. Unabashedly nostalgic, *O Pioneers!* nonetheless succeeds brilliantly as a poignant work of Americana.

Her next novel, *The Song of the Lark* (1915), is also considered one of her best. The story of Thea Kronborg, a Swedish girl from Colorado who becomes a great soprano, initially grew out of a series of articles Cather had written for *McClure's* about opera singers. Yet the novel is also greatly autobiographical, a portrait of the artist—Cather herself—as a young woman. The early parts of the story are fashioned after Cather's childhood in Red Cloud; the youthful artistic aspirations of Thea are Cather's own, and a midsection that takes place in Arizona derives from Cather's first visit to the southwest. And just as Cather broke loose from journalism after years of frustration, Thea in the novel goes west after years of study in Chicago, and for the first time is able to reflect on her life.

Again, one of the main themes she confronts here is the artist's place in society, particularly women artists. But Cather herself wrote within a male tradition, largely because she felt an alienation from the conventional femininity of the day, perhaps best shown in the work of Louisa May Alcott. Her opinion of other women writers past and present was never particularly high: "I have not much faith in women in fiction . . . They are so few, the ones who really did anything worthwhile; there were the great Georges, George Eliot and George Sand, and they were anything but women, and there was Miss Brontë who kept her sentimentality under control, and there was Jane Austen who certainly had more common sense that any of them and was in some respects the greatest of them all. Women are so horribly subjective and they have such scorn for the healthy commonplace. When a woman writes a story of adventure, a stout sea tale, a manly battle yarn, anything without wine, women, and love, then I will begin to hope for something great from them, not before."

My Antonia (1918) followed, completing an informal trilogy about women on the frontier. Antonia Shimerda is for many readers the quintessential Cather character, an embodiment of the strength and endurance associated with those who are at one with the land and nature. Narrated by Jim Burden, an unhappy eastern lawyer who grew up with Antonia, he presents her as the embodiment of the values of the west.

At this point Cather began to turn away from Nebraska as a setting for her fiction. *One of Ours* (1922) was set in World War I, based on the life of her cousin who was killed in France. One of her weaker novels, it nonetheless won the Pulitzer Prize. Her work at this time tended more toward historical novels, set in Civil War Virginia, seventeenth-century Quebec, and the southwest.

Death Comes to the Archbishop (1927) was her last great novel. It is the fictionalized life of Archbishop Lamy, the first bishop appointed to the territory of

New Mexico after its annexation to the United States. Set in the mid-nineteenth century, it is episodic in form, detailing the lives of the bishop and his vicar as they attempt to centralize the church and the religious life of the area. Perhaps most important, Cather's descriptions of the relationship of the people and the land makes this one of the most important portraits of the American southwest.

Cather continued to write all her life, but physical infirmities plagued her in her final years. Her last novel, *Sapphira and the Slave Girl,* was published the week the Japanese bombed Pearl Harbor. When she died in New York, on April 24, 1947, she was working on a novel set in medieval France. According to her wishes, the unfinished manuscript was burned.

Cather was quite popular with both critics and readers in her day, particularly the 1920s. But in her later years and for decades after her death she fell out of favor. Those raised with modernism and post-modernism found her sentimental and anachronistic. It might be said that her resurrection in recent times is coincidental with the rise of both feminism and environmentalism; her fierce individualism, self-reliance, uncompromising artistic vision, and understanding of the forces of nature and how they affect people have made her a wonderful role model for young American artists, male and female. But beyond that, she is now recognized as one of the purest prose stylists in American literature, as well as the chronicler of a time that lives only now in our mythology.

Steven J. Kasdin
1993

O Pioneers!

To the memory of

Sarah Orne Jewett

in whose beautiful and delicate work
there is the perfection
that endures

Contents

Prairie Spring

Evening and the flat land,
Rich and sombre and always silent;
The miles of fresh-plowed soil,
Heavy and black, full of strength and harshness;
The growing wheat, the growing weeds,
The toiling horses, the tired men;
The long empty roads,
Sullen fires of sunset, fading,
The eternal, unresponsive sky.
Against all this, Youth,
Flaming like the wild roses,
Singing like the larks over the plowed fields,
Flashing like a star out of the twilight;
Youth with its insupportable sweetness,
Its fierce necessity,
Its sharp desire,
Singing and singing,
Out of the lips of silence,
Out of the earthy dusk.

Part I

The Wild Land

I

One January day, thirty years ago, the little town of Hanover, anchored on a windy Nebraska tableland, was trying not to be blown away. A mist of fine snowflakes was curling and eddying about the cluster of low drab buildings huddled on the gray prairie, under a gray sky. The dwelling-houses were set about haphazard on the tough prairie sod; some of them looked as if they had been moved in overnight, and others as if they were straying off by themselves, headed straight for the open plain. None of them had any appearance of permanence, and the howling wind blew under them as well as over them. The main street was a deeply rutted road, now frozen hard, which ran from the squat red railway station and the grain "elevator" at the north end of the town to the lumber yard and the horse pond at the south end. On either side of this road straggled two uneven rows of wooden buildings; the general merchandise stores, the two banks, the drug store, the feed store, the saloon, the post-office. The board sidewalks were gray with trampled snow, but at two o'clock in the afternoon the shopkeepers, having come back from dinner, were keeping well behind their frosty windows. The children were all in school, and there was nobody abroad in the streets but a few rough-looking countrymen in coarse overcoats, with their long caps pulled down to their noses. Some of them had brought their wives to town, and now and then a red or a plaid shawl flashed out of one store into the shelter of another. At the hitch-bars along the street a few heavy work-horses, harnessed to farm wagons, shivered under their blankets. About the station everything was quiet, for there would not be another train in until night.

On the sidewalk in front of one of the stores sat a little Swede boy, crying bitterly. He was about five years old. His black cloth coat was much too big for him and made him look like a little old man. His shrunken brown flannel dress had been washed many times and left a long stretch of stocking between the hem of his skirt and the tops of his clumsy, copper-toed shoes. His cap was pulled down over his ears; his nose and his chubby cheeks were chapped and red with cold. He cried quietly, and the few people who hurried by did not notice him. He was afraid to stop any one, afraid to go into the store and ask for help, so he sat wringing his long sleeves and looking up a telegraph pole beside him, whimpering, "My kitten, oh, my kitten! Her will fweeze!" At the top of the pole crouched a shivering gray kitten, mewing faintly and clinging desperately to the wood with her claws. The boy had been left at the store while his sister went to the doctor's office, and in her absence a dog had chased his kitten up the pole. The little creature had never been so high before, and she was too frightened to move. Her master was sunk in despair. He was a little country boy, and this village was to him a very strange and perplexing place, where people wore fine clothes and had hard hearts. He always felt shy and awkward here, and wanted to hide behind things for fear some one might laugh at him. Just now, he was too unhappy to care who laughed. At last he seemed to see a ray of hope: his sister was coming, and he got up and ran toward her in his heavy shoes.

His sister was a tall, strong girl, and she walked rapidly and resolutely, as if she knew exactly where she was going and what she was going to do next. She wore a man's long ulster (not as if it were an affliction, but as if it were very comfortable and belonged to her; carried it like a young soldier), and a round plush cap, tied down with a thick veil. She had a serious, thoughtful face, and her clear, deep blue eyes were fixed intently on the distance, without seeming to see anything, as if she were in trouble. She did not notice the little boy until he pulled her by the coat. Then she stopped short and stooped down to wipe his wet face.

"Why, Emil! I told you to stay in the store and not to come out. What is the matter with you?"

"My kitten, sister, my kitten! A man put her out, and a dog chased her up there." His forefinger, projecting from the sleeve of his coat, pointed up to the wretched little creature on the pole.

"Oh, Emil! Didn't I tell you she'd get us into trouble of some kind, if you brought her? What made you tease me so? But there, I ought to have known better myself." She went to the foot of the pole and held out her arms, crying, "Kitty, kitty, kitty," but the kitten only mewed and faintly waved its tail. Alexandra turned away decidedly. "No, she won't come down. Somebody will have to go up after her. I saw the Linstrums' wagon in town. I'll go and see if I can find Carl. Maybe he can do something. Only you must stop crying, or I won't go a step. Where's your comforter? Did you leave it in the store? Never mind. Hold still, till I put this on you."

She unwound the brown veil from her head and tied it about his throat. A shabby little traveling man, who was just then coming out of the store on his way to the saloon, stopped and gazed stupidly at the shining mass of hair she bared when she took off her veil; two thick braids, pinned about her head in the German way, with a fringe of reddish-yellow curls blowing out from under her cap. He took his cigar out of his mouth and held the wet end between the fingers of his woolen glove. "My God, girl, what a head of hair!" he exclaimed, quite innocently and foolishly. She stabbed him with a glance of Amazonian fierceness and drew in her lower lip—most unnecessary severity. It gave the little clothing drummer such a start that he actually let his cigar fall to the sidewalk and went off weakly in the teeth of the wind to the saloon. His hand was still unsteady when he took his glass from the bartender. His feeble flirtatious instincts had been crushed before, but never so mercilessly. He felt cheap and ill-used, as if some one had taken advantage of him. When a drummer had been knocking about in little drab towns and crawling across the wintry country in dirty smoking-cars, was he to be blamed if, when he chanced upon a fine human creature, he suddenly wished himself more of a man?

While the little drummer was drinking to recover his nerve, Alexandra hurried to the drug store as the most likely place to find Carl Linstrum. There he was, turning over a portfolio of chromo "studies" which the druggist sold to the Hanover women who did china-painting. Alexandra explained her predicament, and the boy followed her to the corner, where Emil still sat by the pole.

"I'll have to go up after her, Alexandra. I think at the depot they have some spikes I can strap on my feet. Wait a minute." Carl thrust his hands into his pockets, lowered his head, and darted up the street against the north wind. He was a tall boy of fifteen, slight and narrow-chested. When he came back with the spikes, Alexandra asked him what he had done with his overcoat.

"I left it in the drug store. I couldn't climb in it, anyhow. Catch me if I fall, Emil," he called back as he began his ascent. Alexandra watched him anxiously; the cold was bitter enough on the ground. The kitten would not budge an inch. Carl had to go to the very top of the pole, and then had some difficulty in tearing her from her hold. When he reached the ground, he handed the cat to her tearful little master. "Now go into the store with her, Emil, and get warm." He opened the door for the child. "Wait a minute, Alexandra. Why can't I drive for you as far as our place? It's getting colder every minute. Have you seen the doctor?"

"Yes. He is coming over to-morrow. But he says father can't get better; can't get well." The girl's lip trembled. She looked fixedly up the bleak street as if she were gathering her strength to face something, as if she were trying with all her might to grasp a situation which, no matter how painful, must be met and dealt with somehow. The wind flapped the skirts of her heavy coat about her.

Carl did not say anything, but she felt his sympathy. He, too, was lonely. He was a thin, frail boy, with brooding dark eyes, very quiet in all his movements. There was a delicate pallor in his thin face, and his mouth was too sensitive for a boy's. The lips had already a little curl of bitterness and skepticism. The two friends stood for a few moments on the windy street corner, not speaking a word, as two travelers, who have lost their way, sometimes stand and admit their perplexity in silence. When Carl turned away he said, "I'll see to your team." Alexandra went into the store to have her purchases packed in the egg-boxes, and to get warm before she set out on her long cold drive.

When she looked for Emil, she found him sitting on a step of the staircase that led up to the clothing and carpet department. He was playing with a little Bohemian girl, Marie Tovesky, who was tying her handkerchief over the kitten's head for a bonnet. Marie was a stranger in the country, having come from Omaha with her mother to visit her uncle, Joe Tovesky. She was a dark child, with brown curly hair, like a brunette doll's, a coaxing little red mouth, and round, yellow-brown eyes. Every one noticed her eyes; the brown iris had golden glints that made them look like gold-stone, or, in softer lights, like that Colorado mineral called tiger-eye.

The country children thereabouts wore their dresses to their shoe-tops, but this city child was dressed in what was then called the "Kate Greenaway" manner, and her red cashmere frock, gathered full from the yoke, came almost to the floor. This, with her poke bonnet, gave her the look of a quaint little woman. She had a white fur tippet about her neck and made no fussy objections when Emil fingered it admiringly. Alexandra had not the heart to take him away from so pretty a playfellow, and she let them tease the kitten together until Joe Tovesky came in noisily and picked up his little niece, setting her on his shoulder for every one to see. His children were all boys, and he adored this little creature. His cronies formed a circle about him, admiring and teasing the little girl, who took their jokes with great good nature. They were all delighted with her, for they seldom saw so pretty and carefully nurtured a child. They told her that she must choose one of them for a sweetheart, and each began pressing his suit and offering her bribes: candy, and little pigs, and spotted calves. She looked archly into the big, brown, mustached faces, smelling of spirits and tobacco, then she ran her tiny forefinger delicately over Joe's bristly chin and said, "Here is my sweetheart."

The Bohemians roared with laughter, and Marie's uncle hugged her until she cried, "Please don't, Uncle Joe! You hurt me." Each of Joe's friends gave her a bag of candy, and she kissed them all around, though she did not like country candy very well. Perhaps that was why she bethought herself of Emil. "Let me down, Uncle Joe," she said, "I want to give some of my candy to that nice little boy I found." She walked graciously over to Emil, followed by her lusty admirers, who formed a new circle and teased the little boy until he hid his face in his sister's skirts, and she had to scold him for being such a baby.

The farm people were making preparations to start for home. The women were checking over their groceries and pinning their big red shawls about their heads. The men were buying tobacco and candy with what money they had left, were showing each other new boots and gloves and blue flannel shirts. Three big Bohemians were drinking raw alcohol, tinctured with oil of cinnamon. This was said to fortify one effectually against the cold, and they smacked their lips after each pull at the flask. Their volubility drowned every other noise in the place, and the overheated store sounded of their spirited language as it reeked of pipe smoke, damp woolens, and kerosene.

Carl came in, wearing his overcoat and carrying a wooden box with a brass handle. "Come," he said, "I've fed and watered your team and the wagon is ready." He carried Emil out and tucked him down in the straw in the wagon-box. The heat had made the little boy sleepy, but he still clung to his kitten.

"You were awful good to climb so high and get my kitten, Carl. When I get big I'll climb and get little boys' kittens for them," he murmured drowsily. Before the horses were over the first hill, Emil and his cat were both fast asleep.

Although it was only four o'clock, the winter day was fading. The road led southwest, toward the streak of pale, watery light that glimmered in the leaden sky. The light fell upon the two sad young faces that were turned mutely toward it: upon the eyes of the girl, who seemed to be looking with such anguished perplexity into the future; upon the sombre eyes of the boy, who seemed already to be looking into the past. The little town behind them had vanished as if it had never been, had fallen behind the swell of the prairie, and the stern frozen country received them into its bosom. The homesteads were few and far apart; here and there a windmill gaunt against the sky, a sod house crouching in a hollow. But the great fact was the land itself, which seemed to overwhelm the little beginnings of human society that struggled in its sombre wastes. It was from facing this vast hardness that the boy's mouth had become so bitter; because he felt that men were too weak to make any mark here, that the land wanted to be let alone, to preserve its own fierce strength, its peculiar, savage kind of beauty, its uninterrupted mournfulness.

The wagon jolted along over the frozen road. The two friends had less to say to each other than usual, as if the cold had somehow penetrated to their hearts.

"Did Lou and Oscar go to the Blue to cut wood to-day?" Carl asked.

"Yes. I'm almost sorry I let them go, it's turned so cold. But mother frets if the wood gets low." She stopped and put her hand to her forehead, brushing back her hair. "I don't know what is to become of us, Carl, if father has to die. I don't dare to think about it. I wish we could all go with him and let the grass grow back over everything."

Carl made no reply. Just ahead of them was the Norwegian graveyard, where the grass had, indeed, grown back over everything, shaggy and red, hiding even the wire fence. Carl realized that he was not a very helpful companion, but there was nothing he could say.

"Of course," Alexandra went on, steadying her voice a little, "the boys are strong and work hard, but we've always depended so on father that I don't see how we can go ahead. I almost feel as if there were nothing to go ahead for."

"Does your father know?"

"Yes, I think he does. He lies and counts on his fingers all day. I think he is trying to count up what he is leaving for us. It's a comfort to him that my chickens are laying right on through the cold weather and bringing in a little money. I wish we could keep his mind off such things, but I don't have much time to be with him now."

"I wonder if he'd like to have me bring my magic lantern over some evening?"

Alexandra turned her face toward him. "Oh, Carl! Have you got it?"

"Yes. It's back there in the straw. Didn't you notice the box I was carrying? I tried it all morning in the drug-store cellar, and it worked ever so well, makes fine big pictures."

"What are they about?"

"Oh, hunting pictures in Germany, and Robinson Crusoe and funny pictures about cannibals. I'm going to paint some slides for it on glass, out of the Hans Andersen book."

Alexandra seemed actually cheered. There is often a good deal of the child left in people who have had to grow up too soon. "Do bring it over, Carl. I can hardly wait to see it, and I'm sure it will please father. Are the pictures colored? Then I know he'll like them. He likes the calendars I get him in town. I wish I could get more. You must leave me here, mustn't you? It's been nice to have company."

Carl stopped the horses and looked dubiously up at the black sky. "It's pretty dark. Of course the horses will take you home, but I think I'd better light your lantern, in case you should need it."

He gave her the reins and climbed back into the wagon-box, where he crouched down and made a tent of his overcoat. After a dozen trials he succeeded in lighting the lantern, which he placed in front of Alexandra, half covering it with a blanket so that the light would not shine in her eyes. "Now, wait until I find my box. Yes, here it is. Good-night, Alexandra. Try not to worry." Carl sprang to the ground and ran off across the fields toward the Linstrum homestead. "Hoo, hoo-o-o-o!" he called back as he disappeared over a ridge and dropped into a sand gully. The wind answered him like an echo, "Hoo, hoo-o-o-o-o-o!" Alexandra drove off alone. The rattle of her wagon was lost in the howling of the wind, but her lantern, held firmly between her feet, made a moving point of light along the highway, going deeper and deeper into the dark country.

II

On one of the ridges of that wintry waste stood the low log house in which John Bergson was dying. The Bergson homestead was easier to find than many another, because it overlooked Norway Creek, a shallow, muddy stream that sometimes flowed, and sometimes stood still, at the bottom of a winding ravine with steep, shelving sides overgrown with brush and cottonwoods and dwarf ash. This creek gave a sort of identity to the farms that bordered upon it. Of all the bewildering things about a new country, the absence of human landmarks is one of the most depressing and disheartening. The houses on the Divide were small and were usually tucked away in low places; you did not see them until you came directly upon them. Most of them were built of the sod itself, and were only the unescapable ground in another form. The roads were but faint tracks in the grass, and the fields were scarcely noticeable. The record of the plow was insignificant, like the feeble scratches on stone left by prehistoric races, so indeterminate that they may, after all, be only the markings of glaciers, and not a record of human strivings.

In eleven long years John Bergson had made but little impression upon the wild land he had come to tame. It was still a wild thing that had its ugly moods; and no one knew when they were likely to come, or why. Mischance hung over it. Its Genius was unfriendly to man. The sick man was feeling this as he lay looking out of the window, after the doctor had left him, on the day following Alexandra's trip to town. There it lay outside his door, the same land, the same lead-colored miles. He knew every ridge and draw and gully between him and the horizon. To the south, his plowed fields; to the east, the sod stables, the cattle corral, the pond,—and then the grass.

Bergson went over in his mind the things that had held him back. One winter his cattle had perished in a blizzard. The next summer one of his plow horses broke its leg in a prairie-dog hole and had to be shot. Another summer he lost his hogs from cholera, and a valuable stallion died from a rattlesnake bite. Time and again his crops had failed. He had lost two children, boys, that came between Lou and Emil, and there had been the cost of sickness and death. Now, when he had at last struggled out of debt, he was going to die himself. He was only forty-six, and had, of course, counted upon more time.

Bergson had spent his first five years on the Divide getting into debt, and the last six getting out. He had paid off his mortgages and had ended pretty much where he began, with the land. He owned exactly six hundred and forty acres of what stretched outside his door; his own original homestead and timber claim, making three hundred and twenty acres, and the half-section adjoining, the homestead of a younger brother who had given up the fight, gone back to Chicago to work in a fancy bakery and distinguish himself in a Swedish athletic club. So far John had not attempted to cultivate the second half-section, but used it for pasture land, and one of his sons rode herd there in open weather.

John Bergson had the Old-World belief that land, in itself, is desirable. But this land was an enigma. It was like a horse that no one knows how to break to harness, that runs wild and kicks things to pieces. He had an idea that no one understood how to farm it properly, and this he often discussed with Alexandra. Their neighbors, certainly, knew even less about farming than he did. Many of them had never worked on a farm until they took up their hor esteads. They had been *handwerkers* at home; tailors, locksmiths, joiners, cigar-makers, etc. Bergson himself had worked in a shipyard.

For weeks, John Bergson had been thinking about these things. His bed stood in the sitting-room, next to the kitchen. Through the day, while the baking and washing and ironing were going on, the father lay and looked up at the roof beams that he himself had hewn, or out at the cattle in the corral. He counted the cattle over and over. It diverted him to speculate as to how much weight each of the steers would probably put on by spring. He often called his daughter in to talk to her about this. Before Alexandra was twelve years old she had begun to be a help to him, and as she grew older he had come to depend more and more upon her resourcefulness and good judgment. His boys were willing enough to work, but when he talked with them they usually irritated him. It was Alexandra who read the papers and followed the markets, and who learned by the mistakes of their neighbors. It was Alexandra who could always tell about what it had cost to fatten each steer, and who could guess the weight of a hog before it went on the scales closer than John Bergson himself. Lou and Oscar were industrious, but he could never teach them to use their heads about their work.

Alexandra, her father often said to himself, was like her grandfather; which was his way of saying that she was intelligent. John Bergson's father had been a shipbuilder, a man of considerable force and of some fortune. Late in life he married a second time, a Stockholm woman of questionable character, much younger than he, who goaded him into every sort of extravagance. On the shipbuilder's part, this marriage was an infatuation, the despairing folly of a powerful man who cannot bear to grow old. In a few years his unprincipled wife warped the probity of a lifetime. He speculated, lost his own fortune and funds entrusted to him by poor seafaring men, and died disgraced, leaving his children nothing. But when all was said, he had come up from the sea himself, had built up a proud little business with no capital but his own skill and foresight, and had proved himself a man. In his daughter, John Bergson recognized the strength of will, and the simple direct way of thinking things out, that had characterized his father in his better days. He would much rather, of course, have seen this likeness in one of his sons, but it was not a question of choice. As he lay there day after day he had to accept the situation as it was, and to be thankful that there was one among his children to whom he could entrust the future of his family and the possibilities of his hard-won land.

The winter twilight was fading. The sick man heard his wife strike a match in the kitchen, and the light of a lamp glimmered through the cracks of the door. It seemed like a light shining far away. He turned painfully in his bed and looked at his white hands, with all the work gone out of them. He was ready to give up, he felt. He did not know how it had come about, but he was quite willing to go deep under his fields and rest, where the plow could not find him. He was tired of making mistakes. He was content to leave the tangle to other hands; he thought of his Alexandra's strong ones.

"Dotter," he called feebly, *"dotter!"* He heard her quick step and saw her tall figure appear in the doorway, with the light of the lamp behind her. He felt her youth and strength, how easily she moved and stooped and lifted. But he would not have had it again if he could, not he! He knew the end too well to wish to begin again. He knew where it all went to, what it all became.

His daughter came and lifted him up on his pillows. She called him by an old Swedish name that she used to call him when she was little and took his dinner to him in the shipyard.

"Tell the boys to come here, daughter. I want to speak to them."

"They are feeding the horses, father. They have just come back from the Blue. Shall I call them?"

He sighed. "No, no. Wait until they come in. Alexandra, you will have to do the best you can for your brothers. Everything will come on you."

"I will do all I can, father."

"Don't let them get discouraged and go off like Uncle Otto. I want them to keep the land."

"We will, father. We will never lose the land."

There was a sound of heavy feet in the kitchen. Alexandra went to the door and beckoned to her brothers, two strapping boys of seventeen and nineteen. They came in and stood at the foot of the bed. Their father looked at them searchingly, though it was too dark to see their faces; they were just the same boys, he told himself, he had not been mistaken in them. The square head and heavy shoulders belonged to Oscar, the elder. The younger boy was quicker, but vacillating.

"Boys," said the father wearily, "I want you to keep the land together and to be guided by your sister. I have talked to her since I have been sick, and she knows all my wishes. I want no quarrels among my children, and so long as there is one house there must be one head. Alexandra is the ol lest, and she knows my wishes. She will do the best she can. If she makes mistakes, she will not make so many as I have made. When you marry, and want a house of your own, the land will be divided fairly, according to the courts. But for the next few years you will have it hard, and you must all keep together. Alexandra will manage the best she can."

Oscar, who was usually the last to speak, replied because he was the older, "Yes, father. It would be so anyway, without your speaking. We will all work the place together."

"And you will be guided by your sister, boys, and be good brothers to her, and good sons to your mother? That is good. And Alexandra must not work in the fields any more. There is no necessity now. Hire a man when you need help. She can make much more with her eggs and butter than the wages of a man. It was one of my mistakes that I did not find that out sooner. Try to break a little more land every year; sod corn is good for fodder. Keep turning the land, and always put up more hay than you need. Don't grudge your mother a little time for plowing her garden and setting out fruit trees, even if it comes in a busy season. She has been a good mother to you, and she has always missed the old country."

When they went back to the kitchen the boys sat down silently at the table. Throughout the meal they looked down at their plates and did not lift their red eyes. They did not eat much, although they had been working in the cold all day, and there was a rabbit stewed in gravy for supper, and prune pies.

John Bergson had married beneath him, but he had married a good housewife. Mrs. Bergson was a fair-skinned, corpulent woman, heavy and placid like her son, Oscar, but there was something comfortable about her; perhaps it was her own love of comfort. For eleven years she had worthily striven to maintain some semblance of household order amid conditions that made order very difficult. Habit was very strong with Mrs. Bergson, and her unremitting efforts to repeat the routine of her old life among new surroundings had done a great deal to keep the family from disintegrating morally and getting careless in their ways. The Bergsons had a log house, for instance, only because Mrs. Bergson would not live in a sod house. She missed the fish diet of her own country, and twice every summer she sent the boys to the river, twenty miles to the southward, to fish for channel cat. When the children were little she used to load them all into the wagon, the baby in its crib, and go fishing herself.

Alexandra often said that if her mother were cast upon a desert island, she would thank God for her deliverance, make a garden, and find something to preserve. Preserving was almost a mania with Mrs. Bergson. Stout as she was, she roamed the scrubby banks of Norway Creek looking for fox grapes and goose plums, like a wild creature in search of prey. She made a yellow jam of the insipid ground-cherries that grew on the prairie, flavoring it with lemon peel; and she made a sticky dark conserve of garden tomatoes. She had experimented even with the rank buffalo-pea, and she could not see a fine bronze luster of them without shaking her head and murmuring, "What a pity!" When there was nothing more to preserve, she began to pickle. The amount of sugar she used in these processes was sometimes a serious drain upon the family resources. She was a good mother, but she was glad when her children were old enough not to be in her way in the kitchen. She had never quite forgiven John Bergson for bringing her to the end of the earth; but, now that she was there, she wanted to be let alone to reconstruct her old life in so far as that was possible. She could still take some comfort in the world if she had bacon in the cave, glass jars on the shelves, and sheets in the press. She disapproved of all her neighbors because of their slovenly housekeeping, and the women thought her very proud. Once when Mrs. Bergson, on her way to Norway Creek, stopped to see old Mrs. Lee, the old woman hid in the haymow "for fear Mis' Bergson would catch her barefoot."

III

One Sunday afternoon in July, six months after John Bergson's death, Carl was sitting in the doorway of the Linstrum kitchen, dreaming over an illustrated paper, when he heard the rattle of a wagon along the hill road. Looking up he recognized the Bergsons' team, with two seats in the wagon, which meant they were off for a pleasure excursion. Oscar and Lou, on the front seat, wore their cloth hats and coats, never worn except on Sundays, and Emil, on the second seat with Alexandra, sat proudly in his new trousers, made from a pair of his father's, and a pink-striped shirt, with a wide ruffled collar. Oscar stopped the horses and waved to Carl, who caught up his hat and ran through the melon patch to join them.

"Want to go with us?" Lou called. "We're going to Crazy Ivar's to buy a hammock."

"Sure." Carl ran up panting, and clambering over the wheel sat down beside Emil. "I've always wanted to see Ivar's pond. They say it's the biggest in all the country. Aren't you afraid to go to Ivar's in that new shirt, Emil? He might want it and take it right off your back."

Emil grinned. "I'd be awful scared to go," he admitted, "if you big boys weren't along to take care of me. Did you ever hear him howl, Carl? People say sometimes he runs about the country howling at night because he is afraid the Lord will destroy him. Mother thinks he must have done something awful wicked."

Lou looked back and winked at Carl. "What would you do, Emil, if you was out on the prairie by yourself and seen him coming?"

Emil stared. "Maybe I could hide in a badger-hole," he suggested doubtfully.

"But suppose there wasn't any badger-hole," Lou persisted. "Would you run?"

"No, I'd be too scared to run," Emil admitted mournfully, twisting his fingers. "I guess I'd sit right down on the ground and say my prayers."

The big boys laughed, and Oscar brandished his whip over the broad backs of the horses.

"He wouldn't hurt you, Emil," said Carl persuasively. "He came to doctor our mare when she ate green corn and swelled up most as big as the water-tank. He petted her just like you do your cats. I couldn't understand much he said, for he don't talk any English, but he kept patting her and groaning as if he had the pain himself, and saying, 'There now, sister, that's easier, that's better!'"

Lou and Oscar laughed, and Emil giggled delightedly and looked up at his sister.

"I don't think he knows anything at all about doctoring," said Oscar scornfully. "They say when horses have distemper he takes the medicine himself, and then prays over the horses."

Alexandra spoke up. "That's what the Crows said, but he cured their horses, all the same. Some days his mind is cloudy, like. But if you can get him on a clear day, you can learn a great deal from him. He understands animals. Didn't I see him take the horn off the Berquist's cow when she had torn it loose and went crazy? She was tearing all over the place, knocking herself against things. And at last she ran out on the roof of the old dugout and her legs went through and there she stuck, bellowing. Ivar came running with his white bag, and the moment he got to her she was quiet and let him saw her horn off and daub the place with tar."

Emil had been watching his sister, his face reflecting the sufferings of the cow. "And then didn't it hurt her any more?" he asked.

Alexandra patted him. "No, not any more. And in two days they could use her milk again."

The road to Ivar's homestead was a very poor one. He had settled in the rough country across the county line, where no one lived but some Russians—half a dozen families who dwelt together in one long house, divided off like barracks. Ivar had explained his choice by saying that the fewer neighbors he had, the fewer temptations. Nevertheless, when one considered that his chief business was horse-doctoring, it seemed rather short-sighted of him to live in the most inaccessible place he could find. The Bergson wagon lurched along over the rough hummocks and grass banks, followed the bottom of winding draws, or skirted the margin of wide lagoons, where the golden coreopsis grew up out of the clear water and the wild ducks rose with a whirr of wings.

Lou looked after them helplessly. "I wish I'd brought my gun, anyway, Alexandra," he said fretfully. "I could have hidden it under the straw in the bottom of the wagon."

"Then we'd have had to lie to Ivar. Besides, they say he can smell dead birds. And if he knew, we wouldn't get anything out of him, not even a hammock. I want to talk to him, and he won't talk sense if he's angry. It makes him foolish."

Lou sniffed. "Whoever heard of him talking sense, anyhow! I'd rather have ducks for supper than Crazy Ivar's tongue."

Emil was alarmed. "Oh, but, Lou, you don't want to make him mad! He might howl!"

They all laughed again, and Oscar urged the horses up the crumbling side of a clay bank. They had left the lagoons and the red grass behind them. In Crazy Ivar's country the grass was short and gray, the draws deeper than they were in the Bergsons' neighborhood, and the land was all broken up into hillocks and clay ridges. The wild flowers disappeared, and only in the bottom of the draws and gullies grew a few of the very toughest and hardiest: shoestring, and ironweed, and snow-on-the-mountain.

"Look, look, Emil, there's Ivar's big pond!" Alexandra pointed to a shining sheet of water that lay at the bottom of a shallow draw. At one end of the pond was an earthen dam, planted with green willow bushes, and above it a door and a single window were set into the hillside. You would not have seen them at all but for the reflection of the sunlight upon the four panes of window-glass. And that was all you saw. Not a shed, not a corral, not a well, not even a path broken in the curly grass. But for the piece of rusty stovepipe sticking up through the sod, you could have walked over the roof of Ivar's dwelling without dreaming that you were near a human habitation. Ivar had lived for three years in the clay bank, without defiling the face of nature any more than the coyote that had lived there before him had done.

When the Bergsons drove over the hill, Ivar was sitting in the doorway of his house, reading the Norwegian Bible. He was a queerly shaped old man, with a thick, powerful body set on short bow-legs. His shaggy white hair, falling in a thick mane about his ruddy cheeks, made him look older than he was. He was barefoot, but he wore a clean shirt of unbleached cotton, open at the neck. He always put on a clean shirt when Sunday morning came round, though he never went to church. He had a peculiar religion of his own and could not get on with any of the denominations. Often he did not see anybody from one week's end to another. He kept a calendar, and every morning he checked off a day, so that he was never in any doubt as to which day of the week it was. Ivar hired himself out in threshing and corn-husking time, and he doctored sick animals when he was sent for. When he was at home, he made hammocks out of twine and committed chapters of the Bible to memory.

Ivar found contentment in the solitude he had sought out for himself. He disliked the litter of human dwellings: the broken food, the bits of broken china, the old wash-boilers and tea-kettles thrown into the sunflower patch. He preferred the cleanness and tidiness of the wild sod. He always said that the badgers had cleaner houses than people, and that when he took a housekeeper her name would be Mrs. Badger. He best expressed his preference for his wild homestead by saying that his Bible seemed truer to him there. If one stood in the doorway of his cave, and looked off at the rough land, the smiling sky, the curly grass white in the hot sunlight; if one listened to the rapturous song of the lark, the drumming of the quail, the burr of the locust against that vast silence, one understood what Ivar meant.

On this Sunday afternoon his face shone with happiness. He closed the book on his knee, keeping the place with his horny finger, and repeated softly:

He sendeth the springs into the valleys, which
        run among the hills;
They give drink to every beast of the field; the
        wild asses quench their thirst.
The trees of the Lord are full of sap; the cedars
        of Lebanon which he hath planted;
Where the birds make their nests: as for the stork the
        fir trees are her house.
The high hills are a refuge for the wild goats;
        and the rocks for the conies.

Before he opened his Bible again, Ivar heard the Bergsons' wagon approaching, and he sprang up and ran toward it.

"No guns, no guns!" he shouted, waving his arms distractedly.

"No, Ivar, no guns," Alexandra called reassuringly.

He dropped his arms and went up to the wagon, smiling amiably and looking at them out of his pale blue eyes.

"We want to buy a hammock, if you have one," Alexandra explained, "and my little brother, here, wants to see your big pond, where so many birds come."

Ivar smiled foolishly, and began rubbing the horses' noses and feeling about their mouths behind the bits. "Not many birds just now. A few ducks this morning; and some snipe come to drink. But there was a crane last week. She spent one night and came back the next evening. I don't know why. It is not her season, of course. Many of them go over in the fall. Then the pond is full of strange voices every night."

Alexandra translated for Carl, who looked thoughtful. "Ask him, Alexandra, if it is true that a sea gull came here once. I have heard so."

She had some difficulty in making the old man understand.

He looked puzzled at first, then smote his hands together as he remembered. "Oh, yes, yes! A big white bird with long wings and pink feet. My! what a voice she had! She came in the afternoon and kept flying about the pond and screaming until dark. She was in trouble of some sort, but I could not understand her. She was going over to the other ocean, maybe, and did not know how far it was. She was afraid of never getting there. She was more mournful than our birds here; she cried in the night. She saw the light from my window and darted up to it. Maybe she thought my house was a boat, she was such a wild thing. Next morning, when the sun rose, I went out to take her food, but she flew up into the sky and went on her way." Ivar ran his fingers through his thick hair. "I have many strange birds stop with me here. They come from very far away and are great company. I hope you boys never shoot wild birds?"

Lou and Oscar grinned, and Ivar shook his bushy head. "Yes, I know boys are thoughtless. But these wild things are God's birds. He watches over them and counts them, as we do our cattle; Christ says so in the New Testament."

"Now, Ivar," Lou asked, "may we water our horses at your pond and give them some feed? It's a bad road to your place."

"Yes, yes, it is." The old man scrambled about and began to loose the tugs. "A bad road, eh, girls? And the bay with a colt at home!"

Oscar brushed the old man aside. "We'll take care of the horses, Ivar. You'll be finding some disease on them. Alexandra wants to see your hammocks."

Ivar led Alexandra and Emil to his little cave house. He had but one room, neatly plastered and whitewashed, and there was a wooden floor. There was a kitchen stove, a table covered with oilcloth, two chairs, a clock, a calendar, a few books on the window-shelf; nothing more. But the place was as clean as a cupboard.

"But where do you sleep, Ivar?" Emil asked, looking about.

Ivar unslung a hammock from a hook on the wall; in it was rolled a buffalo robe. "There, my son. A hammock is a good bed, and in winter I wrap up in this skin. Where I go to work, the beds are not half so easy as this."

By this time Emil had lost all his timidity. He thought a cave a very superior kind of house. There was something pleasantly unusual about it and about Ivar. "Do the birds know you will be kind to them, Ivar? Is that why so many come?" he asked.

Ivar sat down on the floor and tucked his feet under him. "See, little brother, they have come from a long way, and they are very tired. From up there where they are flying, our country looks dark and flat. They must have water to drink and to bathe in before they can go on with their journey. They look this way and that, and far below them they see something shining, like a piece of glass set in the dark earth. That is my pond. They come to it and are not disturbed. Maybe I sprinkle a little corn. They tell the other birds, and next year more come this way. They have their roads up there, as we have down here."

Emil rubbed his knees thoughtfully. "And is that true, Ivar, about the head ducks falling back when they are tired, and the hind ones taking their place?"

"Yes. The point of the wedge gets the worst of it; they cut the wind. They can only stand it there a little while—half an hour, maybe. Then they fall back and the wedge splits a little, while the rear ones come up the middle to the front. Then it closes up and they fly on, with a new edge. They are always changing like that, up in the air. Never any confusion; just like soldiers who have been drilled."

Alexandra had selected her hammock by the time the boys came up from the pond. They would not come in, but sat in the shade of the bank outside while Alexandra and Ivar talked about the birds and about his housekeeping, and why he never ate meat, fresh or salt.

Alexandra was sitting on one of the wooden chairs, her arms resting on the table. Ivar was sitting on the floor at her feet. "Ivar," she said suddenly, beginning to trace the pattern on the oilcloth with her forefinger, "I came to-day more because I wanted to talk to you than because I wanted to buy a hammock."

"Yes?" The old man scraped his bare feet on the plank floor.

"We have a big bunch of hogs, Ivar. I wouldn't sell in the spring, when everybody advised me to, and now so many people are losing their hogs that I am frightened. What can be done?"

Ivar's little eyes began to shine. They lost their vagueness.

"You feed them swill and such stuff? Of course! And sour milk? Oh, yes! And keep them in a stinking pen? I tell you, sister, the hogs of this country are put upon! They become unclean, like the hogs in the Bible. If you kept your chickens like that, what would happen? You have a little sorghum patch, maybe? Put a fence around it, and turn the hogs in. Build a shed to give them shade, a thatch on poles. Let the boys haul water to them in barrels, clean water, and plenty. Get them off the old stinking ground, and do not let them go back there until winter. Give them only grain and clean feed, such as you would give horses or cattle. Hogs do not like to be filthy."

The boys outside the door had been listening. Lou nudged his brother. "Come, the horses are done eating. Let's hitch up and get out of here. He'll fill her full of notions. She'll be for having the pigs sleep with us, next."

Oscar grunted and got up. Carl, who could not understand what Ivar said, saw that the two boys were displeased. They did not mind hard work, but they hated experiments and could never see the use of taking pains. Even Lou, who was more elastic than his older brother, disliked to do anything different from their neighbors. He felt that it made them conspicuous and gave people a chance to talk about them.

Once they were on the homeward road, the boys forgot their ill-humor and joked about Ivar and his birds. Alexandra did not propose any reforms in the care of the pigs, and they hoped she had forgotten Ivar's talk. They agreed that he was crazier than ever, and would never be able to prove up on his land because he worked it so little. Alexandra privately resolved that she would have a talk with Ivar about this and stir him up. The boys persuaded Carl to stay for supper and go swimming in the pasture pond after dark.

That evening, after she had washed the supper dishes, Alexandra sat down on the kitchen doorstep, while her mother was mixing the bread. It was a still, deep-breathing summer night, full of the smell of the hay fields. Sounds of laughter and splashing came up from the pasture, and when the moon rose rapidly above the bare rim of the prairie, the pond glittered like polished metal, and she could see the flash of white bodies as the boys ran about the edge, or jumped into the water. Alexandra watched the shimmering pool dreamily, but eventually her eyes went back to the sorghum patch south of the barn, where she was planning to make her new pig corral.

IV

*F*or the first three years after John Bergson's death, the affairs of his family prospered. Then came the hard times that brought every one on the Divide to the brink of despair; three years of drouth and failure, the last struggle of a wild soil against the encroaching plowshare. The first of these fruitless summers the Bergson boys bore courageously. The failure of the corn crop made labor cheap. Lou and Oscar hired two men and put in bigger crops than ever before. They lost everything they spent. The whole country was discouraged. Farmers who were already in debt had to give up their land. A few foreclosures demoralized the county. The settlers sat about on the wooden sidewalks in the little town and told each other that the country was never meant for men to live in; the thing to do was to get back to Iowa, to Illinois, to any place that had been proved habitable. The Bergson boys, certainly, would have been happier with their uncle Otto, in the bakery shop in Chicago. Like most of their neighbors, they were meant to follow in paths already marked out for them, not to break trails in a new country. A steady job, a few holidays, nothing to think about, and they would have been very happy. It was no fault of theirs that they had been dragged into the wilderness when they were little boys. A pioneer should have imagination, should be able to enjoy the idea of things more than the things themselves.

The second of these barren summers was passing. One September afternoon Alexandra had gone over to the garden across the draw to dig sweet potatoes—they had been thriving upon the weather that was fatal to everything else. But when Carl Linstrum came up the garden rows to find her, she was not working. She was standing lost in thought, leaning upon her pitchfork, her sunbonnet lying beside her on the ground. The dry garden patch smelled of drying vines and was strewn with yellow seed-cucumbers and pumpkins and citrons. At one end, next the rhubarb, grew feathery asparagus, with red berries. Down the middle of the garden was a row of gooseberry and currant bushes. A few tough zenias and marigolds and a row of scarlet sage bore witness to the buckets of water that Mrs. Bergson had carried there after sundown, against the prohibition of her sons. Carl came quietly and slowly up the garden path, looking intently at Alexandra. She did not hear him. She was standing perfectly still, with that serious ease so characteristic of her. Her thick, reddish braids, twisted about her head, fairly burned in the sunlight. The air was cool enough to make the warm sun pleasant on one's back and shoulders, and so clear that the eye could follow a hawk up and up, into the blazing blue depths of the sky. Even Carl, never a very cheerful boy, and considerably darkened by these last two bitter years, loved the country on days like this, felt something strong and young and wild come out of it, that laughed at care.

"Alexandra," he said as he approached her, "I want to talk to you. Let's sit down by the gooseberry bushes." He picked up her sack of potatoes and they crossed the garden. "Boys gone to town?" he asked as he sank down on the warm, sun-baked earth. "Well, we have made up our minds at last, Alexandra. We are really going away."

She looked at him as if she were a little frightened. "Really, Carl? Is it settled?"

"Yes, father has heard from St. Louis, and they will give him back his old job in the cigar factory. He must be there by the first of November. They are taking on new men then. We will sell the place for whatever we can get, and auction the stock. We haven't enough to ship. I am going to learn engraving with a German engraver there, and then try to get work in Chicago."

Alexandra's hands dropped in her lap. Her eyes became dreamy and filled with tears.

Carl's sensitive lower lip trembled. He scratched in the soft earth beside him with a stick. "That's all I hate about it, Alexandra," he said slowly. "You've stood by us through so much and helped father out so many times, and now it seems as if we were running off and leaving you to face the worst of it. But it isn't as if we could really ever be of any help to you. We are only one more drag, one more thing you look out for and feel responsible for. Father was never meant for a farmer, you know that. And I hate it. We'd only get in deeper and deeper."

"Yes, yes, Carl, I know. You are wasting your life here. You are able to do much better things. You are nearly nineteen now, and I wouldn't have you stay. I've always hoped you would get away. But I can't help feeling scared when I think how I will miss you—more than you will ever know." She brushed the tears from her checks, not trying to hide them.

"But, Alexandra," he said sadly and wistfully, "I've never been any real help to you, beyond sometimes trying to keep the boys in a good humor."

Alexandra smiled and shook her head. "Oh, it's not that. Nothing like that. It's by understanding me, and the boys, and mother, that you've helped me. I expect that is the only way one person ever really can help another. I think you are about the only one that ever helped me. Somehow it will take more courage to bear your going than everything that has happened before."

Carl looked at the ground. "You see, we've all depended so on you," he said, "even father. He makes me laugh. When anything comes up he always says, 'I wonder what the Bergsons are going to do about that? I guess I'll go and ask her.' I'll never forget that time, when we first came here, and our horse had the colic, and I ran over to your place—your father was away, and you came home with me and showed father how to let the wind out of the horse. You were only a little girl then, but you knew ever so much more about farm work than poor father. You remember how homesick I used to get, and what long talks we used to have coming from school? We've someway always felt alike about things."

"Yes, that's it; we've liked the same things and we've liked them together, without anybody else knowing. And we've had good times, hunting for Christmas trees and going for ducks and making our plum wine together every year. We've never either of us had any other close friend. And now—" Alexandra wiped her eyes with the corner of her apron, "and now I must remember that you are going where you will have many friends, and will find the work you were meant to do. But you'll write to me, Carl? That will mean a great deal to me here."

"I'll write as long as I live," cried the boy impetuously. "And I'll be working for you as much as for myself, Alexandra. I want to do something you'll like and be proud of. I'm a fool here, but I know I can do something!" He sat up and frowned at the red grass.

Alexandra sighed. "How discouraged the boys will be when they hear. They always come home from town discouraged, anyway. So many people are trying to leave the country, and they talk to our boys and make them low-spirited. I'm afraid they are beginning to feel hard toward me because I won't listen to any talk about going. Sometimes I feel like I'm getting tired of standing up for this country."

"I won't tell the boys yet, if you'd rather not."

"Oh, I'll tell them myself, to-night, when they come home. They'll be talking wild, anyway, and no good comes of keeping bad news. It's all harder on them than it is on me. Lou wants to get married, poor boy, and he can't until times are better. See, there goes the sun, Carl. I must be getting back. Mother will want her potatoes. It's really chilly already, the moment the light goes."

Alexandra rose and looked about. A golden afterglow throbbed in the west, but the country already looked empty and mournful. A dark moving mass came over the western hill, the Lee boy was bringing in the herd from the other half-section. Emil ran from the windmill to open the corral gate. From the log house, on the little rise across the draw, the smoke was curling. The cattle lowed and bellowed. In the sky the pale half-moon was slowly silvering. Alexandra and Carl walked together down the potato rows. "I have to keep telling myself what is going to happen," she said softly. "Since you have been here, ten years now, I have never really been lonely. But I can remember what it was like before. Now I shall have nobody but Emil. But he is my boy, and he is tender-hearted."

That night, when the boys were called to supper, they sat down moodily. They had worn their coats to town, but they ate in their striped shirts and suspenders. They were grown men now, and, as Alexandra said, for the last few years they had been growing more and more like themselves. Lou was still the slighter of the two, the quicker and more intelligent, but apt to go off at half-cock. He had a lively blue eye, a thin, fair skin (always burned red to the neckband of his shirt in summer), stiff, yellow hair that would not lie down on his head, and a bristly little yellow mustache, of which he was very proud. Oscar could not grow a mustache; his pale face was as bare as an egg, and his white eyebrows gave it an empty look. He was a man of powerful body and unusual endurance; the sort of man you could attach to a corn-sheller as you would an engine. He would turn it all day, without hurrying, without slowing down. But he was as indolent of mind as he was unsparing of his body. His love of routine amounted to a vice. He worked like an insect, always doing the same thing over in the same way, regardless of whether it was best or not. He felt that there was a sovereign virtue in mere bodily toil, and he rather liked to do things in the hardest way. If a field had once been in corn, he couldn't bear to put it into wheat. He liked to begin his corn-planting at the same time every year, whether the season were backward or forward. He seemed to feel that by his own irreproachable regularity he would clear himself of blame and reprove the weather. When the wheat crop failed, he threshed the straw at a dead loss to demonstrate how little grain there was, and thus prove his case against Providence.

Lou, on the other hand, was fussy and flighty; always planned to get through two days' work in one, and often got only the least important things done. He liked to keep the place up, but he never got round to doing odd jobs until he had to neglect more pressing work to attend to them. In the middle of the wheat harvest, when the grain was over-ripe and every hand was needed, he would stop to mend fences or to patch the harness; then dash down to the field and overwork and be laid up in bed for a week. The two boys balanced each other, and they pulled well together. They had been good friends since they were children. One seldom went anywhere, even to town, without the other.

To-night, after they sat down to supper, Oscar kept looking at Lou as if he expected him to say something, and Lou blinked his eyes and frowned at his plate. It was Alexandra herself who at last opened the discussion.

"The Linstrums," she said calmly, as she put another plate of hot biscuit on the table, "are going back to St. Louis. The old man is going to work in the cigar factory again."

At this Lou plunged in. "You see, Alexandra, everybody who can crawl out is going away. There's no use of us trying to stick it out, just to be stubborn. There's something in knowing when to quit."

"Where do you want to go, Lou?"

"Any place where things will grow," said Oscar grimly.

Lou reached for a potato. "Chris Arnson has traded his half-section for a place down on the river."

"Who did he trade with?"

"Charley Fuller, in town."

"Fuller the real estate man? You see, Lou, that Fuller has a head on him. He's buying and trading for every bit of land he can get up here. It'll make him a rich man, some day."

"He's rich now, that's why he can take a chance."

"Why can't we? We'll live longer than he will. Some day the land itself will be worth more than all we can ever raise on it."

Lou laughed. "It could be worth that, and still not be worth much. Why, Alexandra, you don't know what you're talking about. Our place wouldn't bring now what it would six years ago. The fellows that settled up here just made a mistake. Now they're beginning to see this high land wasn't never meant to grow nothing on, and everybody who ain't fixed to graze cattle is trying to crawl out. It's too high to farm up here. All the Americans are skinning out. That man Percy Adams, north of town, told me that he was going to let Fuller take his land and stuff for four hundred dollars and a ticket to Chicago."

"There's Fuller again!" Alexandra exclaimed. "I wish that man would take me for a partner. He's feathering his nest! If only poor people could learn a little from rich people! But all these fellows who are running off are bad farmers, like poor Mr. Linstrum. They couldn't get ahead even in good years, and they all got into debt while father was getting out. I think we ought to hold on as long as we can on father's account. He was so set on keeping this land. He must have seen harder times than this, here. How was it in the early days, mother?"

Mrs. Bergson was weeping quietly. These family discussions always depressed her, and made her remember all that she had been torn away from. "I don't see why the boys are always taking on about going away," she said, wiping her eyes. "I don't want to move again; out to some raw place, maybe, where we'd be worse off than we are here, and all to do over again. I won't move! If the rest of you go, I will ask some of the neighbors to take me in, and stay and be buried by father. I'm not going to leave him by himself on the prairie, for cattle to run over." She began to cry more bitterly.

The boys looked angry. Alexandra put a soothing hand on her mother's shoulder. "There's no question of that, mother. You don't have to go if you don't want to. A third of the place belongs to you by American law, and we can't sell without your consent. We only want you to advise us. How did it use to be when you and father first came? Was it really as bad as this, or not?"

"Oh, worse! Much worse," moaned Mrs. Bergson. "Drouth,

chince-bugs, hail, everything! My garden all cut to pieces like sauerkraut. No grapes on the creek, no nothing. The people all lived just like coyotes."

Oscar got up and tramped out of the kitchen. Lou followed him. They felt that Alexandra had taken an unfair advantage in turning their mother loose on them. The next morning they were silent and reserved. They did not offer to take the women to church, but went down to the barn immediately after breakfast and stayed there all day. When Carl Linstrum came over in the afternoon, Alexandra winked to him and pointed toward the barn. He understood her and went down to play cards with the boys. They believed that a very wicked thing to do on Sunday, and it relieved their feelings.

Alexandra stayed in the house. On Sunday afternoon Mrs. Bergson always took a nap, and Alexandra read. During the week she read only the newspaper, but on Sunday, and in the long evenings of winter, she read a good deal; read a few things over a great many times. She knew long portions of the "Frithjof Saga" by heart, and, like most Swedes who read at all, she was fond of Longfellow's verse,—the ballads and the "Golden Legend" and "The Spanish Student." To-day she sat in the wooden rocking chair with the Swedish Bible open on her knees, but she was not reading. She was looking thoughtfully away at the point where the upland road disappeared over the rim of the prairie. Her body was in an attitude of perfect repose, such as it was apt to take when she was thinking earnestly. Her mind was slow, truthful, steadfast. She had not the least spark of cleverness.

All afternoon the sitting-room was full of quiet and sunlight. Emil was making rabbit traps in the kitchen shed. The hens were clucking and scratching brown holes in the flower beds, and the wind was teasing the prince's feather by the door.

That evening Carl came in with the boys to supper.

"Emil," said Alexandra, when they were all seated at the table, "how would you like to go traveling? Because I am going to take a trip, and you can go with me if you want to."

The boys looked up in amazement; they were always afraid of Alexandra's schemes. Carl was interested.

"I've been thinking, boys," she went on, "that maybe I am too set against making a change. I'm going to take Brigham and the buckboard to-morrow and drive down to the river country and spend a few days looking over what they've got down there. If I find anything good, you boys can go down and make a trade."

"Nobody down there will trade for anything up here," said Oscar gloomily.

"That's just what I want to find out. Maybe they are just as discontented down there as we are up here. Things away from home often look better than they are. You know what your Hans Andersen book says, Carl, about the Swedes liking to buy Danish bread and the Danes liking to buy Swedish bread, because people always think the bread of another country is better than their own. Anyway, I've heard so much about the river farms, I won't be satisfied till I've seen for myself."

Lou fidgeted. "Look out! Don't agree to anything. Don't let them fool you."

Lou was apt to be fooled himself. He had not yet learned to keep away from the shell-game wagons that followed the circus.

After supper Lou put on a necktie and went across the fields to court Annie Lee, and Carl and Oscar sat down to a game of checkers, while Alexandra read "The Swiss Family Robinson" aloud to her mother and Emil. It was not long before the two boys at the table neglected their game to listen. They were all big children together, and they found the adventures of the family in the tree house so absorbing that they gave them their undivided attention.

V

*A*lexandra and Emil spent five days down among the river farms, driving up and down the valley. Alexandra talked to the men about their crops and to the women about their poultry. She spent a whole day with one young farmer who had been away at school, and who was experimenting with a new kind of clover hay. She learned a great deal. As they drove along, she and Emil talked and planned. At last, on the sixth day, Alexandra turned Brigham's head northward and left the river behind.

"There's nothing in it for us down there, Emil. There are a few fine farms, but they are owned by the rich men in town, and couldn't be bought. Most of the land is rough and hilly. They can always scrape along down there, but they can never do anything big. Down there they have a little certainty, but up with us there is a big chance. We must have faith in the high land, Emil. I want to hold on harder than ever, and when you're a man you'll thank me." She urged Brigham forward.

When the road began to climb the first long swells of the Divide, Alexandra hummed an old Swedish hymn, and Emil wondered why his sister looked so happy. Her face was so radiant that he felt shy about asking her. For the first time, perhaps, since that land emerged from the waters of geologic ages, a human face was set toward it with love and yearning. It seemed beautiful to her, rich and strong and glorious. Her eyes drank in the breadth of it, until her tears blinded her. Then the Genius of the Divide, the great, free spirit which breathes across it, must have bent lower than it ever bent to a human will before. The history of every country begins in the heart of a man or a woman.

Alexandra reached home in the afternoon. That evening she held a family council and told her brothers all that she had seen and heard.

"I want you boys to go down yourselves and look it over. Nothing will convince you like seeing with your own eyes. The river land was settled before this, and so they are a few years ahead of us, and have learned more about farming. The land sells for three times as much as this, but in five years we will double it. The rich men down there own all the best land, and they are buying all they can get. The thing to do is to sell our cattle and what little old corn we have, and buy the Linstrum place. Then the next thing to do is to take out two loans on our half-sections, and buy Peter Crow's place; raise every dollar we can, and buy every acre we can."

"Mortgage the homestead again?" Lou cried. He sprang up and began to wind the clock furiously. "I won't slave to pay off another mortgage. I'll never do it. You'd just as soon kill us all, Alexandra, to carry out some scheme!"

Oscar rubbed his high, pale forehead. "How do you propose to pay off your mortgages?"

Alexandra looked from one to the other and bit her lip. They had never seen her so nervous. "See here," she brought out at last. "We borrow the money for six years. Well, with the money we buy a half-section from Linstrum and a half from Crow, and a quarter from Struble, maybe. That will give us upwards of fourteen hundred acres, won't it? You won't have to pay off your mortgages for six years. By that time, any of this land will be worth thirty dollars an acre—it will be worth fifty, but we'll say thirty; then you can sell a garden patch anywhere, and pay off a debt of sixteen hundred dollars. It's not the principal I'm worried about, it's the interest and taxes. We'll have to strain to meet the payments. But as sure as we are sitting here to-night, we can sit down here ten years from now independent landowners, not struggling farmers any longer. The chance that father was always looking for has come."

Lou was pacing the floor. "But how do you *know* that land is going to go up enough to pay the mortgages and—"

"And make us rich besides?" Alexandra put in firmly. "I can't explain that, Lou. You'll have to take my word for it. I *know,* that's all. When you drive about over the country you can feel it coming."

Oscar had been sitting with his head lowered, his hands hanging between his knees. "But we can't work so much land," he said dully, as if he were talking to himself. "We can't even try. It would just lie there and we'd work ourselves to death." He sighed, and laid his calloused fist on the table.

Alexandra's eyes filled with tears. She put her hand on his shoulder. "You poor boy, you won't have to work it. The men in town who are buying up other people's land don't try to farm it. They are the men to watch, in a new country. Let's try to do like the shrewd ones and not like these stupid fellows. I don't want you boys always to have to work like this. I want you to be independent, and Emil to go to school."

Lou held his head as if it were splitting. "Everybody will say we are crazy. It must be crazy, or everybody would be doing it."

"If they were, we wouldn't have much chance. No, Lou, I was talking about that with the smart young man who is raising the new kind of clover. He says the right thing is usually just what everybody don't do. Why are we better fixed than any of our neighbors? Because father had more brains. Our people were better people than these in the old country. We *ought* to do more than they do, and see further ahead. Yes, mother, I'm going to clear the table now."

Alexandra rose. The boys went to the stable to see to the stock, and they were gone a long while. When they came back Lou played on his *dragharmonika* and Oscar sat figuring at his father's secretary all evening. They said nothing more about Alexandra's project, but she felt sure now that they would consent to it. Just before bedtime Oscar went out for a pail of water. When he did not come back, Alexandra threw a shawl over her head and ran down the path to the windmill. She found him sitting there with his head in his hands, and she sat down beside him.

"Don't do anything you don't want to do, Oscar," she whispered. She waited a moment, but he did not stir. "I won't say any more about it, if you'd rather not. What makes you so discouraged?"

"I dread signing my name to them pieces of paper," he said slowly. "All the time I was a boy we had a mortgage hanging over us."

"Then don't sign one. I don't want you to, if you feel that way."

Oscar shook his head. "No, I can see there's a chance that way. I've thought a good while there might be. We're in so deep now, we might as well go deeper. But it's hard work pulling out of debt. Like pulling a threshing-machine out of the mud; breaks your back. Me and Lou's worked hard, and I can't see it's got us ahead much."

"Nobody knows about that as well as I do, Oscar. That's why I want to try an easier way. I don't want you to have to grub for every dollar."

"Yes, I know what you mean. Maybe it'll come out right. But signing papers is signing papers. There ain't no maybe about that." He took his pail and trudged up the path to the house.

Alexandra drew her shawl closer about her and stood leaning against the frame of the mill, looking at the stars which glittered so keenly through the frosty autumn air. She always loved to watch them, to think of their vastness and distance, and of their ordered march. It fortified her to reflect upon the great operations of nature, and when she thought of the law that lay behind them, she felt a sense of personal security. That night she had a new consciousness of the country, felt almost a new relation to it. Even her talk with the boys had not taken away the feeling that had overwhelmed her when she drove back to the Divide that afternoon. She had never known before how much the country meant to her. The chirping of the insects down in the long grass had been like the sweetest music. She had felt as if her heart were hiding down there, somewhere, with the quail and the plover and all the little wild things that crooned or buzzed in the sun. Under the long shaggy ridges, she felt the future stirring.

Part II

Neighboring Fields

I

*I*t is sixteen years since John Bergson died. His wife now lies beside him, and the white shaft that marks their graves gleams across the wheatfields. Could he rise from beneath it, he would not know the country under which he has been asleep. The shaggy coat of the prairie, which they lifted to make him a bed, has vanished forever. From the Norwegian graveyard one looks out over a vast checker-board, marked off in squares of wheat and corn; light and dark, dark and light. Telephone wires hum along the white roads, which always run at right angles. From the graveyard gate one can count a dozen gayly painted farmhouses; the gilded weather-vanes on the big red barns wink at each other across the green and brown and yellow fields. The light steel wind-mills tremble throughout their frames and tug at their moorings, as they vibrate in the wind that often blows from one week's end to another across that high, active, resolute stretch of country.

The Divide is now thickly populated. The rich soil yields heavy harvests; the dry, bracing climate and the smoothness of the land make labor easy for men and beasts. There are few scenes more gratifying than a spring plowing in that country, where the furrows of a single field often lie a mile in length, and the brown earth, with such a strong, clean smell, and such a power of growth and fertility in it, yields itself eagerly to the plow; rolls away from the shear, not even dimming the brightness of the metal, with a soft, deep sigh of happiness. The wheat-cutting sometimes goes on all night as well as all day, and in good seasons there are scarcely men and horses enough to do the harvesting. The grain is so heavy that it bends toward the blade and cuts like velvet.

There is something frank and joyous and young in the open face of the country. It gives itself ungrudgingly to the moods of the season, holding nothing back. Like the plains of Lombardy, it seems to rise a little to meet the sun. The air and the earth are curiously mated and intermingled, as if the one were the breath of the other. You feel in the atmosphere the same tonic, puissant quality that is in the tilth, the same strength and resoluteness.

One June morning a young man stood at the gate of the Norwegian graveyard, sharpening his scythe in strokes unconsciously timed to the tune he was whistling. He wore a flannel cap and duck trousers, and the sleeves of his white flannel shirt were rolled back to the elbow. When he was satisfied with the edge of his blade, he slipped the whetstone into his hip pocket and began to swing his scythe, still whistling, but softly, out of respect to the quiet folk about him. Unconscious respect, probably, for he seemed intent upon his own thoughts, and, like the Gladiator's, they were far away. He was a splendid figure of a boy, tall and straight as a young pine tree, with a handsome head, and stormy gray eyes, deeply set under a serious brow. The space between his two front teeth, which were unusually far apart, gave him the proficiency in whistling for which he was distinguished at college. (He also played the cornet in the University band.)

When the grass required his close attention, or when he had to stoop to cut about a headstone, he paused in his lively air,—the "Jewel" song,—taking it up where he had left it when his scythe swung free again. He was not thinking about the tired pioneers over whom his blade glittered. The old wild country, the struggle in which his sister was destined to succeed while so many men broke their hearts and died, he can scarcely remember. That is all among the dim things of childhood and has been forgotten in the brighter pattern life weaves to-day, in the bright facts of being captain of the track team, and holding the interstate record for the high jump, in the all-suffusing brightness of being twenty-one. Yet sometimes, in the pauses of his work, the young man frowned and looked at the ground with an intentness which suggested that even twenty-one might have its problems.

When he had been mowing the better part of an hour, he heard the rattle of a light cart on the road behind him. Supposing that it was his sister coming back from one of her farms, he kept on with his work. The cart stopped at the gate and a merry contralto voice called, "Almost through, Emil?" He dropped his scythe and went toward the fence, wiping his face and neck with his handkerchief. In the cart sat a young woman who wore driving gauntlets and a wide shade hat, trimmed with red poppies. Her face, too, was rather like a poppy, round and brown, with rich color in her cheeks and lips, and her dancing yellow-brown eyes bubbled with gayety. The wind was flapping her big hat and teasing a curl of her chestnut-colored hair. She shook her head at the tall youth.

"What time did you get over here? That's not much of a job for an athlete. Here I've been to town and back. Alexandra lets you sleep late.

Oh, I know! Lou's wife was telling me about the way she spoils you. I was going to give you a lift, if you were done." She gathered up her reins.

"But I will be, in a minute. Please wait for me, Marie," Emil coaxed. "Alexandra sent me to mow our lot, but I've done half a dozen others, you see. Just wait till I finish off the Kourdnas'. By the way, they were Bohemians. Why aren't they up in the Catholic graveyard?"

"Free-thinkers," replied the young woman laconically.

"Lots of the Bohemian boys at the University are," said Emil, taking up his scythe again. "What did you ever burn John Huss for, anyway? It's made an awful row. They still jaw about it in history classes."

"We'd do it right over again, most of us," said the young woman hotly. "Don't they ever teach you in your history classes that you'd all be heathen Turks if it hadn't been for the Bohemians?"

Emil had fallen to mowing. "Oh, there's no denying you're a spunky little bunch, you Czechs," he called back over his shoulder.

Marie Shabata settled herself in her seat and watched the rhythmical movement of the young man's long arms, swinging her foot as if in time to some air that was going through her mind. The minutes passed. Emil mowed vigorously and Marie sat sunning herself and watching the long grass fall. She sat with the ease that belongs to persons of an essentially happy nature, who can find a comfortable spot almost anywhere; who are supple, and quick in adapting themselves to circumstances. After a final swish, Emil snapped the gate and sprang into the cart, holding his scythe well out over the wheel. "There," he sighed. "I gave old man Lee a cut or so, too. Lou's wife needn't talk. I never see Lou's scythe over here."

Marie clucked to her horse. "Oh, you know Annie!" She looked at the young man's bare arms. "How brown you've got since you came home. I wish I had an athlete to mow my orchard. I get wet to my knees when I go down to pick cherries."

"You can have one, any time you want him. Better wait until after it rains." Emil squinted off at the horizon as if he were looking for clouds.

"Will you? Oh, there's a good boy!" She turned her head to him with a quick, bright smile. He felt it rather than saw it. Indeed, he had looked away with the purpose of not seeing it. "I've been up looking at Angélique's wedding clothes," Marie went on, "and I'm so excited I can hardly wait until Sunday. Amédée will be a handsome bridegroom. Is anybody but you going to stand up with him? Well, then it will be a handsome wedding party." She made a droll face at Emil, who flushed.

"Frank," Marie continued, flicking her horse, "is cranky at me because I loaned his saddle to Jan Smirka, and I'm terribly afraid he won't take me to the dance in the evening. Maybe the supper will tempt him. All Angélique's folks are baking for it, and all Amédée's twenty cousins. There will be barrels of beer. If once I get Frank to the supper, I'll see that I stay for the dance. And by the way, Emil, you mustn't dance with me but once or twice. You must dance with all the French girls. It hurts their feelings if you don't. They think you're proud because you've been away to school or something."

Emil sniffed. "How do you know they think that?"

"Well, you didn't dance with them much at Raoul Marcel's party, and I could tell how they took it by the way they looked at you—and at me."

"All right," said Emil shortly, studying the glittering blade of his scythe.

They drove westward toward Norway Creek, and toward a big white house that stood on a hill, several miles across the fields. There were so many sheds and outbuildings grouped about it that the place looked not unlike a tiny village. A stranger, approaching it, could not help noticing the beauty and fruitfulness of the outlying fields. There was something individual about the great farm, a most unusual trimness and care for detail. On either side of the road, for a mile before you reached the foot of the hill, stood tall osage orange hedges, their glossy green marking off the yellow fields. South of the hill, in a low, sheltered swale, surrounded by a mulberry hedge, was the orchard, its fruit trees knee-deep in timothy grass. Any one thereabouts would have told you that this was one of the richest farms on the Divide, and that the farmer was a woman, Alexandra Bergson.

If you go up the hill and enter Alexandra's big house, you will find that it is curiously unfinished and uneven in comfort. One room is papered, carpeted, over-furnished; the next is almost bare. The pleasantest rooms in the house are the kitchen—where Alexandra's three young Swedish girls chatter and cook and pickle and preserve all summer long—and the sitting-room, in which Alexandra has brought together the old homely furniture that the Bergsons used in their first log house, the family portraits, and the few things her mother brought from Sweden.

When you go out of the house into the flower garden, there you feel again the order and fine arrangement manifest all over the great farm; in the fencing and hedging, in the windbreaks and sheds, in the symmetrical pasture ponds, planted with scrub willows to give shade to the cattle in fly-time. There is even a white row of beehives in the orchard, under the walnut trees. You feel that, properly, Alexandra's house is the big out-of-doors, and that it is in the soil that she expresses herself best.

II

*E*mil reached home a little past noon, and when he went into the kitchen Alexandra was already seated at the head of the long table, having dinner with her men, as she always did unless there were visitors. He slipped into his empty place at his sister's right. The three pretty young Swedish girls who did Alexandra's housework were cutting pies, refilling coffee-cups, placing platters of bread and meat and potatoes upon the red tablecloth, and continually getting in each other's way between the table and the stove. To be sure they always wasted a good deal of time getting in each other's way and giggling at each other's mistakes. But, as Alexandra had pointedly told her sisters-in-law, it was to hear them giggle that she kept three young things in her kitchen; the work she could do herself, if it were necessary. These girls, with their long letters from home, their finery, and their love-affairs, afforded her a great deal of entertainment, and they were company for her when Emil was away at school.

Of the youngest girl, Signa, who has a pretty figure, mottled pink cheeks, and yellow hair, Alexandra is very fond, though she keeps a sharp eye upon her. Signa is apt to be skittish at mealtime, when the men are about, and to spill the coffee or upset the cream. It is supposed that Nelse Jensen, one of the six men at the dinner-table, is courting Signa, though he has been so careful not to commit himself that no one in the house, least of all Signa, can tell just how far the matter has progressed. Nelse watches her glumly as she waits upon the table, and in the evening he sits on a bench behind the stove with his *dragharmonika*, playing mournful airs and watching her as she goes about her work. When Alexandra asked Signa whether she thought Nelse was in earnest, the poor child hid her hands under her apron and murmured, "I don't know, ma'm. But he scolds me about everything, like as if he wanted to have me!"

At Alexandra's left sat a very old man, barefoot and wearing a long blue blouse, open at the neck. His shaggy head is scarcely whiter than it was sixteen years ago, but his little blue eyes have become pale and watery, and his ruddy face is withered, like an apple that has clung all winter to the tree. When Ivar lost his land through mismanagement a dozen years ago, Alexandra took him in, and he has been a member of her household ever since. He is too old to work in the fields, but he hitches and unhitches the work-teams and looks after the health of the stock. Sometimes of a winter evening Alexandra calls him into the sitting-room to read the Bible aloud to her, for he still reads very well. He dislikes human habitations, so Alexandra has fitted him up a room in the barn, where he is very comfortable, being near the horses and, as he says, further from temptations. No one has ever found out what his temptations are. In cold weather he sits by the kitchen fire and makes hammocks or mends harness until it is time to go to bed. Then he says his prayers at great length behind the stove, puts on his buffalo-skin coat and goes out to his room in the barn.

Alexandra herself has changed very little. Her figure is fuller, and she has more color. She seems sunnier and more vigorous than she did as a young girl. But she still has the same calmness and deliberation of manner, the same clear eyes, and she still wears her hair in two braids wound round her head. It is so curly that fiery ends escape from the braids and make her head look like one of the big double sunflowers that fringe her vegetable garden. Her face is always tanned in summer, for her sunbonnet is oftener on her arm than on her head. But where her collar falls away from her neck, or where her sleeves are pushed back from her wrist, the skin is of such smoothness and whiteness as none but Swedish women ever possess; skin with the freshness of the snow itself.

Alexandra did not talk much at the table, but she encouraged her men to talk, and she always listened attentively, even when they seemed to be talking foolishly.

To-day Barney Flinn, the big red-headed Irishman who had been with Alexandra for five years and who was actually her foreman, though he had no such title, was grumbling about the new silo she had put up that spring. It happened to be the first silo on the Divide, and Alexandra's neighbors and her men were skeptical about it. "To be sure, if the thing don't work, we'll have plenty of feed without it, indeed," Barney conceded.

Nelse Jensen, Signa's gloomy suitor, had his word. "Lou, he says he wouldn't have no silo on his place if you'd give it to him. He says the feed outen it gives the stock the bloat. He heard of somebody lost four head of horses, feedin' 'em that stuff."

Alexandra looked down the table from one to another. "Well, the only way we can find out is to try. Lou and I have different notions about feeding stock, and that's a good thing. It's bad if all the members of a family think alike. They never get anywhere. Lou can learn by my mistakes and I can learn by his. Isn't that fair, Barney?"

The Irishman laughed. He had no love for Lou, who was always uppish with him and who said that Alexandra paid her hands too much. "I've no thought but to give the thing an honest try, mum. 'Twould be only right, after puttin' so much expense into it. Maybe Emil will come out an' have a look at it wid me." He pushed back his chair, took his hat from the nail, and marched out with Emil, who, with his university ideas, was supposed to have instigated the silo. The other hands followed them, all except old Ivar. He had been depressed throughout the meal and had paid no heed to the talk of the men, even when they mentioned cornstalk bloat, upon which he was sure to have opinions.

"Did you want to speak to me, Ivar?" Alexandra asked as she rose from the table. "Come into the sitting-room."

The old man followed Alexandra, but when she motioned him to a chair he shook his head. She took up her workbasket and waited for him to speak. He stood looking at the carpet, his bushy head bowed, his hands clasped in front of him. Ivar's bandy legs seemed to have grown shorter with years, and they were completely misfitted to his broad, thick body and heavy shoulders.

"Well, Ivar, what is it?" Alexandra asked after she had waited longer than usual.

Ivar had never learned to speak English and his Norwegian was quaint and grave, like the speech of the more old-fashioned people. He always addressed Alexandra in terms of the deepest respect, hoping to set a good example to the kitchen girls, whom he thought too familiar in their manners.

"Mistress," he began faintly, without raising his eyes, "the folk have been looking coldly at me of late. You know there has been talk."

"Talk about what, Ivar?"

"About sending me away; to the asylum."

Alexandra put down her sewing-basket. "Nobody has come to me with such talk," she said decidedly. "Why need you listen? You know I would never consent to such a thing."

Ivar lifted his shaggy head and looked at her out of his little eyes. "They say that you cannot prevent it if the folk complain of me, if your brothers complain to the authorities. They say that your brothers are afraid—God forbid!—that I may do you some injury when my spells are on me. Mistress, how can any one think that?—that I could bite the hand that fed me!" The tears trickled down on the old man's beard.

Alexandra frowned. "Ivar, I wonder at you, that you should come bothering me with such nonsense. I am still running my own house, and other people have nothing to do with either you or me. So long as I am suited with you, there is nothing to be said."

Ivar pulled a red handkerchief out of the breast of his blouse and wiped his eyes and beard. "But I should not wish you to keep me if, as they say, it is against your interests, and if it is hard for you to get hands because I am here."

Alexandra made an impatient gesture, but the old man put out his hand and went on earnestly:

"Listen, mistress, it is right that you should take these things into account. You know that my spells come from God, and that I would not harm any living creature. You believe that every one should worship God in the way revealed to him. But that is not the way of this country. The way here is for all to do alike. I am despised because I do not wear shoes, because I do not cut my hair, and because I have visions. At home, in the old country, there were many like me, who had been touched by God, or who had seen things in the graveyard at night and were different afterward. We thought nothing of it, and let them alone. But here, if a man is different in his feet or in his head, they put him in the asylum. Look at Peter Kralik; when he was a boy, drinking out of a creek, he swallowed a snake, and always after that he could eat only such food as the creature liked, for when he ate anything else, it became enraged and gnawed him. When he felt it whipping about in him, he drank alcohol to stupefy it and get some ease for himself. He could work as good as any man, and his head was clear, but they locked him up for being different in his stomach. That is the way; they have built the asylum for people who are different, and they will not even let us live in the holes with the badgers. Only your great prosperity has protected me so far. If you had had ill-fortune, they would have taken me to Hastings long ago."

As Ivar talked, his gloom lifted. Alexandra had found that she could often break his fasts and long penances by talking to him and letting him pour out the thoughts that troubled him. Sympathy always cleared his mind, and ridicule was poison to him.

"There is a great deal in what you say, Ivar. Like as not they will be wanting to take me to Hastings because I have built a silo; and then I may take you with me. But at present I need you here. Only don't come to me again telling me what people say. Let people go on talking as they like, and we will go on living as we think best. You have been with me now for twelve years, and ˈ have gone to you for advice oftener than I have ever gone to any one. That ought to satisfy you."

Ivar bowed humbly. "Yes, mistress, I shall not trouble you with their talk again. And as for my feet, I have observed your wishes all these years, though you have never questioned me; washing them every night, even in winter."

Alexandra laughed. "Oh, never mind about your feet, Ivar. We can remember when half our neighbors went barefoot in summer. I expect old Mrs. Lee would love to slip her shoes off now sometimes, if she dared. I'm glad I'm not Lou's mother-in-law."

Ivar looked about mysteriously and lowered his voice almost to a whisper. "You know what they have over at Lou's house? A great white tub, like the stone water-troughs in the old country, to wash themselves in. When you sent me over with the strawberries, they were all in town but the old woman Lee and the baby. She took me in and showed me the thing, and she told me it was impossible to wash yourself clean in it, because, in so much water, you could not make a strong suds. So when they fill it up and send her in there, she pretends, and makes a splashing noise. Then, when they are all asleep, she washes herself in a little wooden tub she keeps under her bed."

Alexandra shook with laughter. "Poor old Mrs. Lee! They won't let her wear nightcaps, either. Never mind; when she comes to visit me, she can do all the old things in the old way, and have as much beer as she wants. We'll start an asylum for old-time people, Ivar."

Ivar folded his big handkerchief carefully and thrust it back into his blouse. "This is always the way, mistress. I come to you sorrowing, and you send me away with a light heart. And will you be so good as to tell the Irishman that he is not to work the brown gelding until the sore on its shoulder is healed?"

"That I will. Now go and put Emil's mare to the cart. I am going to drive up to the north quarter to meet the man from town who is to buy my alfalfa hay."

III

Alexandra was to hear more of Ivar's case, however. On Sunday her married brothers came to dinner. She had asked them for that day because Emil, who hated family parties, would be absent, dancing at Amédée Chevalier's wedding, up in the French country. The table was set for company in the dining-room, where highly varnished wood and colored glass and useless pieces of china were conspicuous enough to satisfy the standards of the new prosperity. Alexandra had put herself into the hands of the Hanover furniture dealer, and he had conscientiously done his best to make her dining-room look like his display window. She said frankly that she knew nothing about such things, and she was willing to be governed by the general conviction that the more useless and utterly unusable objects were, the greater their virtue as ornament. That seemed reasonable enough. Since she liked plain things herself, it was all the more necessary to have jars and punch-bowls and candlesticks in the company rooms for people who did appreciate them. Her guests liked to see about them these reassuring emblems of prosperity.

The family party was complete except for Emil, and Oscar's wife who, in the country phrase, "was not going anywhere just now." Oscar sat at the foot of the table and his four tow-headed little boys, aged from twelve to five, were ranged at one side. Neither Oscar nor Lou has changed much; they have simply, as Alexandra said of them long ago, grown to be more and more like themselves. Lou now looks the older of the two; his face is thin and shrewd and wrinkled about the eyes, while Oscar's is thick and dull. For all his dullness, however, Oscar makes more money than his brother, which adds to Lou's sharpness and uneasiness and tempts him to make a show. The trouble with Lou is that he is tricky, and his neighbors have found out that, as Ivar says, he has not a fox's face for nothing. Politics being the natural field for such talents, he neglects his farm to attend conventions and to run for county offices.

Lou's wife, formerly Annie Lee, has grown to look curiously like her husband. Her face has become longer, sharper, more aggressive. She wears her yellow hair in a high pompadour, and is bedecked with rings and

chains and "beauty pins." Her tight, high-heeled shoes give her an awkward walk, and she is always more or less preoccupied with her clothes. As
she sat at the table, she kept telling her youngest daughter to "be careful
now, and not drop anything on mother."

The conversation at the table was all in English. Oscar's wife,
from the malaria district of Missouri, was ashamed of marrying a foreigner,
and his boys do not understand a word of Swedish. Annie and Lou sometimes speak Swedish at home, but Annie is almost as much afraid of being
"caught" at it as ever her mother was of being caught barefoot. Oscar still
has a thick accent, but Lou speaks like anybody from Iowa.

"When I was in Hastings to attend the convention," he was
saying, "I saw the superintendent of the asylum, and I was telling him about
Ivar's symptoms. He says Ivar's case is one of the most dangerous kind, and
it's a wonder he hasn't done something violent before this."

Alexandra laughed good-humoredly. "Oh, nonsense, Lou! The
doctors would have us all crazy if they could. Ivar's queer, certainly, but he
has more sense than half the hands I hire."

Lou flew at his fried chicken. "Oh, I guess the doctor knows his
business, Alexandra. He was very much surprised when I told him how
you'd put up with Ivar. He says he's likely to set fire to the barn any night,
or to take after you and the girls with an axe."

Little Signa, who was waiting on the table, giggled and fled to
the kitchen. Alexandra's eyes twinkled. "That was too much for Signa, Lou.
We all know that Ivar's perfectly harmless. The girls would as soon expect
me to chase them with an axe."

Lou flushed and signaled to his wife. "All the same, the neighbors will be having a say about it before long. He may burn anybody's barn.
It's only necessary for one property-owner in the township to make complaint, and he'll be taken up by force. You'd better send him yourself and
not have any hard feelings."

Alexandra helped one of her little nephews to gravy. "Well,
Lou, if any of the neighbors try that, I'll have myself appointed Ivar's
guardian and take the case to court, that's all. I am perfectly satisfied with
him."

"Pass the preserves, Lou," said Annie in a warning tone. She had
reasons for not wishing her husband to cross Alexandra too openly. "But
don't you sort of hate to have people see him around here, Alexandra?" she
went on with persuasive smoothness. "He is a disgraceful object, and you're
fixed up so nice now. It sort of makes people distant with you, when they

never know when they'll hear him scratching about. My girls are afraid as death of him, aren't you, Milly, dear?"

Milly was fifteen, fat and jolly and pompadoured, with a creamy complexion, square white teeth, and a short upper lip. She looked like her grandmother Bergson, and had her comfortable and comfort-loving nature. She grinned at her aunt, with whom she was a great deal more at ease than she was with her mother. Alexandra winked a reply.

"Milly needn't be afraid of Ivar. She's an especial favorite of his. In my opinion Ivar has just as much right to his own way of dressing and thinking as we have. But I'll see that he doesn't bother other people. I'll keep him at home, so don't trouble any more about him, Lou. I've been wanting to ask you about your new bathtub. How does it work?"

Annie came to the fore to give Lou time to recover himself. "Oh, it works something grand! I can't keep him out of it. He washes himself all over three times a week now, and uses all the hot water. I think it's weakening to stay in as long as he does. You ought to have one, Alexandra."

"I'm thinking of it. I might have one put in the barn for Ivar, if it will ease people's minds. But before I get a bathtub, I'm going to get a piano for Milly."

Oscar, at the end of the table, looked up from his plate. "What does Milly want of a pianny? What's the matter with her organ? She can make some use of that, and play in church."

Annie looked flustered. She had begged Alexandra not to say anything about this plan before Oscar, who was apt to be jealous of what his sister did for Lou's children. Alexandra did not get on with Oscar's wife at all. "Milly can play in church just the same, and she'll still play on the organ. But practising on it so much spoils her touch. Her teacher says so," Annie brought out with spirit.

Oscar rolled his eyes. "Well, Milly must have got on pretty good if she's got past the organ. I know plenty of grown folks that ain't," he said bluntly.

Annie threw up her chin. "She has got on good, and she's going to play for her commencement when she graduates in town next year."

"Yes," said Alexandra firmly, "I think Milly deserves a piano. All the girls around here have been taking lessons for years, but Milly is the only one of them who can ever play anything when you ask her. I'll tell you when I first thought I would like to give you a piano, Milly, and that was when you learned that book of old Swedish songs that your grandfather used to sing. He had a sweet tenor voice, and when he was a young man he loved to sing. I can remember hearing him singing with the sailors down in the shipyard, when I was no bigger than Stella here," pointing to Annie's younger daughter.

Milly and Stella both looked through the door into the sitting-room, where a crayon portrait of John Bergson hung on the wall. Alexandra had had it made from a little photograph, taken for his friends just before he left Sweden; a slender man of thirty-five, with soft hair curling about his high forehead, a drooping mustache, and wondering, sad eyes that looked forward into the distance, as if they already beheld the New World.

After dinner Lou and Oscar went to the orchard to pick cher-ries—they had neither of them had the patience to grow an orchard of their own—and Annie went down to gossip with Alexandra's kitchen girls while they washed the dishes. She could always find out more about Alexandra's domestic economy from the prattling maids than from Alexandra herself, and what she discovered she used to her own advantage with Lou. On the Divide, farmers' daughters no longer went out into service, so Alexandra got her girls from Sweden, by paying their fare over. They stayed with her until they married, and were replaced by sisters or cousins from the old country.

Alexandra took her three nieces into the flower garden. She was fond of the little girls, especially of Milly, who came to spend a week with her aunt now and then, and read aloud to her from the old books about the house, or listened to stories about the early days on the Divide. While they were walking among the flower beds, a buggy drove up the hill and stopped in front of the gate. A man got out and stood talking to the driver. The little girls were delighted at the advent of a stranger, some one from very far away, they knew by his clothes, his gloves, and the sharp, pointed cut of his dark beard. The girls fell behind their aunt and peeped out at him from among the castor beans. The stranger came up to the gate and stood holding his hat in his hand, smiling, while Alexandra advanced slowly to meet him. As she approached he spoke in a low, pleasant voice.

"Don't you know me, Alexandra? I would have known you, anywhere."

Alexandra shaded her eyes with her hand. Suddenly she took a quick step forward. "Can it be!" she exclaimed with feeling; "can it be that it is Carl Linstrum? Why, Carl, it is!" She threw out both her hands and caught him across the gate. "Sadie, Milly, run tell your father and Uncle Oscar that our old friend Carl Linstrum is here. Be quick! Why, Carl, how did it happen? I can't believe this!" Alexandra shook the tears from her eyes and laughed.

The stranger nodded to his driver, dropped his suitcase inside the fence, and opened the gate. "Then you are glad to see me, and you can put me up overnight? I couldn't go through this country without stopping off to have a look at you. How little you have changed! Do you know, I was sure it would be like that. You simply couldn't be different. How fine you are!" He stepped back and looked at her admiringly.

Alexandra blushed and laughed again. "But you yourself, Carl—with that beard—how could I have known you? You went away a little boy." She reached for his suitcase and when he intercepted her she threw up her hands. "You see, I give myself away. I have only women come to visit me, and I do not know how to behave. Where is your trunk?"

"It's in Hanover. I can stay only a few days. I am on my way to the coast."

They started up the path. "A few days? After all these years!" Alexandra shook her finger at him. "See this, you have walked into a trap. You do not get away so easy." She put her hand affectionately on his shoulder. "You owe me a visit for the sake of old times. Why must you go to the coast at all?"

"Oh, I must! I am a fortune hunter. From Seattle I go on to Alaska."

"Alaska?" She looked at him in astonishment. "Are you going to paint the Indians?"

"Paint?" the young man frowned. "Oh! I'm not a painter, Alexandra. I'm an engraver. I have nothing to do with painting."

"But on my parlor wall I have the paintings—"

He interrupted nervously. "Oh, watercolor sketches—done for amusement. I sent them to remind you of me, not because they were good. What a wonderful place you have made of this, Alexandra." He turned and looked back at the wide, map-like prospect of field and hedge and pasture. "I would never have believed it could be done. I'm disappointed in my own eye, in my imagination."

At this moment Lou and Oscar came up the hill from the orchard. They did not quicken their pace when they saw Carl; indeed, they did not openly look in his direction. They advanced distrustfully, and as if they wished the distance were longer.

Alexandra beckoned to them. "They think I am trying to fool them. Come, boys, it's Carl Linstrum, our old Carl!"

Lou gave the visitor a quick, sidelong glance and thrust out his hand. "Glad to see you." Oscar followed with "How d' do." Carl could not tell whether their offishness came from unfriendliness or from embarrassment. He and Alexandra led the way to the porch.

"Carl," Alexandra explained, "is on his way to Seattle. He is going to Alaska."

Oscar studied the visitor's yellow shoes. "Got business there?" he asked.

Carl laughed. "Yes, very pressing business. I'm going there to get rich. Engraving's a very interesting profession, but a man never makes any money at it. So I'm going to try the gold-fields."

Alexandra felt that this was a tactful speech, and Lou looked up with some interest. "Ever done anything in that line before?"

"No, but I'm going to join a friend of mine who went out from New York and has done well. He has offered to break me in."

"Turrible cold winters, there, I hear," remarked Oscar. "I thought people went up there in the spring."

"They do. But my friend is going to spend the winter in Seattle and I am going to stay with him there and learn something about prospecting before we start north next year."

Lou looked skeptical. "Let's see, how long have you been away from here?"

"Sixteen years. You ought to remember that, Lou, for you were married just after we went away."

"Going to stay with us some time?" Oscar asked.

"A few days, if Alexandra can keep me."

"I expect you'll be wanting to see your old place," Lou observed more cordially. "You won't hardly know it. But there's a few chunks of your old sod house left. Alexandra wouldn't never let Frank Shabata plough over it."

Annie Lee, who, ever since the visitor was announced, had been touching up her hair and settling her lace and wishing she had worn another dress, now emerged with her three daughters and introduced them. She was greatly impressed by Carl's urban appearance, and in her excitement talked very loud and threw her head about. "And you ain't married yet? At your age, now! Think of that! You'll have to wait for Milly. Yes, we've got a boy, too. The youngest. He's at home with his grandma. You must come over to see mother and hear Milly play. She's the musician of the family. She does pyrography, too. That's burnt wood, you know. You wouldn't believe what she can do with her poker. Yes, she goes to school in town, and she is the youngest in her class by two years."

Milly looked uncomfortable and Carl took her hand again. He liked her creamy skin and happy, innocent eyes, and he could see that her mother's way of talking distressed her. "I'm sure she's a clever little girl," he murmured, looking at her thoughtfully. "Let me see—Ah, it's your mother that she looks like, Alexandra. Mrs. Bergson must have looked just like this when she was a little girl. Does Milly run about over the country as you and Alexandra used to, Annie?"

Milly's mother protested. "Oh, my, no! Things has changed since we was girls. Milly has it very different. We are going to rent the place and move into town as soon as the girls are old enough to go out into company. A good many are doing that here now. Lou is going into business."

Lou grinned. "That's what she says. You better go get your things on. Ivar's hitching up," he added, turning to Annie.

Young farmers seldom address their wives by Dame. It is always "you," or "she."

Having got his wife out of the way, Lou sat down on the step and began to whittle. "Well, what do folks in New York think of William Jennings Bryan?" Lou began to bluster, as he always did when he talked politics. "We gave Wall Street a scare in ninety-six, all right, and we're fixing another to hand them. Silver wasn't the only issue," he nodded mysteriously. "There's a good many things got to be changed. The West is going to make itself heard."

Carl laughed. "But, surely, it did do that, if nothing else."

Lou's thin face reddened up to the roots of his bristly hair. "Oh, we've only begun. We're waking up to a sense of our responsibilities, out here, and we ain't afraid, neither. You fellows back there must be a tame lot. If you had any nerve you'd get together and march down to Wall Street and blow it up. Dynamite it, I mean," with a threatening nod.

He was so much in earnest that Carl scarcely knew how to answer him. "That would be a waste of powder. The same business would go on in another street. The street doesn't matter. But what have you fellows out here got to kick about? You have the only safe place there is. Morgan himself couldn't touch you. One only has to drive through this country to see that you're all as rich as barons."

"We have a good deal more to say than we had when we were poor," said Lou threateningly. "We're getting on to a whole lot of things."

As Ivar drove a double carriage up to the gate, Annie came out in a hat that looked like the model of a battleship. Carl rose and took her down to the carriage, while Lou lingered for a word with his sister.

"What do you suppose he's come for?" he asked, jerking his head toward the gate.

"Why, to pay us a visit. I've been begging him to for years."

Oscar looked at Alexandra. "He didn't let you know he was coming?"

"No. Why should he? I told him to come at any time."

Lou shrugged his shoulders. "He doesn't seem to have done much for himself. Wandering around this way!"

Oscar spoke solemnly, as from the depths of a cavern. "He never was much account."

Alexandra left them and hurried down to the gate where Annie was rattling on to Carl about her new dining-room furniture. "You must bring Mr. Linstrum over real soon, only be sure to telephone me first," she called back, as Carl helped her into the carriage. Old Ivar, his white head bare, stood holding the horses. Lou came down the path and climbed into the front seat, took up the reins, and drove off without saying anything further to any one. Oscar picked up his youngest boy and trudged off down the road, the other three trotting after him. Carl, holding the gate open for Alexandra, began to laugh. "Up and coming on the Divide, eh, Alexandra?" he cried gayly.

IV

Carl had changed, Alexandra felt, much less than one might have expected. He had not become a trim, self-satisfied city man. There was still something homely and wayward and definitely personal about him. Even his clothes, his Norfolk coat and his very high collars, were a little unconventional. He seemed to shrink into himself as he used to do; to hold himself away from things, as if he were afraid of being hurt. In short, he was more self-conscious than a man of thirty-five is expected to be. He looked older than his years and not very strong. His black hair, which still hung in a triangle over his pale forehead, was thin at the crown, and there were fine, relentless lines about his eyes.

His back, with its high, sharp shoulders, looked like the back of an over-worked German professor off on his holiday. His face was intelligent, sensitive, unhappy.

That evening after supper, Carl and Alexandra were sitting by the clump of castor beans in the middle of the flower garden. The gravel paths glittered in the moonlight, and below them the fields lay white and still.

"Do you know, Alexandra," he was saying, "I've been thinking how strangely things work out. I've been away engraving other men's pictures, and you've stayed at home and made your own." He pointed with his cigar toward the sleeping landscape. "How in the world have you done it? How have your neighbors done it?"

"We hadn't any of us much to do with it, Carl. The land did it. It had its little joke. It pretended to be poor because nobody knew how to work it right; and then, all at once, it worked itself. It woke up out of its sleep and stretched itself, and it was so big, so rich, that we suddenly found we were rich, just from sitting still. As for me, you remember when I began to buy land. For years after that I was always squeezing and borrowing until I was ashamed to show my face in the banks. And then, all at once, men began to come to me offering to lend me money—and I didn't need it! Then I went ahead and built this house. I really built it for Emil. I want you to see Emil, Carl. He is so different from the rest of us!"

"How different?"

"Oh, you'll see! I'm sure it was to have sons like Emil, and to give them a chance, that father left the old country. It's curious, too; on the outside Emil is just like an American boy—he graduated from the State University in June, you know—but underneath he is more Swedish than any of us. Sometimes he is so like father that he frightens me; he is so violent in his feelings like that."

"Is he going to farm here with you?"

"He shall do whatever he wants to," Alexandra declared warmly. "He is going to have a chance, a whole chance; that's what I've worked for. Sometimes he talks about studying law, and sometimes, just lately, he's been talking about going out into the sand hills and taking up more land. He has his sad times, like father. But I hope he won't do that. We have land enough, at last!" Alexandra laughed.

"How about Lou and Oscar? They've done well, haven't they?"

"Yes, very well; but they are different, and now that they have farms of their own I do not see so much of them. We divided the land equally when Lou married. They have their own way of doing things, and they do not altogether like my way, I am afraid. Perhaps they think me too independent. But I have had to think for myself a good many years and am not likely to change. On the whole, though, we take as much comfort in each other as most brothers and sisters do. And I am very fond of Lou's oldest daughter."

"I think I liked the old Lou and Oscar better, and they probably feel the same about me. I even, if you can keep a secret"—Carl leaned forward and touched her arm, smiling—"I even think I liked the old country better. This is all very splendid in its way, but there was something about this country when it was a wild old beast that has haunted me all these years. Now, when I come back to all this milk and honey, I feel like the old German song, 'Wo bist du, wo bist du, mein geliebtest Land?'—Do you ever feel like that, I wonder?"

"Yes, sometimes, when I think about father and mother and those who are gone; so many of our old neighbors." Alexandra paused and looked up thoughtfully at the stars. "We can remember the graveyard when it was wild prairie, Carl, and now—"

"And now the old story has begun to write itself over there," said Carl softly. "Isn't it queer: there are only two or three human stories, and they go on repeating themselves as fiercely as if they had never happened before; like the larks in this country, that have been singing the same five notes over for thousands of years."

"Oh, yes! The young people, they live so hard. And yet I sometimes envy them. There is my little neighbor, now; the people who bought your old place. I wouldn't have sold it to any one else, but I was always fond of that girl. You must remember her, little Marie Tovesky, from Omaha, who used to visit here? When she was eighteen she ran away from the convent school and got married, crazy child! She came out here a bride, with her father and husband. He had nothing, and the old man was willing to buy them a place and set them up. Your farm took her fancy, and I was glad to have her so near me. I've never been sorry, either. I even try to get along with Frank on her account."

"Is Frank her husband?"

"Yes. He's one of these wild fellows. Most Bohemians are good-natured, but Frank thinks we don't appreciate him here, I guess. He's jealous about everything, his farm and his horses and his pretty wife. Everybody likes her, just the same as when she was little. Sometimes I go up to the Catholic church with Emil, and it's funny to see Marie standing there laughing and shaking hands with people, looking so excited and gay, with Frank sulking behind her as if he could eat everybody alive. Frank's not a bad neighbor, but to get on with him you've got to make a fuss over him and act as if you thought he was a very important person all the time, and different from other people. I find it hard to keep that up from one year's end to another."

"I shouldn't think you'd be very successful at that kind of thing, Alexandra." Carl seemed to find the idea amusing.

"Well," said Alexandra firmly, "I do the best I can, on Marie's account. She has it hard enough, anyway. She's too young and pretty for this sort of life. We're all ever so much older and slower. But she's the kind that won't be downed easily. She'll work all day and go to a Bohemian wedding and dance all night, and drive the hay wagon for a cross man next morning. I could stay by a job, but I never had the go in me that she has, when I was going my best. I'll have to take you over to see her to-morrow."

Carl dropped the end of his cigar softly among the castor beans and sighed. "Yes, I suppose I must see the old place. I'm cowardly about things that remind me of myself. It took courage to come at all, Alexandra. I wouldn't have, if I hadn't wanted to see you very, very much."

Alexandra looked at him with her calm, deliberate eyes. "Why do you dread things like that, Carl?" she asked earnestly. "Why are you dissatisfied with yourself?"

Her visitor winced. "How direct you are, Alexandra! Just like you used to be. Do I give myself away so quickly? Well, you see, for one thing, there's nothing to look forward to in my profession. Wood-engraving is the only thing I care about, and that had gone out before I began. Everything's cheap metal work nowadays, touching up miserable photographs, forcing up poor drawings, and spoiling good ones. I'm absolutely sick of it all." Carl frowned. "Alexandra, all the way out from New York I've been planning how I could deceive you and make you think me a very enviable fellow, and here I am telling you the truth the first night. I waste a lot of time pretending to people, and the joke of it is, I don't think I ever deceive any one. There are too many of my kind; people know us on sight."

Carl paused. Alexandra pushed her hair back from her brow with a puzzled, thoughtful gesture. "You see," he went on calmly, "measured by your standards here, I'm a failure. I couldn't buy even one of your cornfields. I've enjoyed a great many things, but I've got nothing to show for it all."

"But you show for it yourself, Carl. I'd rather have had your freedom than my land."

Carl shook his head mournfully. "Freedom so often means that one isn't needed anywhere. Here you are an individual, you have a background of your own, you would be missed. But off there in the cities there are thousands of rolling stones like me. We are all alike; we have no ties, we know nobody, we own nothing. When one of us dies, they scarcely know where to bury him. Our landlady and the delicatessen man are our mourners, and we leave nothing behind us but a frock-coat and a fiddle, or an easel, or a typewriter, or whatever tool we got our living by. All we have ever managed to do is to pay our rent, the exorbitant rent that one has to pay for a few square feet of space near the heart of things. We have no house, no place, no people of our own. We live in the streets, in the parks, in the theatres. We sit in restaurants and concert halls and look about at the hundreds of our own kind and shudder."

Alexandra was silent. She sat looking at the silver spot the moon made on the surface of the pond down in the pasture. He knew that she understood what he meant. At last she said slowly, "And yet I would rather have Emil grow up like that than like his two brothers. We pay a high rent, too, though we pay differently. We grow hard and heavy here. We don't move lightly and easily as you do, and our minds get stiff. If the world were no wider than my cornfields, if there were not something beside this, I wouldn't feel that it was much worth while to work. No, I would rather have Emil like you than like them. I felt that as soon as you came."

"I wonder why you feel like that?" Carl mused.

"I don't know. Perhaps I am like Carrie Jensen, the sister of one of my hired men. She had never been out of the cornfields, and a few years ago she got despondent and said life was just the same thing over and over, and she didn't see the use of it. After she had tried to kill herself once or twice, her folks got worried and sent her over to Iowa to visit some relations. Ever since she's come back she's been perfectly cheerful, and she says she's contented to live and work in a world that's so big and interesting. She said that anything as big as the bridges over the Platte and the Missouri reconciled her. And it's what goes on in the world that reconciles me."

V

*A*lexandra did not find time to go to her neighbor's the next day, nor the next. It was a busy season on the farm, with the corn-plowing going on, and even Emil was in the field with a team and cultivator. Carl went about over the farms with Alexandra in the morning, and in the afternoon and evening they found a great deal to talk about. Emil, for all his track practice, did not stand up under farmwork very well, and by night he was too tired to talk or even to practise on his cornet.

On Wednesday morning Carl got up before it was light, and stole downstairs and out of the kitchen door just as old Ivar was making his morning ablutions at the pump. Carl nodded to him and hurried up the draw, past the garden, and into the pasture where the milking cows used to be kept.

The dawn in the east looked like the light from some great fire that was burning under the edge of the world. The color was reflected in the globules of dew that sheathed the short gray pasture grass. Carl walked rapidly until he came to the crest of the second hill, where the Bergson pasture joined the one that had belonged to his father. There he sat down and waited for the sun to rise. It was just there that he and Alexandra used to do their milking together, he on his side of the fence, she on hers. He could remember exactly how she looked when she came over the close-cropped grass, her skirts pinned up, her head bare, a bright tin pail in either hand, and the milky light of the early morning all about her. Even as a boy he used to feel, when he saw her coming with her free step, her upright head and calm shoulders, that she looked as if she had walked straight out of the morning itself. Since then, when he had happened to see the sun come up in the country or on the water, he had often remembered the young Swedish girl and her milking pails.

Carl sat musing until the sun leaped above the prairie, and in the grass about him all the small creatures of day began to tune their tiny instruments. Birds and insects without number began to chirp, to twitter, to snap and whistle, to make all manner of fresh shrill noises. The pasture was flooded with light; every clump of ironweed and snow-on-the-mountain threw a long shadow, and the golden light seemed to be rippling through the curly grass like the tide racing in.

He crossed the fence into the pasture that was now the Shabatas' and continued his walk toward the pond. He had not gone far, however, when he discovered that he was not the only person abroad. In the draw below, his gun in his hands, was Emil, advancing cautiously, with a young woman beside him. They were moving softly, keeping close together, and Carl knew that they expected to find ducks on the pond. At the moment when they came in sight of the bright spot of water, he heard a whirr of wings and the ducks shot up into the air. There was a sharp crack from the gun, and five of the birds fell to the ground. Emil and his companion laughed delightedly, and Emil ran to pick them up. When he came back, dangling the ducks by their feet, Marie held her apron and he dropped them into it. As she stood looking down at them, her face changed. She took up one of the birds, a rumpled ball of feathers with the blood dripping slowly from its mouth, and looked at the live color that still burned on its plumage.

As she let it fall, she cried in distress, "Oh, Emil, why did you?"

"I like that!" the boy exclaimed indignantly. "Why, Marie, you asked me to come yourself."

"Yes, yes, I know," she said tearfully, "but I didn't think. I hate to see them when they are first shot. They were having such a good time, and we've spoiled it all for them."

Emil gave a rather sore laugh. "I should say we had! I'm not going hunting with you any more. You're as bad as Ivar. Here, let me take them." He snatched the ducks out of her apron.

"Don't be cross, Emil. Only—Ivar's right about wild things. They're too happy to kill. You can tell just how they felt when they flew up. They were scared, but they didn't really think anything could hurt them. No, we won't do that any more."

"All right," Emil assented. "I'm sorry I made you feel bad." As he looked down into her tearful eyes, there was a curious, sharp young bitterness in his own.

Carl watched them as they moved slowly down the draw. They had not seen him at all. He had not overheard much of their dialogue, but he felt the import of it. It made him, somehow, unreasonably mournful to find two young things abroad in the pasture in the early morning. He decided that he needed his breakfast.

VI

*A*t dinner that day Alexandra said she thought they must really manage to go over to the Shabatas' that afternoon. "It's not often I let three days go by without seeing Marie. She will think I have forsaken her, now that my old friend has come back."

After the men had gone back to work, Alexandra put on a white dress and her sun-hat, and she and Carl set forth across the fields. "You see we have kept up the old path, Carl. It has been so nice for me to feel that there was a friend at the other end of it again."

Carl smiled a little ruefully. "All the same, I hope it hasn't been *quite* the same."

Alexandra looked at him with surprise. "Why, no, of course not. Not the same. She could not very well take your place, if that's what you mean. I'm friendly with all my neighbors, I hope. But Marie is really a companion, some one I can talk to quite frankly. You wouldn't want me to be more lonely than I have been, would you?"

Carl laughed and pushed back the triangular lock of hair with the edge of his hat. "Of course I don't. I ought to be thankful that this path hasn't been worn by—well, by friends with more pressing errands than your little Bohemian is likely to have." He paused to give Alexandra his hand as she stepped over the stile. "Are you the least bit disappointed in our coming together again?" he asked abruptly. "Is it the way you hoped it would be?"

Alexandra smiled at this. "Only better. When I've thought about your coming, I've sometimes been a little afraid of it. You have lived where things move so fast, and everything is slow here; the people slowest of all. Our lives are like the years, all made up of weather and crops and cows. How you hated cows!" She shook her head and laughed to herself.

"I didn't when we milked together. I walked up to the pasture corners this morning. I wonder whether I shall ever be able to tell you all that I was thinking about up there. It's a strange thing, Alexandra; I find it easy to be frank with you about everything under the sun except—yourself!"

"You are afraid of hurting my feelings, perhaps." Alexandra looked at him thoughtfully.

"No, I'm afraid of giving you a shock. You've seen yourself for so long in the dull minds of the people about you, that if I were to tell you how you seem to me, it would startle you. But you must see that you astonish me. You must feel when people admire you."

Alexandra blushed and laughed with some confusion. "I felt that you were pleased with me, if you mean that."

"And you've felt when other people were pleased with you?" he insisted.

"Well, sometimes. The men in town, at the banks and the county offices, seem glad to see me. I think, myself, it is more pleasant to do business with people who are clean and healthy-looking," she admitted blandly.

Carl gave a little chuckle as he opened the Shabatas' gate for her. "Oh, do you?" he asked dryly.

There was no sign of life about the Shabatas' house except a big yellow cat, sunning itself on the kitchen doorstep.

Alexandra took the path that led to the orchard. "She often sits there and sews. I didn't telephone her we were coming, because I didn't want her to go to work and bake cake and freeze ice-cream. She'll always make a party if you give her the least excuse. Do you recognize the apple trees, Carl?"

Linstrum looked about him. "I wish I had a dollar for every bucket of water I've carried for those trees. Poor father, he was an easy man, but he was perfectly merciless when it came to watering the orchard."

"That's one thing I like about Germans; they make an orchard grow if they can't make anything else. I'm so glad these trees belong to some one who takes comfort in them. When I rented this place, the tenants never kept the orchard up, and Emil and I used to come over and take care of it ourselves. It needs mowing now. There she is, down in the corner. Maria-a-a!" she called.

A recumbent figure started up from the grass and came running toward them through the flickering screen of light and shade.

"Look at her! Isn't she like a little brown rabbit?" Alexandra laughed.

Marie ran up panting and threw her arms about Alexandra. "Oh, I had begun to think you were not coming at all, maybe. I knew you were so busy. Yes, Emil told me about Mr. Linstrum being here. Won't you come up to the house?"

"Why not sit down there in your corner? Carl wants to see the orchard. He kept all these trees alive for years, watering them with his own back."

Marie turned to Carl. "Then I'm thankful to you, Mr. Linstrum. We'd never have bought the place if it hadn't been for this orchard, and then I wouldn't have had Alexandra, either." She gave Alexandra's arm a little squeeze as she walked beside her. "How nice your dress smells, Alexandra; you put rosemary leaves in your chest, like I told you."

She led them to the northwest corner of the orchard, sheltered on one side by a thick mulberry hedge and bordered on the other by a wheatfield, just beginning to yellow. In this corner the ground dipped a little, and the bluegrass, which the weeds had driven out in the upper part of the orchard, grew thick and luxuriant. Wild roses were flaming in the tufts of bunchgrass along the fence. Under a white mulberry tree there was an old wagon-seat. Beside it lay a book and a workbasket.

"You must have the seat, Alexandra. The grass would stain your dress," the hostess insisted. She dropped down on the ground at Alexandra's side and tucked her feet under her. Carl sat at a little distance from the two women, his back to the wheatfield, and watched them. Alexandra took off her shade-hat and threw it on the ground. Marie picked it up and played with the white ribbons, twisting them about her brown fingers as she talked. They made a pretty picture in the strong sunlight, the leafy pattern surrounding them like a net; the Swedish woman so white and gold, kindly and amused, but armored in calm, and the alert brown one, her full lips parted, points of yellow light dancing in her eyes as she laughed and chattered. Carl had never forgotten little Marie Tovesky's eyes, and he was glad to have an opportunity to study them. The brown iris, he found, was curiously slashed with yellow, the color of sunflower honey, or of old amber. In each eye one of these streaks must have been larger than the others, for the effect was that of two dancing points of light, two little yellow bubbles, such as rise in a glass of champagne. Sometimes they seemed like the sparks from a forge. She seemed so easily excited, to kindle with a fierce little flame if one but breathed upon her. "What a waste," Carl reflected. "She ought to be doing all that for a sweetheart. How awkwardly things come about!"

It was not very long before Marie sprang up out of the grass again. "Wait a moment. I want to show you something." She ran away and disappeared behind the low-growing apple trees.

"What a charming creature," Carl murmured. "I don't wonder that her husband is jealous. But can't she walk? Does she always run?"

Alexandra nodded. "Always. I don't see many people, but I don't believe there are many like her, anywhere."

Marie came back with a branch she had broken from an apricot tree, laden with pale-yellow, pink-cheeked fruit. She dropped it beside Carl. "Did you plant those, too? They are such beautiful little trees."

Carl fingered the blue-green leaves, porous like blotting-paper and shaped like birch leaves, hung on waxen red stems. "Yes, I think I did. Are these the circus trees, Alexandra?"

"Shall I tell her about them?" Alexandra asked. "Sit down like a good girl, Marie, and don't ruin my poor hat, and I'll tell you a story. A long time ago, when Carl and I were, say, sixteen and twelve, a circus came to Hanover and we went to town in our wagon, with Lou and Oscar, to see the parade. We hadn't money enough to go to the circus. We followed the parade out to the circus grounds and hung around until the show began and the crowd went inside the tent. Then Lou was afraid we looked foolish standing outside in the pasture, so we went back to Hanover feeling very sad. There was a man in the streets selling apricots, and we had never seen any before. He had driven down from somewhere up in the French country, and he was selling them twenty-five cents a peck. We had a little money our fathers had given us for candy, and I bought two pecks and Carl bought one. They cheered us a good deal, and we saved all the seeds and planted them. Up to the time Carl went away, they hadn't borne at all."

"And now he's come back to eat them," cried Marie, nodding at Carl. "That *is* a good story. I can remember you a little, Mr. Linstrum. I used to see you in Hanover sometimes, when Uncle Joe took me to town. I remember you because you were always buying pencils and tubes of paint at the drug store. Once, when my uncle left me at the store, you drew a lot of little birds and flowers for me on a piece of wrapping-paper. I kept them for a long while. I thought you were very romantic because you could draw and had such black eyes."

Carl smiled. "Yes, I remember that time. Your uncle bought you some kind of a mechanical toy, a Turkish lady sitting on an ottoman and smoking a hookah, wasn't it? And she turned her head backwards and forwards."

"Oh, yes! Wasn't she splendid! I knew well enough I ought not to tell Uncle Joe I wanted it, for he had just come back from the saloon and was feeling good. You remember how he laughed? She tickled him, too. But when we got home, my aunt scolded him for buying toys when she needed so many things. We wound our lady up every night, and when she began to move her head my aunt used to laugh as hard as any of us. It was a music-box, you know, and the Turkish lady played a tune while she smoked. That was how she made you feel so jolly. As I remember her, she was lovely, and had a gold crescent on her turban."

Half an hour later, as they were leaving the house, Carl and Alexandra were met in the path by a strapping fellow in overalls and a blue shirt. He was breathing hard, as if he had been running, and was muttering to himself.

Marie ran forward, and, taking him by the arm, gave him a little push toward her guests. "Frank, this is Mr. Linstrum."

Frank took off his broad straw hat and nodded to Alexandra. When he spoke to Carl, he showed a fine set of white teeth. He was burned a dull red down to his neckband, and there was a heavy three-days' stubble on his face. Even in his agitation he was handsome, but he looked a rash and violent man.

Barely saluting the callers, he turned at once to his wife and began, in an outraged tone, "I have to leave my team to drive the old woman Hiller's hogs out-a my wheat. I go to take dat old woman to de court if she ain't careful, I tell you!"

His wife spoke soothingly. "But, Frank, she has only her lame boy to help her. She does the best she can."

Alexandra looked at the excited man and offered a suggestion. "Why don't you go over there some afternoon and hog-tight her fences? You'd save time for yourself in the end."

Frank's neck stiffened. "Not-a-much, I won't. I keep my hogs home. Other peoples can do like me. See? If that Louis can mend shoes, he can mend fence."

"Maybe," said Alexandra placidly; "but I've found it sometimes pays to mend other people's fences. Good-bye, Marie. Come to see me soon."

Alexandra walked firmly down the path and Carl followed her.

Frank went into the house and threw himself on the sofa, his face to the wall, his clenched fist on his hip. Marie, having seen her guests off, came in and put her hand coaxingly on his shoulder.

"Poor Frank! You've run until you've made your head ache, now haven't you? Let me make you some coffee."

"What else am I to do?" he cried hotly in Bohemian. "Am I to let any old woman's hogs root up my wheat? Is that what I work myself to death for?"

"Don't worry about it, Frank. I'll speak to Mrs. Hiller again. But, really, she almost cried last time they got out, she was so sorry."

Frank bounced over on his other side. "That's it; you always side with them against me. They all know it. Anybody here feels free to borrow the mower and break it, or turn their hogs in on me. They know you won't care!"

Marie hurried away to make his coffee. When she came back, he was fast asleep. She sat down and looked at him for a long while, very thoughtfully. When the kitchen clock struck six she went out to get supper, closing the door gently behind her. She was always sorry for Frank when he worked himself into one of these rages, and she was sorry to have him rough and quarrelsome with his neighbors. She was perfectly aware that the neighbors had a good deal to put up with, and that they bore with Frank for her sake.

VII

Marie's father, Albert Tovesky, was one of the more intelligent Bohemians who came West in the early seventies. He settled in Omaha and became a leader and adviser among his people there. Marie was his youngest child, by a second wife, and was the apple of his eye. She was barely sixteen, and was in the graduating class of the Omaha High School, when Frank Shabata arrived from the old country and set all the Bohemian girls in a flutter. He was easily the buck of the beer-gardens, and on Sunday he was a sight to see, with his silk hat and tucked shirt and blue frock-coat, wearing gloves and carrying a little wisp of a yellow cane. He was tall and fair, with splendid teeth and close-cropped yellow curls, and he wore a slightly disdainful expression, proper for a young man with high connections, whose mother had a big farm in the Elbe valley. There was often an interesting discontent in his blue eyes, and every Bohemian girl he met imagined herself the cause of that unsatisfied expression. He had a way of drawing out his cambric handkerchief slowly, by one corner, from his breast-pocket, that was melancholy and romantic in the extreme. He took a little flight with each of the more eligible Bohemian girls, but it was when he was with little Marie Tovesky that he drew his handkerchief out most slowly, and, after he had lit a fresh cigar, dropped the match most despairingly. Any one could see, with half an eye, that his proud heart was bleeding for somebody.

One Sunday, late in the summer after Marie's graduation, she met Frank at a Bohemian picnic down the river and went rowing with him all the afternoon. When she got home that evening she went straight to her father's room and told him that she was engaged to Shabata. Old Tovesky was having a comfortable pipe before he went to bed. When he heard his daughter's announcement, he first prudently corked his beer bottle and then leaped to his feet and had a turn of temper. He characterized Frank Shabata by a Bohemian expression which is the equivalent of stuffed shirt.

"Why don't he go to work like the rest of us did? His farm in the Elbe valley, indeed! Ain't he got plenty brothers and sisters? It's his mother's farm, and why don't he stay at home and help her? Haven't I seen his mother out in the morning at five o'clock with her ladle and her big bucket on wheels, putting liquid manure on the cabbages? Don't I know the look of old Eva Shabata's hands? Like an old horse's hoofs they are—and this fellow wearing gloves and rings! Engaged, indeed! You aren't fit to be out of school, and that's what's the matter with you. I will send you off to the Sisters of the Sacred Heart in St. Louis, and they will teach you some sense, *I* guess!"

Accordingly, the very next week, Albert Tovesky took his daughter, pale and tearful, down the river to the convent. But the way to make Frank want anything was to tell him he couldn't have it. He managed to have an interview with Marie before she went away, and whereas he had been only half in love with her before, he now persuaded himself that he would not stop at anything. Marie took with her to the convent, under the canvas lining of her trunk, the results of a laborious and satisfying morning on Frank's part; no less than a dozen photographs of himself, taken in a dozen different love-lorn attitudes. There was a little round photograph for her watch-case, photographs for her wall and dresser, and even long narrow ones to be used as bookmarks. More than once the handsome gentleman was torn to pieces before the French class by an indignant nun.

Marie pined in the convent for a year, until her eighteenth birthday was passed. Then she met Frank Shabata in the Union Station in St. Louis and ran away with him. Old Tovesky forgave his daughter because there was nothing else to do, and bought her a farm in the country that she had loved so well as a child. Since then her story had been a part of the history of the Divide. She and Frank had been living there for five years when Carl Linstrum came back to pay his long deferred visit to Alexandra.

Frank had, on the whole, done better than one might have expected. He had flung himself at the soil with savage energy. Once a year he went to Hastings or to Omaha, on a spree. He stayed away for a week or two, and then came home and worked like a demon. He did work; if he felt sorry for himself, that was his own affair.

VIII

On the evening of the day of Alexandra's call at the Shabatas', a heavy rain set in. Frank sat up until a late hour reading the Sunday newspapers. One of the Goulds was getting a divorce, and Frank took it as a personal affront. In printing the story of the young man's marital troubles, the knowing editor gave a sufficiently colored account of his career, stating the amount of his income and the manner in which he was supposed to spend it. Frank read English slowly, and the more he read about this divorce case, the angrier he grew. At last he threw down the page with a snort. He turned to his farm-hand who was reading the other half of the paper.

"By God! if I have that young feller in de hayfield once, I show him something. Listen here what he do wit his money." And Frank began the catalogue of the young man's reputed extravagances.

Marie sighed. She thought it hard that the Goulds, for whom she had nothing but good will, should make her so much trouble. She hated to see the Sunday newspapers come into the house. Frank was always reading about the doings of rich people and feeling outraged. He had an inexhaustible stock of stories about their crimes and follies, how they bribed the courts and shot down their butlers with impunity whenever they chose. Frank and Lou Bergson had very similar ideas, and they were two of the political agitators of the county.

The next morning broke clear and brilliant, but Frank said the ground was too wet to plough, so he took the cart and drove over to Sainte-Agnes to spend the day at Moses Marcel's saloon. After he was gone, Marie went out to the back porch to begin her butter-making. A brisk wind had come up and was driving puffy white clouds across the sky. The orchard was sparkling and rippling in the sun. Marie stood looking toward it wistfully, her hand on the lid of the churn, when she heard a sharp ring in the

air, the merry sound of the whetstone on the scythe. That invitation
decided her. She ran into the house, put on a short skirt and a pair of her
husband's boots, caught up a tin pail and started for the orchard. Emil had
already begun work and was mowing vigorously. When he saw her coming, he stopped and wiped his brow. His yellow canvas leggings and khaki
trousers were splashed to the knees.

"Don't let me disturb you, Emil. I'm going to pick cherries. Isn't
everything beautiful after the rain? Oh, but I'm glad to get this place
mowed! When I heard it raining in the night, I thought maybe you would
come and do it for me to-day. The wind wakened me. Didn't it blow
dreadfully? Just smell the wild roses! They are always so spicy after a rain.
We never had so many of them in here before. I suppose it's the wet season.
Will you have to cut them, too?"

"If I cut the grass, I will," Emil said teasingly. "What's the matter
with you? What makes you so flighty?"

"Am I flighty? I suppose that's the wet season, too, then. It's
exciting to see everything growing so fast,—and to get the grass cut! Please
leave the roses till last, if you must cut them. Oh, I don't mean all of them,
I mean that low place down by my tree, where there are so many. Aren't
you splashed! Look at the spider-webs all over the grass. Good-bye. I'll call
you if I see a snake."

She tripped away and Emil stood looking after her. In a few
moments he heard the cherries dropping smartly into the pail, and he began
to swing his scythe with that long, even stroke that few American boys ever
learn. Marie picked cherries and sang softly to herself, stripping one glittering branch after another, shivering when she caught a shower of raindrops
on her neck and hair. And Emil mowed his way slowly down toward the
cherry trees.

That summer the rains had been so many and opportune that it
was almost more than Shabata and his man could do to keep up with the
corn; the orchard was a neglected wilderness. All sorts of weeds and herbs
and flowers had grown up there; splotches of wild larkspur, pale green-and-
white spikes of hoarhound, plantations of wild cotton, tangles of foxtail and
wild wheat. South of the apricot trees, cornering on the wheatfield, was
Frank's alfalfa, where myriads of white and yellow butterflies were always
fluttering above the purple blossoms. When Emil reached the lower corner
by the hedge, Marie was sitting under her white mulberry tree, the pailful
of cherries beside her, looking off at the gentle, tireless swelling of the
wheat.

"Emil," she said suddenly—he was mowing quietly about under the tree so as not to disturb her—"what religion did the Swedes have away back, before they were Christians?"

Emil paused and straightened his back. "I don't know. About like the Germans', wasn't it?"

Marie went on as if she had not heard him. "The Bohemians, you know, were tree worshipers before the missionaries came. Father says the people in the mountains still do queer things, sometimes,—they believe that trees bring good or bad luck."

Emil looked superior. "Do they? Well, which are the lucky trees? I'd like to know."

"I don't know all of them, but I know lindens are. The old people in the mountains plant lindens to purify the forest, and to do away with the spells that come from the old trees they say have lasted from heathen times. I'm a good Catholic, but I think I could get along with caring for trees, if I hadn't anything else."

"That's a poor saying," said Emil, stooping over to wipe his hands in the wet grass.

"Why is it? If I feel that way, I feel that way. I like trees because they seem more resigned to the way they have to live than other things do. I feel as if this tree knows everything I ever think of when I sit here. When I come back to it, I never have to remind it of anything; I begin just where I left off."

Emil had nothing to say to this. He reached up among the branches and began to pick the sweet, insipid fruit,—long ivory-colored berries, tipped with faint pink, like white coral, that fall to the ground unheeded all summer through. He dropped a handful into her lap.

"Do you like Mr. Linstrum?" Marie asked suddenly.

"Yes. Don't you?"

"Oh, ever so much; only he seems kind of staid and school-teachery. But, of course, he is older than Frank, even. I'm sure I don't want to live to be more than thirty, do you? Do you think Alexandra likes him very much?"

"I suppose so. They were old friends."

"Oh, Emil, you know what I mean!" Marie tossed her head impatiently. "Does she really care about him? When she used to tell me about him, I always wondered whether she wasn't a little in love with him."

"Who, Alexandra?" Emil laughed and thrust his hands into his trousers pockets. "Alexandra's never been in love, you crazy!" He laughed again. "She wouldn't know how to go about it. The idea!"

Marie shrugged her shoulders. "Oh, you don't know Alexandra as well as you think you do! If you had any eyes, you would see that she is very fond of him. It would serve you all right if she walked off with Carl. I like him because he appreciates her more than you do."

Emil frowned. "What are you talking about, Marie? Alexandra's all right. She and I have always been good friends. What more do you want? I like to talk to Carl about New York and what a fellow can do there."

"Oh, Emil! Surely you are not thinking of going off there?"

"Why not? I must go somewhere, mustn't I?" The young man took up his scythe and leaned on it. "Would you rather I went off in the sand hills and lived like Ivar?"

Marie's face fell under his brooding gaze. She looked down at his wet leggings. "I'm sure Alexandra hopes you will stay on here," she murmured.

"Then Alexandra will be disappointed," the young man said roughly. "What do I want to hang around here for? Alexandra can run the farm all right, without me. I don't want to stand around and look on. I want to be doing something on my own account."

"That's so," Marie sighed. "There are so many, many things you can do. Almost anything you choose."

"And there are so many, many things I can't do." Emil echoed her tone sarcastically. "Sometimes I don't want to do anything at all, and sometimes I want to pull the four corners of the Divide together"—he threw out his arm and brought it back with a jerk—"so, like a tablecloth. I get tired of seeing men and horses going up and down, up and down."

Marie looked up at his defiant figure and her face clouded. "I wish you weren't so restless, and didn't get so worked up over things," she said sadly.

"Thank you," he returned shortly.

She sighed despondently. "Everything I say makes you cross, don't it? And you never used to be cross to me."

Emil took a step nearer and stood frowning down at her bent head. He stood in an attitude of self-defense, his feet well apart, his hands clenched and drawn up at his sides, so that the cords stood out on his bare arms. "I can't play with you like a little boy any more," he said slowly. "That's what you miss, Marie. You'll have to get some other little boy to play with." He stopped and took a deep breath. Then he went on in a low tone, so intense that it was almost threatening: "Sometimes you seem to understand perfectly, and then sometimes you pretend you don't. You don't help things any by pretending. It's then that I want to pull the corners of the Divide together. If you *won't* understand, you know, I could make you!"

Marie clasped her hands and started up from her seat. She had grown very pale and her eyes were shining with excitement and distress. "But, Emil, if I understand, then all our good times are over, we can never do nice things together any more. We shall have to behave like Mr. Linstrum. And, anyhow, there's nothing to understand!" She struck the ground with her little foot fiercely. "That won't last. It will go away, and things will be just as they used to. I wish you were a Catholic. The Church helps people, indeed it does. I pray for you, but that's not the same as if you prayed yourself."

She spoke rapidly and pleadingly, looked entreatingly into his face. Emil stood defiant, gazing down at her.

"I can't pray to have the things I want," he said slowly, "and I won't pray not to have them, not if I'm damned for it."

Marie turned away, wringing her hands. "Oh, Emil, you won't try! Then all our good times are over."

"Yes, over. I never expect to have any more."

Emil gripped the hand-holds of his scythe and began to mow. Marie took up her cherries and went slowly toward the house, crying bitterly.

IX

On Sunday afternoon, a month after Carl Linstrum's arrival, he rode with Emil up into the French country to attend a Catholic fair. He sat for most of the afternoon in the basement of the church, where the fair was held, talking to Marie Shabata, or strolled about the gravel terrace, thrown up on the hillside in front of the basement doors, where the French boys were jumping and wrestling and throwing the discus. Some of the boys were in their white baseball suits; they had just come up from a Sunday practice game down in the ball-grounds. Amédée, the newly married, Emil's best friend, was their pitcher, renowned among the country towns for his dash and skill. Amédée was a little fellow, a year younger than Emil and much more boyish in appearance; very lithe and active and neatly made, with a clear brown and white skin, and flashing white teeth. The Sainte-Agnes boys were to play the Hastings nine in a fortnight, and Amédée's lightning balls were the hope of his team. The little Frenchman seemed to get every ounce there was in him behind the ball as it left his hand.

"You'd have made the battery at the University for sure, 'Médée," Emil said as they were walking from the ball-grounds back to the church on the hill. "You're pitching better than you did in the spring."

Amédée grinned. "Sure! A married man don't lose his head no more." He slapped Emil on the back as he caught step with him. "Oh, Emil, you wanna get married right off quick! It's the greatest thing ever!"

Emil laughed. "How am I going to get married without any girl?"

Amédée took his arm. "Pooh! There are plenty girls will have you. You wanna get some nice French girl, now. She treat you well; always be jolly. See"—he began checking off on his fingers—"there is Séverine, and Alphosen, and Joséphine, and Hectorine, and Louise, and Malvina— why, I could love any of them girls! Why don't you get after them? Are you stuck up, Emil, or is anything the matter with you? I never did know a boy twenty-two years old before that didn't have no girl. You wanna be a priest, maybe? Not-a for me!" Amédée swaggered. "I bring many good Catholics into this world, I hope, and that's a way I help the Church."

Emil looked down and patted him on the shoulder. "Now you're windy, 'Médée. You Frenchies like to brag."

But Amédée had the zeal of the newly married, and he was not to be lightly shaken off. "Honest and true, Emil, don't you want *any* girl? Maybe there's some young lady in Lincoln, now, very grand"—Amédée waved his hand languidly before his face to denote the fan of heartless beauty—"and you lost your heart up there. Is that it?"

"Maybe," said Emil.

But Amédée saw no appropriate glow in his friend's face. "Bah!" he exclaimed in disgust. "I tell all the French girls to keep 'way from you. You gotta rock in there," thumping Emil on the ribs.

When they reached the terrace at the side of the church, Amédée, who was excited by his success on the ball-grounds, challenged Emil to a jumping-match, though he knew he would be beaten. They belted themselves up, and Raoul Marcel, the choir tenor and Father Duchesne's pet, and Jean Bordelau, held the string over which they vaulted.

All the French boys stood round, cheering and humping themselves up when Emil or Amédée went over the wire, as if they were helping in the lift. Emil stopped at five-feet-five, declaring that he would spoil his appetite for supper if he jumped any more.

Angélique, Amédée's pretty bride, as blonde and fair as her name, who had come out to watch the match, tossed her head at Emil and said:

" 'Médée could jump much higher than you if he were as tall. And anyhow, he is much more graceful. He goes over like a bird, and you have to hump yourself all up."

"Oh, I do, do I?" Emil caught her and kissed her saucy mouth squarely, while she laughed and struggled and called, " 'Médée! 'Médée!"

"There, you see your 'Médée isn't even big enough to get you away from me. I could run away with you right now and he could only sit down and cry about it. I'll show you whether I have to hump myself!" Laughing and panting, he picked Angélique up in his arms and began running about the rectangle with her. Not until he saw Marie Shabata's tiger eyes flashing from the gloom of the basement doorway did he hand the disheveled bride over to her husband. "There, go to your graceful; I haven't the heart to take you away from him."

Angélique clung to her husband and made faces at Emil over the white shoulder of Amédée's ball-shirt. Emil was greatly amused at her air of proprietorship and at Amédée's shameless submission to it. He was delighted with his friend's good fortune. He liked to see and to think about Amédée's sunny, natural, happy love.

He and Amédée had ridden and wrestled and larked together since they were lads of twelve. On Sundays and holidays they were always arm in arm. It seemed strange that now he should have to hide the thing that Amédée was so proud of, that the feeling which gave one of them such happiness should bring the other such despair. It was like that when Alexandra tested her seed-corn in the spring, he mused. From two ears that had grown side by side, the grains of one shot up joyfully into the light, projecting themselves into the future, and the grains from the other lay still in the earth and rotted; and nobody knew why.

X

*W*hile Emil and Carl were amusing themselves at the fair, Alexandra was at home, busy with her account-books, which had been neglected of late. She was almost through with her figures when she heard a cart drive up to the gate, and looking out of the window she saw her two older brothers. They had seemed to avoid her ever since Carl Linstrum's arrival, four weeks ago that day, and she hurried to the door to welcome them. She saw at once that they had come with some very definite purpose. They followed her stiffly into the sitting-room. Oscar sat down, but Lou walked over to the window and remained standing, his hands behind him.

"You are by yourself?" he asked, looking toward the doorway into the parlor.

"Yes. Carl and Emil went up to the Catholic fair."

For a few moments neither of the men spoke.

Then Lou came out sharply. "How soon does he intend to go away from here?"

"I don't know, Lou. Not for some time, I hope." Alexandra spoke in an even, quiet tone that often exasperated her brothers. They felt that she was trying to be superior with them.

Oscar spoke up grimly. "We thought we ought to tell you that people have begun to talk," he said meaningly.

Alexandra looked at him. "What about?"

Oscar met her eyes blankly. "About you, keeping him here so long. It looks bad for him to be hanging on to a woman this way. People think you're getting taken in."

Alexandra shut her account-book firmly. "Boys," she said seriously, "don't let's go on with this. We won't come out anywhere. I can't take advice on such a matter. I know you mean well, but you must not feel responsible for me in things of this sort. If we go on with this talk it will only make hard feeling."

Lou whipped about from the window. "You ought to think a little about your family. You're making us all ridiculous."

"How am I?"

"People are beginning to say you want to marry the fellow."

"Well, and what is ridiculous about that?"

Lou and Oscar exchanged outraged looks. "Alexandra! Can't you see he's just a tramp and he's after your money? He wants to be taken care of, he does!"

"Well, suppose I want to take care of him? Whose business is it but my own?"

"Don't you know he'd get hold of your property?"

"He'd get hold of what I wished to give him, certainly."

Oscar sat up suddenly and Lou clutched at his bristly hair.

"Give him?" Lou shouted. "Our property, our homestead?"

"I don't know about the homestead," said Alexandra quietly. "I know you and Oscar have always expected that it would be left to your children, and I'm not sure but what you're right. But I'll do exactly as I please with the rest of my land, boys."

"The rest of your land!" cried Lou, growing more excited every minute. "Didn't all the land come out of the homestead? It was bought with money borrowed on the homestead, and Oscar and me worked ourselves to the bone paying interest on it."

"Yes, you paid the interest. But when you married we made a division of the land, and you were satisfied. I've made more on my farms since I've been alone than when we all worked together."

"Everything you've made has come out of the original land that us boys worked for, hasn't it? The farms and all that comes out of them belongs to us as a family."

Alexandra waved her hand impatiently. "Come now, Lou. Stick to the facts. You are talking nonsense. Go to the county clerk and ask him who owns my land, and whether my titles are good."

Lou turned to his brother. "This is what comes of letting a woman meddle in business," he said bitterly. "We ought to have taken things in our own hands years ago. But she liked to run things, and we humored her. We thought you had good sense, Alexandra. We never thought you'd do anything foolish."

Alexandra rapped impatiently on her desk with her knuckles. "Listen, Lou. Don't talk wild. You say you ought to have taken things into your own hands years ago. I suppose you mean before you left home. But how could you take hold of what wasn't there? I've got most of what I have now since we divided the property; I've built it up myself, and it has nothing to do with you."

Oscar spoke up solemnly. "The property of a family really

belongs to the men of the family, no matter about the title. If anything goes wrong, it's the men that are held responsible."

"Yes, of course," Lou broke in. "Everybody knows that. Oscar and me have always been easy-going and we've never made any fuss. We were willing you should hold the land and have the good of it, but you got no right to part with any of it. We worked in the fields to pay for the first land you bought, and whatever's come out of it has got to be kept in the family."

Oscar reinforced his brother, his mind fixed on the one point he could see. "The property of a family belongs to the men of the family, because they are held responsible, and because they do the work."

Alexandra looked from one to the other, her eyes full of indignation. She had been impatient before, but now she was beginning to feel angry. "And what about my work?" she asked in an unsteady voice.

Lou looked at the carpet. "Oh, now, Alexandra, you always took it pretty easy! Of course we wanted you to. You liked to manage round, and we always humored you. We realize you were a great deal of help to us. There's no woman anywhere around that knows as much about business as you do, and we've always been proud of that, and thought you were pretty smart. But, of course, the real work always fell on us. Good advice is all right, but it don't get the weeds out of the corn."

"Maybe not, but it sometimes puts in the crop, and it sometimes keeps the fields for corn to grow in," said Alexandra dryly. "Why, Lou, I can remember when you and Oscar wanted to sell this homestead and all the improvements to old preacher Ericson for two thousand dollars. If I'd consented, you'd have gone down to the river and scraped along on poor farms for the rest of your lives. When I put in our first field of alfalfa you both opposed me, just because I first heard about it from a young man who had been to the University. You said I was being taken in then, and all the neighbors said so. You know as well as I do that alfalfa has been the salvation of this country. You all laughed at me when I said our land here was about ready for wheat, and I had to raise three big wheat crops before the neighbors quit putting all their land in corn. Why, I remember you cried, Lou, when we put in the first big wheat-planting, and said everybody was laughing at us."

Lou turned to Oscar. "That's the woman of it; if she tells you to put in a crop, she thinks she's put it in. It makes women conceited to meddle in business. I shouldn't think you'd want to remind us how hard you were on us, Alexandra, after the way you baby Emil."

"Hard on you? I never meant to be hard. Conditions were hard. Maybe I would never have been very soft, anyhow; but I certainly didn't choose to be the kind of girl I was. If you take even a vine and cut it back again and again, it grows hard, like a tree."

Lou fel that they were wandering from the point, and that in digression Alexandra might unnerve him. He wiped his forehead with a jerk of his handkerchief. "We never doubted you, Alexandra. We never questioned anything you did. You've always had your own way. But you can't expect us to sit like stumps and see you done out of the property by any loafer who happens along, and making yourself ridiculous into the bargain."

Oscar rose. "Yes," he broke in, "everybody's laughing to see you get took in; at your age, too. Everybody knows he's nearly five years younger than you, and is after your money. Why, Alexandra, you are forty years old!"

"All that doesn't concern anybody but Carl and me. Go to town and ask your lawyers what you can do to restrain me from disposing of my own property. And I advise you to do what they tell you; for the authority you can exert by law is the only influence you will ever have over me again." Alexandra rose. "I think I would rather not have lived to find out what I have to-day," she said quietly, closing her desk.

Lou and Oscar looked at each other questioningly. There seemed to be nothing to do but to go, and they walked out.

"You can't do business with women," Oscar said heavily as he clambered into the cart. "But anyhow, we've had our say, at last."

Lou scratched his head. "Talk of that kind might come too high, you know; but she's apt to be sensible. You hadn't ought to said that about her age, though, Oscar. I'm afraid that hurt her feelings; and the worst thing we can do is to make her sore at us. She'd marry him out of contrariness."

"I only meant," said Oscar, "that she is old enough to know better, and she is. If she was going to marry, she ought to done it long ago, and not go making a fool of herself now."

Lou looked anxious, nevertheless. "Of course," he reflected hopefully and inconsistently, "Alexandra ain't much like other women-folks. Maybe it won't make her sore. Maybe she'd as soon be forty as not!"

XI

*E*mil came home at about half-past seven o'clock that evening. Old Ivar met him at the windmill and took his horse, and the young man went directly into the house. He called to his sister and she answered from her bedroom, behind the sitting-room, saying that she was lying down.

Emil went to her door.

"Can I see you for a minute?" he asked. "I want to talk to you about something before Carl comes."

Alexandra rose quickly and came to the door. "Where is Carl?"

"Lou and Oscar met us and said they wanted to talk to him, so he rode over to Oscar's with them. Are you coming out?" Emil asked impatiently.

"Yes, sit down. I'll be dressed in a moment."

Alexandra closed her door, and Emil sank down on the old slat lounge and sat with his head in his hands. When his sister came out, he looked up, not knowing whether the interval had been short or long, and he was surprised to see that the room had grown quite dark. That was just as well; it would be easier to talk if he were not under the gaze of those clear, deliberate eyes, that saw so far in some directions and were so blind in others. Alexandra, too, was glad of the dusk. Her face was swollen from crying.

Emil started up and then sat down again. "Alexandra," he said slowly, in his deep young baritone, "I don't want to go away to law school this fall. Let me put it off another year. I want to take a year off and look around. It's awfully easy to rush into a profession you don't really like, and awfully hard to get out of it. Linstrum and I have been talking about that."

"Very well, Emil. Only don't go off looking for land." She came up and put her hand on his shoulder. "I've been wishing you could stay with me this winter."

"That's just what I don't want to do, Alexandra. I'm restless. I want to go to a new place. I want to go down to the City of Mexico to join one of the University fellows who's at the head of an electrical plant. He wrote me he could give me a little job, enough to pay my way, and I could look around and see what I want to do. I want to go as soon as harvest is over. I guess Lou and Oscar will be sore about it."

"I suppose they will." Alexandra sat down on the lounge beside him. "They are very angry with me, Emil. We have had a quarrel. They will not come here again."

Emil scarcely heard what she was saying; he did not notice the sadness of her tone. He was thinking about the reckless life he meant to live in Mexico.

"What about?" he asked absently.

"About Carl Linstrum. They are afraid I am going to marry him, and that some of my property will get away from them."

Emil shrugged his shoulders. "What nonsense!" he murmured. "Just like them."

Alexandra drew back. "Why nonsense, Emil?"

"Why, you've never thought of such a thing, have you? They always have to have something to fuss about."

"Emil," said his sister slowly, "you ought not to take things for granted. Do you agree with them that I have no right to change my way of living?"

Emil looked at the outline of his sister's head in the dim light. They were sitting close together and he somehow felt that she could hear his thoughts. He was silent for a moment, and then said in an embarrassed tone, "Why, no, certainly not. You ought to do whatever you want to. I'll always back you."

"But it would seem a little bit ridiculous to you if I married Carl?"

Emil fidgeted. The issue seemed to him too far-fetched to warrant discussion. "Why, no. I should be surprised if you wanted to. I can't see exactly why. But that's none of my business. You ought to do as you please. Certainly you ought not to pay any attention to what the boys say."

Alexandra sighed. "I had hoped you might understand, a little, why I do want to. But I suppose that's too much to expect. I've had a pretty lonely life, Emil. Besides Marie, Carl is the only friend I have ever had."

Emil was awake now; a name in her last sentence roused him. He put out his hand and took his sister's awkwardly. "You ought to do just as you wish, and I think Carl's a fine fellow. He and I would always get on. I don't believe any of the things the boys say about him, honest I don't. They are suspicious of him because he's intelligent. You know their way.

They've been sore at me ever since you let me go away to college. They're always trying to catch me up. If I were you, I wouldn't pay any attention to them. There's nothing to get upset about. Carl's a sensible fellow. He won't mind them."

"I don't know. If they talk to him the way they did to me, I think he'll go away."

Emil grew more and more uneasy. "Think so? Well, Marie said it would serve us all right if you walked off with him."

"Did she? Bless her little heart! *She* would." Alexandra's voice broke.

Emil began unlacing his leggings. "Why don't you talk to her about it? There's Carl, I hear his horse. I guess I'll go upstairs and get my boots off. No, I don't want any supper. We had supper at five o'clock, at the fair."

Emil was glad to escape and get to his own room. He was a little ashamed for his sister, though he had tried not to show it. He felt that there was something indecorous in her proposal, and she did seem to him somewhat ridiculous. There was trouble enough in the world, he reflected, as he threw himself upon his bed, without people who were forty years old imagining they wanted to get married. In the darkness and silence Emil was not likely to think long about Alexandra. Every image slipped away but one. He had seen Marie in the crowd that afternoon. She sold candy at the fair. *Why* had she ever run away with Frank Shabata, and how could she go on laughing and working and taking an interest in things? Why did she like so many people, and why had she seemed pleased when all the French and Bohemian boys, and the priest himself, crowded round her candy stand? Why did she care about any one but him? Why could he never, never find the thing he looked for in her playful, affectionate eyes?

Then he fell to imagining that he looked once more and found it there, and what it would be like if she loved him—she who, as Alexandra said, could give her whole heart. In that dream he could lie for hours, as if in a trance. His spirit went out of his body and crossed the fields to Marie Shabata.

At the University dances the girls had often looked wonderingly at the tall young Swede with the fine head, leaning against the wall and frowning, his arms folded, his eyes fixed on the ceiling or the floor. All the girls were a little afraid of him. He was distinguished-looking, and not the jollying kind. They felt that he was too intense and preoccupied. There was something queer about him. Emil's fraternity rather prided itself upon its dances, and sometimes he did his duty and danced every dance. But whether he was on the floor or brooding in a corner, he was always thinking about Marie Shabata. For two years the storm had been gathering in him.

XII

Carl came into the sitting-room while Alexandra was lighting the lamp. She looked up at him as she adjusted the shade. His sharp shoulders stooped as if he were very tired, his face was pale, and there were bluish shadows under his dark eyes. His anger had burned itself out and left him sick and disgusted.

"You have seen Lou and Oscar?" Alexandra asked.

"Yes." His eyes avoided hers.

Alexandra took a deep breath. "And now you are going away. I thought so."

Carl threw himself into a chair and pushed the dark lock back from his forehead with his white, nervous hand. "What a hopeless position you are in, Alexandra!" he exclaimed feverishly. "It is your fate to be always surrounded by little men. And I am no better than the rest. I am too little to face the criticism of even such men as Lou and Oscar. Yes, I am going away; to-morrow. I cannot even ask you to give me a promise until I have something to offer you. I thought, perhaps, I could do that; but I find I can't."

"What good comes of offering people things they don't need?" Alexandra asked sadly. "I don't need money. But I have needed you for a great many years. I wonder why I have been permitted to prosper, if it is only to take my friends away from me."

"I don't deceive myself," Carl said frankly. "I know that I am going away on my own account. I must make the usual effort. I must have something to show for myself. To take what you would give me, I should have to be either a very large man or a very small one, and I am only in the middle class."

Alexandra sighed. "I have a feeling that if you go away, you will not come back. Something will happen to one of us, or to both. People have to snatch at happiness when they can, in this world. It is always easier to lose than to find. What I have is yours, if you care enough about me to take it."

Carl rose and looked up at the picture of John Bergson. "But I can't, my dear, I can't! I will go North at once. Instead of idling about in California all winter, I shall be getting my bearings up there. I won't waste another week. Be patient with me, Alexandra. Give me a year!"

"As you will," said Alexandra wearily. "All at once, in a single day, I lose everything; and I do not know why. Emil, too, is going away." Carl was still studying John Bergson's face and Alexandra's eyes followed his. "Yes," she said, "if he could have seen all that would come of the task he gave me, he would have been sorry. I hope he does not see me now. I hope that he is among the old people of his blood and country, and that tidings do not reach him from the New World."

Part III

Winter Memories

I

*W*inter has settled down over the Divide again; the season in which Nature recuperates, in which she sinks to sleep between the fruitfulness of autumn and the passion of spring. The birds have gone. The teeming life that goes on down in the long grass is exterminated. The prairie-dog keeps his hole. The rabbits run shivering from one frozen garden patch to another and are hard put to it to find frost-bitten cabbage-stalks. At night the coyotes roam the wintry waste, howling for food. The variegated fields are all one color now; the pastures, the stubble, the roads, the sky are the same leaden gray. The hedgerows and trees are scarcely perceptible against the bare earth, whose slaty hue they have taken on. The ground is frozen so hard that it bruises the foot to walk in the roads or in the ploughed fields. It is like an iron country, and the spirit is oppressed by its rigor and melancholy. One could easily believe that in that dead landscape the germs of life and fruitfulness were extinct forever.

Alexandra has settled back into her old routine. There are weekly letters from Emil. Lou and Oscar she has not seen since Carl went away. To avoid awkward encounters in the presence of curious spectators, she has stopped going to the Norwegian Church and drives up to the Reform Church at Hanover, or goes with Marie Shabata to the Catholic Church, locally known as "the French Church." She has not told Marie about Carl, or her differences with her brothers. She was never very communicative about her own affairs, and when she came to the point, an instinct told her that about such things she and Marie would not understand one another.

Old Mrs. Lee had been afraid that family misunderstandings might deprive her of her yearly visit to Alexandra. But on the first day of December Alexandra telephoned Annie that to-morrow she would send Ivar over for her mother, and the next day the old lady arrived with her bundles. For twelve years Mrs. Lee had always entered Alexandra's sitting-room with the same exclamation, "Now we be yust-a like old times!" She enjoyed the liberty Alexandra gave her, and hearing her own language about her all day long. Here she could wear her nightcap and sleep with all her windows shut, listen to Ivar reading the Bible, and here she could run about among the stables in a pair of Emil's old boots. Though she was bent almost double, she was as spry as a gopher. Her face was as brown as if it had been varnished, and as full of wrinkles as a washerwoman's hands. She had three jolly old teeth left in the front of her mouth, and when she grinned she looked very knowing, as if when you found out how to take it, life wasn't half bad. While she and Alexandra patched and pieced and quilted, she talked incessantly about stories she read in a Swedish family paper, telling the plots in great detail; or about her life on a dairy farm in Gottland when she was a girl. Sometimes she forgot which were the printed stories and which were the real stories, it all seemed so far away. She loved to take a little brandy, with hot water and sugar, before she went to bed, and Alexandra always had it ready for her. "It sends good dreams," she would say with a twinkle in her eye.

When Mrs. Lee had been with Alexandra for a week, Marie Shabata telephoned one morning to say that Frank had gone to town for the day, and she would like them to come over for coffee in the afternoon. Mrs. Lee hurried to wash out and iron her new cross-stitched apron, which she had finished only the night before; a checked gingham apron worked with a design ten inches broad across the bottom; a hunting scene, with fir trees and a stag and dogs and huntsmen. Mrs. Lee was firm with herself at dinner, and refused a second helping of apple dumplings. "I ta-ank I save up," she said with a giggle.

At two o'clock in the afternoon Alexandra's cart drove up to the Shabatas' gate, and Marie saw Mrs. Lee's red shawl come bobbing up the path. She ran to the door and pulled the old woman into the house with a hug, helping her to take off her wraps while Alexandra blanketed the horse outside. Mrs. Lee had put on her best black satin dress—she abominated woolen stuffs, even in winter—and a crocheted collar, fastened with a big pale gold pin, containing faded daguerreotypes of her father and mother. She had not worn her apron for fear of rumpling it, and now she shook it out and tied it round her waist with a conscious air. Marie drew back and threw up her hands, exclaiming, "Oh, what a beauty! I've never seen this one before, have I, Mrs. Lee?"

The old woman giggled and ducked her head. "No, yust las' night I ma-ake. See dis tread; verra strong, no wa-ash out, no fade. My sister send from Sveden. I yust-a ta-ank you like dis."

Marie ran to the door again. "Come in, Alexandra. I have been looking at Mrs. Lee's apron. Do stop on your way home and show it to Mrs. Hiller. She's crazy about cross-stitch."

While Alexandra removed her hat and veil, Mrs. Lee went out to the kitchen and settled herself in a wooden rocking-chair by the stove, looking with great interest at the table, set for three, with a white cloth, and a pot of pink geraniums in the middle. "My, a-an't you gotta fine plants; such-a much flower. How you keep from freeze?"

She pointed to the window-shelves, full of blooming fuchsias and geraniums.

"I keep the fire all night, Mrs. Lee, and when it's very cold I put them all on the table, in the middle of the room. Other nights I only put newspapers behind them. Frank laughs at me for fussing, but when they don't bloom he says, 'What's the matter with the darned things?'—What do you hear from Carl, Alexandra?"

"He got to Dawson before the river froze, and now I suppose I won't hear any more until spring. Before he left California he sent me a box of orange flowers, but they didn't keep very well. I have brought a bunch of Emil's letters for you." Alexandra came out from the sitting-room and pinched Marie's cheek playfully. "You don't look as if the weather ever froze you up. Never have colds, do you? That's a good girl. She had dark red cheeks like this when she was a little girl, Mrs. Lee. She looked like some queer foreign kind of a doll. I've never forgot the first time I saw you in Mieklejohn's store, Marie, the time father was lying sick. Carl and I were talking about that before he went away."

"I remember, and Emil had his kitten along. When are you going to send Emil's Christmas box?"

"It ought to have gone before this. I'll have to send it by mail now, to get it there in time."

Marie pulled a dark purple silk necktie from her workbasket. "I knit this for him. It's a good color, don't you think? Will you please put it in with your things and tell him it's from me, to wear when he goes serenading."

Alexandra laughed. "I don't believe he goes serenading much. He says in one letter that the Mexican ladies are said to be very beautiful, but that don't seem to me very warm praise."

Marie tossed her head. "Emil can't fool me. If he's bought a guitar, he goes serenading. Who wouldn't, with all those Spanish girls dropping flowers down from their windows! I'd sing to them every night, wouldn't you, Mrs. Lee?"

The old lady chuckled. Her eyes lit up as Marie bent down and opened the oven door. A delicious hot fragrance blew out into the tidy kitchen. "My, somet'ing smell good!" She turned to Alexandra with a wink, her three yellow teeth making a brave show, "I ta-ank dat stop my yaw from ache no more!" she said contentedly.

Marie took out a pan of delicate little rolls, stuffed with stewed apricots, and began to dust them over with powdered sugar. "I hope you'll like these, Mrs. Lee; Alexandra does. The Bohemians always like them with their coffee. But if you don't, I have a coffee-cake with nuts and poppy seeds. Alexandra, will you get the cream jug? I put it in the window to keep cool."

"The Bohemians," said Alexandra, as they drew up to the table, "certainly know how to make more kinds of bread than any other people in the world. Old Mrs. Hiller told me once at the church supper that she could make seven kinds of fancy bread, but Marie could make a dozen."

Mrs. Lee held up one of the apricot rolls between her brown thumb and forefinger and weighed it critically. "Yust like-a fedders," she pronounced with satisfaction. "My, a-an't dis nice!" she exclaimed as she stirred her coffee. "I yust ta-ake a liddle yelly now, too, I ta-ank."

Alexandra and Marie laughed at her forehandedness, and fell to talking of their own affairs. "I was afraid you had a cold when I talked to you over the telephone the other night, Marie. What was the matter, had you been crying?"

"Maybe I had," Marie smiled guiltily. "Frank was out late that night. Don't you get lonely sometimes in the winter, when everybody has gone away?"

"I thought it was something like that. If I hadn't had company, I'd have run over to see for myself. If you get down-hearted, what will become of the rest of us?" Alexandra asked.

"I don't, very often. There's Mrs. Lee without any coffee!"

Later, when Mrs. Lee declared that her powers were spent, Marie and Alexandra went upstairs to look for some crochet patterns the old lady wanted to borrow. "Better put on your coat, Alexandra. It's cold up there, and I have no idea where those patterns are. I may have to look through my old trunks." Marie caught up a shawl and opened the stair door, running up the steps ahead of her guest. "While I go through the bureau drawers, you might look in those hat-boxes on the closet-shelf, over where Frank's clothes hang. There are a lot of odds and ends in them."

She began tossing over the contents of the drawers, and Alexandra went into the clothes-closet. Presently she came back, holding a slender elastic yellow stick in her hand.

"What in the world is this, Marie? You don't mean to tell me Frank ever carried such a thing?"

Marie blinked at it with astonishment and sat down on the floor. "Where did you find it? I didn't know he had kept it. I haven't seen it for years."

"It really is a cane, then?"

"Yes. One he brought from the old country. He used to carry it when I first knew him. Isn't it foolish? Poor Frank!"

Alexandra twirled the stick in her fingers and laughed. "He must have looked funny!"

Marie was thoughtful. "No, he didn't, really. It didn't seem out of place. He used to be awfully gay like that when he was a young man. I guess people always get what's hardest for them, Alexandra." Marie gathered the shawl closer about her and still looked hard at the cane. "Frank would be all right in the right place," she said reflectively. "He ought to have a different kind of wife, for one thing. Do you know, Alexandra, I could pick out exactly the right sort of woman for Frank—now. The trouble is you almost have to marry a man before you can find out the sort of wife he needs; and usually it's exactly the sort you are not. Then what are you going to do about it?" she asked candidly.

Alexandra confessed she didn't know. "However," she added, "it seems to me that you get along with Frank about as well as any woman I've ever seen or heard of could."

Marie shook her head, pursing her lips and blowing her warm breath softly out into the frosty air. "No; I was spoiled at home. I like my own way, and I have a quick tongue. When Frank brags, I say sharp things, and he never forgets. He goes over and over it in his mind; I can feel him. Then I'm too giddy. Frank's wife ought to be timid, and she ought not to care about another living thing in the world but just Frank! I did when I married him, but I suppose I was too young to stay like that." Marie sighed.

Alexandra had never heard Marie speak so frankly about her husband before, and she felt that it was wiser not to encourage her. No good, she reasoned, ever came from talking about such things, and while Marie was thinking aloud, Alexandra had been steadily searching the hatboxes. "Aren't these the patterns, Marie?"

Marie sprang up from the floor. "Sure enough, we were looking for patterns, weren't we? I'd forgot about everything but Frank's other wife. I'll put that away."

She poked the cane behind Frank's Sunday clothes, and though she laughed, Alexandra saw there were tears in her eyes.

When they went back to the kitchen, the snow had begun to fall, and Marie's visitors thought they must be getting home. She went out

to the cart with them, and tucked the robes about old Mrs. Lee while
Alexandra took the blanket off her horse. As they drove away, Marie turned
and went slowly back to the house. She took up the package of letters
Alexandra had brought, but she did not read them. She turned them over
and looked at the foreign stamps, and then sat watching the flying snow
while the dusk deepened in the kitchen and the stove sent out a red glow.

Marie knew perfectly well that Emil's letters were written more
for her than for Alexandra. They were not the sort of letters that a young
man writes to his sister. They were both more personal and more painstak-
ing; full of descriptions of the gay life in the old Mexican capital in the days
when the strong hand of Porfirio Diaz was still strong. He told about
bull-fights and cock-fights, churches and *fiestas,* the flower-markets and the
fountains, the music and dancing, the people of all nations he met in the
Italian restaurants on San Francisco Street. In short, they were the kind of
letters a young man writes to a woman when he wishes himself and his life
to seem interesting to her, when he wishes to enlist her imagination in his
behalf.

Marie, when she was alone or when she sat sewing in the
evening, often thought about what it must be like down there where Emil
was; where there were flowers and street bands everywhere, and carriages
rattling up and down, and where there was a little blind boot-black in front
of the cathedral who could play any tune you asked for by dropping the lids
of blacking-boxes on the stone steps. When everything is done and over for
one at twenty-three, it is pleasant to let the mind wander forth and follow
a young adventurer who has life before him. "And if it had not been for
me," she thought, "Frank might still be free like that, and having a good
time making people admire him. Poor Frank, getting married wasn't very
good for him either. I'm afraid I do set people against him, as he says. I seem,
somehow, to give him away all the time. Perhaps he would try to be
agreeable to people again, if I were not around. It seems as if I always make
him just as bad as he can be."

Later in the winter, Alexandra looked back upon that afternoon
as the last satisfactory visit she had had with Marie. After that day the
younger woman seemed to shrink more and more into herself. When she
was with Alexandra she was not spontaneous and frank as she used to be.
She seemed to be brooding over something, and holding something back.
The weather had a good deal to do with their seeing less of each other than
usual. There had not been such snowstorms in twenty years, and the path
across the fields was drifted deep from Christmas until March. When the

two neighbors went to see each other, they had to go round by the wagon-road, which was twice as far. They telephoned each other almost every night, though in January there was a stretch of three weeks when the wires were down, and when the postman did not come at all.

Marie often ran in to see her nearest neighbor, old Mrs. Hiller, who was crippled with rheumatism and had only her son, the lame shoe-maker, to take care of her; and she went to the French Church, whatever the weather. She was a sincerely devout girl. She prayed for herself and for Frank, and for Emil, among the temptations of that gay, corrupt old city. She found more comfort in the Church that winter than ever before. It seemed to come closer to her, and to fill an emptiness that ached in her heart. She tried to be patient with her husband. He and his hired man usually played California Jack in the evening. Marie sat sewing or crochet-ing and tried to take a friendly interest in the game, but she was always thinking about the wide fields outside, where the snow was drifting over the fences; and about the orchard, where the snow was falling and packing, crust over crust. When she went out into the dark kitchen to fix her plants for the night, she used to stand by the window and look out at the white fields, or watch the currents of snow whirling over the orchard. She seemed to feel the weight of all the snow that lay down there. The branches had become so hard that they wounded your hand if you but tried to break a twig. And yet, down under the frozen crusts, at the roots of the trees, the secret of life was still safe, warm as the blood in one's heart; and the spring would come again! Oh, it would come again!

II

If Alexandra had had much imagina-tion she might have guessed what was going on in Marie's mind, and she would have seen long before what was going on in Emil's. But that, as Emil himself had more than once reflected, was Alexandra's blind side, and her life had not been of the kind to sharpen her vision. Her training had all been toward the end of making her proficient in what she had undertaken to do. Her personal life, her own realization of herself, was almost a subconscious existence; like an underground river that came to the surface only here and there, at intervals months apart, and then sank again to flow on under her own fields. Nevertheless, the underground stream was there, and it was because she had so much personality to put into her enterprises and succeeded in putting it into them so completely, that her affairs prospered better than those of her neighbors.

There were certain days in her life, outwardly uneventful, which Alexandra remembered as peculiarly happy; days when she was close to the flat, fallow world about her, and felt, as it were, in her own body the joyous germination in the soil. There were days, too, which she and Emil had spent together, upon which she loved to look back. There had been such a day when they were down on the river in the dry year, looking over the land. They had made an early start one morning and had driven a long way before noon. When Emil said he was hungry, they drew back from the road, gave Brigham his oats among the bushes, and climbed up to the top of a grassy bluff to eat their lunch under the shade of some little elm trees. The river was clear there, and shallow, since there had been no rain, and it ran in ripples over the sparkling sand. Under the overhanging willows of the opposite bank there was an inlet where the water was deeper and flowed so slowly that it seemed to sleep in the sun. In this little bay a single wild duck was swimming and diving and preening her feathers, disporting herself very happily in the flickering light and shade. They sat for a long time, watching the solitary bird take its pleasure. No living thing had ever seemed to Alexandra as beautiful as that wild duck. Emil must have felt about it as she did, for afterward, when they were at home, he used sometimes to say, "Sister, you know our duck down there—" Alexandra remembered that day as one of the happiest in her life. Years afterward she thought of the duck as still there, swimming and diving all by herself in the sunlight, a kind of enchanted bird that did not know age or change.

Most of Alexandra's happy memories were as impersonal as this one; yet to her they were very personal. Her mind was a white book, with clear writing about weather and beasts and growing things. Not many people would have cared to read it; only a happy few. She had never been in love, she had never indulged in sentimental reveries. Even as a girl she had looked upon men as work-fellows. She had grown up in serious times.

There was one fancy indeed, which persisted through her girlhood. It most often came to her on Sunday mornings, the one day in the week when she lay late abed listening to the familiar morning sounds; the windmill singing in the brisk breeze, Emil whistling as he blacked his boots down by the kitchen door. Sometimes, as she lay thus luxuriously idle, her eyes closed, she used to have an illusion of being lifted up bodily and carried lightly by some one very strong. It was a man, certainly, who carried her, but he was like no man she knew; he was much larger and stronger and swifter, and he carried her as easily as if she were a sheaf of wheat. She never saw him, but, with eyes closed, she could feel that he was yellow like the sunlight, and there was the smell of ripe cornfields about him. She could feel him approach, bend over her and lift her, and then she could feel herself being carried swiftly off across the fields. After such a reverie she would rise hastily, angry with herself, and go down to the bath-house that was partitioned off the kitchen shed. There she would stand in a tin tub and prosecute her bath with vigor, finishing it by pouring buckets of cold well-water over her gleaming white body which no man on the Divide could have carried very far.

As she grew older, this fancy more often came to her when she was tired than when she was fresh and strong. Sometimes, after she had been in the open all day, overseeing the branding of the cattle or the loading of the pigs, she would come in chilled, take a concoction of spices and warm home-made wine, and go to bed with her body actually aching with fatigue. Then, just before she went to sleep, she had the old sensation of being lifted and carried by a strong being who took from her all her bodily weariness.

Part IV

The White Mulberry Tree

I

*T*he French Church, properly the Church of Sainte-Agnes, stood upon a hill. The high, narrow, red-brick building, with its tall steeple and steep roof, could be seen for miles across the wheatfields, though the little town of Sainte-Agnes was completely hidden away at the foot of the hill. The church looked powerful and triumphant there on its eminence, so high above the rest of the landscape, with miles of warm color lying at its feet, and by its position and setting it reminded one of some of the churches built long ago in the wheat-lands of middle France.

Late one June afternoon Alexandra Bergson was driving along one of the many roads that led through the rich French farming country to the big church. The sunlight was shining directly in her face, and there was a blaze of light all about the red church on the hill. Beside Alexandra lounged a strikingly exotic figure in a tall Mexican hat, a silk sash, and a black velvet jacket sewn with silver buttons. Emil had returned only the night before, and his sister was so proud of him that she decided at once to take him up to the church supper, and to make him wear the Mexican costume he had brought home in his trunk. "All the girls who have stands are going to wear fancy costumes," she argued, "and some of the boys. Marie is going to tell fortunes, and she sent to Omaha for a Bohemian dress her father brought back from a visit to the old country. If you wear those clothes, they will all be pleased. And you must take your guitar. Everybody ought to do what they can to help along, and we have never done much. We are not a talented family."

The supper was to be at six o'clock, in the basement of the church, and afterward there would be a fair, with charades and an auction. Alexandra had set out from home early, leaving the house to Signa and Nelse Jensen, who were to be married next week. Signa had shyly asked to have the wedding put off until Emil came home.

Alexandra was well satisfied with her brother. As they drove through the rolling French country toward the westering sun and the stalwart church, she was thinking of that time long ago when she and Emil drove back from the river valley to the still unconquered Divide. Yes, she told herself, it had been worth while; both Emil and the country had become what she had hoped. Out of her father's children there was one who was fit to cope with the world, who had not been tied to the plow, and who had a personality apart from the soil. And that, she reflected, was what she had worked for. She felt well satisfied with her life.

When they reached the church, a score of teams were hitched in front of the basement doors that opened from the hillside upon the sanded terrace, where the boys wrestled and had jumping-matches. Amédée Chevalier, a proud father of one week, rushed out and embraced Emil. Amédée was an only son—hence he was a very rich young man—but he meant to have twenty children himself, like his uncle Xavier. "Oh, Emil," he cried, hugging his old friend rapturously, "why ain't you been up to see my boy? You come to-morrow, sure? Emil, you wanna get a boy right off! It's the greatest thing ever! No, no, no! Angel not sick at all. Everything just fine. That boy he come into this world laughin', and he been laughin' ever since. You come an' see!" He pounded Emil's ribs to emphasize each announcement.

Emil caught his arms. "Stop, Amédée. You're knocking the wind out of me. I brought him cups and spoons and blankets and moccasins enough for an orphan asylum. I'm awful glad it's a boy, sure enough!"

The young men crowded round Emil to admire his costume and to tell him in a breath everything that had happened since he went away. Emil had more friends up here in the French country than down on Norway Creek. The French and Bohemian boys were spirited and jolly, liked variety, and were as much predisposed to favor anything new as the Scandinavian boys were to reject it. The Norwegian and Swedish lads were much more self-centred, apt to be egotistical and jealous. They were cautious and reserved with Emil because he had been away to college, and were prepared to take him down if he should try to put on airs with them. The French boys liked a bit of swagger, and they were always delighted to hear about anything new: new clothes, new games, new songs, new dances. Now they carried Emil off to show him the club room they had just fitted up over the post-office, down in the village. They ran down the hill in a drove, all laughing and chattering at once, some in French, some in English.

Alexandra went into the cool, whitewashed basement where the women were setting the tables. Marie was standing on a chair, building a little tent of shawls where she was to tell fortunes. She sprang down and ran toward Alexandra, stopping short and looking at her in disappointment. Alexandra nodded to her encouragingly.

"Oh, he will be here, Marie. The boys have taken him off to show him something. You won't know him. He is a man now, sure enough. I have no boy left. He smokes terrible-smelling Mexican cigarettes and talks Spanish. How pretty you look, child. Where did you get those beautiful earrings?"

"They belonged to father's mother. He always promised them to me. He sent them with the dress and said I could keep them."

Marie wore a short red skirt of stoutly woven cloth, a white bodice and kirtle, a yellow silk turban wound low over her brown curls, and long coral pendants in her ears. Her ears had been pierced against a piece of cork by her great-aunt when she was seven years old. In those germless days she had worn bits of broom-straw, plucked from the common sweeping-broom, in the lobes until the holes were healed and ready for little gold rings.

When Emil came back from the village, he lingered outside on the terrace with the boys. Marie could hear him talking and strumming on his guitar while Raoul Marcel sang falsetto. She was vexed with him for staying out there. It made her very nervous to hear him and not to see him; for, certainly, she told herself, she was not going out to look for him. When the supper bell rang and the boys came trooping in to get seats at the first table, she forgot all about her annoyance and ran to greet the tallest of the crowd, in his conspicuous attire. She didn't mind showing her embarrassment at all. She blushed and laughed excitedly as she gave Emil her hand, and looked delightedly at the black velvet coat that brought out his fair skin and fine blond head. Marie was incapable of being lukewarm about anything that pleased her. She simply did not know how to give a half-hearted response. When she was delighted, she was as likely as not to stand on her tip-toes and clap her hands. If people laughed at her, she laughed with them.

"Do the men wear clothes like that every day, in the street?" She caught Emil by his sleeve and turned him about. "Oh, I wish I lived where people wore things like that! Are the buttons real silver? Put on the hat, please. What a heavy thing! How do you ever wear it? Why don't you tell us about the bull-fights?"

She wanted to wring all his experiences from him at once, without waiting a moment. Emil smiled tolerantly and stood looking down at her with his old, brooding gaze, while the French girls fluttered about him in their white dresses and ribbons, and Alexandra watched the scene with pride. Several of the French girls, Marie knew, were hoping that Emil would take them to supper, and she was relieved when he took only his sister. Marie caught Frank's arm and dragged him to the same table, managing to get seats opposite the Bergsons, so that she could hear what they were talking about. Alexandra made Emil tell Mrs. Xavier Chevalier, the mother of the twenty, about how he had seen a famous matador killed in the bull-ring. Marie listened to every word, only taking her eyes from Emil to watch Frank's plate and keep it filled. When Emil finished his account— bloody enough to satisfy Mrs. Xavier and to make her feel thankful that she was not a matador—Marie broke out with a volley of questions. How did the women dress when they went to bull-fights? Did they wear mantillas? Did they never wear hats?

After supper the young people played charades for the amusement of their elders, who sat gossiping between their guesses. All the shops in Sainte-Agnes were closed at eight o'clock that night, so that the merchants and their clerks could attend the fair. The auction was the liveliest part of the entertainment, for the French boys always lost their heads when they began to bid, satisfied that their extravagance was in a good cause. After all the pincushions and sofa pillows and embroidered slippers were sold, Emil precipitated a panic by taking out one of his turquoise shirt studs, which every one had been admiring, and handing it to the auctioneer. All the French girls clamored for it, and their sweethearts bid against each other recklessly. Marie wanted it, too, and she kept making signals to Frank, which he took a sour pleasure in disregarding. He didn't see the use of making a fuss over a fellow just because he was dressed like a clown. When the turquoise went to Malvina Sauvage, the French banker's daughter, Marie shrugged her shoulders and betook herself to her little tent of shawls, where she began to shuffle her cards by the light of a tallow candle, calling out, "Fortunes, fortunes!"

The young priest, Father Duchesne, went first to have his fortune read. Marie took his long white hand, looked at it, and then began to run off her cards. "I see a long journey across water for you, Father. You will go to a town all cut up by water; built on islands, it seems to be, with rivers and green fields all about. And you will visit an old lady with a white cap and gold hoops in her ears, and you will be very happy there."

"Mais, oui," said the priest, with a melancholy smile. "C'est L'Isle-Adam, chez ma mère. Vous êtes très savante, ma fille." He patted her yellow turban, calling, "Venez donc, mes garçons! Il y a ici une véritable clairvoyante!"

Marie was clever at fortune-telling, indulging in a light irony that amused the crowd. She told old Brunot, the miser, that he would lose all his money, marry a girl of sixteen, and live happily on a crust. Sholte, the fat Russian boy, who lived for his stomach, was to be disappointed in love, grow thin, and shoot himself from despondency. Amédée was to have twenty children, and nineteen of them were to be girls. Amédée slapped Frank on the back and asked him why he didn't see what the fortune-teller would promise him. But Frank shook off his friendly hand and grunted, "She tell my fortune long ago; bad enough!" Then he withdrew to a corner and sat glowering at his wife.

Frank's case was all the more painful because he had no one in particular to fix his jealousy upon. Sometimes he could have thanked the man who would bring him evidence against his wife. He had discharged a good farm-boy, Jan Smirka, because he thought Marie was fond of him; but she had not seemed to miss Jan when he was gone, and she had been just as kind to the next boy. The farm-hands would always do anything for Marie; Frank couldn't find one so surly that he would not make an effort to please her. At the bottom of his heart Frank knew well enough that if he could once give up his grudge, his wife would come back to him. But he could never in the world do that. The grudge was fundamental. Perhaps he could not have given it up if he had tried. Perhaps he got more satisfaction out of feeling himself abused than he would have got out of being loved. If he could once have made Marie thoroughly unhappy, he might have relented and raised her from the dust. But she had never humbled herself. In the first days of their love she had been his slave; she had admired him abandonedly. But the moment he began to bully her and to be unjust, she began to draw away; at first in tearful amazement, then in quiet, unspoken disgust. The distance between them had widened and hardened. It no longer contracted and brought them suddenly together. The spark of her life went somewhere else, and he was always watching to surprise it. He knew that somewhere she must get a feeling to live upon, for she was not a woman who could live without loving. He wanted to prove to himself the wrong he felt. What did she hide in her heart? Where did it go? Even Frank had his churlish delicacies; he never reminded her of how much she had once loved him. For that Marie was grateful to him.

While Marie was chattering to the French boys, Amédée called Emil to the back of the room and whispered to him that they were going to play a joke on the girls. At eleven o'clock, Amédée was to go up to the switchboard in the vestibule and turn off the electric lights, and every boy would have a chance to kiss his sweetheart before Father Duchesne could find his way up the stairs to turn the current on again. The only difficulty was the candle in Marie's tent; perhaps, as Emil had no sweetheart, he would oblige the boys by blowing out the candle. Emil said he would undertake to do that.

At five minutes to eleven he sauntered up to Marie's booth, and the French boys dispersed to find their girls. He leaned over the card-table and gave himself up to looking at her. "Do you think you could tell my fortune?" he murmured. It was the first word he had had alone with her for almost a year. "My luck hasn't changed any. It's just the same."

Marie had often wondered whether there was anyone else who could look his thoughts to you as Emil could. To-night, when she met his steady, powerful eyes, it was impossible not to feel the sweetness of the dream he was dreaming; it reached her before she could shut it out, and hid itself in her heart. She began to shuffle her cards furiously. "I'm angry with you, Emil," she broke out with petulance. "Why did you give them that lovely blue stone to sell? You might have known Frank wouldn't buy it for me, and I wanted it awfully!"

Emil laughed shortly. "People who want such little things surely ought to have them," he said dryly. He thrust his hand into the pocket of his velvet trousers and brought out a handful of uncut turquoises, as big as marbles. Leaning over the table he dropped them into her lap. "There, will those do? Be careful, don't let any one see them. Now, I suppose you want me to go away and let you play with them?"

Marie was gazing in rapture at the soft blue color of the stones. "Oh, Emil! Is everything down there beautiful like these? How could you ever come away?"

At that instant Amédée laid hands on the switchboard. There was a shiver and a giggle, and every one looked toward the red blur that Marie's candle made in the dark. Immediately that, too, was gone. Little shrieks and currents of soft laughter ran up and down the dark hall. Marie started up—directly into Emil's arms. In the same instant she felt his lips. The veil that had hung uncertainly between them for so long was dissolved. Before she knew what she was doing, she had committed herself to that kiss that was at once a boy's and a man's, as timid as it was tender; so like Emil and so unlike any one else in the world. Not until it was over did she realize what it meant. And Emil, who had so often imagined the shock of this first kiss, was surprised at its gentleness and naturalness. It was like a sigh which they had breathed together; almost sorrowful, as if each were afraid of wakening something in the other.

When the lights came on again, everybody was laughing and shouting, and all the French girls were rosy and shining with mirth. Only

Marie, in her little tent of shawls, was pale and quiet. Under her yellow turban the red coral pendants swung against white cheeks. Frank was still staring at her, but he seemed to see nothing. Years ago, he himself had had the power to take the blood from her cheeks like that. Perhaps he did not remember—perhaps he had never noticed! Emil was already at the other end of the hall, walking about with the shoulder-motion he had acquired among the Mexicans, studying the floor with his intent, deep-set eyes. Marie began to take down and fold her shawls. She did not glance up again. The young people drifted to the other end of the hall where the guitar was sounding. In a moment she heard Emil and Raoul singing:

"Across the Rio Grand-e
There lies a sunny land-e,
My bright-eyed Mexico!"

Alexandra Bergson came up to the card booth. "Let me help you, Marie. You look tired."

She placed her hand on Marie's arm and felt her shiver. Marie stiffened under that kind, calm hand. Alexandra drew back, perplexed and hurt.

There was about Alexandra something of the impervious calm of the fatalist, always disconcerting to very young people, who cannot feel that the heart lives at all unless it is still at the mercy of storms; unless its strings can scream to the touch of pain.

II

Signa's wedding supper was over. The guests, and the tiresome little Norwegian preacher who had performed the marriage ceremony, were saying good-night. Old Ivar was hitching the horses to the wagon to take the wedding presents and the bride and groom up to their new home, on Alexandra's north quarter. When Ivar drove up to the gate, Emil and Marie Shabata began to carry out the presents, and Alexandra went into her bedroom to bid Signa good-bye and to give her a few words of good counsel. She was surprised to find that the bride had changed her slippers for heavy shoes and was pinning up her skirts. At that

moment Nelse appeared at the gate with the two milk cows that Alexandra
had given Signa for a wedding present.

Alexandra began to laugh. "Why, Signa, you and Nelse are to
ride home. I'll send Ivar over with the cows in the morning."

Signa hesitated and looked perplexed. When her husband called
her, she pinned her hat on resolutely. "I ta-ank I better do yust like he say,"
she murmured in confusion.

Alexandra and Marie accompanied Signa to the gate and saw the
party set off, old Ivar driving ahead in the wagon and the bride and groom
following on foot, each leading a cow. Emil burst into a laugh before they
were out of hearing.

"Those two will get on," said Alexandra as they turned back to
the house. "They are not going to take any chances. They will feel safer
with those cows in their own stable. Marie, I am going to send for an old
woman next. As soon as I get the girls broken in, I marry them off."

"I've no patience with Signa, marrying that grumpy fellow!"
Marie declared. "I wanted her to marry that nice Smirka boy who worked
for us last winter. I think she liked him, too."

"Yes, I think she did," Alexandra assented, "but I suppose she
was too much afraid of Nelse to marry any one else. Now that I think of
it, most of my girls have married men they were afraid of. I believe there
is a good deal of the cow in most Swedish girls. You high-strung Bohemians
can't understand us. We're a terribly practical people, and I guess we think
a cross man makes a good manager."

Marie shrugged her shoulders and turned to pin up a lock of hair
that had fallen on her neck. Somehow Alexandra had irritated her of late.
Everybody irritated her. She was tired of everybody. "I'm going home
alone, Emil, so you needn't get your hat," she said as she wound her scarf
quickly about her head. "Good-night, Alexandra," she called back in a
strained voice, running down the gravel walk.

Emil followed with long strides until he overtook her. Then she
began to walk slowly. It was a night of warm wind and faint starlight, and
the fireflies were glimmering over the wheat.

"Marie," said Emil after they had walked for a while, "I wonder
if you know how unhappy I am?"

Marie did not answer him. Her head, in its white scarf, drooped
forward a little.

Emil kicked a clod from the path and went on:

"I wonder whether you are really shallow-hearted, like you

seem? Sometimes I think one boy does just as well as another for you. It never seems to make much difference whether it is me or Raoul Marcel or Jan Smirka. Are you like that?"

"Perhaps I am. What do you want me to do? Sit around and cry all day? When I've cried until I can't cry any more, then—I must do something else."

"Are you sorry for me?" he persisted.

"No, I'm not. If I were big and free like you, I wouldn't let anything make me unhappy. As old Napoleon Brunot said at the fair, I wouldn't go lovering after no woman. I'd take the first train and go off and have all the fun there is."

"I tried that, but it didn't do any good. Everything reminded me. The nicer the place was, the more I wanted you." They had come to the stile and Emil pointed to it persuasively. "Sit down a moment, I want to ask you something." Marie sat down on the top step and Emil drew nearer. "Would you tell me something that's none of my business if you thought it would help me out? Well, then, tell me, *please* tell me, why you ran away with Frank Shabata!"

Marie drew back. "Because I was in love with him," she said firmly.

"Really?" he asked incredulously.

"Yes, indeed. Very much in love with him. I think I was the one who suggested our running away. From the first it was more my fault than his."

Emil turned away his face.

"And now," Marie went on, "I've got to remember that. Frank is just the same now as he was then, only then I would see him as I wanted him to be. I would have my own way. And now I pay for it."

"You don't do all the paying."

"That's it. When one makes a mistake, there's no telling where it will stop. But you can go away; you can leave all this behind you."

"Not everything. I can't leave you behind. Will you go away with me, Marie?"

Marie started up and stepped across the stile. "Emil! How wickedly you talk! I am not that kind of a girl, and you know it. But what am I going to do if you keep tormenting me like this!" she added plaintively.

"Marie, I won't bother you any more if you will tell me just one thing. Stop a minute and look at me. No, nobody can see us. Everybody's asleep. That was only a firefly. Marie, *stop* and tell me!"

Emil overtook her and catching her by the shoulders shook her gently, as if he were trying to awaken a sleepwalker.

Marie hid her face on his arm. "Don't ask me anything more. I don't know anything except how miserable I am. And I thought it would be all right when you came back. Oh, Emil," she clutched his sleeve and began to cry, "what am I to do if you don't go away? I can't go, and one of us must. Can't you see?"

Emil stood looking down at her, holding his shoulders stiff and stiffening the arm to which she clung. Her white dress looked gray in the darkness. She seemed like a troubled spirit, like some shadow out of the earth, clinging to him and entreating him to give her peace. Behind her the fireflies were weaving in and out over the wheat. He put his hand on her bent head. "On my honor, Marie, if you will say you love me, I will go away."

She lifted her face to his. "How could I help it? Didn't you know?"

Emil was the one who trembled, through all his frame. After he left Marie at her gate, he wandered about the fields all night, till morning put out the fireflies and the stars.

III

One evening, a week after Signa's wedding, Emil was kneeling before a box in the sitting-room, packing his books. From time to time he rose and wandered about the house, picking up stray volumes and bringing them listlessly back to his box. He was packing without enthusiasm. He was not very sanguine about his future. Alexandra sat sewing by the table. She had helped him pack his trunk in the afternoon. As Emil came and went by her chair with his books, he thought to himself that it had not been so hard to leave his sister since he first went away to school. He was going directly to Omaha, to read law in the office of a Swedish lawyer until October, when he would enter the law school at Ann Arbor. They had planned that Alexandra was to come to Michigan—a long journey for her—at Christmas time, and spend several weeks with him. Nevertheless, he felt that this leavetaking would be more final than his earlier ones had been; that it meant a definite break with his old home and the beginning of something new—he did not know what. His ideas about the future would not crystallize; the more he tried to think about it, the vaguer his conception of it became. But one thing was clear, he told himself; it was high time that he made good to Alexandra, and that ought to be incentive enough to begin with.

As he went about gathering up his books he felt as if he were uprooting things. At last he threw himself down on the old slat lounge where he had slept when he was little, and lay looking up at the familiar cracks in the ceiling.

"Tired, Emil?" his sister asked.

"Lazy," he murmured, turning on his side and looking at her. He studied Alexandra's face for a long time in the lamplight. It had never occurred to him that his sister was a handsome woman until Marie Shabata had told him so. Indeed, he had never thought of her as being a woman at all, only a sister. As he studied her bent head, he looked up at the picture of John Bergson above the lamp. "No," he thought to himself, "she didn't get it there. I suppose I am more like that."

"Alexandra," he said suddenly, "that old walnut secretary you use for a desk was father's, wasn't it?"

Alexandra went on stitching. "Yes. It was one of the first things he bought for the old log house. It was a great extravagance in those days. But he wrote a great many letters back to the old country. He had many friends there, and they wrote to him up to the time he died. No one ever blamed him for grandfather's disgrace. I can see him now, sitting there on Sundays, in his white shirt, writing pages and pages, so carefully. He wrote a fine, regular hand, almost like engraving. Yours is something like his, when you take pains."

"Grandfather was really crooked, was he?"

"He married an unscrupulous woman, and then—then I'm afraid he was really crooked. When we first came here father used to have dreams about making a great fortune and going back to Sweden to pay back to the poor sailors the money grandfather had lost."

Emil stirred on the lounge. "I say, that would have been worth while, wouldn't it? Father wasn't a bit like Lou or Oscar, was he? I can't remember much about him before he got sick."

"Oh, not at all!" Alexandra dropped her sewing on her knee. "He had better opportunities; not to make money, but to make something of himself. He was a quiet man, but he was very intelligent. You would have been proud of him, Emil."

Alexandra felt that he would like to know there had been a man of his kin whom he could admire. She knew that Emil was ashamed of Lou and Oscar, because they were bigoted and self-satisfied. He never said much about them, but she could feel his disgust. His brothers had shown their disapproval of him ever since he first went away to school. The only thing that would have satisfied them would have been his failure at the University. As it was, they resented every change in his speech, in his dress, in his point of view; though the latter they had to conjecture, for Emil avoided talking to them about any but family matters. All his interests they treated as affectations.

Alexandra took up her sewing again. "I can remember father when he was quite a young man. He belonged to some kind of a musical society, a male chorus, in Stockholm. I can remember going with mother to hear them sing. There must have been a hundred of them, and they all wore long black coats and white neckties. I was used to seeing father in a blue coat, a sort of jacket, and when I recognized him on the platform, I was very proud. Do you remember that Swedish song he taught you, about the ship boy?"

"Yes. I used to sing it to the Mexicans. They like anything different." Emil paused. "Father had a hard fight here, didn't he?" he added thoughtfully.

"Yes, and he died in a dark time. Still, he had hope. He believed in the land."

"And in you, I guess," Emil said to himself. There was another period of silence; that warm, friendly silence, full of perfect understanding, in which Emil and Alexandra had spent many of their happiest half-hours.

At last Emil said abruptly, "Lou and Oscar would be better off if they were poor, wouldn't they?"

Alexandra smiled. "Maybe. But their children wouldn't. I have great hopes of Milly."

Emil shivered. "I don't know. Seems to me it gets worse as it goes on. The worst of the Swedes is that they're never willing to find out how much they don't know. It was like that at the University. Always so pleased with themselves! There's no getting behind that conceited Swedish grin. The Bohemians and Germans were so different."

"Come, Emil, don't go back on your own people. Father wasn't conceited, Uncle Otto wasn't. Even Lou and Oscar weren't when they were boys."

Emil looked incredulous, but he did not dispute the point. He turned on his back and lay still for a long time, his hands locked under his head, looking up at the ceiling. Alexandra knew that he was thinking of many things. She felt no anxiety about Emil. She had always believed in him, as she had believed in the land. He had been more like himself since he got back from Mexico; seemed glad to be at home, and talked to her as he used to do. She had no doubt that his wandering fit was over, and that he would soon be settled in life.

"Alexandra," said Emil suddenly, "do you remember the wild duck we saw down on the river that time?"

His sister looked up. "I often think of her. It always seems to me she's there still, just like we saw her."

"I know. It's queer what things one remembers and what things one forgets." Emil yawned and sat up. "Well, it's time to turn in." He rose, and going over to Alexandra stooped down and kissed her lightly on the cheek. "Good-night, sister. I think you did pretty well by us."

Emil took up his lamp and went upstairs. Alexandra sat finishing his new nightshirt, that must go in the top tray of his trunk.

IV

The next morning Angélique, Amédée's wife, was in the kitchen baking pies, assisted by old Mrs. Chevalier. Between the mixing-board and the stove stood the old cradle that had been Amédée's, and in it was his black-eyed son. As Angélique, flushed and excited, with flour on her hands, stopped to smile at the baby, Emil Bergson rode up to the kitchen door on his mare and dismounted.

" 'Médée is out in the field, Emil," Angélique called as she ran across the kitchen to the oven. "He begins to cut his wheat to-day; the first wheat ready to cut anywhere about here. He bought a new header, you know, because all the wheat's so short this year. I hope he can rent it to the neighbors, it cost so much. He and his cousins bought a steam thresher on shares. You ought to go out and see that header work. I watched it an hour this morning, busy as I am with all the men to feed. He has a lot of hands, but he's the only one that knows how to drive the header or how to run the engine, so he has to be everywhere at once. He's sick, too, and ought to be in his bed."

Emil bent over Hector Baptiste, trying to make him blink his round, bead-like black eyes. "Sick? What's the matter with your daddy, kid? Been making him walk the floor with you?"

Angélique sniffed. "Not much! We don't have that kind of babies. It was his father that kept Baptiste awake. All night I had to be getting up and making mustard plasters to put on his stomach. He had an awful colic. He said he felt better this morning, but I don't think he ought to be out in the field, overheating himself."

Angélique did not speak with much anxiety, not because she was indifferent, but because she felt so secure in their good fortune. Only good things could happen to a rich, energetic, handsome young man like Amédée, with a new baby in the cradle and a new header in the field.

Emil stroked the black fuzz on Baptiste's head. "I say, Angélique, one of 'Médée's grandmothers, 'way back, must have been a squaw. This kid looks exactly like the Indian babies."

Angélique made a face at him, but old Mrs. Chevalier had been touched on a sore point, and she let out such a stream of fiery *patois* that Emil fled from the kitchen and mounted his mare.

Opening the pasture gate from the saddle, Emil rode across the field to the clearing where the thresher stood, driven by a stationary engine and fed from the header boxes. As Amédée was not on the engine, Emil rode on to the wheatfield, where he recognized, on the header, the slight, wiry figure of his friend, coatless, his white shirt puffed out by the wind, his straw hat stuck jauntily on the side of his head. The six big work-horses that drew, or rather pushed, the header, went abreast at a rapid walk, and as they were still green at the work they required a good deal of management on Amédée's part; especially when they turned the corners, where they divided, three and three, and then swung round into line again with a movement that looked as complicated as a wheel of artillery. Emil felt a new thrill of admiration for his friend, and with it the old pang of envy at the way in which Amédée could do with his might what his hand found to do, and feel that, whatever it was, it was the most important thing in the world. "I'll have to bring Alexandra up to see this thing work," Emil thought; "it's splendid!"

When he saw Emil, Amédée waved to him and called to one of his twenty cousins to take the reins. Stepping off the header without stopping it, he ran up to Emil who had dismounted. "Come along," he called. "I have to go over to the engine for a minute. I gotta green man running it, and I gotta to keep an eye on him."

Emil thought the lad was unnaturally flushed and more excited than even the cares of managing a big farm at a critical time warranted. As they passed behind a last year's stack, Amédée clutched at his right side and sank down for a moment on the straw.

"Ouch! I got an awful pain in me, Emil. Something's the matter with my insides, for sure."

Emil felt his fiery cheek. "You ought to go straight to bed, 'Médée, and telephone for the doctor; that's what you ought to do."

Amédée staggered up with a gesture of despair. "How can I? I got no time to be sick. Three thousand dollars' worth of new machinery to manage, and the wheat so ripe it will begin to shatter next week. My wheat's short, but it's gotta grand full berries. What's he slowing down for? We haven't got header boxes enough to feed the thresher, I guess."

Amédée started hot-foot across the stubble, leaning a little to the right as he ran, and waved to the engineer not to stop the engine.

Emil saw that this was no time to talk about his own affairs. He mounted his mare and rode on to Sainte-Agnes, to bid his friends there good-bye. He went first to see Raoul Marcel, and found him innocently practising the "Gloria" for the big confirmation service on Sunday while he polished the mirrors of his father's saloon.

As Emil rode homewards at three o'clock in the afternoon, he saw Amédée staggering out of the wheatfield, supported by two of his cousins. Emil stopped and helped them put the boy to bed.

V

*W*hen Frank Shabata came in from work at five o'clock that evening, old Moses Marcel, Raoul's father, telephoned him that Amédée had had a seizure in the wheatfield, and that Doctor Paradis was going to operate on him as soon as the Hanover doctor got there to help. Frank dropped a word of this at the table, bolted his supper, and rode off to Sainte-Agnes, where there would be sympathetic discussion of Amédée's case at Marcel's saloon.

As soon as Frank was gone, Marie telephoned Alexandra. It was a comfort to hear her friend's voice. Yes, Alexandra knew what there was to be known about Amédée. Emil had been there when they carried him out of the field, and had stayed with him until the doctors operated for appendicitis at five o'clock. They were afraid it was too late to do much good; it should have been done three days ago. Amédée was in a very bad way. Emil had just come home, worn out and sick himself. She had given him some brandy and put him to bed.

Marie hung up the receiver. Poor Amédée's illness had taken on a new meaning to her, now that she knew Emil had been with him. And it might so easily have been the other way—Emil who was ill and Amédée who was sad! Marie looked about the dusky sitting-room. She had seldom felt so utterly lonely. If Emil was asleep, there was not even a chance of his coming; and she could not go to Alexandra for sympathy. She meant to tell Alexandra everything, as soon as Emil went away. Then whatever was left between them would be honest.

But she could not stay in the house this evening. Where should she go? She walked slowly down through the orchard, where the evening air was heavy with the smell of wild cotton. The fresh, salty scent of the wild roses had given way before this more powerful perfume of midsummer. Wherever those ashes-of-rose balls hung on their milky stalks, the air about them was saturated with their breath. The sky was still red in the west and the evening star hung directly over the Bergsons' windmill. Marie crossed the fence at the wheatfield corner, and walked slowly along the path that led to Alexandra's. She could not help feeling hurt that Emil had not come to tell her about Amédée. It seemed to her most unnatural that he should not have come. If she were in trouble, certainly he was the one person in the world she would want to see. Perhaps he wished her to understand that for her he was as good as gone already.

Marie stole slowly, flutteringly, along the path, like a white night-moth out of the fields. The years seemed to stretch before her like the land; spring, summer, autumn, winter, spring; always the same patient fields, the patient little trees, the patient lives; always the same yearning, the same pulling at the chain—until the instinct to live had torn itself and bled and weakened for the last time, until the chain secured a dead woman, who might cautiously be released. Marie walked on, her face lifted toward the remote, inaccessible evening star.

When she reached the stile she sat down and waited. How terrible it was to love people when you could not really share their lives!

Yes, in so far as she was concerned, Emil was already gone. They couldn't meet any more. There was nothing for them to say. They had spent the last penny of their small change; there was nothing left but gold. The day of love-tokens was past. They had now only their hearts to give each other. And Emil being gone, what was her life to be like? In some ways, it would be easier. She would not, at least, live in perpetual fear. If Emil were once away and settled at work, she would not have the feeling that she was spoiling his life. With the memory he left her, she could be as rash as she chose. Nobody could be the worse for it but herself; and that, surely, did not matter. Her own case was clear. When a girl had loved one man, and then loved another while that man was still alive, everybody knew what to think of her. What happened to her was of little consequence, so long as she did not drag other people down with her. Emil once away, she could let everything else go and live a new life of perfect love.

Marie left the stile reluctantly. She had, after all, thought he might come. And how glad she ought to be, she told herself, that he was asleep. She left the path and went across the pasture. The moon was almost full. An owl was hooting somewhere in the fields. She had scarcely thought about where she was going when the pond glittered before her, where Emil had shot the ducks. She stopped and looked at it. Yes, there would be a dirty way out of life, if one chose to take it. But she did not want to die. She wanted to live and dream—a hundred years, forever! As long as this sweetness welled up in her heart, as long as her breast could hold this treasure of pain! She felt as the pond must feel when it held the moon like that; when it encircled and swelled with that image of gold.

In the morning, when Emil came downstairs, Alexandra met him in the sitting-room and put her hands on his shoulders. "Emil, I went to your room as soon as it was light, but you were sleeping so sound I hated to wake you. There was nothing you could do, so I let you sleep. They telephoned from Sainte-Agnes that Amédée died at three o'clock this morning."

VI

*T*he Church has always held that life is for the living. On Saturday, while half the village of Sainte-Agnes was mourning for Amédée and preparing the funeral black for his burial on Monday, the other half was busy with white dresses and white veils for the great confirmation service to-morrow, when the bishop was to confirm a class of one hundred boys and girls. Father Duchesne divided his time between the living and the dead. All day Saturday the church was a scene of bustling activity, a little hushed by the thought of Amédée. The choir were busy rehearsing a mass of Rossini, which they had studied and practised for this occasion. The women were trimming the altar, the boys and girls were bringing flowers.

On Sunday morning the bishop was to drive overland to Sainte-Agnes from Hanover, and Emil Bergson had been asked to take the place of one of Amédée's cousins in the cavalcade of forty French boys who were to ride across country to meet the bishop's carriage. At six o'clock on Sunday morning the boys met at the church. As they stood holding their horses by the bridle, they talked in low tones of their dead comrade. They kept repeating that Amédée had always been a good boy, glancing toward the red brick church which had played so large a part in Amédée's life, had been the scene of his most serious moments and of his happiest hours. He had played and wrestled and sung and courted under its shadow. Only three weeks ago he had proudly carried his baby there to be christened. They could not doubt that that invisible arm was still about Amédée; that through the church on earth he had passed to the church triumphant, the goal of the hopes and faith of so many hundred years.

When the word was given to mount, the young men rode at a walk out of the village; but once out among the wheatfields in the morning sun, their horses and their own youth got the better of them. A wave of zeal and fiery enthusiasm swept over them. They longed for a Jerusalem to deliver. The thud of their galloping hoofs interrupted many a country breakfast and brought many a woman and child to the door of the farmhouses as they passed. Five miles east of Sainte-Agnes they met the bishop in his open carriage, attended by two priests. Like one man the boys swung off their hats in a broad salute, and bowed their heads as the handsome old man lifted his two fingers in the episcopal blessing. The horsemen closed about the carriage like a guard, and whenever a restless horse broke from control and shot down the road ahead of the body, the bishop laughed and rubbed his plump hands together. "What fine boys!" he said to his priests. "The Church still has her cavalry."

As the troop swept past the graveyard half a mile east of the town,—the first frame church of the parish had stood there,—old Pierre Séguin was already out with his pick and spade, digging Amédée's grave. He knelt and uncovered as the bishop passed. The boys with one accord looked away from old Pierre to the red church on the hill, with the gold cross flaming on its steeple.

Mass was at eleven. While the church was filling, Emil Bergson waited outside, watching the wagons and buggies drive up the hill. After the bell began to ring, he saw Frank Shabata ride up on horseback and tie his horse to the hitch-bar. Marie, then, was not coming. Emil turned and went into the church. Amédée's was the only empty pew, and he sat down in it. Some of Amédée's cousins were there, dressed in black and weeping. When all the pews were full, the old men and boys packed the open space at the back of the church, kneeling on the floor. There was scarcely a family in town that was not represented in the confirmation class, by a cousin, at least. The new communicants, with their clear, reverent faces, were beautiful to look upon as they entered in a body and took the front benches reserved for them. Even before the Mass began, the air was charged with feeling. The choir had never sung so well and Raoul Marcel, in the "Gloria," drew even the bishop's eyes to the organ loft. For the offertory he sang Gounod's "Ave Maria,"—always spoken of in Sainte-Agnes as "the Ave Maria."

Emil began to torture himself with questions about Marie. Was she ill? Had she quarreled with her husband? Was she too unhappy to find comfort even here? Had she, perhaps, thought that he would come to her? Was she waiting for him? Overtaxed by excitement and sorrow as he was, the rapture of the service took hold upon his body and mind. As he listened to Raoul, he seemed to emerge from the conflicting emotions which had been whirling him about and sucking him under. He felt as if a clear light broke upon his mind, and with it a conviction that good was, after all, stronger than evil, and that good was possible to men. He seemed to discover that there was a kind of rapture in which he could love forever without faltering and without sin. He looked across the heads of the people at Frank Shabata with calmness. That rapture was for those who could feel it; for people who could not, it was non-existent. He coveted nothing that was Frank Shabata's. The spirit he had met in music was his own. Frank Shabata had never found it; would never find it if he lived beside it a thousand years; would have destroyed it if he had found it, as Herod slew the innocents, as Rome slew the martyrs.

San—cta Mari-i-i-a,

wailed Raoul from the organ loft;

O—ra pro no-o-bis!

And it did not occur to Emil that any one had ever reasoned thus before, that music had ever before given a man this equivocal revelation.

The confirmation service followed the Mass. When it was over, the congregation thronged about the newly confirmed. The girls, and even the boys, were kissed and embraced and wept over. All the aunts and grandmothers wept with joy. The housewives had much ado to tear themselves away from the general rejoicing and hurry back to their kitchens. The country parishioners were staying in town for dinner, and nearly every house in Sainte-Agnes entertained visitors that day. Father Duchesne, the bishop, and the visiting priests dined with Fabien Sauvage, the banker. Emil and Frank Shabata were both guests of old Moïse Marcel. After dinner Frank and old Moïse retired to the rear room of the saloon to play California Jack and drink their cognac, and Emil went over to the banker's with Raoul, who had been asked to sing for the bishop.

At three o'clock, Emil felt that he could stand it no longer. He slipped out under cover of "The Holy City," followed by Malvina's wistful eye, and went to the stable for his mare. He was at that height of excitement from which everything is foreshortened, from which life seems short and simple, death very near, and the soul seems to soar like an eagle. As he rode past the graveyard he looked at the brown hole in the earth where Amédée was to lie, and felt no horror. That, too, was beautiful, that simple doorway into forgetfulness. The heart, when it is too much alive, aches for that brown earth, and ecstasy has no fear of death. It is the old and the poor and the maimed who shrink from that brown hole; its wooers are found among the young, the passionate, the gallant-hearted. It was not until he had passed the graveyard that Emil realized where he was going. It was the hour for saying good-bye. It might be the last time that he would see her alone, and to-day he could leave her without rancor, without bitterness.

Everywhere the grain stood ripe and the hot afternoon was full of the smell of the ripe wheat, like the smell of bread baking in an oven. The breath of the wheat and the sweet clover passed him like pleasant things in a dream. He could feel nothing but the sense of diminishing distance. It seemed to him that his mare was flying, or running on wheels, like a railway train. The sunlight, flashing on the window-glass of the big red barns, drove him wild with joy. He was like an arrow shot from the bow. His life poured itself out along the road before him as he rode to the Shabata farm.

When Emil alighted at the Shabatas' gate, his horse was in a lather. He tied her in the stable and hurried to the house. It was empty. She might be at Mrs. Hiller's or with Alexandra. But anything that reminded him of her would be enough, the orchard, the mulberry tree . . . When he reached the orchard the sun was hanging low over the wheatfield. Long fingers of light reached through the apple branches as through a net; the orchard was riddled and shot with gold; light was the reality, the trees were merely interferences that reflected and refracted light. Emil went softly down between the cherry trees toward the wheatfield. When he came to the corner, he stopped short and put his hand over his mouth. Marie was lying on her side under the white mulberry tree, her face half hidden in the grass, her eyes closed, her hands lying limply where they had happened to fall. She had lived a day of her new life of perfect love, and it had left her like this. Her breast rose and fell faintly, as if she were asleep. Emil threw himself down beside her and took her in his arms. The blood came back to her cheeks, her amber eyes opened slowly, and in them Emil saw his own face and the orchard and the sun. "I was dreaming this," she whispered, hiding her face against him, "don't take my dream away!"

VII

*W*hen Frank Shabata got home that night, he found Emil's mare in his stable. Such an impertinence amazed him. Like everybody else, Frank had had an exciting day. Since noon he had been drinking too much, and he was in a bad temper. He talked bitterly to himself while he put his own horse away, and as he went up the path and saw that the house was dark he felt an added sense of injury. He approached quietly and listened on the doorstep. Hearing nothing, he opened the kitchen door and went softly from one room to another. Then he went through the house again, upstairs and down, with no better result. He sat down on the bottom step of the box stairway and tried to get his wits together. In that unnatural quiet there was no sound but his own heavy breathing. Suddenly an owl began to hoot out in the fields. Frank lifted his head. An idea flashed into his mind, and his sense of injury and outrage grew. He went into his bedroom and took his murderous 405 Winchester from the closet.

When Frank took up his gun and walked out of the house, he had not the faintest purpose of doing anything with it. He did not believe that he had any real grievance. But it gratified him to feel like a desperate man. He had got into the habit of seeing himself always in desperate straits. His unhappy temperament was like a cage; he could never get out of it; and he felt that other people, his wife in particular, must have put him there. It had never more than dimly occurred to Frank that he made his own unhappiness. Though he took up his gun with dark projects in his mind, he would have been paralyzed with fright had he known that there was the slightest probability of his ever carrying any of them out.

Frank went slowly down to the orchard gate, stopped and stood for a moment lost in thought. He retraced his steps and looked through the barn and the hayloft. Then he went out to the road, where he took the footpath along the outside of the orchard hedge. The hedge was twice as tall as Frank himself, and so dense that one could see through it only by peering closely between the leaves. He could see the empty path a long way in the moonlight. His mind traveled ahead to the stile, which he always thought of as haunted by Emil Bergson. But why had he left his horse?

At the wheatfield corner, where the orchard hedge ended and the path led across the pasture to the Bergsons', Frank stopped. In the warm, breathless night air he heard a murmuring sound, perfectly inarticulate, as low as the sound of water coming from a spring, where there is no fall, and where there are no stones to fret it. Frank strained his ears. It ceased. He held his breath and began to tremble. Resting the butt of his gun on the ground, he parted the mulberry leaves softly with his fingers and peered through the hedge at the dark figures on the grass, in the shadow of the mulberry tree. It seemed to him that they must feel his eyes, that they must hear him breathing. But they did not. Frank, who had always wanted to see things blacker than they were, for once wanted to believe less than he saw. The woman lying in the shadow might so easily be one of the Bergsons' farm-girls. . . . Again the murmur, like water welling out of the ground. This time he heard it more distinctly, and his blood was quicker than his brain. He began to act, just as a man who falls into the fire begins to act. The gun sprang to his shoulder, he sighted mechanically and fired three times without stopping, stopped without knowing why. Either he shut his eyes or he had vertigo. He did not see anything while he was firing. He thought he heard a cry simultaneous with the second report, but he was not sure. He peered again through the hedge, at the two dark figures under the tree. They had fallen a little apart from each other, and were perfectly still—No, not quite; in a white patch of light, where the moon shone through the branches, a man's hand was plucking spasmodically at the grass.

Suddenly the woman stirred and uttered a cry, then another, and another. She was living! She was dragging herself toward the hedge! Frank dropped his gun and ran back along the path, shaking, stumbling, gasping. He had never imagined such horror. The cries followed him. They grew fainter and thicker, as if she were choking. He dropped on his knees beside the hedge and crouched like a rabbit, listening; fainter, fainter; a sound like a whine; again—a moan—another—silence. Frank scrambled to his feet and ran on, groaning and praying. From habit he went toward the house, where he was used to being soothed when he had worked himself into a frenzy, but at the sight of the black, open door, he started back. He knew that he had murdered somebody, that a woman was bleeding and moaning in the orchard, but he had not realized before that it was his wife. The gate stared him in the face. He threw his hands over his head. Which way to turn? He lifted his tormented face and looked at the sky. "Holy Mother of God, not to suffer! She was a good girl—not to suffer!"

Frank had been wont to see himself in dramatic situations; but now, when he stood by the windmill, in the bright space between the barn and the house, facing his own black doorway, he did not see himself at all. He stood like the hare when the dogs are approaching from all sides. And he ran like a hare, back and forth about that moonlit space, before he could make up his mind to go into the dark stable for a horse. The thought of going into a doorway was terrible to him. He caught Emil's horse by the bit and led it out. He could not have buckled a bridle on his own. After two or three attempts, he lifted himself into the saddle and started for Hanover. If he could catch the one o'clock train, he had money enough to get as far as Omaha.

While he was thinking dully of this in some less sensitized part of his brain, his acuter faculties were going over and over the cries he had heard in the orchard. Terror was the only thing that kept him from going back to her, terror that she might still be she, that she might still be suffering. A woman, mutilated and bleeding in his orchard—it was because it was a woman that he was so afraid. It was inconceivable that he should have hurt a woman. He would rather be eaten by wild beasts than see her move on the ground as she had moved in the orchard. Why had she been so careless? She knew he was like a crazy man when he was angry. She had more than once taken that gun away from him and held it, when he was angry with other people. Once it had gone off while they were struggling over it! She was never afraid. But, when she knew him, why hadn't she been more careful? Didn't she have all summer before her to love Emil Bergson in, without taking such chances? Probably she had met the Smirka boy, too, down there in the orchard. He didn't care. She could have met all the men on the Divide there, and welcome, if only she hadn't brought this horror on him.

There was a wrench in Frank's mind. He did not honestly

believe that of her. He knew that he was doing her wrong. He stopped his horse to admit this to himself the more directly, to think it out the more clearly. He knew that he was to blame. For three years he had been trying to break her spirit. She had a way of making the best of things that seemed to him a sentimental affectation. He wanted his wife to resent that he was wasting his best years among these stupid and unappreciative people; but she had seemed to find the people quite good enough. If he ever got rich he meant to buy her pretty clothes and take her to California in a Pullman car, and treat her like a lady; but in the mean time he wanted her to feel that life was as ugly and as unjust as he felt it. He had tried to make her life ugly. He had refused to share any of the little pleasures she was so plucky about making for herself. She could be gay about the least thing in the world; but she must be gay! When she first came to him, her faith in him, her adoration—Frank struck the mare with his fist. Why had Marie made him do this thing; why had she brought this upon him? He was overwhelmed by sickening misfortune. All at once he heard her cries again—he had forgotten for a moment. "Maria," he sobbed aloud, "Maria!"

When Frank was halfway to Hanover, the motion of his horse brought on a violent attack of nausea. After it had passed, he rode on again, but he could think of nothing except his physical weakness and his desire to be comforted by his wife. He wanted to get into his own bed! Had his wife been at home, he would have turned and gone back to her meekly enough.

VIII

*W*hen old Ivar climbed down from his loft at four o'clock the next morning, he came upon Emil's mare, jaded and lather-stained, her bridle broken, chewing the scattered tufts of hay outside the stable door. The old man was thrown into a fright at once. He put the mare in her stall, threw her a measure of oats, and then set out as fast as his bow-legs could carry him on the path to the nearest neighbor.

"Something is wrong with that boy. Some misfortune has come upon us. He would never have used her so, in his right senses. It is not his way to abuse his mare," the old man kept muttering, as he scuttled through the short, wet pasture grass on his bare feet.

While Ivar was hurrying across the fields, the first long rays of the sun were reaching down between the orchard boughs to those two dew-drenched figures. The story of what had happened was written plainly on the orchard grass, and on the white mulberries that had fallen in the night and were covered with dark stain. For Emil the chapter had been short. He was shot in the heart, and had rolled over on his back and died. His face was turned up to the sky and his brows were drawn in a frown, as if he had realized that something had befallen him. But for Marie Shabata it had not been so easy. One ball had torn through her right lung, another had shattered the carotid artery. She must have started up and gone toward the hedge, leaving a trail of blood. There she had fallen and bled. From that spot there was another trail, heavier than the first, where she must have dragged herself back to Emil's body. Once there, she seemed not to have struggled any more. She had lifted her head to her lover's breast, taken his hand in both her own, and bled quietly to death. She was lying on her right side in an easy and natural position, her cheek on Emil's shoulder. On her face there was a look of ineffable content. Her lips were parted a little; her eyes were lightly closed, as if in a day-dream or a light slumber. After she lay down there, she seemed not to have moved an eyelash. The hand she held was covered with dark stains, where she had kissed it.

But the stained, slippery grass, the darkened mulberries, told only half the story. Above Marie and Emil, two white butterflies from Frank's alfalfa-field were fluttering in and out among the interlacing shadows; diving and soaring, now close together, now far apart; and in the long grass by the fence the last wild roses of the year opened their pink hearts to die.

When Ivar reached the path by the hedge, he saw Shabata's rifle lying in the way. He turned and peered through the branches, falling upon his knees as if his legs had been mowed from under him. "Merciful God!" he groaned; "merciful, merciful God!"

Alexandra, too, had risen early that morning, because of her anxiety about Emil. She was in Emil's room upstairs when, from the window, she saw Ivar coming along the path that led from the Shabatas'. He was running like a spent man, tottering and lurching from side to side. Ivar never drank, and Alexandra thought at once that one of his spells had come upon him, and that he must be in a very bad way indeed. She ran downstairs and hurried out to meet him, to hide his infirmity from the eyes of her household. The old man fell in the road at her feet and caught her hand, over which he bowed his shaggy head. "Mistress, mistress," he sobbed, "it has fallen! Sin and death for the young ones! God have mercy upon us!"

Part V

Alexandra

I

Ivar was sitting at a cobbler's bench in the barn, mending harness by the light of a lantern and repeating to himself the 101st Psalm. It was only five o'clock of a mid-October day, but a storm had come up in the afternoon, bringing black clouds, a cold wind and torrents of rain. The old man wore his buffalo-skin coat, and occasionally stopped to warm his fingers at the lantern. Suddenly a woman burst into the shed, as if she had been blown in, accompanied by a shower of rain-drops. It was Signa, wrapped in a man's overcoat and wearing a pair of boots over her shoes. In time of trouble Signa had come back to stay with her mistress, for she was the only one of the maids from whom Alexandra would accept much personal service. It was three months now since the news of the terrible thing that had happened in Frank Shabata's orchard had first run like a fire over the Divide. Signa and Nelse were staying on with Alexandra until winter.

"Ivar," Signa exclaimed as she wiped the rain from her face, "do you know where she is?"

The old man put down his cobbler's knife. "Who, the mistress?"

"Yes. She went away about three o'clock. I happened to look out of the window and saw her going across the fields in her thin dress and sun-hat! And now this storm has come on. I thought she was going to Mrs. Hiller's, and I telephoned as soon as the thunder stopped, but she had not been there. I'm afraid she is out somewhere and will get her death of cold."

Ivar put on his cap and took up the lantern. "*Ja, ja,* we will see. I will hitch the boy's mare to the cart and go."

Signa followed him across the wagon-shed to the horses' stable. She was shivering with cold and excitement. "Where do you suppose she can be, Ivar?"

The old man lifted a set of single harness carefully from its peg. "How should I know?"

"But you think she is at the graveyard, don't you?" Signa persisted. "So do I. Oh, I wish she would be more like herself! I can't believe it's Alexandra Bergson come to this, with no head about anything. I have to tell her when to eat and when to go to bed."

"Patience, patience, sister," muttered Ivar as he settled the bit in the horse's mouth. "When the eyes of the flesh are shut, the eyes of the spirit are open. She will have a message from those who are gone, and that will bring her peace. Until then we must bear with her. You and I are the only ones who have weight with her. She trusts us."

"How awful it's been these last three months." Signa held the lantern so that he could see to buckle the straps. "It don't seem right that we must all be so miserable. Why do we all have to be punished? Seems to me like good times would never come again."

Ivar expressed himself in a deep sigh, but said nothing. He stooped and took a sandburr from his toe.

"Ivar," Signa asked suddenly, "will you tell me why you go barefoot? All the time I lived here in the house I wanted to ask you. Is it for a penance, or what?"

"No, sister. It is for the indulgence of the body. From my youth up I have had a strong, rebellious body, and have been subject to every kind of temptation. Even in age my temptations are prolonged. It was necessary to make some allowances; and the feet, as I understand it, are free members. There is no divine prohibition for them in the Ten Commandments. The hands, the tongue, the eyes, the heart, all the bodily desires we are commanded to subdue; but the feet are free members. I indulge them without harm to any one, even to trampling in filth when my desires are low. They are quickly cleaned again."

Signa did not laugh. She looked thoughtful as she followed Ivar out to the wagon-shed and held the shafts up for him, while he backed in the mare and buckled the hold-backs. "You have been a good friend to the mistress, Ivar," she murmured.

"And you, God be with you," replied Ivar as he clambered into the cart and put the lantern under the oilcloth lap-cover. "Now for a ducking, my girl," he said to the mare, gathering up the reins.

As they emerged from the shed, a stream of water, running off the thatch, struck the mare on the neck. She tossed her head indignantly, then struck out bravely on the soft ground, slipping back again and again as she climbed the hill to the main road. Between the rain and the darkness Ivar could see very little, so he let Emil's mare have the rein, keeping her head in the right direction. When the ground was level, he turned her out of the dirt road upon the sod, where she was able to trot without slipping.

Before Ivar reached the graveyard, three miles from the house, the storm had spent itself, and the downpour had died into a soft, dripping rain. The sky and the land were a dark smoke color, and seemed to be coming together, like two waves. When Ivar stopped at the gate and swung out his lantern, a white figure rose from beside John Bergson's white stone.

The old man sprang to the ground and shuffled toward the gate calling, "Mistress, mistress!"

Alexandra hurried to meet him and put her hand on his shoulder. *"Tyst!* Ivar. There's nothing to be worried about. I'm sorry if I've scared you all. I didn't notice the storm till it was on me, and I couldn't walk against it. I'm glad you've come. I am so tired I didn't know how I'd ever get home!"

Ivar swung the lantern up so that it shone in her face. *"Gud!* You are enough to frighten us, mistress. You look like a drowned woman. How could you do such a thing!"

Groaning and mumbling he led her out of the gate and helped her into the cart, wrapping her in the dry blankets on which he had been sitting.

Alexandra smiled at his solicitude. "Not much use in that, Ivar. You will only shut the wet in. I don't feel so cold now; but I'm heavy and numb. I'm glad you came."

Ivar turned the mare and urged her into a sliding trot. Her feet sent back a continual spatter of mud.

Alexandra spoke to the old man as they jogged along through the sullen gray twilight of the storm. "Ivar, I think it has done me good to get cold clear through like this, once. I don't believe I shall suffer so much any more. When you get so near the dead, they seem more real than the living. Worldly thoughts leave one. Ever since Emil died, I've suffered so when it rained. Now that I've been out in it with him, I shan't dread it. After you once get cold clear through, the feeling of the rain on you is sweet. It seems to bring back feelings you had when you were a baby. It carries you back into the dark, before you were born; you can't see things, but they come to you, somehow, and you know them and aren't afraid of them. Maybe it's like that with the dead. If they feel anything at all, it's the old things, before they were born, that comfort people like the feeling of their own bed does when they are little."

"Mistress," said Ivar reproachfully, "those are bad thoughts. The dead are in Paradise."

Then he hung his head, for he did not believe that Emil was in Paradise.

When they got home, Signa had a fire burning in the sitting-

room stove. She undressed Alexandra and gave her a hot footbath, while
Ivar made ginger tea in the kitchen. When Alexandra was in bed, wrapped
in hot blankets, Ivar came in with his tea and saw that she drank it. Signa
asked permission to sleep on the slat lounge outside her door. Alexandra
endured their attentions patiently, but she was glad when they put out the
lamp and left her. As she lay alone in the dark, it occurred to her for the
first time that perhaps she was actually tired of life. All the physical operations of life seemed difficult and painful. She longed to be free from her
own body, which ached and was so heavy. And longing itself was heavy:
she yearned to be free of that.

As she lay with her eyes closed, she had again, more vividly than
for many years, the old illusion of her girlhood, of being lifted and carried
lightly by some one very strong. He was with her a long while this time,
and carried her very far, and in his arms she felt free from pain. When he
laid her down on her bed again, she opened her eyes, and, for the first time
in her life, she saw him, saw him clearly, though the room was dark, and
his face was covered. He was standing in the doorway of her room. His
white cloak was thrown over his face, and his head was bent a little forward.
His shoulders seemed as strong as the foundations of the world. His right
arm, bared from the elbow, was dark and gleaming, like bronze, and she
knew at once that it was the arm of the mightiest of all lovers. She knew
at last for whom it was she had waited, and where he would carry her. That,
she told herself, was very well. Then she went to sleep.

Alexandra wakened in the morning with nothing worse than a
hard cold and a stiff shoulder. She kept her bed for several days, and it was
during that time that she formed a resolution to go to Lincoln to see Frank
Shabata. Ever since she last saw him in the courtroom, Frank's haggard face
and wild eyes had haunted her. The trial had lasted only three days. Frank
had given himself up to the police in Omaha and pleaded guilty of killing
without malice and without premeditation. The gun was, of course, against
him, and the judge had given him the full sentence—ten years. He had now
been in the State Penitentiary for a month.

Frank was the only one, Alexandra told herself, for whom anything could be done. He had been less in the wrong than any of them, and
he was paying the heaviest penalty. She often felt that she herself had been
more to blame than poor Frank. From the time the Shabatas had first moved
to the neighboring farm, she had omitted no opportunity of throwing
Marie and Emil together. Because she knew Frank was surly about doing
little things to help his wife, she was always sending Emil over to spade or

plant or carpenter for Marie. She was glad to have Emil see as much as possible of an intelligent, city-bred girl like their neighbor; she noticed that it improved his manners. She knew that Emil was fond of Marie, but it had never occurred to her that Emil's feeling might be different from her own. She wondered at herself now, but she had never thought of danger in that direction. If Marie had been unmarried,—oh, yes. Then she would have kept her eyes open. But the mere fact that she was Shabata's wife, for Alexandra, settled everything. That she was beautiful, impulsive, barely two years older than Emil, these facts had had no weight with Alexandra. Emil was a good boy, and only bad boys ran after married women.

Now, Alexandra could in a measure realize that Marie was, after all, Marie; not merely a "married woman." Sometimes, when Alexandra thought of her, it was with an aching tenderness. The moment she had reached them in the orchard that morning, everything was clear to her. There was something about those two lying in the grass, something in the way Marie had settled her cheek on Emil's shoulder, that told her everything. She wondered then how they could have helped loving each other; how she could have helped knowing that they must. Emil's cold, frowning face, the girl's content—Alexandra had felt awe of them, even in the first shock of her grief.

The idleness of those days in bed, the relaxation of body which attended them, enabled Alexandra to think more calmly than she had done since Emil's death. She and Frank, she told herself, were left out of that group of friends who had been overwhelmed by disaster. She must certainly see Frank Shabata. Even in the courtroom her heart had grieved for him. He was in a strange country, he had no kinsmen or friends, and in a moment he had ruined his life. Being what he was, she felt, Frank could not have acted otherwise. She could understand his behavior more easily than she could understand Marie's. Yes, she must go to Lincoln to see Frank Shabata.

The day after Emil's funeral, Alexandra had written to Carl Linstrum; a single page of notepaper, a bare statement of what had happened. She was not a woman who could write much about such a thing, and about her own feelings she could never write very freely. She knew that Carl was away from post-offices, prospecting somewhere in the interior. Before he started he had written her where he expected to go, but her ideas about Alaska were vague. As the weeks went by and she heard nothing from him, it seemed to Alexandra that her heart grew hard against Carl. She began to wonder whether she would not do better to finish her life alone. What was left of life seemed unimportant.

II

*L*ate in the afternoon of a brilliant October day, Alexandra Bergson, dressed in a black suit and traveling-hat, alighted at the Burlington depot in Lincoln. She drove to the Lindell Hotel, where she had stayed two years ago when she came up for Emil's Commencement. In spite of her usual air of sureness and self-possession, Alexandra felt ill at ease in hotels, and she was glad, when she went to the clerk's desk to register, that there were not many people in the lobby. She had her supper early, wearing her hat and black jacket down to the dining-room and carrying her handbag. After supper she went out for a walk.

It was growing dark when she reached the university campus. She did not go into the grounds, but walked slowly up and down the stone walk outside the long iron fence, looking through at the young men who were running from one building to another, at the lights shining from the armory and the library. A squad of cadets were going through their drill behind the armory, and the commands of their young officer rang out at regular intervals, so sharp and quick that Alexandra could not understand them. Two stalwart girls came down the library steps and out through one of the iron gates. As they passed her, Alexandra was pleased to hear them speaking Bohemian to each other. Every few moments a boy would come running down the flagged walk and dash out into the street as if he were rushing to announce some wonder to the world. Alexandra felt a great tenderness for them all. She wished one of them would stop and speak to her. She wished she could ask them whether they had known Emil.

As she lingered by the south gate she actually did encounter one of the boys. He had on his drill cap and was swinging his books at the end of a long strap. It was dark by this time; he did not see her and ran against her. He snatched off his cap and stood bareheaded and panting. "I'm awfully sorry," he said in a bright, clear voice, with a rising inflection, as if he expected her to say something.

"Oh, it was my fault!" said Alexandra eagerly. "Are you an old student here, may I ask?"

"No, ma'am. I'm a Freshie, just off the farm. Cherry County. Were you hunting somebody?"

"No, thank you. That is——" Alexandra wanted to detain him. "That is, I would like to find some of my brother's friends. He graduated two years ago."

"Then you'd have to try the Seniors, wouldn't you? Let's see; I don't know any of them yet, but there'll be sure to be some of them around the library. That red building right there," he pointed.

"Thank you, I'll try there," said Alexandra lingeringly.

"Oh, that's all right! Good-night." The lad clapped his cap on his head and ran straight down Eleventh Street. Alexandra looked after him wistfully.

She walked back to her hotel unreasonably comforted. "What a nice voice that boy had, and how polite he was. I know Emil was always like that to women." And again, after she had undressed and was standing in her nightgown, brushing her long, heavy hair by the electric light, she remembered him and said to herself: "I don't think I ever heard a nicer voice than that boy had. I hope he will get on well here. Cherry County; that's where the hay is so fine, and the coyotes can scratch down to water."

At nine o'clock the next morning Alexandra presented herself at the warden's office in the State Penitentiary. The warden was a German, a ruddy, cheerful-looking man who had formerly been a harness-maker. Alexandra had a letter to him from the German banker in Hanover. As he glanced at the letter, Mr. Schwartz put away his pipe.

"That big Bohemian, is it? Sure, he's gettin' along fine," said Mr. Schwartz cheerfully.

"I am glad to hear that. I was afraid he might be quarrelsome and get himself into more trouble. Mr. Schwartz, if you have time, I would like to tell you a little about Frank Shabata, and why I am interested in him."

The warden listened genially while she told him briefly something of Frank's history and character, but he did not seem to find anything unusual in her account.

"Sure, I'll keep an eye on him. We'll take care of him all right," he said, rising. "You can talk to him here, while I go to see to things in the kitchen. I'll have him sent in. He ought to be done washing out his cell by this time. We have to keep 'em clean, you know."

The warden paused at the door, speaking back over his shoulder to a pale young man in convicts' clothes who was seated at a desk in the corner, writing in a big ledger.

"Bertie, when 1037 is brought in, you just step out and give this lady a chance to talk."

The young man bowed his head and bent over his ledger again.

When Mr. Schwartz disappeared, Alexandra thrust her black-edged handkerchief nervously into her handbag. Coming out on the street-car she had not had the least dread of meeting Frank. But since she had been here the sounds and smells in the corridor, the look of the men in convicts' clothes who passed the glass door of the warden's office, affected her unpleasantly.

The warden's clock ticked, the young convict's pen scratched busily in the big book, and his sharp shoulders were shaken every few seconds by a loose cough which he tried to smother. It was easy to see that he was a sick man. Alexandra looked at him timidly, but he did not once raise his eyes. He wore a white shirt under his striped jacket, a high collar, and a necktie, very carefully tied. His hands were thin and white and well cared for, and he had a seal ring on his little finger. When he heard steps approaching in the corridor, he rose, blotted his book, put his pen in the rack, and left the room without raising his eyes. Through the door he opened a guard came in, bringing Frank Shabata.

"You the lady that wanted to talk to 1037? Here he is. Be on your good behavior, now. He can set down, lady," seeing that Alexandra remained standing. "Push that white button when you're through with him, and I'll come."

The guard went out and Alexandra and Frank were left alone.

Alexandra tried not to see his hideous clothes. She tried to look straight into his face, which she could scarcely believe was his. It was already bleached to a chalky gray. His lips were colorless, his fine teeth looked yellowish. He glanced at Alexandra sullenly, blinked as if he had come from a dark place, and one eyebrow twitched continually. She felt at once that this interview was a terrible ordeal to him. His shaved head, showing the conformation of his skull, gave him a criminal look which he had not had during the trial.

Alexandra held out her hand. "Frank," she said, her eyes filling suddenly, "I hope you'll let me be friendly with you. I understand how you did it. I don't feel hard toward you. They were more to blame than you."

Frank jerked a dirty blue handkerchief from his trousers pocket. He had begun to cry. He turned away from Alexandra. "I never did mean to do not'ing to dat woman," he muttered. "I never mean to do not'ing to dat boy. I ain't had not'ing ag'in' dat boy. I always like dat boy fine. An' then I find him—" He stopped. The feeling went out of his face and eyes. He dropped into a chair and sat looking stolidly at the floor, his hands hanging loosely between his knees, the handkerchief lying across his striped leg. He seemed to have stirred up in his mind a disgust that had paralyzed his faculties.

"I haven't come up here to blame you, Frank. I think they were more to blame than you." Alexandra, too, felt benumbed.

Frank looked up suddenly and stared out of the office window. "I guess dat place all go to hell what I work so hard on," he said with a slow, bitter smile. "I not care a damn." He stopped and rubbed the palm of his hand over the light bristles on his head with annoyance. "I no can t'ink without my hair," he complained. "I forget English. We not talk here, except swear."

Alexandra was bewildered. Frank seemed to have undergone a change of personality. There was scarcely anything by which she could recognize her handsome Bohemian neighbor. He seemed, somehow, not altogether human. She did not know what to say to him.

"You do not feel hard to me, Frank?" she asked at last.

Frank clenched his fist and broke out in excitement. "I not feel hard at no woman. I tell you I not that kind-a man. I never hit my wife. No, never I hurt her when she devil me something awful!" He struck his fist down on the warden's desk so hard that he afterward stroked it absently. A pale pink crept over his neck and face. "Two, t'ree years I know dat woman don' care no more 'bout me, Alexandra Bergson. I know she after some other man. I know her, oo-oo! An' I ain't never hurt her. I never would-a done dat, if I ain't had dat gun along. I don' know what in hell make me take dat gun. She always say I ain't no man to carry gun. If she been in dat house, where she ought-a been—But das a foolish talk."

Frank rubbed his head and stopped suddenly, as he had stopped before. Alexandra felt that there was something strange in the way he chilled off, as if something came up in him that extinguished his power of feeling or thinking.

"Yes, Frank," she said kindly. "I know you never meant to hurt Marie."

Frank smiled at her queerly. His eyes filled slowly with tears. "You know, I most forgit dat woman's name. She ain't got no name for me no more. I never hate my wife, but dat woman what make me do dat— Honest to God, but I hate her! I no man to fight. I don' want to kill no boy and no woman. I not care how many men she take under dat tree. I no care for not'ing but dat fine boy I kill, Alexandra Bergson. I guess I go crazy sure 'nough."

Alexandra remembered the little yellow cane she had found in

Frank's clothes-closet. She thought of how he had come to this country a gay young fellow, so attractive that the prettiest Bohemian girl in Omaha had run away with him. It seemed unreasonable that life should have landed him in such a place as this. She blamed Marie bitterly. And why, with her happy, affectionate nature, should she have brought destruction and sorrow to all who had loved her, even to poor old Joe Tovesky, the uncle who used to carry her about so proudly when she was a little girl? That was the strangest thing of all. Was there, then, something wrong in being warm-hearted and impulsive like that? Alexandra hated to think so. But there was Emil, in the Norwegian graveyard at home, and here was Frank Shabata. Alexandra rose and took him by the hand.

"Frank Shabata, I am never going to stop trying until I get you pardoned. I'll never give the Governor any peace. I know I can get you out of this place."

Frank looked at her distrustfully, but he gathered confidence from her face. "Alexandra," he said earnestly, "if I git out-a here, I not trouble dis country no more. I go back where I come from; see my mother."

Alexandra tried to withdraw her hand, but Frank held on to it nervously. He put out his finger and absently touched a button on her black jacket. "Alexandra," he said in a low tone, looking steadily at the button, "you ain' t'ink I use dat girl awful bad before—"

"No, Frank. We won't talk about that," Alexandra said, pressing his hand. "I can't help Emil now, so I'm going to do what I can for you. You know I don't go away from home often, and I came up here on purpose to tell you this."

The warden at the glass door looked inquiringly. Alexandra nodded, and he came in and touched the white button on his desk. The guard appeared, and with a sinking heart Alexandra saw Frank led away down the corridor. After a few words with Mr. Schwartz, she left the prison and made her way to the street-car. She had refused with horror the warden's cordial invitation to "go through the institution." As the car lurched over its uneven roadbed, back toward Lincoln, Alexandra thought of how she and Frank had been wrecked by the same storm and of how, although she could come out into the sunlight, she had not much more left in her life than he. She remembered some lines from a poem she had liked in her schooldays:

> Henceforth the world will only be
> A wider prison-house to me—

and sighed. A disgust of life weighed upon her heart; some such feeling as had twice frozen Frank Shabata's features while they talked together. She wished she were back on the Divide.

When Alexandra entered her hotel, the clerk held up one finger and beckoned to her. As she approached his desk, he handed her a telegram. Alexandra took the yellow envelope and looked at it in perplexity, then stepped into the elevator without opening it. As she walked down the corridor toward her room, she reflected that she was, in a manner, immune from evil tidings. On reaching her room she locked the door, and sitting down on a chair by the dresser, opened the telegram. It was from Hanover, and it read:

ARRIVED HANOVER LAST NIGHT. SHALL WAIT
HERE UNTIL YOU COME. PLEASE HURRY.
                              CARL LINSTRUM.

Alexandra put her head down on the dresser and burst into tears.

III

*T*he next afternoon Carl and Alexandra were walking across the fields from Mrs. Hiller's. Alexandra had left Lincoln after midnight, and Carl had met her at the Hanover station early in the morning. After they reached home, Alexandra had gone over to Mrs. Hiller's to leave a little present she had bought for her in the city. They stayed at the old lady's door but a moment, and then came out to spend the rest of the afternoon in the sunny fields.

Alexandra had taken off her black traveling-suit and put on a white dress; partly because she saw that her black clothes made Carl uncomfortable and partly because she felt oppressed by them herself. They seemed a little like the prison where she had worn them yesterday, and to be out of place in the open fields. Carl had changed very little. His cheeks were browner and fuller. He looked less like a tired scholar than when he went away a year ago, but no one, even now, would have taken him for a man of business. His soft, lustrous black eyes, his whimsical smile, would be less against him in the Klondike than on the Divide. There are always dreamers on the frontier.

Carl and Alexandra had been talking since morning. Her letter had never reached him. He had first learned of her misfortune from a San Francisco paper, four weeks old, which he had picked up in a saloon, and which contained a brief account of Frank Shabata's trial. When he put down the paper, he had already made up his mind that he could reach Alexandra as quickly as a letter could; and ever since he had been on the way; day and night, by the fastest boats and trains he could catch. His steamer had been held back two days by rough weather.

As they came out of Mrs. Hiller's garden they took up their talk again where they had left it.

"But could you come away like that, Carl, without arranging things? Could you just walk off and leave your business?" Alexandra asked.

Carl laughed. "Prudent Alexandra! You see, my dear, I happen to have an honest partner. I trust him with everything. In fact, it's been his enterprise from the beginning, you know. I'm in it only because he took me in. I'll have to go back in the spring. Perhaps you will want to go with me then. We haven't turned up millions yet, but we've got a start that's worth following. But this winter I'd like to spend with you. You won't feel that we ought to wait longer, on Emil's account, will you, Alexandra?"

Alexandra shook her head. "No, Carl; I don't feel that way about it. And surely you needn't mind anything Lou and Oscar say now. They are much angrier with me about Emil, now, than about you. They say it was all my fault. That I ruined him by sending him to college."

"No, I don't care a button for Lou or Oscar. The moment I knew you were in trouble, the moment I thought you might need me, it all looked different. You've always been a triumphant kind of person." Carl hesitated, looking sidewise at her strong, full figure. "But you do need me now, Alexandra?"

She put her hand on his arm. "I needed you terribly when it happened, Carl. I cried for you at night. Then everything seemed to get hard inside of me, and I thought perhaps I should never care for you again. But when I got your telegram yesterday, then—then it was just as it used to be. You are all I have in the world, you know."

Carl pressed her hand in silence. They were passing the Shabatas' empty house now, but they avoided the orchard path and took one that led over by the pasture pond.

"Can you understand it, Carl?" Alexandra murmured. "I have had nobody but Ivar and Signa to talk to. Do talk to me. Can you understand it? Could you have believed that of Marie Tovesky? I would have been cut to pieces, little by little, before I would have betrayed her trust in me!"

Carl looked at the shining spot of water before them. "Maybe she was cut to pieces, too, Alexandra. I am sure she tried hard; they both did. That was why Emil went to Mexico, of course. And he was going away again, you tell me, though he had only been home three weeks. You remember that Sunday when I went with Emil up to the French Church fair? I thought that day there was some kind of feeling, something unusual, between them. I meant to talk to you about it. But on my way back I met Lou and Oscar and got so angry that I forgot everything else. You mustn't be hard on them, Alexandra. Sit down here by the pond a minute. I want to tell you something."

They sat down on the grass-tufted bank and Carl told her how he had seen Emil and Marie out by the pond that morning, more than a year ago, and how young and charming and full of grace they had seemed to him. "It happens like that in the world sometimes, Alexandra," he added earnestly. "I've seen it before. There are women who spread ruin around them through no fault of theirs, just by being too beautiful, too full of life and love. They can't help it. People come to them as people go to a warm fire in winter. I used to feel that in her when she was a little girl. Do you remember how all the Bohemians crowded round her in the store that day, when she gave Emil her candy? You remember those yellow sparks in her eyes?"

Alexandra sighed. "Yes. People couldn't help loving her. Poor Frank does, even now, I think; though he's got himself in such a tangle that for a long time his love has been bitterer than his hate. But if you saw there was anything wrong, you ought to have told me, Carl."

Carl took her hand and smiled patiently. "My dear, it was something one felt in the air, as you feel the spring coming, or a storm in summer. I didn't *see* anything. Simply, when I was with those two young things, I felt my blood go quicker, I felt—how shall I say it?—an acceleration of life. After I got away, it was all too delicate, too intangible, to write about."

Alexandra looked at him mournfully. "I try to be more liberal about such things than I used to be. I try to realize that we are not all made alike. Only, why couldn't it have been Raoul Marcel, or Jan Smirka? Why did it have to be my boy?"

"Because he was the best there was, I suppose. They were both the best you had here."

The sun was dropping low in the west when the two friends rose and took the path again. The straw-stacks were throwing long shadows, the owls were flying home to the prairie-dog town. When they came to the corner where the pastures joined, Alexandra's twelve young colts were galloping in a drove over the brow of the hill.

"Carl," said Alexandra, "I should like to go up there with you in the spring. I haven't been on the water since we crossed the ocean, when I was a little girl. After we first came out here I used to dream sometimes about the shipyard where father worked, and a little sort of inlet, full of masts." Alexandra paused. After a moment's thought she said, "But you would never ask me to go away for good, would you?"

"Of course not, my dearest. I think I know how you feel about this country as well as you do yourself." Carl took her hand in both his own and pressed it tenderly.

"Yes, I still feel that way, though Emil is gone. When I was on the train this morning, and we got near Hanover, I felt something like I did when I drove back with Emil from the river that time, in the dry year. I was glad to come back to it. I've lived here a long time. There is great peace here, Carl, and freedom. . . . I thought when I came out of that prison, where poor Frank is, that I should never feel free again. But I do, here." Alexandra took a deep breath and looked off into the red west.

"You belong to the land," Carl murmured, "as you have always said. Now more than ever."

"Yes, now more than ever. You remember what you once said about the graveyard, and the old story writing itself over? Only it is we who write it, with the best we have."

They paused on the last ridge of the pasture, overlooking the house and the windmill and the stables that marked the site of John Bergson's homestead. On every side the brown waves of the earth rolled away to meet the sky.

"Lou and Oscar can't see those things," said Alexandra suddenly. "Suppose I do will my land to their children, what difference will that make? The land belongs to the future, Carl; that's the way it seems to me. How many of the names on the county clerk's plat will be there in fifty years? I might as well try to will the sunset over there to my brother's children. We come and go, but the land is always here. And the people who love it and understand it are the people who own it—for a little while."

Carl looked at her wonderingly. She was still gazing into the west, and in her face there was that exalted serenity that sometimes came to her at moments of deep feeling. The level rays of the sinking sun shone in her clear eyes.

"Why are you thinking of such things now, Alexandra?"

"I had a dream before I went to Lincoln—But I will tell you about that afterward, after we are married. It will never come true, now, in the way I thought it might." She took Carl's arm and they walked toward the gate. "How many times we have walked this path together, Carl. How many times we will walk it again! Does it seem to you like coming back to your own place? Do you feel at peace with the world here? I think we shall be very happy. I haven't any fears. I think when friends marry, they are safe. We don't suffer like—those young ones." Alexandra ended with a sigh.

They had reached the gate. Before Carl opened it, he drew Alexandra to him and kissed her softly, on her lips and on her eyes.

She leaned heavily on his shoulder. "I am tired," she murmured. "I have been very lonely, Carl."

They went into the house together, leaving the Divide behind them, under the evening star. Fortunate country, that is one day to receive hearts like Alexandra's into its bosom, to give them out again in the yellow wheat, in the rustling corn, in the shining eyes of youth!

The Song
of the Lark

To

Isabelle McClung

"It was a wond'rous lovely storm
that drove me!"

Lenau's *Don Juan*

Contents

Part I

Friends of Childhood

I

*D*octor Howard Archie had just come up from a game of pool with the Jewish clothier and two travelling men who happened to be staying overnight in Moonstone. His offices were in the Duke Block, over the drugstore. Larry, the doctor's man, had lit the overhead light in the waiting-room and the double student's lamp on the desk in the study. The isinglass sides of the hard-coal burner were aglow, and the air in the study was so hot that as he came in the doctor opened the door into his little operating-room, where there was no stove. The waiting-room was carpeted and stiffly furnished, something like a country parlour. The study had worn, unpainted floors, but there was a look of winter comfort about it. The doctor's flat-top desk was large and well made; the papers were in orderly piles, under glass weights. Behind the stove a wide bookcase, with double glass doors, reached from the floor to the ceiling. It was filled with medical books of every thickness and colour. On the top shelf stood a long row of thirty or forty volumes, bound all alike in dark mottled board covers, with imitation leather backs.

As the doctor in New England villages is proverbially old, so the doctor in small Colorado towns twenty-five years ago was generally young. Doctor Archie was barely thirty. He was tall, with massive shoulders which he held stiffly, and a large, well-shaped head. He was a distinguished-looking man, for that part of the world, at least. There was something individual in the way in which his reddish-brown hair, parted cleanly at the side, bushed over his high forehead. His nose was straight and thick, and his eyes were intelligent. He wore a curly, reddish moustache and an imperial, cut trimly, which made him look a little like the pictures of Napoleon III. His hands were large and well kept, but ruggedly formed, and the backs were shaded with crinkly reddish hair. He wore a blue suit of woolly, wide-waled serge; the travelling men had known at a glance that it was made by a Denver tailor. The doctor was always well dressed.

Doctor Archie turned up the student's lamp and sat down in the swivel chair before his desk. He sat uneasily, beating a tattoo on his knees with his fingers, and looked about him as if he were bored. He glanced at his watch, then absently took from his pocket a bunch of small keys, selected one and looked at it. A contemptuous smile, barely perceptible, played on his lips, but his eyes remained meditative. Behind the door that led into the hall, under his buffalo-skin driving-coat, was a locked cupboard. This the doctor opened mechanically, kicking aside a pile of muddy overshoes. Inside, upon the shelves, were whisky glasses and decanters, lemons, sugar, and bitters. Hearing a step in the empty, echoing hall without, the doctor closed the cupboard again, snapping the Yale lock. The door of the waiting-room opened, a man entered and came on into the consulting-room.

"Good evening, Mr. Kronborg," said the doctor carelessly. "Sit down."

His visitor was a tall, loosely built man, with a thin brown beard, streaked with grey. He wore a frock coat, a broad-brimmed black hat, a white lawn necktie, and steel-rimmed spectacles. Altogether there was a pretentious and important air about him, as he lifted the skirts of his coat and sat down.

"Good evening, doctor. Can you step around to the house with me? I think Mrs. Kronborg will need you this evening." This was said with profound gravity and, curiously enough, with a slight embarrassment.

"Any hurry?" the doctor asked over his shoulder as he went into his operating-room.

Mr. Kronborg coughed behind his hand, and contracted his brows. His face threatened at every moment to break into a smile of foolish excitement. He controlled it only by calling upon his habitual pulpit manner. "Well, I think it would be as well to go immediately. Mrs. Kronborg will be more comfortable if you are there. She has been suffering for some time."

The doctor came back and threw a black bag upon his desk. He wrote some instructions for his man on a prescription pad and then drew on his overcoat. "All ready," he announced, putting out his lamp. Mr. Kronborg rose and they tramped through the empty hall and down the stairway to the street. The drugstore below was dark, and the saloon next door was just closing. Every other light on Main Street was out.

On either side of the road and at the outer edge of the board sidewalk, the snow had been shovelled into breastworks. The town looked small and black, flattened down in the snow, muffled and all but extinguished. Overhead the stars shone gloriously. It was impossible not to notice them. The air was so clear that the white sand hills to the east of Moonstone gleamed softly. Following the Reverend Mr. Kronborg along the narrow walk, past the little dark, sleeping houses, the doctor looked up at the flashing night and whistled softly. It did seem that people were stupider than they need be; as if on a night like this there ought to be something better to do than to sleep nine hours, or to assist Mrs. Kronborg in functions which she could have performed so admirably unaided. He wished he had gone down to Denver to hear Fay Templeton sing "See-Saw." Then he remembered that he had a personal interest in this family, after all. They turned into another street and saw before them lighted windows; a low storey-and-a-half house, with a wing built on at the right and a kitchen addition at the back, everything a little on the slant—roofs, windows, and doors. As they approached the gate, Peter Kronborg's pace grew brisker. His nervous, ministerial cough annoyed the doctor. "Exactly as if he were going to give out a text," he thought. He drew off his glove and felt in his vest pocket. "Have a troche, Kronborg," he said, producing some. "Sent me for samples. Very good for a rough throat."

"Ah, thank you, thank you. I was in something of a hurry. I neglected to put on my overshoes. Here we are, doctor." Kronborg opened his front door—seemed delighted to be at home again.

The front hall was dark and cold; the hat-rack was hung with an astonishing number of children's hats and caps and cloaks. They were even piled on the table beneath the hat-rack. Under the table was a heap of rubbers and overshoes. While the doctor hung up his coat and hat, Peter Kronborg opened the door into the living-room. A glare of light greeted them, and a rush of hot, stale air, smelling of warming flannels.

At three o'clock in the morning, Doctor Archie was in the parlour putting on his cuffs and coat—there was no spare bedroom in that house. Peter Kronborg's seventh child, a boy, was being soothed and cosseted by his aunt, Mrs. Kronborg was asleep, and the doctor was going home. But he wanted first to speak to Kronborg, who, coatless and fluttery, was pouring coal into the kitchen stove. As the doctor crossed the dining-room, he paused and listened. From one of the wing rooms, off to the left, he heard rapid, distressed breathing. He went to the kitchen door.

"One of the children sick in there?" he asked, nodding toward the partition.

Kronborg hung up the stove-lifter and dusted his fingers. "It must be Thea. I meant to ask you to look at her. She has a croupy cold. But in my excitement—Mrs. Kronborg is doing finely, eh, doctor? Not many of your patients with such a constitution, I expect."

"Oh, yes. She's a fine mother." The doctor took up the lamp from the kitchen table and unceremoniously went into the wing room. Two chubby little boys were asleep in a double bed, with the coverlids over their noses and their feet drawn up. In a single bed, next to theirs, lay a little girl of eleven, wide awake, two yellow braids sticking up on the pillow behind her. Her face was scarlet and her eyes were blazing.

The doctor shut the door behind him. "Feel pretty sick, Thea?" he asked as he took out his thermometer. "Why didn't you call somebody?"

She looked at him with greedy affection. "I thought you were here"—she spoke between quick breaths. "There is a new baby, isn't there? Which?"

"Which?" repeated the doctor.

"Brother or sister?"

He smiled and sat down on the edge of the bed. "Brother," he said, taking her hand. "Open."

"Good. Brothers are better," she murmured as he put the glass tube under her tongue.

"Now, be still, I want to count." Doctor Archie reached for her hand and took out his watch. When he put her hand back under the quilt, he went over to one of the windows—they were both tight shut—and lifted it a little way. He reached up and ran his hand along the cold, unpapered wall. "Keep under the covers; I'll come back to you in a moment," he said, bending over the glass lamp with his thermometer. He winked at her from the door before he shut it.

Peter Kronborg was sitting in his wife's room, holding the bundle which contained his son. His air of cheerful importance, his beard and glasses, even his shirt-sleeves, annoyed the doctor. He beckoned Kronborg into the living-room and said sternly:

"You've got a very sick child in there. Why didn't you call me before? It's pneumonia, and she must have been sick for several days. Put the baby down somewhere, please, and help me make up the bed-lounge here in the parlour. She's got to be in a warm room, and she's got to be quiet. You must keep the other children out. Here, this thing opens up, I see," swinging back the top of the carpet lounge. "We can lift her mattress and carry her in just as she is. I don't want to disturb her more than is necessary."

Kronborg was all concern immediately. The two men took up the mattress and carried the sick child into the parlour. "I'll have to go down to my office to get some medicine, Kronborg. The drugstore won't be open. Keep the covers on her. I shan't be gone long. Shake down the stove and put on a little coal, but not too much; so it'll catch quickly, I mean. Find an old sheet for me, and put it there to warm."

The doctor caught his coat and hurried out into the dark street. Nobody was stirring yet, and the cold was bitter. He was tired and hungry and in no mild humour. "The idea!" he muttered; "to be such an ass at his age about the seventh! And to feel no responsibility about the little girl. Silly old goat! The baby would have got into the world somehow; they always do. But a nice little girl like that—she's worth the whole litter. Where she ever got it from—" He turned into the Duke Block and ran up the stairs to his office.

Thea Kronborg, meanwhile, was wondering why she happened to be in the parlour, where nobody but company—usually visiting preachers—ever slept. She had moments of stupor when she did not see anything, and moments of excitement when she felt that something unusual and pleasant was about to happen, when she saw everything clearly in the red light from the isinglass sides of the hard-coal burner—the nickel trimmings on the stove itself, the pictures on the wall, which she thought very beautiful, the flowers on the Brussels carpet, Czerny's "Daily Studies" which stood open on the upright piano. She forgot, for the time being, all about the new baby.

When she heard the front door open, it occurred to her that the pleasant thing which was going to happen was Doctor Archie himself. He came in and warmed his hands at the stove. As he turned to her, she threw herself wearily toward him, half out of her bed. She would have tumbled to the floor had he not caught her. He gave her some medicine and went to the kitchen for something he needed. She drowsed and lost the sense of his being there. When she opened her eyes again, he was kneeling before the stove, spreading something dark and sticky on a white cloth, with a big spoon; batter, perhaps. Presently she felt him taking off her night-gown. He wrapped the hot plaster about her chest. There seemed to be straps which he pinned over her shoulders. Then he took out a thread and needle and began to sew her up in it. That, she felt, was too strange; she must be dreaming, anyhow, so she succumbed to her drowsiness.

Thea had been moaning with every breath since the doctor came back, but she did not know it. She did not realize that she was suffering pain. When she was conscious at all, she seemed to be separated from her body; to be perched on top of the piano, or on the hanging lamp, watching the doctor sew her up. It was perplexing and unsatisfactory, like dreaming. She wished she could waken up and see what was going on.

The doctor thanked God that he had persuaded Peter Kronborg to keep out of the way. He could do better by the child if he had her to himself. He had no children of his own. His marriage was a very unhappy one. As he lifted and undressed Thea, he thought to himself what a beautiful thing a little girl's body was—like a flower. It was so neatly and delicately fashioned, so soft, and so milky white. Thea must have got her hair and her silky skin from her mother. She was a little Swede, through and through. Doctor Archie could not help thinking how he would cherish a little creature like this if she were his. Her hands, so little and hot, so clever, too—he glanced at the open exercise-book on the piano. When he had stitched up the flax-seed jacket, he wiped it neatly about the edges, where the paste had worked out on the skin. He put on her the clean night-gown he had warmed before the fire, and tucked the blankets about her. As he pushed back the hair that had fuzzed down over her eyebrows, he felt her head thoughtfully with the tips of his fingers. No, he couldn't say that it was different from any other child's head, though he believed that there was something very different about her. He looked intently at her wide, flushed face, freckled nose, fierce little mouth, and her delicate, tender chin—the one soft touch in her hard little Scandinavian face, as if some fairy god-mother had caressed her there and left a cryptic promise. Her brows were usually drawn together defiantly, but never when she was with Doctor Archie. Her affection for him was prettier than most of the things that went to make up the doctor's life in Moonstone.

The windows grew grey. He heard a tramping on the attic floor, on the back stairs, then cries: "Give me my shirt!" "Where's my other stocking?"

"I'll have to stay till they get off to school," he reflected, "or they'll be in here tormenting her, the whole lot of them."

II

For the next four days it seemed to Doctor Archie that his patient might slip through his hands, do what he might. But she did not. On the contrary, after that she recovered very rapidly. As her father remarked, she must have inherited the "constitution" which he was never tired of admiring in her mother.

One afternoon, when her new brother was a week old, the doctor found Thea very comfortable and happy in her bed in the parlour. The sunlight was pouring in over her shoulders, the baby was asleep on a pillow in a big rocking-chair beside her. Whenever he stirred, she put out her hand and rocked him. Nothing of him was visible but a flushed, puffy forehead and an uncompromisingly big, bald cranium. The door into her mother's room stood open, and Mrs. Kronborg was sitting up in bed darning stockings. She was a short, stalwart woman, with a short neck and a determined-looking head. Her skin was very fair, her face calm and unwrinkled, and her yellow hair, braided down her back as she lay in bed, still looked like a girl's. She was a woman whom Doctor Archie respected; active, practical, unruffled; good-humoured, but determined. Exactly the sort of woman to take care of a flighty preacher. She had brought her husband some property, too—one fourth of her father's broad acres in Nebraska—but this she kept in her own name. She had profound respect for her husband's erudition and eloquence. She sat under his preaching with deep humility, and was as much taken in by his stiff shirt and white neckties as if she had not ironed them herself by lamplight the night before they appeared correct and spotless in the pulpit. But for all this, she had no confidence in his administration of worldly affairs. She looked to him for morning prayers and grace at table; she expected him to name the babies and to supply whatever parental sentiment there was in the house, to remember birthdays and anniversaries, to point the children to moral and patriotic ideals. It was her work to keep their bodies, their clothes, and their conduct in some sort of order, and this she accomplished with a success that was a source of wonder to her neighbours. As she used to remark, and her husband admiringly to echo, she "had never lost one." With all his flightiness, Peter Kronborg appreciated the matter-of-fact, punctual way in which his wife got her children into the world and along in it. He believed, and he was right in believing, that the sovereign State of Colorado was much indebted to Mrs. Kronborg and women like her.

Mrs. Kronborg believed that the size of every family was decided in heaven. More modern views would not have startled her; they would simply have seemed foolish—thin chatter, like the boasts of the men who built the Tower of Babel, or like Axel's plan to breed ostriches in the chicken-yard. From what evidence Mrs. Kronborg formed her opinions on this and other matters, it would have been difficult to say, but once formed, they were unchangeable. She would no more have questioned her convictions than she would have questioned revelation. Calm and even-tempered, naturally kind, she was capable of strong prejudices, and she never forgave.

When the doctor came in to see Thea, Mrs. Kronborg was reflecting that the washing was a week behind, and deciding what she had better do about it. The arrival of a new baby meant a revision of her entire domestic schedule, and as she drove her needle along she had been working out new sleeping arrangements and cleaning days. The doctor had entered the house without knocking, after making noise enough in the hall to prepare his patients. Thea was reading, her book propped up before her in the sunlight.

"Mustn't do that; bad for your eyes," he said, as Thea shut the book quickly and slipped it under the covers.

Mrs. Kronborg called from her bed: "Bring the baby here, doctor, and have that chair. She wanted him in there for company."

Before the doctor picked up the baby, he put a yellow paper bag down on Thea's coverlid and winked at her. They had a code of winks and grimaces. When he went in to chat with her mother, Thea opened the bag cautiously, trying to keep it from crackling. She drew out a long bunch of white grapes, with a little of the sawdust in which they had been packed still clinging to them. They were called Malaga grapes in Moonstone, and once or twice during the winter the leading grocer got a keg of them. They were used mainly for table decoration, about Christmas time. Thea had never had more than one grape at a time before. When the doctor came back, she was holding the almost transparent fruit up in the sunlight, feeling the pale-green skins softly with the tips of her fingers. She did not thank him; she only snapped her eyes at him in a special way which he understood, and, when he gave her his hand, put it quickly and shyly under her cheek, as if she were trying to do so without knowing it—and without his knowing it.

Doctor Archie sat down in the rocking-chair. "And how's Thea feeling to-day?"

He was quite as shy as his patient, especially when a third person overheard his conversation. Big and handsome and superior to his fellow townsmen as Doctor Archie was, he was seldom at his ease, and like Peter Kronborg he often dodged behind a professional manner. There was some-times a contraction of embarrassment and self-consciousness all over his big body, which made him awkward—likely to stumble, to kick up rugs, or to knock over chairs. If anyone was very sick, he forgot himself, but he had a clumsy touch in convalescent gossip.

Thea curled up on her side and looked at him with pleasure. "All right. I like to be sick. I have more fun then than other times."

"How's that?"

"I don't have to go to school, and I don't have to practise. I can read all I want to, and have good things"—she patted the grapes. "I had lots of fun that time I mashed my finger and you wouldn't let Professor Wunsch make me practise. Only I had to do left hand, even then. I think that was mean."

The doctor took her hand and examined the forefinger, where the nail had grown back a little crooked. "You mustn't trim it down close at the corner there, and then it will grow straight. You won't want it crooked when you're a big girl and wear rings and have sweethearts."

She made a mocking little face at him and looked at his new scarf-pin. "That's the prettiest one you ev-*er* had. I wish you'd stay a long while and let me look at it. What is it?"

Doctor Archie laughed. "It's an opal. Spanish Johnny brought it up for me from Chihuahua in his shoe. I had it set in Denver, and I wore it to-day for your benefit."

Thea had a curious passion for jewellery. She wanted every shining stone she saw, and in summer she was always going off into the sand hills to hunt for crystals and agates and bits of pink chalcedony. She had two cigar-boxes full of stones that she had found or traded for, and she imagined that they were of enormous value. She was always planning how she would have them set.

"What are you reading?" The doctor reached under the covers and pulled out a book of Byron's poems. "Do you like this?"

She looked confused, turned over a few pages rapidly, and pointed to "My native land, good night." "That," she said sheepishly.

"How about 'Maid of Athens'?"

She blushed and looked at him suspiciously. "I like 'There was a sound of revelry,' " she muttered.

The doctor laughed and closed the book. It was clumsily bound in padded leather and had been presented to the Reverend Peter Kronborg by his Sunday-School class as an ornament for his parlour table.

"Come into the office some day, and I'll lend you a nice book. You can skip the parts you don't understand. You can read it in vacation. Perhaps you'll be able to understand all of it by then."

Thea frowned and looked fretfully toward the piano. "In vacation I have to practise four hours every day, and then there'll be Thor to take care of." She pronounced it "Tor."

"Thor? Oh, you've named the baby Thor?" exclaimed the
doctor.

Thea frowned again, still more fiercely, and said quickly, "That's
a nice name, only maybe it's a little—old-fashioned." She was very sensitive
about being thought a foreigner, and was proud of the fact that, in town,
her father always preached in English; very bookish English, at that, one
might add.

Born in an old Scandinavian colony in Minnesota, Peter Kronborg had been sent to a small divinity school in Indiana by the women of
a Swedish evangelical mission, who were convinced of his gifts and who
skimped and begged and gave church suppers to get the long, lazy youth
through the seminary. He could still speak enough Swedish to exhort and
to bury the members of his country church out at Copper Hole, and he
wielded in his Moonstone pulpit a somewhat pompous English vocabulary
he had learned out of books at college. He always spoke of "the infant
Saviour," "our Heavenly Father," etc. The poor man had no natural,
spontaneous human speech. If he had his sincere moments, they were
perforce inarticulate. Probably a good deal of his pretentiousness was due
to the fact that he habitually expressed himself in a book-learned language,
wholly remote from anything personal, native, or homely. Mrs. Kronborg
spoke Swedish to her own sisters and to her sister-in-law Tillie, and colloquial English to her neighbours. Thea, who had a rather sensitive ear, until
she went to school never spoke at all, except in monosyllables, and her
mother was convinced that she was tongue-tied. She was still inept in
speech for a child so intelligent. Her ideas were usually clear, but she seldom
attempted to explain them, even at school, where she excelled in "written
work" and never did more than mutter a reply.

"Your music professor stopped me on the street to-day and
asked me how you were," said the doctor, rising. "He'll be sick himself,
trotting around in this slush with no overcoat or overshoes."

"He's poor," said Thea simply.

The doctor sighed. "I'm afraid he's worse than that. Is he always
all right when you take your lessons? Never acts as if he'd been drinking?"

Thea looked angry and spoke excitedly. "He knows a lot. More
than anybody. I don't care if he does drink; he's old and poor." Her voice
shook a little.

Mrs. Kronborg spoke up from the next room. "He's a good
teacher, doctor. It's good for us he does drink. He'd never be in a little place
like this if he didn't have some weakness. These women that teach music

around here don't know nothing. I wouldn't have my child wasting time with them. If Professor Wunsch goes away, Thea'll have nobody to take from. He's careful with his scholars; he don't use bad language. Mrs. Kohler is always present when Thea takes her lesson. It's all right." Mrs. Kronborg spoke calmly and judicially. One could see that she had thought the matter out before.

"I'm glad to hear that, Mrs. Kronborg. I wish we could get the old man off his bottle and keep him tidy. Do you suppose if I gave you an old overcoat you could get him to wear it?" The doctor went to the bedroom door and Mrs. Kronborg looked up from her darning.

"Why, yes, I guess he'd be glad of it. He'll take 'most anything from me. He won't buy clothes, but I guess he'd wear 'em if he had 'em. I've never had any clothes to give him, having so many to make over for."

"I'll have Larry bring the coat around to-night. You aren't cross with me, Thea?" taking her hand.

Thea grinned warmly. "Not if you give Professor Wunsch a coat—and things," she tapped the grapes significantly. The doctor bent over and kissed her.

III

*B*eing sick was all very well, but Thea knew from experience that starting back to school again was attended by depressing difficulties. One Monday morning she got up early with Axel and Gunner, who shared her wing room, and hurried into the back living-room, between the dining-room and the kitchen. There, beside a soft-coal stove, the younger children of the family undressed at night and dressed in the morning. The older daughter, Anna, and the two big boys slept upstairs, where the rooms were theoretically warmed by stovepipes from below. The first (and the worst!) thing that confronted Thea was a suit of clean, prickly red flannel, fresh from the wash. Usually the torment of breaking in a clean suit of flannel came on Sunday, but yesterday, as she was staying in the house, she had begged off. Their winter underwear was a trial to all the children, but it was bitterest to Thea because she happened to have the most sensitive skin. While she was tugging it on, her Aunt Tillie brought in warm water from the boiler and filled the tin pitcher. Thea washed her face,

brushed and braided her hair, and got into her blue cashmere dress. Over
this she buttoned a long apron, with sleeves, which would not be removed
until she put on her cloak to go to school. Gunner and Axel, on the
soap-box behind the stove, had their usual quarrel about which should wear
the tightest stockings, but they exchanged reproaches in low tones, for they
were wholesomely afraid of Mrs. Kronborg's rawhide whip. She did not
chastise her children often, but she did it thoroughly. Only a somewhat
stern system of discipline could have kept any degree of order and quiet in
that overcrowded house.

Mrs. Kronborg's children were all trained to dress themselves at
the earliest possible age, to make their own beds—the boys as well as the
girls—to take care of their clothes, to eat what was given them, and to keep
out of the way. Mrs. Kronborg would have made a good chess-player; she
had a head for moves and positions.

Anna, the elder daughter, was her mother's lieutenant. All the
children knew that they must obey Anna, who was an obstinate contender
for proprieties and not always fair-minded. To see the young Kronborgs
headed for Sunday-School was like watching a military drill. Mrs. Kronborg
let her children's minds alone. She did not pry into their thoughts or nag
them. She respected them as individuals, and outside of the house they had
a great deal of liberty. But their communal life was definitely ordered.

In the winter the children breakfasted in the kitchen; Gus and
Charley and Anna first, while the younger children were dressing. Gus was
nineteen and was a clerk in a drygoods store. Charley, eighteen months
younger, worked in a feed store. They left the house by the kitchen door
at seven o'clock, and then Anna helped her Aunt Tillie get the breakfast for
the younger ones. Without the help of this sister-in-law, Tillie Kronborg,
Mrs. Kronborg's life would have been a hard one. Mrs. Kronborg often
reminded Anna that "no hired help would ever have taken the same
interest."

Mr. Kronborg came of a poorer stock than his wife; from a
lowly, ignorant family that had lived in a poor part of Sweden. His great-
grandfather had gone to Norway to work as a farm labourer and had
married a Norwegian girl. This strain of Norwegian blood came out somewhere in each generation of the Kronborgs. The intemperance of one of
Peter Kronborg's uncles, and the religious mania of another, had been alike
charged to the Norwegian grandmother. Both Peter Kronborg and his sister
Tillie were more like the Norwegian root of the family than like the
Swedish, and this same Norwegian strain was strong in Thea, though in her
it took a very different character.

Tillie was a queer, addle-pated thing, at thirty-five as flighty as a girl, and overweeningly fond of gay clothes—which taste, as Mrs. Kronborg philosophically said, did nobody any harm. Tillie was always cheerful, and her tongue was still for scarcely a minute during the day. She had been cruelly overworked on her father's Minnesota farm when she was a young girl, and she had never been so happy as she was now; had never before, as she said, had such social advantages. She thought her brother the most important man in Moonstone. She never missed a church service, and, much to the embarrassment of the children, she always "spoke a piece" at the Sunday-School concerts. She had a complete set of *Standard Recitations,* which she conned on Sundays. This morning, when Thea and her two younger brothers sat down to breakfast, Tillie was remonstrating with Gunner because he had not learned a recitation assigned to him for George Washington Day at school. The unmemorized text lay heavily on Gunner's conscience as he attacked his buckwheat cakes and sausage. He knew that Tillie was in the right, and that "when the day came he would be ashamed of himself."

"I don't care," he muttered, stirring his coffee; "they oughtn't to make boys speak. It's all right for girls. They like to show off."

"No showing off about it. Boys ought to like to speak up for their country. And what was the use of your father buying you a new suit, if you're not going to take part in anything?"

"That was for Sunday-School. I'd rather wear my old one, anyhow. Why didn't they give the piece to Thea?" Gunner grumbled.

Tillie was turning buckwheat cakes at the griddle. "Thea can play and sing, she don't need to speak. But you've got to know how to do something, Gunner, that you have. What are you going to do when you git big and want to git into society, if you can't do nothing? Everybody'll say, 'Can you sing? Can you play? Can you speak? Then git right out of society.' An' that's what they'll say to you, Mr. Gunner."

Gunner and Axel grinned at Anna, who was preparing her mother's breakfast. They never made fun of Tillie, but they understood well enough that there were subjects upon which her ideas were rather foolish. When Tillie struck the shallows, Thea was usually prompt in turning the conversation.

"Will you and Axel let me have your sled at recess?" she asked.

"All the time?" asked Gunner dubiously.

"I'll work your examples for you to-night, if you do."

"Oh, all right. There'll be a lot of 'em."

"I don't mind, I can work 'em fast. How about yours, Axel?"

Axel was a fat little boy of seven, with pretty, lazy blue eyes. "I don't care," he murmured, buttering his last buckwheat cake without ambition; "too much trouble to copy 'em down. Jenny Smiley'll let me have hers."

The boys were to pull Thea to school on their sled, as the snow was deep. The three set off together. Anna was now in the high school, and she no longer went with the family party, but walked to school with some of the older girls who were her friends, and wore a hat, not a hood like Thea.

IV

*A*nd it was Summer, beautiful Summer!" Those were the closing words of Thea's favourite fairy tale, and she thought of them as she ran out into the world one Saturday morning in May, her music-book under her arm. She was going to the Kohlers' to take her lesson, but she was in no hurry.

It was in the summer that one really lived. Then all the little overcrowded houses were opened wide, and the wind blew through them with sweet, earthy smells of garden-planting. The town looked as if it had just been washed. People were out painting their fences. The cottonwood trees were a-flicker with sticky, yellow little leaves, and the feathery tamarisks were in pink bud. With the warm weather came freedom for everybody. People were dug up, as it were. The very old people, whom one had not seen all winter, came out and sunned themselves in the yard. The double windows were taken off the houses, the tormenting flannels in which children had been encased all winter were put away in boxes, and the youngsters felt a pleasure in the cool cotton things next their skin.

Thea had to walk more than a mile to reach the Kohlers' house, a very pleasant mile out of town toward the glittering sand hills—yellow this morning, with lines of deep violet where the clefts and valleys were. She followed the sidewalk to the depot at the south end of the town; then took the road east to the little group of adobe houses where the Mexicans lived, and then dropped into a deep ravine; a dry sand creek, across which the railroad track ran on a trestle. Beyond that gulch, on a little rise of ground that faced the open sandy plain, was the Kohlers' house, where Professor

Wunsch lived. Fritz Kohler was the town tailor, one of the first settlers. He had moved there, built a little house and made a garden, when Moonstone was first marked down on the map. He had three sons, but they now worked on the railroad and were stationed in distant cities. One of them had gone to work for the Santa Fé, and lived in New Mexico.

Mrs. Kohler seldom crossed the ravine and went into the town except at Christmas time, when she had to buy presents and Christmas cards to send to her old friends in Freeport, Illinois. As she did not go to church, she did not possess such a thing as a hat. Year after year she wore the same red hood in winter and a black sunbonnet in summer. She made her own dresses; the skirts came barely to her shoe-tops, and were gathered as full as they could possibly be to the waistband. She preferred men's shoes, and usually wore the cast-offs of one of her sons. She had never learned much English, and her plants and shrubs were her companions. She lived for her men and her garden. Beside that sand gulch she had tried to reproduce a bit of her own village in the Rhine Valley. She hid herself behind the growth she had fostered, lived under the shade of what she had planted and watered and pruned. In the blaze of the open plain she was stupid and blind like an owl. Shade, shade; that was what she was always planning and making. Behind the high tamarisk hedge, her garden was a jungle of verdure in summer. Above the cherry trees and peach trees and golden plums stood the windmill, with its tank on stilts, which kept all this verdure alive. Outside, the sagebrush grew up to the very edge of the garden, and the sand was always drifting up to the tamarisks.

Everyone in Moonstone was astonished when the Kohlers took the wandering music-teacher to live with them. In seventeen years old Fritz had never had a crony, except the harness-maker and Spanish Johnny. This Wunsch came from God knew where—followed Spanish Johnny into town when that wanderer came back from one of his tramps. Wunsch played in the dance orchestra, tuned pianos, and gave lessons. When Mrs. Kohler rescued him, he was sleeping in a dirty, unfurnished room over one of the saloons, and he had only two shirts in the world. Once he was under her roof, the old woman went at him as she did at her garden. She sewed and washed and mended for him, and made him so clean and respectable that he was able to get a large class of pupils and to rent a piano. As soon as he had money ahead, he sent to the Narrow-Gauge lodging-house, in Denver, for a trunkful of music which had been held there for unpaid board. With tears in his eyes the old man—he was not over fifty, but sadly battered—told Mrs. Kohler that he asked nothing better of God than to end his days with her, and to be buried in the garden, under her linden trees. They were not American basswood, but the European linden, which has honey-coloured blooms in summer, with a fragrance that surpasses all trees and flowers and drives young people wild with joy.

Thea was reflecting as she walked along that had it not been for Professor Wunsch she might have lived on for years in Moonstone without ever knowing the Kohlers, without ever seeing their garden or the inside of their house. Besides the cuckoo clock, which was wonderful enough, and which Mrs. Kohler said she kept for "company when she was lonesome," the Kohlers had in their house the most wonderful thing Thea had ever seen—but of that later.

Professor Wunsch went to the houses of his other pupils to give them their lessons, but one morning he told Mrs. Kronborg that Thea had talent, and that if she came to him he could teach her in his slippers, and that would be better. Mrs. Kronborg was a strange woman. That word "talent," which no one else in Moonstone, not even Doctor Archie, would have understood, she comprehended perfectly. To any other woman there, it would have meant that a child must have her hair curled every day and must play in public. Mrs. Kronborg knew it meant that Thea must practise four hours a day. A child with talent must be kept at the piano, just as a child with measles must be kept under the blankets. Mrs. Kronborg and her three sisters had all studied piano, and all sang well, but none of them had talent. Their father had played the oboe in an orchestra in Sweden, before he came to America to better his fortunes. He had even known Jenny Lind. A child with talent had to be kept at the piano; so twice a week in summer and once a week in winter Thea went over the gulch to the Kohlers', though the Ladies' Aid Society thought it was not proper for their preacher's daughter to go "where there was so much drinking." Not that the Kohler sons ever so much as looked at a glass of beer. They were ashamed of their old folks and got out into the world as fast as possible; had their clothes made by a Denver tailor and their necks shaved up under their hair and forgot the past. Old Fritz and Wunsch, however, indulged in a friendly bottle pretty often. The two men were like comrades; perhaps the bond between them was the glass wherein lost hopes are found; perhaps it was common memories of another country; perhaps it was the grapevine in the garden—the knotty, fibrous shrub, full of homesickness and sentiment, which the Germans have carried around the world with them.

As Thea approached the house she peeped between the pink sprays of the tamarisk hedge and saw the professor and Mrs. Kohler in the garden, spading and raking. The garden looked like a relief-map now, and gave no indication of what it would be in August; such a jungle! Pole beans and potatoes and corn and leeks and kale and red cabbage—there would even be vegetables for which there is no American name. Mrs. Kohler was always getting by mail packages of seeds from Freeport and from the old country. Then the flowers! There were big sunflowers for the canary bird, tiger lilies and phlox and zinnias and lady's-slippers and portulaca and hollyhocks—giant hollyhocks. Besides the fruit trees there was a great umbrella shaped catalpa, and a balm of Gilead, two lindens, and even a ginkgo—a rigid, pointed tree with leaves shaped like butterflies, which shivered, but never bent to the wind.

This morning Thea saw to her delight that the two oleander trees, one white and one red, had been brought up from their winter quarters in the cellar. There is hardly a German family in the most arid parts of Utah, New Mexico, or Arizona, but has its oleander trees. However loutish the American-born sons of the family may be, there was never one who refused to give his muscle to the back-breaking task of getting those tubbed trees down into the cellar in the fall and up into the sunlight in the spring. They may strive to avert the day, but they grapple with the tub at last.

When Thea entered the gate, her professor leaned his spade against the white post that supported the turreted dove-house, and wiped his face with his shirt-sleeve; someway he never managed to have a handkerchief about him. Wunsch was short and stocky, with something rough and bearlike about his shoulders. His face was a dark, bricky red, deeply creased rather than wrinkled, and the skin was like loose leather over his neckband—he wore a brass collar button but no collar. His hair was cropped close; iron-grey bristles on a bullet-like head. His eyes were always suffused and bloodshot. He had a coarse, scornful mouth, and irregular, yellow teeth, much worn at the edges. His hands were square and red, seldom clean, but always alive, impatient, even sympathetic.

"*Morgen,*" he greeted his pupil in a businesslike way, put on a black alpaca coat, and conducted her at once to the piano in Mrs. Kohler's sitting-room. He twirled the stool to the proper height, pointed to it, and sat down in a wooden chair beside Thea.

"The scale of B flat major," he directed, and then fell into an attitude of deep attention. Without a word his pupil set to work.

To Mrs. Kohler, in the garden, came the cheerful sound of effort, of vigorous striving. Unconsciously she wielded her rake more

lightly. Occasionally she heard the teacher's voice. "Scale of E minor.
. . . *Weiter, weiter!* . . . *Immer* I hear the thumb, like a lame foot. *Weiter*
. . . *weiter*, once; . . . *Schön!* The chords, quick!"

The pupil did not open her mouth until they began the second
movement of the Clementi sonata, when she remonstrated in low tones
about the way he had marked the fingering of a passage.

"It makes no matter what you think," replied her teacher coldly.
"There is only one right way. The thumb there. *Eins, zwei, drei, vier,*" etc.
Then for an hour there was no further interruption.

At the end of the lesson, Thea turned on her stool and leaned her
arm on the keyboard. They usually had a little talk after the lesson.

Herr Wunsch grinned. "How soon is it you are free from
school? Then we make ahead faster, eh?"

"First week in June. Then will you give me the 'Invitation to the
Dance'?"

He shrugged his shoulders. "It makes no matter. If you want
him, you play him out of lesson hours."

"All right." Thea fumbled in her pocket and brought out a
crumpled slip of paper. "What does this mean, please? I guess it's Latin."

Wunsch blinked at the line pencilled on the paper. "Wherefrom
you get this?" he asked gruffly.

"Out of a book Doctor Archie gave me to read. It's all English
but that. Did you ever see it before?" she asked, watching his face.

"Yes. A long time ago," he muttered, scowling. "Ovidius!" He
took a stub of lead pencil from his vest pocket, steadied his hand by a visible
effort, and under the words

"Lente currite, lente currite, noctis equi,"

he wrote in a clear, elegant Gothic hand,

"Go slowly, go slowly, ye steeds of the night."

He put the pencil back in his pocket and continued to stare at
the Latin. It recalled the poem, which he had read as a student, and thought
very fine. There were treasures of memory which no lodging-house keeper
could attach. One carried things about in one's head, long after one's linen
could be smuggled out in a tuning-bag. He handed the paper back to Thea.
"There is the English, quite elegant," he said, rising.

Mrs. Kohler stuck her head in at the door, and Thea slid off the stool. "Come in, Mrs. Kohler," she called, "and show me the piece-picture."

The old woman laughed, pulled off her big gardening-gloves, and pushed Thea to the lounge before the object of her delight. The "piece-picture," which hung on the wall and nearly covered one whole end of the room, was the handiwork of Fritz Kohler. He had learned his trade under an old-fashioned tailor in Magdeburg who required from each of his apprentices a thesis: that is, before they left his shop, each apprentice had to copy in cloth some well-known German painting, stitching bits of coloured stuff together on a linen background; a kind of mosaic. The pupil was allowed to select his subject, and Fritz Kohler had chosen a popular painting of Napoleon's retreat from Moscow. The gloomy Emperor and his staff were represented as crossing a stone bridge, and behind them was the blazing city, the walls and fortresses done in grey cloth with orange tongues of flame darting about the domes and minarets. Napoleon rode his white horse; Murat, in Oriental dress, a bay charger. Thea was never tired of examining this work, of hearing how long it had taken Fritz to make it, how much it had been admired, and what narrow escapes it had had from moths and fire. Silk, Mrs. Kohler explained, would have been much easier to manage than woolen cloth, in which it was often hard to get the right shades. The reins of the horses, the wheels of the spurs, the brooding eyebrows of the Emperor, Murat's fierce moustaches, the great shakos of the Guard, were all worked out with the minutest fidelity. Thea's admiration for this picture had endeared her to Mrs. Kohler. It was now many years since she used to point out its wonders to her own little boys. As Mrs. Kohler did not go to church, she never heard any singing, except the songs that floated over from Mexican Town, and Thea often sang for her after the lesson was over. This morning Wunsch pointed to the piano.

"On Sunday, when I go by the church, I hear you sing something."

Thea obediently sat down on the stool again and began, "Come, ye Disconsolate." Thoughtfully Wunsch listened, his hands on his knees. Such a beautiful child's voice! Old Mrs. Kohler's face relaxed in a smile of happiness; she half-closed her eyes. A big fly was darting in and out of the window; the sunlight made a golden pool on the rag carpet and bathed the faded cretonne pillows on the lounge, under the piece-picture. "Earth has no sorrow that Heaven cannot heal," the song died away.

"That is a good thing to remember." Wunsch shook himself. "You believe that?" looking quizzically at Thea.

She became confused and pecked nervously at a black key with her middle finger. "I don't know. I guess so," she murmured.

Her teacher rose abruptly. "Remember, for next time, thirds. You ought to get up earlier."

That night the air was so warm that Fritz and Herr Wunsch had their after-supper pipe in the grape arbour, smoking in silence while the sound of fiddles and guitars came across the ravine from Mexican town. Long after Fritz and his old Paulina had gone to bed, old Wunsch sat motionless in the arbour, looking up through the woolly vine leaves at the glittering machinery of heaven.

> *"Lente currite, lente currite, noctis equi."*

That line awoke many memories. He was thinking of youth; of his own, so long gone by, and of his pupil's, just beginning. He would even have cherished hopes for her, except that he had become superstitious. He believed that whatever he hoped for was destined not to be; that his affection brought ill fortune, especially to the young; that if he held anything in his thoughts, he harmed it. He had taught in music schools in St. Louis and in Kansas City, where the shallowness and complacency of the young misses had maddened him. He had encountered bad manners and bad faith, had been the victim of sharpers of all kinds, was dogged by bad luck. He had played in orchestras that were never paid and wandering opera troupes which disbanded penniless. And there was always the old enemy, more relentless than the others. It was long since he had wished anything or desired anything beyond the necessities of the body. Now that he was tempted to hope for another, he felt alarmed and shook his head.

It was his pupil's power of application, her rugged will, that interested him. He had lived for so long among people whose sole ambition was to get something for nothing that he had learned not to look for seriousness in anyone. Now that he by chance encountered it, it recalled standards, ambitions, a society long forgot. What was it she reminded him of? A yellow flower, full of sunlight, perhaps. No; a thin glass full of sweet-smelling, sparkling Moselle wine. He seemed to see such a glass before him in the arbour, to watch the bubbles rising and breaking, like the silent discharge of energy in the nerves and brain, the rapid florescence in young blood—Wunsch felt ashamed and dragged his slippers along the path to the kitchen, his eyes on the ground.

V

The children in the primary grades were sometimes required to make relief-maps of Moonstone in sand. Had they used coloured sands, as the Navajo medicine-men do in their sand mosaics, they could easily have indicated the social classifications of Moonstone, since these conformed to certain topographical boundaries, and every child understood them perfectly.

The main business street ran, of course, through the centre of the town. To the west of this street lived all the people who were, as Tillie Kronborg said, "in society." Sylvester Street, the third parallel with Main Street on the west, was the longest in town, and the best dwellings were built along it. Far out at the north end, nearly a mile from the court-house and its cottonwood grove, was Doctor Archie's house, its big yard and garden surrounded by a white paling fence. The Methodist Church was in the centre of the town, facing the court-house square. The Kronborgs lived half a mile south of the church, on the long street that stretched out like an arm to the depot settlement. This was the first street west of Main, and was built up only on one side. The preacher's house faced the backs of the brick and frame store buildings and a draw full of sunflowers and scraps of old iron. The sidewalk which ran in front of the Kronborgs' house was the one continuous sidewalk to the depot, and all the train men and roundhouse employees passed the front gate every time they came uptown. Thea and Mrs. Kronborg had many friends among the railroad men, who often paused to chat across the fence, and of one of these we shall have more to say.

In the part of Moonstone that lay east of Main Street, toward the deep ravine which, farther south, wound by Mexican Town, lived all the humbler citizens, the people who voted but did not run for office. The houses were little storey-and-a-half cottages, with none of the fussy architectural efforts that marked those on Sylvester Street. They nestled modestly behind their cottonwoods and Virginia creeper; their occupants had no social pretensions to keep up. There were no half-glass front doors with doorbells, or formidable parlours behind closed shutters. Here the old women washed in the back yard, and the men sat in the front doorway and smoked their pipes. The people on Sylvester Street scarcely knew that this part of the town existed. Thea liked to take Thor and her express wagon and explore these quiet, shady streets, where the people never tried to have lawns or to grow elms and pine trees, but let the native timber have its way and spread in luxuriance. She had many friends there, old women who gave her a yellow rose or a spray of trumpet-vine and appeased Thor with a cooky or a doughnut. They called Thea "that preacher's girl," but the demonstrative was misplaced, for when they spoke of Mr. Kronborg they called him "the Methodist preacher."

Doctor Archie was very proud of his yard and garden, which he worked himself. He was the only man in Moonstone who was successful at growing tea roses, and his strawberries were famous. One morning when Thea was downtown on an errand, the doctor stopped her, took her hand and went over her with a quizzical eye, as he nearly always did when they met.

"You haven't been up to my place to get any strawberries yet, Thea. They're at their best just now. Mrs. Archie doesn't know what to do with them all. Come up this afternoon. Just tell Mrs. Archie I sent you. Bring a big basket and pick till you are tired."

When she got home, Thea told her mother that she didn't want to go, because she didn't like Mrs. Archie.

"She is certainly one queer woman," Mrs. Kronborg assented, "but he's asked you so often, I guess you'll have to go this time. She won't bite you."

After dinner Thea took a basket, put Thor in his baby-buggy, and set out for Doctor Archie's house at the other end of town. As soon as she came within sight of the house, she slackened her pace. She approached it very slowly, stopping often to pick dandelions and sand-peas for Thor to crush up in his fist.

It was his wife's custom, as soon as Doctor Archie left the house in the morning, to shut all the doors and windows to keep the dust out, and to pull down the shades to keep the sun from fading the carpets. She thought, too, that neighbours were less likely to drop in if the house was closed up. She was one of those people who are stingy without motive or reason, even when they can gain nothing by it. She must have known that skimping the doctor in heat and food made him more extravagant than he would have been had she made him comfortable. He never came home for lunch, because she gave him such miserable scraps and shreds of food. No matter how much milk he bought, he could never get thick cream for his strawberries. Even when he watched his wife lift it from the milk in smooth, ivory-coloured blankets, she managed, by some sleight-of-hand, to dilute it before it got to the breakfast table. The butcher's favourite joke was about the kind of meat he sold Mrs. Archie. She liked nothing better than to have Doctor Archie go to Denver for a few days—he often went chiefly because he was hungry—and to be left alone to eat canned salmon and to keep the house shut up from morning until night.

Mrs. Archie would not have a servant because, she said, "they ate too much and broke too much"; she even said they knew too much. She used what mind she had in devising shifts to minimize her housework. She used to tell her neighbours that if there were no men, there would be no housework. When Mrs. Archie was first married, she had been always in a panic for fear she would have children. Now that her apprehensions on that score had grown paler, she was almost as much afraid of having dust in the house as she had once been of having children in it. If dust did not get in, it did not have to be got out, she said. She would take any amount of trouble to avoid trouble. Why, nobody knew. Certainly her husband had never been able to make her out. Such little, mean natures are among the darkest and most baffling of created things. There is no law by which they can be explained. The ordinary incentives of pain and pleasure do not account for their behaviour. They live like insects, absorbed in petty activities that seem to have nothing to do with any genial aspect of human life.

Mrs. Archie, as Mrs. Kronborg said, "liked to gad." She liked to have her house clean, empty, dark, locked, and to be out of it—anywhere. A church social, a prayer-meeting, a ten-cent show; she seemed to have no preference. When there was nowhere else to go, she used to sit for hours in Mrs. Smiley's millinery and notion store, listening to the talk of the women who came in, watching them while they tried on hats, blinking at them from her corner with her sharp, restless little eyes. She never talked much herself, but she knew all the gossip of the town and she had a sharp ear for racy anecdotes—"travelling men's stories," they used to be called in Moonstone. Her clicking laugh sounded like a typewriting machine in action, and, for very pointed stories, she had a little screech.

Mrs. Archie had been Mrs. Archie for only eight years, and when she was Belle White she was one of the "pretty" girls in Lansing, Michigan. She had then a train of suitors. She could truly remind Archie that "the boys hung around her." They did. They thought her very spirited and were always saying, "Oh, that Belle White, she's a case!" She used to play heavy practical jokes which the young men thought very clever. Archie was considered the most promising young man in "the young crowd," so Belle selected him. She let him see, made him fully aware, that she had selected him, and Archie was the sort of boy who could not withstand such enlightenment. Belle's family were sorry for him. On his wedding day her sisters looked at the big, handsome boy—he was twenty-four—as he walked down the aisle with his bride, and then they looked at each other. His besotted confidence, his sober, radiant face, his gentle, protecting arm, made them uncomfortable. Well, they were glad that he was going West at once, to fulfill his doom where they would not be onlookers. Anyhow, they consoled themselves, they had got Belle off their hands.

More than that, Belle seemed to have got herself off her own hands. Her reputed prettiness must have been entirely the result of determination, of a fierce little ambition. Once she had married, fastened herself on someone, come to port—it vanished like the ornamental plumage which drops away from some birds after the mating season. The one aggressive action of her life was over. She began to shrink in face and stature. Of her harum-scarum spirit there was nothing left but the little screech. Within a few years she looked as small and mean as she was.

Thor's chariot crept along. Thea approached the house unwillingly. She didn't care about the strawberries, anyhow. She had come only because she did not want to hurt Doctor Archie's feelings. She not only disliked Mrs. Archie, she was a little afraid of her. While she was getting the heavy baby-buggy through the iron gate, she heard someone call, "Wait a minute!" and Mrs. Archie came running around the house from the back door, her apron over her head. She came to help with the buggy, because she was afraid the wheels might scratch the paint off the gateposts. She was a skinny little woman with a great pile of frizzy light hair on a small head.

"Doctor Archie told me to come up and pick some strawberries," Thea muttered, wishing she had stayed at home.

Mrs. Archie led the way to the back door, squinting and shading her eyes with her hand. "Wait a minute," she said again, when Thea explained why she had come.

She went into her kitchen and Thea sat down on the porch step. When Mrs. Archie reappeared, she carried in her hand a little wooden butter-basket trimmed with fringed tissue paper, which she must have brought home from some church supper. "You'll have to have something to put them in," she said, ignoring the yawning willow basket which stood empty at Thor's feet. "You can have this, and you needn't mind about returning it. You know about not trampling the vines, don't you?"

Mrs. Archie went back into the house and Thea leaned over in the sand and picked a few strawberries. As soon as she was sure that she was not going to cry, she tossed the little basket into the big one and ran Thor's buggy along the gravel walk and out of the gate as fast as she could push it. She was angry, and she was ashamed for Doctor Archie. She could not help thinking how uncomfortable he would be if he ever found out about it. Little things like that were the ones that cut him most. She slunk home by the back way, and again almost cried when she told her mother about it.

Mrs. Kronborg was frying doughnuts for her husband's supper. She laughed as she dropped a new lot into the hot grease. "It's wonderful, the way some people are made," she declared. "But I wouldn't let that upset me if I was you. Think what it would be to live with it all the time. You look in the black pocketbook inside my handbag and take a dime and go downtown and get an ice-cream soda. That'll make you feel better. Thor can have a little of the ice cream if you feed it to him with a spoon. He likes it, don't you, son?"

She stooped to wipe his chin. Thor was only six months old and inarticulate, but it was quite true that he liked ice cream.

VI

Seen from a balloon, Moonstone would have looked like a Noah's Ark town set out in the sand and lightly shaded by grey-green tamarisks and cottonwoods. A few people were trying to make soft maples grow in their turfed lawns, but the fashion of planting incongruous trees from the North Atlantic States had not become general then, and the frail, brightly painted desert town was shaded by the light-reflecting, wind-loving trees of the desert, whose roots are always seeking water and whose leaves are always talking about it, making the sound of rain. The long, porous roots of the cottonwood are irrepressible. They break into the wells as rats do into granaries, and thieve the water.

The long street which connected Moonstone with the depot settlement traversed in its course a considerable stretch of rough open country, staked out in lots, but not built up at all, a weedy hiatus between the town and the railroad. When you set out along this street to go to the station, you noticed that the houses became smaller and farther apart, until they ceased altogether, and the board sidewalk continued its uneven course through sunflower patches, until you reached the solitary, new brick Catholic Church. The church stood there because the land was given to the parish by the man who owned the adjoining waste lots, in the hope of making them more saleable—"Farrier's Addition," this patch of prairie was called in the clerk's office. An eighth of a mile beyond the church was a washout, a deep sand gully, where the board sidewalk became a bridge for perhaps fifty feet.

Just beyond the gully was old Uncle Billy Beemer's grove— twelve town lots set out in fine, well-grown cottonwood trees, delightful to look upon, or to listen to, as they swayed and rippled in the wind. Uncle Billy had been one of the most worthless old drunkards who ever sat on a store box and told filthy stories. One night he played hide-and-seek with a switch engine and got his sodden brains knocked out. But his grove, the one creditable thing he had ever done in his life, rustled on. Beyond this grove the houses of the depot settlement began, and the naked board walk, that had run in out of the sunflowers, again became a link between human dwellings.

One afternoon, late in the summer, Doctor Howard Archie was fighting his way back to town along this walk through a blinding sandstorm, a silk handkerchief tied over his mouth. He had been to see a sick woman down in the depot settlement, and he was walking because his ponies had been out for a hard drive that morning.

As he passed the Catholic Church, he came upon Thea and Thor. Thea was sitting in a child's express wagon, her feet out behind, kicking the wagon along and steering by the tongue. Thor was on her lap and she held him with one arm. He had grown to be a big cub of a baby, with a constitutional grievance, and he had to be continually amused. Thea took him philosophically, and tugged and pulled him about, getting as much fun as she could under her encumbrance. Her hair was blowing about her face, and her eyes were squinting so intently at the uneven board sidewalk in front of her that she did not see the doctor until he spoke to her.

"Look out, Thea. You'll steer that youngster into the ditch."

The wagon stopped. Thea released the tongue, wiped her hot, sandy face, and pushed back her hair. "Oh, no, I won't! I never ran off but once, and then he didn't get anything but a bump. He likes this better than a baby-buggy, and so do I."

"Are you going to kick that cart all the way home?"

"Of course. We take long trips; wherever there is a sidewalk. It's no good on the road."

"Looks to me like working pretty hard for your fun. Are you going to be busy tᵣ -night? Want to make a call with me? Spanish Johnny's come home again, all used up. His wife sent me word this morning, and I said I'd go over to see him to-night. He's an old chum of yours, isn't he?"

"Oh, I'm glad. She's been crying her eyes out. When did he come?"

"Last night, on Number Six. Paid his fare, they tell me. Too sick to beat it. There'll come a time when that boy won't get back, I'm afraid. Come around to my office about eight o'clock—and you needn't bring that!"

Thor seemed to understand that he had been insulted, for he scowled and began to kick the side of the wagon, shouting, "Go-go, go-go!" Thea leaned forward and grabbed the wagon-tongue. Doctor Archie stepped in front of her and blocked the way. "Why don't you make him wait? What do you let him boss you like that for?"

"If he gets mad he throws himself, and then I can't do anything with him. When he's mad he's lots stronger than me, aren't you, Thor?" Thea spoke with pride, and the idol was appeased. He grunted approvingly as his sister began to kick rapidly behind her, and the wagon rattled off and soon disappeared in the flying currents of sand.

That evening Doctor Archie was seated in his office, his desk chair tilted back, reading by the light of a hot coal-oil lamp. All the windows were open, but the night was breathless after the sandstorm, and his hair was moist where it hung over his forehead. He was deeply engrossed in his book and sometimes smiled thoughtfully as he read. When Thea Kronborg entered quietly and slipped into a seat, he nodded, finished his paragraph, inserted a bookmark, and rose to put the book back into the case. It was one out of the long row of uniform volumes on the top shelf.

"Nearly every time I come in, when you're alone, you're reading one of those books," Thea remarked thoughtfully. "They must be very nice."

The doctor dropped back into his swivel chair, the mottled volume still in his hand. "They aren't exactly books, Thea," he said seriously. "They're a city."

"A history, you mean?"

"Yes, and no. They're a history of a live city, not a dead one.

A Frenchman undertook to write about a whole cityful of people, all the kinds he knew. And he got them nearly all in, I guess. Yes, it's very interesting. You'll like to read it some day, when you're grown up."

Thea leaned forward and made out the title on the back, *A Distinguished Provincial in Paris.*

"It doesn't sound very interesting."

"Perhaps not, but it is." The doctor scrutinized her broad face, low enough to be in the direct light from under the green lampshade. "Yes," he went on with some satisfaction, "I think you'll like them some day. You're always curious about people, and I expect this man knew more about people than anybody that ever lived."

"City people or country people?"

"Both. People are pretty much the same everywhere."

"Oh, no, they're not. The people who go through in the dining-car aren't like us."

"What makes you think they aren't, my girl? Their clothes?"

Thea shook her head. "No, it's something else. I don't know." Her eyes shifted under Doctor Archie's searching gaze and she glanced up at the row of books. "How soon will I be old enough to read them?"

"Soon enough, soon enough, little girl." The doctor patted her hand and looked at her index finger. "The nail's coming all right, isn't it? But I think that man makes you practise too much. You have it on your mind all the time." He had noticed that when she talked to him she was always opening and shutting her hands. "It makes you nervous."

"No, he don't," Thea replied stubbornly, watching Doctor Archie return the book to its niche.

He took up a black leather case, put on his hat, and they went down the dark stairs into the street. The summer moon hung full in the sky. For the time being it was the great fact in the world. Beyond the edge of the town the plain was so white that every clump of sage stood out distinct from the sand, and the dunes looked like a shining lake. The doctor took off his straw hat and carried it in his hand as they walked toward Mexico Town, across the sand.

North of Pueblo, Mexican settlements were rare in Colorado then. This one had come about accidentally. Spanish Johnny was the first Mexican who came to Moonstone. He was a painter and decorator, and had been working in Trinidad, when Ray Kennedy told him there was a "boom" on in Moonstone, and a good many new buildings were going up. A year after Johnny settled in Moonstone, his cousin, Famos Serreños, came to work in the brickyard; then Serreños's cousins came to help him. During the strike, the master mechanic put a gang of Mexicans to work in the roundhouse. The Mexicans had arrived so quietly, with their blankets and musical instruments, that before Moonstone was awake to the fact, there was a Mexican quarter; a dozen families or more.

As Thea and the doctor approached the 'dobe houses, they heard a guitar, and a rich baritone voice—that of Famos Serreños—singing "La Golandrina." All the Mexican houses had neat little yards, with tamarisk hedges and flowers, and walks bordered with shells or whitewashed stones. Johnny's house was dark. His wife, Mrs. Tellamantez, was sitting on the doorstep, combing her long, blue-black hair. (Mexican women are like the Spartans; when they are in trouble, in love, under stress of any kind, they comb and comb their hair.) She rose without embarrassment or apology, comb in hand, and greeted the doctor.

"Good evening; will you go in?" she asked in a low, musical voice. "He is in the back room. I will make a light."

She followed them indoors, lit a candle and handed it to the doctor, pointing toward the bedroom. Then she went back and sat down on her doorstep.

Doctor Archie and Thea went into the bedroom, which was dark and quiet. There was a bed in the corner, and a man was lying on the clean sheets. On the table beside him was a glass pitcher, half-full of water. Spanish Johnny looked younger than his wife, and when he was in health he was very handsome: slender, gold-coloured, with wavy black hair, a round, smooth throat, white teeth, and burning black eyes. His profile was strong and severe, like an Indian's. What was termed his "wildness" showed itself only in his feverish eyes and in the colour that burned on his tawny cheeks. That night he was a coppery green, and his eyes were like black holes. He opened them when the doctor held the candle before his face.

"*Mi testa!*" he muttered, "*mi testa, doctor. La fiebre!*" Seeing the doctor's companion at the foot of the bed, he attempted a smile. "*Muchacha!*" he exclaimed deprecatingly.

Doctor Archie stuck a thermometer into his mouth. "Now, Thea, you can run outside and wait for me."

Thea slipped noiselessly through the dark house and joined Mrs. Tellamantez. The sombre Mexican woman did not seem inclined to talk, but her nod was friendly. Thea sat down on the warm sand, her back to the moon, facing Mrs. Tellamantez on her doorstep, and began to count the moonflowers on the vine that ran over the house. Mrs. Tellamantez was

always considered a very homely woman. Her face was of a strongly marked
type not sympathetic to Americans. Such long, oval faces, with a full chin,
a large, mobile mouth, a high nose, are not uncommon in Spain. Mrs.
Tellamantez could not write her name, and could read but little. Her strong
nature lived upon itself. She was chiefly known in Moonstone for her
forbearance with her incorrigible husband.

    Nobody knew exactly what was the matter with Johnny, and
everybody liked him. His popularity would have been unusual for a white
man; for a Mexican it was unprecedented. His talents were his undoing. He
had a high, uncertain tenor voice, and he played the mandolin with excep-
tional skill. Periodically he went crazy. There was no other way to explain
his behaviour. He was a clever workman, and, when he worked, as regular
and faithful as a burro. Then some night he would fall in with a crowd at
the saloon and begin to sing. He would go on until he had no voice left,
until he wheezed and rasped. Then he would play his mandolin furiously,
and drink until his eyes sank back into his head. At last, when he was put
out of the saloon at closing time, and could get nobody to listen to him, he
would run away—along the railroad track, straight across the desert. He
always managed to get aboard a freight somewhere. Once beyond Denver,
he played his way southward from saloon to saloon until he got across the
border. He never wrote to his wife; but she would soon begin to get
newspapers from La Junta, Albuquerque, Chihuahua, with marked para-
graphs announcing that Juan Tellamantez and his wonderful mandolin
could be heard at the Jack Rabbit Grill or the Pearl of Cadiz Saloon. Mrs.
Tellamantez waited and wept and combed her hair. When he was completely wrung out and burned up—all but destroyed—her Juan always came
back to her to be taken care of—once with an ugly knife wound in the
neck, once with a finger missing from his right hand—but he played just
as well with three fingers as he had with four.

    Public sentiment was lenient toward Johnny, but everybody was
disgusted with Mrs. Tellamantez for putting up with him. She ought to
discipline him, people said; she ought to leave him; she had no self-respect.
In short, Mrs. Tellamantez got all the blame. Even Thea thought she was
much too humble. To-night, as she sat with her back to the moon, looking
at the moonflowers and Mrs. Tellamantez's sombre face, she was thinking
that there is nothing so sad in the world as that kind of patience and
resignation. It was much worse than Johnny's craziness. She even wondered
whether it did not help to make Johnny crazy. People had no right to be
so passive and resigned. She would like to roll over and over in the sand and

screech at Mrs. Tellamantez. She was glad when the doctor came out.

The Mexican woman rose and stood respectful and expectant. The doctor held his hat in his hand and looked kindly at her.

"Same old thing, Mrs. Tellamantez. He's no worse than he's been before. I've left some medicine. Don't give him anything but toast water until I see him again. You're a good nurse; you'll get him out." Doctor Archie smiled encouragingly. He glanced about the little garden and wrinkled his brows. "I can't see what makes him behave so. He's killing himself, and he's not a rowdy sort of fellow. Can't you tie him up someway? Can't you tell when these fits are coming on?"

Mrs. Tellamantez put her hand on her forehead.

"The saloon, doctor, the excitement; that is what makes him. People listen to him, and it excites him."

The doctor shook his head. "Maybe. He's too much for my calculations. I don't see what he gets out of it."

"He is always fooled"—the Mexican woman spoke rapidly and tremulously, her long under lip quivering. "He is good at heart, but he has no head. He fools himself. You do not understand in this country, you are progressive. But he has no judgement, and he is fooled." She stooped quickly, took up one of the white conch-shells that bordered the walk, and, with an apologetic inclination of her head, held it to Dcotor Archie's ear. "Listen, doctor. You hear something in there? You hear the sea; and yet the sea is very far from here. You have judgment, and you know that. But he is fooled. To him, it is the sea itself. A little thing is big to him." She bent and placed the shell in the white row, with its fellows. Thea took it up softly and pressed it to her own ear. The sound in it startled her; it was like something calling one. So that was why Johnny ran away. There was something awe-inspiring about Mrs. Tellamantez and her shell.

Thea caught Doctor Archie's hand and squeezed it hard as she skipped along beside him back toward Moonstone. She went home, and the doctor went back to his lamp and his book. He never left his office until after midnight. If he did not play whist or pool in the evening, he read. It had become a habit with him to lose himself.

*T*hea's twelfth birthday had passed a few weeks before her memorable call upon Mrs. Tellamantez. There was a worthy man in Moonstone who was already planning to marry Thea as soon as she should be old enough. His name was Ray Kennedy, his age was thirty, and he was conductor on a freight train, his run being from Moonstone to Denver. Ray was a big fellow, with a square, open American face, a rock chin, and features that one would never happen to remember. He was an aggressive idealist, a free-thinker, and, like most railroad men, deeply sentimental. Thea liked him for reasons that had to do with the adventurous life he had led in Mexico and the Southwest, rather than for anything very personal. She liked him, too, because he was the only one of her friends who ever took her to the sand hills. The sand hills were a constant tantalization; she loved them better than anything near Moonstone, and yet she could so seldom get to them. The first dunes were accessible enough; they were only a few miles beyond the Kohlers', and she could run out there any day when she could do her practising in the morning and get Thor off her hands for an afternoon. But the real hills—the Turquoise Hills, the Mexicans called them—were ten good miles away, and one reached them by a heavy, sandy road. Doctor Archie sometimes took Thea on his long drives, but as nobody lived in the sand hills, he never had calls to make in that direction. Ray Kennedy was her only hope of getting there.

This summer Thea had not been to the hills once, though Ray had planned several Sunday expeditions. Once Thor was sick, and once the organist in her father's church was away and Thea had to play the organ for the three Sunday services. But on the first Sunday in September, Ray drove up to the Kronborgs' front gate at nine o'clock in the morning and the party actually set off. Gunner and Axel went with Thea, and Ray had asked Spanish Johnny to come and to bring Mrs. Tellamantez and his mandolin. Ray was artlessly fond of music, especially of Mexican music. He and Mrs. Tellamantez had got up the lunch between them, and they were to make coffee in the desert.

When they left Mexican Town, Thea was on the front seat with

Ray and Johnny, and Gunner and Axel sat behind with Mrs. Tellamantez. They objected to this, of course, but there were some things about which Thea would have her own way. "As stubborn as a Finn," Mrs. Kronborg sometimes said of her, quoting an old Swedish saying. When they passed the Kohlers', old Fritz and Wunsch were cutting grapes at the arbour. Thea gave them a business-like nod. Wunsch came to the gate and looked after them. He divined Ray Kennedy's hopes, and he distrusted every expedition that led away from the piano. Unconsciously he made Thea pay for frivolousness of this sort.

As Ray Kennedy's party followed the faint road across the sagebrush, they heard behind them the sound of church bells, which gave them a sense of escape and boundless freedom. Every rabbit that shot across the path, every sage hen that flew up by the trail, was like a runaway thought, a message that one sent into the desert. As they went farther, the illusion of the mirage became more instead of less convincing; a shallow silver lake that spread for many miles, a little misty in the sunlight. Here and there one saw reflected the image of a heifer, turned loose to live upon the sparse sand grass. They were magnified to a preposterous height and looked like mammoths, prehistoric beasts standing solitary in the waters that for many thousands of years actually washed over that desert: the mirage itself may be the ghost of that long-vanished sea. Beyond the phantom lake lay the line of many-coloured hills; rich, sun-baked yellow, glowing turquoise, lavender, purple; all the open, pastel colours of the desert.

After the first five miles the road grew heavier. The horses had to slow down to a walk and the wheels sank deep into the sand, which now lay in long ridges, like waves, where the last high wind had drifted it. Two hours brought the party to Pedro's Cup, named for a Mexican desperado who had once held the sheriff at bay there. The Cup was a great amphitheatre, cut out in the hills, its floor smooth and packed hard, dotted with sagebrush and greasewood.

On either side of the Cup the yellow hills ran north and south, with winding ravines between them, full of soft sand which drained down from the crumbling banks. On the surface of this fluid sand, one could find bits of brilliant stone, crystals and agates and onyx, and petrified wood as red as blood. Dried toads and lizards were to be found there, too. Birds, decomposing more rapidly, left only feathered skeletons.

After a little reconnoitering, Mrs. Tellamantez declared that it was time for lunch, and Ray took his hatchet and began to cut greasewood, which burns fiercely in its green state. The little boys dragged the bushes to the spot that Mrs. Tellamantez had chosen for her fire. Mexican women like to cook out-of-doors.

After lunch Thea sent Gunner and Axel to hunt for agates. "If you see a rattlesnake, run. Don't try to kill it," she enjoined.

Gunner hesitated. "If Ray would let me take the hatchet, I could kill one all right."

Mrs. Tellamantez smiled and said something to Johnny in Spanish.

"Yes," her husband replied, translating, "they say in Mexico, kill a snake but never hurt his feelings. Down in the hot country, *muchacha,*" turning to Thea, "people keep a pet snake in the house to kill rats and mice. They call him the house snake. They keep a little mat for him by the fire, and at night he curl up there and sit with the family, just as friendly!"

Gunner sniffed with disgust. "Well, I think that's a dirty Mexican way to keep house; so there!"

Johnny shrugged his shoulders. "Perhaps," he muttered. A Mexican learns to dive below insults or soar above them, after he crosses the border.

By this time the south wall of the amphitheatre cast a narrow shelf of shadow, and the party withdrew to this refuge. Ray and Johnny began to talk about the Grand Cañon and Death Valley, two places much shrouded in mystery in those days, and Thea listened intently. Mrs. Tellamantez took out her drawn-work and pinned it to her knee. Ray could talk well about the large part of the continent over which he had been knocked about, and Johnny was appreciative.

"You been all over, pretty near. Like a Spanish boy," he commented respectfully.

Ray, who had taken off his coat, whetted his pocket knife thoughtfully on the sole of his shoe. "I began to browse around early. I had a mind to see something of this world, and I ran away from home before I was twelve. Rustled for myself ever since."

"Ran away?" Johnny looked hopeful. "What for?"

"Couldn't make it go with my old man, and didn't take to farming. There were plenty of boys at home. I wasn't missed."

Thea wriggled down in the hot sand and rested her chin on her arm. "Tell Johnny about the melons, Ray, please do!"

Ray's solid, sunburned cheeks grew a shade redder, and he looked reproachfully at Thea. "You're stuck on that story, kid. You like to get the laugh on me, don't you? That was the finishing split I had with my old man, John. He had a claim along the creek, not far from Denver, and raised a little garden stuff for market. One day he had a load of melons and he decided to take 'em to town and sell 'em along the street, and he made me go along and drive for him. Denver wasn't the queen city it is now, by any means, but it seemed a terrible big place to me; and when we got there, if he didn't make me drive right up Capitol Hill! Pap got out and stopped at folkses houses to ask if they didn't want to buy any melons, and I was to drive along slow. The farther I went the madder I got, but I was trying to look unconscious, when the end-gate came loose and one of the melons fell out and squashed. Just then a swell girl, all dressed up, comes out of one of the big houses and calls out, 'Hello, boy, you're losing your melons!' Some dudes on the other side of the street took their hats off to her and began to laugh. I couldn't stand it any longer. I grabbed the whip and lit into that team, and they tore up the hill like jack-rabbits, them damned melons bouncing out the back every jump, the old man cussin' an' yellin' behind and everybody laughin'. I never looked behind, but the whole of Capitol Hill must have been a mess with them squashed melons. I didn't stop the team till I got out of sight of town. Then I pulled up an' left 'em with a rancher I was acquainted with, and I never went home to get the lickin' that was waitin' for me. I expect it's waitin' for me yet."

Thea rolled over in the sand. "Oh, I wish I could have seen those melons fly, Ray! I'll never see anything as funny as that. Now, tell Johnny about your first job."

Ray had a collection of good stories. He was observant, truthful, and kindly—perhaps the chief requisites in a good storyteller. Occasionally he used newspaper phrases, conscientiously learned in his efforts at self-instruction, but when he talked naturally he was always worth listening to. Never having had any schooling to speak of, he had, almost from the time he first ran away, tried to make good his loss. As a sheep-herder he had worried an old grammar to tatters, and read instructive books with the help of a pocket dictionary. By the light of many campfires he had pondered upon Prescott's histories, and the works of Washington Irving, which he bought at a high price from a book agent. Mathematics and physics were easy for him, but general culture came hard, and he was determined to get it. Ray was a free-thinker, and inconsistently believed himself damned for being one. When he was braking, down on the Santa Fé, at the end of his run he used to climb into the upper bunk of the caboose, while a noisy gang played poker about the stove below him, and by the roof-lamp read Robert Ingersoll's speeches and *The Age of Reason*.

Ray was a loyal-hearted fellow, and it had cost him a great deal to give up his God. He was one of the step-children of Fortune, and he had very little to show for all his hard work; the other fellow always got the best of it. He had come in too late, or too early, on several schemes that had made money. He brought with him from all his wanderings a good deal of information (more or less correct in itself, but unrelated, and therefore misleading), a high standard of personal honour, a sentimental veneration for all women, bad as well as good, and a bitter hatred of Englishmen. Thea often thought that the nicest thing about Ray was his love for Mexico and the Mexicans, who had been kind to him when he drifted, a homeless boy, over the border. In Mexico, Ray was Señor Ken-ay-dy, and when he answered to that name he was somehow a different fellow. He could speak Spanish fluently, and the sunny warmth of that tongue kept him from being quite as hard as his chin, or as narrow as his popular science.

While Ray was smoking his cigar, he and Johnny fell to talking about the great fortunes that had been made in the Southwest, and about fellows they knew who had "struck it rich."

"I guess you been in on some big deals down there?" Johnny asked trustfully.

Ray smiled and shook his head. "I've been out on some, Johnny. I've never been exactly in on any. So far, I've either held on too long or let go too soon. But mine's coming to me, all right." Ray looked reflective. He leaned back in the shadow and dug out a rest for his elbow in the sand. "The narrowest escape I ever had was in the Bridal Chamber. If I hadn't let go there, it would have made me rich. That was a close call."

Johnny looked delighted. "You don't say! She was silver mine, I guess?"

"I guess she was! Down at Lake Valley. I put up a few hundred for the prospector, and he gave me a bunch of stock. Before we'd got anything out of it, my brother-in-law died of the fever in Cuba. My sister was beside herself to get his body back to Colorado to bury him. Seemed foolish to me, but she's the only sister I got. It's expensive for dead folks to travel, and I had to sell my stock in the mine to raise the money to get Elmer on the move. Two months afterward, the boys struck that big pocket in the rock, full of virgin silver. They named her the Bridal Chamber. It wasn't ore, you remember. It was pure, soft metal you could have melted right down into dollars. The boys cut it out with chisels. If old Elmer hadn't played that trick on me, I'd have been in for about fifty thousand. That was a close call, Spanish."

"I recollec'. When the pocket gone, the town go bust."

"You bet. Higher'n a kite. There was no vein, just a pocket in the rock that had sometime or another got filled up with molten silver. You'd think there would be more somewhere about, but *nada*. There's fools digging holes in that mountain yet."

When Ray had finished his cigar, Johnny took his mandolin and began Kennedy's favourite, "Ultimo Amor." It was now three o'clock in the afternoon, the hottest hour in the day. The narrow shelf of shadow had widened until the floor of the amphitheatre was marked off in two halves, one glittering yellow, and one purple. The little boys had come back and were making a robbers' cave to enact the bold deeds of Pedro the bandit. Johnny, stretched gracefully on the sand, passed from "Ultimo Amor" to "Fluvia de Oro," and then to "Noches de Algeria," playing languidly.

Everyone was busy with his own thoughts. Mrs. Tellamantez was thinking of the square in the little town in which she was born; of the white church steps, with people genuflecting as they passed, and the round-topped acacia trees, and the band playing in the plaza. Ray Kennedy was thinking of the future, dreaming the large Western dream of easy money, of a fortune kicked up somewhere in the hills—an oil well, a gold mine, a ledge of copper. He always told himself, when he accepted a cigar from a newly married railroad man, that he knew enough not to marry until he had found his ideal, and could keep her like a queen. He believed that in the yellow head over there in the sand he had found his ideal, and that by the time she was old enough to marry, he would be able to keep her like a queen. He would kick it up from somewhere, when he got loose from the railroad.

Thea, stirred by tales of adventure, of the Grand Cañon and Death Valley, was recalling a great adventure of her own. Early in the summer her father had been invited to conduct a reunion of old frontiersmen, up in Wyoming, near Laramie, and he took Thea along with him to play the organ and sing patriotic songs. There they stayed at the house of an old ranchman who told them about a ridge up in the hills called Laramie Plain, where the wagon-trails of the forty-niners and the Mormons were still visible. The old man even volunteered to take Mr. Kronborg up into the hills to see this place, though it was a very long drive to make in one day. Thea had begged frantically to go along, and the old rancher, flattered by her rapt attention to his stories, had interceded for her. They set out from Laramie before daylight, behind a strong team of mules. All the way there was much talk of the forty-niners. The old rancher had been a teamster in

a freight train that used to crawl back and forth across the plains between
Omaha and Cherry Creek, as Denver was then called, and he had met many
a wagon-train bound for California. He told of Indians and buffaloes, thirst
and slaughter, wanderings in snowstorms, and lonely graves in the desert.

The road they followed was a wild and beautiful one. It led up
and up, by granite rocks and stunted pines, around deep ravines and echoing
gorges. The top of the ridge, when they reached it, was a great flat plain,
strewn with white boulders, with the wind howling over it. There was not
one trail, as Thea had expected; there were a score: deep furrows, cut in the
earth by heavy wagon-wheels, and now grown over with dry, whitish grass.
The furrows ran side by side; when one trail had been worn too deep, the
next party had abandoned it and made a new trail to the right or left. They
were, indeed, only old wagon-ruts, running east and west, and grown over
with grass. But as Thea ran about among the white stones, her skirts
blowing this way and that, the wind brought to her eyes tears that might
have come, anyway. The old rancher picked up an iron ox-shoe from one
of the furrows and gave it to her for a keepsake. To the west one could see
range after range of blue mountains, and at last the snowy range, with its
white, windy peaks, the clouds caught here and there on their spurs. Again
and again Thea had to hide her face from the cold for a moment. The wind
never slept on this plain, the old man said. Every little while eagles flew
over.

Coming up from Laramie, the old man had told them that he
was in Brownsville, Nebraska, when the first telegraph wires were put
across the Missouri River, and that the first message that ever crossed the
river was, "Westward the course of Empire takes its way." He had been in
the room when the instrument began to click, and all the men there had,
without thinking what they were doing, taken off their hats, waiting bareheaded to hear the message translated. Thea remembered that message
when she sighted down the wagon-tracks toward the blue mountains. She
told herself she would never, never forget it. The spirit of human courage
seemed to live up there with the eagles. For long after, when she was moved
by a Fourth-of-July oration, or a band, or a circus parade, she was apt to
remember that windy ridge.

To-day she went to sleep while she was thinking about it. When
Ray wakened her, the horses were hitched to the wagon and Gunner and
Axel were begging for a place on the front seat. The air had cooled, the sun
was setting, and the desert was on fire. Thea contentedly took the back seat
with Mrs. Tellamantez. As they drove homeward, the stars began to come

out, pale yellow in a yellow sky, and Ray and Johnny began to sing one of those railroad ditties that are usually born on the Southern Pacific and run the length of the Santa Fé and the "Q" system before they die to give place to a new one. This was a song about a Greaser dance, the refrain being something like this:

> "Pedró, Pedró, swing high, swing low,
> And it's allamand left again;
> For there's boys that's bold and there's some
>   that's cold,
> But the góld boys come from Spain,
> Oh, the góld boys come from Spain!"

VIII

*W*inter was long in coming that year. Throughout October the days were bathed in sunlight and the air was clear as crystal. The town kept its cheerful summer aspect, the desert glistened with light, the sand hills every day went through magical changes of colour. The scarlet sage bloomed late in the front yards, the cottonwood leaves were bright gold long before they fell, and it was not until November that the green on the tamarisks began to cloud and fade. There was a flurry of snow about Thanksgiving, and then December came on warm and clear.

Thea had three music-pupils now, little girls whose mothers declared that Professor Wunsch was "much too severe." They took their lessons on Saturday, and this, of course, cut down her time for play. She did not really mind this because she was allowed to use the money—her pupils paid her twenty-five cents a lesson—to fit up a little room for herself upstairs in the half-storey. It was the end room of the wing, and was not plastered, but was snugly lined with soft pine. The ceiling was so low that a grown person could reach it with the palm of the hand, and it sloped down on either side. There was only one window, but it was a double one and went to the floor. In October, while the days were still warm, Thea and Tillie papered the room, walls and ceiling in the same paper, small red and brown roses on a yellowish ground. Thea bought a brown cotton carpet, and her big brother, Gus, put it down for her one Sunday. She made white cheese-cloth curtains and hung them on a tape. Her mother gave her an old walnut dresser with a broken mirror, and she had her own dumpy walnut single bed, and a blue washbowl and pitcher which she had drawn at a church-fair lottery. At the head of her bed she had a tall round wooden hat-crate, from the clothing store. This, standing on end and draped with cretonne, made a fairly steady table for her lantern. She was not allowed to take a lamp upstairs, so Ray Kennedy gave her a railroad lantern by which she could read at night.

In winter this loft room of Thea's was bitterly cold, but against her mother's advice—and Tillie's—she always left her window open a little way. Mrs. Kronborg declared that she "had no patience with American physiology," though the lessons about the injurious effects of alcohol and tobacco were well enough for the boys. Thea asked Doctor Archie about the window, and he told her that a girl who sang must always have plenty of fresh air, or her voice would get husky, and that the cold would harden her throat. The important thing, he said, was to keep your feet warm. On very cold nights Thea always put a brick in the oven after supper, and when she went upstairs she wrapped it in an old flannel petticoat and put it in her bed. The boys, who would never heat bricks for themselves, sometimes carried off Thea's, and thought it a good joke to get ahead of her.

When Thea first plunged in between her red blankets, the cold sometimes kept her awake for a good while, and she comforted herself by remembering all she could of *Polar Explorations,* a fat, calf-bound volume her father had bought from a book-agent, and by thinking about the members of Greely's party: how they lay in their frozen sleeping-bags, each man hoarding the warmth of his own body and trying to make it last as long as possible against the oncoming cold that would be everlasting. After half an hour or so, a warm wave crept over her body and round, sturdy legs; she glowed like a little stove with the warmth of her own blood, and the heavy quilts and the red blankets grew warm wherever they touched her, though her breath sometimes froze on the coverlid. Before daylight, her internal fires went down a little, and she often wak-ened to find herself drawn up into a tight ball, somewhat stiff in the legs. But that made it all the easier to get up.

The acquisition of this room was the beginning of a new era in Thea's life. It was one of the most important things that ever happened to her. Hitherto, except in summer, when she could be out-of-doors, she had lived in constant turmoil; the family, the day school, the Sunday-School.

The clamour about her drowned the voice within herself. In the end of the wing, separated from the other upstairs sleeping-rooms by a long, cold, unfinished lumber-room, her mind worked better. She thought things out more clearly. Pleasant plans and ideas occurred to her which had never come before. She had certain thoughts which were like companions, ideas which were like older and wiser friends. She left them there in the morning, when she finished dressing in the cold, and at night, when she came up with her lantern and shut the door after a busy day, she found them awaiting her. There was no possible way of heating the room, but that was fortunate, for otherwise it would have been occupied by one of her older brothers.

From the time when she moved up into the wing, Thea began to live a double life. During the day, when the hours were full of tasks, she was one of the Kronborg children, but at night she was a different person. On Friday and Saturday nights she always read for a long while after she was in bed. She had no clock, and there was no one to nag her.

Ray Kennedy, on his way from the depot to his boarding-house, often looked up and saw Thea's light burning when the rest of the house was dark, and felt cheered as by a friendly greeting. He was a faithful soul, and many disappointments had not changed his nature. He was still, at heart, the same boy who, when he was sixteen, had settled down to freeze with his sheep in a Wyoming blizzard, and had been rescued only to play the losing game of fidelity to other charges.

Ray had no very clear idea of what might be going on in Thea's head, but he knew that something was. He used to remark to Spanish Johnny, "That girl is developing something fine." Thea was patient with Ray, even in regard to the liberties he took with her name. Outside the family, everyone in Moonstone, except Wunsch and Doctor Archie, called her "Thee-a," but this seemed cold and distant to Ray, so he called her "Thee." Once, in a moment of exasperation, Thea asked him why he did this, and he explained that he once had a chum, Theodore, whose name was always abbreviated thus, and that since he was killed down on the Santa Fé, it seemed natural to call somebody "Thee." Thea sighed and submitted. She was always helpless before homely sentiment and usually changed the subject.

It was the custom for each of the different Sunday-Schools in Moonstone to give a concert on Christmas Eve. But this year all the churches were to unite and give, as was announced from the pulpits, "a semi-sacred concert of picked talent" at the opera house. The Moonstone Orchestra, under the direction of Professor Wunsch, was to play, and the most talented members of each Sunday-School were to take part in the programme. Thea was put down by the committee "for instrumental." This made her indignant, for the vocal numbers were always more popular. Thea went to the president of the committee and demanded hotly if her rival, Lily Fisher, were going to sing. The president was a big, florid, powdered woman, a fierce W.C.T.U. worker, one of Thea's natural enemies. Her name was Johnson; her husband kept the livery stable, and she was called Mrs. Livery Johnson, to distinguish her from other families of the same surname. Mrs. Johnson was a prominent Baptist, and Lily Fisher was the Baptist prodigy. There was a not very Christian rivalry between the Baptist Church and Mr. Kronborg's church.

When Thea asked Mrs. Johnson whether her rival was to be allowed to sing, Mrs. Johnson, with an eagerness which told how she had waited for this moment, replied that "Lily was going to recite to be obliging, and to give other children a chance to sing." As she delivered this thrust, her eyes glittered more than the Ancient Mariner's, Thea thought. Mrs. Johnson disapproved of a child whose chosen associates were Mexicans and sinners, and who was, as she pointedly put it, "bold with men." She so enjoyed an opportunity to rebuke Thea, that, tightly corseted as she was, she could scarcely control her breathing, and her lace and her gold watch-chain rose and fell "with short, uneasy motion." Frowning, Thea turned away and walked slowly homeward. She suspected guile. Lily Fisher was the most stuck-up doll in the world, and it was certainly not like her to recite to be obliging. Nobody who could sing ever recited, because the warmest applause always went to the singers.

However, when the programme was printed in the Moonstone *Gleam,* there it was: "Instrumental solo, Thea Kronborg; Recitation, Lily Fisher."

Because his orchestra was to play for the concert, Mr. Wunsch imagined that he had been put in charge of the music, and he became arrogant. He insisted that Thea should play a "Ballade" by Reinecke. When Thea consulted her mother, Mrs. Kronborg agreed with her that the "Ballade" would "never take" with a Moonstone audience.

"It makes no matter what they like," Wunsch replied to Thea's entreaties. "It is time already that they learn something."

Thea's fighting powers had been impaired by an ulcerated tooth and consequent loss of sleep, so she gave in. She finally had the molar pulled, though it was a second tooth and should have been saved. The dentist was a clumsy, ignorant country boy, and Mr. Kronborg would not hear of

Doctor Archie's taking Thea to a dentist in Denver, though Ray Kennedy said he could get a pass for her. What with the pain of the tooth, and family discussions about it, with trying to make Christmas presents and to keep up her school work and practising, and giving lessons on Saturdays, Thea was fairly worn out.

On Christmas Eve she was nervous and excited. It was the first time she had ever played in the opera house, and she had never before had to face so many people. Wunsch would not let her play with her notes, and she was afraid of forgetting. Before the concert began, all the participants had to assemble on the stage and sit there to be looked at. Thea wore her white summer dress and a blue sash, but Lily Fisher had a new pink silk, trimmed with white swansdown.

The hall was packed. It seemed as if everyone in Moonstone was there, even Mrs. Kohler, in her hood, and old Fritz. The seats were wooden kitchen chairs, numbered, and nailed to long planks which held them together in rows. As the floor was not raised, the chairs were all on the same level. The more interested persons in the audience peered over the heads of the people in front of them to get a good view of the stage. From the platform Thea picked out many friendly faces. There was Doctor Archie, who never went to church entertainments; there was the friendly jeweller who ordered her music for her—he sold accordions and guitars as well as watches—and the druggist who often lent her books, and her favourite teacher from the school. There was Ray Kennedy, with a party of freshly barbered railroad men he had brought along with him. There was Mrs. Kronborg with all the children, even Thor, who had been brought out in a new white plush coat. At the back of the hall sat a little group of Mexicans, and among them Thea caught the gleam of Spanish Johnny's white teeth, and of Mrs. Tellamantez's lustrous, smoothly coiled black hair.

After the orchestra played "Selections from Erminie," and the Baptist preacher made a long prayer, Tillie Kronborg came on with a highly coloured recitation, "The Polish Boy." When it was over, everyone breathed more freely. No committee had the courage to leave Tillie off a programme. She was accepted as a trying feature of every entertainment. The Progressive Euchre Club was the only social organization in the town that entirely escaped Tillie. After Tillie sat down, the Ladies' Quartet sang, "Beloved, it is Night," and then it was Thea's turn.

The "Ballade" took ten minutes, which was five minutes too long. The audience grew restive and fell to whispering. Thea could hear Mrs. Livery Johnson's bracelets jangling as she fanned herself, and she could hear her father's nervous, ministerial cough. Thor behaved better than anyone else. When Thea bowed and returned to her seat at the back of the stage, there was the usual applause, but it was vigorous only from the back of the house where the Mexicans sat, and from Ray Kennedy's *claqueurs*. Anyone could see that a good-natured audience had been bored.

Because Mr. Kronborg's sister was on the programme, it had also been necessary to ask the Baptist preacher's wife's cousin to sing. She was a "deep alto" from McCook, and she sang, "Thy Sentinel Am I." After her came Lily Fisher. Thea's rival was also a blonde, but her hair was much heavier than Thea's, and fell in long round curls over her shoulders. She was the angel-child of the Baptists, and looked exactly like the beautiful children on soap calendars. Her pink-and-white face, her set smile of innocence, were surely born of a colour-press. She had long, drooping eyelashes, a little pursed-up mouth, and narrow pointed teeth, like a squirrel's.

Lily began:

> "*Rock of Ages, cleft for me,* carelessly the maiden
> sang."

Thea drew a long breath. That was the game: it was a recitation and a song in one. Lily trailed the hymn through half a dozen verses with great effect. The Baptist preacher had announced at the beginning of the concert that, "owing to the length of the programme, there would be no encores." But the applause which followed Lily to her seat was such an unmistakable expression of enthusiasm that Thea had to admit Lily was justified in going back. She was attended this time by Mrs. Livery Johnson herself, crimson with triumph and gleaming-eyed, nervously rolling and unrolling a sheet of music. She took off her bracelets and played Lily's accompaniment. Lily had the effrontery to come out with "She sang the song of Home, Sweet Home, the song that touched my heart." But this did not surprise Thea; as Ray said later in the evening, "the cards had been stacked against her from the beginning." The next issue of the *Gleam* correctly stated that "unquestionably the honours of the evening must be accorded to Miss Lily Fisher." The Baptists had everything their own way.

After the concert, Ray Kennedy joined the Kronborgs' party and walked home with them. Thea was grateful for his silent sympathy, even while it irritated her. She inwardly vowed that she would never take another lesson from old Wunsch. She wished that her father would not keep cheerfully singing, "When Shepherds Watched," as he marched ahead, carrying Thor. She felt that silence would become the Kronborgs for a while. As a family, they somehow seemed a little ridiculous, trooping along in the starlight. There were so many of them, for one thing. Then Tillie was so absurd. She was giggling and talking to Anna just as if she had not made, as even Mrs. Kronborg admitted, an exhibition of herself.

When they got home, Ray took a box from his overcoat pocket and slipped it into Thea's hand as he said good night. They all hurried in to the glowing stove in the parlour. The sleepy children were sent to bed. Mrs. Kronborg and Anna stayed up to fill the stockings.

"I guess you're tired, Thea. You needn't stay up." Mrs. Kronborg's clear and seemingly indifferent eye usually measured Thea pretty accurately.

Thea hesitated. She glanced at the presents laid out on the dining-room table, but they looked unattractive. Even the brown plush monkey she had bought for Thor with such enthusiasm seemed to have lost his wise and humorous expression. She murmured, "All right," to her mother, lit her lantern, and went upstairs.

Ray's box contained a hand-painted white satin fan, with pond-lilies—an unfortunate reminder. Thea smiled grimly and tossed it into her upper drawer. She was not to be consoled by toys. She undressed quickly and stood for some time in the cold, frowning in the broken looking-glass at her flaxen pig-tails, at her white neck and arms. Her own broad, resolute face set its chin at her, her eyes flashed into her own defiantly. Lily Fisher was pretty, and she was willing to be just as big a fool as people wanted her to be. Very well; Thea Kronborg wasn't. She would rather be hated than be stupid, any day. She popped into bed and read stubbornly at a queer paper book the drugstore man had given her because he couldn't sell it. She had trained herself to put her mind on what she was doing, otherwise she would have come to grief with her complicated daily schedule. She read, as intently as if she had not been flushed with anger, the strange *Musical Memories* of the Reverend H. R. Haweis. At last she blew out the lantern and went to sleep. She had many curious dreams that night. In one of them Mrs. Tellamantez held her shell to Thea's ear, and she heard the roaring, as before, and distant voices calling, "Lily Fisher! Lily Fisher!"

IX

Mr. Kronborg considered Thea a remarkable child; but so were all his children remarkable. If one of the business men downtown remarked to him that he "had a mighty bright little girl, there," he admitted it, and at once began to explain what a "long head for business" his son Gus had, or that Charley was "a natural electrician," and had put in a telephone from the house to the preacher's study behind the church.

Mrs. Kronborg watched her daughter thoughtfully. She found her more interesting than her other children, and she took her more seriously, without thinking much about why she did so. The other children had to be guided, directed, kept from conflicting with one another. Charley and Gus were likely to want the same thing, and to quarrel about it. Anna often demanded unreasonable service from her older brothers; that they should sit up until after midnight to bring her home from parties when she did not like the youth who had offered himself as her escort; or that they should drive twelve miles into the country, on a winter night, to take her to a ranch dance, after they had been working hard all day. Gunner often got bored with his own clothes or stilts or sled, and wanted Axel's. But Thea, from the time she was a little thing, had her own routine. She kept out of everyone's way, and was hard to manage only when the other children interfered with her. Then there was trouble indeed: bursts of temper which used to alarm Mrs. Kronborg. "You ought to know enough to let Thea alone. She lets you alone," she often said to the other children.

One may have staunch friends in one's own family, but one seldom has admirers. Thea, however, had one in the person of her addle-pated aunt, Tillie Kronborg. In older countries, where dress and opinions and manners are not so thoroughly standardized as in our own West, there is a belief that people who are foolish about the more obvious things of life are apt to have peculiar insight into what lies beyond the obvious. The old woman who can never learn not to put the kerosene can on the stove may yet be able to tell fortunes, to persuade a backward child to grow, to cure warts, or to tell people what to do with a young girl who has gone melancholy. Tillie's mind was a curious machine; when she was awake it went round like a wheel when the belt has slipped off, and when she was asleep she dreamed follies. But she had intuitions. She knew, for instance, that Thea was different from the other Kronborgs, worthy though they all were. Her romantic imagination found possibilities in her niece. When she was sweeping or ironing, or turning the ice-cream freezer at a furious rate, she often built up brilliant futures for Thea, adapting freely the latest novel she had read. Tillie made enemies for her niece among the church people because, at sewing societies and church suppers, she sometimes spoke vauntingly, with a toss of her head, just as if Thea's "wonderfulness" were an accepted fact in Moonstone, like Mrs. Archie's stinginess, or Mrs. Livery Johnson's duplicity. People declared that, on this subject, Tillie made them tired.

Tillie belonged to a dramatic club that once a year performed in the Moonstone Opera House such plays as *Among the Breakers,* and *The Veteran of 1812.* Tillie played character parts, the flirtatious old maid or the spiteful *intrigante.* She used to study her parts up in the attic at home. While she was committing the lines, she got Gunner or Anna to hold the book for her, but when she began "to bring out the expression," as she said, she used, very timorously, to ask Thea to hold the book. Thea was usually—not always—agreeable about it. Her mother had told her that, since she had some influence with Tillie, it would be a good thing for them all if she could tone her down a shade and "keep her from taking on any worse than need be." Thea would sit on the foot of Tillie's bed, her feet tucked under her, and stare at the silly text. "I wouldn't make so much fuss, there, Tillie," she would remark occasionally; "I don't see the point in it"; or, "What do you pitch your voice so high for? It don't carry half as well."

"I don't see how it comes Thea is so patient with Tillie," Mrs. Kronborg more than once remarked to her husband. "She ain't patient with most people, but it seems like she's got a peculiar patience for Tillie."

Tillie always coaxed Thea to go "behind the scenes" with her when the club presented a play, and help her with her make-up. Thea hated it, but she always went. She felt as if she had to do it. There was something in Tillie's adoration of her that compelled her. There was no family impropriety that Thea was so much ashamed of as Tillie's "acting" and yet she was always being dragged in to assist her. Tillie simply had her, there. She didn't know why, but it was so. There was a string in her somewhere that Tillie could pull; a sense of obligation to Tillie's misguided aspirations. The saloon-keepers had some such feeling of responsibility toward Spanish Johnny.

The dramatic club was the pride of Tillie's heart, and her enthusiasm was the principal factor in keeping it together. Sick or well, Tillie always attended rehearsals, and was always urging the young people, who took rehearsals lightly, to "stop fooling and begin now." The young men—bank clerks, grocery clerks, insurance agents—played tricks, laughed at Tillie, and "put it up on each other" about seeing her home; but they often went to tiresome rehearsals just to oblige her. They were good-natured young fellows. Their trainer and stage-manager was young Upping, the jeweller who ordered Thea's music for her. Though barely thirty, he had followed half a dozen professions, and had once been a violinist in the orchestra of the Andrews Opera Company, then well known in little towns throughout Colorado and Nebraska.

By one amazing indiscretion Tillie very nearly lost her hold upon the Moonstone Drama Club. The club had decided to put on *The Drummer Boy of Shiloh,* a very ambitious undertaking because of the many supers needed and the scenic difficulties of the act which took place in Andersonville Prison. The members of the club consulted together in Tillie's absence as to who should play the part of the drummer boy. It must be taken by a very young person, and village boys of that age are self-conscious and are not apt at memorizing. The part was a long one, and clearly it must be given to a girl. Some members of the club suggested Thea Kronborg, others advocated Lily Fisher. Lily's partisans urged that she was much prettier than Thea, and had a much "sweeter disposition." Nobody denied these facts. But there was nothing in the least boyish about Lily, and she sang all songs and played all parts alike. Lily's simper was popular, but it seemed not quite the right thing for the heroic drummer boy.

Upping, the trainer, talked to one and another: "Lily's all right for girl parts," he insisted, "but you've got to get a girl with some ginger in her for this. Thea's got the voice, too. When she sings, 'Just Before the Battle, Mother,' she'll bring down the house."

When all the members of the club had been privately consulted, they announced their decision to Tillie at the first regular meeting that was called to cast the parts. They expected Tillie to be overcome with joy, but, on the contrary, she seemed embarrassed. "I'm afraid Thea hasn't got time for that," she said jerkily. "She is always so busy with her music. Guess you'll have to get somebody else."

The club lifted its eyebrows. Several of Lily Fisher's friends coughed. Mr. Upping flushed. The stout woman who always played the injured wife called Tillie's attention to the fact that this would be a fine opportunity for her niece to show what she could do. Her tone was condescending.

Tillie threw up her head and laughed; there was something sharp and wild about Tillie's laugh—when it was not a giggle. "Oh, I guess Thea hasn't got time to do any showing off. Her time to show off ain't come yet. I expect she'll make us all sit up when it does. No use asking her to take the part. She'd turn her nose up at it. I guess they'd be glad to get her in the Denver Dramatics, if they could."

The company broke up into groups and expressed their amazement. Of course all Swedes were conceited, but they would never have believed that all the conceit of all the Swedes put together would reach such a pitch as this. They confided to each other that Tillie was "just a little off, on the subject of her niece," and agreed that it would be as well not to excite her further. Tillie got a cold reception at rehearsals for a long while afterward, and Thea had a new crop of enemies without even knowing it.

X

*W*unsch and old Fritz and Spanish Johnny celebrated Christmas together, so joyously that Wunsch was unable to give Thea her lesson the next day. In the middle of the vacation week, Thea went to the Kohlers' through a soft, beautiful snowstorm. The air was a tender blue-grey, like the colour on the doves that flew in and out of the white dove-house on the post in the Kohlers' garden. The sand hills looked dim and sleepy. The tamarisk hedge was full of snow, like a foam of blossoms drifted over it. When Thea opened the gate, old Mrs. Kohler was just coming in from the chicken-yard, with five fresh eggs in her apron and a pair of old top-boots on her feet. She called Thea to come and look at a bantam egg, which she held up proudly. Her bantam hens were remiss in zeal, and she was always delighted when they accomplished anything. She took Thea into the sitting-room, very warm and smelling of food, and brought her a plateful of little Christmas cakes, made according to old and hallowed formulae, and put them before her while she warmed her feet.

Then she went to the door of the kitchen stairs and called: "Herr Wunsch! Herr Wunsch!"

Wunsch came down wearing an old wadded jacket, with a velvet collar. The brown silk was so worn that the white wadding stuck out almost everywhere. He avoided Thea's eyes when he came in, nodded without speaking, and pointed directly to the piano-stool. He was not so

insistent upon the scales as usual, and throughout the little sonata of Mozart's she was studying, he remained languid and absent-minded. His eyes
looked very heavy, and he kept wiping them with one of the new silk
handkerchiefs Mrs. Kohler had given him for Christmas. When the lesson
was over, he did not seem inclined to talk. Thea, loitering on the stool,
reached for a tattered book she had taken off the music-rest when she sat
down. It was a very old Leipsic edition of the piano score of Gluck's
"Orpheus." She turned over the pages curiously.

"Is it nice?" she asked.

"It is the most beautiful opera ever made," Wunsch declared
solemnly. "You know the story, eh? How, when she die, Orpheus went
down below for his wife?"

"Oh, yes, I know. I didn't know there was an opera about it,
though. Do people sing this now?"

"*Aber ja!* What else? You like to try? See." He drew her from
the stool and sat down at the piano. Turning over the leaves to the third
act, he handed the score to Thea. "Listen, I play it through and you get the
Rhythmus. Eins, zwei, drei, vier." He played through Orpheus' lament, then
pushed back his cuffs with awakening interest and nodded at Thea. "Now,
vom Blatt, mit mir."

> *"Ach, ich habe sie verloren,*
> *All' mein Glück ist nun dahin."*

Wunsch sang the aria with much feeling. It was evidently one that was very
dear to him.

"*Noch einmal,* alone, yourself." He played the introductory measures, then nodded at her vehemently, and she began:

> *"Ach, ich habe sie verloren."*

When she finished, Wunsch nodded again. "*Schön,*" he muttered as he finished the accompaniment softly. He dropped his hands on his
knees and looked up at Thea. "That is very fine, eh? There is no such
beautiful melody in the world. You can take the book for one week and
learn something, to pass the time. It is good to know—always. *Euridice,
Eu—ri—di—ce, weh dass ich auf Erden bin!*" he sang softly, playing the
melody with his right hand.

Thea, who was turning over the pages of the third act, stopped and scowled at a passage. The old German's blurred eyes watched her curiously.

"For what do you look so, *immer?*" puckering up his own face. "You see something a little difficult, may-be, and you make such a face like it was an enemy."

Thea laughed, disconcerted. "Well, difficult things are enemies, aren't they? When you have to get them?"

Wunsch lowered his head and threw it up as if he were butting something. "Not at all! By no means." He took the book from her and looked at it. "Yes, that is not so easy, there. This is an old book. They do not print it so now any more, I think. They leave it out, may-be. Only one woman could sing that good."

Thea looked at him in perplexity.

Wunsch went on. "It is written for alto, you see. A woman sings the part, and there was only one to sing that good in there. You understand? Only one!" He glanced at her quickly and lifted his red forefinger upright before her eyes.

Thea looked at the finger as if she were hypnotized. "Only one?" she asked breathlessly; her hands, hanging at her sides, were opening and shutting rapidly.

Wunsch nodded and still held up that compelling finger. When he dropped his hands, there was a look of satisfaction in his face.

"Was she very great?"

Wunsch nodded.

"Was she beautiful?"

"*Aber gar nicht!* Not at all. She was ugly; big mouth, big teeth, no figure, nothing at all," indicating a luxuriant bosom by sweeping his hands over his chest. "A pole, a post! But for the voice—*ach!* She have something in there, behind the eyes," tapping his temples.

Thea followed all his gesticulations intently. "Was she German?"

"No, *Spanisch.*" He looked down and frowned for a moment. "*Ach,* I tell you, she look like the Frau Tellamantez, some-thing. Long face, long chin, and ugly al-so."

"Did she die a long while ago?"

"Die? I think not. I never hear, anyhow. I guess she is alive somewhere in the world; Paris, may-be. But old, of course. I hear her when I was a youth. She is too old to sing now any more."

"Was she the greatest singer you ever heard?"

Wunsch nodded gravely. "Quite so. She was the most—" He hunted for an English word, lifted his hand over his head and snapped his fingers noiselessly in the air, enunciating fiercely, *"künst-le-risch!"* The word seemed to glitter in his uplifted hand, his voice was so full of emotion.

Wunsch rose from the stool and began to button his wadded jacket, preparing to return to his half-heated room in the loft.

Thea regretfully put on her cloak and hood and set out for home.

When Wunsch looked for his score late that afternoon, he found that Thea had not forgotten to take it with her. He smiled his loose, sarcastic smile, and thoughtfully rubbed his stubbly chin with his red fingers.

When Fritz came home in the early blue twilight, the snow was flying faster, Mrs. Kohler was cooking *Hasenpfeffer* in the kitchen, and the professor was seated at the piano, playing the Gluck, which he knew by heart. Old Fritz took off his shoes quietly behind the stove and lay down on the lounge before his masterpiece, where the firelight was playing over the walls of Moscow. He listened, while the room grew darker and the windows duller. Wunsch always came back to the same thing:

> *"Ach, ich habe sie verloren,*
>
> .   .   .   .
>
> *Euridice, Euridice!"*

From time to time Fritz sighed softly. He, too, had lost a Euridice.

XI

One Saturday, late in June, Thea arrived early for her lesson. As she perched herself upon the piano-stool—a wobbly, old-fashioned thing that worked on a creaky screw—she gave Wunsch a side glance, smiling. "You must not be cross to me to-day. This is my birthday."

"So?" he pointed to the keyboard.

After the lesson they went out to join Mrs. Kohler, who had asked Thea to come early, so that she could stay and smell the linden bloom.

It was one of those still days of intense light, when every particle of mica in the soil flashed like a little mirror, and the glare from the plain below seemed more intense than the rays from above. The sand ridges ran glittering gold out to where the mirage licked them up, shining and steaming like a lake in the tropics. The sky looked like blue lava, forever incapable of clouds—a turquoise bowl that was the lid of the desert. And yet within Mrs. Kohler's green patch the water dripped, the beds had all been hosed, and the air was fresh with rapidly evaporating moisture.

The two symmetrical linden trees were the proudest things in the garden. Their sweetness embalmed all the air. At every turn of the paths—whether one went to see the hollyhocks or the bleeding-heart, or to look at the purple morning-glories that ran over the bean-poles—wherever one went, the sweetness of the lindens struck one afresh and one always came back to them. Under the round leaves, where the waxen yellow blossoms hung, bevies of wild bees were buzzing. The tamarisks were still pink, and the flower-beds were doing their best in honour of the linden festival. The white dove-house was shining with a fresh coat of paint, and the pigeons were crooning contentedly, flying down often to drink at the drip from the water-tank. Mrs. Kohler, who was transplanting pansies, came up with her trowel and told Thea it was lucky to have your birthday when the lindens were in bloom, and that she must go and look at the sweet peas.

Wunsch accompanied her, and as they walked between the flower-beds he took Thea's hand.

"Es flüstern und sprechen die Blumen,"

he muttered. "You know that von Heine? *Im leuchtenden Sommermorgen?"* He looked down at Thea and softly pressed her hand.

"No, I don't know it. What does *flüstern* mean?"

"Flüstern?—to whisper. You must begin now to know such things. That is necessary. How many birthdays?"

"Thirteen. I'm in my 'teens now. But how can I know words like that? I only know what you say at my lessons. They don't teach German at school. How can I learn?"

"It is always possible to learn when one likes," said Wunsch. His words were peremptory, as usual, but his tone was mild, even confidential. "There is always a way. And if some day you are going to sing, it is necessary to know well the German language."

Thea stooped over to pick a leaf of rosemary. How did Wunsch know that, when the very roses on her wall-paper had never heard it? "But am I going to?" she asked, still stooping.

"That is for you to say," returned Wunsch coldly. "You would better marry some *Jacob* here and keep the house for him, maybe? That is as one desires."

Thea flashed up at him a clear, laughing look. "No, I don't want to do that. You know"—she brushed his coat-sleeve quickly with her yellow head. "Only how can I learn anything here? It's so far from Denver."

Wunsch's loose lower lip curled in amusement.

Then, as if he suddenly remembered something, he spoke seriously. "Nothing is far and nothing is near, if one desires. The world is little, people are little, human life is little. There is only one big thing—desire. And before it, when it is big, all is little. It brought Columbus across the sea in a little boat, *und so weiter.*" Wunsch made a grimace, took his pupil's hand and drew her toward the grape arbour. "Hereafter I will more speak to you in German. Now, sit down and I will teach you for your birthday that little song. Ask me the words you do not know already. Now: *Im leuchtenden Sommermorgen.*"

Thea memorized quickly because she had the power of listening intently. In a few moments she could repeat the eight lines for him. Wunsch nodded encouragingly and they went out of the arbour into the sunlight again. As they went up and down the gravel paths between the flower-beds, the white and yellow butterflies kept darting before them, and the pigeons were washing their pink feet at the drip and crooning in their husky bass. Over and over again Wunsch made her say the lines to him. "You see it is nothing. If you learn a great many of the *Lieder,* you will know the German language already. *Weiter, nun.*" He would incline his head gravely and listen.

> "Im leuchtenden Sommermorgen
> Geh' ich im Garten herum;
> Es flüstern und sprechen die Blumen,
> Ich aber, ich wandle stumm.
>
> "Es flüstern und sprechen die Blumen
> Und schau'n mitleidig mich an:
> 'Sei unserer Schwester nicht böse,
> Du trauriger, blasser Mann!' "

(In the soft-shining summer morning
I wandered the garden within.
The flowers they whispered and murmured,
But I, I wandered dumb.

The flowers they whisper and murmur,
And me with compassion they scan:
"Oh, be not harsh to our sister,
Thou sorrowful, death-pale man!")

Wunsch had noticed before that when his pupil read anything in verse the character of her voice changed altogether; it was no longer the voice which spoke the speech of Moonstone. It was a soft, rich contralto, and she read quietly; the feeling was in the voice itself, not indicated by emphasis or change of pitch. She repeated the little verses musically, like a song, and the entreaty of the flowers was even softer than the rest, as the shy speech of flowers might be, and she ended with the voice suspended, almost with a rising inflection. It was a nature-voice, Wunsch told himself, breathed from the creature and apart from language, like the sound of the wind in the trees, or the murmur of water.

"What is it the flowers mean when they ask him not to be harsh to their sister, eh?" he asked, looking down at her curiously and wrinkling his dull red forehead.

Thea glanced at him in surprise. "I suppose he thinks they are asking him not to be harsh to his sweetheart—or some girl they remind him of."

"And why *trauriger, blasser Mann?*"

They had come back to the grape arbour, and Thea picked out a sunny place on the bench, where a tortoise-shell cat was stretched at full length. She sat down, bending over the cat and teasing his whiskers. "Because he had been awake all night, thinking about her, wasn't it? Maybe that was why he was up so early."

Wunsch shrugged his shoulders. "If he think about her all night already, why do you say the flowers remind him?"

Thea looked up at him in perplexity. A flash of comprehension lit her face and she smiled eagerly. "Oh, I didn't mean 'remind' in that way! I didn't mean they brought her to his mind! I meant it was only when he came out in the morning that she seemed to him like that—like one of the flowers."

"And before he came out, how did she seem?"

This time it was Thea who shrugged her shoulders. The warm smile left her face. She lifted her eyebrows in annoyance and looked off at the sand hills.

Wunsch persisted. "Why you not answer me?"

"Because it would be silly. You are just trying to make me say things. It spoils things to ask questions."

Wunsch bowed mockingly; his smile was disagreeable. Suddenly his face grew grave, grew fierce, indeed. He pulled himself up from his clumsy stoop and folded his arms. "But it is necessary to know if you know some things. Some things cannot be taught. If you not know in the beginning, you not know in the end. For a singer there must be something in the inside from the beginning. I shall not be long in this place, may-be, and I like to know. Yes"—he ground his heel in the gravel—"yes, when you are barely six, you must know that already. That is the beginning of all things; *der Geist, die Phantasie*. It must be in the baby, when it makes its first cry, like *der Rhythmus,* or it is not to be. You have some voice already, and if in the beginning, when you are with things-to-play, you know that what you will not tell me, then you can learn to sing, may-be."

Wunsch began to pace the arbour, rubbing his hands together. The dark flush of his face had spread up under the iron-grey bristles on his head. He was talking to himself, not to Thea. Insidious power of the linden bloom! "Oh, much you can learn! *Aber nicht die amerikanischen Fräulein.* They have nothing inside them," striking his chest with both fists. "They are like the ones in the *Märchen,* a grinning face and hollow in the insides. Something they can learn, oh, yes, may-be! But the secret—what make the rose to red, the sky to blue, the man to love—*in der Brust, in der Brust* it is, *und ohne dieses gibt es keine Kunst, gibt es keine Kunst!''* He threw up his square hand and shook it, all the fingers apart and wagging. Purple and breathless he went out of the arbour and into the house, without saying good-bye. These outbursts frightened Wunsch. They were always harbingers of ill.

Thea got her music-book and stole quietly out of the garden. She did not go home, but wandered off into the sand dunes, where the prickly pear was in blossom and the green lizards were racing each other in the glittering light. She was shaken by a passionate excitement. She did not altogether understand what Wunsch was talking about; and yet, in a way she knew. She knew, of course, that there was something about her that was different. But it was more like a friendly spirit than like anything that was a part of herself. She brought everything to it, and it answered her; happiness consisted of that backward and forward movement of herself. The something came and went, she never knew how. Sometimes she hunted for it and could not find it; again, she lifted her eyes from a book, or stepped out-of-doors, or wakened in the morning, and it was there—under her cheek, it usually seemed to be, or over her breast—a kind of warm sureness. And when it was there, everything was more interesting and beautiful, even people. When this companion was with her, she could get the most wonderful things out of Spanish Johnny, or Wunsch, or Doctor Archie.

On her thirteenth birthday she wandered for a long while about the sand ridges, picking up crystals and looking into the yellow prickly-pear blossoms with their thousand stamens. She looked at the sand hills until she wished she *were* a sand hill. And yet she knew that she was going to leave them all behind some day. They would be changing all day long, yellow and purple and lavender, and she would not be there. From that day on, she felt there was a secret between her and Wunsch. Together they had lifted a lid, pulled out a drawer, and looked at something. They hid it away and never spoke of what they had seen; but neither of them forgot it.

XII

One July night, when the moon was full, Doctor Archie was coming up from the depot, restless and discontented, wishing there were something to do. He carried his straw hat in his hand, and kept brushing his hair back from his forehead with a purposeless, unsatisfied gesture. After he passed Uncle Billy Beemer's cottonwood grove, the sidewalk ran out of the shadow into the white moonlight and crossed the sand gully on high posts, like a bridge. As the doctor approached this trestle, he saw a white figure, and recognized Thea Kronborg. He quickened his pace and she came to meet him.

"What are you doing out so late, my girl?" he asked as he took her hand.

"Oh, I don't know. What do people go to bed so early for? I'd like to run along before the houses and screech at them. Isn't it glorious out here?"

The young doctor gave a melancholy laugh and pressed her hand.

"Think of it," Thea snorted impatiently. "Nobody up but us

and the rabbits! I've started up half a dozen of 'em. Look at that little one down there now"—she stooped and pointed. In the gully below them there was, indeed, a little rabbit with a white spot of a tail, crouching down on the sand, quite motionless. It seemed to be lapping up the moonlight like cream. On the other side of the walk, down in the ditch, there was a patch of tall, rank sunflowers, their shaggy leaves white with dust. The moon stood over the cottonwood grove. There was no wind, and no sound but the wheezing of an engine down on the tracks.

"Well, we may as well watch the rabbits." Doctor Archie sat down on the sidewalk and let his feet hang over the edge. He pulled out a smooth linen handkerchief that smelled of German cologne water. "Well, how goes it? Working hard? You must know about all Wunsch can teach you by this time."

Thea shook her head. "Oh, no, I don't, Doctor Archie. He's hard to get at, but he's been a real musician in his time. Mother says she believes he's forgotten more than the music-teachers down in Denver ever knew."

"I'm afraid he won't be around here much longer," said Doctor Archie. "He's been making a tank of himself lately. He'll be pulling his freight one of these days. That's the way they do, you know, I'll be sorry on your account." He paused and ran his fresh handkerchief over his face. "What the deuce are we all here for, anyway, Thea?" he said abruptly.

"On earth, you mean?" Thea asked in a low voice.

"Well, primarily, yes. But secondarily, why are we in Moonstone? It isn't as if we'd been born here. You were, but Wunsch wasn't, and I wasn't. I suppose I'm here because I married as soon as I got out of medical school and had to get a practice quick. If you hurry things, you always get left in the end. I don't learn anything here, and as for the people—In my own town in Michigan, now, there were people who liked me on my father's account, who had even known my grandfather. That meant something. But here it's all like the sand: blows north one day and south the next. We're all a lot of gamblers without much nerve, playing for small stakes. The railroad is the one real fact in this country. That has to be; the world has to be got back and forth. But the rest of us are here just because it's the end of a run and the engine has to have a drink. Some day I'll get up and find my hair turning grey, and I'll have nothing to show for it."

Thea slid closer to him and caught his arm. "No, no. I won't let you get grey. You've got to stay young for me. I'm getting young now, too."

Archie laughed. "Getting?"

"Yes. People aren't young when they're children. Look at Thor, now; he's just a little old man. But Gus has a sweetheart, and he's young!"

"Something in that!" Doctor Archie patted her head, and then felt the shape of h'r skull gently, with the tips of his fingers. "When you were little, Thea, I used always to be curious about the shape of your head. You seemed to have more inside it than most youngsters. I haven't examined it for a long time. Seems to be the usual shape, but uncommonly hard, somehow. What are you going to do with yourself, anyway?"

"I don't know."

"Honest, now?" He lifted her chin and looked into her eyes.

Thea laughed and edged away from him.

"You've got something up your sleeve, haven't you? Anything you like; only don't marry and settle down here without giving yourself a chance, will you?"

"Not much. See, there's another rabbit!"

"That's all right about the rabbits, but I don't want you to get tied up. Remember that."

Thea nodded. "Be nice to Wunsch, then. I don't know what I'd do if he went away."

"You've got older friends than Wunsch here, Thea."

"I know." Thea spoke seriously and looked up at the moon, propping her chin on her hand. "But Wunsch is the only one that can teach me what I want to know. I've got to learn to do something well, and that's the thing I can do best."

"Do you want to be a music-teacher?"

"Maybe, but I want to be a good one. I'd like to go to Germany to study, some day. Wunsch says that's the best place—the only place you can really learn." Thea hesitated and then went on nervously: "I've got a book that says so, too. It's called *My Musical Memories*. It made me want to go to Germany even before Wunsch said anything. Of course it's a secret. You're the first one I've told."

Doctor Archie smiled indulgently. "That's a long way off. Is that what you've got in your hard noddle?" He put his hand on her hair, but this time she shook him off.

"No, I don't think much about it. But you talk about going, and a body has to have something to go *to!*"

"That's so." Doctor Archie sighed. "You're lucky if you have. Poor Wunsch, now, he hasn't. What do such fellows come out here for?

He's been asking me about my mining stock, and about mining towns. What would he do in a mining town? He wouldn't know a piece of ore if he saw one. He's got nothing to sell that a mining town wants to buy. Why don't those old fellows stay at home? We won't need them for another hundred years. An engine-wiper can get a job, but a piano-player! Such people can't make good."

"My grandfather Alstrom was a musician, and he made good."

Doctor Archie chuckled. "Oh, a Swede can make good anywhere, at anything! You've got that in your favour, miss. Come, you must be getting home."

Thea rose. "Yes, I used to be ashamed of being a Swede, but I'm not any more. Swedes are kind of common, but I think it's better to be *something*."

"It surely is! How tall you are getting! You come above my shoulder now."

"I'll keep on growing, don't you think? I particularly want to be tall. Yes, I guess I must go home. I wish there'd be a fire."

"A fire?"

"Yes, so the fire-bell would ring and the roundhouse whistle would blow, and everybody would come running out. Sometime I'm going to ring the fire-bell myself and stir them all up."

"You'd be arrested."

"Well, that would be better than going to bed."

"I'll have to lend you some more books."

Thea shook herself impatiently. "I can't read every night."

Doctor Archie gave one of his low, sympathetic chuckles as he opened the gate for her. "You're beginning to grow up, that's what's the matter with you. I'll have to keep an eye on you. Now you'll have to say good night to the moon."

"No, I won't. I sleep on the floor now, right in the moonlight. My window comes down to the floor, and I can look at the sky all night."

She shot round the house to the kitchen door, and Doctor Archie watched her disappear with a sigh. He thought of the hard, mean, frizzy little woman who kept his house for him; once the belle of a Michigan town, now dry and withered up at thirty. "If I had a daughter like Thea to watch," he reflected, "I wouldn't mind anything. I wonder if all of my life's going to be a mistake just because I made a big one then? Hardly seems fair."

Howard Archie was "respected" rather than popular in Moonstone. Everyone recognized that he was a good physician, and a progressive Western town likes to be able to point to a handsome, well-set-up, well-dressed man among its citizens. But a great many people thought Archie "distant," and they were right. He had the uneasy manner of a man who is not among his own kind, and who has not seen enough of the world to feel that all people are in some sense his own kind. He knew that everyone was curious about his wife, that she played a sort of character part in Moonstone, and that people made fun of her, not very delicately. Her own friends—most of them women who were distasteful to Archie—liked to ask her to contribute to church charities, just to see how mean she could be. The little, lopsided cake at the church supper, the cheapest pincushion, the skimpiest apron at the bazaar were always Mrs. Archie's contribution.

All this hurt the doctor's pride. But if there was one thing he had learned, it was that there was no changing Belle's nature. He had married a mean woman; and he must accept the consequences. Even in Colorado he would have had no pretext for divorce, and, to do him justice, he had never thought of such a thing. The tenets of the Presbyterian Church in which he had grown up, though he had long ceased to believe in them, still influenced his conduct and his conception of propriety. To him there was something vulgar about divorce. A divorced man was a disgraced man; at least, he had exhibited his hurt, and made it a matter for common gossip. Respectability was so necessary to Archie that he was willing to pay a high price for it. As long as he could keep up a decent exterior, he could manage to get on; and if he could have concealed his wife's littleness from all his friends, he would scarcely have complained. He was more afraid of pity than he was of any unhappiness. Had there been another woman for whom he cared greatly, he might have had plenty of courage; but he was not likely to meet such a woman in Moonstone.

There was a puzzling timidity in Archie's make-up. The thing that held his shoulders stiff, that made him resort to a mirthless little laugh when he was talking to dull people, that made him sometimes stumble over rugs and carpets, had its counterpart in his mind. He had not the courage to be an honest thinker. He could comfort himself by evasions and compromises. He consoled himself for his own marriage by telling himself that other people's were not much better. In his work he saw pretty deeply into marital relations in Moonstone, and he could honestly say that there were not many of his friends whom he envied. Their wives seemed to suit them well enough, but they would never have suited him.

Although Doctor Archie could not bring himself to regard marriage merely as a social contract, but looked upon it as somehow made sacred by a church in which he did not believe—as a physician he knew that a young man whose marriage is merely nominal must yet go on living his life. When he went to Denver or to Chicago, he drifted about in careless company where gaiety and good-humour can be bought, not because he had any taste for such society, but because he honestly believed that anything was better than divorce. He often told himself that "hanging and wiving go by destiny." If wiving went badly with a man—and it did oftener than not—then he must do the best he could to keep up appearances and help the tradition of domestic happiness along. The Moonstone gossips, assembled in Mrs. Smiley's millinery and notion store, often discussed Doctor Archie's politeness to his wife, and his pleasant manner of speaking about her. "Nobody has ever got a thing out of him yet," they agreed. And it was certainly not because no one had ever tried.

When he was down in Denver, feeling a little jolly, Archie could forget how unhappy he was at home, and could even make himself believe that he missed his wife. He always bought her presents, and would have liked to send her flowers if she had not repeatedly told him never to send her anything but bulbs—which did not appeal to him in his expansive moments. At the Denver Athletic Club banquets, or at dinner with his colleagues at the Brown Palace Hotel, he sometimes spoke sentimentally about "little Mrs. Archie," and he always drank the toast, "To our wives, God bless them!" with gusto.

The determining factor about Doctor Archie was that he was romantic. He had married Belle White because he was romantic—too romantic to know anything about women, except what he wished them to be, or to repulse a pretty girl who had set her cap for him. At medical school, though he was a rather wild boy in behaviour, he had always disliked coarse jokes and vulgar stories. In his old Flint's *Physiology* there was still a poem he had pasted there when he was a student; some verses by Doctor Oliver Wendell Holmes about the ideals of the medical profession. After so much and such disillusioning experience with it, he still had a romantic feeling about the human body; a sense that finer things dwelt in it than could be explained by anatomy. He never jested about birth or death or marriage, and did not like to hear other doctors do it. He was a good nurse, and had a reverence for the bodies of women and children. When he was tending them, one saw him at his best. Then his constraint and self-consciousness fell away from him. He was easy, gentle, competent, master of himself and of other people. Then the idealist in him was not afraid of being discovered and ridiculed.

In his tastes, too, the doctor was romantic. Though he read Balzac all the year through, he still enjoyed the Waverley Novels as much as when he had first come upon them, in thick leather-bound volumes, in his grandfather's library. He nearly always read Scott on Christmas and holidays, because it brought back the pleasures of his boyhood so vividly. He liked Scott's women. Constance de Beverley and the minstrel girl in *The Fair Maid of Perth,* not the Duchesse de Langeais, were his heroines. But better than anything that ever got from the heart of a man into printer's ink, he loved the poetry of Robert Burns. "Death and Doctor Hornbook" and "The Jolly Beggars," Burns's "Reply to his Tailor," he often read aloud to himself in his office, late at night, after a glass of hot toddy. He used to read "Tam o'Shanter" to Thea Kronborg, and he got her some of the songs, set to the old airs for which they were written. He loved to hear her sing them. Sometimes when she sang, "Oh, wert thou in the cauld blast," the doctor and even Mr. Kronborg joined in. Thea never minded if people could not sing; she directed them with her head and somehow carried them along. When her father got off the pitch, she let her own voice out and covered him.

XIII

*A*t the beginning of June, when school closed, Thea had told Wunsch that she didn't know how much practising she could get in this summer because Thor had his worst teeth still to cut.

"My God! all last summer he was doing that!" exclaimed Wunsch furiously.

"I know, but it takes them two years, and Thor is slow," Thea answered reprovingly.

The summer went well beyond her hopes, however. She told herself that it was the best summer of her life, so far. Nobody was sick at home, and her lessons were uninterrupted. Now that she had four pupils of her own and made a dollar a week, her practising was regarded more seriously by the household. Her mother had always arranged things so that she could have the parlour four hours a day in summer. Thor proved a friendly ally. He behaved handsomely about his molars, and never objected to being pulled off into remote places in his cart. When Thea dragged him over the hill and made a camp under the shade of a bush or a bank, he would waddle about and play with his blocks, or bury his monkey in the sand and dig him up again. Sometimes he got into the cactus and set up a howl, but usually he let his sister read peacefully, while he coated his hands and face, first with an all-day sucker and then with gravel.

Life was pleasant and uneventful until the first of September, when Wunsch began to drink so hard that he was unable to appear when Thea went to take her mid-week lesson, and Mrs. Kohler had to send her home after a tearful apology. On Saturday morning she set out for the Kohlers' again, but on her way, when she was crossing the ravine, she noticed a woman sitting at the bottom of the gulch, under the railroad trestle. She turned from her path and saw that it was Mrs. Tellamantez, and she seemed to be doing drawn-work. Then Thea noticed that there was something beside her, covered up with a purple-and-yellow Mexican blanket. She ran up the gulch and called to Mrs. Tellamantez. The Mexican woman held up a warning finger. Thea glanced at the blanket and recognized a square red hand which protruded. The middle finger twitched slightly.

"Is he hurt?" she gasped.

Mrs. Tellamantez shook her head. "No; very sick. He knows nothing," she said quietly, folding her hands over her drawn-work.

Thea learned that Wunsch had been out all night, that this morning Mrs. Kohler had gone to look for him and found him under the trestle covered with dirt and cinders. Probably he had been trying to get home and had lost his way. Mrs. Tellamantez was watching beside the unconscious man while Mrs. Kohler and Johnny went to get help.

"You better go home now, I think," said Mrs. Tellamantez, in closing her narration.

Thea hung her head and looked wistfully toward the blanket.

"Couldn't I just stay till they come?" she asked. "I'd like to know if he's very bad."

"Bad enough," sighed Mrs. Tellamantez, taking up her work again.

Thea sat down under the narrow shade of one of the trestle posts and listened to the locusts rasping in the hot sand while she watched Mrs. Tellamantez evenly draw her threads. The blanket looked as if it were over a heap of bricks.

"I don't see him breathing any," she said anxiously.

"Yes, he breathes," said Mrs. Tellamantez, not lifting her eyes. It seemed to Thea that they waited for hours. At last they heard voices, and a party of men came down the hill and up the gulch. Doctor Archie and Fritz Kohler came first; behind were Johnny and Ray, and several men from the roundhouse. Ray had the canvas litter that was kept at the station for accidents on the road. Behind them trailed half a dozen boys who had been hanging round the depot.

When Ray saw Thea, he dropped his canvas roll and hurried forward. "Better run along home, Thee. This is ugly business." Ray was indignant that anybody who gave Thea music-lessons should behave in such a manner.

Thea resented both his proprietary tone and his superior virtue. "I won't! I want to know how bad he is. I'm not a baby!" she exclaimed indignantly, stamping her foot into the sand.

Doctor Archie, who had been kneeling by the blanket, got up and came toward Thea, dusting his knees. He smiled and nodded confidentially. "He'll be all right when we get him home. But he wouldn't want you to see him like this, poor old chap! Understand? Now, skip!"

Thea ran down the gulch and looked back only once, to see them lifting the canvas litter with Wunsch upon it, still covered with the blanket.

The men carried Wunsch up the hill and down the road to the Kohlers'. Mrs. Kohler had gone home and made up a bed in the sitting-room, as she knew the litter could not be got round the turn in the narrow stairway. Wunsch was like a dead man. He lay unconscious all day. Ray Kennedy stayed with him till two o'clock in the afternoon, when he had to go out on his run. It was the first time he had ever been inside the Kohlers' house, and he was so much impressed by Napoleon that the piece-picture formed a new bond between him and Thea.

Doctor Archie went back at six o'clock, and found Mrs. Kohler and Spanish Johnny with Wunsch, who was in a high fever, muttering and groaning.

"There ought to be someone here to look after him to-night, Mrs. Kohler," he said. "I'm on a confinement case, and I can't be here, but there ought to be somebody. He may get violent."

Mrs. Kohler insisted that she could always do anything with Wunsch, but the doctor shook his head and Spanish Johnny grinned. He said he would stay. The doctor laughed at him. "Ten fellows like you couldn't hold him, Spanish, if he got obstreperous; an Irishman would have his hands full. Guess I'd better put the soft pedal on him." He pulled out his hypodermic.

Spanish Johnny stayed, however, and the Kohlers went to bed.

At about two o'clock in the morning, Wunsch rose from his ignominious cot. Johnny, who was dozing on the lounge, awoke to find the German standing in the middle of the room in his undershirt and drawers, his arms bare, his heavy body seeming twice its natural girth. His face was snarling and savage, and his eyes were crazy. He had risen to avenge himself, to wipe out his shame, to destroy his enemy. One look was enough for Johnny. Wunsch raised a chair threateningly, and Johnny, with the lightness of a *picador,* darted under the missile and out of the open window. He shot across the gully to get help, meanwhile leaving the Kohlers to their fate.

Fritz, upstairs, heard the chair crash upon the stove. Then he heard doors opening and shutting, and someone stumbling about in the shrubbery of the garden. He and Paulina sat up in bed and held a consultation. Fritz slipped from under the covers, and going cautiously over to the window, poked out his head. Then he rushed to the door and bolted it.

"*Mein Gott,* Paulina," he gasped, "he has the axe, he will kill us!"

"The dresser," cried Mrs. Kohler; "push the dresser before the door. *Ach,* if you had your rabbit gun, now!"

"It is in the barn," said Fritz sadly. "It would do no good; he would not be afraid of anything now. Stay you in the bed, Paulina." The dresser had lost its casters years ago, but he managed to drag it in front of the door. "He is in the garden. He makes nothing. He will get sick again, may-be."

Fritz went back to bed and his wife pulled the quilt over him and made him lie down. They heard stumbling in the garden again, then a smash of glass.

"*Ach, das Mistbeet!*" gasped Paulina, hearing her hot-bed shivered. "The poor soul, Fritz, he will cut himself. *Ach,* what is that?" They both sat up in bed. "*Wieder! Ach!* What is he doing?"

The noise came steadily, a sound of chopping. Paulina tore off her night-cap. "*Die Bäume, die Bäume!* He is cutting our trees, Fritz!" Before her husband could prevent her, she had sprung from the bed and rushed to the window. "*Der Taubenschlag! Gerechter Himmel,* he is chopping the dove-house down!"

Fritz reached her side before she had got her breath again, and poked his head out beside hers. There, in the faint starlight, they saw a bulky man, barefoot, half-dressed, chopping away at the white post that formed the pedestal of the dove-house. The startled pigeons were croaking and flying about his head, even beating their wings in his face, so that he struck at them furiously with the axe. In a few seconds there was a crash, and Wunsch had actually felled the dove-house.

"Oh, if only it is not the trees next!" prayed Paulina. "The dove-house you can make new again, but not *die Bäume.*"

They watched breathlessly. In the garden below Wunsch stood in the attitude of a woodman, contemplating the fallen cote. Suddenly he threw the axe over his shoulder and went out of the front gate toward the town.

"The poor soul, he will meet his death!" Mrs. Kohler wailed. She ran back to her feather bed and hid her face in the pillow.

Fritz kept watch at the window. "No, no, Paulina," he called presently; "I see lanterns coming. Johnny must have gone for somebody. Yes, four lanterns, coming along the gulch. They stop; they must have seen him already. Now they are under the hill and I cannot see them, but I think they have him. They will bring him back. I must dress and go down." He caught his trousers and began pulling them on by the window. "Yes, here they come, half a dozen men. And they have tied him with a rope, Paulina!"

"*Ach,* the poor man! To be led like a cow," groaned Mrs. Kohler. "Oh, it is good that he has no wife!"

She was reproaching herself for nagging Fritz when he drank himself into foolish pleasantry or mild sulks, and felt that she had never before appreciated her blessings.

Wunsch was in bed for ten days, during which time he was gossiped about and even preached about in Moonstone. The Baptist preacher took a shot at the fallen man from his pulpit, with Mrs. Livery Johnson nodding approvingly from her pew. The mothers of Wunsch's pupils sent him notes informing him that their daughters would discontinue their music-lessons. The old maid who had rented him her piano sent the town dray for her contaminated instrument, and ever afterward declared that Wunsch had ruined its tone and scarred its glossy finish. The Kohlers were unremitting in their kindness to their friend. Mrs. Kohler made him soups and broths without stint, and Fritz repaired the dove-house and mounted it on a new post, lest it might be a sad reminder.

As soon as Wunsch was strong enough to sit about in his slippers and wadded jacket, he told Fritz to bring him some stout thread from the shop. When Fritz asked what he was going to sew, he produced the tattered score of "Orpheus" and said he would like to fix it up for a little present.

Fritz carried it over to the shop and stitched it into pasteboards,

covered with dark suiting-cloth. Over the stitches he glued a strip of thin
red leather which he got from his friend, the harnessmaker. After Paulina
had cleaned the pages with fresh bread, Wunsch was amazed to see what a
fine book he had. It opened stiffly, but that was no matter.

Sitting in the arbour one morning, under the ripe grapes and the
brown, curling leaves, with a pen and ink on the bench beside him and the
Gluck score on his knee, Wunsch pondered for a long while. Several times
he dipped the pen in the ink, and then put it back again in the cigar-box
in which Mrs. Kohler kept her writing utensils. His thoughts wandered
over a wide territory; over many countries and many years. There was no
order or logical sequence in his ideas. Pictures came and went without
reason. Faces, mountains, rivers, autumn days in other vineyards far away.
He thought of a *Fuszreise* he had made through the Hartz Mountains in his
student days; of the innkeeper's pretty daughter who had lighted his pipe
for him in the garden one summer evening, of the woods above Wiesbaden,
haymakers on an island in the river. The roundhouse whistle woke him
from his reveries. Ah, yes, he was in Moonstone, Colorado. He frowned for
a moment and looked at the book on his knee. He had thought of a great
many appropriate things to write in it, but suddenly he rejected all of them,
opened the book, and at the top of the much-engraved title-page he wrote
rapidly in purple ink:

> *Einst, O Wunder!*—
> > *A. Wunsch.*
>
> *Moonstone, Colo.*
> *September 30, 18—*

Nobody in Moonstone ever found what Wunsch's first name
was. That "A" may have stood for Adam, or August, or even Amadeus; he
got very angry if anyone asked him. He remained A. Wunsch to the end
of his chapter there.

When he presented this score to Thea, he told her that in ten
years she would either know what the inscription meant, or she would not
have the least idea, in which case it would not matter.

When Wunsch began to pack his trunk, both the Kohlers were
very unhappy. He said he was coming back some day, but that for the
present, since he had lost all his pupils, it would be better for him to try
some "new town." Mrs. Kohler darned and mended all his clothes, and
gave him two new shirts she had made for Fritz. Fritz made him a new pair

of trousers and would have made him an overcoat but for the fact that overcoats were so easy to pawn.

Wunsch would not go across the ravine to the town until he went to take the morning train for Denver. He said that after he got to Denver he would "look around." He left Moonstone one bright October morning, without telling anyone good-bye. He bought his ticket and went directly into the smoking-car. When the train was beginning to pull out, he heard his name called frantically, and looking out of the window he saw Thea Kronborg standing on the siding, bareheaded and panting.

Some boys had brought word to school that they had seen Wunsch's trunk going over to the station, and Thea had run away from school. She was at the end of the station platform, her hair in two braids, her blue gingham dress wet to the knees because she had run across lots through the weeds. It had rained during the night, and the tall sunflowers behind her were fresh and shining.

"Good-bye, Herr Wunsch, good-bye!" she called, waving to him.

He thrust his head out at the car window and called back, *"Leb' wohl, leb' wohl, mein Kind!"* He watched her until the train swept around the curve beyond the roundhouse, and then sank back into his seat, muttering, "She had been running. Ah, she will run a long way; they cannot stop her!"

What was it about the child that one believed in? Was it her dogged industry, so unusual in this free-and-easy country? Was it her imagination? More likely it was because she had both imagination and a stubborn will, curiously balancing and interpenetrating each other. There was something unconscious and unawakened about her, that tempted curiosity. She had a kind of seriousness that he had not met with in a pupil before. She hated difficult things, and yet she could never pass one by. They seemed to challenge her; she had no peace until she had mastered them. She had the power to make a great effort, to lift a weight heavier than herself. Wunsch hoped he would always remember her as she stood by the track, looking up at him; her broad eager face, so fair in colour, with its high cheek-bones, its yellow eyebrows and greenish-hazel eyes.

It was a face full of light and energy, of the unquestioning hopefulness of first youth. Yes, she was like a flower full of sun, but not the soft German flowers of his childhood. He had it now, the comparison he had absently reached for before: she was like the yellow prickly-pear blossoms that open there in the desert; thornier and sturdier than the maiden flowers he remembered; not so sweet, but wonderful.

* ★ *

That night Mrs. Kohler brushed away many a tear as she got supper and set the table for two. When they sat down, Fritz was more silent than usual. People who have lived long together need a third at table: they know each other's thoughts so well that they have nothing left to say. Mrs. Kohler stirred and stirred her coffee and clattered the spoon, but she had no heart for her supper. She felt, for the first time in years, that she was tired of her own cooking. She looked across the glass lamp at her husband and asked him if the butcher liked his new overcoat, and whether he had got the shoulders right in a ready-made suit he was patching over for Ray Kennedy. After supper Fritz offered to wipe the dishes for her, but she told him to go about his business, and not to act as if she were sick or getting helpless.

When her work in the kitchen was all done, she went out to cover the oleanders against frost, and to take a last look at her chickens. As she came back from the hen-house she stopped by one of the linden trees and stood resting her hand on the trunk. Wunsch would never come back, the poor man; she knew that. He would drift on from new town to new town, from catastrophe to catastrophe. He would hardly find a good home for himself again. He would die at last in some rough place, and be buried in the desert or on the wild prairie, far enough from any linden tree!

Fritz, smoking his pipe on the kitchen doorstep, watched his Paulina and guessed her thoughts. He, too, was sorry to lose his friend. But Fritz was getting old; he had lived a long while and had learned to lose without struggle.

XIV

Mother," said Peter Kronborg to his wife one morning about two weeks after Wunsch's departure, "how would you like to drive out to Copper Hole with me to-day?"

Mrs. Kronborg said she thought she would enjoy the drive. She put on her grey cashmere dress and gold watch and chain, as befitted a minister's wife, and while her husband was dressing, she packed a black oil-cloth satchel with such clothing as she and Thor would need overnight.

Copper Hole was a settlement fifteen miles north-west of Moonstone where Mr. Kronborg preached every Friday evening. There was a big spring there and a creek and a few irrigating ditches. It was a community of discouraged agriculturists who had disastrously experimented with dry farming. Mr. Kronborg always drove out one day and back the next, spending the night with one of his parishioners. Often, when the weather was fine, his wife accompanied him. To-day they set out from home after the midday meal, leaving Tillie in charge of the house. Mrs. Kronborg's maternal feeling was always garnered up in the baby, whoever the baby happened to be. If she had the baby with her, the others could look out for themselves. Thor, of course, was not, accurately speaking, a baby any longer. In the matter of nourishment he had long been quite independent of his mother, though this independence had not been won without a struggle. Thor was conservative in all things, and the whole family had anguished with him when he was being weaned. Being the youngest, he was still the baby for Mrs. Kronborg, though he was nearly four years old and sat up boldly on her lap this afternoon, holding on to the ends of the lines and shouting, " 'mup, 'mup, horsey." His father watched him affectionately and hummed hymn tunes in the jovial way that was sometimes such a trial to Thea.

Mrs. Kronborg was enjoying the sunshine and the brilliant sky and all the faintly marked features of the dazzling, monotonous landscape. She had a rather unusual capacity for getting the flavour of places and of people. Although she was so enmeshed in family cares most of the time, she could emerge serene when she was away from them. For a mother of seven, she had a singularly unprejudiced point of view. She was, moreover, a fatalist, and as she did not attempt to direct things beyond her control, she found a good deal of time to enjoy the ways of man and nature.

When they were well upon their road, out where the first lean pasture lands began and the sand grass made a faint showing between the sagebushes, Mr. Kronborg dropped his tune and turned to his wife. "Mother, I've been thinking about something."

"I guessed you had. What is it?" She shifted Thor to her left knee, where he would be less in the way.

"Well, it's about Thea. Mr. Follansbee came to my study at the church the other day and said they would like to have their two girls take lessons of Thea. Then I sounded Miss Meyers" (Miss Meyers was the organist in Mr. Kronborg's church) "and she said there was a good deal of talk about whether Thea wouldn't take over Wunsch's pupils. She said if Thea stopped school she wouldn't wonder if she could get pretty much all Wunsch's class. People think Thea knows about all Wunsch could teach."

Mrs. Kronborg looked thoughtful. "Do you think we ought to take her out of school so young?"

"She is young, but next year would be her last year, anyway. She's far along for her age. And she can't learn much under the principal we've got now, can she?"

"No, I'm afraid she can't," his wife admitted. "She frets a good deal and says that man always has to look in the back of the book for the answers. She hates all that diagramming they have to do, and I think myself it's a waste of time."

Mr. Kronborg settled himself back into the seat and slowed the mare to a walk. "You see, it occurs to me that we might raise Thea's prices, so it would be worth her while. Seventy-five cents for hour lessons, fifty cents for half-hour lessons. If she got, say two thirds of Wunsch's class, that would bring her in upwards of ten dollars a week. Better pay than teaching a country school, and there would be more work in vacation than in winter. Steady work twelve months in the year; that's an advantage. And she'd be living at home, with no expenses."

"There'd be talk if you raised her prices," said Mrs. Kronborg dubiously.

"At first there would. But Thea is so much the best musician in town that they'd all come into line after a while. A good many people in Moonstone have been making money lately, and have bought new pianos. There were ten new pianos shipped in here from Denver in the last year. People ain't going to let them stand idle; too much money invested. I believe Thea can have as many scholars as she can handle, if we set her up a little."

"How set her up, do you mean?" Mrs. Kronborg felt a certain reluctance about accepting this plan, though she had not yet had time to think out her reasons.

"Well, I've been thinking for some time we could make good use of another room. We couldn't give up the parlour to her all the time. If we built another room on the ell and put the piano in there, she could give lessons all day long and it wouldn't bother us. We could build a clothes-press in it, and put in a bed-lounge and a dresser and let Anna have it for her sleeping-room. She needs a place of her own, now that she's beginning to be dressy."

"Seems like Thea ought to have the choice of the room, herself," said Mrs. Kronborg.

"But, my dear, she don't want it. Won't have it. I sounded her coming home from church on Sunday; asked her if she would like to sleep

in a new room, if we built on. She fired up like a little wildcat and said she'd
made her own room all herself, and she didn't think anybody ought to take
it away from her."

"She don't mean to be impertinent, father. She's made decided
that way, like my father." Mrs. Kronborg spoke up warmly. "I never have
any trouble with the child. I remember my father's ways and go at her
carefully. Thea's all right."

Mr. Kronborg laughed indulgently and pinched Thor's full
cheek. "Oh, I didn't mean anything against your girl, mother! She's all
right, but she's a little wildcat, just the same. I think Ray Kennedy's
planning to spoil a born old maid."

"Huh! She'll get something a good sight better than Ray
Kennedy, you see! Thea's an awful smart girl. I've seen a good many girls
take music-lessons in my time, but I ain't seen one that took to it so.
Wunsch said so, too. She's got the making of something in her."

"I don't deny that, and the sooner she gets at it in a businesslike
way, the better. She's the kind that takes responsibility, and it'll be good for
her."

Mrs. Kronborg was thoughtful. "In some ways it will, maybe.
But there's a good deal of strain about teaching youngsters, and she's always
worked so hard with the scholars she has. I've often listened to her pounding it into 'em. I don't want to work her too hard. She's so serious that she's
never had what you might call any real childhood. Seems like she ought to
have the next few years sort of free and easy. She'll be tied down with
responsibilities soon enough."

Mr. Kronborg patted his wife's arm. "Don't you believe it,
mother. Thea is not the marrying kind. I've watched 'em. Anna will marry
before long and make a good wife, but I don't see Thea bringing up a
family. She's got a good deal of her mother in her, but she hasn't got all.
She's too peppery and too fond of having her own way. Then she's always
got to be ahead in everything. That kind make good church-workers and
missionaries and school-teachers, but they don't make good wives. They
fret all their energy away, like colts, and get cut on the wire."

Mrs. Kronborg laughed. "Give me the graham crackers I put in
your pocket for Thor. He's hungry. You're a funny man, Peter. A body
wouldn't think, to hear you, you was talking about your own daughters. I
guess you see through 'em. Still, even if Thea ain't apt to have children of
her own, I don't know as that's a good reason why she should wear herself
out on other people's."

"That's just the point, mother. A girl with all that energy has got to do something, same as a boy, to keep her out of mischief. If you don't want her to marry Ray, let her do something to make herself independent."

"Well, I'm not against it. It might be the best thing for her. I wish I felt sure she wouldn't worry. She takes things hard. She nearly cried herself sick about Wunsch's going away. She's the smartest child of 'em all, Peter, by a long ways."

Peter Kronborg smiled. "There you go, Anna. That's you all over again. Now, I have no favourites; they all have their good points. But you," with a twinkle, "always did go in for brains."

Mrs. Kronborg chuckled as she wiped the cracker crumbs from Thor's chin and fists. "Well, you are mighty conceited, Peter! But I don't know as I ever regretted it. I prefer having a family of my own to fussing with other folks' children, that's the truth."

Before the Kronborgs reached Copper Hole, Thea's destiny was pretty well mapped out for her. Mr. Kronborg was always delighted to have an excuse for enlarging the house.

Mrs. Kronborg was quite right in her conjecture that there would be unfriendly comment in Moonstone when Thea raised her prices for music-lessons. People said she was getting too conceited for anything. Mrs. Livery Johnson put on a new bonnet and paid up all her back calls to have the pleasure of announcing in each parlour she entered that her daughters, at least, would "never pay professional prices to Thea Kronborg."

Thea raised no objection to quitting school. She was now in the "high room," as it was called, in next to the highest class, and was studying geometry and beginning Caesar. She no longer recited her lessons to the teacher she liked, but to the principal, a man who belonged, as did Mrs. Livery Johnson, to the camp of Thea's natural enemies. He taught school because he was too lazy to work among grown-up people, and he made an easy job of it. He got out of real work by inventing useless activities for his pupils, such as the "tree-diagramming system." Thea had spent hours making trees out of the "Thanatopsis," Hamlet's soliloquy, Cato on "Immortality." She agonized under this waste of time, and was only too glad to accept her father's offer of liberty.

So Thea left school the first of November. By the first of January she had eight one-hour pupils and ten half-hour pupils, and there would be more in the summer. She spent her earnings generously. She bought a new Brussels carpet for the parlour, and a rifle for Gunner and Axel, and an imitation tiger-skin coat and cap for Thor. She enjoyed being able to add to the family possessions, and she thought Thor looked quite as handsome in his spots as the rich children she had seen in Denver. Thor was most complacent in his conspicuous apparel. He could walk anywhere by this time—though he always preferred to sit, or to be pulled in his cart. He was a blissfully lazy child, and had a number of long, dull plays, such as making nests for his china duck and waiting for her to lay him an egg. Thea thought him very intelligent, and she was proud that he was so big and burly. She found him restful, loved to hear him call her "sitter," and really liked his companionship, especially when she was tired. On Saturday, for instance, when she taught from nine in the morning until five in the afternoon, she liked to get off in a corner with Thor after supper, away from all the bathing and dressing and joking and talking that went on in the house, and ask him about his duck, or hear him tell one of his rambling stories.

XV

*B*y the time Thea's fifteenth birthday came round, she was established as a music-teacher in Moonstone. The new room had been added to the house early in the spring, and Thea had been giving her lessons there since the middle of May. She liked the personal independence which was accorded her as a wage-earner. The family questioned her comings and goings very little. She could go buggy-riding with Ray Kennedy, for instance, without taking Gunner or Axel. She could go to Spanish Johnny's and sing part songs with the Mexicans, and nobody objected.

Thea was still under the first excitement of teaching, and was terribly in earnest about it. If a pupil did not get on well, she fumed and fretted. She counted until she was hoarse. She listened to scales in her sleep. Wunsch had taught only one pupil seriously, but Thea taught twenty. The duller they were, the more furiously she poked and prodded them. With the little girls she was nearly always patient, but with pupils older than herself, she sometimes lost her temper. One of her mistakes was to let herself in for a calling-down from Mrs. Livery Johnson. That lady appeared at the Kronborgs' one morning and announced that she would allow no girl to stamp her foot at her daughter Grace. She added that Thea's bad manners with the older girls were being talked about all over town, and that if her temper did not speedily improve she would lose all her advanced pupils. Thea was frightened. She felt she could never bear the disgrace, if such a thing happened. Besides, what would her father say, after he had gone to the expense of building an addition to the house? Mrs. Johnson demanded an apology to Grace. Thea said she was willing to make it. Mrs. Johnson said that hereafter, since she had taken lessons of the best piano teacher in Grinnell, Iowa, she herself would decide what pieces Grace should study. Thea readily consented to that, and Mrs. Johnson rustled away to tell a neighbour woman that Thea Kronborg could be meek enough when you went at her right.

Thea was telling Ray about this unpleasant encounter as they were driving out to the sand hills the next Sunday.

"She was stuffing you, all right, Thee," Ray reassured her. "There's no general dissatisfaction among your scholars. She just wanted to get in a knock. I talked to the piano-tuner the last time he was here, and he said all the people he tuned for expressed themselves very favourably about your teaching. I wish you didn't take so much pains with them, myself."

"But I have to, Ray. They're all so dumb. They've got no ambition," Thea exclaimed irritably. "Jenny Smiley is the only one who isn't stupid. She can read pretty well, and she has such good hands. But she don't care a rap about it. She has no pride."

Ray's face was full of complacent satisfaction as he glanced sidewise at Thea, but she was looking off intently into the mirage, at one of those mammoth cattle that are nearly always reflected there. "Do you find it easier to teach in your new room?" he asked.

"Yes; I'm not interrupted so much. Of course, if I ever happen to want to practise at night, that's always the night Anna chooses to go to bed early."

"It's a darned shame, Thee, you didn't cop that room for yourself. I'm sore at the *padre* about that. He ought to give you that room. You could fix it up so pretty."

"I didn't want it, honest I didn't. Father would have let me have it. I like my own room better. Somehow I can think better in a little room. Besides, up there I am away from everybody, and I can read as late as I please and nobody nags me."

"A growing girl needs lots of sleep," Ray providently remarked.

Thea moved restlessly on the buggy cushions. "They need other things more," she muttered. "Oh, I forgot. I brought something to show you. Look here, it came on my birthday. Wasn't it nice of him to remember?"

She took from her pocket a postcard, bent in the middle and folded, and handed it to Ray. On it was a white dove, perched on a wreath of very blue forget-me-nots and "Birthday Greetings" in gold letters. Under this was written, "From A. Wunsch."

Ray turned the card over, examined the postmark, and then began to laugh.

"Concord, Kansas. He has my sympathy!"

"Why, is that a poor town?"

"It's the jumping-off place, no town at all. Some houses dumped down in the middle of a cornfield. You get lost in the corn. Not even a saloon to keep things going; sell whisky without a licence at the butcher shop, beer on ice with the liver and beefsteak. I wouldn't stay there over Sunday for a ten-dollar bill."

"Oh, dear! What do you suppose he's doing there? Maybe he just stopped off there a few days to tune pianos," Thea suggested hopefully.

Ray gave her back the card. "He's headed in the wrong direction. What does he want to get back into a grass country for? Now, there are lots of good live towns down on the Santa Fé, and everybody down there is musical. He could always get a job playing in saloons if he was dead-broke. I've figured out that I've got no years of my life to waste in a Methodist country where they raise pork."

"We must stop on our way back and show this card to Mrs. Kohler. She misses him so."

"By the way, Thee, I hear the old woman goes to church every Sunday to hear you sing. Fritz tells me he has to wait till two o'clock for his Sunday dinner these days. The church people ought to give you credit for that, when they go for you."

Thea shook her head and spoke in a tone of resignation. "They'll always go for me, just as they did for Wunsch. It wasn't because he drank they went for him; not really. It was something else."

"You want to salt your money down, Thee, and go to Chicago and take some lessons. Then you come back, and wear a long feather and high heels and put on a few airs, and that will fix 'em. That is what they like."

"I'll never have money enough to go to Chicago. Mother meant to lend me some, I think, but now they have got hard times back in Nebraska, and her farm don't bring her in anything. Takes all the tenant can raise to pay the taxes. Don't let's talk about that. You promised to tell me about the play you went to see in Denver."

Anyone would have liked to hear Ray's simple and clear account of the performance he had seen at the Tabor Grand Opera House—Maggie Mitchell in *Little Barefoot*—and anyone would have liked to watch his kind face. Ray looked his best out-of-doors, when his thick red hands were covered by gloves, and the dull red of his sunburned face somehow seemed right in the light and wind. He looked better, too, with his hat on; his hair was thin and dry, with no particular colour or character, "regular Willy-boy hair," as he himself described it. His eyes were pale beside the reddish bronze of his skin. They had the faded look often seen in the eyes of men who have lived much in the sun and wind and who have been accustomed to train their vision upon distant objects.

Ray realized that Thea's life was dull and exacting, and that she missed Wunsch. He knew she worked hard, that she put up with a great many little annoyances, and that her duties as a teacher separated her more than ever from the boys and girls of her own age. He did everything he could to provide recreation for her. He brought her candy and magazines and pineapples—of which she was very fond—from Denver, and kept his eyes and ears open for anything that might interest her. He was, of course, living for Thea. He had thought it all out carefully and had made up his mind just when he would speak to her. When she was seventeen, then he would tell her his plan and ask her to marry him. He would be willing to wait two, or even three years, until she was twenty, if she thought best. By that time he would surely have got in on something: copper, oil, gold, silver, sheep—something.

Meanwhile, it was pleasure enough to feel that she depended on him more and more, that she leaned upon his steady kindness. He never broke faith with himself about her; he never hinted to her of his hopes for the future, never suggested that she might be more intimately confidential with him, or talked to her of the thing he thought about so constantly. He had the chivalry which is perhaps the proudest possession of his race. He had never embarrassed her by so much as a glance. Sometimes, when they drove out to the sand hills, he let his left arm lie along the back of the buggy seat, but it never came any nearer to Thea than that, never touched her. He often turned to her a face full of pride, and frank admiration, but his glance was never so intimate or so penetrating as Doctor Archie's. His blue eyes were clear and shallow, friendly, uninquiring. He rested Thea because he was so different; because, though he often told her interesting things, he never set lively fancies going in her head; because he never misunderstood her, and because he never, by any chance, for a single instant, understood her! Yes, with Ray she was safe; by him she would never be discovered!

XVI

*T*he pleasantest experience Thea had that summer was a trip that she and her mother made to Denver in Ray Kennedy's caboose. Mrs. Kronborg had been looking forward to this excursion for a long while, but as Ray never knew at what hour his freight would leave Moonstone, it was difficult to arrange. The call-boy was as likely to summon him to start on his run at twelve o'clock midnight as at twelve o'clock noon. The first week in June started out with all the scheduled trains running on time, and a light freight business. Tuesday evening Ray, after consulting with the dispatcher, stopped at the Kronborgs' front gate to tell Mrs. Kronborg—who was helping Tillie water the flowers—that if she and Thea could be at the depot at eight o'clock the next morning, he thought he could promise them a pleasant ride and get them into Denver before nine o'clock in the evening. Mrs. Kronborg told him cheerfully, across the fence, that she would "take him up on it," and Ray hurried back to the yards to scrub out his car.

The one complaint Ray's brakemen had to make of him was that he was too fussy about his caboose. His former brakeman had asked to be transferred because, he said, "Kennedy was as fussy about his car as an old maid about her bird-cage." Joe Giddy, who was braking with Ray now, called him "the bride," because he kept the caboose and bunks so clean.

It was properly the brakeman's business to keep the car clean, but when Ray got back to the depot, Giddy was nowhere to be found. Muttering that all his brakemen seemed to consider him "easy," Ray went down to his car alone. He built a fire in the stove and put water on to heat while he got into his overalls and jumper. Then he set to work with a scrubbing-brush and plenty of soap and "cleaner." He scrubbed the floor and seats, blacked the stove, put clean sheets on the bunks, and then began to demolish Giddy's picture gallery. Ray found that his brakemen were likely to have what he termed "a taste for the nude in art," and Giddy was no exception. Ray took down half a dozen girls in tights and ballet skirts—

premiums for cigarette coupons—and some racy calendars advertising saloons and sporting clubs, which had cost Giddy both time and trouble; he
even removed Giddy's particular pet, a naked girl lying on a couch with her
knee carelessly poised in the air. Underneath the picture was printed the
title, "The Odalisque." Giddy was under the happy delusion that this title
meant something wicked—there was a wicked look about the conso-
nants—but Ray, of course, had looked it up, and Giddy was indebted to the
dictionary for the privilege of keeping his lady. If "odalisque" had been
what Ray called an objectionable word, he would have thrown the picture
out in the first place. He deposited all these pictures under the mattress of
Giddy's bunk, and stood admiring his clean car in the lamplight; the walls
now exhibited only a wheatfield, advertising agricultural implements, a map
of Colorado, and some pictures of race-horses and hunting-dogs. At this
moment Giddy, freshly shaved and shampooed, his shirt shining with the
highest polish known to Chinese laundrymen, his straw hat tipped over his
right eye, thrust his head in at the door.

"What in hell—" he brought out furiously. His good-humoured, sunburned face seemed fairly to swell with amazement and anger.

"That's all right, Giddy," Ray called in a conciliatory tone.
"Nothing injured. I'll put 'em all up again as I found 'em. Going to take
some ladies down in the car to-morrow."

Giddy scowled. He did not dispute the propriety of Ray's measures, if there were to be ladies on board, but he felt injured. "I suppose
you'll expect me to behave like a Y.M.C.A. secretary," he growled. "I can't
do my work and serve tea at the same time."

"No need to have a tea-party," said Ray with determined cheerfulness. "Mrs. Kronborg will bring the lunch, and it will be a darned good
one."

Giddy lounged against the car, holding his cigar between two
thick fingers. "Then I guess she'll get it," he observed knowingly. "I don't
think your musical friend is much on the grub-box. Has to keep her hands
white to tickle the ivories." Giddy had nothing against Thea, but he felt
cantankerous and wanted to get a rise out of Kennedy.

"Every man to his own job," Ray replied agreeably, pulling his
white shirt on over his head.

Giddy emitted smoke disdainfully. "I suppose so. The man that
gets her will have to wear an apron and bake the pancakes. Well, some men
like to mess about the kitchen." He paused, but Ray was intent on getting
into his clothes as quickly as possible. Giddy thought he could go a little

further. "Of course, I don't dispute your right to haul women in this car if you want to; but personally, so far as I'm concerned, I'd a good deal rather drink a can of tomatoes and do without the women *and* their lunch. I was never much enslaved to hard-boiled eggs, anyhow."

"You'll eat 'em to-morrow, all the same." Ray's tone had a steely glitter as he jumped out of the car, and Giddy stood aside to let him pass. He knew that Kennedy's next reply would be delivered by hand. He had once seen Ray beat up a nasty fellow for insulting a Mexican woman who helped about the grub-car in the work-train, and his fists had worked like two steel hammers. Giddy wasn't looking for trouble.

At eight o'clock the next morning Ray greeted his ladies and helped them into the car. Giddy had put on a clean shirt and yellow pig-skin gloves and was whistling his best. He considered Kennedy a fluke as a ladies' man, and if there was to be a party, the honours had to be done by someone who wasn't a blacksmith at small-talk. Giddy had, as Ray sarcastically admitted, "a local reputation as a jollier," and he was fluent in gallant speeches of a not too-veiled nature. He insisted that Thea should take his seat in the cupola, opposite Ray's, where she could look out over the country. Thea told him, as she clambered up, that she cared a good deal more about riding in that seat than about going to Denver. Ray was never so companionable and easy as when he sat chatting in the lookout of his little house on wheels. Good stories came to him, and interesting recollections. Thea had a great respect for the reports he had to write out, and for the telegrams that were handed to him at stations; for all the knowledge and experience it must take to run a freight train.

Giddy, down in the car, in the pauses of his work made himself agreeable to Mrs. Kronborg.

"It's a great rest to be where my family can't get at me, Mr. Giddy," she told him. "I thought you and Ray might have some house-work here for me to look after, but I couldn't improve any on this car."

"Oh, we like to keep her neat," returned Giddy glibly, winking up at Ray's expressive back. "If you want to see a clean icebox, look at this one. Yes, Kennedy always carries fresh cream to eat on his oatmeal. I'm not particular. The tin cow's good enough for me."

"Most of you boys smoke so much that all victuals taste alike to you," said Mrs. Kronborg. "I've got no religious scruples against smoking, but I couldn't take as much interest cooking for a man that used tobacco. I guess it's all right for bachelors who have to eat round."

Mrs. Kronborg took off her hat and veil and made herself comfortable. She seldom had an opportunity to be idle, and she enjoyed it. She could sit for hours and watch the sage-hens fly up and the jack-rabbits dart away from the track, without being bored. She wore a tan bombazine dress, made very plainly, and carried a roomy, worn, mother-of-the-family handbag.

Ray Kennedy always insisted that Mrs. Kronborg was "a fine-looking lady," but this was not the common opinion in Moonstone. Ray had lived long enough among the Mexicans to dislike fussiness, to feel that there was something more attractive in ease of manner than in absent-minded concern about hairpins and dabs of lace. He had learned to think that the way a woman stood, moved, sat in her chair, looked at you, was more important than the absence of wrinkles from her skirt. Ray had, indeed, such unusual perceptions in some directions, that one could not help wondering what he would have been if he had ever, as he said, had "half a chance."

He was right; Mrs. Kronborg was a fine-looking woman. She was short and square, but her head was a real head, not a mere jerky termination of the body. It had some individuality apart from hats and hairpins. Her hair, Moonstone women admitted, would have been very pretty "on anybody else." Frizzy bangs were worn then, but Mrs. Kronborg always dressed her hair in the same way, parted in the middle, brushed smoothly back from her low, white forehead, pinned loosely on the back of her head in two thick braids. It was growing grey about the temples, but after the manner of yellow hair it seemed only to have grown paler there, and had taken on a colour like that of English primroses. Her eyes were clear and untroubled; her face was smooth and calm, and, as Ray said, "strong."

Thea and Ray, up in the sunny cupola, were laughing and talking. Ray got great pleasure out of seeing her face there in the little box where he so often imagined it. They were crossing a plateau where great red sandstone boulders lay about, most of them much wider at the top than at the base, so that they looked like great toadstools.

"The sand has been blowing against them for a good many hundred years," Ray explained, directing Thea's eyes with his gloved hand. "You see the sand blows low, being so heavy, and cuts them out underneath. Wind and sand are pretty high-class architects. That's the principle of most of the Cliff-Dweller remains down at Cañon de Chelly. The sandstorms had dug out big depressions in the face of a cliff, and the Indians built their houses back in that depression."

"You told me that before, Ray, and of course you know. But the geography says their houses were cut out of the face of the living rock, and I like that better."

Ray sniffed. "What nonsense does get printed! It's enough to give a man disrespect for learning. How could them Indians cut houses out of the living rock, when they knew nothing about the art of forging metals?" Ray leaned back in his chair, swung his foot, and looked thoughtful and happy. He was in one of his favourite fields of speculation, and nothing gave him more pleasure than talking these things over with Thea Kronborg. "I'll tell you, Thee, if those old fellows had learned to work metals once, your ancient Egyptians and Assyrians wouldn't have beat them very much. Whatever they did do, they did well. Their masonry's standing there to-day, the corners as true as the Denver Capitol. They were clever at most everything but metals; and that one failure kept them from getting across. It was the quicksand that swallowed 'em up, as a race. I guess civilization proper began when men mastered metals."

Ray was not vain about his bookish phrases. He did not use them to show off, but because they seemed to him more adequate than colloquial speech. He felt strongly about these things, and groped for words, as he said, "to express himself." He had the lamentable American belief that "expression" is obligatory. He still carried in his trunk, among the unrelated possessions of a railroad man, a notebook on the title-page of which was written "Impressions on First Viewing the Grand Cañon, Ray H. Kennedy." The pages of that book were like a battlefield; the labouring author had fallen back from metaphor after metaphor, abandoned position after position. He would have admitted that the art of forging metals was nothing to this treacherous business of recording impressions, in which the material you were so full of vanished mysteriously under your striving hand. "Escaping steam!" he had said to himself, the last time he tried to read that notebook.

Thea didn't mind Ray's travel-lecture expressions. She dodged them unconsciously, as she did her father's professional palaver. The light in Ray's pale-blue eyes and the feeling in his voice more than made up for the stiffness of his language.

"Were the Cliff-Dwellers really clever with their hands, Ray, or do you always have to make allowance and say, 'That was pretty good for an Indian'?" she asked.

Ray went down into the car to give some instructions to Giddy.

"Well," he said when he returned, "about the aborigines: once or twice I have been with some fellows who were cracking burial mounds. Always felt a little ashamed of it, but we did pull out some remarkable things. We got some pottery out whole; seemed pretty fine to me. I guess their women were their artists. We found lots of old shoes and sandals made out of yucca fibre, neat and strong; and feather blankets, too."

"Feather blankets? You never told me about them."

"Didn't I? The old fellows—or the squaws—wove a close net-ting of yucca fibre, and then tied on little bunches of down feathers, overlapping, just the way feathers grow on a bird. Some of them were feathered on both sides. You can't get anything warmer than that, now, can you?—or prettier. What I like about those old aborigines is, that they got all their ideas from nature."

Thea laughed. "That means you're going to say something about girls' wearing corsets. But some of your Indians flattened their babies' heads, and that's worse than wearing corsets."

"Give me an Indian girl's figure for beauty," Ray insisted. "And a girl with a voice like yours ought to have plenty of lung-action. But you know my sentiments on that subject. I was going to tell you about the handsomest thing we ever looted out of those burial mounds. It was on a woman, too, I regret to say. She was preserved as perfect as any mummy that ever came out of the pyramids. She had a big string of turquoises around her neck, and she was wrapped in a fox-fur cloak, lined with yellow feathers that must have come off wild canaries. Can you beat that, now? The fellow that claimed it sold it to a Boston man for a hundred and fifty dollars."

Thea looked at him admiringly. "Oh, Ray, and didn't you get anything off her, to remember her by, even? She must have been a prin-cess."

Ray took a wallet from the pocket of the coat that was hanging beside him, and drew from it a little lump wrapped in worn tissue paper. In a moment a stone, soft and blue as a robin's egg, lay in the hard palm of his hand. It was a turquoise, rubbed smooth in the Indian finish, which is so much more beautiful than the incongruous high polish the white man gives that tender stone.

"I got this from her necklace. See the hole where the string went through? You know how the Indians drill them? Work the drill with their teeth. You like it, don't you? They're just right for you. Blue and yellow are the Swedish colours." Ray looked intently at her head, bent over his hand, and then gave his whole attention to the track.

"I'll tell you, Thee," he began after a pause, "I'm going to form a camping party one of these days and persuade your *padre* to take you and your mother down to that country, and we'll live in the rock-houses—they are as comfortable as can be—and start the cook fires up in 'em once again. I'll go into the burial mounds and get you more keepsakes than any girl ever had before." Ray had planned such an expedition for his wedding journey, and it made his heart thump to see how Thea's eyes kindled when he talked about it. "I have learned more down there about what makes history," he went on, "than in all the books I've ever read. When you sit in the sun and let your heels hang out of a doorway that drops a thousand feet, ideas come to you. You begin to feel what the human race has been up against from the beginning. There's something mighty elevating about those old habitations. You feel like it's up to you to do your best, on account of those fellows having it so hard. You feel like you owed them something."

At Wassiwappa, Ray got instructions to sidetrack until Thirty-Six went by. After reading the message, he turned to his guests. "I'm afraid this will hold us up about two hours, Mrs. Kronborg, and we won't get into Denver till near midnight."

"That won't trouble me," said Mrs. Kronborg contentedly. "They know me at the Y.W.C.A., and they'll let me in any time of night. I came to see the country, not to make time. I've always wanted to get out at this white place and look around, and now I'll have a chance. What makes it so white?"

"Some kind of chalky rock." Ray sprang to the ground and gave Mrs. Kronborg his hand. "You can get soil of any colour in Colorado; match most any ribbon."

While Ray was getting his train onto a side track, Mrs. Kronborg strolled off to examine the post-office and station house; these, with the water-tank, made up the town. The station agent "batched" and raised chickens. He ran out to meet Mrs. Kronborg, clutched at her feverishly, and began telling her at once how lonely he was and what bad luck he was having with his poultry. She went to his chicken yard with him, and prescribed for gapes.

Wassiwappa seemed a dreary place enough to people who looked for verdure, a brilliant place to people who liked colour. Beside the station house there was a blue-grass plot, protected by a red plank fence, and six fly-bitten box-elder trees, not much larger than bushes, were kept alive by frequent hosings from the waterplug. Over the windows some dusty morning-glory vines were trained on strings. All the country about was broken up into low chalky hills, which were so intensely white, and spotted so evenly with sage, that they looked like white leopards crouching. White dust powdered everything, and the light was so intense that the station agent usually wore blue glasses. Behind the station there was a watercourse, which roared in flood time, and a basin in the soft white rock where a pool of alkali water flashed in the sun like a mirror. The agent looked almost as sick as his chickens, and Mrs. Kronborg at once invited him to lunch with her party. He had, he confessed, a distaste for his own cooking, and lived mainly on soda crackers and canned beef. He laughed apologetically when Mrs. Kronborg said she guessed she'd look about for a shady place to eat lunch.

She walked up the track to the water-tank, and there, in the narrow shadows cast by the uprights on which the tank stood, she found two tramps. They sat up and stared at her, heavy with sleep. When she asked them where they were going, they told her "to the coast." They rested by day and travelled by night; walked the ties unless they could steal a ride, they said; adding that "these Western roads were getting strict." Their faces were blistered, their eyes bloodshot, and their shoes looked fit only for the trash pile.

"I suppose you're hungry?" Mrs. Kronborg asked. "I suppose you both drink?" she went on thoughtfully, not censoriously.

The huskier of the two hoboes, a bushy, bearded fellow, rolled his eyes and said, "I wonder?" But the other, who was old and spare, with a sharp nose and watery eyes, sighed. "Some has one affliction, some another," he said.

Mrs. Kronborg reflected. "Well," she said at last, "you can't get liquor here, anyway. I am going to ask you to vacate, because I want to have a little picnic under this tank for the freight crew that brought me along. I wish I had lunch enough to provide you, but I ain't. The station agent says he gets his provisions over there at the post-office store, and if you are hungry you can get some canned stuff there." She opened her handbag and gave each of the tramps a half-dollar.

The old man wiped his eyes with his forefinger. "Thank 'ee, ma'am. A can of tomatters will taste pretty good to me. I wasn't always walkin' ties; I had a good job in Cleveland before—"

The hairy tramp turned on him fiercely. "Aw, shut up on that, grandpaw! Ain't you got no gratitude? What do you want to hand the lady that fur?"

The old man hung his head and turned away. As he went off, his comrade looked after him and said to Mrs. Kronborg: "It's true, what

he says. He had a job in the car shops; but he had bad luck." They both
limped away toward the store, and Mrs. Kronborg sighed. She was not
afraid of tramps. She always talked to them, and never turned one away. She
hated to think how many of them there were, crawling along the tracks
over that vast cou'' try.

Her reflections were cut short by Ray and Giddy and Thea, who
came bringing the lunch-box and water bottles. Although there was not
shadow enough to accommodate all the party at once, the air under the tank
was distinctly cooler than the surrounding air, and the drip made a pleasant
sound in that breathless noon. The station agent ate as if he had never been
fed before, apologizing every time he took another piece of fried chicken.
Giddy was unabashed before the devilled eggs of which he had spoken so
scornfully last night. After lunch the men lit their pipes and lay back against
the uprights that supported the tank.

"This is the sunny side of railroading, all right," Giddy drawled
luxuriously.

"You fellows grumble too much," said Mrs. Kronborg as she
corked the pickle jar. "Your job has its drawbacks, but it don't tie you
down. Of course there's the risk; but I believe a man's watched over,
and he can't be hurt on the railroad or anywhere else if it's intended he
shouldn't be."

Giddy laughed. "Then the trains must be operated by fellows the
Lord has it in for, Mrs. Kronborg. They figure it out that a railroad man's
only due to last eleven years; then it's his turn to be smashed."

"That's a dark Providence, I don't deny," Mrs. Kronborg admitted. "But there's lots of things in life that's hard to understand."

"I guess!" murmured Giddy, looking off at the spotted white
hills.

Ray smoked his pipe in silence, watching Thea and her mother
clear away the lunch. He was thinking that Mrs. Kronborg had in her face
the same serious look that Thea had; only hers was calm and satisfied, and
Thea's was intense and questioning. But in both it was a large kind of look,
that was not all the time being broken up and convulsed by trivial things.
They both carried their heads like Indian women, with a kind of noble
unconsciousness. He got so tired of women who were always nodding and
jerking; apologizing, deprecating, coaxing, insinuating with their heads.

When Ray's party set off again that afternoon, the sun beat
fiercely into the cupola, and Thea curled up in one of the seats at the back
of the car and had a nap.

As the short twilight came on, Giddy took a turn in the cupola, and Ray came down and sat with Thea on the rear platform of the caboose and watched the darkness come in soft waves over the plain. They were now about thirty miles from Denver, and the mountains looked very near. The great toothed wall behind which the sun had gone down now separated into four distinct ranges, one behind the other. They were a very pale blue, a colour scarcely stronger than wood smoke, and the sunset had left bright streaks in the snow-filled gorges. In the clear, yellow-streaked sky the stars were coming out, flickering like newly lighted lamps, growing steadier and more golden as the sky darkened and the land beneath them fell into complete shadow. It was a cool, restful darkness that was not black or forbidding, but somehow open and free; the night of high plains where there is no moistness or mistiness in the atmosphere.

Ray lit his pipe. "I never get tired of them old stars, Thee. I miss 'em up in Washington and Oregon where it's misty. Like 'em best down in Mother Mexico, where they have everything their own way. I'm not for any country where the stars are dim." Ray paused and drew on his pipe. "I don't know as I ever really noticed 'em much till that first year I herded sheep up in Wyoming. That was the year the blizzard caught me."

"And you lost all your sheep, didn't you, Ray?" Thea spoke sympathetically. "Was the man who owned them nice about it?"

"Yes, he was a good loser. But I didn't get over it for a long while. Sheep are so damned resigned. Sometimes, to this day, when I'm dog-tired, I try to save them sheep all night long. It comes kind of hard on a boy when he first finds out how little he is, and how big everything else is."

Thea moved restlessly toward him and dropped her chin on her hand, looking at a low star that seemed to rest just on the rim of the earth. "I don't see how you stood it. I don't believe I could. I don't see how people can stand it to get knocked out, anyhow!"

She spoke with such fierceness that Ray glanced at her in surprise. She was sitting on the floor of the car, crouching like a little animal about to spring.

"No occasion for you to see," he said warmly. "There'll always be plenty of other people to take the knocks for you."

"That's nonsense, Ray." Thea spoke impatiently and leaned lower still, frowning at the red star. "Everybody's up against it for himself, succeeds or fails—himself."

"In one way, yes," Ray admitted, knocking the sparks from his pipe out into the soft darkness that seemed to flow like a river beside the car. "But when you look at it another way, there are a lot of halfway people in this world who help the winners win, and the failers fail. If a man stumbles, there's plenty of people to push him down. But if he's like "the youth who bore," those same people are foreordained to help him along. They may hate to, worse than blazes, and they may do a lot of cussin' about it, but they have to help the winners and they can't dodge it. It's a natural law, like what keeps the big clock up there going, little wheels and big, and no mix up." Ray's hand and his pipe were suddenly outlined against the sky. "Ever occur to you, Thea, that they have to be on time close enough to *make time?* The Dispatcher up there must have a long head." Pleased with his similitude, Ray went back to the lookout. Going into Denver, he had to keep a sharp watch.

Giddy came down, cheerful at the prospect of getting into port, and singing a new topical ditty that had come up from the Santa Fé by way of La Junta.

Nobody knows who makes these songs; they seem to follow events automatically. Mrs. Kronborg made Giddy sing the whole twelve verses of this one, and laughed until she wiped her eyes. The story was that of Katie Casey, head dining-room girl at Winslow, Arizona, who was unjustly discharged by the Harvey House manager. Her suitor, the yardmaster, took the switchmen out on a strike until she was reinstated. Freight trains from the east and the west piled up at Winslow until the yards looked like a log-jam. The division superintendent, who was in California, had to wire instructions for Katie Casey's restoration before he could get his trains running. Giddy's song told all this with much detail, both tender and technical, and after each of the dozen verses came the refrain:

> "Oh, who would think that Katie Casey owned
>   the Santa Fé?
> But it really looks that way,
> The dispatcher's turnin' gray,
> All the crews is off their pay;
> She can hold the freight from Albuquerq' to
>   Needles any day;
> The division superintendent, he come home
>   from Monterey,
> Just to see if things was pleasin' Katie
>   Ca-a-a-sey."

Thea laughed with her mother and applauded Giddy. Everything was so kindly and comfortable; Giddy and Ray, and their hospitable little house, and the easy-going country, and the stars. She curled up on the seat again with that warm, sleepy feeling of the friendliness of the world—which nobody keeps very long, and which she was to lose early and irrevocably.

XVII

*T*he summer flew by. Thea was glad when Ray Kennedy had a Sunday in town and could take her driving. Out among the sand hills she could forget the "new room" which was the scene of wearing and fruitless labour. Doctor Archie was away from home a good deal that year. He had put all his money into mines above Colorado Springs, and he hoped for great returns from them.

In the fall of that year, Mr. Kronborg decided that Thea ought to show more interest in church work. He put it to her frankly, one night at supper, before the whole family. "How can I insist on the other girls in the congregation being active in the work, when one of my own daughters manifests so little interest?"

"But I sing every Sunday morning, and I have to give up one night a week to choir practice," Thea declared rebelliously, pushing back her plate with an angry determination to eat nothing more.

"One night a week is not enough for the pastor's daughter," her father replied. "You won't do anything in the sewing society, and you won't take part in the Christian Endeavour or the Band of Hope. Very well, you must make it up in other ways. I want someone to play the organ and lead the singing at prayer-meeting this winter. Deacon Potter told me some time ago that he thought there would be more interest in our prayer-meetings if we had the organ. And there ought to be somebody to start the hymns. Mrs. Potter is getting old, and she always starts them too high. It won't take much of your time, and it will keep people from talking."

This argument conquered Thea, though she left the table sullenly. The fear of the tongue, that terror of little towns, is usually felt more keenly by the minister's family than by other households. Whenever the Kronborgs wanted to do anything, even to buy a new carpet, they had to take counsel together as to whether people would talk. Mrs. Kronborg had her own conviction that people talked when they felt like it, and said what they chose, no matter how the minister's family conducted themselves. But she did not impart these dangerous ideas to her children. Thea was still under the belief that public opinion could be placated; that if you clucked often enough, the hens would mistake you for one of themselves.

Mrs. Kronborg did not have any particular zest for prayer-meetings, and she stayed at home whenever she had a valid excuse. Thor was too old to furnish such an excuse now, so every Wednesday night, unless one of the children was sick, she trudged off with Thea, behind Mr. Kronborg. At first Thea was terribly bored. But she got used to prayer-meeting, got even to feel a mournful interest in it.

The exercises were always pretty much the same. After the first hymn her father read a passage from the Bible, usually a Psalm. Then there was another hymn, and then her father commented upon the passage he had read and, as he said, "applied the Word to our necessities." After a third hymn, the meeting was declared open, and the old men and women took turns at praying and talking. Mrs. Kronborg never spoke in meeting. She told people firmly that she had been brought up to keep silent and let the men talk, but she gave respectful attention to the others, sitting with her hands folded in her lap.

The prayer-meeting audience was always small. The young and energetic members of the congregation came only once or twice a year, "to keep people from talking." The usual Wednesday night gathering was made up of old women, with perhaps six or eight old men, and a few sickly girls who had not much interest in life; two of them, indeed, were already preparing to die. Thea accepted the mournfulness of the prayer-meetings as a kind of spiritual discipline, like funerals. She always read late after she went home and felt a stronger wish than usual to live and to be happy.

The meetings were conducted in the Sunday-School room, where there were wooden chairs instead of pews; an old map of Palestine hung on the wall, and the bracket lamps gave out only a dim light. The old women sat motionless as Indians in their shawls and bonnets; some of them wore long black mourning veils. The old men drooped in their chairs. Every back, every face, every head said "resignation." Often there were long silences, when you could hear nothing but the crackling of the soft coal in the stove and the muffled cough of one of the sick girls.

There was one nice old lady—tall, erect, self-respecting, with a delicate white face and a soft voice. She never whined, and what she said was always cheerful, though she spoke so nervously that Thea knew she dreaded getting up, and that she made a real sacrifice to, as she said, "testify to the goodness of her Saviour." She was the mother of the girl who coughed, and Thea used to wonder how she explained things to herself. There was, indeed, only one woman who talked because she was, as Mr. Kronborg said, "tonguey." The others were somehow impressive. They told about the sweet thoughts that came to them while they were at their work; how, amid their household tasks, they were suddenly lifted by the sense of a divine Presence. Sometimes they told of their first conversion, of how in their youth that higher Power had made itself known to them. Old Mr. Carsen, the carpenter, who gave his services as janitor to the church, used often to tell how, when he was a young man and a scoffer, bent on the destruction of both body and soul, his Saviour had come to him in the Michigan woods and had stood, it seemed to him, beside the tree he was felling; and how he dropped his axe and knelt in prayer "to Him who died for us upon the tree." Thea always wanted to ask him more about it; about his mysterious wickedness, and about the vision.

        Sometimes the old people would ask for prayers for their absent children. Sometimes they asked their brothers and sisters in Christ to pray that they might be stronger against temptations. One of the sick girls used to ask them to pray that she might have more faith in the times of depression that came to her, "when all the way before seemed dark." She repeated that husky phrase so often that Thea always remembered it.

        One old woman, who never missed a Wednesday night, and who nearly always took part in the meeting, came all the way up from the depot settlement. She always wore a black crocheted "fascinator" over her thin white hair, and she made long, tremulous prayers, full of railroad terminology. She had six sons in the service of different railroads, and she always prayed "for the boys on the road, who know not at what moment they may be cut off. When, in Thy divine wisdom, their hour is upon them, may they, O our Heavenly Father, see only white lights along the road to Eternity." She used to speak, too, of "the engines that race with death"; and though she looked so old and little when she was on her knees, and her voice was so shaky, her prayers had a thrill of speed and danger in them; they made one think of the deep black cañons, the slender trestles, the pounding trains. Thea liked to look at her sunken eyes that seemed full of wisdom, at her black thread gloves, much too long in the fingers and so meekly folded one over the other. Her face was brown, and worn away as rocks are worn by water. There are many ways of describing that colour of age, but in reality it is not like parchment, or like any of the things it is said to be like. That brownness and that texture of skin are found only in the faces of old human creatures, who have worked hard and who have always been poor.

One bir'erly cold night in December the prayer-meeting seemed to Thea longer than usual. The prayers and the talks went on and on. It was as if the old people were afraid to go out into the cold, or were stupefied by the hot air of the room. She had left a book at home that she was impatient to get back to. At last the Doxology was sung, but the old people lingered about the stove to greet each other, and Thea took her mother's arm and hurried out to the frozen sidewalk, before her father could get away. The wind was whistling up the street and whipping the naked cottonwood trees against the telegraph poles and the sides of the houses. Thin snow clouds were flying overhead, so that the sky looked grey, with a dull phosphorescence. The icy streets and the shingle roofs of the houses were grey, too. All along the street, shutters banged or windows rattled, or gates wobbled, held by their latch but shaking on loose hinges. There was not a cat or a dog in Moonstone that night that was not given a warm shelter; the cats under the kitchen stove, the dogs in barns or coal-sheds. When Thea and her mother reached home, their mufflers were covered with ice, where their breath had frozen. They hurried into the house and made a dash for the parlour and the hard-coal burner, behind which Gunner was sitting on a stool, reading his Jules Verne book. The door stood open into the dining-room, which was heated from the parlour. Mr. Kronborg always had a lunch when he came home from prayer-meeting, and his pumpkin pie and milk were set out on the dining-table. Mrs. Kronborg said she thought she felt hungry, too, and asked Thea if she didn't want something to eat.

"No, I am not hungry, mother. I guess I'll go upstairs."

"I expect you've got some book up there," said Mrs. Kronborg, bringing out another pie. "You had better bring it down here to read. Nobody'll disturb you, and it's terrible cold up in that loft."

Thea was always assured that no one would disturb her if she read downstairs, but the boys talked when they came in, and her father fairly delivered discourses after he had been renewed by half a pie and a pitcher of milk.

"I don't mind the cold. I'll take a hot brick up for my feet. I put one in the stove before I left, if one of the boys hasn't stolen it. Good night, mother." Thea got her brick and lantern, and dashed upstairs through the windy loft. She undressed at top speed and got into bed with her brick. She put a pair of white knitted gloves on her hands, and pinned over her head a piece of soft flannel that had been one of Thor's long petticoats when he was a baby. Thus equipped, she was ready for business. She took from her table a thick paper-backed volume, one of the "line" of paper novels the druggist kept to sell to travelling men. She had bought it, only yesterday, because the first sentence interested her very much, and because she saw, as she glanced over the pages, the magical names of two Russian cities. The book was a poor translation of *Anna Karenina*. Thea opened it at a mark, and fixed her eyes intently upon the small print. The hymns, the sick girl, the resigned black figures were forgotten. It was the night of the ball in Moscow.

Thea would have been astonished if she could have known how, years afterward, when she had need of them, those old faces were to come back to her, long after they were hidden away under the earth; that they would seem to her then as full of meaning, as mysteriously marked by Destiny, as the people who danced the mazurka under the elegant Korsunsky.

XVIII

Mr. Kronborg was too fond of his ease and too sensible to worry his children much about religion. He was more sincere than many preachers, but when he spoke to his family about matters of conduct, it was usually with a regard for keeping up appearances. The church and church work were discussed in the family like the routine of any other business. Sunday was the hard day of the week with them, just as Saturday was the busy day with the merchants on Main Street. Revivals were seasons of extra work and pressure, just as threshing-time was on the farms. Visiting elders had to be lodged and cooked for, the folding-bed in the parlour was let down, and Mrs. Kronborg had to work in the kitchen all day long and attend the night meetings.

During one of these revivals, Thea's sister Anna professed religion with, as Mrs. Kronborg said, "a good deal of fluster." While Anna was going up to the mourners' bench nightly and asking for the prayers of the congregation, she disseminated a general gloom throughout the household, and after she joined the church she took on an air of "set-apartness" that was extremely trying to her brothers and her sister, though they realized that Anna's sanctimoniousness was perhaps a good thing for their father. A preacher ought to have one child who did more than merely acquiesce in religious observances, and Thea and the boys were glad enough that it was Anna and not one of themselves who assumed this obligation.

"Anna, she's American," Mrs. Kronborg used to say. The Scandinavian mould of countenance, more or less marked in each of the other children, was scarcely discernible in her, and she looked enough like other Moonstone girls to be thought pretty. Anna's nature was conventional, like her face. Her position as the minister's eldest daughter was important to her, and she tried to live up to it. She read sentimental religious story-books and emulated the spiritual struggles and magnanimous behaviour of their persecuted heroines. Everything had to be interpreted for Anna. Her opinions about the smallest and most commonplace things were gleaned from the Denver papers, from the church weeklies, from sermons and Sunday-School addresses. Scarcely anything was attractive to her in its natural state—indeed, scarcely anything was decent until it was clothed by the opinion of some authority. Her ideas about habit, character, duty, love, marriage, were grouped under heads, like a book of popular quotations, and were totally unrelated to the emergencies of human living. She discussed all these subjects with other Methodist girls of her age. They would spend hours, for instance, in deciding what they would or would not tolerate in a suitor or a husband, and the frailties of masculine nature were too often a subject of discussion among them. In her behaviour Anna was a harmless girl, mild except where her prejudices were concerned, neat and industrious, with no graver fault than priggishness; but her mind had really shocking habits of classification. The wickedness of Denver and of Chicago, and even of Moonstone, occupied her thoughts too much. She had none of the delicacy that goes with a nature of warm impulses, but the kind of fishy curiosity which justifies itself by an expression of horror.

Thea, and all Thea's ways and friends, seemed indecorous to Anna. She not only felt a grave social discrimination against the Mexicans; she could not forget that Spanish Johnny was a drunkard and that "nobody knew what he did when he ran away from home." Thea pretended, of course, that she liked the Mexicans because they were fond of music; but everyone knew that music was nothing very real, and that it did not matter in a girl's relations with people. What was real, then, and what did matter? Poor Anna!

Anna approved of Ray Kennedy as a young man of steady habits and blameless life, but she regretted that he was an atheist, and that he was not a passenger conductor with brass buttons on his coat. On the whole, she wondered what such an exemplary young man found to like in Thea. Doctor Archie she treated respectfully because of his position in Moonstone, but she *knew* he had kissed the Mexican baritone's pretty daughter, and she had a whole *dossier* of evidence about his behaviour in his hours of relaxation in Denver. He was "fast," and it was because he was "fast" that Thea liked him. Thea always liked that kind of people. Doctor Archie's whole manner with Thea, Anna often told her mother, was too free. He was always putting his hand on Thea's head, or holding her hand while he laughed and looked down at her. The kindlier manifestations of human nature (about which Anna sang and talked, in the interests of which she went to conventions and wore white ribbons) were never realities to her after all. She did not believe in them. It was only in attitudes of protest or reproof, clinging to the cross, that human beings could be even temporarily decent.

Preacher Kronborg's secret convictions were very much like Anna's. He believed that his wife was absolutely good, but there was not a man or woman in his congregation whom he trusted all the way.

Mrs. Kronborg, on the other hand, was likely to find something to admire in almost any human conduct that was positive and energetic. She could always be taken in by the stories of tramps and runaway boys. She went to the circus and admired the bareback riders, who were "likely good enough women in their way." She admired Doctor Archie's fine physique and well-cut clothes as much as Thea did, and said she "felt it was a privilege to be handled by such a gentleman when she was sick."

Soon after Anna became a church member, she began to remonstrate with Thea about practising—playing "secular music"—on Sunday. On one Sunday the dispute in the parlour grew warm and was carried to Mrs. Kronborg in the kitchen. She listened judicially and told Anna to read the chapter about how Naaman the leper was permitted to bow down in the house of Rimmon. Thea went back to the piano, and Anna lingered to say that, since she was in the right, her mother should have supported her.

"No," said Mrs. Kronborg, rather indifferently, "I can't see it that way, Anna. I never forced you to practise, and I don't see as I should keep Thea from it. I like to hear her, and I guess your father does. You and Thea will likely follow different lines, and I don't see as I'm called upon to bring you up alike."

Anna looked meek and abused. "Of course all the church people must hear her. Ours is the only noisy house on this street. You hear what she's playing now, don't you?"

Mrs. Kronborg rose from browning her coffee. "Yes; it's the Blue Danube waltzes. I'm familiar with 'em. If any of the church people come at you, you just send 'em to me. I ain't afraid to speak out on occasion, and I wouldn't mind one bit telling the Ladies' Aid a few things about standard composers." Mrs. Kronborg smiled, and added thoughtfully, "No, I wouldn't mind that one bit."

Anna went about with a reserved and distant air for a week, and Mrs. Kronborg suspected that she held a larger place than usual in her daughter's prayers; but that was another thing she didn't mind.

Although revivals were merely a part of the year's work, like examination week at school, and although Anna's piety impressed her very little, a time came when Thea was perplexed about religion. A scourge of typhoid broke out in Moonstone and several of Thea's schoolmates died of it. She went to their funerals, saw them put into the ground, and wondered a good deal about them. But a certain grim incident, which caused the epidemic, troubled her even more than the death of her friends.

Early in July, soon after Thea's fifteenth birthday, a particularly disgusting sort of tramp came into Moonstone in an empty box-car. Thea was sitting in the hammock in the front yard when he first crawled up to the town from the depot, carrying a bundle wrapped in dirty ticking under one arm, and under the other a wooden box with rusty screening nailed over one end. He had a thin, hungry face covered with black hair. It was just before supper time when he came along, and the street smelled of fried potatoes and fried onions and coffee. Thea saw him sniffing the air greedily and walking slower and slower. He looked over the fence. She hoped he would not stop at their gate, for her mother never turned anyone away, and this was the dirtiest and most utterly wretched-looking tramp she had ever seen. There was a terrible odour about him, too. She caught it even at that distance, and put her handkerchief to her nose. A moment later she was sorry, for she knew that he had noticed it. He looked away and shuffled a little faster.

A few days later, Thea heard that the tramp had camped in an empty shack over on the east edge of town, beside the ravine, and was trying to give a miserable sort of show there. He told the boys who went to see what he was doing that he had travelled with a circus. His bundle contained a filthy clown's suit, and his box held half a dozen rattlesnakes.

Saturday night, when Thea went to the butcher shop to get the chickens for Sunday, she heard the whine of an accordion and saw a crowd before one of the saloons. There she found the tramp, his bony body grotesquely attired in the clown's suit, his face shaved and painted white—the sweat trickling through the paint and washing it away—and his eyes wild and feverish. Pulling the accordion in and out seemed to be almost too great an effort for him, and he panted to the tune of "Marching Through Georgia." After a considerable crowd had gathered, the tramp exhibited his box of snakes, announced that he would now pass the hat, and that when the onlookers had contributed the sum of one dollar, he would eat "one of these living reptiles." The crowd began to cough and murmur, and the saloon-keeper rushed off for the marshal, who arrested the wretch for giving a show without a licence and hurried him away to the calaboose.

The calaboose stood in a sunflower patch—an old hut with a barred window and a padlock on the door. The tramp was utterly filthy and there was no way to give him a bath. The law made no provision to grubstake vagrants, so after the constable had detained the tramp for twenty-four hours, he released him and told him to "get out of town, and get quick." The fellow's rattlesnakes had been killed by the saloon-keeper. He hid in a box-car in the freight yard, probably hoping to get a ride to the next station, but he was found and put out. After that he was seen no more. He had disappeared and left no trace except an ugly, stupid word, chalked on the black paint of the seventy-five-foot standpipe which was the reservoir for the Moonstone watersupply; the same word, in another tongue, that the French soldier shouted at Waterloo to the English officer who bade the Old Guard surrender; a comment on life which the defeated, along the hard roads of the world, sometimes bawl at the victorious.

A week after the tramp excitement had passed over, the city water began to smell and to taste. The Kronborgs had a well in their back yard and did not use city water, but they heard the complaints of their neighbours. At first people said that the town well was full of rotting cottonwood roots, but the engineer at the pumping-station convinced the mayor that the water left the well untainted. Mayors reason slowly, but, the well being eliminated, the official mind had to travel toward the standpipe—there was no other track for it to go in. The standpipe amply rewarded investigation. The tramp had got even with Moonstone. He had climbed the standpipe by the handholds and let himself down into seventy-five feet of cold water, with his shoes and hat and roll of ticking. The city council had a mild panic and passed a new ordinance about tramps. But the fever had already broken out, and several adults and half a dozen children died of it.

Thea had always found everything that happened in Moonstone exciting, disasters particularly so. It was gratifying to read sensational Moonstone items in the Denver paper. But she wished she had not chanced to see the tramp as he came into town that evening, sniffing the supper-laden air. His face remained unpleasantly clear in her memory, and her mind struggled with the problem of his behaviour as if it were a hard page in arithmetic. Even when she was practising, the drama of the tramp kept going on in the back of her head, and she was constantly trying to make herself realize what pitch of hatred or despair could drive a man to do such a hideous thing. She kept seeing him in his bedraggled clown suit, the white paint on his roughly shaven face, playing his accordion before the saloon. She had noticed his lean body, his high, bald forehead that sloped back like a curved metal lid. How could people fall so far out of fortune? She tried to talk to Ray Kennedy about her perplexity, but Ray would not discuss things of that sort with her. It was in his sentimental conception of women that they should be deeply religious, though men were at liberty to doubt and finally to deny. A picture called "The Soul Awakened," popular in Moonstone parlours, pretty well interpreted Ray's idea of woman's spiritual nature.

One evening when she was haunted by the figure of the tramp, Thea went up to Doctor Archie's office. She found him sewing up two bad gashes in the face of a little boy who had been kicked by a mule. After the boy had been bandaged and sent away with his father, Thea helped the doctor wash and put away the surgical instruments. Then she dropped into her accustomed seat beside his desk and began to talk about the tramp. Her eyes were hard and green with excitement, the doctor noticed.

"It seems to me, Doctor Archie, that the whole town's to blame. I'm to blame, myself. I know he saw me hold my nose when he went by. Father's to blame. If he believes the Bible, he ought to have gone to the calaboose and cleaned that man up and taken care of him. That's what I can't understand; do people believe the Bible, or don't they? If the next life is all that matters, and we're put here to get ready for it, then why do we try to make money, or learn things, or have a good time? There's not one person in Moonstone that really lives the way the New Testament says. Does it matter, or doesn't it?"

Doctor Archie swung round in his chair and looked at her, honestly and leniently. "Well, Thea, it seems to me like this. Every people has had its religion. All religions are good, and all are pretty much alike. But I don't see how we could live up to them in the sense you mean. I've thought about it a good deal, and I can't help feeling that while we are in this world we have to live for the best things of this world, and those things are material and positive. Now, most religions are passive, and they tell us chiefly what we should not do." The doctor moved restlessly, and his eyes hunted for something along the opposite wall: "See here, my girl, take out the years of early childhood and the time we spend in sleep and dull old age, and we only have about twenty able, waking years. That's not long enough to get acquainted with half the fine things that have been done in the world, much less to do anything ourselves. I think we ought to keep the Commandments and help other people all we can; but the main thing is to live those twenty splendid years; to do all we can and enjoy all we can."

Doctor Archie met his little friend's searching gaze, the look of acute inquiry which always touched him.

"But poor fellows like that tramp—" She hesitated and wrinkled her forehead.

The doctor leaned forward and put his hand protectingly over hers, which lay clenched on the green felt desk top. "Ugly accidents happen, Thea; always have and always will. But the failures are swept back into the pile and forgotten. They don't leave any lasting scar in the world, and they don't affect the future. The things that last are the good things. The people who forge ahead and do something, they really count."

He saw tears on her cheeks, and he remembered that he had never seen her cry before, not even when she crushed her finger when she was little. He rose and walked to the window, came back and sat down on the edge of his chair.

"Forget the tramp, Thea. This is a great big world, and I want you to get about and see it all. You're going to Chicago some day, and do something with that fine voice of yours. You're going to be a number one musician and make us proud of you. Take Mary Anderson, now; even the tramps are proud of her. There isn't a tramp along the "Q" system who hasn't heard of her. We all like people who do things, even if we only see their faces on a cigar-box lid."

They had a long talk. Thea felt that Doctor Archie had never let himself out to her so much before. It was the most grown-up conversation she had ever had with him. She left his office happy, flattered and stimulated. She ran for a long while about the white, moonlit streets, looking up at the stars and the bluish night, at the quiet houses sunk in black shade, the glittering sand hills. She loved the familiar trees, and the people in those little houses, and she loved the unknown world beyond Denver. She felt as if she were being pulled in two, between the desire to go away forever and the desire to stay forever. She had only twenty years—no time to lose.

Many a night that summer she left Doctor Archie's office with a desire to run and run about those quiet streets until she wore out her shoes, or wore out the streets themselves; when her chest ached and it seemed as if her heart were spreading all over the desert. When she went home, it was not to go to sleep. She used to drag her mattress beside her low window and lie awake for a long while, vibrating with excitement, as a machine vibrates from speed. Life rushed in upon her through that window—or so it seemed. In reality, of course, life rushes from within, not from without. There is no work of art so big or so beautiful that it was not once all contained in some youthful body, like this one which lay on the floor in the moonlight, pulsing with ardour and anticipation. It was on such nights that Thea Kronborg learned the thing that old Dumas meant when he told the Romanticists that to make a drama he needed but one passion and four walls.

XIX

*I*t is well for its peace of mind that the travelling public takes railroads so much for granted. The only men who are incurably nervous about railway travel are the railroad operatives. A railroad man never forgets that the next run may be his turn.

On a single-track road, like that upon which Ray Kennedy worked, the freight trains make their way as best they can between passenger trains. Even when there is such a thing as a freight time-schedule, it is merely a form. Along the one track dozens of fast and slow trains dash in both directions, kept from collision only by the brains in the dispatcher's office. If one passenger train is late, the whole schedule must be revised in an instant; the trains following must be warned, and those moving toward the belated train must be assigned new meeting-places.

Between the shifts and modifications of the passenger schedule, the freight trains play a game of their own. They have no right to the track at any given time, but are supposed to be on it when it is free, and to make the best time they can between passenger trains. A freight train, on a single-track road, gets anywhere at all only by stealing bases.

Ray Kennedy had stuck to the freight service, although he had had opportunities to go into the passenger service at higher pay. He always regarded railroading as a temporary makeshift, until he "got into something," and he disliked the passenger service. No brass buttons for him, he said; too much like a livery. While he was railroading he would wear a jumper, thank you!

The wreck that "caught" Ray was a very commonplace one; nothing thrilling about it, and it got only six lines in the Denver papers. It happened about daybreak one morning, only thirty-two miles from home.

At four o'clock in the morning Ray's train had stopped to take water at Saxony, having just rounded the long curve which lies south of that station. It was Joe Giddy's business to walk back along the curve about three hundred yards and put out torpedoes to warn any train which might be coming up from behind—a freight crew is not notified of trains following, and the brakeman is supposed to protect his train. Ray was so fussy about the punctilious observance of orders that almost any brakeman would take a chance once in a while, from natural perversity.

When the train stopped for water that morning, Ray was at the desk in his caboose, making out his report. Giddy took his torpedoes, swung off the rear platform, and glanced back at the curve. He decided that he would not go back to flag this time. If anything was coming up behind, he could hear it in plenty of time. So he ran forward to look after a hot journal that had been bothering him. In a general way, Giddy's reasoning was sound. If a freight train, or even a passenger train, had been coming up behind them, he could have heard it in time. But as it happened, a light engine, which made no noise at all, was coming—ordered out to help with the freight that was piling up at the other end of the division. This engine got no warning, came round the curve, and struck the caboose, went straight through it, and crashed into the heavy lumber car ahead.

The Kronborgs were just sitting down to breakfast when the night telegraph operator dashed into the yard at a run and hammered on the front door. Gunner answered the knock, and the telegraph operator told him he wanted to see his father a minute, quick. Mr. Kronborg appeared at the door, napkin in hand. The operator was pale and panting.

"Fourteen was wrecked down at Saxony this morning," he shouted, "and Kennedy's all broke up. We're sending an engine down with the doctor, and the operator at Saxony says Kennedy wants you to come along with us and bring your girl."

He stopped for breath.

Mr. Kronborg took off his glasses and began rubbing them with his napkin.

"Bring—I don't understand," he muttered. "How did this happen?"

"No time for that, sir. Getting the engine out now. Your girl, Thea. You'll surely do that for the poor chap. Everybody knows he thinks the world of her." Seeing that Mr. Kronborg showed no indication of having made up his mind, the operator turned to Gunner. "Call your sister, kid. I'm going to ask the girl herself," he blurted out.

"Yes, yes, certainly. Thea," Mr. Kronborg called. He had somewhat recovered himself and reached to the hall hat-rack for his hat.

Just as Thea came out on the front porch, before the operator had had time to explain to her, Doctor Archie's ponies came up to the gate at a brisk trot. The doctor jumped out the moment his driver stopped the team and came up to the bewildered girl without so much as saying good morning to anyone. He took her hand with the sympathetic, reassuring graveness which had helped her at more than one hard time in her life. "Get your hat, my girl. Kennedy's hurt down the road, and he wants you to run down with me. They'll have a car for us. Get into my buggy, Mr. Kronborg. I'll drive you down, and Larry can come for the team."

The driver jumped out of the buggy and Mr. Kronborg and the doctor got in. Thea, still bewildered, sat on her father's knee. Doctor Archie gave his ponies a smart cut with the whip.

When they reached the depot, the engine, with one car attached, was standing on the main track. The engineer had got his steam up, and was leaning out of the cab impatiently. In a moment they were off. The run to Saxony took forty minutes. Thea sat still in her seat while Doctor Archie and her father talked about the wreck. She took no part in the conversation and asked no questions, but occasionally she looked at Doctor Archie with a frightened, inquiring glance, which he answered by an encouraging nod. Neither he nor her father said anything about how badly Ray was hurt.

When the engine stopped near Saxony, the main track was already cleared. As they got out of the car, Doctor Archie pointed to a pile of ties.

"Thea, you'd better sit down here and watch the wreck crew

while your father and I go up and look Kennedy over. I'll come back for you when I get him fixed up."

The two men went off up the sand gulch, and Thea sat down and looked at the pile of splintered wood and twisted iron that had lately been Ray's caboose. She was frightened and absent-minded. She felt that she ought to be thinking about Ray, but her mind kept racing off to all sorts of trivial and irrelevant things. She wondered whether Grace Johnson would be furious when she came to take her music-lesson and found nobody there to give it to her; whether she had forgotten to close the piano last night and whether Thor would get into the new room and mess the keys all up with his sticky fingers; whether Tillie would go upstairs and make her bed for her. Her mind worked fast, but she could fix it upon nothing. The grasshoppers, the lizards, distracted her attention and seemed more real to her than poor Ray.

On their way to the sand bank where Ray had been carried, Doctor Archie and Mr. Kronborg met the Saxony doctor. He shook hands with them.

"Nothing you can do, doctor. I couldn't count the fractures. His back is broken, too. He would not be alive now if he weren't so confoundedly strong, poor chap. No use bothering him. I've given him morphia, one and a half, in eighths."

Doctor Archie hurried on. Ray was lying on a flat canvas litter, under the shelter of a shelving bank, lightly shaded by a slender cottonwood tree. When the doctor and the preacher approached, he looked at them intently.

"Didn't—" he closed his eyes to hide his bitter disappointment.

Doctor Archie knew what was the matter. "Thea's back there, Ray. I'll bring her as soon as I've had a look at you."

Ray looked up. "You might clean me up a trifle, doc. Won't need you for anything else, thank you all the same."

However little there was left of him, that little was certainly Ray Kennedy. His personality was as positive as ever, and the blood and dirt on his face seemed merely accidental, to have nothing to do with the man himself. Doctor Archie told Mr. Kronborg to bring a pail of water, and he began to sponge Ray's face and neck. Mr. Kronborg stood by, nervously rubbing his hands together and trying to think of something to say. Serious situations always embarrassed him and made him formal, even when he felt real sympathy.

"In times like this, Ray," he brought out at last, crumpling up his handkerchief in his long fingers—"in times like this, we don't want to forget the Friend that sticketh closer than a brother."

Ray looked up at him; a lonely, disconsolate smile played over his mouth and his square cheeks. "Never mind about all that, *padre,*" he said quietly. "Christ and me fell out long ago."

There was a moment of silence. Then Ray took pity on Mr. Kronborg's embarrassment. "You go back for the little girl, *padre.* I want a word with the doc in private."

Ray talked to Doctor Archie for a few moments, then stopped suddenly, with a broad smile. Over the doctor's shoulder he saw Thea coming up the gulch, in her pink chambray dress, carrying her sun-hat by the strings. Such a yellow head! He often told himself that he was "perfectly foolish about her hair." The sight of her, coming, went through him softly, like the morphia. "There she is," he whispered. "Get the old preacher out of the way, doc. I want to have a little talk with her."

Doctor Archie looked up. Thea was hurrying and yet hanging back. She was more frightened than he had thought she would be. She had gone with him to see very sick people and had always been steady and calm. As she came up, she looked at the ground, and he could see that she had been crying.

Ray Kennedy made an unsuccessful effort to put out his hand.

"Hello, little kid, nothing to be afraid of. Darned if I don't believe they've gone and scared you! Nothing to cry about. I'm the same old goods, only a little dented. Sit down on my coat there, and keep me company. I've got to lay still a bit."

Doctor Archie and Mr. Kronborg disappeared. Thea cast a timid glance after them, but she sat down resolutely and took Ray's hand.

"You ain't scared now, are you?" he asked affectionately. "You were a regular brick to come, Thee. Did you get any breakfast?"

"No, Ray, I'm not scared. Only I'm dreadful sorry you're hurt, and I can't help crying."

His broad, earnest face, languid from the opium and smiling with such simple happiness, reassured her. She drew nearer to him and lifted his hand to her knee. He looked at her with his clear, shallow blue eyes. How he loved everything about that face and head! How many nights in his cupola, looking up the track, he had seen that face in the darkness; through the sleet and snow, or in the soft blue air when the moonlight slept on the desert.

"You needn't bother to talk, Thee. The doctor's medicine

makes me sort of dopey. But it's nice to have company. Kind of cosy, don't you think? Pull my coat under you more. It's a darned shame I can't wait on you."

"No, no, Ray. I'm all right. Yes, I like it here. And I guess you ought not to talk much, ought you? If you can sleep, I'll stay right here, and be awful quiet. I feel just as much at home with you as ever, now."

That simple, humble, faithful something in Ray's eyes went straight to Thea's heart. She did feel comfortable with him, and happy to give him so much happiness. It was the first time she had ever been conscious of that power to bestow intense happiness by simply being near anyone. She always remembered this day as the beginning of that knowledge. She bent over him and put her lips softly to his cheek.

Ray's eyes filled with light. "Oh, do that again, kid!" he said impulsively. Thea kissed him on the forehead, blushing faintly. Ray held her hand fast and closed his eyes with a deep sigh of happiness. The morphia and the sense of her nearness filled him with content. The gold mine, the oil well, the copper ledge—all pipe-dreams, he mused, and this was a dream, too. He might have known it before. It had always been like that; the things he admired had always been away out of his reach: a college education, a gentleman's manner, an Englishman's accent—things over his head. And Thea was farther out of his reach than all the rest put together. He had been a fool to imagine it, but he was glad he had been a fool. She had given him one grand dream. Every mile of his run, from Moonstone to Denver, was painted with the colours of that hope. Every cactus knew about it. But now that it was not to be, he knew the truth. Thea was never meant for any rough fellow like him—hadn't he really known that all along, he asked himself? She wasn't meant for common men. She was like wedding cake, a thing to dream on. He raised his eyelids a little. She was stroking his hand and looking off into the distance. He felt in her face that look of unconscious power that Wunsch had seen there. Yes, she was bound for the big terminals of the world; no way stations for her. His lids drooped. In the dark he could see her as she would be after a while; in a box at the Tabor Grand in Denver, with diamonds on her neck and a tiara in her yellow hair, with all the people looking at her through their opera-glasses, and a United States Senator, maybe, talking to her. "Then you'll remember me!" He opened his eyes, and they were full of tears.

Thea leaned closer. "What did you say, Ray? I couldn't hear."

"Then you'll remember me," he whispered.

The spark in his eye, which is one's very self, caught the spark in hers that was herself, and for a moment they looked into each other's natures. Thea realized how good and how great-hearted he was, and he realized about her many things. When that elusive spark of personality retreated in each of them, Thea still saw in his wet eyes her own face, very small, but much prettier than the cracked glass at home had ever shown it. It was the first time she had seen her face in that kindest mirror a woman can ever find.

Ray had felt things in that moment when he seemed to be looking into the very soul of Thea Kronborg. Yes, the gold mine, the oil well, the copper ledge, they had all got away from him, as things will; but he had backed a winner once in his life! With all his might he gave his faith to the broad little hand he held. He wished he could leave her the rugged strength of his body to help her through with it all. He would have liked to tell her a little about his old dream—there seemed long years between him and it already—but to tell her now would somehow be unfair; wouldn't be quite the straightest thing in the world. Probably she knew, anyway.

He looked up quickly. "You know, don't you, Thee, that I think you are just the finest thing I've struck in this world?"

The tears ran down Thea's cheeks. "You're too good to me, Ray. You're a lot too good to me," she faltered.

"Why, kid," he murmured, "everybody in this world's going to be good to you!"

Doctor Archie came to the gulch and stood over his patient. "How's it going?"

"Can't you give me another punch with your pacifier, doc? The little girl had better run along now." Ray released Thea's hand. "See you later, Thee."

She got up and moved away aimlessly, carrying her hat by the strings. Ray looked after her with the exaltation born of bodily pain and said between his teeth, "Always look after that girl, doc. She's a queen!"

Thea and her father went back to Moonstone on the one-o'clock passenger. Doctor Archie stayed with Ray Kennedy until he died, late in the afternoon.

XX

On Monday morning, the day after Ray Kennedy's funeral, Doctor Archie called at Mr. Kronborg's study, a little room behind the church. Mr. Kronborg did not write out his sermons, but spoke from notes jotted upon small pieces of cardboard in a kind of shorthand of his own. As sermons go, they were not worse than most. His conventional rhetoric pleased the majority of his congregation, and Mr. Kronborg was generally regarded as a model preacher. He did not smoke, he never touched spirits. His indulgence in the pleasures of the table was an endearing bond between him and the women of his congregation. He ate enormously, with a zest which seemed incongruous with his spare frame.

This morning the doctor found him opening his mail and reading a pile of advertising circulars with deep attention.

"Good morning, Mr. Kronborg," said Doctor Archie, sitting down. "I came to see you on business. Poor Kennedy asked me to look after his affairs for him. Like most railroad men he spent his wages, except for a few investments in mines which don't look to me very promising. But his life was insured for six hundred dollars in Thea's favour."

Mr. Kronborg wound his feet about the standard of his desk chair. "I assure you, doctor, this is a complete surprise to me."

"Well, it's not very surprising to me," Doctor Archie went on. "He talked to me about it the day he was hurt. He said he wanted the money to be used in a particular way, and in no other." Doctor Archie paused meaningly.

Mr. Kronborg fidgeted. "I am sure Thea would observe his wishes in every respect."

"No doubt; but he wanted me to see that you agreed to his plan. It seems that for some time Thea has wanted to go away to study music. It was Kennedy's wish that she should take this money and go to Chicago this winter. He felt that it would be an advantage to her in a business way; that even if she came back here to teach, it would give her more authority and make her position here more comfortable."

Mr. Kronborg looked a little startled. "She is very young," he hesitated; "she is barely seventeen. Chicago is a long way from home. We would have to consider. I think, Doctor Archie, we had better consult Mrs. Kronborg."

"I think I can bring Mrs. Kronborg around, if I have your consent. I've always found her pretty level-headed. I have several old classmates practising in Chicago. One is a throat specialist. He has a good deal to do with singers. He probably knows the best piano-teachers and could recommend a boarding-house where music students stay. I think Thea needs to get among a lot of young people who are clever like herself. Here she has no companions but old fellows like me. It's not a natural life for a young girl. She'll either get warped, or wither up before her time. If it will make you and Mrs. Kronborg feel any easier, I'll be glad to take Thea to Chicago and see that she gets started right. This throat man I speak of is a big fellow in his line, and if I can get him interested, he may be able to put her in the way of a good many things. At any rate, he'll know the right teachers. Of course, six hundred dollars won't take her very far, but even one winter there would be a great advantage. I think Kennedy sized the situation up exactly."

"Perhaps; I don't doubt it. You are very kind, Doctor Archie." Mr. Kronborg was ornamenting his desk-blotter with hieroglyphics. "I should think Denver might be better. There we could watch over her. She is very young."

Doctor Archie rose. "Kennedy didn't mention Denver. He said Chicago, repeatedly. Under the circumstances, it seems to me we ought to try to carry out his wishes exactly, if Thea is willing."

"Certainly, certainly. Thea is conscientious. She would not waste her opportunities." Mr. Kronborg paused. "If Thea were your own daughter, doctor, would you consent to such a plan, at her present age?"

"I most certainly should. In fact, if she were my daughter, I'd have sent her away before this. She's a most unusual child, and she's only wasting herself here. At her age she ought to be learning, not teaching. She will never learn so quickly and easily as she will right now."

"Well, doctor, you had better talk it over with Mrs. Kronborg. I make it a point to defer to her wishes in such matters. She understands all her children perfectly. I may say that she has all a mother's insight, and more."

Doctor Archie smiled. "Yes, and then some. I feel quite confident about Mrs. Kronborg. We usually agree. Good morning."

Doctor Archie stepped out into the hot sunshine and walked

rapidly toward his office, with a determined look on his face. He found his waiting-room full of patients, and it was one o'clock before he had dismissed the last one.

Then he shut his door and took a drink before going over to the hotel for his lunch. He smiled as he locked his cupboard. "I feel almost as gay as if I were going to get away for a winter myself," he thought.

Afterward Thea could never remember much about that summer, or how she lived through her impatience. She was to set off with Doctor Archie on the fifteenth of October, and she gave lessons until the first of September. Then she began to get her clothes ready, and spent whole afternoons in the village dressmaker's stuffy, littered little sewing-room. Thea and her mother made a trip to Denver to buy the materials for her dresses. Ready-made clothes for girls were not to be had in those days. Miss Spencer, the dressmaker, declared that she could do handsomely by Thea if they would only let her carry out her own ideas. But Mrs. Kronborg and Thea felt that Miss Spencer's most daring productions might seem out of place in Chicago, so they restrained her with a firm hand. Tillie, who always helped Mrs. Kronborg with the family sewing, was for letting Miss Spencer challenge Chicago on Thea's person. Since Ray Kennedy's death Thea had become more than ever one of Tillie's heroines. Tillie swore each of her friends to secrecy, and, coming home from church or leaning over the fence, told them the most touching stories about Ray's devotion, and how Thea would "never get over it."

Tillie's confidences stimulated the general discussion of Thea's venture. This discussion went on, upon front porches and in back yards, pretty much all summer. Some people approved of Thea's going to Chicago, but most people did not. There were others who changed their minds about it every day.

Tillie said she wanted Thea to have a ball dress "above all things." She bought a fashion book especially devoted to evening clothes and looked hungrily over the coloured plates, picking out costumes that would be becoming to "a blonde." She wanted Thea to have all the gay clothes she herself had always longed for—clothes she often told herself she needed "to recite in."

"Tillie," Thea used to cry impatiently, "can't you see that if Miss Spencer tried to make one of those things, she'd make me look like a circus girl? Anyhow, I don't know anybody in Chicago. I won't be going to parties."

Tillie always replied with a knowing toss of her head: "You see!

You'll be in society before you know it. There ain't many girls as accomplished as you."

On the morning of the fifteenth of October the Kronborg family—all of them but Gus, who couldn't leave the store—started for the station an hour before train time. Charley had taken Thea's trunk and "telescope" to the depot in his delivery wagon early that morning. Thea wore her new blue serge travelling-dress, chosen for its serviceable qualities. She had done her hair up carefully, and had put a pale-blue ribbon around her throat, under a little lace collar that Mrs. Kohler had crocheted for her. As they went out of the gate, Mrs. Kronborg looked her over thoughtfully. Yes, that blue ribbon went very well with the dress, and with Thea's eyes. Thea had a rather unusual touch about such things, she reflected comfortably. Tillie always said that Thea was "so indifferent to dress," but her mother noticed that she usually put her clothes on well. She felt the more at ease about letting Thea go away from home, because she had good sense about her clothes and never tried to dress up too much. Her colouring was so individual, she was so unusually fair, that in the wrong clothes she might easily have been "conspicuous."

It was a fine morning, and the family set out from the house in good spirits. Thea was quiet and calm. She had forgotten nothing, and she clung tightly to her handbag, which held her trunk-key and all of her money that was not in an envelope pinned to her chemise. Thea walked behind the others, holding Thor by the hand, and this time she did not feel that the procession was too long. Thor was uncommunicative that morning, and would only talk about how he would rather get a sand burr in his toe every day than wear shoes and stockings. As they passed the cottonwood grove where Thea often used to bring him in his cart, she asked him who would take him for nice long walks after sister went away.

"Oh, I can walk in our yard," he replied unappreciatively. "I guess I can make a pond for my duck."

Thea leaned down and looked into his face. "But you won't forget about sister, will you?" Thor shook his head. "And won't you be glad when sister comes back and can take you over to Mrs. Kohler's to see the pigeons?"

"Yes, I'll be glad. But I'm going to have a pigeon my own self."

"But you haven't got any little house for one. Maybe Axel would make you a little house."

"Oh, her can live in the barn, her can." Thor drawled indifferently.

Thea laughed and squeezed his hand. She always liked his sturdy matter-of-factness. Boys ought to be like that, she thought.

When they reached the depot, Mr. Kronborg paced the platform somewhat ceremoniously with his daughter. Any member of his flock would have gathered that he was giving her good counsel about meeting the temptations of the world. He did, indeed, begin to admonish her not to forget that talents come from our Heavenly Father and are to be used for His glory, but he cut his remarks short and looked at his watch. He believed that Thea was a religious girl, but when she looked at him with that intent, that passionately inquiring gaze which used to move even Wunsch, Mr. Kronborg suddenly felt his eloquence fail. Thea was like her mother, he reflected; you couldn't put much sentiment across with her. As a usual thing, he liked girls to be a little more responsive. He liked them to blush at his compliments; as Mrs. Kronborg candidly said, "Father could be very soft with the girls." But this morning he was thinking that hard-headedness was a reassuring quality in a daughter who was going to Chicago alone.

Mr. Kronborg believed that big cities were places where people went to lose their identity and to be wicked. He himself, when he was a student at the seminary—he coughed and opened his watch again. He knew, of course, that a great deal of business went on in Chicago, that there was an active Board of Trade, and that hogs and cattle were slaughtered there. But when, as a young man, he had stopped over in Chicago, he had not interested himself in the commercial activities of the city. He remembered it as a place full of cheap shows and dance-halls and boys from the country who were behaving disgustingly.

Doctor Archie drove up to the station about ten minutes before the train was due. His man tied the ponies and stood holding the doctor's alligator-skin bag—very elegant, Thea thought it. Mrs. Kronborg did not burden the doctor with warnings and cautions. She said again that she hoped he could get Thea a comfortable place to stay, where they had good beds, and she hoped the landlady would be a woman who'd had children of her own. "I don't go much on old maids looking after girls," she remarked as she took a pin out of her own hat and thrust it into Thea's blue turban. "You'll be sure to lose your hatpins on the train, Thea. It's better to have an extra one in case." She tucked in a little curl that had escaped from Thea's careful twist. "Don't forget to brush your dress often, and pin it up to the curtains of your berth to-night, so it won't wrinkle. If you get it wet, have a tailor press it before it draws."

She turned Thea about by the shoulders and looked her over a last time. Yes, she looked very well. She wasn't pretty, exactly—her face was too broad and her nose was too big. But she had that lovely skin, and she looked fresh and sweet. She had always been a sweet-smelling child. Her mother had always liked to kiss her, when she happened to think of it.

The train whistled in, and Mr. Kronborg carried the canvas "telescope" into the car. Thea kissed them all good-bye. Tillie cried, but she was the only one who did. They all shouted things up at the closed window of the Pullman car, from which Thea looked down at them as from a frame, her face glowing with excitement, her turban a little tilted in spite of three hatpins. She had already taken off her new gloves to save them. Mrs. Kronborg reflected that she would never see just that same picture again, and as Thea's car slid off along the rails, she wiped a tear from her eye. "She won't come back a little girl," Mrs. Kronborg said to her husband as they turned to go home. "Anyhow, she's been a sweet one."

While the Kronborg family were trooping slowly homeward, Thea was sitting in the Pullman, her telescope in the seat beside her, and her handbag tightly gripped in her fingers. Doctor Archie had gone into the smoker. He thought she might be a little tearful, and that it would be kinder to leave her alone for a while. Her eyes did fill once, when she saw the last of the sand hills and realized that she was going to leave them behind for a long while. They always made her think of Ray, too. She had had such good times with him out there.

But, of course, it was herself and her own adventure that mattered to her. If youth did not matter so much to itself, it would never have the heart to go on. Thea was surprised that she did not feel a deeper sense of loss at leaving her old life behind her. It seemed, on the contrary, as she looked out at the yellow desert speeding by, that she had left very little. Everything that was essential seemed to be right there in the car with her. She lacked nothing. She even felt more compact and confident than usual. She was all there, and something else was there, too—in her heart, was it, or under her cheek? Anyhow, it was about her somewhere, that warm sureness, that sturdy little companion with whom she shared a secret.

When Doctor Archie came in from the smoker, she was sitting still, looking intently out of the window and smiling, her lips a little parted, her hair in a blaze of sunshine. The doctor thought she was the prettiest thing he had ever seen, and very funny, with her telescope and big handbag. She made him feel jolly, and a little mournful, too. He knew that the splendid things of life are few, after all, and so very easy to miss.

Part II

The Song of
The Lark

I

Thea and Doctor Archie had been gone from Moonstone four days. On the afternoon of the nineteenth of October they were in a street-car, riding through the depressing, unkept wastes of North Chicago, on their way to call upon the Reverend Lars Larsen, a friend to whom Mr. Kronborg had written. Thea was still staying at the rooms of the Young Women's Christian Association, and was miserable and homesick there. The housekeeper watched her in a way that made her uncomfortable. Things had not gone very well, so far. The noise and confusion of a big city tired and disheartened her. She had not had her trunk sent to the Christian Association rooms because she did not want to double cartage charges, and now she was running up a bill for storage on it. The contents of her grey telescope were becoming untidy, and it seemed impossible to keep one's face and hands clean in Chicago. She felt as if she were still on the train, travelling without enough clothes to keep clean. She wanted another nightgown, and it did not occur to her that she could buy one. There were other clothes in her trunk that she needed very much, and she seemed no nearer a place to stay than when she arrived in the rain, on that first disillusioning morning.

Doctor Archie had gone at once to his friend Hartley Evans, the throat specialist, and had asked him to tell him of a good piano-teacher and direct him to a good boarding-house. Doctor Evans said he could easily tell him who was the best piano-teacher in Chicago but that most students' boarding-houses were "abominable places, where girls got poor food for body and mind." He gave Doctor Archie several addresses, however, and the doctor went to look the places over. He left Thea in her room, for she seemed tired and was not at all like herself. His inspection of boarding-houses was not encouraging. The only place that seemed to him at all desirable was full, and the mistress of the house could not give Thea a room in which she could have a piano. She said Thea might use the piano in her parlour; but when Doctor Archie went to look at the parlour he found a girl talking to a young man on one of the corner sofas. Learning that the boarders received all their callers there, he gave up that house, too, as hopeless.

So when they set out to make the acquaintance of Mr. Larsen on the afternoon he had appointed, the question of a lodging was still undecided. The Swedish Reform Church was in a sloughy, weedy district, near a group of factories. The church itself was a very neat little building. The parsonage, next door, looked clean and comfortable, and there was a well-kept yard about it, with a picket fence. Thea saw several little children playing under a swing, and wondered why ministers always had so many. When they rang at the parsonage door, a capable-looking Swedish servant girl answered the bell and told them that Mr. Larsen's study was in the church, and that he was waiting for them there.

Mr. Larsen received them very cordially. The furniture in his study was so new and the pictures were so heavily framed that Thea thought it looked more like the waiting-room of the fashionable Denver dentist to whom Doctor Archie had taken her that summer than like a preacher's study. There were even flowers in a glass vase on the desk. Mr. Larsen was a small, plump man, with a short, yellow beard, very white teeth, and a little turned-up nose on which he wore gold-rimmed eye-glasses. He looked about thirty-five, but he was growing bald, and his thin hair was parted above his left ear and brought up over the bare spot on the top of his head. He looked cheerful and agreeable. He wore a blue coat and no cuffs.

After Doctor Archie and Thea sat down on a slippery leather couch, the minister asked for an outline of Thea's plans. Doctor Archie explained that she meant to study piano with Andor Harsanyi; that they had already seen him, that Thea had played for him and he said he would be glad to teach her.

Mr. Larsen lifted his pale eyebrows and rubbed his plump white hands together. "But he is a concert pianist already. He will be very expensive."

"That's why Miss Kronborg wants to get a church position if possible. She has not money enough to see her through the winter. There's no use her coming all the way from Colorado and studying with a second-rate teacher. My friends here tell me Harsanyi is the best."

"Oh, very likely! I have heard him play with Thomas. You Western people do things on a big scale. There are half a dozen teachers that I should think—However, you know what you want." Mr. Larsen showed his contempt for such extravagant standards by a shrug. He felt that Doctor Archie was trying to impress him. He had succeeded, indeed, in bringing out the doctor's stiffest manner. Mr. Larsen went on to explain that he managed the music in his church himself, and drilled his choir, though the tenor was the official choirmaster. Unfortunately, there were no vacancies in his choir just now. He had four voices, very good ones. He looked away from Doctor Archie and glanced at Thea. She looked troubled, even a little frightened when he said this, and drew in her lower lip. She, certainly, was not pretentious, if 'her protector was. He continued to study her. She was sitting on the lounge, her knees far apart, her gloved hands lying stiffly in her lap, like a country girl. Her turban, which seemed a little too big for her, had got tilted in the wind—it was always windy in that part of Chicago—and she looked tired. She wore no veil, and her hair, too, was the worse for the wind and dust. When he said he had all the voices he required, he noticed that her gloved hands shut tightly. Mr. Larsen reflected that she was not, after all, responsible for the lofty manner of her father's physician; that she was not even responsible for her father, whom he remembered as a tiresome fellow. As he watched her tired, worried face, he felt sorry for her.

"All the same, I would like to try your voice," he said, turning pointedly away from her companion. "I am interested in voices. Can you sing to the violin?"

"I guess so," Thea replied dully. "I don't know. I never tried."

Mr. Larsen took his violin out of the case and began to tighten the keys. "We might go into the lecture-room and see how it goes. I can't tell much about a voice by the organ. The violin is really the proper instrument to try a voice." He opened a door at the back of his study, pushed Thea gently through it, and looking over his shoulder to Doctor Archie said, "Excuse us, sir. We will be back soon."

Doctor Archie chuckled. All preachers were alike, officious and on their dignity; liked to deal with women and girls, but not with men. He took up a thin volume from the minister's desk. To his amusement it proved to be a book of *Devotional and Kindred Poems; by Mrs. Aurelia S. Larsen*. He looked them over, thinking that the world changed very little. He could remember when the wife of his father's minister had published a volume of verses, which all the church members had to buy and all the children were encouraged to read. His grandfather had made a face at the book and said, "Puir body!" Both ladies seemed to have chosen the same subjects, too: Jephthah's Daughter, Rizpah, David's Lament for Absalom, etc. The doctor found the book very amusing.

The Reverend Mr. Lars Larsen was a reactionary Swede. His father came to Iowa in the sixties, married a Swedish girl who was ambitious, like himself, and they had moved to Kansas and taken up land under the Homestead Act. After that, they had bought land and leased it from the

Government, acquired land in every possible way. They worked like horses, both of them; indeed, they would never have used any horse-flesh they owned as they used themselves. They reared a large family and worked their sons and daughters as mercilessly as they worked themselves; all of them but Lars. Lars was the fourth son, and he was born lazy. He seemed to bear the mark of overstrain on the part of his parents. Even in his cradle he was an example of physical inertia; anything to lie still. When he was a growing boy, his mother had to drag him out of bed every morning, and he had to be driven to his chores. At school he had a model "attendance record," because he found getting his lessons easier than farm work. He was the only one of the family who went through the high school, and by the time he graduated he had already made up his mind to study for the ministry, because it seemed to him the least laborious of all callings. In so far as he could see, it was the only business in which there was practically no competition, in which a man was not all the time pitted against other men who were willing to work themselves to death. His father stubbornly opposed Lars's plan, but after keeping the boy at home for a year and finding how useless he was on the farm, he sent him to a theological seminary—as much to conceal his laziness from the neighbours as because he did not know what else to do with him.

Larsen, like Peter Kronborg, got on well in the ministry, because he got on well with the women. His English was no worse than that of most young preachers of American parentage, and he made the most of his skill with the violin. He was supposed to exert a very desirable influence over young people and to stimulate their interest in church work. He married an American girl, and when his father died he got his share of the property—which was very considerable. He invested his money carefully and was that rare thing, a preacher of independent means. His white, well-kept hands were his result—the evidence that he worked out his life successfully in the way that pleased him. His Kansas brothers hated the sight of his hands.

Larsen liked all the softer things of life—in so far as he knew about them. He slept late in the morning, was fussy about his food, and read a great many novels, preferring sentimental ones. He did not smoke, but he ate a great deal of candy "for his throat," and always kept a box of chocolate drops in the upper right-hand drawer of his desk. He always bought season tickets for the symphony concerts, and he played his violin for women's culture clubs. He did not wear cuffs, except on Sunday, because he believed that a free wrist facilitated his violin practice. When he drilled his choir, he always held his hand with the little and index fingers curved higher than the other two, like a noted German conductor he had heard. On the whole, the

Reverend Larsen was not an insincere man; he merely spent his life resting and playing, to make up for the time his forebears had wasted grubbing in the earth. He was simple-hearted and kind; he enjoyed his candy and his children and his sacred cantatas. He could work energetically at almost any form of play.

Doctor Archie was deep in "The Lament of Mary Magdalen" when Mr. Larsen and Thea came back to the study. From the minister's expression he judged that Thea had succeeded in interesting him.

Mr. Larsen seemed to have forgotten his hostility toward him, and addressed him frankly as soon as he entered. He stood holding his violin, and as Thea sat down he pointed to her with his bow:

"I have just been telling Miss Kronborg that though I cannot promise her anything permanent, I might give her something for the next few months. My soprano is a young married woman and is temporarily indisposed. She would be glad to be excused from her duties for a while. I like Miss Kronborg's singing very much, and I think she would benefit by the instruction in my choir. Singing here might very well lead to something else. We pay our soprano only eight dollars a Sunday, but she always gets ten dollars for singing at funerals. Miss Kronborg has a sympathetic voice, and I think there would be a good deal of demand for her at funerals. Several American churches apply to me for a soloist on such occasions, and I could help her to pick up quite a little money that way."

This sounded lugubrious to Doctor Archie, who had a physician's dislike of funerals, but he tried to accept the suggestion cordially.

"Miss Kronborg tells me she is having some trouble getting located," Mr. Larsen went on with animation, still holding his violin. "I would advise her to keep away from boarding-houses altogether. Among my parishioners there are two German women, a mother and daughter. The daughter is a Swede by marriage, and clings to the Swedish Church. They live near here and they rent some of their rooms. They have now a large room vacant, and have asked me to recommend someone. They have never taken boarders, but Mrs. Lorch, the mother, is a good cook—at least, I am always glad to take supper with her—and I think I could persuade her to let this young woman partake of the family table. The daughter, Mrs. Andersen, is musical, too, and sings in the Mozart Society. I think they might like to have a music student in the house. You speak German, I suppose?" he turned to Thea.

"Oh, no; a few words. I don't know the grammar," she murmured.

Doctor Archie noticed that her eyes looked alive again, not

frozen as they had looked all morning. "If this fellow can help her, it's not for me to be stand-offish," he said to himself.

"Do you think you would like to stay in such a quiet place, with old-fashioned people?" Mr. Larsen asked. "I shouldn't think you could find a better place to work if that's what you want."

"I think mother would like to have me with people like that," Thea replied. "And I'd be glad to settle down 'most anywhere. I'm losing time."

"Very well, there's no time like the present. Let us go to see Mrs. Lorch and Mrs. Andersen."

The minister put his violin in its case and caught up a black-and-white checked travelling-cap that he wore when he rode his high Columbia wheel. The three left the church together.

II

So Thea did not go to a boarding-house after all. When Doctor Archie left Chicago she was comfortably settled with Mrs. Lorch, and her happy reunion with her trunk somewhat consoled her for his departure.

Mrs. Lorch and her daughter lived half a mile from the Swedish Reform Church, in an old square frame house, with a porch supported by frail pillars, set in a damp yard full of big lilac bushes. The house, which had been left over from country times, needed paint badly, and looked gloomy and despondent among its smart Queen Anne neighbours. There was a big back yard with two rows of apple trees and a grape arbour, and a warped walk, two planks wide, which led to the coal-bins at the back of the lot. Thea's room was on the second floor, overlooking this back yard, and she understood that in the winter she must carry up her own coal and kindling from the bin. There was no furnace in the house, no running water except in the kitchen, and that was why the room rent was small. All the rooms were heated by stoves, and the lodgers pumped the water they needed from the cistern under the porch, or from the well at the entrance of the grape arbour. Old Mrs. Lorch could never bring herself to have costly improvements made in her house; indeed, she had very little money. She preferred to keep the house just as her husband built it, and she thought her way of living good enough for plain people.

Thea's room was large enough to admit a rented upright piano without crowding. It was, the widowed daughter said, "a double room that had always before been occupied by two gentlemen"; the piano now took the place of a second occupant. There was an ingrain carpet on the floor, green ivy leaves on a red ground, and clumsy, old-fashioned walnut furniture. The bed was very wide, and the mattress thin and hard. Over the fat pillows were "shams" embroidered in Turkey red, each with a flowering scroll—one with "Gute' Nacht," the other with "Guten Morgen." The dresser was so huge that Thea wondered how it had ever been got into the house and up the narrow stairs. Besides an old horsehair armchair, there were two low plush "spring-rockers," against the massive pedestals of which one was always stumbling in the dark. Thea sat in the dark a good deal those first weeks, and sometimes a painful bump against one of those brutally immovable pedestals roused her temper and pulled her out of a heavy hour. The wall-paper was brownish yellow, with blue flowers. When it was put on, the carpet, certainly, had not been consulted. There was only one picture on the wall when Thea moved in: a large coloured print of a brightly lighted church in a snow-storm, on Christmas Eve, with greens hanging about the stone doorway and arched windows. There was something warm and home-like about this picture, and Thea grew fond of it. One day, on her way into town to take her lesson, she stopped at a bookstore and bought a photograph of the Naples bust of Julius Caesar. This she had framed, and hung it on the big bare wall behind her stove. It was a curious choice, but she was at the age when people do inexplicable things. She had been interested in Caesar's *Commentaries* when she left school to begin teaching, and she loved to read about great generals; but these facts would scarcely explain her wanting that grim bald head to share her daily existence. It seemed a strange freak, when she bought so few things, and when she had, as Mrs. Andersen said to Mrs. Lorch, "no pictures of the composers at all."

Both the widows were kind to her, but Thea liked the mother better. Old Mrs. Lorch was fat and jolly, with a red face, always shining as if she had just come from the stove, bright little eyes, and hair of several colours. Her own hair was one cast of iron-grey, her switch another, and her false front still another. Her clothes always smelled of savoury cooking, except when she was dressed for church or *Kaffeeklatsch,* and then she smelled of bay rum or of the lemon-verbena sprig which she tucked inside her puffy black kid glove. Her cooking justified all that Mr. Larsen had said of it, and Thea had never been so well nourished before.

The daughter, Mrs. Andersen—Irene, her mother called her—
was a different sort of woman altogether. She was perhaps forty years old,
angular, big-boned, with large, thin features, light-blue eyes, and dry,
yellow hair, the bang tightly frizzed. She was pale, anaemic, and sentimental. She had married the youngest son of a rich, arrogant Swedish family
who were lumber merchants in St. Paul. There she dwelt during her
married life. Oscar Andersen was a strong, full-blooded fellow who had
counted on a long life and had been rather careless about his business affairs.
He was killed by the explosion of a steam boiler in the mills, and his brothers
managed to prove that he had very little stock in the big business. They had
strongly disapproved of his marriage and they agreed among themselves that
they were entirely justified in defrauding his widow, who, they said,
"would only marry again and give some fellow a good thing of it." Mrs.
Andersen would not go to law with the family which had always snubbed
and wounded her—she felt the humiliation of being thrust out more than
she felt her impoverishment; so she went back to Chicago to live with her
widowed mother on an income of five hundred a year. This experience had
given her sentimental nature an incurable hurt. Something withered away
in her. Her head had a downward droop; her step was soft and apologetic,
even in her mother's house, and her smile had the sickly, uncertain flicker
that so often comes from a secret humiliation. She was affable and yet
shrinking, like one who has come down in the world, who has known
better clothes, better carpets, better people, brighter hopes. Her husband
was buried in the Andersen lot in St. Paul, with a locked iron fence around
it. She had to go to his eldest brother for the key when she went to say
good-bye to his grave. She clung to the Swedish Church because it had
been her husband's church.

As her mother had no room for her household belongings, Mrs.
Andersen had brought home with her only her bedroom set, which now
furnished her own room at Mrs. Lorch's. There she spent most of her time,
doing fancy-work or writing letters to sympathizing German friends in St.
Paul, surrounded by keepsakes and photographs of the burly Oscar Andersen. Thea, when she was admitted to this room, and shown these photographs, found herself wondering, like the Andersen family, why such a
lusty, gay-looking fellow ever thought he wanted this pallid, long-cheeked
woman, whose manner was always that of withdrawing, and who must
have been rather thin-blooded even as a girl.

Mrs. Andersen was certainly a depressing person. It sometimes
annoyed Thea very much to hear her insinuating knock on the door, her

flurried explanation of why she had come, as she backed toward the stairs. Mrs. Andersen admired Thea greatly. She thought it a distinction to be even a "temporary soprano"—Thea called herself so quite seriously—in the Swedish Church. She also thought it distinguished to be a pupil of Harsanyi's. She consid' red Thea very handsome, very Swedish, very talented. She fluttered about the upper floor when Thea was practising. In short, she tried to make a heroine of her, just as Tillie Kronborg had always done, and Thea was conscious of something of the sort. When she was working and heard Mrs. Andersen tiptoeing past her door, she used to shrug her shoulders and wonder whether she was always to have a Tillie diving furtively about her in some disguise or other.

At the dressmaker's Mrs. Andersen recalled Tillie even more painfully. After her first Sunday in Mr. Larsen's choir, Thea saw that she must have a proper dress for morning service. Her Moonstone party dress might do to wear in the evening, but she must have one frock that could stand the light of day. She, of course, knew nothing about Chicago dressmakers, so she let Mrs. Andersen take her to a German woman whom she recommended warmly. The German dressmaker was excitable and dramatic. Concert dresses, she said, were her specialty. In her fitting-room there were photographs of singers in the dresses she had made them for this or that *Sängerfest*. She and Mrs. Andersen together achieved a costume which would have warmed Tillie Kronborg's heart. It was clearly intended for a woman of forty, with violent tastes. There seemed to be a piece of every known fabric in it somewhere. When it came home, and was spread out on her huge bed, Thea looked it over and told herself candidly that it was "a horror." However, her money was gone, and there was nothing to do but make the best of the dress. She never wore it except, as she said, "to sing in," as if it were an unbecoming uniform. When Mrs. Lorch and Irene told her that she "looked like a little bird-of-Paradise in it," Thea shut her teeth and repeated to herself words she had learned from Joe Giddy and Spanish Johnny.

In these two good women Thea found faithful friends, and in their house she found the quiet and peace which helped her to support the great experiences of that winter.

III

*A*ndor Harsanyi had never had a pupil in the least like Thea Kronborg. He had never had one more intelligent, and he had never had one so ignorant. When Thea sat down to take her first lesson from him, she had never heard a work by Beethoven or a composition by Chopin. She knew their names vaguely. Wunsch had been a musician once, long before he wandered into Moonstone, but when Thea awoke his interest there was not much left of him. From him Thea had learned something about the works of Gluck and Bach, and he used to play her some of the compositions of Schumann. In his trunk he had a mutilated score of the F sharp minor sonata, which he had heard Clara Schumann play at a festival in Leipsic. Though his powers of execution were at such a low ebb, he used to play at this sonata for his pupil and managed to give her some idea of its beauty. When Wunsch was a young man, it was still daring to like Schumann; enthusiasm for his work was considered an expression of youthful waywardness. Perhaps that was why Wunsch remembered him best. Thea studied some of the *Kinderszenen* with him, as well as some little sonatas by Mozart and Clementi. But for the most part Wunsch stuck to Czerny and Hummel.

Harsanyi found in Thea a pupil with sure, strong hands, one who read rapidly and intelligently, who had, he felt, a richly gifted nature. But she had been given no direction, and her ardour was unawakened. She had never heard a symphony orchestra. The literature of the piano was an undiscovered world to her. He wondered how she had been able to work so hard when she knew so little of what she was working toward. She had been taught according to the old Stuttgart method; stiff back, stiff elbows, a very formal position of the hands. The best thing about her preparation was that she had developed an unusual power of work. He noticed at once her way of charging at difficulties. She ran to meet them as if they were foes she had long been seeking, seized them as if they were destined for her and she for them. Whatever she did well, she took for granted. Her eagerness aroused all the young Hungarian's chivalry. Instinctively one went to the rescue of a creature who had so much to overcome and who struggled so hard. He used to tell his wife that Miss Kronborg's hour took more out of him than half a dozen other lessons. He usually kept her long over time; he changed her lessons about so that he could do so, and often gave her time at the end of the day when he could talk to her afterward and play for her a little from what he happened to be studying. It was always interesting to play for her. Sometimes she was so silent that he wondered, when she left him, whether she had got anything out of it. But a week later, two weeks later, she would give back his idea again in a way that set him vibrating.

All this was very well for Harsanyi; an interesting variation in the routine of teaching. But for Thea Kronborg, that winter was almost beyond enduring. She always remembered it as the happiest and wildest and saddest of her life. Things came too fast for her; she had not had enough preparation. There were times when she came home from her lesson and lay upon her bed hating Wunsch and her family, hating a world that had let her grow up so ignorant; when she wished that she could die then and there, and be born over again to begin anew. She said something of this kind once to her teacher, in the midst of a bitter struggle. Harsanyi turned the light of his wonderful eye upon her—poor fellow, he had but one, though that was set in such a handsome head—and said slowly: "Every artist makes himself born. It is very much harder than the other time, and longer. Your mother did not bring anything into the world to play piano. That you must bring into the world yourself."

This comforted Thea temporarily, for it seemed to give her a chance. But a great deal of the time she was comfortless. Her letters to Doctor Archie were brief and business-like. She was not apt to chatter much, even in the stimulating company of people she liked, and to chatter on paper was simply impossible for her. If she tried to write him anything definite about her work, she immediately scratched it out as being only partially true, or not true at all. Nothing that she could say about her studies seemed unqualifiedly true, once she put it down on paper.

Late one afternoon, when she was thoroughly tired and wanted to struggle on into the dusk, Harsanyi, tired too, threw up his hands and laughed at her. "Not to-day, Miss Kronborg. That sonata will keep: it won't run away. Even if you and I should not waken up to-morrow, it will be there."

Thea turned to him fiercely. "No, it isn't here unless I have it—not for me," she cried passionately. "Only what I hold in my two hands is there for me!"

Harsanyi made no reply. He took a deep breath and sat down

again. "The second movement now, quietly, with the shoulders relaxed."

There were hours, too, of great exaltation; when she was at her best and became a part of what she was doing and ceased to exist in any other sense. There were other times when she was so shattered by ideas that she could do nothing worth while; when they trampled over her like an army and she felt as if she were bleeding to death under them. She sometimes came home from a late lesson so exhausted that she could eat no supper. If she tried to eat, she was ill afterward. She used to throw herself upon the bed and lie there in the dark, not thinking, not feeling, but evaporating. That same night, perhaps, she would waken up rested and calm, and as she went over her work in her mind, the passages seemed to become something of themselves, to take a sort of pattern in the darkness. She had never learned to work away from the piano until she came to Harsanyi, and it helped her more than anything had ever helped her before.

She almost never worked now with the sunny, happy contentment that had filled the hours when she worked with Wunsch—"like a fat horse turning a sorghum mill," she said bitterly to herself. Then, by sticking to it, she could always do what she set out to do. Now, everything that she really wanted was impossible; a *cantabile* like Harsanyi's, for instance, instead of her own cloudy tone. No use telling her she might have it in ten years. She wanted it now. She wondered how she had ever found other things interesting: books, *Anna Karenina*—all that seemed so unreal and on the outside of things. She was not born a musician, she decided; there was no other way of explaining it.

Sometimes she got so nervous at the piano that she left it, and snatching up her hat and cape went out and walked, hurrying through the streets like Christian fleeing from the City of Destruction. And while she walked she cried. There was scarcely a street in the neighbourhood that she had not cried up and down before that winter was over. The thing that used to lie under her cheek, that sat so warmly over her heart when she glided away from the sand hills that autumn morning, was far from her. She had come to Chicago to be with it, and it had deserted her, leaving in its place a painful longing, an unresigned despair.

Harsanyi knew that his interesting pupil—"the savage blonde," one of his male students called her—was sometimes very unhappy. He saw in her discontent a curious definition of character. He would have said that a girl with so much musical feeling, so intelligent, with good training of eye and hand, would, when thus suddenly introduced to the great literature of the piano, have found boundless happiness. But he soon learned that she was not able to forget her own poverty in the richness of the world he opened to her. Often, when he played to her, her face was the picture of restless misery. She would sit crouching forward, her elbows on her knees, her brows drawn together and her grey-green eyes smaller than ever, reduced to mere pinpoints of cold, piercing light. Sometimes, while she listened, she would swallow hard, two or three times, and look nervously from left to right, drawing her shoulders together. "Exactly," he thought, "as if she were being watched, or as if she were naked and heard someone coming."

On the other hand, when she came several times to see Mrs. Harsanyi and the two babies, she was like a little girl, jolly and gay and eager to play with the children, who loved her. The little daughter, Tanya, liked to touch Miss Kronborg's yellow hair and pat it, saying, "Dolly, dolly," because it was of a colour much oftener seen on dolls than on people. But if Harsanyi opened the piano and sat down to play, Miss Kronborg gradually drew away from the children, retreated to a corner and became sullen or troubled. Mrs. Harsanyi noticed this, also, and thought it very strange behaviour.

Another thing that puzzled Harsanyi was Thea's apparent lack of curiosity. Several times he offered to give her tickets to concerts, but she said she was too tired or that it "knocked her out to be up late." Harsanyi did not know that she was singing in a choir, and had often to sing at funerals, neither did he realize how much her work with him stirred her and exhausted her. Once, just as she was leaving his studio, he called her back and told her he could give her some tickets that had been sent him for Emma Juch that evening. Thea fingered the black wool on the edge of her plush cape and replied, "Oh, thank you, Mr. Harsanyi, but I have to wash my hair to-night."

Mrs. Harsanyi liked Miss Kronborg thoroughly. She saw in her the making of a pupil who would reflect credit upon Harsanyi. She felt that the girl could be made to look strikingly handsome, and that she had the kind of personality which takes hold of audiences. Moreover, Miss Kronborg was not in the least sentimental about her husband. Sometimes from the show pupils one had to endure a good deal. "I like that girl," she used to say, when Harsanyi told her of one of Thea's *gaucheries*. "She doesn't sigh every time the wind blows. With her one swallow doesn't make a summer."

Thea told them very little about herself. She was not naturally communicative, and she found it hard to feel confidence in new people.

She did not know why, but she could not talk to Harsanyi as she could to Doctor Archie, or to Johnny and Mrs. Tellamantez. With Mr. Larsen she felt more at home, and when she was walking, she sometimes stopped at his study to eat candy with him or to hear the plot of the novel he happened to be reading.

One evening, toward the middle of December, Thea was to dine with the Harsanyis. She arrived early, to have time to play with the children before they went to bed. Mrs. Harsanyi took her into her own room and helped her take off her country "fascinator" and her clumsy plush cape. Thea had bought this cape at a big department store and had paid sixteen dollars and fifty cents for it. As she had never paid more than ten dollars for a coat before, that seemed to her a large price. It was very heavy and not very warm, ornamented with a showy pattern in black disks, and trimmed around the collar and the edges with some kind of black wool that "crocked" badly in snow or rain. It was lined with a cotton stuff called "farmer's satin." Mrs. Harsanyi was one woman in a thousand. As she lifted this cape from Thea's shoulders and laid it on her white bed, she wished that her husband did not have to charge pupils like this one for their lessons. Thea wore her Moonstone party dress, white organdie, made with a "V" neck and elbow sleeves, and a blue sash. She looked very pretty in it, and around her throat she had a string of pink coral and tiny white shells that Ray once brought her from Los Angeles. Mrs. Harsanyi noticed that she wore high heavy shoes which needed blacking. The choir in Mr. Larsen's church stood behind a railing, so Thea did not pay much attention to her shoes.

"You have nothing to do to your hair," Mrs. Harsanyi said kindly, as Thea turned to the mirror. "However it happens to lie, it's always pretty. I admire it as much as Tanya does."

Thea glanced awkwardly away from her and looked stern, but Mrs. Harsanyi knew that she was pleased. They went into the living-room, behind the studio, where the two children were playing on the big rug before the coal grate. Andor, the boy, was six, a sturdy, handsome child, and the little girl was four. She came tripping to meet Thea, looking like a little doll in her white net dress—her mother made all her clothes. Thea picked her up and hugged her. Mrs. Harsanyi excused herself and went to the dining-room. She kept only one maid and did a good deal of the housework herself, besides cooking her husband's favourite dishes for him. She was still under thirty, a slender, graceful woman, gracious, intelligent, and capable. She adapted herself to circumstances with a well-bred ease which solved many of her husband's difficulties, and kept him, as he said, from feeling cheap and down at the heel. No musician ever had a better wife. Unfortunately her beauty was of a very frail and impressionable kind, and she was beginning to lose it. Her face was too thin now, and there were often dark circles under her eyes.

Left alone with the children, Thea sat down on Tanya's little chair—she would rather have sat on the floor, but was afraid of rumpling her dress—and helped them play "cars" with Andor's iron railway set. She showed him new ways to lay his tracks and how to make switches, set up his Noah's Ark village for stations and packed the animals in the open coal cars to send them to the stockyards. They worked out their shipment so realistically that when Andor put the two little reindeer into the stock car, Tanya snatched them out and began to cry, saying she wasn't going to have all their animals killed.

Harsanyi came in, jaded and tired, and asked Thea to go on with her game, as he was not equal to talking much before dinner. He sat down and made pretence of glancing at the evening paper, but he soon dropped it. After the railroad began to grow tiresome, Thea went with the children to the lounge in the corner, and played for them the game with which she used to amuse Thor for hours together behind the parlour stove at home, making shadow pictures against the wall with her hands. Her fingers were very supple, and she could make a duck and a cow and a sheep and a fox and a rabbit and even an elephant. Harsanyi, from his low chair, watched them, smiling. The boy was on his knees, jumping up and down with the excitement of guessing the beasts, and Tanya sat with her feet tucked under her and clapped her frail little hands. Thea's profile, in the lamplight, teased his fancy. Where had he seen a head like it before?

When dinner was announced, little Andor took Thea's hand and walked to the dining-room with her. The children always had dinner with their parents and behaved very nicely at table. "Mamma," said Andor seriously as he climbed into his chair and tucked his napkin into the collar of his blouse, "Miss Kronborg's hands are every kind of animal there is."

His father laughed. "I wish somebody would say that about my hands, Andor."

When Thea dined at the Harsanyis' before, she noticed that there was an intense suspense from the moment they took their places at the table until the master of the house had tasted the soup. He had a theory that if the soup went well, the dinner would go well; but if the soup was poor, all was lost. To-night he tasted his soup and smiled, and Mrs. Harsanyi sat

more easily in her chair and turned her attention to Thea. Thea loved their
dinner table, because it was lighted by candles in silver candlesticks, and she
had never seen a table so lighted anywhere else. There were always flowers,
too. To-night there was a little orange tree, with oranges on it, that one of
Harsanyi's pupils had sent him at Thanksgiving time. After Harsanyi had
finished his soup and a glass of red Hungarian wine, he lost his fagged look
and became cordial and witty. He persuaded Thea to drink a little wine
to-night. The first time she dined with them, when he urged her to taste
the glass of sherry beside her plate, she astonished them by telling them that
she "never drank."

Harsanyi was then a man of thirty-two. He was to have a very
brilliant career, but he did not know it then. Theodore Thomas was perhaps
the only man in Chicago who felt that Harsanyi might have a great future.
Harsanyi belonged to the softer Slavic type, and was more like a Pole than
a Hungarian. He was tall, slender, active, with sloping, graceful shoulders
and long arms. His head was very fine, strongly and delicately modelled,
and, as Thea put it, "so independent." A lock of his thick brown hair usually
hung over his forehead. His eye was wonderful; full of light and fire when
he was interested, soft and thoughtful when he was tired or melancholy.
The meaning and power of two very fine eyes must all have gone into this
one—the right one, fortunately, the one next his audience when he played.
He believed that the glass eye which gave one side of his face such a dull,
blind look, had ruined his career, or rather had made a career impossible for
him. Harsanyi lost his eye when he was twelve years old, in a Pennsylvania
mining town where explosives happened to be kept too near the frame
shanties in which the company packed newly arrived Hungarian families.

His father was a musician and a good one, but he had cruelly
overworked the boy; keeping him at the piano for six hours a day and
making him play in cafés and dance-halls for half the night. Andor ran away
and crossed the ocean with an uncle, who smuggled him through the port
as one of his own many children. The explosion in which Andor was hurt
killed a score of people, and he was thought lucky to get off with an eye.
He still had a clipping from a Pittsburgh paper, giving a list of the dead and
injured. He appeared as "Harsanyi, Andor, left eye and slight injuries about
the head." That was his first American "notice"; and he kept it. He held
no grudge against the coal company; he understood that the accident was
merely one of the things that are bound to happen in the general scramble
of American life, where everyone comes to grab and takes his chance.

While they were having dessert, Thea asked Harsanyi if she

could change her Tuesday lesson from afternoon to morning. "I have to be at a choir rehearsal in the afternoon, to get ready for the Christmas music, and I expect it will last until late."

Harsanyi put down his fork and looked up. "A choir rehearsal? You sing in a church?"

"Yes. A little Swedish church, over on the North Side."

"Why did you not tell us?"

"Oh, I'm only a temporary. The regular soprano is not well."

"How long have you been singing there?"

"Ever since I came. I had to get a position of some kind," Thea explained, flushing, "and the preacher took me on. He runs the choir himself. He knew my father, and I guess he took me to oblige."

Harsanyi tapped the tablecloth with the ends of his fingers. "But why did you never tell us? Why are you so reticent with us?"

Thea looked shyly at him from under her brows. "Well, it's certainly not very interesting. It's only a little church. I only do it for business reasons."

"What do you mean? Don't you like to sing? Don't you sing well?"

"I like it well enough, but, of course, I don't know anything about singing. I guess that's why I never said anything about it. Anybody that's got a voice can sing in a little church like that."

Harsanyi laughed softly—a little scornfully, Thea thought. "So you have a voice, have you?"

Thea hesitated, looked intently at the candles and then at Harsanyi. "Yes," she said firmly; "I have got some, anyway."

"Good girl," said Mrs. Harsanyi, nodding and smiling at Thea. "You must let us hear you sing after dinner."

This remark seemingly closed the subject, and when the coffee was brought they began to talk of other things. Harsanyi asked Thea how she happened to know so much about the way in which freight trains are operated, and she tried to give him some idea of how the people in little desert towns live by the railway and order their lives by the coming and going of the trains. When they left the dining-room, the children were sent to bed and Mrs. Harsanyi took Thea into the studio. She and her husband usually sat there in the evening.

Although their apartment seemed so elegant to Thea it was small and cramped. The studio was the only spacious room. The Harsanyis were poor, and it was due to Mrs. Harsanyi's good management that their lives, even in hard times, moved along with dignity and order. She had long ago found out that bills or debts of any kind frightened her husband and crippled his working power. He said they were like bars on the windows, and shut out the future; they meant that just so many hundred dollars' worth of his life was debilitated and exhausted before he got to it. So Mrs. Harsanyi saw to it that they never owed anything. Harsanyi was not extravagant, although he was sometimes careless about money. Quiet and order and his wife's good taste were the things that meant most to him. After these, good food, good cigars, a little good wine. He wore his clothes until they were shabby, until his wife had to ask the tailor to come to the house and measure him for new ones. His neckties she usually made herself, and when she was in the shops she always kept her eye open for silks in very dull or pale shades, greys and olives, warm blacks and browns.

When they went into the studio, Mrs. Harsanyi took up her embroidery and Thea sat down beside her on a low stool, her hands clasped about her knees. While his wife and his pupil talked, Harsanyi sank into a *chaise longue* in which he sometimes snatched a few moments' rest between his lessons, and smoked. He sat well out of the circle of the lamplight, his feet to the fire. His feet were slender and well shaped, always elegantly shod. Much of the grace of his movements was due to the fact that his feet were almost as sure and flexible as his hands. He listened to the conversation with amusement. He admired his wife's tact and kindness with crude young people; she taught them so much without seeming to be instructing. When the clock struck nine, Thea said she must be going home.

Harsanyi rose and flung away his cigarette. "Not yet. We have just begun the evening. Now you are going to sing for us. I have been waiting for you to recover from dinner. Come, what shall it be?" He crossed to the piano.

Thea laughed and shook her head, locking her elbows still tighter about her knees. "Thank you, Mr. Harsanyi, but if you really make me sing, I'll accompany myself. You couldn't stand it to play the sort of things I have to sing."

As Harsanyi still pointed to the chair at the piano, she left her stool and went to it, while he returned to his *chaise longue*. Thea looked at the keyboard uneasily for a moment, then she began "Come, ye Disconsolate," the hymn Wunsch had always liked to hear her sing. Mrs. Harsanyi glanced questioningly at her husband, but he was looking intently at the toes of his boots, shading his forehead with his long white hand. When Thea finished the hymn, she did not turn around, but immediately began

"The Ninety and Nine." Mrs. Harsanyi kept trying to catch her husband's eye; but his chin only sank lower on his collar.

> "There were ninety and nine that safely lay
> In the shelter of the fold,
> But one was out on the hills away,
> Far off from the gates of gold."

Harsanyi looked at her, then back at the fire.

> "Rejoice, for the Shepherd has found his
>   sheep."

Thea turned on the chair and grinned. "That's about enough, isn't it? That song got me my job. The preacher said it was sympathetic," she minced the word, remembering Mr. Larsen's manner.

Harsanyi drew himself up in his chair, resting his elbows on the low arms. "Yes? That is better suited to your voice. Your upper tones are good, above G. I must teach you some songs. Don't you know anything—pleasant?"

Thea shook her head ruefully. "I'm afraid I don't. Let me see Perhaps" she turned to the piano and put her hands on the keys. "I used to sing this for Mr. Wunsch a long while ago. It's for contralto, but I'll try it." She frowned at the keyboard a moment, played the few introductory measures, and began

> *"Ach, ich habe sie verloren."*

She had not sung it for a long time, and it came back like an old friendship. When she finished, Harsanyi sprang from his chair and dropped lightly upon his toes, a kind of *entre-chat* that he sometimes executed when he formed a sudden resolution, or when he was about to follow a pure intuition, against reason. His wife knew from his manner that he was intensely interested. He went quickly to the piano.

"Sing that again. There is nothing the matter with your low voice, my girl. I will play for you. Let your voice out." Without looking at her, he began the accompaniment. Thea drew back her shoulders, relaxed them instinctively, and sang.

When she finished the aria, Harsanyi beckoned her nearer.

"Sing *ah—ah* for me, as I indicate." He kept his right hand on the keyboard and put his left to her throat, placing the tips of his delicate fingers over her larynx. "Again—until your breath is gone.—Trill between the two tones, always; good! Again; excellent!—Now up—stay there. E and F. Not so good, is it? F is always a hard one.—Now, try the half-tone.—That's right, there's nothing difficult about it. Now, pianissimo, *ah—ah*. Now, swell it, *ah—ah*.—Again, follow my hand.—Now, carry it down.—Anybody ever tell you anything about your breathing?"

"Mr. Larsen says I have an unusually long breath," Thea replied with spirit.

Harsanyi smiled. "So you have, so you have. That was what I meant. Now, once more; carry it up and then down, *ah—ah*." He put his hand back to her throat and sat with his head bent, his one eye closed. He loved to hear a big voice throb in a relaxed, natural throat, and he was thinking that no one had ever felt this voice vibrate before. It was like a wild bird that had flown into his studio on Middleton Street from goodness knew how far! No one knew that it had come, or even that it existed; least of all the strange, crude girl in whose throat it beat its passionate wings. What a simple thing it was, he reflected; why had he never guessed it before? Everything about her indicated it—the big mouth, the wide jaw and chin, the strong white teeth, the deep laugh. The machine was so simple and strong, seemed to be so easily operated. She sang from the bottom of herself. Her breath came from down where her laugh came from, the deep laugh which Mrs. Harsanyi had once called "the laugh of the people." A relaxed throat, a voice that lay on the breath, that had never been forced off the breath; it rose and fell in the air-column like the little balls which are put to shine in the jet of a fountain. The voice did not thin as it went up; the upper tones were as full and rich as the lower, produced in the same way and as unconsciously, only with deeper breath.

At last Harsanyi threw back his head and rose. "You must be tired, Miss Kronborg."

When she replied, she startled him; he had forgotten how hard and full of burrs her speaking voice was. "No," she said, "singing never tires me."

Harsanyi pushed back his hair with a nervous hand. "I don't know much about the voice, but I shall take liberties and teach you some good songs. I think you have a very interesting voice."

"I'm glad if you like it. Good night, Mr. Harsanyi." Thea went with Mrs. Harsanyi to get her wraps.

When Mrs. Harsanyi came back to her husband, she found him walking restlessly up and down the room.

"Don't you think her voice wonderful, dear?" she asked.

"I scarcely know what to think. All I really know about that girl is that she tires me to death. We must not have her often. If I did not have my living to make, then—" He dropped into a chair and closed his eyes. "How tired I am! What a voice!"

IV

After that evening Thea's work with Harsanyi changed somewhat. He insisted that she should study some songs with him, and after almost every lesson he gave up half an hour of his own time to practising them with her. He did not pretend to know much about voice production, but so far, he thought, she had acquired no really injurious habits. A healthy and powerful organ had found its own method, which was not a bad one. He wished to find out a good deal before he recommended a vocal teacher. He never told Thea what he thought about her voice, and made her general ignorance of anything worth singing his pretext for the trouble he took. That was in the beginning. After the first few lessons his own pleasure and hers were pretext enough. The singing came at the end of the lesson hour, and they both treated it as a form of relaxation.

Harsanyi did not say much even to his wife about his discovery. He brooded upon it in a curious way. He found that these unscientific singing lessons stimulated him in his own study. After Miss Kronborg left him, he often lay down in his studio for an hour before dinner, with his head full of musical ideas, with an effervescence in his brain which he had sometimes lost for weeks together under the grind of teaching. He had never got so much back for himself from any pupil as he did from Miss Kronborg. From the first she had stimulated him; something in her personality invariably affected him. Now that he was feeling his way toward her voice, he found her more interesting than ever before. She lifted the tedium of the winter for him, gave him curious fancies and reveries. Musically, she was sympathetic to him. Why all this was true, he never asked himself. He had learned that one must take where and when one can the mysterious mental irritant that rouses one's imagination; that it is not to be had by

order. She often wearied him, but she never bored him. Under her crude-
ness and brusque hardness, he felt there was a nature quite different, of
which he never got so much as a hint except when she was at the piano,
or when she sang. It was toward this hidden creature that he was trying, for
his own pleasure, to find his way. In short, Harsanyi looked forward to his
hour with Thea for the same reason that poor Wunsch had sometimes
dreaded his; because she stirred him more than anything she did could
adequately explain.

One afternoon Harsanyi, after the lesson, was standing by the
window putting some collodion on a cracked finger, and Thea was at the
piano trying over "Die Lorelei" which he had given her last week to
practise. It was scarcely a song which a singing master would have given her,
but he had his own reasons. How she sang it mattered only to him and to
her. He was playing his own game now, without interference; he suspected
that he could not do so always.

When she finished the song, she looked back over her shoulder
at him and spoke thoughtfully. "That wasn't right, at the end, was it?"

"No, that should be an open, flowing tone, something like
this"—he waved his fingers rapidly in the air. "You get the idea?"

"No, I don't. Seems a queer ending, after the rest."

Harsanyi corked his little bottle and dropped it into the pocket
of his velvet coat. "Why so? Shipwrecks come and go, *Märchen* come and
go, but the river keeps right on. There you have your open, flowing tone."

Thea looked intently at the music. "I see," she said dully. "Oh,
I see!" she repeated quickly and turned to him a glowing countenance. "It
is the river.—Oh, yes, I get it now!" She looked at him but long enough
to catch his glance, then turned to the piano again. Harsanyi was never quite
sure where the light came from when her face suddenly flashed out at him
in that way. Her eyes were too small to account for it, though they glittered
like green ice in the sun. At such moments her hair was yellower, her skin
whiter, her cheeks pinker, as if a lamp had suddenly been turned up inside
of her. She went at the song again:

> *"Ich weiss nicht, was soll es bedeuten,*
> *Dass ich so traurig bin."*

A kind of happiness vibrated in her voice. Harsanyi noticed how
much and how unhesitatingly she changed her delivery of the whole song,
the first part as well as the last. He had often noticed that she could not think

a thing out in passages. Until she saw it as a whole, she wandered like a blind man surrounded by torments. After she once had her "revelation," after she got the idea that to her—not always to him—explained everything, then she went forward rapidly. But she was not always easy to help. She was sometimes impervious to suggestion; she would stare at him as if she were deaf and ignore everything he told her to do. Then, all at once, something would happen in her brain and she would begin to do all that he had been for weeks telling her to do, without realizing that he had ever told her.

To-night Thea forgot Harsanyi and his finger. She finished the song only to begin it with fresh enthusiasm.

> *"Und das hat mit ihrem Singen*
> *Die Lorelei gethan."*

She sat there singing it until the darkening room was so flooded with it that Harsanyi threw open a window.

"You really must stop it, Miss Kronborg. I shan't be able to get it out of my head to-night."

Thea laughed tolerantly as she began to gather up her music. "Why, I thought you had gone, Mr. Harsanyi. I like that song."

That evening at dinner Harsanyi sat looking intently into a glass of heavy yellow wine; boring into it, indeed, with his one eye, when his face suddenly broke into a smile.

"What is it, Andor?" his wife asked.

He smiled again, this time at her, and took up the nutcrackers and a Brazil nut. "Do you know," he said in a tone so intimate and confidential that he might have been speaking to himself—"do you know, I like to see Miss Kronborg get hold of an idea. In spite of being so talented, she's not quick. But when she does get an idea, it fills her up to the eyes. She had my room so reeking of a song this afternoon that I couldn't stay there."

Mrs. Harsanyi looked up quickly, " 'Die Lorelei,' you mean? One couldn't think of anything else anywhere in the house. I thought she was possessed. But don't you think her voice is wonderful sometimes?"

Harsanyi tasted his wine slowly. "My dear, I've told you before that I don't know what I think about Miss Kronborg, except that I'm glad there are not two of her. I sometimes wonder whether she is not glad. Fresh as she is at it all, I've occasionally fancied that, if she knew how, she would like to—diminish." He moved his left hand out into the air as if he were suggesting a *diminuendo* to an orchestra.

V

*B*y the first of February Thea had
been in Chicago almost four months, and she did not know much more
about the city than if she had never quitted Moonstone. She was, as
Harsanyi said, incurious. Her work took most of her time, and she found
that she had to sleep a good deal. It had never before been so hard to get
up in the morning. She had the bother of caring for her room, and she had
to build her fire and bring up her coal. Her routine was frequently interrupted by a message from Mr. Larsen summoning her to sing at a funeral.
Every funeral took half a day, and the time had to be made up. When Mrs.
Harsanyi asked her if it did not depress her to sing at funerals, she replied
that she "had been brought up to go to funerals and didn't mind."

Thea never went into shops unless she had to, and she felt no
interest in them. Indeed, she shunned them, as places where one was sure
to be parted from one's money in some way. She was nervous about
counting her change, and she could not accustom herself to having her
purchases sent to her address. She felt much safer with her bundles under
her arm.

During this first winter Thea got no city consciousness. Chicago
was simply a wilderness through which one had to find one's way. She felt
no interest in the general briskness and zest of the crowds. The crash and
scramble of that big, rich, appetent Western city she did not take in at all,
except to notice that the noise of the drays and street-cars tired her. The
brilliant window displays, the splendid furs and stuffs, the gorgeous flower
shops, the gay candy shops, she scarcely noticed. At Christmas time she did
feel some curiosity about the toy stores, and she wished she held Thor's little
mittened fist in her hand as she stood before the windows. The jewellers'
windows, too, had a strong attraction for her—she had always liked bright
stones. When she went into the city, she used to brave the biting lake winds
and stand gazing in at the displays of diamonds and pearls and emeralds; the
tiaras and necklaces and earrings, on white velvet. These seemed very well
worth while to her, things worth coveting.

Mrs. Lorch and Mrs. Andersen often told each other it was

strange that Miss Kronborg had so little initiative about "visiting points of interest." When Thea came to live with them, she had expressed a wish to see two places: Montgomery Ward and Company's big mail-order store, and the packing-houses, to which all the hogs and cattle that went through Moonstone were bound. One of Mrs. Lorch's lodgers worked in a packing-house, and Mrs. Andersen brought Thea word that she had spoken to Mr. Eckman and he would gladly take her to Packingtown. Eckman was a toughish young Swede, and he thought it would be something of a lark to take a pretty girl through the slaughter-houses. But he was disappointed. Thea neither grew faint nor clung to the arm he kept offering her. She asked innumerable questions and was impatient because he knew so little of what was going on outside of his own department. When they got off the street-car and walked back to Mrs. Lorch's house in the dusk, Eckman put her hand in his overcoat pocket—she had no muff—and kept squeezing it ardently until she said, "Don't do that; my ring cuts me." That night he told his roommate that he "could have kissed her as easy as rolling off a log, but she wasn't worth the trouble." As for Thea, she had enjoyed the afternoon very much, and wrote her father a brief but clear account of what she had seen.

One night at supper, Mrs. Andersen was talking about the ex-hibit of students' work she had seen at the Art Institute that afternoon. Several of her friends had sketches in the exhibit. Thea, who always felt that she was behindhand in courtesy to Mrs. Andersen, thought that here was an opportunity to show interest without committing herself to anything. "Where is that, the Institute?" she asked absently.

Mrs. Andersen clasped her napkin in both hands. "The Art Institute? Our beautiful Art Institute on Michigan Avenue? Do you mean to say you have never visited it?"

"Oh, is it the place with the big lions out in front? I remember; I saw it when I went to Montgomery Ward's. Yes, I thought the lions were beautiful."

"But the pictures! Didn't you visit the galleries?"

"No. The sign outside said it was a pay day. I've always meant to go back, but I haven't happened to be down that way since."

Mrs. Lorch and Mrs. Andersen looked at each other. The old mother spoke, fixing her shining little eyes upon Thea across the table. "Ah, but Miss Kronborg, there are old masters! Oh, many of them, such as you could not see anywhere out of Europe."

"And Corots," breathed Mrs. Andersen, tilting her head feel-ingly. "Such examples of the Barbizon school!" This was meaningless to Thea, who did not read the art columns of the Sunday *Inter-Ocean* as Mrs. Andersen did.

"Oh, I'm going there some day," she reassured them. "I like to look at oil paintings."

One bleak day in February, when the wind was blowing clouds of dirt like a Moonstone sandstorm, dirt that filled your eyes and ears and mouth, Thea fought her way across the unprotected space in front of the Art Institute and into the doors of the building. She did not come out again until the closing hour. In the street-car, on the long cold ride home, while she sat staring at the waistcoat buttons of a fat strap-hanger, she had a serious reckoning with herself. She seldom thought about her way of life, about what she ought or ought not to do; usually there was but one obvious and important thing to be done. But that afternoon she remonstrated with herself severely. She told herself that she was missing a great deal; that she ought to be more willing to take advice and to go to see things. She was sorry that she had let months pass without going to the Art Institute. After this she would go once a week.

The Institute proved, indeed, a place of retreat, as the sand hills or the Kohlers' garden used to be; a place where she could forget Mrs. Andersen's tiresome overtures of friendship, the stout contralto in the choir whom she so unreasonably hated, and even, for a little while, the torment of her work. That building was a place in which she could relax and play, and she could hardly ever play now. On the whole, she spent more time with the casts than with the pictures. They were at once more simple and more perplexing; and some way they seemed more important, harder to overlook. It never occurred to her to buy a catalogue, so she called most of the casts by names she made up for them. Some of them she knew; the Dying Gladiator she had read about in "Childe Harold" almost as long ago as she could remember; he was strongly associated with Doctor Archie and childish illnesses. The Venus di Milo puzzled her; she could not see why people thought her so beautiful. She told herself over and over that she did not think the Apollo Belvedere "at all handsome." Better than anything else she liked a great equestrian statue of an evil, cruel-looking general with an unpronounceable name. She used to walk round and round this terrible man and his terrible horse, frowning at him, brooding upon him, as if she had to make some momentous decision about him.

The casts, when she lingered long among them, always made her gloomy. It was with a lightening of the heart, a feeling of throwing off the old miseries and old sorrows of the world, that she ran up the wide staircase to the pictures. There she liked best the ones that told stories. There was a painting by Gérôme called "The Pasha's Grief" which always made her wish for Gunner and Axel. The Pasha was seated on a rug, beside a green candle almost as big as a telegraph pole, and before him was stretched his dead tiger, a splendid beast, and there were pink roses scattered about him. She loved, too, a picture of some boys bringing in a newborn calf on a litter, the cow walking beside it and licking it. The Corot which hung next to this painting she did not like or dislike; she never saw it.

But in that same room there was a picture—oh, that was the thing she ran upstairs so fast to see! That was her picture. She imagined that nobody cared for it but herself, and that it waited for her. That was a picture indeed. She liked even the name of it, "The Song of the Lark." The flat country, the early morning light, the wet fields, the look in the girl's heavy face—well, they were all hers, anyhow, whatever was there. She told herself that that picture was "right." Just what she meant by this, it would take a clever person to explain. But to her the word covered the almost boundless satisfaction she felt when she looked at the picture.

Before Thea had any idea how fast the weeks were flying, before Mr. Larsen's "permanent" soprano had returned to her duties, spring came; windy, dusty, strident, shrill; a season almost more violent in Chicago than the winter from which it releases one, or the heat to which it eventually delivers one. One sunny morning the apple trees in Mrs. Lorch's back yard burst into bloom, and for the first time in months Thea dressed without building a fire. The morning shone like a holiday, and for her it was to be a holiday. There was in the air that sudden, treacherous softness which makes the Poles who work in the packing-houses get drunk. At such times beauty is necessary, and in Packingtown there is no place to get it except at the saloons, where one can buy for a few hours the illusion of comfort, hope, love—whatever one most longs for.

Harsanyi had given Thea a ticket for the symphony concert that afternoon, and when she looked out at the white apple trees her doubts as to whether she ought to go vanished at once. She would make her work light that morning, she told herself. She would go to the concert full of energy. When she set off, after dinner, Mrs. Lorch, who knew Chicago weather, prevailed upon her to take her cape. The old lady said that such sudden mildness, so early in April, presaged a sharp return of winter, and she was anxious about her apple trees.

The concert began at two-thirty, and Thea was in her seat in the Auditorium at ten minutes after two—a fine seat in the first row of the balcony, on the side, where she could see the house as well as the orchestra. She had been to so few concerts that the great house, the crowd of people, and the lights, all had a stimulating effect. She was surprised to see so many men in the audience, and wondered how they could leave their business in the afternoon. During the first number Thea was so much interested in the orchestra itself, in the men, the instruments, the volume of sound, that she paid little attention to what they were playing. Her excitement impaired her power of listening. She kept saying to herself, "Now I must stop this foolishness and listen; I may never hear this again"; but her mind was like a glass that is hard to focus. She was not ready to listen until the second number, Dvorak's Symphony in E minor, called on the programme, "From the New World." The first theme had scarcely been given out when her mind became clear; instant composure fell upon her, and with it came the power of concentration. This was music she could understand, music from the New World indeed! Strange how, as the first movement went on, it brought back to her that high tableland above Laramie; the grass-grown wagon-trails, the far-away peaks of the snowy range, the wind and the eagles, that old man and the first telegraph message.

When the first movement ended, Thea's hands and feet were cold as ice. She was too much excited to know anything except that she wanted something desperately, and when the English horns gave out the theme of the Largo, she knew that what she wanted was exactly that. Here were the sand hills, the grasshoppers and locusts, all the things that wakened and chirped in the early morning; the reaching and reaching of high plains, the immeasurable yearning of all flat lands. There was home in it, too; first memories, first mornings long ago; the amazement of a new soul in a new world; a soul new and yet old, that had dreamed something despairing, something glorious, in the dark before it was born; a soul obsessed by what it did not know, under the cloud of a past it could not recall.

If Thea had had much experience in concert-going, and had known her own capacity, she would have left the hall when the symphony was over. But she sat still, scarcely knowing where she was, because her mind had been far away and had not yet come back to her. She was startled when the orchestra began to play again—the entry of the gods into Walhalla. She heard it as people hear things in their sleep. She knew scarcely anything about the Wagner operas. She had a vague idea that "Rhinegold" was about the strife between gods and men; she had read something about it in Mr. Haweis's book long ago. Too tired to follow the orchestra with much understanding, she crouched down in her seat and closed her eyes. The cold, stately measures of the Walhalla music rang out, far away; the rainbow bridge throbbed out into the air, under it the wailing of the Rhine daughters and the singing of the Rhine. But Thea was sunk in twilight; it was all going on in another world. So it happened that with a dull, almost listless ear she heard for the first time that troubled music, ever-darkening, ever-brightening, which was to flow through so many years of her life.

When Thea emerged from the concert hall, Mrs. Lorch's predictions had been fulfilled. A furious gale was beating over the city from Lake Michigan. The streets were full of cold, hurrying, angry people, running for street-cars and barking at each other. The sun was setting in a clear, windy sky, that flamed with red as if there were a great fire somewhere on the edge of the city. For almost the first time Thea was conscious of the city itself, of the congestion of life all about her, of the brutality and power of those streams that flowed in the streets, threatening to drive one under. People jostled her, ran into her, poked her aside with their elbows, uttering angry exclamations. She got on the wrong car and was roughly ejected by the conductor at a windy corner, in front of a saloon. She stood there dazed and shivering. The cars passed, screaming as they rounded curves, but either they were full to the doors, or were bound for places where she did not want to go. Her hands were so cold that she took off her tight kid gloves. The street lights began to gleam in the dusk. A young man came out of the saloon and stood eyeing her questioningly while he lit a cigarette. "Looking for a friend to-night?" he asked. Thea drew up the collar of her cape and walked on a few paces. The young man shrugged his shoulders and drifted away.

Thea came back to the corner and stood there irresolutely. An old man approached her. He, too, seemed to be waiting for a car. He wore an overcoat with a black fur collar, his grey moustache was waxed into little points, and his eyes were watery. He kept thrusting his face up near hers. Her hat blew off and he ran after it—a stiff, pitiful skip he had—and brought it back to her. Then, while she was pinning her hat on, her cape blew up, and he held it down for her, looking at her intently. His face worked as if he were going to cry or were frightened. He leaned over and whispered something to her. It struck her as curious that he was really quite timid, like an old beggar. "Oh, let me *alone!*" she cried miserably between her teeth. He vanished, disappeared like the Devil in a play. But in the meantime something had got away from her; she could not remember how the violins came in after the horns, just there. When her cape blew up, perhaps—Why did these men torment her? A cloud of dust blew in her face and blinded her. There was some power abroad in the world bent upon taking away from her that feeling with which she had come out of the concert hall. Everything seemed to sweep down on her to tear it out from under her cape. If one had that, the world became one's enemy; people, buildings, wagons, cars, rushed at one to crush it under, to make one let go of it. Thea glared round her at the crowds, the ugly, sprawling streets, the long lines of lights, and she was not crying now. Her eyes were brighter than even Harsanyi had ever seen them. All these things and people were no longer remote and negligible; they had to be met, they were lined up against her, they were there to take something from her. Very well; they should never have it. They might trample her to death, but they should never have it. As long as she lived that ecstasy was going to be hers. She would live for it, work for it, die for it; but she was going to have it, time after time, height after height. She could hear the crash of the orchestra again, and she rose on the brasses. She would have it, what the trumpets were singing! She would have it, have it—it! Under the old cape she pressed her hands upon her heaving bosom, that was a little girl's no longer.

VI

One afternoon in April, Theodore Thomas, the conductor of the Chicago Symphony Orchestra, had turned out his desk light and was about to leave his office in the Auditorium Building, when Harsanyi appeared in the doorway. The conductor welcomed him with a hearty hand-grip and threw off the overcoat he had just put on. He pushed Harsanyi into a chair and sat down at his burdened desk, pointing to the piles of papers and railway folders upon it.

"Another tour, clear to the coast. This travelling is the part of my work that grinds me, Andor. You know what it means: bad food, dirt, noise, exhaustion for the men and for me. I'm not so young as I once was. It's time I quit the highway. This is the last tour, I swear!"

"Then I'm sorry for the 'highway.' I remember when I first heard you in Pittsburgh, long ago. It was a life-line you threw me. It's about one of the people along your highway that I've come to see you. Whom do you consider the best teacher for voice in Chicago?"

Mr. Thomas frowned and pulled his heavy moustache. "Let me see; I suppose on the whole Madison Bowers is the best. He's intelligent, and he had good training. I don't like him."

Harsanyi nodded. "I thought there was no one else. I don't like him, either, so I hesitated. But I suppose he must do, for the present."

"Have you found anything promising? One of your own students?"

"Yes, sir. A young Swedish girl from somewhere in Colorado. She is very talented, and she seems to me to have a remarkable voice."

"High voice?"

"I think it will be; though her low voice has a beautiful quality, very individual. She has had no instruction in voice at all, and I shrink from handing her over to anybody; her own instinct about it has been so good. It is one of those voices that manages itself easily, without thinning as it goes up; good breathing and perfect relaxation. But she must have a teacher, of course. There is a break in the middle voice, so that the voice does not all work together; an unevenness."

Thomas looked up. "So? Curious; that cleft often happens with the Swedes. Some of their best singers have had it. It always reminds me of the space you so often see between their front teeth. Is she strong physically?"

Harsanyi's eye flashed. He lifted his hand before him and clenched it. "Like a horse, like a tree! Every time I give her a lesson, I lose a pound. She goes after what she wants."

"Intelligent, you say? Musically intelligent?"

"Yes; but no cultivation whatever. She came to me like a fine young savage, a book with nothing written in it. That is why I feel the responsibility of directing her." Harsanyi paused and crushed his soft grey hat over his knee. "She would interest you, Mr. Thomas," he added slowly. "She has a quality—very individual."

"Yes; the Scandinavians are apt to have that, too. She can't go to Germany, I suppose?"

"Not now, at any rate. She is poor."

Thomas frowned again.

"I don't think Bowers a really first-rate man. He's too petty to be really first-rate; in his nature, I mean. But I dare say he's the best you can do, if you can't give her time enough yourself."

Harsanyi waved his hand. "Oh, the time is nothing—she may

have all she wants. But I cannot teach her to sing."

"Might not come amiss if you made a musician of her, however," said Mr. Thomas dryly.

"I have done my best. But I can only play with a voice, and this is not a voice to be played with. I think she will be a musician, whatever happens. She is not quick, but she is solid, real; not like these others. My wife says that with that girl one swallow does not make a summer."

Mr. Thomas laughed. "Tell Mrs. Harsanyi that her remark conveys something to me. Don't let yourself get too much interested. Voices are so often disappointing; especially women's voices. So much chance about it, so many factors."

"Perhaps that is why they interest one. All the intelligence and talent in the world can't make a singer. The voice is a wild thing. It can't be bred in captivity. It is a sport, like the silver fox. It happens."

Mr. Thomas smiled into Harsanyi's gleaming eye. "Why haven't you brought her to sing for me?"

"I've been tempted to, but I knew you were driven to death, with this tour confronting you."

"Oh, I can always find time to listen to a girl who has a voice, if she means business. I'm sorry I'm leaving so soon. I could advise you better if I had heard her. I can sometimes give a singer suggestions. I've worked so much with them."

"You're the only conductor I know who is not snobbish about singers," Harsanyi spoke warmly.

"Dear me, why should I be? They've learned from me, and I've learned from them."

As they rose, Thomas took the younger man affectionately by the arm. "Tell me about that wife of yours. Is she well, and as lovely as ever? And such fine children! Come to see me oftener, when I get back. I miss it when you don't."

The two men left the Auditorium Building together. Harsanyi walked home. Even a short talk with Theodore Thomas always stimulated him. As he walked, he was recalling an evening they once spent together in Cincinnati.

Harsanyi was the soloist at one of Thomas's concerts there, and after the performance the conductor had taken him off to a *Rathskeller* where there was excellent German cooking, and where the proprietor saw to it that Thomas had the best wines procurable. Thomas had been working with the great chorus of the Festival Association and was speaking of it with enthusiasm when Harsanyi asked him how it was that he was able to feel such an interest in choral directing and in voices generally.

Thomas seldom spoke of his youth or his early struggles, but that night he had turned back the pages and told Harsanyi a long story.

He said he had spent the summer of his fifteenth year wandering about alone in the South, giving violin concerts in little towns. He travelled on horseback. When he came into a town, he went about all day tacking up posters announcing his concert in the evening. Before the concert, he stood at the door taking in the admission money until his audience had arrived, and then he went on the platform and played. It was a lazy, hand-to-mouth existence, and Thomas said he must have got to like that easy way of living and the relaxing Southern atmosphere. At any rate, when he got back to New York in the fall, he was rather torpid; perhaps he had been growing too fast. From this adolescent drowsiness the lad was awakened by two voices, by two women who sang in New York in 1851—Jenny Lind and Henrietta Sontag. They were the first great artists he had ever heard, and he never forgot his debt to them.

As he said: "It was not voice and execution alone. There was a greatness about them. They were great women, great artists. They opened a new world to me." Night after night he went to hear them, striving to reproduce the quality of their tone upon his violin. From that time his idea about strings was completely changed, and on his violin he tried always for the singing, vibrating tone, instead of the loud and somewhat harsh tone then prevalent among even the best German violinists. In later years he often advised violinists to study singing, and singers to study violin. He told Harsanyi that he got his first conception of tone quality from Jenny Lind.

"But, of course," he added, "the great thing I got from Lind and Sontag was the indefinite, not the definite, thing. For an impressionable boy, their inspiration was incalculable. They gave me my first feeling for the Italian style—but I could never say how much they gave me. At that age, such influences are actually creative. I always think of my artistic consciousness as beginning then."

All his life Thomas did his best to repay what he felt he owed to the singer's art. No other man could get such singing from choruses, and no man worked harder to raise the standard of singing in schools and churches and choral societies.

VII

*A*ll through the lesson Thea had felt that Harsanyi was restless and abstracted. Before the hour was over, he pushed back his chair and said resolutely: "I am not in the mood, Miss Kronborg. I have something on my mind and I must talk to you. When do you intend to go home?"

Thea turned to him in surprise. "The first of June, about. Mr. Larsen will not need me after that, and I have not much money ahead. I shall work hard this summer, though."

"And to-day is the first of May; May Day." Harsanyi leaned forward, his elbows on his knees, his hands locked between them. "Yes, I must talk to you about something. I have asked Madison Bowers to let me bring you to him on Thursday, at your usual lesson time. He is the best vocal teacher in Chicago, and it is time you began to work seriously with your voice."

Thea's brow wrinkled. "You mean take lessons of Bowers?"

Harsanyi nodded, without lifting his head.

"But I can't, Mr. Harsanyi. I haven't got the time, and, be-sides"—she blushed and drew her shoulders up stiffly—"besides, I can't afford to pay two teachers." Thea felt that she had blurted this out in the worst possible way, and she turned back to the keyboard to hide her chagrin.

"I know that. I don't mean that you shall pay two teachers. After you go to Bowers, you will not need me. I need scarcely tell you that I shan't be happy at losing you."

Thea turned to him, hurt and angry. "But I don't want to go to Bowers. I don't want to leave you. What's the matter? Don't I work hard enough? I'm sure you teach people that don't try half as hard."

Harsanyi rose to his feet. "Don't misunderstand me, Miss Kronborg. You interest me more than any pupil I have. I have been thinking for months about what you ought to do, since that night when you first sang for me." He walked over to the window, turned, and came toward her again. "I believe that your voice is worth all that you can put into it. I have not come to this decision rashly. I have studied you, and I have become more and more convinced, against my own desires. I cannot make a singer of you, so it was my business to find a man who could. I have even consulted Theodore Thomas about it."

"But suppose I don't want to be a singer? I want to study with you. What's the matter? Do you really think I've no talent? Can't I be a pianist?"

Harsanyi paced up and down the long rug in front of her. "My girl, you are very talented. You could be a pianist, a good one. But the early training of a pianist, such a pianist as you would want to be, must be something tremendous. He must have had no other life than music. At your age he must be the master of his instrument. Nothing can ever take the place of that first training. You know very well that your technique is good, but it is not remarkable. It will never overtake your intelligence. You have a fine power of work, but you are not by nature a student. You are not by nature, I think, a pianist. You would never find yourself. In the effort to do so, I'm afraid your playing would become warped, eccentric." He threw back his head and looked at his pupil intently with that one eye which sometimes seemed to see deeper than any two eyes, as if its singleness gave it privileges. "Oh, I have watched you very carefully, Miss Kronborg. Because you had had so little and had yet done so much for yourself, I had a great wish to help you. I believe that the strongest need of your nature is to find yourself, to emerge *as* yourself. Until I heard you sing, I wondered how you were to do this, but it has grown clearer to me every day."

Thea looked away toward the window with hard, narrow eyes. "You mean I can be a singer because I haven't brains enough to be a pianist."

"You have brains enough and talent enough. But to do what you will want to do, it takes more than these—it takes vocation. Now, I think you have vocation, but for the voice, not for the piano. If you knew"—he stopped and sighed—"if you knew how fortunate I sometimes think you. With the voice the way is so much shorter, the rewards are more easily won. In your voice I think Nature herself did for you what it would take you many years to do at the piano. Perhaps you were not born in the wrong place after all. Let us talk frankly now. We have never done so before, and I have respected your reticence. What you want more than anything else in the world is to be an artist; is that true?"

She turned her face away from him and looked down at the keyboard. Her answer came in a thickened voice. "Yes, I suppose so."

"When did you first feel that you wanted to be an artist?"

"I don't know. There was always—something."

"Did you never think that you were going to sing?"

"Yes."

"How long ago was that?"

"Always, until I came to you. It was you who made me want to play piano." Her voice trembled. "Before, I tried to think I did, but I was pretending."

Harsanyi reached out and caught the hand that was hanging at her side. He pressed it as if to give her something. "Can't you see, my dear girl, that was only because I happened to be the first artist you have ever known? If I had been a trombone player, it would have been the same; you would have wanted to play trombone. But all the while you have been working with such good will, something has been struggling against me. See, here we were, you and I and this instrument"—he tapped the piano—"three good friends, working so hard. But all the while there was something fighting us: your gift, and the woman you were meant to be. When you find your way to that gift and to that woman, you will be at peace. In the beginning it was an artist that you wanted to be; well, you may be an artist, always."

Thea drew a long breath. Her hands fell in her lap. "So I'm just where I began. No teacher, nothing done. No money."

Harsanyi turned away. "Feel no apprehension about the money, Miss Kronborg. Come back in the fall and we shall manage that. I shall even go to Mr. Thomas if necessary. This year will not be lost. If you but knew what an advantage this winter's study, all your study of the piano, will give you over most singers. Perhaps things have come out better for you than if we had planned them knowingly."

"You mean they have *if* I can sing."

Thea spoke with a heavy irony, so heavy, indeed, that it was coarse. It grated upon Harsanyi because he felt that it was not sincere, an awkward affectation.

He wheeled toward her. "Miss Kronborg, answer me this. *You know that you can sing,* do you not? You have always known it. While we worked here together you sometimes said to yourself, 'I have something you know nothing about; I could surprise you.' Is that also true?"

Thea nodded and hung her head.

"Why were you not frank with me? Did I not deserve it?"

She shuddered. Her bent shoulders trembled. "I don't know,"

she muttered. "I didn't mean to be like that. I couldn't. I can't. It's different."

"You mean it is very personal?" he asked kindly.

She nodded. "Not at church or funerals, or with people like Mr. Larsen. But with you it was—personal. I'm not like you and Mrs. Harsanyi. I come of rough people. I'm rough. But I'm independent, too. It was—all I had. There is no use my talking, Mr. Harsanyi. I can't tell you."

"You needn't tell me. I know. Every artist knows." Harsanyi stood looking at his pupil's back, bent as if she were pushing something, at her lowered head. "You can sing for those people because with them you do not commit yourself. But the reality, one cannot uncover *that* until one is sure. One can fail one's self, but one must not live to see that fail; better never reveal it. Let me help you to make yourself sure of it. That I can do better than Bowers."

Thea lifted her face and threw out her hands.

Harsanyi shook his head and smiled. "Oh, promise nothing! You will have much to do. There will not be voice only, but French, German, Italian. You will have work enough. But sometimes you will need to be understood; what you never show to anyone will need companionship. And then you must come to me." He peered into her face with that searching, intimate glance. "You know what I mean, the thing in you that has no business with what is little, that will have to do only with beauty and power."

Thea threw out her hands fiercely, as if to push him away. She made a sound in her throat, but it was not articulate. Harsanyi took one of her hands and kissed it lightly upon the back. His salute was one of greeting, not of farewell, and it was for some one he had never seen.

When Mrs. Harsanyi came in at six o'clock, she found her husband sitting listlessly by the window. "Tired?" she asked.

"A little. I've just got through a difficulty. I've sent Miss Kronborg away; turned her over to Bowers, for voice."

"Sent Miss Kronborg away? Andor, what is the matter with you?"

"It's nothing rash. I've known for a long while I ought to do it. She is made for a singer, not a pianist."

Mrs. Harsanyi sat down on the piano-chair. She spoke a little bitterly: "How can you be sure of that? She was, at least, the best you had. I thought you meant to have her play at your students' recital next fall. I am sure she would have made an impression. I could have dressed her so that she would have been very striking. She had so much individuality."

Harsanyi bent forward, looking at the floor. "Yes, I know. I shall miss her, of course."

Mrs. Harsanyi looked at her husband's fine head against the grey window. She had never felt deeper tenderness for him than she did at that moment. Her heart ached for him. "You will never get on, Andor," she said mournfully.

Harsanyi sat motionless. "No, I shall never get on," he repeated quietly. Suddenly he sprang up with that light movement she knew so well, and stood in the window, with folded arms. "But some day I shall be able to look her in the face and laugh because I did what I could for her. I believe in her. She will do nothing common. She is uncommon, in a common, common world. That is what I get out of it. It means more to me than if she played at my concert and brought me a dozen pupils. All this drudgery will kill me if once in a while I cannot hope something, for somebody! If I cannot sometimes see a bird fly and wave my hand to it."

His tone was angry and injured. Mrs. Harsanyi understood that this was one of the times when his wife was a part of the drudgery, of the "common, common world." He had let something he cared for go, and he felt bitterly about whatever was left. The mood would pass, and he would be sorry. She knew him. It wounded her, of course, but that hurt was not new. It was as old as her love for him. She went out and left him alone.

VIII

One warm damp June night the Denver Express was speeding westward across the earthy-smelling plains of Iowa. The lights in the day-coach were turned low and the ventilators were open, admitting showers of soot and dust upon the occupants of the narrow green plush chairs which were tilted at various angles of discomfort. In each of these chairs some uncomfortable human being lay drawn up, or stretched out, or writhing from one position to another. There were tired men in rumpled shirts, their necks bare and their suspenders down; old women with their heads tied up in black handkerchiefs; bedraggled young women who went to sleep while they were nursing their babies and forgot to button up their dresses; dirty boys who added to the general discomfort by taking off their boots. The brakeman, when he came through at midnight, sniffed the heavy air disdainfully and looked up at the ventilators. As he glanced down the double rows of contorted figures, he saw one pair of eyes that were wide open and bright, a yellow head that was not overcome by the stupefying heat and smell in the car. "There's a girl for you," he thought as he stopped by Thea's chair.

"Like to have the window up a little?" he asked.

Thea smiled up at him, not misunderstanding his friendliness. "The girl behind me is sick; she can't stand a draught. What time is it, please?"

He took out his open-faced watch and held it before her eyes with a knowing look. "In a hurry?" he asked. "I'll leave the end door open and air you out. Catch a wink; the time'll go faster."

Thea nodded good night to him and settled her head back on her pillow, looking up at the oil lamps. She was going back to Moonstone for her summer vacation, and she was sitting up all night in a day-coach because that seemed such an easy way to save money. At her age discomfort was a small matter, when one made five dollars a day by it. She had confidently expected to sleep after the car got quiet, but in the two chairs behind her were a sick girl and her mother, and the girl had been coughing steadily since ten o'clock. They had come from somewhere in Pennsylvania, and this was their second night on the road. The mother said they were going to Colorado "for her daughter's lungs." The daughter was a little older than Thea, perhaps nineteen, with patient dark eyes and curly brown hair. She was pretty in spite of being so sooty and travel-stained. She had put on an ugly figured sateen kimono over her loosened clothes. Thea, when she boarded the train in Chicago, happened to stop and plant her heavy telescope on this seat. She had not intended to remain there, but the sick girl had looked up at her with an eager smile and said, "Do sit there, miss. I'd so much rather not have a gentleman in front of me."

After the girl began to cough there were no empty seats left, and if there had been Thea could scarcely have changed without hurting her feelings. The mother turned on her side and went to sleep; she was used to the cough. But the girl lay wide awake, her eyes fixed on the roof of the car, as Thea's were. The two girls must have seen very different things there.

Thea fell to going over her winter in Chicago. It was only under unusual or uncomfortable conditions like these that she could keep her mind fixed upon herself or her own affairs for any length of time. The rapid motion and the vibration of the wheels under her seemed to give her thoughts rapidity and clearness. She had taken twenty very expensive lessons from Madison Bowers, but she did not yet know what he thought of her or of her ability. He was different from any man with whom she had ever had to do. With her other teachers she had felt a personal relation; but with him she did not. Bowers was a cold, bitter, avaricious man, but he knew a great deal about voices. He worked with a voice as if he were in a laboratory, conducting a series of experiments. He was conscientious and industrious, even capable of a certain cold fury when he was working with an interesting voice, but Harsanyi declared that he had the soul of a shrimp, and could no more make an artist than a throat specialist could. Thea realized that he had taught her a great deal in twenty lessons.

Although she cared so much less for Bowers than for Harsanyi, she was, on the whole, happier since she had been studying with him than she had been before. She had always told herself that she studied piano to fit herself to be a music-teacher. But she never asked herself why she was studying voice. Her voice, more than any other part of her, had to do with that confidence, that sense of wholeness and inner well-being that she had felt at moments ever since she could remember.

Of this feeling Thea had never spoken to any human being until that day when she told Harsanyi that "there had always been—something." Hitherto she had felt but one obligation toward it—secrecy; to protect it even from herself. She had always believed that by doing all that was required of her by her family, her teachers, her pupils, she kept that part of herself from being caught up in the meshes of common things. She took it for granted that some day, when she was older, she would know a great deal more about it. It was as if she had an appointment to meet the rest of herself sometime, somewhere. It was moving to meet her and she was moving to meet it. That meeting awaited her, just as surely as, for the poor girl in the seat behind her, there awaited a hole in the earth, already dug.

For Thea, so much had begun with a hole in the earth. Yes, she reflected, this new part of her life had all begun that morning when she sat on the clay bank beside Ray Kennedy, under the flickering shade of the cottonwood tree. She remembered the way Ray had looked at her that morning. Why had he cared so much? And Wunsch, and Doctor Archie, and Spanish Johnny, why had they? It was something that had to do with her that made them care, but it was not she. It was something they believed in, but it was not she. Perhaps each of them concealed another person in himself, just as she did. Why was it that they seemed to feel and to hunt for a second person in her and not in each other? Thea frowned up at the dull

lamp in the roof of the car. What if one's second self could somehow speak
to all these second selves? What if one could bring them out, as whiskey did
Spanish Johnny's? How deep they lay, these second persons, and how little
one knew about them, except to guard them fiercely. It was to music, more
than to anything else, that these hidden things in people responded. Her
mother—even her mother had something of that sort which replied to
music.

     Thea found herself listening for the coughing behind her and not
hearing it. She turned cautiously and looked back over the head-rest of her
chair. The poor girl had fallen asleep. Thea looked at her intently. Why was
she so afraid of men? Why did she shrink into herself and avert her face
whenever a man passed her chair? Thea thought she knew; of course, she
knew. How horrible to waste away like that, in the time when one ought
to be growing fuller and stronger and rounder every day. Suppose there
were such a dark hole open for her, between to-night and that place where
she was to meet herself? Her eyes narrowed. She put her hand on her breast
and felt how warm it was; and within it there was a full, powerful pulsation.
She smiled—though she was ashamed of it—with the natural contempt of
strength for weakness, with the sense of physical security which makes the
savage merciless. Nobody could die while he felt like that inside. The
springs there were wound so tight that it would be a long while before there
was any slack in them. The life in there was rooted deep. She was going to
have a few things before she died. She realized that there were a great many
trains dashing east and west on the face of the continent that night, and that
they all carried young people who meant to have things. But the difference
was that *she was going to get them!* That was all. Let people try to stop her!
She glowered at the rows of feckless bodies that lay sprawled in the chairs.
Let them try it once! Along with the yearning that came from some deep
part of her, that was selfless and exalted, Thea had a hard kind of cockiness,
a determination to get ahead. Well, there are passages in life when that
fierce, stubborn self-assertion will stand its ground after the nobler feeling
is overwhelmed and beaten under.

     Having told herself once more that she meant to grab a few
things, Thea went to sleep.

     She was wakened in the morning by the sunlight, which beat
fiercely through the glass of the car window upon her face. She made herself
as clean as she could, and while the people all about her were getting cold
food out of their lunch-baskets, she escaped into the dining-car. Her thrift
did not go to the point of enabling her to carry a lunch-basket. At that early

hour there were few people in the dining-car. The linen was white and fresh, the darkies were trim and smiling, and the sunlight gleamed pleasantly upon the silver and the glass water-bottles. On each table there was a slender vase with a single pink rose in it. When Thea sat down she looked into her rose and thought it the most beautiful thing in the world; it was wide open, recklessly offering its yellow heart, and there were drops of water on the petals. All the future was in that rose, all that one would like to be. The flower put her in an absolutely regal mood. She had a whole pot of coffee, and scrambled eggs with chopped ham, utterly disregarding the astonishing price they cost. She had faith enough in what she could do, she told herself, to have eggs if she wanted them. At the table opposite her sat a man and his wife and little boy—Thea classified them as being "from the East." They spoke in that quick, sure staccato, which Thea, like Ray Kennedy, pretended to scorn and secretly admired. People who could use words in that confident way, and who spoke them elegantly, had a great advantage in life, she reflected. There were so many words which she could not pronounce in speech as she had to do in singing. Language was like clothes; it could be a help to one, or it could give one away. But the most important thing was that one should not pretend to be what one was not.

When she paid her cheque she consulted the waiter. "Waiter, do you suppose I could buy one of those roses? I'm out of the day-coach, and there is a sick girl in there. I'd like to take her a cup of coffee and one of those flowers."

The waiter liked nothing better than advising travellers less sophisticated than himself. He told Thea there were a few roses left in the icebox and he would get one. He took the flower and the coffee into the day-coach. Thea pointed out the girl, but she did not accompany him. She hated thanks and never received them gracefully. She stood outside on the platform to get some fresh air into her lungs. The train was crossing the Platte River now, and the sunlight was so intense that it seemed to quiver in little flames on the glittering sandbars, the scrub willows, and the curling, fretted shallows.

Thea felt that she was coming back to her own land. She had often heard Mrs. Kronborg say that she "believed in immigration," and so did Thea believe in it. This earth seemed to her young and fresh and kindly, a place where refugees from old, sad countries were given another chance. The mere absence of rocks gave the soil a kind of amiability and generosity, and the absence of natural boundaries gave the spirit a wider range. Wire fences might mark the end of a man's pasture, but they could not shut in his thoughts as mountains and forests can. It was over flat lands like this, stretching out to drink the sun, that the larks sang—and one's heart sang there, too. Thea was glad that this was her country, even if one did not learn to speak elegantly there. It was, somehow, an honest country, and there was a new song in that blue air which had never been sung in the world before. It was hard to tell about it, for it had nothing to do with words; it was like the light of the desert at noon, or the smell of the sagebrush after rain; intangible but powerful. She had the sense of going back to a friendly soil, whose friendship was somehow going to strengthen her; a naïve, generous country that gave one its joyous force, its large-hearted, childlike power to love, just as it gave one its coarse, brilliant flowers.

As she drew in that glorious air, Thea's mind went back to Ray Kennedy. He, too, had that feeling of empire; as if all the Southwest really belonged to him because he had knocked about over it so much, and knew it, as he said, "like the blisters on his own hands." That feeling, she reflected, was the real element of companionship between her and Ray. Now that she was going back to Colorado, she realized this as she had not done before.

IX

*T*hea reached Moonstone in the late afternoon, and all the Kronborgs were there to meet her except her two older brothers. Gus and Charley were young men now, and they had declared at noon that it would "look silly if the whole bunch went down to the train." "There's no use making a fuss over Thea just because she's been to Chicago," Charley warned his mother. "She's inclined to think pretty well of herself, anyhow, and if you go treating her like company, there'll be no living in the house with her." Mrs. Kronborg simply levelled her eyes at Charley, and he faded away muttering. She had, as Mr. Kronborg always said with an inclination of his head, good control over her children. Anna, too, wished to absent herself from the party, but in the end her curiosity got the better of her. So when Thea stepped down from the porter's stool, a very creditable Kronborg representation was grouped on the platform to greet her. After they had all kissed her (Gunner and Axel shyly), Mr. Kronborg hurried his flock into the hotel omnibus, in which they were to be driven ceremoniously home, with the neighbours looking out of their windows to see them go by.

All the family talked to her at once, except Thor—impressive in new trousers—who was gravely silent and who refused to sit on Thea's lap. One of the first things Anna told her was that Maggie Evans, the girl who used to cough in prayer-meeting, died yesterday, and had made a request that Thea sing at her funeral.

Thea's smile froze. "I'm not going to sing at all this summer, except my exercises. Bowers says I taxed my voice last winter, singing at funerals so much. If I begin the first day after I get home, there'll be no end to it. You can tell them I caught cold on the train, or something."

Thea saw Anna glance at their mother. Thea remembered having seen that look on Anna's face often before, but she had never thought anything about it because she was used to it. Now she realized that the look was distinctly spiteful, even vindictive. She suddenly realized that Anna had always disliked her.

Mrs. Kronborg seemed to notice nothing, and changed the trend of the conversation, telling Thea that Doctor Archie and Mr. Upping, the jeweller, were both coming in to see her that evening, and that she had asked Spanish Johnny to come, because he had behaved well all winter and ought to be encouraged.

The next morning Thea wakened early in her own room up under the eaves and lay watching the sunlight shine on the roses of her wall-paper. She wondered whether she would ever like a plastered room as well as this one lined with scantlings. It was snug and tight, like the cabin of a little boat. Her bed faced the window and stood against the wall, under the slant of the ceiling. When she went away she could just touch the ceiling with the tips of her fingers; now she could touch it with the palm of her hand. It was so little that it was like a sunny cave, with roses running all over the roof. Through the low window, as she lay there, she could watch people going by on the farther side of the street; men, going downtown to open their stores. Thor was over there, rattling his express wagon along the sidewalk. Tillie had put a bunch of French pinks in a tumbler of water on her dresser, and they gave out a pleasant perfume. The blue jays were fighting and screeching in the cottonwood tree outside her window, as they always did, and she could hear the old Baptist deacon across the street calling his chickens, as she had heard him do every summer morning since she could remember. It was pleasant to waken up in that bed, in that room, and to feel the brightness of the morning, while light quivered about the low, papered ceiling in golden spots, refracted by the broken mirror and the glass of water that held the pinks. *"Im leuchtenden Sommermorgen";* those lines, and the face of her old teacher, came back to Thea, floated to her out of sleep, perhaps. She had been dreaming something pleasant, but she could not remember what. She would go to call upon Mrs. Kohler to-day, and see the pigeons washing their pink feet in the drip under the water-tank, and flying about their house that was sure to have a fresh coat of white paint on it for summer. On the way home she would stop to see Mrs. Tellamantez. On Sunday she would coax Gunner to take her out to the sand hills. She had missed them in Chicago; had been homesick for their brilliant morning gold and for their soft colours at evening. The Lake, somehow, had never taken their place.

While she lay planning, relaxed in warm drowsiness, she heard a knock at her door. She supposed it was Tillie, who sometimes fluttered in on her before she was out of bed to offer some service which the family would have ridiculed. But instead, Mrs. Kronborg herself came in, carrying a tray with Thea's breakfast set out on one of the best white napkins. Thea sat up with some embarrassment and pulled her night-gown together across her chest. Mrs. Kronborg was always busy downstairs in the morning, and Thea could not remember when her mother had come to her room before.

"I thought you'd be tired, after travelling, and might like to take it easy for once." Mrs. Kronborg put the tray on the edge of the bed. "I took some thick cream for you before the boys got at it. They raised a howl." She chuckled and sat down in the big wooden rocking-chair. Her visit made Thea feel grown-up, and, somehow, important.

Mrs. Kronborg asked her about Bowers and the Harsanyis. She felt a great change in Thea, in her face and in her manner. Mr. Kronborg had noticed it, too, and had spoken of it to his wife with great satisfaction while they were undressing last night. Mrs. Kronborg sat looking at her daughter, who lay on her side, supporting herself on her elbow and lazily drinking her coffee from the tray before her. Her short-sleeved night-gown had come open at the throat again, and Mrs. Kronborg noticed how white her arms and shoulders were, as if they had been dipped in new milk. Her chest was fuller than when she went away, her breasts rounder and firmer, and though she was so white where she was uncovered, they looked rosy through the thin muslin. Her body had the elasticity that comes of being highly charged with the desire to live. Her hair, hanging in two loose braids, one by either cheek, was just enough disordered to catch the light in all its curly ends.

Thea always woke with a pink flush on her cheeks, and this morning her mother thought she had never seen her eyes so wide-open and bright; like clear green springs in the wood, when the early sunlight sparkles in them. She would make a very handsome woman, Mrs. Kronborg said to herself, if she would only get rid of that fierce look she had sometimes. Mrs. Kronborg took great pleasure in good looks, wherever she found them. She still remembered that, as a baby, Thea had been the "best-formed" of any of her children.

"I'll have to get you a longer bed," she remarked, as she put the tray on the table. "You're getting too long for that one."

Thea looked up at her mother and laughed, dropping back on her pillow with a magnificent stretch of her whole body. Mrs. Kronborg sat down again.

"I don't like to press you, Thea, but I think you'd better sing at that funeral to-morrow. I'm afraid you'll always be sorry if you don't. Sometimes a little thing like that, that seems nothing at the time, comes back on one afterward and troubles one a good deal. I don't mean the church shall run you to death this summer, like they used to. I've spoken my mind to your father about that, and he's very reasonable. But Maggie talked a good deal about you to people this winter; always asked what word we'd had, and said how she missed your singing and all. I guess you ought to do that much for her."

"All right, mother, if you think so." Thea lay looking at her mother with intensely bright eyes.

"That's right, daughter." Mrs. Kronborg rose and went over to get the tray, stopping to put her hand on Thea's chest. "You're filling out nice," she said, feeling about. "No, I wouldn't bother about the buttons. Leave 'em stay off. This is a good time to harden your chest."

Thea lay still and heard her mother's firm step receding along the bare floor of the trunk loft. There was no sham about her mother, she reflected. Her mother knew a great many things of which she never talked, and all the church people were forever chattering about things of which they knew nothing. She liked her mother.

Now for Mexican Town and the Kohlers! She meant to run in on the old woman without warning, and hug her.

X

Spanish Johnny had no shop of his own, but he kept a table and an order-book in one corner of the drugstore where paints and wall-paper were sold, and he was sometimes to be found there for an hour or so about noon. Thea had gone into the drugstore to have a friendly chat with the proprietor, who used to lend her books from his shelves. She found Johnny there, trimming rolls of wall-paper for the parlour of Banker Smith's new house. She sat down on the top of his table and watched him.

"Johnny," she said suddenly, "I want you to write down the words of that Mexican serenade you used to sing; you know, *"Rosa de Noche."* It's an unusual song. I'm going to study it. I know enough Spanish for that."

Johnny looked up from his roller with his bright, affable smile. *"Si,* but it is low for you, I think; *voz contralto.* It is low for me."

"Nonsense. I can do more with my low voice than I used to. I'll show you. Sit down and write it out for me, please." Thea beckoned him with the short yellow pencil tied to his order-book.

Johnny ran his fingers through his curly black hair. "If you wish. I do not know if that *serenata* all right for young ladies. Down there it is more for married ladies. They sing it for husbands—or somebody else, may-bee." Johnny's eyes twinkled and he apologized gracefully with his shoulders. He sat down at the table, and while Thea looked over his arm, began to write the song down in the long, slanting script, with highly ornamental capitals. Presently he looked up. "This-a song not exactly Mexican," he said thoughtfully. "It come from farther down; Brazil, Venezuela, may-bee. I learn it from some fellow down there, and he learn it from another fellow. It is-a most like Mexican, but not quite." Thea did not release him, but pointed to the paper. There were three verses of the song in all, and when Johnny had written them down, he sat looking at them meditatively, his head on one side. "I don't think for a high voice, *señorita,"* he objected with polite persistence. "How you accompany with piano?"

"Oh, that will be easy enough."

"For you, may-bee!" Johnny smiled and drummed on the table
with the tips of his agile brown fingers. "You know something? Listen, I
tell you." He rose and sat down on the table beside her, putting his foot on
the chair. He loved to talk at the hour of noon. "When you was a little girl,
no bigger than that, you come to my house one day 'bout noon, like this,
and I was in the door, playing guitar. You was barehead, barefoot; you run
away from home. You stand there and make a frown at me an' listen. By 'n
by you say for me to sing. I sing some lil' ting, and then I say for you to
sing with me. You don' know no words, of course, but you take the air and
you sing it just-a beauti-ful! I never see a child do that, outside Mexico. You
was, oh, I do' know—seven year, may-bee. By 'n by the preacher come
look for you and begin for scold. I say, "Don' scold, Meester Kronborg. She
come for hear guitar. She gotta some music in her, that child. Where she
get?" Then he tell me 'bout your gran'papa play oboe in the old country.
I never forgetta that time." Johnny chuckled softly.

Thea nodded. "I remember that day, too. I liked your music
better than the church music. When are you going to have a dance over
there, Johnny?"

Johnny tilted his head. "Well, Saturday night the Spanish boys
have a lil' party, some *danza*. You know Miguel Ramas? He have some
young cousins, two boys, very nice-a, come from Torreon. They going to
Salt Lake for some job-a, and stay off with him two-three days, and he mus'
have a party. You like to come?"

That was how Thea came to go to the Mexican ball. Mexican
Town had been increased by half a dozen new families during the last few
years, and the Mexicans had put up an adobe dance-hall, that looked exactly
like one of their own dwellings, except that it was a little longer, and was
so unpretentious that nobody in Moonstone knew of its existence. The
"Spanish boys" are reticent about their own affairs. Ray Kennedy used to
know about all their little doings, but since his death there was no one
whom the Mexicans considered *simpatico*.

On Saturday evening after supper Thea told her mother that she
was going over to Mrs. Tellamantez's to watch the Mexicans dance for a
while, and that Johnny would bring her home.

Mrs. Kronborg smiled. She noticed that Thea had put on a white
dress and had done her hair up with unusual care, and that she carried her
best blue scarf. "Maybe you'll take a turn yourself, eh? I wouldn't mind
watching them Mexicans. They're lovely dancers."

Thea made a feeble suggestion that her mother might go with

her, but Mrs. Kronborg was too wise for that. She knew that Thea would have a better time if she went alone, and she watched her daughter go out of the gate and down the sidewalk that led to the depot.

Thea walked slowly. It was a soft, rosy evening. The sand hills were lavender. The sun had gone down a glowing copper disk, and the fleecy clouds in the east were a burning rose-colour, flecked with gold. Thea passed the cottonwood grove and then the depot, where she left the sidewalk and took the sandy path toward Mexican Town. She could hear the scraping of violins being tuned, the tinkle of mandolins, and the growl of a double bass. Where had they got a double bass? She did not know there was one in Moonstone. She found later that it was the property of one of Ramas's young cousins, who was taking it to Utah with him to cheer him at his "job-a."

The Mexicans never wait until it is dark to begin to dance, and Thea had no difficulty in finding the new hall, because every other house in the town was deserted. Even the babies had gone to the ball; a neighbour was always willing to hold the baby while the mother danced. Mrs. Tellamantez came out to meet Thea and led her in. Johnny bowed to her from the platform at the end of the room, where he was playing the mandolin along with two fiddles and the bass. The hall was a long low room, with whitewashed walls, a fairly tight plank floor, wooden benches along the sides, and a few bracket lamps screwed to the frame timbers. There must have been fifty people there, counting the children. The Mexican dances were very much family affairs. The fathers always danced again and again with their little daughters, as well as with their wives. One of the girls came up to greet Thea, her dark cheeks glowing with pleasure and cordiality, and introduced her brother, with whom she had just been dancing. "You better take him every time he asks you," she whispered. "He's the best dancer here, except Johnny."

Thea soon decided that the poorest dancer was herself. Even Mrs. Tellamantez, who always held her shoulders so stiffly, danced better than she did. The musicians did not remain long at their post. When one of them felt like dancing, he called some other boy to take his instrument, put on his coat, and went down on the floor. Johnny, who wore a blousy white silk shirt, did not even put on his coat.

The dances the railroad men gave in Firemen's Hall were the only dances Thea had ever been allowed to go to, and they were very different from this. The boys played rough jokes and thought it smart to be clumsy and to run into each other on the floor. For the square dances there was always the bawling voice of the caller, who was also the county auctioneer.

This Mexican dance was soft and quiet. There was no calling, the conversation was very low, the rhythm of the music was smooth and engaging, the men were graceful and courteous. Some of them Thea had never before seen out of their working clothes, smeared with grease from the roundhouse or clay from the brickyard. Sometimes, when the music happened to be a popular Mexican waltz song, the dancers sang it softly as they moved. There were three little girls under twelve, in their first communion dresses, and one of them had an orange marigold in her black hair, just over her ear. They danced with the men and with each other. There was an atmosphere of ease and friendly pleasure in the low, dimly lit room, and Thea could not help wondering whether the Mexicans had no jealousies or neighbourly grudges as the people in Moonstone had. There was no constraint of any kind there to-night, but a kind of natural harmony about their movements, their greetings, their low conversation, their smiles.

Ramas brought up his two young cousins, Silvo and Felipe, and presented them. They were handsome, smiling youths, of eighteen and twenty, with pale-gold skins, smooth cheeks, aquiline features, and wavy black hair, like Johnny's. They were dressed alike, in black velvet jackets and soft silk shirts, with opal shirt-buttons and flowing black ties looped through gold rings. They had charming manners, and low, guitar-like voices. They knew almost no English, but a Mexican boy can pay a great many compliments with a very limited vocabulary. The Ramas boys thought Thea dazzlingly beautiful. They had never seen a Scandinavian girl before, and her hair and fair skin bewitched them. *"Blanco y oro, semejante la Pascua!"* (White and gold, like Easter!) they exclaimed to each other.

Silvo, the younger, declared that he could never go on to Utah; that he and his double bass had reached their ultimate destination. The elder was more crafty; he asked Miguel Ramas whether there would be "plenty more girls like that *a* Salt Lake, may-bee?"

Silvo, overhearing, gave his brother a contemptuous glance. "Plenty more *a Paraíso* may-bee!" he retorted. When they were not dancing with her, their eyes followed her, over the coiffures of their other partners. That was not difficult: one blonde head moving among so many dark ones.

Thea had not meant to dance much, but the Ramas boys danced so well and were so handsome and adoring that she yielded to their entreaties. When she sat out a dance with them, they talked to her about their family at home, and told her how their mother had once punned upon their name. *Rama,* in Spanish, meant a branch, they explained. Once when they were little lads their mother took them along when she went to help the women decorate the church for Easter. Someone asked her whether she had brought any flowers, and she replied that she had brought her "ramas." This was evidently a cherished family story.

When it was nearly midnight, Johnny announced that everyone was going to his house to have "some lil' ice cream and some lil' *musica.*" He began to put out the lights and Mrs. Tellamantez led the way across the square to her *casa.* The Ramas brothers escorted Thea, and as they stepped out of the door, Silvo exclaimed, *"Hace frio!"* and threw his velvet coat about her shoulders.

Most of the company followed Mrs. Tellamantez, and they sat about on the gravel in her little yard while she and Johnny and Mrs. Miguel Ramas served the ice cream. Thea sat on Felipe's coat, since Silvo's was already about her shoulders. The youths lay down on the shining gravel beside her, one on her right and one on her left. Johnny already called them *"los acolitos,"* the altar-boys.

The talk all about them was low, and indolent. One of the girls was playing on Johnny's guitar, another was picking lightly at the mandolin. The moonlight was so bright that one could see every glance and smile, and the flash of their teeth. The moonflowers over Mrs. Tellamantez's door were wide open and of an unearthly white. The moon itself looked like a great pale flower in the sky.

After all the ice cream was gone, Johnny approached Thea, his guitar under his arm, and the elder Ramas boy politely gave up his place. Johnny sat down, took a long breath, struck a fierce chord, and then hushed it with his other hand. "Now we have some lil' *serenata,* eh? You wan' a try?"

When Thea began to sing, instant silence fell upon the company. She felt all those dark eyes fix themselves upon her intently. She could see them shine. The faces came out of the shadow like the white flowers over the door. Felipe leaned his head upon his hand. Silvo dropped on his back and lay looking at the moon, under the impression that he was still looking at Thea. When she finished the first verse, Thea whispered to Johnny, "Again, I can do it better than that."

She had sung for churches and funerals and teachers, but she had never before sung for a really musical people, and this was the first time she had ever felt the response that such a people can give. They turned themselves and all they had over to her. For the moment they cared about nothing in the world but what she was doing. Their faces confronted her—open, eager, unprotected. She felt as if all these warm-blooded people débouched into her. Mrs. Tellamantez's fateful resignation, Johnny's madness, the adoration of the boy who lay still in the sand: in an instant these things seemed to be within her instead of without, as if they had come from her in the first place.

When she finished, her listeners broke into excited murmur. The men began hunting feverishly for cigarettes. Famos Serreños, the baritone bricklayer, touched Johnny's arm, gave him a questioning look, then heaved a deep sigh. Johnny dropped on his elbow, wiping his face and neck and hands with his handkerchief. *"Señorita,"* he panted, "if you sing like that once in the City of Mexico, they just-a go crazy. In the City of Mexico they ain't-a sit like stumps when they hear that, not-a much! When they like, they just-a give you the town."

Thea laughed. She, too, was excited. "Think so, Johnny? Come, sing something with me. *El Parreño;* I haven't sung that for a long time."

Johnny laughed and hugged his guitar. "You not-a forget him?" He began teasing his strings. "Come!" He threw back his head, *"Anoche-e-e—"*

> *"Anoche me confesse*
> *Con un padre carmelite.*
> *Y me dio penitencia*
> *Que besaras tu boquita."*

> (Last night I made confession
> To a Carmelite father,
> And he told me to do penance
> By kissing your pretty mouth.)

Johnny had almost every fault that a tenor can have. His voice was thin, unsteady, husky in the middle tones. But it was distinctly a voice, and sometimes he managed to get something very sweet out of it. Certainly it made him happy to sing. Thea kept glancing down at him as he lay there on his elbow. His eyes seemed twice as large as usual and had lights in them like those the moonlight makes on black, running water. Thea remembered the old stories about his "spells." She had never seen him when his madness was on him, but she felt something to-night at her elbow that gave her an idea of what it might be like. For the first time she fully understood the cryptic explanation that Mrs. Tellamantez had made to Doctor Archie long ago. There were the same shells along the walk; she believed she could pick out the very one. There was the same moon up yonder, and panting at her elbow was the same Johnny—fooled by the same old things!

When they had finished, Famos, the baritone, murmured something to Johnny; who replied, "Sure we can sing 'Trovatore.' We have no alto, but all the girls can sing alto and make some noise."

The women laughed. Mexican women of the poorer class do not sing like the men. Perhaps they are too indolent. In the evening, when the men are singing their throats dry on the doorstep, or around the campfire beside the work-train, the women usually sit and comb their hair.

While Johnny was gesticulating and telling everybody what to sing and how to sing it, Thea put out her foot and touched the corpse of Silvo with the toe of her slipper. "Aren't you going to sing, Silvo?" she asked teasingly.

The boy turned on his side and raised himself on his elbow for a moment. "Not this night, *señorita*," he pleaded softly—"not this night!" He dropped back again, and lay with his cheek on his right arm, the hand lying passive on the sand above his head.

"How does he flatten himself into the ground like that?" Thea asked herself. "I wish I knew. It's very effective, somehow."

Across the gulch the little house of the Kohlers slept among its trees, a dark spot on the white face of the desert. The windows of their upstairs bedroom were open, and Paulina had listened to the dance-music for a long while before she drowsed off. She was a light sleeper, and when she woke again, after midnight, Johnny's concert was at its height. She lay still until she could bear it no longer. Then she wakened Fritz and they went over to the window and leaned out. They could hear clearly there.

"*Die Thea*," whispered Mrs. Kohler; "it must be. *Ach, wunderschön!*"

Fritz was not so wide awake as his wife. He grunted and scratched on the floor with his bare foot. They were listening to a Mexican part-song; the tenor, then the soprano, then both together; the baritone joins them, rages, is extinguished; the tenor expires in sobs, and the soprano finishes alone. When the soprano's last note died away, Fritz nodded to his wife. "*Ja*," he said; "*schön.*"

There was silence for a few moments. Then the guitar sounded fiercely, and several male voices began the sextette from "Lucia." Johnny's reedy tenor they knew well, and the bricklayer's big, opaque baritone; the others might be anybody over there—just Mexican voices. Then at the appointed, at the acute, moment, the soprano voice, like a fountain jet, shot up into the light. *"Horch! Horch!"* whispered the old people, both at once. How it leaped from among those dusky male voices! How it played in and about and around and over them, like a goldfish darting among creek minnows, like a yellow butterfly soaring above a swarm of dark ones. "Ah," said Mrs. Kohler softly, "the dear man; if he could hear her now."

XI

M rs. Kronborg had said that Thea was not to be disturbed on Sunday morning, and she slept until noon. When she came downstairs the family were just sitting down to dinner, Mr. Kronborg at one end of the long table, Mrs. Kronborg at the other. Anna, stiff and ceremonious in her summer silk, sat at her father's right, and the boys were strung along on either side of the table. There was a place left for Thea between her mother and Thor. During the silence which preceded the blessing, Thea felt something uncomfortable in the air. Anna and her older brothers had lowered their eyes when she came in. Mrs. Kronborg nodded cheerfully, and after the blessing, as she began to pour the coffee, turned to her.

"I expect you had a good time at that dance, Thea. I hope you got your sleep out."

"High society, that," remarked Charley, giving the mashed potatoes a vicious swat. Anna's mouth and eyebrows became half-moons.

Thea looked across the table at the uncompromising countenances of her older brothers. "Why, what's the matter with the Mexicans?" she asked, flushing. "They don't trouble anybody, and they are kind to their families and have good manners."

"Nice clean people; got some style about them. Do you really like that kind, Thea, or do you just pretend to? That's what I'd like to know." Gus looked at her with pained inquiry. But he at least looked at her.

"They're just as clean as white people, and they have a perfect right to their own ways. Of course I like 'em. I don't pretend things."

"Everybody according to his own taste," remarked Charley

bitterly. "Quit crumbling your bread up, Thor. Ain't you learned how to eat yet?"

"Children, children!" said Mr. Kronborg nervously, looking up from the chicken he was dismembering. He glanced at his wife, whom he expected to maintain harmony in the family.

"That's all right, Charley. Drop it there," said Mrs. Kronborg. "No use spoiling your Sunday dinner with race prejudices. The Mexicans suit me and Thea very well. They are a useful people. Now you can just talk about something else."

Conversation, however, did not flourish at that dinner. Everybody ate as fast as possible. Charley and Gus said they had engagements and left the table as soon as they finished their apple pie. Anna sat primly and ate with great elegance. When she spoke at all she spoke to her father, about church matters, and always in a commiserating tone, as if he had met with some misfortune. Mr. Kronborg, quite innocent of her intentions, replied kindly and absent-mindedly. After the dessert he went to take his usual Sunday afternoon nap, and Mrs. Kronborg carried some dinner to a sick neighbour. Thea and Anna began to clear the table.

"I should think you would show more consideration for father's position, Thea," Anna began as soon as she and her sister were alone.

Thea gave her a sidelong glance. "Why, what have I done to father?"

"Everybody at Sunday-School was talking about you going over there and singing with the Mexicans all night, when you won't sing for the church. Somebody heard you, and told it all over town. Of course, we all get the blame for it."

"Anything disgraceful about singing?" Thea asked with a provoking yawn.

"I must say you choose your company! You always had that streak in you, Thea. We all hoped that going away would improve you. Of course, it reflects on father when you are scarcely polite to the nice people here and make up to the rowdies."

"Oh, it's my singing with the Mexicans you object to?" Thea put down a trayful of dishes. "Well, I like to sing over there, and I don't like to over here. I'll sing for them any time they ask me to. They know something about what I'm doing. They're a talented people."

"Talented!" Anna made the word sound like escaping steam. "I suppose you think it's smart to come home and throw that at your family!"

Thea picked up the tray. By this time she was as white as the

Sunday tablecloth. "Well," she replied in a cold, even tone, "I'll have to throw it at them sooner or later. It's just a question of when, and it might as well be now as any time." She carried the tray blindly into the kitchen.

Tillie, who was always listening and looking out for her, took the dishes from her with a furtive, frightened glance at her stony face. Thea went slowly up the back stairs to her loft. Her legs seemed as heavy as lead as she climbed the stairs, and she felt as if everything inside her had solidified and grown hard.

After shutting her door and locking it, she sat down on the edge of her bed. This place had always been her refuge, but there was a hostility in the house now which this door could not shut out. This would be her last summer in that room. Its services were over; its time was done. She rose and put her hand on the low ceiling. Two tears ran down her cheeks, as if they came from ice that melted slowly. She was not ready to leave her little shell. She was being pulled out too soon. She would never be able to think anywhere else as well as here. She would never sleep so well or have such dreams in any other bed; even last night, such sweet, breathless dreams— Thea hid her face in the pillow. Wherever she went she would like to take that little bed with her. When she went away from it for good, she would leave something that she could never recover; memories of pleasant excitement, of happy adventures in her mind; of warm sleep on howling winter nights, and joyous awakenings on summer mornings. There were certain dreams that might refuse to come to her at all except in a little morning cave, facing the sun—where they came to her so powerfully, where they beat a triumph in her!

The room was hot as an oven. The sun was beating fiercely on the shingles behind the board ceiling. She undressed, and before she threw herself upon her bed in her chemise, she frowned at herself for a long while in her looking-glass. Yes, she and It must fight it out together. The thing that looked at her out of her own eyes was the only friend she could count on. Oh, she would make these people sorry enough! There would come a time when they would want to make it up to her. But, never again! She had no little vanities, only one big one, and she would never forgive.

Her mother was all right, but her mother was a part of the family, and she was not. In the nature of things, her mother had to be on both sides. Thea felt that she had been betrayed. A truce had been broken behind her back. She had never had much individual affection for any of her brothers except Thor, but she had never been disloyal, never felt scorn or held grudges. As a little girl she had always been good friends with

Gunner and Axel, whenever she had time to play. Even before she got her own room, when they were all sleeping and dressing together, like little cubs, and breakfasting in the kitchen, she had led an absorbing personal life of her own. But she had a cub loyalty to the other cubs. She thought them nice boys and tried to make them get their lessons. She once fought a bully who "picked on" Axel at school. She never made fun of Anna's crimpings and curlings and beauty-rites.

Thea had always taken it for granted that her sister and brothers recognized that she had special abilities, and that they were proud of it. She had done them the honour, she told herself bitterly, to believe that though they had no particular endowments, *they were of her kind,* and not of the Moonstone kind. Now they had all grown up and become persons. They faced each other as individuals, and she saw that Anna and Gus and Charley were among the people whom she had always recognized as her natural enemies. Their ambitions and sacred proprieties were meaningless to her. She had neglected to congratulate Charley upon having been promoted from the grocery department of Commings's store to the drygoods depart-ment. Her mother had reproved her for this omission. And how was she to know, Thea asked herself, that Anna expected to be teased because Bert Rice now came and sat in the hammock with her every night? No, it was all clear enough. Nothing that she would ever do in the world would seem important to them, and nothing they would ever do would seem important to her.

Thea lay thinking intently all through the stifling afternoon. Tillie whispered something outside her door once, but she did not answer. She lay on her bed until the second church bell rang, and she saw the family go trooping up the sidewalk on the opposite side of the street, Anna and her father in the lead. Anna seemed to have taken on a very story-book attitude toward her father; patronizing and condescending, it seemed to Thea. The older boys were not in the family band. They now took their girls to church. Tillie had stayed at home to get supper. Thea got up, washed her hot face and arms, and put on the white organdie dress she had worn last night; it was getting too small for her and she might as well wear it out. After she was dressed she unlocked her door and went cautiously downstairs. She felt as if chilling hostilities might be awaiting her in the trunk loft, on the stairway, almost anywhere. In the dining-room she found Tillie, sitting by the open window, reading the dramatic news in a Denver Sunday paper. Tillie kept a scrapbook in which she pasted clippings about actors and actresses.

"Come look at this picture of Pauline Hall in tights, Thea," she called. "Ain't she cute? It's too bad you didn't go to the theatre more when you was in Chicago; such a good chance! Didn't you even get to see Clara Morris or Modjeska?"

"No; I didn't have time. Besides, it costs money, Tillie," Thea replied wearily, glancing at the paper Tillie held out to her.

Tillie looked up at her niece. "Don't you go and be upset about any of Anna's notions. She's one of these narrow kind. Your father and mother don't pay any attention to what she says. Anna's fussy; she is with me, but I don't mind her."

"Oh, I don't mind her. That's all right, Tillie. I guess I'll take a walk."

Thea knew that Tillie hoped she would stay and talk to her for a while, and she would have liked to please her. But in a house as small as that one, everything was too intimate and mixed up together. The family was the family, an integral thing. One couldn't discuss Anna there. She felt differently toward the house and everything in it, as if the battered old furniture that seemed so kindly, and the old carpets on which she had played, had been nourishing a secret grudge against her and were not to be trusted any more.

She went aimlessly out of the front gate, not knowing what to do with herself. Mexican Town, somehow, was spoiled for her just then, and she felt that she would hide if she saw Silvo or Felipe coming toward her. She walked down through the empty main street. All the stores were closed, their blinds down. On the steps of the bank some idle boys were sitting, telling disgusting stories because there was nothing else to do. Several of them had gone to school with Thea, but when she nodded to them they hung their heads and did not speak. Thea's body was often curiously expressive of what was going on in her mind, and to-night there was something in her walk and carriage that made these boys feel that she was "stuck up." If she had stopped and talked to them, they would have thawed out on the instant and would have been friendly and grateful. But Thea was hurt afresh, and walked on, holding her chin higher than ever. As she passed the Duke Block, she saw a light in Doctor Archie's office, and she went up the stairs and opened the door into his study. She found him with a pile of papers and account-books before him. He pointed her to her old chair at the end of his desk and leaned back in his own, looking at her with satisfaction. How handsome she was growing!

"I'm still chasing the elusive metal, Thea"—he pointed to the papers before him—"I'm up to my neck in mines, and I'm going to be a rich man some day."

"I hope you will; awfully rich. That's the only thing that counts." She looked restlessly about the consulting-room. "To do any of the things one wants to do, one has to have lots and lots of money."

Doctor Archie was direct. "What's the matter? Do you need some?"

Thea shrugged. "Oh, I can get along, in a little way." She looked intently out of the window at the arc street-lamp that was just beginning to sputter. "But it's silly to live at all for little things," she added quietly. "Living's too much trouble unless one can get something big out of it."

Doctor Archie rested his elbows on the arms of his chair, dropped his chin on his clasped hands and looked at her. "Living is no trouble for little people, believe me!" he exclaimed. "What do you want to get out of it?"

"Oh—so many things!" Thea shivered.

"But what? Money? You mentioned that. Well, you can make money, if you care about that more than anything else." He nodded prophetically above his interlacing fingers.

"But I don't. That's only one thing. Anyhow, I couldn't if I did." She pulled her dress lower at the neck as if she were suffocating. "I only want impossible things," she said roughly. "The others don't interest me."

Doctor Archie watched her contemplatively, as if she were a beaker full of chemicals working. A few years ago, when she used to sit there, the light from under his green lampshade used to fall full upon her broad face and yellow pig-tails. Now her face was in the shadow and the line of light fell below her bare throat, directly across her bosom. The shrunken white organdie rose and fell as if she were struggling to be free and to break out of it altogether. He felt that her heart must be labouring heavily in there, but he was afraid to touch her; he was, indeed. He had never seen her like this before. Her hair, piled high on her head, gave her a commanding look, and her eyes, that used to be so inquisitive, were stormy.

"Thea," he said slowly, "I won't say that you can have everything you want—that means having nothing, in reality. But if you decide what it is you want most, *you can get it.*" His eye caught hers for a moment. "Not everybody can, but you can. Only, if you want a big thing, you've got to have nerve enough to cut out all that's easy, everything that's to be had cheap." Doctor Archie paused. He picked up a paper-cutter and, feeling the edge of it softly with his fingers, he added slowly, as if to himself:

> "He either fears his fate too much,
>   Or his deserts are small,
> Who dares not put it to the touch
>   To win . . . or lose it all."

Thea's lips parted; she looked at him from under a frown, searching his face. "Do you mean to break loose, too, and—do something?" she asked in a low voice.

"I mean to get rich, if you call that doing anything. I've found what I can do without. You make such bargains in your mind, first."

Thea sprang up and took the paper-cutter he had put down, twisting it in her hands. "A long while first, sometimes," she said with a short laugh. "But suppose you can never get out what you've got in you? Suppose one makes a mess of it in the end; then what?" She threw the paper-cutter on the desk and took a step toward the doctor, until her dress touched him. She stood looking down at him. "Oh, it's easy to fail!" She was breathing through her mouth and her throat was throbbing with excitement.

As he looked up at her, Doctor Archie's hands tightened on the arms of his chair. He had thought he knew Thea Kronborg pretty well, but he did not know the girl who was standing there. She was beautiful, as his little Swede had never been, but she frightened him. Her pale cheeks, her parted lips, her flashing eyes, seemed suddenly to mean one thing—he did not know what. A light seemed to break upon her from far away—or perhaps from far within. She seemed to grow taller, like a scarf drawn out long; looked as if she were pursued and fleeing, and—yes, she looked tormented. "It's easy to fail," he heard her say again, "and if I fail, you'd better forget about me, for I'll be one of the worst women that ever lived. I'll be an awful woman!"

In the shadowy light above the lampshade he caught her glance again and held it for a moment. Wild as her eyes were, that yellow gleam at the back of them was as hard as a diamond drill-point. He rose with a nervous laugh and dropped his hand lightly on her shoulder. "No, you won't. You'll be a splendid one!"

She shook him off before he could say anything more, and went out of his door with a kind of bound. She left so quickly and so lightly that he could not even hear her footstep in the hallway outside. Archie dropped back into his chair and sat motionless for a long while.

So it went; one loved a quaint little girl, cheerful, industrious, always on the run and hustling through her tasks; and suddenly one lost her. He had thought he knew that child like the glove on his hand. But about this tall girl who threw up her head and glittered like that all over, he knew nothing. She was goaded by desires, ambitions, revulsions that were dark to him. One thing he knew: the old highroad of life, worn safe and easy, hugging the sunny slopes, would scarcely hold her again.

After that night Thea could have asked pretty much anything of him. He could have refused her nothing. Years ago a crafty little bunch of hair and smiles had shown him what she wanted, and he had promptly married her. To-night a very different sort of girl—driven wild by doubts and youth, by poverty and riches—had let him see the fierceness of her nature. She went out still distraught, not knowing or caring what she had shown him. But to Archie knowledge of that sort was obligation. Oh, he was the same old Howard Archie!

That Sunday in July was the turning-point: Thea's peace of mind did not come back. She found it hard even to practise at home. There was something in the air there that froze her throat. In the morning, she walked as far as she could walk. In the hot afternoons she lay on her bed in her night-gown, planning fiercely. She haunted the post-office. She must have worn a path in the sidewalk that led to the post-office, that summer. She was there the moment the mail-sacks came up from the depot, morning and evening, and while the letters were being sorted and distributed she paced up and down outside, under the cottonwood trees, listening to the thump, thump, thump of Mr. Thompson's stamp. She hung upon any sort of word from Chicago: a card from Bowers, a letter from Mrs. Harsanyi, from Mr. Larsen, from her landlady—anything to reassure her that Chicago was still there. She began to feel the same restlessness that had tortured her the last spring when she was teaching in Moonstone. Suppose she never got away again, after all? Suppose one broke a leg and had to lie in bed at home for weeks, or had pneumonia and died there. The desert was so big and thirsty; if one's foot slipped, it could drink one up like a drop of water.

This time, when Thea left Moonstone to go back to Chicago, she went alone. As the train pulled out, she looked back at her mother and father and Thor. They were calm and cheerful; they did not know, they did not understand. Something pulled in her—and broke. She cried all the way to Denver, and that night, in her berth, she kept sobbing and waking herself. But when the sun rose in the morning, she was far away. It was all behind her, and she knew that she would never cry like that again. People live through such pain only once; pain comes again, but it finds a tougher surface. Thea remembered how she had gone away the first time, with what confidence in everything, and what pitiful ignorance. Such a silly! She felt resentful toward that stupid, good-natured child. How much older she was now, and how much harder! She was going away to fight, and she was going away forever.

Part III

Stupid Faces

I

So many grinning, stupid faces! Thea was sitting by the window in Bower's studio, waiting for him to come back from lunch. On her knee was the latest number of an illustrated musical journal in which musicians great and little stridently advertised their wares. Every afternoon she played accompaniments for people who looked and smiled like these. She was getting tired of the human countenance.

Thea had been in Chicago for two months. She had a small church position which partly paid her living expenses, and she paid for her singing-lessons by playing Bowers's accompaniments every afternoon from two until six. She had been compelled to leave her old friends Mrs. Lorch and Mrs. Andersen, because the long ride from North Chicago to Bowers's studio on Michigan Avenue took too much time—an hour in the morning, and at night, when the cars were crowded, an hour and a half. For the first month she had clung to her old room, but the bad air in the cars, at the end of a long day's work, fatigued her greatly and was bad for her voice. Since she left Mrs. Lorch, she had been staying at a students' club to which she was introduced by Miss Adler, Bowers's morning accompanist, an intelligent Jewish girl from Evanston.

Thea took her lesson from Bowers every day from eleven-thirty until twelve. Then she went out to lunch with an Italian grammar under her arm, and came back to the studio to begin her work at two. In the afternoon Bowers coached professionals and taught his advanced pupils. It was his theory that Thea ought to be able to learn a great deal by keeping her ears open while she played for him.

The concert-going public of Chicago still remembers the long, sallow, discontented face of Madison Bowers. He seldom missed an evening concert, and was usually to be seen lounging somewhere at the back of the concert hall, reading a newspaper or review, and conspicuously ignoring the efforts of the performers. At the end of a number he looked up from his paper long enough to sweep the applauding audience with a contemptuous eye. His face was intelligent, with a narrow lower jaw, a thin nose, faded grey eyes, and a close-cut brown moustache. His hair was iron-grey, thin and dead-looking. He went to concerts chiefly to satisfy himself as to how badly things were done and how gullible the public was. He hated the whole race of artists; the work they did, the wages they got, and the way they spent their money. His father, old Hiram Bowers, was still alive and at work, a genial old choirmaster in Boston, full of enthusiasm at seventy. But Madison was of the colder stuff of his grandfathers, a long line of New Hampshire farmers: hard workers, close traders, with good minds, mean natures, and flinty eyes. As a boy Madison had a fine baritone voice, and his father made great sacrifices for him, sending him to Germany at an early age and keeping him abroad at his studies for years. Madison worked under the best teachers, and afterward sang in England in oratorio. His cold nature and academic methods were against him. His audiences were always aware of the contempt he felt for them. A dozen poorer singers succeeded, but Bowers did not.

Bowers had all the qualities which go to make a good teacher—except generosity and warmth. His intelligence was of a high order, his taste never at fault. He seldom worked with a voice without improving it, and in teaching the delivery of oratorio he was without a rival. Singers came from far and near to study Bach and Handel with him. Even the fashionable sopranos and contraltos of Chicago, St. Paul, and St. Louis (they were usually ladies with very rich husbands, and Bowers called them the "pampered jades of Asia") humbly endured his sardonic humour for the sake of what he could do for them. He was not at all above helping a very lame singer across, if her husband's cheque-book warranted it. He had a whole bag of tricks for stupid people, "life-preservers," he called them. "Cheap repairs for a cheap 'un," he used to say, but the husbands never found the repairs very cheap. Those were the days when lumbermen's daughters and brewers' wives contended in song; studied in Germany and then floated from *Sängerfest* to *Sängerfest*. Choral societies flourished in all the rich lake cities and river cities. The soloists came to Chicago to coach with Bowers, and he often took long journeys to hear and instruct a chorus. He was intensely avaricious, and from these semi-professionals he reaped a golden harvest. They fed his pockets and they fed his ever-hungry contempt, his scorn of himself and his accomplices. The more money he made, the more parsimonious he became. His wife was so shabby that she never went anywhere with him, which suited him exactly. Because his clients were luxurious and extravagant, he took a revengeful pleasure in having his shoes half-soled a second time, and in getting the last wear out of a broken collar. He had first been interested in Thea Kronborg because of her bluntness, her country roughness, and her manifest carefulness about money. The mention of Harsanyi's name always made him pull a wry face. For the first time Thea had a friend who, in his own cool and guarded way, liked her for whatever was least admirable in her.

Thea was still looking at the musical paper, her grammar unopened on the window-sill, when Bowers sauntered in a little before two o'clock. He was smoking a cheap cigarette and wore the same soft felt hat he had worn all last winter. He never carried a cane or wore gloves.

Thea followed him from the reception-room into the studio. "I may cut my lesson out to-morrow, Mr. Bowers. I have to hunt a new boarding-place."

Bowers looked up languidly from his desk where he had begun to go over a pile of letters. "What's the matter with the Studio Club? Been fighting with them again?"

"The Club's all right for people who like to live that way. I don't."

Bowers lifted his eyebrows. "Why so tempery?" he asked as he drew a cheque from an envelope postmarked "Minneapolis."

"I can't work with a lot of girls around. They're too familiar. I never could get along with girls of my own age. It's all too chummy. Gets on my nerves. I didn't come here to play kindergarten games." Thea began energetically to arrange the scattered music on the piano.

Bowers grimaced good-humouredly at her over the three cheques he was pinning together. He liked to play at a rough game of banter with her. He flattered himself that he had made her harsher than she was when she first came to him; that he had got off a little of the sugar-coating Harsanyi always put on his pupils.

"The art of making yourself agreeable never comes amiss, Miss Kronborg. I should say you rather need a little practice along that line. When you come to marketing your wares in the world, a little smoothness goes farther than a great deal of talent sometimes. If you happen to be cursed with a real talent, then you've got to be very smooth, indeed, or you'll never get your money back." Bowers snapped the elastic band around his bank-book.

Thea gave him a sharp, recognizing glance. "Well, that's the money I'll have to go without," she replied.

"Just what do you mean?"

"I mean the money people have to grin for. I used to know a railroad man who said there was money in every profession that you couldn't take. He'd tried a good many jobs," Thea added musingly; "perhaps he was too particular about the kind he could take, for he never picked up much. He was proud, but I liked him for that."

Bowers rose and closed his desk. "Mrs. Priest is late again. By the way, Miss Kronborg, remember not to frown when you are playing for Mrs. Priest. You did not remember yesterday."

"You mean when she hits a tone with her breath like that? Why do you let her? You wouldn't let me."

"I certainly would not. But that is a mannerism of Mrs. Priest's. The public like it, and they pay a great deal of money for the pleasure of hearing her do it. There she is. Remember!"

Bowers opened the door of the reception-room and a tall, imposing woman rustled in, bringing with her a glow of animation which pervaded the room as if half a dozen persons, all talking gaily, had come in instead of one. She was large, handsome, expansive, uncontrolled; one felt this the moment she crossed the threshold. She shone with care and cleanliness, mature vigour, unchallenged authority, gracious good-humour, and absolute confidence in her person, her powers, her position, and her way of life; a glowing, overwhelming self-satisfaction, only to be found where human society is young and strong and without yesterdays. Her face had a kind of heavy, thoughtless beauty, like a pink peony just at the point of beginning to fade. Her brown hair was waved in front and done up behind in a great twist, held by a tortoise-shell comb with gold filigree. She wore a beautiful little green hat with three long green feathers sticking straight up in front, a little cape made of velvet and fur with a yellow satin rose on it. Her gloves, her shoes, her veil, somehow made themselves felt. She gave the impression of wearing a cargo of splendid merchandise.

Mrs. Priest nodded graciously to Thea, coquettishly to Bowers, and asked him to untie her veil for her. She threw her splendid wrap on a chair, the yellow lining out. Thea was already at the piano. Mrs. Priest stood behind her.

" 'Rejoice Greatly' first, please. And please don't hurry it in there," she put her arm over Thea's shoulder, and indicated the passage by a sweep of her white glove. She threw out her chest, clasped her hands over her abdomen, lifted her chin, worked the muscles of her cheeks back and forth for a moment, and then began with conviction, "Re-jo-oice! Re-jo-oice!"

Bowers paced the room with his catlike tread. When he checked Mrs. Priest's vehemence at all, he handled her roughly; poked and hammered her massive person with cold satisfaction, almost as if he were taking out a grudge on this splendid creation. Such treatment the imposing lady did not at all resent. She tried harder and harder, her eyes growing all the while more lustrous and her lips redder. Thea played on as she was told, ignoring the singer's struggles.

When she first heard Mrs. Priest sing in church, Thea admired her. Since she had found out how dull the good-natured soprano really was, she felt a deep contempt for her. She felt that Mrs. Priest ought to be reproved and even punished for her shortcomings; that she ought to be exposed—at least to herself—and not be permitted to live and shine in happy ignorance of what a poor thing it was she brought across so radiantly. Thea's cold looks of reproof were lost upon Mrs. Priest; although the lady did murmur one day when she took Bowers home in her carriage, "How handsome your afternoon girl would be if she did not have that unfortunate squint; it gives her that vacant Swede look, like an animal." That amused Bowers. He liked to watch the germination and growth of antipathies.

One of the first disappointments Thea had to face, when she returned to Chicago that fall, was the news that the Harsanyis were not coming back. They had spent the summer in a camp in the Adirondacks and were moving to New York. An old teacher and friend of Harsanyi's, one of the best-known piano-teachers in New York, was about to retire because of failing health and had arranged to turn his pupils over to Harsanyi. Andor was to give two recitals in New York in November, to devote himself to his new students until spring, and then to go on a short concert tour. The Harsanyis had taken a furnished apartment in New York, as they would not attempt to settle a place of their own until Andor's recitals were over. The first of December, however, Thea received a note from Mrs. Harsanyi, asking her to call at the old studio, where she was packing their goods for shipment.

The morning after this invitation reached her, Thea climbed the stairs and knocked at the familiar door. Mrs. Harsanyi herself opened it, and embraced her visitor warmly. Taking Thea into the studio, which was littered with excelsior and packing-cases, she stood holding her hand and looking at her in the strong light from the big window before she allowed her to sit down. Her quick eye saw many changes. The girl was taller, her figure had become definite, her carriage positive. She had got used to living in the body of a young woman, and she no longer tried to ignore it and behave as if she were a little girl. With that increased independence of body there had come a change in her face; an indifference, something hard and sceptical. Her clothes, too, were different, like the attire of a shopgirl who tries to follow the fashions: a purple suit, a piece of cheap fur, a three-cornered purple hat with a pompon sticking up in front. The queer country clothes she used to wear suited her much better, Mrs. Harsanyi thought. But such trifles, after all, were accidental and remediable. She put her hand on the girl's strong shoulder.

"How much the summer has done for you! Yes, you are a young lady at last. Andor will be so glad to hear about you."

Thea looked about at the disorder of the familiar room. The pictures were piled in a corner, the piano and the *chaise longue* were gone. "I suppose I ought to be glad you have gone away," she said, "but I'm not. It's a fine thing for Mr. Harsanyi, I suppose."

Mrs. Harsanyi gave her a quick glance which said more than words. "If you knew how long I have wanted, to get him away from here, Miss Kronborg! He is never tired, never discouraged, now."

Thea sighed. "I'm glad for that, then." Her eyes travelled over the faint discolourations on the walls where the pictures had hung. "I may run away myself. I don't know whether I can stand it here without you."

"We hope that you can come to New York to study before very long. We have thought of that. And you must tell me how you are getting on with Bowers. Andor will want to know all about it."

"I guess I get on more or less. But I don't like my work very well. It never seems serious as my work with Mr. Harsanyi did. I play Bowers's accompaniments in the afternoons, you know. I thought I should learn a good deal from the people who work with him, but I don't think I get much."

Mrs. Harsanyi looked at her inquiringly. Thea took out a carefully folded handkerchief from the bosom of her dress and began to draw the corners apart. "Singing doesn't seem to be a very brainy profession, Mrs. Harsanyi," she said slowly. "The people I see now are not a bit like the ones I used to meet here. Mr. Harsanyi's pupils, even the dumb ones, had more—well, more of everything, it seems to me. The people I have to play accompaniments for are discouraging. The professionals, like Katharine Priest and Miles Murdstone, are worst of all. If I have to play 'The Messiah' much longer for Mrs. Priest, I'll go out of my mind!" Thea brought her foot down sharply on the bare floor.

Mrs. Harsanyi looked down at the foot in perplexity. "You mustn't wear such high heels, my dear. They will spoil your walk and make you mince along. Can't you at least learn to avoid what you dislike in these singers? I was never able to care for Mrs. Priest's singing."

Thea was sitting with her chin lowered. Without moving her head she looked up at Mrs. Harsanyi and smiled; a smile much too cold and desperate to be seen on a young face, Mrs. Harsanyi felt. "Mrs. Harsanyi, it seems to me that what I learn is just *to dislike*. I dislike so much and so hard that it tires me out. I've got no heart for anything." She threw up her head suddenly and sat in defiance, her hand clenched on the arm of the chair. "Mr. Harsanyi couldn't stand these people an hour, I know he couldn't. He'd put them right out of the window there, frizzes and feathers and all. Now, take that new soprano they're all making such a fuss about, Jessie Darcey. She's going on tour with a symphony orchestra and she's working up her repertory with Bowers. She's singing some Schumann songs Mr. Harsanyi used to go over with me. Well, I don't know what he *would* do if he heard her."

"But if your own work goes well, and you know these people are wrong, why do you let them discourage you?"

Thea shook her head. "That's just what I don't understand myself. Only, after I've heard them all afternoon, I come out frozen up. Somehow it takes the shine off of everything. People want Jessie Darcey and the kind of thing she does; so what's the use?"

Mrs. Harsanyi smiled. "That stile you must simply vault over. You must not begin to fret about the successes of cheap people. After all, what have they to do with you?"

"Well, if I had somebody like Mr. Harsanyi, perhaps I shouldn't fret about them. He was the teacher for me. Please tell him so."

Thea rose and Mrs. Harsanyi took her hand again. "I am sorry you have to go through this time of discouragement. I wish Andor could talk to you, he would understand it so well. But I feel like urging you to keep clear of Mrs. Priest and Jessie Darcey and all their kind."

Thea laughed discordantly. "No use urging me. I don't get on with them *at all*. My spine gets like a steel rail when they come near me. I liked them at first, you know. Their clothes and their manners were so fine, and Mrs. Priest *is* handsome. But now I keep wanting to tell them how stupid they are. Seems like they ought to be informed, don't you think so?" There was a flash of the shrewd grin that Mrs. Harsanyi remembered. Thea pressed her hand. "I must go now. I had to give my lesson hour this morning to a Duluth woman who has come on to coach, and I must go and play 'On Mighty Pens' for her. Please tell Mr. Harsanyi that I think oratorio is a great chance for bluffers."

Mrs. Harsanyi detained her. "But he will want to know much more than that about you. You are free at seven? Come back this evening, then, and we will go to dinner somewhere, to some cheerful place. I think you need a party."

Thea brightened. "Oh, I do! I'll love to come; that will be like old times. You see"—she lingered a moment, softening—"I shouldn't mind if there were only *one* of them I could really admire."

"How about Bowers?" Mrs. Harsanyi asked as they were approaching the stairway.

"Well, there's nothing he loves like a good fakir, and nothing he hates like a good artist. I always remember something Mr. Harsanyi said about him. He said Bowers was the cold muffin that had been left on the plate."

Mrs. Harsanyi stopped short at the head of the stairs and said decidedly: "I think Andor made a mistake. I can't believe that is the right atmosphere for you. It would hurt you more than most people. It's all wrong."

"Something's wrong," Thea called back as she clattered down the stairs in her high heels.

II

*D*uring that winter Thea lived in so many places that sometimes at night, when she left Bowers's studio and emerged into the street, she had to stop and think for a moment to remember where she was living now and what was the best way to get there.

When she moved into a new place, her eyes challenged the beds, the carpets, the food, the mistress of the house. The boarding-houses were wretchedly conducted, and Thea's complaints sometimes took an insulting form. She quarrelled with one landlady after another and moved on. When she moved into a new room, she was almost sure to hate it on sight and to begin planning to hunt another place before she had unpacked her trunk. She was moody and contemptuous toward her fellow boarders, except toward the young men, whom she treated with a careless familiarity which they usually misunderstood. They liked her, however, and when she left the house after a storm, they helped her to move her things and came to see her after she got settled in a new place. But she moved so often that they soon ceased to follow her. They could see no reason for keeping up with a girl who, under her jocularity, was cold, self-centered, and unimpressionable. They soon felt that she did not admire them.

Thea used to waken up in the night and wonder why she was so unhappy. She would have been amazed if she had known how much the people whom she met in Bowers's studio had to do with her low spirits. She had never been conscious of those instinctive standards which are called ideals, and she did not know that she was suffering for them. She often found herself sneering when she was on a street-car, or when she was brushing out her hair before her mirror, as some inane remark or too familiar mannerism flitted across her mind.

She felt no creature kindness, no tolerant good will for Mrs. Priest or Jessie Darcey. After one of Jessie Darcey's concerts the glowing press notices, and the admiring comments that floated about Bowers's studio, caused Thea bitter unhappiness. It was not the torment of personal jealousy. She had never thought of herself as even a possible rival of Miss Darcey. She was a poor music student, and Jessie Darcey was a popular and petted professional. Mrs. Priest, whatever one held against her, had a fine, big, showy voice and an impressive presence. She read indifferently, was inaccurate, and was always putting other people wrong, but she at least had the material out of which singers can be made. But people seemed to like Jessie Darcey exactly because she could not sing; because, as they put it, she was "so natural and unprofessional." Her singing was pronounced "artless," her voice "birdlike." Miss Darcey was thin and awkward in person, with a sharp, sallow face. Thea noticed that her plainness was accounted to her credit, and that people spoke of it affectionately. Miss Darcey was singing everywhere just then; one could not help hearing about her. She was backed by some of the packing-house people and by the Chicago Northwestern Railroad. Only one critic raised his voice against her. Thea went to several of Jessie Darcey's concerts. It was the first time she had had an opportunity to observe the whims of the public which singers live by interesting. She saw that people liked in Miss Darcey every quality a singer ought not to have, and especially the nervous complacency that stamped her as a commonplace young woman. They seemed to have a warmer feeling for Jessie than for Mrs. Priest, an affectionate and cherishing regard. Chicago was not so very different from Moonstone, after all, and Jessie Darcey was only Lily Fisher under another name.

Thea particularly hated to accompany for Miss Darcey because she sang off pitch and didn't mind it in the least. It was excruciating to sit there day after day and hear her; there was something shameless and indecent about not singing true.

One morning Miss Darcey came by appointment to go over the programme for her Peoria concert. She was such a frail-looking girl that Thea ought to have felt sorry for her. True, she had an arch, sprightly little manner, and a flash of salmon-pink on either brown cheek. But a narrow upper jaw gave her face a pinched look, and her eyelids were heavy and relaxed. By the morning light, the purplish brown circles under her eyes were pathetic enough, and foretold no long or brilliant future. A singer with a poor digestion and low vitality; she needed no seer to cast her horoscope. If Thea had ever taken the pains to study her, she would have seen that, under all her smiles and archness, poor Miss Darcey was really frightened to death. She could not understand her success any more than Thea could; she kept catching her breath and lifting her eyebrows and trying to believe that it was true. Her loquacity was not natural, she forced herself to it, and when she confided to you how many defects she could overcome by her unusual command of head resonance, she was not so much trying to persuade you as to persuade herself.

When she took a note that was high for her, Miss Darcey always put her right hand out into the air, as if she were indicating height, or giving an exact measurement. Some early teacher had told her that she could "place" a tone more surely by the help of such a gesture, and she firmly believed that it was of great assistance to her. (Even when she was singing in public, she kept her right hand down with difficulty, nervously clasping her white-kid fingers together when she took a high note. Thea could always see her elbows stiffen.) She unvaryingly executed this gesture with a smile of gracious confidence, as if she were actually putting her finger on the note: "There it is, friends!"

This morning, in Gounod's "Ave Maria," as Miss Darcey approached her B natural—

Dans——nos a—lár————mes!

out went the hand, with the sure airy gesture, though it was little above A she got with her voice, whatever she touched with her finger. Often Bowers let such things pass—with the right people—but this morning he snapped his jaws together and muttered, "God!" Miss Darcey tried again, with the same gesture as of putting the crowning touch, tilting her head and smiling radiantly at Bowers, as if to say, "It is for you I do all this!"

Dans———nos a—lár———mes!

This time she made B flat, and went on in the happy belief that she had done well enough, when she suddenly found that her accompanist was not going on with her, and this put her out completely.

She turned to Thea, whose hands had fallen in her lap. "Oh, why did you stop just there! It *is* too trying! Now we'd better go back to that other *crescendo* and try it from there."

"I beg your pardon," Thea muttered. "I thought you wanted to get that B natural." She began again, as Miss Darcey indicated.

After the singer was gone, Bowers walked up to Thea and asked languidly, "Why do you hate Jessie so? Her little variations from pitch are between her and her public; they don't hurt you. Has she ever done anything to you except be very agreeable?"

"Yes, she has done things to me," Thea retorted hotly.

Bowers looked interested. "What, for example?"

"I can't explain, but I've got it in for her."

Bowers laughed. "No doubt about that. I'll have to suggest that you conceal it a little more effectually. That is—necessary, Miss Kronborg," he added, looking back over the shoulder of the overcoat he was putting on.

He went out to lunch and Thea thought the subject closed. But late in the afternoon, when he was taking his dyspepsia tablet and a glass of water between lessons, he looked up at her and said in a voice ironically coaxing:

"Miss Kronborg, I wish you would tell me why you hate Jessie."

Taken by surprise Thea put down the score she was reading and answered before she knew what she was saying, "I hate her for the sake of what I used to think a singer might be."

Bowers balanced the tablet on the end of his long forefinger and whistled softly.

"And how did you form your conception of what a singer ought to be?" he asked.

"I don't know." Thea flushed and spoke under her breath. "But I suppose I got most of it from Harsanyi."

Bowers made no comment upon this reply, but opened the door for the next pupil, who was waiting in the reception-room.

It was dark when Thea left the studio that night. She knew she had offended Bowers. Somehow she had hurt herself, too. She felt unequal to the boarding-house table, the sneaking divinity student who sat next her and had tried to kiss her on the stairs last night. She went over to the waterside of Michigan Avenue and walked along beside the lake. It was a clear, frosty winter night. The great empty space over the water was restful and spoke of freedom. If she had any money at all, she would go away. The stars glittered over the wide black water. She looked up at them wearily and shook her head. She believed that what she felt was despair, but it was only one of the forms of hope. She felt, indeed, as if she were bidding the stars good-bye; but she was merely renewing a promise. Though their challenge is universal and eternal, the stars get no answer but that—the brief light flashed back to them from the eyes of the young who unaccountably aspire.

The rich, noisy city, fat with food and drink, is a spent thing; its chief concern is its digestion and its little game of hide-and-seek with the undertaker. Money and office and success are the consolations of impotence. Fortune turns kind to such solid people and lets them suck their bone in peace. She flicks her whip upon flesh that is more alive, upon that stream of hungry boys and girls who tramp the streets of every city, recognizable by their pride and discontent, who are the Future, and who possess the treasure of creative power.

III

*W*hile her living arrangements were so casual and fortuitous, Bowers's studio was the one fixed thing in Thea's life. She went out from it to uncertainties, and hastened to it from nebulous confusion. She was more influenced by Bowers than she knew. Unconsciously she began to take on something of his dry contempt, and to share his grudge without understanding exactly what it was about. His cynicism seemed to her honest, and the amiability of his pupils artificial. She admired his drastic treatment of his dull pupils. The stupid deserved all they got, and more. Bowers knew that she thought him a very clever man.

One afternoon when Bowers came in from lunch, Thea handed him a card on which he read the name, "Mr. Philip Frederick Ottenburg."

"He said he would be in again to-morrow and that he wanted some time. Who is he? I like him better than the others."

Bowers nodded. "So do I. He's not a singer. He is a beer prince: son of the big brewer in St. Louis. He has been in Germany with his mother. I didn't know he was back."

"Does he take lessons?"

"Now and again. He sings rather well. He's at the head of the Chicago branch of the Ottenburg business, but he can't stick to work and is always running away. He has great ideas in beer, people tell me. He's what they call an imaginative business man; goes over to Bayreuth and seems to do nothing but give parties and spend money, and brings back more good notions for the brewery than the fellows who sit tight dig out in five years. I was born too long ago to be much taken in by these chesty boys with flowered vests, but I like Fred, all the same."

"So do I," said Thea positively.

Bowers made a sound between a cough and a laugh. "Oh, he's a lady-killer, all right! The girls in here are always making eyes at him. You won't be the first." He threw some sheets of music on the piano. "Better look that over; accompaniment's a little tricky. It's for that new woman from Detroit. And Mrs. Priest will be in this afternoon."

Thea sighed.

"'I Know that my Redeemer Liveth'?"

"The same. She starts on her concert tour next week, and we'll have a rest. Until then, I suppose we'll have to be going over her programme."

The next day Thea hurried through her luncheon at a German bakery and got back to the studio at ten minutes past one. She felt sure that the young brewer would come early, before it was time for Bowers to arrive. He had not said he would, but yesterday, when he opened the door to go, he had glanced about the room and at her, and something in his eye had conveyed that suggestion.

Sure enough, at twenty minutes past one the door of the reception-room opened, and a tall, robust young man with a cane and an English hat and ulster looked in expectantly. "Ah—ha!" he exclaimed. "I thought if I came early I might have good luck. And how are you to-day, Miss Kronborg?"

Thea was sitting in the window chair. At her left elbow there was a table, and upon this table the young man sat down, holding his hat and cane in his hand, loosening his long coat so that it fell back from his shoulders. He was a gleaming, florid young fellow. His hair, thick and yellow, was cut very short, and he wore a closely trimmed beard, long enough on the chin to curl a little. Even his eyebrows were thick and yellow, like fleece. He had lively blue eyes—Thea looked up at them with great interest as he sat chatting and swinging his foot rhythmically. He was easily familiar, and frankly so. Wherever people met young Ottenburg—in his office, on shipboard, in a foreign hotel or railway compartment—they always felt (and usually liked) that artless presumption which seemed to say, "In this case we may waive formalities. We really haven't time. This is to-day, but it will soon be to-morrow, and then we may be very different people, and in some other country." He had a way of floating people out of dull or awkward situations, out of their own torpor or constraint or discouragement. It was a marked personal talent, of almost incalculable value in the representative of a great business founded on social amenities. Thea had liked him yesterday for the way in which he had picked her up out of herself and her German grammar for a few exciting moments.

"By the way, will you tell me your first name, please? Thea? Oh, then you *are* a Swede, sure enough! I thought so. Let me call you Miss Thea, after the German fashion. You won't mind? Of course not!" He usually made his assumption of a special understanding seem a tribute to the other person and not to himself.

"How long have you been with Bowers here? Do you like the old grouch? So do I. I've come to tell him about a new soprano I heard at Bayreuth. He'll pretend not to care, but he does. Do you warble with him? Have you anything of a voice? Honest? You look it, you know. What are you going in for, something big? Opera?"

Thea blushed crimson. "Oh, I'm not going in for anything. I'm trying to learn to sing at funerals."

Ottenburg leaned forward. His eyes twinkled. "I'll engage you to sing at mine. You can't fool me, Miss Thea. May I hear you take your lesson this afternoon?"

"No, you may not. I took it this morning."

He picked up a roll of music that lay behind him on the table. "Is this yours? Let me see what you are doing." He snapped back the clasp and began turning over the songs. "All very fine, but tame. What's he got you at this Mozart stuff for? I shouldn't think it would suit your voice. Oh, I can make a pretty good guess at what will suit you! This from "Gioconda" is more in your line. What's this Grieg? It looks interesting. *Tak for dit Råd.* What does that mean?"

" 'Thanks for your Advice.' Don't you know it?"

"No; not at all. Let's try it." He rose, pushed open the door into the music-room, and motioned Thea to enter before him. She hung back.

"I couldn't give you much of an idea of it. It's a big song."

Ottenburg took her gently by the elbow and pushed her into the other room. He sat down carelessly at the piano and looked over the music for a moment.

"I think I can get you through it. But how stupid not to have the German words. Can you really sing the Norwegian? What an infernal language to sing. Translate the text for me." He handed her the music.

Thea looked at it, then at him, and shook her head. "I can't. The truth is I don't know either English or Swedish very well, and Norwegian's still worse," she said confidentially. She not infrequently refused to do what she was asked to do, but it was not like her to explain her refusal, even when she had a good reason.

"I understand. We immigrants never speak any language well. But you know what it means, don't you?"

"Of course I do!"

"Then don't frown at me like that, but tell me."

Thea continued to frown, but she also smiled. She was confused, but not embarrassed. She was not afraid of Ottenburg. He was not one of those people who made her spine like a steel rail. On the contrary, he made one venturesome.

"Well, it goes something like this: 'Thanks for your advice! But I prefer to steer my boat into the din of roaring breakers. Even if the journey is my last, I may find what I have never found before. Onward must I go, for I yearn for the wild sea. I long to fight my way through the angry waves, and to see how far, and how long I can make them carry me.' "

Ottenburg took the music and began: "Wait a moment. Is that too fast? How do you take it? That right?" He pulled up his cuffs and began the accompaniment again. He had become entirely serious, and he played with fine enthusiasm and with understanding.

Fred's talent was worth almost as much to old Otto Ottenburg as the steady industry of his older sons. When Fred sang the Prize Song at an interstate meet of the *Turnverein,* ten thousand *Turners* went forth pledged to Ottenburg beer.

As Thea finished the song, Fred turned back to the first page, without looking up from the music. "Now, once more," he called. They began again, and did not hear Bowers when he came in and stood in the doorway. He stood still, blinking like an owl at their two heads shining in the sun. He could not see their faces, but there was something about his girl's back that he had not noticed before: a very slight and yet very free motion, from the toes up. Her whole back seemed plastic, seemed to be moulding itself to the galloping rhythm of the song. Bowers perceived such things sometimes—unwillingly. He had known to-day that there was something afoot. The river of sound which had its source in his pupil had caught him two flights down. He had stopped and listened with a kind of sneering admiration. From the door he watched her with a half-incredulous, half-malicious smile.

When he had struck the keys for the last time, Ottenburg dropped his hands on his knees and looked up with a quick breath. "I got you through. What a stunning song! Did I play it right?"

Thea studied his excited face. There was a good deal of meaning in it, and there was a good deal in her own as she answered him. "You suited me," she said ungrudgingly.

After Ottenburg was gone, Thea noticed that Bowers was more agreeable than usual. She had heard the young brewer ask Bowers to dine with him at his club that evening, and she saw that he looked forward to the dinner with pleasure. He dropped a remark to the effect that Fred knew as much about food and wines as any man in Chicago. He said this boastfully.

"If he's such a grand business man, how does he have time to run around listening to singing-lessons?" Thea asked suspiciously.

As she went home to her boarding-house through the February slush, she wished she were going to dine with them. At nine o'clock she looked up from her grammar to wonder what Bowers and Ottenburg were having to eat. At that moment they were talking of her.

IV

*T*hea noticed that Bowers took rather more pains with her now that Fred Ottenburg often dropped in at eleven-thirty to hear her lesson. After the lesson the young man took Bowers off to lunch with him, and Bowers liked good food when another man paid for it. He encouraged Fred's visits, and Thea soon saw that Fred knew exactly why.

One morning, after her lesson, Ottenburg turned to Bowers. "If you'll lend me Miss Thea, I think I have an engagement for her. Mrs. Henry Nathanmeyer is going to give three musical evenings in April, the first three Saturdays, and she has consulted me about soloists. For the first evening she has a young violinist, and she would be charmed to have Miss Kronborg. She will pay fifty dollars. Not much, but Miss Thea would meet some people there who might be useful. What do you say?"

Bowers passed the question on to Thea. "I guess you could use the fifty, couldn't you, Miss Kronborg? You can easily work up some songs."

Thea was perplexed. "I need the money awfully," she said frankly; "but I haven't got the right clothes for that sort of thing. I suppose I'd better try to get some."

Ottenburg spoke up quickly: "Oh, you'd make nothing out of it if you went to buying evening clothes. I've thought of that. Mrs. Nathan-meyer has a troop of daughters, a perfect seraglio, all ages and sizes. She'll be glad to fit you out. Let me take you to see her, and you'll find that she'll arrange that easily enough. I told her she must produce something nice, blue or yellow, and properly cut. I brought half a dozen Worth gowns through the customs for her two weeks ago, and she's not ungrateful. When can we go to see her?"

"I haven't any time free, except at night," Thea replied in some confusion.

"To-morrow evening, then? I shall call for you at eight. Bring all your songs along; she will want us to give her a little rehearsal, perhaps. I'll play your accompaniments, if you've no objection. That will save money for you and for Mrs. Nathanmeyer. She needs it." Ottenburg chuckled as he took down the number of Thea's boarding-house.

The Nathanmeyers were so rich and great that even Thea had heard of them, and this seemed a very remarkable opportunity. Ottenburg had brought it about by merely lifting a finger, apparently. He was a beer prince sure enough, as Bowers had said.

The next evening at a quarter to eight Thea was dressed and waiting in the boarding-house parlour. She was nervous and fidgety and found it difficult to sit still on the hard, convex upholstery of the chairs. She tried them one after another, moving about the dimly lighted, musty room, where the gas always leaked gently and sang in the burners. There was no one in the parlour but the medical student, who was playing one of Sousa's marches so vigorously that the china ornaments on the top of the piano rattled. In a few moments some of the pension-office girls would come in and begin to two-step. Thea wished that Ottenburg would come and let her escape. She glanced at herself in the long, sombre mirror. She was wearing her pale-blue broadcloth church dress, which was not unbecoming, but was certainly too heavy to wear to anybody's house in the evening. Her slippers were run over at the heel and she had not had time to have them mended, and her white gloves were not so clean as they should be. However, she knew that she would forget these annoying things as soon as Ottenburg came.

Mary, the Hungarian chambermaid, came to the door, stood between the plush portières, beckoned to Thea, and made an inarticulate sound in her throat. Thea jumped up and ran into the hall, where Ottenburg stood smiling, his caped cloak open, his silk hat in his white-kid hand. The Hungarian girl stood like a monument on her flat heels, staring at the pink carnation in Ottenburg's coat. Her broad, pockmarked face wore the only expression of which it was capable, a kind of animal wonder. As the young man followed Thea out, he glanced back over his shoulder through the crack of the door; the Hun clapped her hands over her stomach, opened her mouth, and made another raucous sound in her throat.

"Isn't she awful?" Thea exclaimed. "I think she's half-witted. Can you understand her?"

Ottenburg laughed as he helped her into the carriage. "Oh, yes; I can understand her!" He settled himself on the front seat opposite Thea. "Now, I want to tell you about the people we are going to see. We may have a musical public in this country some day, but as yet there are only the Germans and the Jews. All the other people go to hear Jessie Darcey sing, 'O, Promise Me!' The Nathanmeyers are the finest kind of Jews. If you do anything for Mrs. Henry Nathanmeyer, you must put yourself into her hands. Whatever she says about music, about clothes, about life, will be correct. And you may feel at ease with her. She expects nothing of people; she has lived in Chicago twenty years. If you were to behave like the Magyar who was so interested in my buttonhole, she would not be surprised. If you were to sing like Jessie Darcey, she would not be surprised; but she would manage not to hear you again."

"Would she? Well, that's the kind of people I want to find." Thea felt herself growing bolder.

"You will be all right with her so long as you do not try to be anything that you are not. Her standards have nothing to do with Chicago. Her perceptions—or her grandmother's, which is the same thing—were keen when all this was an Indian village. So merely be yourself, and you will like her. She will like you because the Jews always sense talent, and," he added ironically, "they admire certain qualities of feeling that are found only in the white-skinned races."

Thea looked into the young man's face as the light of a street-lamp flashed into the carriage. His somewhat academic manner amused her.

"What makes you take such an interest in singers?" she asked curiously. "You seem to have a perfect passion for hearing music-lessons. I wish I could trade jobs with you!"

"I'm not interested in singers." His tone was offended. "I am interested in talent. There are only two interesting things in the world, anyhow; and talent is one of them."

"What's the other?" The question came meekly from the figure opposite him. Another arc-light flashed in at the window.

Fred saw her face and broke into a laugh. "Why, you're guying me, you little wretch! You won't let me behave properly." He dropped his gloved hand lightly on her knee, took it away and let it hang between his own. "Do you know," he said confidentially, "I believe I'm more in earnest about all this than you are."

"About all what?"

"All you've got in your throat there."

"Oh! I'm in earnest all right; only I never was much good at talking. Jessie Darcey is the smooth talker: 'You notice the effect I get there—' If she only got 'em, she'd be a wonder, you know!"

Mr. and Mrs. Nathanmeyer were alone in their great library. Their three unmarried daughters had departed in successive carriages, one to a dinner, one to a Nietzsche club, one to a ball given for the girls employed in the big department stores. When Ottenburg and Thea entered, Henry Nathanmeyer and his wife were sitting at a table at the farther end of the long room, with a reading-lamp and a tray of cigarettes and cordial-glasses between them. The overhead lights were too soft to bring out the colours of the big rugs, and none of the picture lights were on. One could merely see that there were pictures there. Fred whispered that they were Rousseaus and Corots, very fine ones which the old banker had bought long ago for next to nothing. In the hall Ottenburg had stopped Thea before a painting of a woman eating grapes out of a paper bag, and had told her gravely that there was the most beautiful Manet in the world. He made her take off her hat and gloves in the hall, and looked her over a little before he took her in. But once they were in the library, he seemed perfectly satisfied with her and led her down the long room to their hostess.

Mrs. Nathanmeyer was a heavy, powerful old Jewess, with a great pompadour of white hair, a swarthy complexion, an eagle nose, and sharp, glittering eyes. She wore a black velvet dress with a long train, and a diamond necklace and earrings. She took Thea to the other side of the table and presented her to Mr. Nathanmeyer, who apologized for not rising, pointing to a slippered foot on a cushion; he said that he suffered from gout. He had a very soft voice and spoke with an accent which would have been heavy if it had not been so caressing. He kept Thea standing beside him for some time. He noticed that she stood easily, looked straight down into his face, and was not embarrassed. Even when Mrs. Nathanmeyer told Ottenburg to bring a chair for Thea, the old man did not release her hand, and she did not sit down. He admired her just as she was, as she happened to be standing, and she felt it. He was much handsomer than his wife, Thea thought. His forehead was high, his hair soft and white, his skin pink, a little puffy under his clear blue eyes. She noticed how warm and delicate his hands were, pleasant to touch and beautiful to look at. Ottenburg had told her that Mr. Nathanmeyer had a very fine collection of medals and cameos, and his fingers looked as if they had never touched anything but delicately cut surfaces.

He asked Thea where Moonstone was; how many inhabitants it had; what her father's business was; from what part of Sweden her grandfather came; and whether she spoke Swedish as a child. He was interested to hear that her mother's mother was still living, and that her grandfather had played the oboe. Thea felt at home standing there beside him; she felt that he was very wise, and that he some way took one's life up and looked it over kindly, as if it were a story. She was sorry when they left him to go into the music-room.

As they reached the door of the music-room, Mrs. Nathanmeyer turned a switch that threw on many lights. The room was even larger than the library, all glittering surfaces, with two Steinway pianos.

Mrs. Nathanmeyer rang for her own maid. "Selma will take you upstairs, Miss Kronborg, and you will find some dresses on the bed. Try several of them, and take the one you like best. Selma will help you. She has a great deal of taste. When you are dressed, come down and let us go over some of your songs with Mr. Ottenburg."

After Thea went away with the maid, Ottenburg came up to Mrs. Nathanmeyer and stood beside her, resting his hand on the high back of her chair.

"Well, *gnädige Frau,* do you like her?"

"I think so. I liked her when she talked to father. She will always get on better with men."

Ottenburg leaned over her chair. "Prophetess! Do you see what I meant?"

"About her beauty? She has great possibilities, but you can never tell about those Northern women. They look so strong, but they are easily battered. The face falls so early under those wide cheek-bones. A single idea—hate or greed, or even love—can tear them to shreds. She is nineteen? Well, in ten years she may have quite a regal beauty, or she may have a heavy, discontented face, all dug out in channels. That will depend upon the kind of ideas she lives with."

"Or the kind of people?" Ottenburg suggested.

The old Jewess folded her arms over her massive chest, drew back her shoulders, and looked up at the young man.

"With that hard glint in her eye? The people won't matter much, I fancy. They will come and go. She is very much interested in herself—as she should be."

Ottenburg frowned.

"Wait until you hear her sing. Her eyes are different then. That gleam that comes in them is curious, isn't it? As you say, it's impersonal."

The object of this discussion came in, smiling. She had chosen neither the blue nor the yellow gown, but a pale rose-colour, with silver butterflies. Mrs. Nathanmeyer lifted her lorgnette and studied her as she approached. She caught the characteristic things at once: the free, strong walk, the calm carriage of the head, the milky whiteness of the girl's arms and shoulders.

"Yes, that colour is good for you," she said approvingly. "The yellow one probably killed your hair? Yes; this does very well, indeed, so we need think no more about it."

Thea glanced questioningly at Ottenburg. He smiled and bowed, seemed perfectly satisfied. He asked her to stand in the elbow of the piano, in front of him, instead of behind him as she had been taught to do.

"Yes," said the hostess with feeling. "That other position is barbarous."

Thea sang an aria from "Gioconda," some songs by Schumann which she had studied with Harsanyi, and the "Tak for dit Räd," which Ottenburg liked.

"That you must do again," he declared when they finished this song. "You did it much better the other day. You accented it more, like a dance or a galop. How did you do it?"

Thea laughed, glancing sidewise at Mrs. Nathanmeyer. "You want it rough-house, do you? Bowers likes me to sing it more seriously, but it always makes me think about a story my grandmother used to tell."

Fred pointed to the chair behind her. "Won't you rest a moment and tell us about it? I thought you had some notion about it when you first sang it for me."

Thea sat down. "In Norway my grandmother knew a girl who was awfully in love with a young fellow. She went into service on a big dairy farm to make enough money for her outfit. They were married at Christmas time, and everybody was glad, because they'd been sighing around about each other for so long. That very summer, the day before Saint John's Day, her husband caught her carrying on with another farm-hand. The next night all the farm people had a bonfire and a big dance up on the mountain, and everybody was dancing and singing. I guess they were all a little drunk, for they got to seeing how near they could make the girls dance to the edge of the cliff. Ole—he was the girl's husband—seemed the jolliest and the drunkest of anybody. He danced his wife nearer and nearer the edge of the rock, and his wife began to scream so that the others stopped dancing and the music stopped; but Ole went right on singing, and he danced her over the edge of the cliff and they fell hundreds of feet and were all smashed to pieces."

Ottenburg turned back to the piano.

"That's the idea! Now, come, Miss Thea. Let it go!"

Thea took her place. She laughed and drew herself up out of her corsets, threw her shoulders high and let them drop again. She had never sung in a low dress before, and she found it comfortable. Ottenburg jerked his head and they began the song. The accompaniment sounded more than ever like the thumping and scraping of heavy feet.

When they stopped, they heard a sympathetic tapping at the end of the room. Old Mr. Nathanmeyer had come to the door and was sitting back in the shadow, just inside the library, applauding with his cane. Thea threw him a bright smile. He continued to sit there, his slippered foot on a low chair, his cane between his fingers, and she glanced at him from time to time. The doorway made a frame for him, and he looked like a man in a picture, with the long, shadowy room behind him.

Mrs. Nathanmeyer summoned the maid again.

"Selma will pack that gown in a box for you, and you can take it home in Mr. Ottenburg's carriage."

Thea turned to follow the maid, but hesitated. "Shall I wear gloves?" she asked, turning again to Mrs. Nathanmeyer.

"No, I think not. Your arms are good, and you will feel freer without. You will need light slippers, pink—or white, if you have them, will do quite as well."

Thea went upstairs with the maid, and Mrs. Nathanmeyer rose, took Ottenburg's arm, and walked toward her husband.

"That's the first real voice I have heard in Chicago," she said decidedly. "I don't count that stupid Priest woman. What do you say, father?"

Mr. Nathanmeyer shook his white head and smiled softly, as if he were thinking about something very agreeable. *"Svensk sommar,"* he murmured. "She is like a Swedish summer. I spent nearly a year there when I was a young man," he explained to Ottenburg.

When Ottenburg got Thea and her big box into the carriage, it occurred to him that she must be hungry, after singing so much. When he asked her, she admitted that she was very hungry indeed.

He took out his watch. "Would you mind stopping somewhere with me? It's only eleven."

"Mind? Of course, I wouldn't mind. I wasn't brought up like that. I can take care of myself."

Ottenburg laughed. "And I can take care of myself, so we can do lots of jolly things together." He opened the carriage door and spoke to the driver. "I'm stuck on the way you sing that Grieg song," he declared.

When Thea got into bed that night she told herself that this was the happiest evening she had had in Chicago. She had enjoyed the Nathanmeyers and their grand house, her new dress, and Ottenburg, her first real carriage ride, and the good supper when she was so hungry. And Ottenburg *was* jolly! He made you want to come back at him. You weren't always being caught up and mystified. When you started in with him, you went; you cut the breeze, as Ray used to say. He had some go in him.

Philip Frederick Ottenburg was the third son of the great brewer. His mother was Katarina Fürst, the daughter and heiress of a brewing business older and richer than Otto Ottenburg's. As a young woman she had been a conspicuous figure in German-American society in New York, and not untouched by scandal. She was a handsome, headstrong girl, a rebellious and violent force in a provincial society. She was brutally sentimental and heavily romantic. Her free speech, her Continental ideas, and her proclivity for championing new causes, even when she did not know much about them, made her an object of suspicion. She was always going abroad to seek out intellectual affinities, and was one of the group of young women who followed Wagner about in his old age, keeping at a respectful distance, but receiving now and then a gracious acknowledgement that he appreciated their homage. When the composer died, Katarina, then a matron with a family, took to her bed and saw no one for a week.

After having been engaged to an American actor, a Welsh social-ist agitator, and a German army officer, Fräulein Fürst at last placed herself and her great brewery interests into the trustworthy hands of Otto Otten-burg, who had been her suitor ever since he was a clerk, learning his business in her father's office.

Her first two sons were exactly like their father. Even as children they were industrious, earnest little tradesmen. As Frau Ottenburg said, "she had to wait for her Fred, but she got him at last," the first man who had altogether pleased her. Frederick entered Harvard when he was eigh-teen. When his mother went to Boston to visit him, she not only got him everything he wished for, but she made handsome and often embarrassing presents to all his friends. She gave dinners and supper parties for the Glee Club, made the crew break training, and was a generally disturbing influ-ence. In his third year Fred left the university because of a serious escapade which had somewhat hampered his life ever since. He went at once into his father's business, where, in his own way, he had made himself very useful.

Fred Ottenburg was now twenty-eight, and people could only say of him that he had been less hurt by his mother's indulgence than most boys would have been. He had never wanted anything that he could not have it, and he might have had a great many things that he had never wanted. He was extravagant, but not prodigal. He turned most of the money his mother gave him into the business, and lived on his generous salary.

Fred had never been bored for a whole day in his life. When he was in Chicago or St. Louis, he went to ball-games, prize-fights, and horse-races. When he was in Germany, he went to concerts and to the opera. He belonged to a long list of sporting-clubs and hunting-clubs, and was a good boxer. He had so many natural interests that he had no affecta-tions. Physical energy was the thing he was full to the brim of, and music was one of its natural forms of expression. He had a healthy love of sport and art, of eating and drinking. When he was in Germany, he scarcely knew where the soup ended and the symphony began.

V

*M*arch began badly for Thea. She had a cold during the first week, and after she got through her church duties on Sunday, she had to go to bed with tonsillitis. She was still in the boarding-house at which young Ottenburg had called when he took her to see Mrs. Nathanmeyer. She had stayed on there because her room, although it was inconvenient and very small, was at the corner of the house and got the sunlight.

Since she left Mrs. Lorch, this was the first place where she had got away from a north light. Her rooms had all been as damp and mouldy as they were dark, with deep foundations of dirt under the carpets, and dirty walls. In her present room there was no running water and no clothes-closet, and she had to have the dresser moved out to make room for her piano. But there were two windows, one on the south and one on the west, a light wall-paper with morning-glory vines, and on the floor a clean matting. The landlady had tried to make the room look cheerful, because it was hard to let. It was so small that Thea could keep it clean herself, after the Hun had done her worst. She hung her dresses on the door under a sheet, used the washstand for a dresser, slept on a cot, and opened both the windows when she practised. She felt less walled in than she had in the other houses.

Wednesday was her third day in bed. The medical student who lived in the house had been in to see her, had left some tablets and a foamy gargle, and told her that she could probably go back to work on Monday. The landlady stuck her head in once a day, but Thea did not encourage her visits. The Hungarian chambermaid brought her soup and toast. She made a sloppy pretence of putting the room in order, but she was such a dirty creature that Thea would not let her touch her cot; she got up every morning and turned the mattress and made the bed herself. The exertion made her feel miserably ill, but at least she could lie still contentedly for a long while afterward. She hated the poisoned feeling in her throat, and no matter how often she gargled she felt unclean and disgusting. Still, if she had to be ill, she was almost glad that she had a contagious illness. Otherwise she would have been at the mercy of the people in the house. She knew that they disliked her, yet now that she was ill, they took it upon themselves to tap at her door, send her messages, books, even a miserable flower or two. Thea knew that their sympathy was an expression of self-righteousness, and she hated them for it. The divinity student, who was always whispering soft things to her, sent her "The Kreutzer Sonata."

The medical student had been kind to her: he knew that she did not want to pay a doctor. His gargle had helped her, and he gave her things to make her sleep at night. But he had been a cheat, too. He had exceeded his rights. She had no soreness in her chest, and had told him so clearly. All this thumping of her back, and listening to her breathing, was done to satisfy personal curiosity. She had watched him with a contemptuous smile. She was too sick to care; if it amused him—She made him wash his hands before he touched her; he was never very clean. All the same, it wounded her and made her feel that the world was a pretty disgusting place. "The Kreutzer Sonata" did not make her feel any more cheerful. She threw it aside with hatred. She could not believe it was written by the same man who wrote the novel that had thrilled her.

Her cot was beside the south window, and on Wednesday afternoon she lay thinking about the Harsanyis, about old Mr. Nathanmeyer, and about how she was missing Fred Ottenburg's visits to the studio. That was much the worst thing about being sick. If she were going to the studio every day, she might be having pleasant encounters with Fred. He was always running away, Bowers said, and he might be planning to go away as soon as Mrs. Nathanmeyer's evenings were over. And here she was losing all this time!

After a while she heard the Hun's clumsy trot in the hall, and then a pound on the door. Mary came in, making her usual uncouth sounds, carrying a long box and a big basket. Thea sat up in bed and tore off the strings and paper. The basket was full of fruit, with a big Hawaiian pineapple in the middle, and in the box there were layers of pink roses with long, woody stems and dark-green leaves. They filled the room with a cool smell that made another air to breathe. Mary stood with her apron full of paper and cardboard. When she saw Thea take an envelope out from under the flowers, she uttered an exclamation, pointed to the roses, and then to the bosom of her own dress, on the left side. Thea laughed and nodded. She understood that Mary associated the colour with Ottenburg's *boutonnière*. She pointed to the water-pitcher—she had nothing else big enough to hold the flowers—and made Mary put it on the window-sill beside her.

After Mary was gone, Thea locked the door. When the landlady knocked, she pretended that she was asleep. She lay still all afternoon and with drowsy eyes watched the roses open. They were the first hothouse flowers she had ever had. The cool fragrance they released was soothing, and as the pink petals curled back, they were the only things between her and the gray sky. She lay on her side, putting the room and the boarding-house behind her. Fred knew where all the pleasant things in the world were, she reflected, and knew the road to them. He had keys to all the nice places in his pocket, and seemed to jingle them from time to time. And then, he was young; and her friends had always been old. Her mind went back over them. They had all been teachers; wonderfully kind, but still teachers. Ray Kennedy, she knew, had wanted to marry her, but he was the most protecting and teacher-like of them all. She moved impatiently in her cot and threw her braids away from her hot neck, over her pillow. "I don't want him for a teacher," she thought, frowning petulantly out of the window. "I've had such a string of them. I want him for a sweetheart."

VI

*T*hea," said Fred Ottenburg one driz-zly afternoon in April, while they sat waiting for their tea at a restaurant in the Pullman Building, overlooking the lake, "what are you going to do this summer?"

"I don't know. Work, I suppose."

"With Bowers, you mean? Even Bowers goes fishing for a month. Chicago's no place to work, in the summer. Haven't you made any plans?"

Thea shrugged her shoulders. "No use having any plans when you haven't any money. They are unbecoming."

"Aren't you going home?"

She shook her head. "No. It won't be comfortable there till I've got something to show for myself. I'm not getting on at all, you know. This year has been mostly wasted."

"You're stale; that's what's the matter with you. And just now you're dead tired. You'll talk more rationally after you've had some tea. Rest your throat until it comes." They were sitting by a window. As

Ottenburg looked at her in the grey light, he remembered what Mrs. Nathanmeyer had said about the Swedish face "breaking early." Thea was as grey as the weather. Her skin looked sick. Her hair, too, though on a damp day it curled charmingly about her face, looked pale.

Fred beckoned the waiter and increased his order for food. Thea did not hear him. She was staring out of the window, down at the roof of the Art Institute and the green lions, dripping in the rain. The lake was all rolling mist, with a soft shimmer of robin's-egg blue in the grey. A lumber boat, with two very tall masts, was emerging gaunt and black out of the fog. When the tea came, Thea ate hungrily, and Fred watched her. He thought her eyes became a little less bleak. The kettle sang cheerfully over the spirit lamp, and she seemed to concentrate her attention upon that pleasant sound. She kept looking toward it listlessly and indulgently, in a way that gave him a realization of her loneliness. Fred lighted a cigarette and smoked thoughtfully. He and Thea were alone in the quiet, dusky room full of white tables. In those days Chicago people never stopped for tea.

"Come," he said at last, "what would you do this summer, if you could do whatever you wished?"

"I'd go a long way from here! West, I think. Maybe I could get some of my spring back. All this cold, cloudy weather"—she looked out at the lake and shivered—"I don't know, it does things to me," she ended abruptly.

Fred nodded. "I know. You've been going down ever since you had tonsillitis. I've seen it. What you need is to sit in the sun and bake for three months. You've got the right idea. I remember once, when we were having dinner somewhere, you kept asking me about the Cliff-Dweller ruins. Do they still interest you?"

"Of course they do. I've always wanted to go down there—long before I ever got in for this."

"I don't think I told you, but my father owns a whole cañon full of Cliff-Dweller ruins. He has a big worthless ranch down in Arizona, near a Navajo reservation, and there's a cañon on the place they call Panther Cañon, chock full of that sort of thing. I often go down there to hunt. Henry Biltmer and his wife live there and keep a tidy place. He's an old German who worked in the brewery until he lost his health. Now he runs a few cattle. Henry likes to do me a favour. I've done a few for him." Fred drowned his cigarette in his saucer and studied Thea's expression, which was wistful and intent, envious and admiring. He continued with satisfaction: "If you went down there and stayed with them for two or three months, they wouldn't let you pay anything. I might send Henry a new gun, but even I couldn't offer him money for putting up a friend of mine. I'll get you transportation. It would make a new girl of you. Let me write to Henry, and you pack your trunk. That's all that's necessary. No red tape about it. What do you say, Thea?"

She bit her lip, and sighed as if she were waking up.

Fred crumpled his napkin impatiently. "Well, isn't it easy enough?"

"That's the trouble; it's *too* easy. Doesn't sound probable. I'm not used to getting things for nothing."

Ottenburg laughed. "Oh, if that's all, I'll show you how to begin. You won't get this for nothing, quite. I'll ask you to let me stop off and see you on my way to California. Perhaps by that time you will be glad to see me. Better let me break the news to Bowers. I can manage him. He needs a little transportation himself now and then. You must get corduroy riding-things and leather leggings. There are a few snakes about. Why do you keep frowning?"

"Well, I don't exactly see why you take the trouble. What do you get out of it? You haven't liked me so well the last two or three weeks."

Fred dropped his cigarette and looked at his watch. "If you don't see that, it's because you need a tonic. I'll show you what I'll get out of it. Now I'm going to get a cab and take you home. You are too tired to walk a step. You'd better get to bed as soon as you get there. Of course, I don't like you so well when you're half anaesthetized all the time. What have you been doing to yourself?"

Thea rose. "I don't know. Being bored eats the heart out of me, I guess." She walked meekly in front of him to the elevator. Fred noticed for the hundredth time how vehemently her body proclaimed her state of feeling. He remembered how remarkably brilliant and beautiful she had been when she sang at Mrs. Nathanmeyer's: flushed and gleaming, round and supple, something that couldn't be dimmed or downed. And now she seemed a moving figure of discouragement. The very waiters glanced at her apprehensively. It was not that she made a fuss, but her back was most extraordinarily vocal. One never needed to see her face to know what she was full of that day. Yet she was certainly not mercurial. Her flesh seemed to take a mood and to "set," like plaster. As he put her into the cab, Fred reflected once more that he "gave her up." He would attack her when his lance was brighter.

Part IV

The Ancient People

I

*T*he San Francisco Mountain lies in northern Arizona, above Flagstaff, and its blue slopes and snowy summit entice the eye for a hundred miles across the desert. About its base lie the pine forests of the Navajos, where the great red-trunked trees live out their peaceful centuries in that sparkling air. The *piñons* and scrub begin only where the forest ends, where the country breaks into open, stony clearings and the surface of the earth cracks into deep cañons. The great pines stand at a considerable distance from each other. Each tree grows alone, murmurs alone, thinks alone. They do not intrude upon each other. The Navajos are not much in the habit of giving or of asking help. Their language is not a communicative one, and they never attempt an interchange of personality in speech. Over their forests there is the same inexorable reserve. Each tree has its exalted power to bear.

That was the first thing Thea Kronborg felt about the forest, as she drove through it one May morning in Henry Biltmer's democrat wagon—and it was the first great forest she had ever seen. She had got off the train at Flagstaff that morning, rolled off into the high, chill air when all the pines on the mountain were fired by sunrise, so that she seemed to fall from sleep directly into the forest.

Old Biltmer followed a faint wagon-trail which ran southeast, and which, as they travelled, continually dipped lower, falling away from the high plateau on the slope of which Flagstaff sits. The white peak of the mountain, the snow gorges above the timber, now disappeared from time to time as the road dropped and dropped, and the forest closed behind the wagon. More than the mountain disappeared as the forest closed thus. Thea seemed to be taking very little through the wood with her. The personality of which she was so tired seemed to let go of her. The high, sparkling air drank it up like blotting-paper. It was lost in the thrilling blue of the new sky and the song of the thin wind in the *piñons*. The old, fretted lines which marked one off, which defined her—made her Thea Kronborg, Bowers's accompanist, a soprano with a faulty middle voice—were all erased.

So far she had failed. Her two years in Chicago had not resulted in anything. She had failed with Harsanyi, and she had made no great progress with her voice. She had come to believe that whatever Bowers had taught her was of secondary importance, and that in the essential things she had made no advance. Her student life closed behind her, like the forest, and she doubted whether she could go back to it if she tried.

Probably she would teach music in little country towns all her life. Failure was not so tragic as she would have supposed; she was tired enough not to care.

She was getting back to the earliest sources of gladness that she could remember. She had loved the sun, and the brilliant solitudes of sand and sun, long before these other things had come along to fasten themselves upon her and torment her. That night, when she clambered into her big German feather bed, she felt completely released from the enslaving desire to get on in the world. Darkness had once again the sweet wonder that it had in childhood.

II

*T*hea's life at the Ottenburg ranch was simple and full of light, like the days themselves. She awoke every morning when the first fierce shafts of sunlight darted through the curtainless windows of her room at the ranch-house. After breakfast she took her lunch-basket and went down to the cañon. Usually she did not return until sunset.

Panther Cañon was like a thousand others—one of those abrupt fissures with which the earth in the Southwest is riddled; so abrupt that you might walk over the edge of any one of them on a dark night and never know what had happened to you. This cañon headed on the Ottenburg ranch, about a mile from the ranch-house, and it was accessible only at its head. The cañon walls, for the first two hundred feet below the surface, were perpendicular cliffs, striped with even-running strata of rock. From there on to the bottom the sides were less abrupt, were shelving, and lightly fringed with *piñons* and dwarf cedars. The effect was that of a gentler cañon within a wilder one. The dead city lay at the point where the perpendicular outer wall ceased and the V-shaped inner gorge began. There a stratum of rock, softer than those above, had been hollowed out by the action of time until it was like a deep groove running along the sides of the cañon. In this hollow (like a great fold in the rock) the Ancient People had built their houses of yellowish stone and mortar. The overhanging cliff above made a roof two hundred feet thick. The hard stratum below was an everlasting floor. The houses stood along in a row, like the buildings in a city block, or like a barracks.

In both walls of the cañon the same streak of soft rock had been washed out, and the long horizontal groove had been built up with houses. The dead city had thus two streets, one set in either cliff, facing each other across the ravine, with a river of blue air between them.

The cañon twisted and wound like a snake, and these two streets went on for four miles or more, interrupted by the abrupt turnings of the gorge, but beginning again within each turn. The cañon had a dozen of these false endings near its head. Beyond, the windings were larger and less perceptible, and it went on for a hundred miles, too narrow, precipitous, and terrible for man to follow it. The Cliff-Dwellers liked wide cañons, where the great cliffs caught the sun. Panther Cañon had been deserted for hundreds of years when the first Spanish missionaries came into Arizona, but the masonry of the houses was still wonderfully firm; had crumbled only where a landslide or a rolling boulder had torn it.

All the houses in the cañon were clean with the cleanness of sun-baked, wind-swept places, and they all smelled of the tough little cedars that twisted themselves into the very doorways. One of these rock-rooms Thea took for her own. Fred had told her how to make it comfortable. The day after she came, old Henry brought over on one of the pack-ponies a roll of Navajo blankets that belonged to Fred, and Thea lined her cave with them. The room was not more than eight by ten feet, and she could touch the stone roof with her finger-tips. This was her old idea: a nest in a high cliff, full of sun. All morning long the sun beat upon her cliff, while the ruins on the opposite side of the cañon were in shadow. In the afternoon, when she had the shade of two hundred feet of rock wall, the ruins on the other side of the gulf stood out in the blazing sunlight. Before her door ran the narrow, winding path that had been the street of the Ancient People. The yucca and niggerhead cactus grew everywhere. From her doorstep she looked out on the ochre-coloured slope that ran down several hundred feet to the stream, and this hot rock was sparsely grown with dwarf trees. Their colours were so pale that the shadows of the little trees on the rock stood out sharper than the trees themselves. When Thea first came, the choke-cherry bushes were in blossom, and the scent of them was almost sickeningly sweet after a shower. At the very bottom of the cañon, along the stream, there was a thread of bright, flickering, golden-green—cottonwood seedlings. They made a living, chattering screen behind which she took her bath every morning.

Thea went down to the stream by the Indian water-trail. She had found a bathing-pool with a sand bottom, where the creek was dammed by fallen trees. The climb back was long and steep, and when she reached her little house in the cliff, she always felt fresh delight in its comfort and inaccessibility. By the time she got there, the woolly red-and-grey blankets were saturated with sunlight, and she sometimes fell asleep as soon as she stretched her body on their warm surfaces. She used to wonder at her own inactivity. She could lie there hour after hour in the sun and listen to the strident whirr of the big locusts, and to the light, ironical laughter of the quaking asps. All her life she had been hurrying and sputtering, as if she had been born behind time and had been trying to catch up. Now, she reflected, as she drew herself out long upon the rugs, it was as if she were waiting for something to catch up with her. She had got to a place where she was out of the stream of meaningless activity and undirected effort.

Here she could lie for half a day undistracted, holding pleasant and incomplete conceptions in her mind—almost in her hands. They were scarcely clear enough to be called ideas. They had something to do with fragrance and colour and sound, but almost nothing to do with words. She was singing very little now, but a song would go through her head all morning, as a spring keeps welling up, and it was like a pleasant sensation indefinitely prolonged. It was much more like a sensation than like an idea, or an act of remembering.

Music had never before come to her in that sensuous form. It had always been a thing to be struggled with, had always brought anxiety and exaltation and chagrin—never content and indolence. Thea began to wonder whether people could not utterly lose the power to work, as they can lose their voice or their memory. She had always been a little drudge, hurrying from one task to another—as if it mattered! And now her power to think seemed converted into a power of sustained sensation. She could become a mere receptacle for heat, or become a colour, like the bright lizards that darted about on the hot stones outside her door; or she could become a continuous repetition of sound, like the cicadas.

III

*T*he faculty of observation was never highly developed in Thea Kronborg. A great deal escaped her eye as she passed through the world. But the things which were for her, she saw; she experienced them physically and remembered them as if they had once been a part of herself. The roses she used to see in the florists' shops in Chicago were merely roses. But when she thought of the moonflowers that grew over Mrs. Tellamantez's door, it was as if she had been that vine and had opened up in white flowers every night. There were memories of light on the sand hills, of masses of prickly-pear blossoms she had found in the desert in early childhood, of the late afternoon sun pouring through the grape leaves and the mint bed in Mrs. Kohler's garden, which she would never lose. These recollections were a part of her mind and personality. In Chicago she had got almost nothing that went into her subconscious self and took root there. But here, in Panther Cañon, there were again things which seemed destined for her.

Panther Cañon was the home of innumerable swallows. They built nests in the wall far above the hollow groove in which Thea's own rock-chamber lay. They seldom ventured above the rim of the cañon, to the flat, wind-swept tableland. Their world was the blue air-river between the cañon walls. In that blue gulf the arrow-shaped birds swam all day long, with only an occasional movement of the wings. The only sad thing about them was their timidity: the way in which they lived their lives between the echoing cliffs and never dared to rise out of the shadow of the cañon walls. As they swam past her door, Thea often felt how easy it would be to dream one's life out in some cleft in the world.

From the ancient dwelling there came always a dignified, unobtrusive sadness; now stronger, now fainter—like the aromatic smell which the dwarf cedars gave out in the sun—but always present, a part of the air one breathed. At night, when Thea dreamed about the cañon—or in the early morning when she hurried toward it, anticipating it—her conception of it was of yellow rocks baking in sunlight, the swallows, the cedar smell, and that peculiar sadness—a voice out of the past, not very loud, that went on saying a few simple things to the solitude eternally.

Standing up in her lodge, Thea with her thumb-nail could dislodge flakes of carbon from the rock-roof—the cooking-smoke of the Ancient People. They were that near! A timid, nest-building folk, like the swallows. How often Thea remembered Ray Kennedy's moralizing about the cliff cities. He used to say that he never felt the hardness of the human struggle or the sadness of history as he felt it among those ruins. He used to say, too, that it made one feel an obligation to do one's best. On the first day that Thea climbed the water-trail, she began to have intuitions about the women who had worn the path, and who had spent so great a part of their lives going up and down it. She found herself trying to walk as they must have walked, with a feeling in her feet and knees and loins which she had never known before—which must have come up to her out of the accustomed dust of that rocky trail. She could feel the weight of an Indian baby hanging to her back as she climbed.

The empty houses, among which she wandered in the afternoon, the blanketed one in which she lay all morning, were haunted by certain fears and desires; feelings about warmth and cold and water and physical strength. It seemed to Thea that a certain understanding of those old people came up to her out of the rock-shelf on which she lay; that certain feelings were transmitted to her, suggestions that were simple, insistent, and monotonous, like the beating of Indian drums. They were not expressible in words, but seemed rather to translate themselves into attitudes of body, into degrees of muscular tension or relaxation; the naked strength of youth, sharp as the sun-shafts; the crouching timorousness of age, the sullenness of women who waited for their captors. At the first turning of the cañon there was a half-ruined tower of yellow masonry, a watch-tower upon which the young men used to entice eagles and snare them with nets. Sometimes for a whole morning Thea could see the coppery breast and shoulders of an Indian youth there against the sky; see him throw the net, and watch the struggle with the eagle.

Old Henry Biltmer, at the ranch, had been a great deal among the Pueblo Indians who are the descendants of the Cliff-Dwellers. After supper he used to sit and smoke his pipe by the kitchen stove and talk to Thea about them. He had never found anyone before who was interested in his ruins. Every Sunday the old man prowled about in the cañon, and he had come to know a good deal more about it than he could account for. He had gathered up a whole chestful of Cliff-Dweller relics which he meant to take back to Germany with him some day. He taught Thea how to find things among the ruins: grinding-stones, and drills and needles made of turkey-bones. There were fragments of pottery everywhere. Old Henry explained to her that the Ancient People had developed masonry and pottery far beyond any other crafts. After they had made houses for themselves, the next thing was to house the precious water. He explained to her how all their customs and ceremonies and their religion went back to water. The men provided the food, but water was the care of the women. The stupid women carried water for most of their lives; the cleverer ones made the vessels to hold it. Their pottery was their most direct appeal to water, the envelope and sheath of the precious element itself. The strongest Indian need was expressed in those graceful jars, fashioned slowly by hand, without the aid of a wheel.

When Thea took her bath at the bottom of the cañon, in the sunny pool behind the screen of cottonwoods, she sometimes felt as if the water must have sovereign qualities, from having been the object of so much service and desire. That stream was the only living thing left of the drama that had been played out in the cañon centuries ago. In the rapid, restless heart of it, flowing swifter than the rest, there was a continuity of life that reached back into the old time. The glittering thread of current had a kind of lightly worn, loosely knit personality, graceful and laughing. Thea's bath came to have a ceremonial gravity. The atmosphere of the cañon was ritualistic.

One morning, as she was standing upright in the pool, splashing water between her shoulder-blades with a big sponge, something flashed through her mind that made her draw herself up and stand still until the water had quite dried upon her flushed skin. The stream and the broken pottery: what was any art but an effort to make a sheath, a mould in which to imprison for a moment the shining, elusive element which is life itself— life hurrying past us and running away, too strong to stop, too sweet to lose? The Indian women had held it in their jars. In the sculpture she had seen in the Art Institute, it had been caught in a flash of arrested motion. In singing, one made a vessel of one's throat and nostrils and held it on one's breath, caught the stream in a scale of natural intervals.

IV

*T*hea had a superstitious feeling about the potsherds, and liked better to leave them in the dwellings where she found them. If she took a few bits back to her own lodge and hid them under the blankets, she did it guiltily, as if she were being watched. She was a guest in these houses, and ought to behave as such. Nearly every afternoon she went to the chambers which contained the most interesting fragments of pottery, sat and looked at them for a while. Some of them were beautifully decorated. This care, expended upon vessels that could not hold food or water any better for the additional labour put upon them, made her heart go out to those ancient potters. They had not only expressed their desire, but they had expressed it as beautifully as they could. Food, fire, water, and something else—even here, in this crack in the world, so far back in the night of the past! Down here at the beginning, that painful thing was already stirring; the seed of sorrow, and of so much delight.

There were jars done in a delicate overlay, like pine cones; and there were many patterns in a low relief, like basket-work. Some of the pottery was decorated in colour, red and brown, black and white, in graceful geometrical patterns. One day, on a fragment of a shallow bowl, she found a crested serpent's head, painted in red on terra-cotta. Again she found half a bowl with a broad band of white cliff-houses painted on a black ground. They were scarcely conventionalized at all; there they were in the black border, just as they stood in the rock before her. It brought her centuries nearer to these people to find that they saw their houses exactly as she saw them.

Yes, Ray Kennedy was right. All these things made one feel that one ought to do one's best, and help to fulfill some desire of the dust that slept there. A dream had been dreamed there long ago, in the night of ages, and the wind had whispered some promise to the sadness of the savage. In their own way, those people had felt the beginnings of what was to come. These potsherds were like fetters that bound one to a long chain of human endeavour.

Not only did the world seem older and richer to Thea now, but she herself seemed older. She had never been alone for so long before, or thought so much. Nothing had ever engrossed her so deeply as the daily contemplation of that line of pale-yellow houses tucked into the wrinkle of the cliff. Moonstone and Chicago had become vague. Here everything was simple and definite, as things had been in childhood. Her mind was like a ragbag into which she had been frantically thrusting whatever she could grab. And here she must throw this lumber away. The things that were really hers separated themselves from the rest. Her ideas were simplified, became sharper and clearer. She felt united and strong.

When Thea had been at the Ottenburg ranch for two months, she got a letter from Fred announcing that he "might be along at almost any time now." The letter came at night, and the next morning she took it down into the cañon with her. She was delighted that he was coming soon. She had never felt so grateful to anyone, and she wanted to tell him everything that had happened to her since she had been there—more than had happened in all her life before. Certainly she liked Fred better than anyone else in the world. There was Harsanyi, of course—but Harsanyi was always tired. Just now, and here, she wanted someone who had never been tired, who could catch an idea and run with it.

She was ashamed to think what an apprehensive drudge she must always have seemed to Fred, and she wondered why he had concerned himself about her at all. Perhaps she would never be so happy or so good-looking again, and she would like Fred to see her, for once, at her best. She had not been singing much, but she knew that her voice was more interesting than it had ever been before. She had begun to understand that—with her, at least—voice was, first of all, vitality; a lightness in the body and a driving power in the blood. If she had that, she could sing. When she felt so keenly alive, lying on that insensible shelf of stone, when her body bounded like a rubber ball away from its hardness, then she could sing. This, too, she could explain to Fred. He would know what she meant.

Another week passed. Thea did the same things as before, felt the same influences, went over the same ideas; but there was a livelier movement in her thoughts, and a freshening of sensation, like the brightness which came over the underbrush after a shower. A persistent affirmation—or denial—was going on in her, like the tapping of the woodpecker in the one tall pine tree across the chasm. Musical phrases drove each other rapidly through her mind, and the song of the cicada was now too long and too sharp. Everything seemed suddenly to take the form of a desire for action.

It was while she was in this abstracted state, waiting for the clock to strike, that Thea at last made up her mind what she was going to try to do in the world, and that she was going to Germany to study without further loss of time. Only by the merest chance had she ever got to Panther Cañon. There was certainly no kindly Providence that directed one's life; and one's parents did not in the least care what became of one, so long as one did not misbehave and endanger their comfort. One's life was at the mercy of blind chance. She had better take it in her own hands and lose everything than meekly draw the plough under the rod of parental guidance. She had seen it when she was at home last summer—the hostility of comfortable, self-satisfied people toward any serious effort. Even to her father it seemed indecorous. Whenever she spoke seriously, he looked apologetic. Yet she had clung fast to whatever was left of Moonstone in her mind. No more of that! The Cliff-Dwellers had lengthened her past. She had older and higher obligations.

V

One Sunday afternoon late in July, old Henry Biltmer was rheumatically descending into the head of the cañon. The Sunday before had been one of those cloudy days—fortunately rare—when the life goes out of that country and it becomes a grey ghost, an empty, shivering uncertainty. Henry had spent the day in the barn; his cañon was a reality only when it was flooded with the light of its great lamp, when the yellow rocks cast purple shadows, and the resin was fairly cooking in the corkscrew cedars. The yuccas were in blossom now. Out of each clump of sharp bayonet leaves rose a tall stalk hung with greenish-white bells with thick, fleshy petals. The niggerhead cactus was thrusting its crimson blooms up out of every crevice in the rocks.

Henry had come out on the pretext of hunting a spade and pick-axe that young Ottenburg had borrowed, but he was keeping his eyes open. He was really very curious about the new occupants of the cañon, and what they found to do there all day long. He let his eye travel along the gulf for a mile or so to the first turning, where the fissure zigzagged out and then receded behind a stone promontory on which stood the yellowish, crumbling ruin of the old watch-tower.

From the base of this tower, which now threw its shadow forward, bits of rock kept flying out into the open gulf—skating upon the air until they lost their momentum, then falling like chips until they rang upon the ledges at the bottom of the gorge or splashed into the stream. Biltmer shaded his eyes with his hand. There on the promontory, against the cream-coloured cliff, were two figures nimbly moving in the light, both slender and agile, entirely absorbed in their game. They looked like two boys. Both were hatless and both wore white shirts.

Henry forgot his pick-axe and followed the trail before the cliff-houses toward the tower. Behind the tower, as he well knew, were heaps of stones, large and small, piled against the face of the cliff. He had always believed that the Indian watchmen piled them there for ammunition. Thea and Fred had come upon these missiles and were throwing them for distance. As Biltmer approached, he could hear them laughing, and he caught Thea's voice, high and excited, with a ring of vexation in it. Fred was teaching her to throw a heavy stone like a discus. When it was Fred's turn, he sent a triangular-shaped stone out into the air with considerable skill. Thea watched it enviously, standing in a half-defiant posture, her sleeves rolled above her elbows and her face flushed with heat and excitement. After Fred's third missile had rung upon the rocks below, she snatched up a stone and stepped impatiently out on the ledge in front of him. He caught her by the elbows and pulled her back.

"Not so close, you silly! You'll spin yourself off in a minute."

"You went that close. There's your heel-mark," she retorted.

"Well, I know how. That makes a difference." He drew a mark in the dust with his toe. "There, that's right. Don't step over that. Pivot yourself on your spine, and make a half-turn. When you've swung your length, let it go."

Thea settled the flat piece of rock between her wrist and fingers, faced the cliff wall, stretched her arm in position, whirled round on her left foot to the full stretch of her body, and let the missile spin out over the gulf. She hung expectantly in the air, forgetting to draw back her arm, her eyes following the stone as if it carried her fortunes with it. Her comrade watched her; there weren't many girls who could show a line like that from the toe to the thigh, from the shoulder to the tip of the outstretched hand. The stone spent itself and began to fall. Thea drew back and struck her knee furiously with her palm.

"There it goes again! Not nearly so far as yours. What *is* the matter with me? Give me another."

She faced the cliff and whirled again. The stone spun out, not quite so far as before.

Ottenburg laughed. "Why do you keep on working *after* you've thrown it? You can't help it along then."

Without replying, Thea stooped and selected another stone, took a deep breath and made another turn. Fred watched the disk, exclaiming, "Good girl! You got past the pine that time. That's a good throw."

She took out her handkerchief and wiped her glowing face and throat, pausing to feel her right shoulder with her left hand.

"Ah—ha, you've made yourself sore, haven't you? What did I tell you? You go at things too hard. I'll tell you what I'm going to do, Thea"—Fred dusted his hands and began tucking in the blouse of his shirt—"I'm going to make some single-sticks and teach you to fence. You'd be all right there. You're light and quick and you've got lots of drive in you. I'd like to have you come at me with foils; you'd look so fierce," he chuckled.

She turned away from him and stubbornly sent out another stone, hanging in the air after its flight. Her fury amused Fred, who took all games lightly and played them well. She was breathing hard, and little beads of moisture had gathered on her upper lip. He slipped his arm about her. "If you will look as pretty as that—" He bent his head and kissed her. Thea was startled, gave him an angry push, drove at him with her free hand in a manner quite hostile. Fred was on his mettle in an instant. He pinned both her arms down and kissed her resolutely.

When he released her, she turned away and spoke over her shoulder. "That was mean of you, but I suppose I deserved what I got."

"I should say you did deserve it," Fred panted, "turning savage on me like that! I should say you did deserve it!"

He saw her shoulders harden. "Well, I just said I deserved it, didn't I? What more do you want?"

"I want you to tell me why you flew at me like that! You weren't playing; you looked as if you'd like to murder me."

She brushed back her hair impatiently. "I didn't mean anything, really. You interrupted me when I was watching the stone. I can't jump from one thing to another. I pushed you without thinking."

Fred thought her back expressed contrition. He went up to her, stood behind her with his chin above her shoulder, and said something in her ear. Thea laughed and turned toward him. They left the stone-pile carelessly, as if they had never been interested in it, rounded the yellow tower, and disappeared into the second turn of the cañon, where the dead city, interrupted by the jutting promontory, began again.

Old Biltmer had been somewhat embarrassed by the turn the game had taken. He had not heard their conversation, but the pantomime against the rocks was clear enough. When the two young people disappeared, their host retreated rapidly toward the head of the cañon.

"I guess that young lady can take care of herself," he chuckled. "Young Fred, though, he has quite a way with them."

VI

Day was breaking over Panther Cañon. The gulf was cold and full of heavy, purplish twilight. The wood smoke which drifted from one of the cliff-houses hung in a blue scarf across the chasm, until the draught caught it and whirled it away. Thea was crouching in the doorway of her rock-house, while Fred looked after the crackling fire in the next cave. He was waiting for it to burn down to coals before he put the coffee on to boil.

They had left the ranch-house that morning a little after three o'clock, having packed their camp equipment the day before, and had crossed the open pasture land with their lantern while the stars were still bright. During the descent into the cañon by lantern-light, they were chilled through their coats and sweaters. The lantern crept slowly along the rock trail, where the heavy air seemed to offer resistance. The voice of the stream at the bottom of the gorge was hollow and threatening, much louder and deeper than it ever was by day—another voice altogether. The sullenness of the place seemed to say that the world could get on very well without people, red or white; that under the human world there was a geological world, conducting its silent, immense operations which were indifferent to man. Thea had often seen the desert sunrise—a light-hearted affair, where the sun springs out of bed and the world is golden in an instant. But this cañon seemed to waken like an old man, with rheum and stiffness of the joints, with heaviness, and a dull, malignant mind. She crouched against the wall while the stars faded, and thought what courage the early races must have had to endure so much for the little they got out of life.

At last a kind of hopefulness broke in the air. In a moment the

pine trees up on the edge of the rim were flashing with coppery fire. The
thin red clouds which hung above their pointed tops began to boil and
move rapidly, weaving in and out like smoke. The swallows darted out of
their rock-houses as at a signal, and flew upward, toward the rim. Little
brown birds began to chirp in the bushes along the watercourse down at the
bottom of the ravine, where everything was still dusky and pale. At first the
golden light seemed to hang like a wave upon the rim of the cañon; the trees
and bushes up there, which one scarcely noticed at noon, stood out magnified by the slanting rays. Long, thin streaks of light began to reach quiver-
ingly down into the gorge. The red sun rose rapidly above the tops of the
blazing pines, and its glow burst into the gulf, about the very doorstep on
which Thea sat. It bored into the wet, dark underbrush. The dripping
cherry bushes, the pale aspens, and the frosty *piñons* were glittering and
trembling, swimming in the liquid gold. All the pale, dusty little herbs of
the bean family, never seen by anyone but a botanist, became for a moment
individual and important, their silky leaves quite beautiful with dew and
light. The arch of sky overhead, heavy as lead a little while before, lifted,
became more and more transparent, and one could look up into depths of
pearly blue.

The savour of coffee and bacon mingled with the smell of wet
cedars drying, and Fred called to Thea that he was ready for her. They sat
down in the doorway of his kitchen, with the warmth of the live coals
behind them and the sunlight on their faces, and began their breakfast, Mrs.
Biltmer's thick coffee-cups and the cream-bottle between them, the coffee-pot and frying-pan conveniently keeping hot among the embers.

"I thought you were going back on the whole proposition,
Thea, when you were crawling along with that lantern. I couldn't get a
word out of you."

"I know. I was cold and hungry, and I didn't believe there was
going to be any morning anyway. Didn't you feel queer, at all?"

Fred squinted above his smoking cup. "Well, I am never strong
for getting up before the sun. The world looks unfurnished. When I first
lit the fire and had a square look at you, I thought I'd got the wrong girl.
Pale, grim—you were a sight!"

Thea leaned back into the shadow of the rock-room and
warmed her hands over the coals. "It was dismal enough. How warm these
walls are, all the way round; and your breakfast is so good. I'm all right now,
Fred."

"Yes, you're all right now." Fred lit a cigarette and looked at her critically as her head emerged into the sun again. "You get up every morning just a little bit handsomer than you were the day before. I'd love you just as much if you were not turning into one of the loveliest women I've ever seen; but you are, and that's a fact to be reckoned with." He watched her across the thin line of smoke he blew from his lips. "What are you going to do with all that beauty and all that talent, Miss Kronborg?"

She turned away to the fire again. "I don't know what you're talking about," she muttered with an awkwardness which did not conceal her pleasure.

Ottenburg laughed softly. "Oh, yes, you do! Nobody better! You're a close one, but you give yourself away sometimes, like everybody else. Do you know, I've decided that you never do a single thing without an ulterior motive." He threw away his cigarette, took out his tobacco-pouch and began to fill his pipe. "You ride and fence and walk and climb, but I know that all the while you're getting somewhere in your mind. All these things are instruments; and I, too, am an instrument." He looked up in time to intercept a quick, startled glance from Thea. "Oh, I don't mind," he chuckled; "not a bit. Every woman, every interesting woman, has ulterior motives, many of 'em less creditable than yours. It's your constancy that amuses me. You must have been doing it ever since you were two feet high."

Thea looked slowly up at her companion's good-humoured face. His eyes, sometimes too restless and sympathetic in town, had grown steadier and clearer in the open air. His short curly beard and yellow hair had reddened in the sun and wind. The pleasant vigour of his person was always delightful to her, something to signal to and laugh with in a world of negative people. With Fred she was never becalmed. There was always life in the air, always something coming and going, a rhythm of feeling and action—stronger than the natural accord of youth. As she looked at him, leaning against the sunny wall, she felt a desire to be frank with him. She was not wilfully holding anything back. But, on the other hand, she could not force things that held themselves back. "Yes, it was like that when I was little," she said at last. "I had to be close, as you call it, or go under. But I didn't know I had been like that since you came. I've had nothing to be close about. I haven't thought about anything but having a good time with you. I've just drifted."

Fred blew a trail of smoke out into the breeze and looked knowing. "Yes, you drift like a rifle ball, my dear. It's your—your direction that I like best of all. Most fellows wouldn't, you know. I'm unusual."

They both laughed, but Thea frowned questioningly. "Why wouldn't most fellows? Other fellows have liked me."

"Yes, serious fellows. You told me yourself they were all old, or solemn. But jolly fellows want to be the whole target. They would say you were all brain and muscle; that you have no feeling."

She glanced at him sidewise.

"Oh, they would, would they?"

"Of course they would," Fred continued blandly. "Jolly fellows have no imagination. They want to be the animating force. When they are not around, they want a girl to be—extinct," he waved his hand. "Old fellows like Mr. Nathanmeyer understand your kind; but among the young ones, you are rather lucky to have found me. Even I wasn't always so wise. I've had my time of thinking it would not bore me to be the Apollo of a homey flat, and I've paid out a trifle to learn better. All those things get very tedious unless they are hooked up with an idea of some sort. It's because we *don't* come out here only to look at each other and drink coffee that it's so pleasant to—look at each other." Fred drew on his pipe for a while, studying Thea's abstraction. She was staring up at the far wall of the cañon with a troubled expression that drew her eyes narrow and her mouth hard. Her hands lay in her lap, one over the other, the fingers interlacing.

"Suppose," Fred came out at length—"suppose I were to offer you what most of the young men I know would offer a girl they'd been sitting up nights about: a comfortable flat in Chicago, a summer camp up in the woods, musical evenings, and a family to bring up. Would it look attractive to you?"

Thea sat up straight and stared at him in alarm, glared into his eyes.

"Perfectly hideous!" she exclaimed.

Fred dropped back against the old stonework and laughed deep in his chest. "Well, don't be frightened. I won't offer them. You're not a nest-building bird. You know I always liked your song, 'Me for the jolt of the breakers!' I understand."

She rose impatiently and walked to the edge of the cliff. "It's not that so much. It's waking up every morning with the feeling that your life is your own, and your strength is your own, and your talent is your own; that you're all there, and there's no sag in you." She stood for a moment as if she were tortured by uncertainty, then turned suddenly back to him. "Don't talk about these things any more now," she entreated. "It isn't that I want to keep anything from you. The trouble is that I've got nothing to keep—except (you know as well as I) that feeling. I told you about it in Chicago once. But it always makes me unhappy to talk about it. It will spoil the day. Will you go for a climb with me?" She held out her hands with a smile so eager that it made Ottenburg feel how much she needed to get away from herself.

He sprang up and caught the hands she put out so cordially, and stood swinging them back and forth. "I won't tease you. A word's enough to me. But I love it, all the same. Understand?" He pressed her hands and dropped them. "Now, where are you going to drag me?"

"I want you to drag me. Over there, to the other houses. They are more interesting than these." She pointed across the gorge to the row of white houses in the other cliff. "The trail is broken away, but I got up there once. It's possible. You have to go to the bottom of the cañon, cross the creek, and then go up hand-over-hand."

Ottenburg, lounging against the sunny wall, his hands in the pockets of his jacket, looked across at the distant dwellings.

"It's an awful climb," he sighed, "when I could be perfectly happy here with my pipe. However—" He took up his stick and hat and followed Thea down the water-trail. "Do you climb this path every day? You surely earn your bath. I went down and had a look at your pool the other afternoon. Neat place, with all those little cottonwoods. Must be very becoming."

"Think so?" Thea said over her shoulder, as she swung round a turn.

"Yes, and so do you, evidently. I'm becoming expert at reading your meaning in your back. I'm behind you so much on these single-foot trails. You don't wear stays, do you?"

"Not here."

"I wouldn't, anywhere, if I were you. They will make you less elastic. The side muscles get flabby. If you go in for opera, there's a fortune in a flexible body. Most of the German singers are clumsy, even when they're well set up."

Thea switched a *piñon* branch back at him. "Oh, I'll never get fat! That I can promise you."

Fred smiled, looking after her. "Keep that promise, no matter how many others you break," he drawled.

The upward climb, after they had crossed the stream, was at first a breathless scramble through underbrush. When they reached the big boulders, Ottenburg went first because he had the longer leg-reach, and gave Thea a hand when the step was quite beyond her, swinging her up until she could get a foothold. At last they reached a little platform among the rocks, with only a hundred feet of jagged, sloping wall between them and the cliff-houses.

Ottenburg lay down under a pine tree and declared that he was going to have a pipe before he went any farther. "It's a good thing to know when to stop, Thea," he said meaningly.

"I'm not going to stop now until I get there," Thea insisted. "I'll go on alone."

Fred settled his shoulder against the tree-trunk. "Go on if you like, but I'm here to enjoy myself. If you meet a rattler on the way, have it out with him."

She hesitated, fanning herself with her felt hat. "I never have met one."

"There's reasoning for you," Fred murmured languidly.

Thea turned away resolutely and began to go up the wall, using an irregular cleft in the rock for a path. The cliff, which looked almost perpendicular from the bottom, was really made up of ledges and boulders, and behind these she soon disappeared. For a long while Fred smoked with half-closed eyes, smiling to himself now and again. Occasionally he lifted an eyebrow as he heard the rattle of small stones among the rocks above. "In a temper," he concluded; "do her good." Then he subsided into warm drowsiness and listened to the locusts in the yuccas, and the tap-tap of the old woodpecker that was never weary of assaulting the big pine.

Fred had finished his pipe and was wondering whether he wanted another, when he heard a call from the cliff far above him. Looking up, he saw Thea standing on the edge of a projecting crag. She waved to him and threw her arm over her head, as if she were snapping her fingers in the air.

As he saw her there between the sky and the gulf, with that great wash of air and the morning light about her, Fred recalled the brilliant figure at Mrs. Nathanmeyer's. Thea was one of those people who emerge, unexpectedly, larger than we are accustomed to see them. Even at this distance one got the impression of muscular energy and audacity—a kind of brilliancy of motion—of a personality that carried across big spaces and expanded among big things. Lying still, with his hands under his head, Ottenburg rhetorically addressed the figure in the air. "You are the sort that used to run wild in Germany, dressed in their hair and a piece of skin. Soldiers caught 'em in nets. Old Nathanmeyer," he mused, "would like a peep at her now. Knowing old fellow. Always buying those Zorn etchings of peasant girls bathing. No sag in them either. Must be the cold climate." He sat up. "She'll begin to pitch rocks on me if I don't move." In response to another impatient gesture from the crag, he rose and began swinging slowly up the trail.

It was the afternoon of that long day. Thea was lying on a blanket in the door of her rock-house. She and Ottenburg had come back from their climb and had lunch, and he had gone off for a nap in one of the cliff-houses farther down the path. He was sleeping peacefully, his coat under his head and his face turned toward the wall.

Thea, too, was drowsy, and lay looking through half-closed eyes up at the blazing blue arch over the rim of the cañon. She was thinking of nothing at all. Her mind, like her body, was full of warmth, lassitude, physical content. Suddenly an eagle, tawny and of great size, sailed over the cleft in which she lay, across the arch of sky. He dropped for a moment into the gulf between the walls, then wheeled, and mounted until his plumage was so steeped in light that he looked like a golden bird. He swept on, following the course of the cañon a little way and then disappearing beyond the rim. Thea sprang to her feet as if she had been thrown up from the rock by volcanic action. She stood rigid on the edge of the stone shelf, straining her eyes after that strong, tawny flight. O eagle of eagles! Endeavour, achievement, desire, glorious striving of human art! From a cleft in the heart of the world she saluted it. . . . It had come all the way; when men lived in caves, it was there. A vanished race; but along the trails, in the stream, under the spreading cactus, there still glittered in the sun the bits of their frail clay vessels, fragments of their desire.

VII

*F*rom the day of Fred's arrival, he and Thea were unceasingly active. They took long rides into the Navajo pine forests, bought turquoises and silver bracelets from the wandering Indian herdsmen, and rode twenty miles to Flagstaff upon the slightest pretext. Thea had never felt this pleasant excitement about any man before, and she found herself trying very hard to please young Ottenburg. She was never tired, never dull. There was a zest about waking up in the morning and dressing, about walking, riding, even about sleep.

One morning when Thea came out from her room at seven o'clock, she found Henry and Fred on the porch, looking up at the sky. The day was already hot and there was no breeze. The sun was shining, but heavy brown clouds were hanging in the west, like the smoke of a forest fire. She and Fred had meant to ride to Flagstaff that morning, but Biltmer advised against it, foretelling a storm. After breakfast they lingered about the house, waiting for the weather to make up its mind. Fred had brought his guitar, and as they had the dining-room to themselves, he made Thea go over some songs with him. They got interested and kept it up until Mrs. Biltmer came to set the table for dinner. Ottenburg knew some of the Mexican things Spanish Johnny used to sing. Thea had never before happened to tell him about Spanish Johnny, and he seemed more interested in Johnny than in Doctor Archie or Wunsch.

After dinner they were too restless to endure the ranch-house any longer, and ran away to the cañon to practise with single-sticks. Fred carried a slicker and a sweater, and he made Thea wear one of the rubber hats that hung in Biltmer's gun-room. As they crossed the pasture land, the clumsy slicker kept catching in the lacings of his leggings.

"Why don't you drop that thing?" Thea asked. "I won't mind a shower. I've been wet before."

"No use taking chances."

From the cañon they were unable to watch the sky, since only a strip of the zenith was visible. The flat ledge about the watch-tower was the only level spot large enough for single-stick exercise, and they were still practising there when, at about four o'clock, a tremendous roll of thunder echoed between the cliffs and the atmosphere suddenly became thick.

Fred thrust the sticks in a cleft in the rock. "We're in for it, Thea. Better make for your cave where there are blankets."

He caught her elbow and hurried her along the path before the cliff-houses. They made the half-mile at a quick trot, and as they ran the rocks and the sky and the air between the cliffs turned a turbid green, like the colour in a moss agate. When they reached the blanketed rock-room, they looked at each other and laughed. Their faces had taken on a greenish pallor. Thea's hair, even, was green.

"Dark as pitch in here," Fred exclaimed as they hurried over the old rock doorstep. "But it's warm. The rocks hold the heat. It's going to be terribly cold outside, all right." He was interrupted by a deafening peal

of thunder. "Lord, what an echo! Lucky you don't mind. It's worth watching out there. We needn't come in yet."

The green light grew murkier and murkier. The smaller vegeta-
tion was blotted out. The yuccas, the cedars, and *piñons* stood dark and
rigid, like bronze. The swallows flew up with sharp, terrified twitterings.
Even the quaking asps were still. While Fred and Thea watched from the
doorway, the light changed to purple. Clouds of dark vapour, like chlorine
gas, began to float down from the head of the cañon and hung between
them and the cliff-houses in the opposite wall. Before they knew it, the wall
itself had disappeared. The air was positively venomous-looking, and grew
colder every minute. The thunder seemed to crash against one cliff, then
against the other, and to go shrieking off into the inner cañon.

The moment the rain broke, it beat the vapours down. In the
gulf before them the water fell in spouts, and dashed from the high cliffs
overhead. It tore aspens and chokecherry bushes out of the ground and left
the yuccas hanging by their tough roots. Only the little cedars stood black
and unmoved in the torrents that fell from so far above. The rock-chamber
was full of fine spray from the streams of water that shot over the doorway.
Thea crept to the back wall and rolled herself in a blanket, and Fred threw
the heavier blankets over her. The wool of the Navajo sheep was soon
kindled by the warmth of her body, and was impenetrable to dampness. Her
hair, where it hung below the rubber hat, gathered the moisture like a
sponge. Fred put on the slicker, tied the sweater about his neck, and settled
himself cross-legged beside her. The chamber was so dark that, although he
could see the outline of her head and shoulders, he could not see her face.
He struck a wax match to light his pipe. As he sheltered it between his
hands, it sizzled and sputtered, throwing a yellow flicker over Thea and her
blankets.

"You look like a gipsy," he said as he dropped the match.
"Anyone you'd rather be shut up with than me? No? Sure about that?"

"I think I am. Aren't you cold?"

"Not especially." Fred smoked in silence, listening to the roar
of the water outside. "We may not get away from here right away," he
remarked.

"I shan't mind. Shall you?"

He laughed grimly and pulled on his pipe. "Do you know where
you're at, Miss Thea Kronborg?" he said at last. "You've got me going
pretty hard, I suppose you know. I've had a lot of sweethearts, but I've
never been so much—engrossed before. What are you going to do about

it?" He heard nothing from the blankets. "Are you going to play fair, or is it about my cue to cut away?"

"I'll play fair. I don't see why you want to go."

"What do you want me around for?—to play with?"

Thea struggled up among the blankets. "I want you for everything. I don't know whether I'm what people call in love with you or not. In Moonstone that meant sitting in a hammock with somebody. I don't want to sit in a hammock with you, but I want to do almost everything else. Oh, hundreds of things!"

"If I run away, will you go with me?"

"I don't know. I'll have to think about that. Maybe I would." She freed herself from her wrappings and stood up. "It's not raining so hard now. Hadn't we better start this minute? It will be night before we get to Biltmer's."

Fred struck another match. "It's seven. I don't know how much of the path may be washed away. I don't even know whether I ought to let you try it without a lantern."

Thea went to the doorway and looked out. "There's nothing else to do. The sweater and the slicker will keep me dry, and this will be my chance to find out whether these shoes are really water-tight. They cost a week's salary." She retreated to the back of the cave. "It's getting blacker every minute."

Ottenburg took a brandy-flask from his coat-pocket. "Better have some of this before we start. Can you take it without water?"

Thea lifted it obediently to her lips. She put on the sweater and Fred helped her to get the clumsy slicker on over it. He buttoned it and fastened the high collar. She could feel that his hands were hurried and clumsy. The coat was too big, and he took off his necktie and belted it in at the waist. While she tucked her hair more securely under the rubber hat, he stood in front of her, between her and the grey doorway, without moving.

"Are you ready to go?" she asked carelessly.

"If you are," he spoke quietly, without moving, except to bend his head forward a little.

Thea laughed and put her hands on his shoulders. "You know how to handle me, don't you?" she whispered. For the first time, she kissed him without constraint or embarrassment.

"Thea, Thea, Thea!" Fred whispered her name three times, shaking her a little as if to waken her. It was too dark to see, but he could feel that she was smiling.

When she kissed him she had not hidden her face on his shoulder—she had risen a little on her toes, and stood straight and free. In that moment when he came close to her actual personality, he felt in her the same expansion that he had noticed at Mrs. Nathanmeyer's. She became freer and stronger under impulses. When she rose to meet him like that, he felt her flash into everything that she had ever suggested to him, as if she filled out her own shadow.

She pushed him away and shot past him out into the rain. "Now for it, Fred," she called back exultantly. The rain was pouring steadily down through the dying gray twilight, and muddy streams were spouting and foaming over the cliff.

Fred caught her and held her back. "Keep behind me, Thea. I don't know about the path. It may be gone altogether. Can't tell what there is under this water."

But the path was older than the white man's Arizona. The rush of water had washed away the dust and stones that lay on the surface, but the rock skeleton of the Indian trail was there, ready for the foot. Where the streams poured down through gullies, there was always a cedar or a *piñon* to cling to. By wading and slipping and climbing, they got along. As they neared the head of the cañon, where the path lifted and rose in steep loops to the surface of the plateau, the climb was more difficult. The earth above had broken away and washed down over the trail, bringing rocks and bushes and even young trees with it. The last ghost of daylight was dying and there was no time to lose. The cañon behind them was already black.

"We've got to go right through the top of this pine tree, Thea. No time to hunt a way around. Give me your hand." After they had crashed through the mass of branches, Fred stopped abruptly. "Gosh, what a hole! Can you jump it? Wait a minute."

He cleared the washout, slipped on the wet rock at the farther side, and caught himself just in time to escape a tumble. "If I could only find something to hold to, I could give you a hand. It's so cursed dark, and there are no trees here where they're needed. Here's something; it's a root. It will hold all right." He braced himself on the rock, gripped the crooked root with one hand and swung himself across toward Thea, holding out his arm. "Good jump! I must say you don't lose your nerve in a tight place. Can you keep at it a little longer? We're almost out. Have to make that next ledge. Put your foot on my knee and catch something to pull by."

Thea went up over his shoulder. "It's hard ground up here," she panted. "Did I wrench your arm when I slipped then? It was a cactus I grabbed, and it startled me."

"Now, one more pull and we're on the level."

They emerged gasping upon the black plateau. In the last five minutes the darkness had solidified and it seemed as if the skies were pouring black water. They could not see where the sky ended or the plain began. The light at the ranch-house burned a steady spark through the rain. Fred drew Thea's arm through his and they struck off toward the light. They could not see each other, and the rain at their backs seemed to drive them along. They kept laughing as they stumbled over tufts of grass or stepped into slippery pools. They were delighted with each other and with the adventure which lay behind them.

"I can't even see the whites of your eyes, Thea. But I'd know who was here stepping out with me, anywhere. Part coyote you are, by the feel of you. When you make up your mind to jump, you jump! My gracious, what's the matter with your hand?"

"Cactus spines. Didn't I tell you when I grabbed the cactus? I thought it was a root. Are we going straight?"

"I don't know. Somewhere near it, I think. I'm very comfortable, aren't you? You're warm, except your cheeks. How funny they are when they're wet. Still, you always feel like you. I like this. I could walk to Flagstaff. It's fun, not being able to see anything. I feel surer of you when I can't see you. Will you run away with me?"

Thea laughed. "I won't run far to-night. I'll think about it. Look, Fred, there's somebody coming."

"Henry, with his lantern. Good enough! Halloo! Hallo-o-o!" Fred shouted.

The moving light bobbed toward them. In half an hour Thea was in her big feather bed, drinking hot lentil soup, and almost before the soup was swallowed she was asleep.

VIII

On the first day of September Fred Ottenburg and Thea Kronborg left Flagstaff by the east-bound express. As the bright morning advanced, they sat alone on the rear platform of the observation car, watching the yellow miles unfold and disappear. With complete content they saw the brilliant, empty country flash by. They were tired of the desert and the dead races, of a world without change or ideas. Fred said he was glad to sit back and let the Santa Fé do the work for a while.

"And where are we going, anyhow?" he added.

"To Chicago, I suppose. Where else would we be going?" Thea hunted for a handkerchief in her handbag.

"I wasn't sure, so I had the trunks checked to Albuquerque. We can recheck there to Chicago, if you like. Why Chicago? You'll never go back to Bowers. Why wouldn't this be a good time to make a run for it? We could take the southern branch at Albuquerque, down to El Paso, and then over into Mexico. We are exceptionally free. Nobody waiting for us anywhere."

Thea sighted along the steel rails that quivered in the light behind them.

"I don't see why I couldn't marry you in Chicago as well as any place," she brought out, with some embarrassment.

Fred took the handbag out of her nervous clasp and swung it about on his finger. "You've no particular love for that spot, have you? Besides, as I've told you, my family would make a row. They are an excitable lot. They discuss and argue everlastingly. The only way I can ever put anything through is to go ahead, and convince them afterward."

"Yes, I understand. I don't mind that. I don't want to marry your family. I'm sure you wouldn't want to marry mine. But I don't see why we have to go so far."

"When we get to Winslow, you look about the freight yards and you'll probably see several yellow cars with my name on them. That's why, my dear. When your visiting-card is on every beer-bottle, you can't do things quietly. Things get into the papers." As he watched her troubled expression, he grew anxious. He leaned forward on his camp-chair, and kept twirling the handbag between his knees. "Here's a suggestion, Thea," he said presently. "Dismiss it if you don't like it: suppose we go down to Mexico on the chance. You've never seen anything like Mexico City; it will be a lark for you, anyhow. If you change your mind, and don't want to marry me, you can go back to Chicago, and I'll take a steamer from Vera Cruz and go up to New York. When I get to Chicago, you'll be at work, and nobody will ever be the wiser. No reason why we should not both travel in Mexico, is there? You'll be travelling alone. I'll merely tell you the right places to stop, and come to take you driving. I won't put any pressure on you. Have I ever?" He swung the bag toward her and looked up under her hat.

"No, you haven't," she murmured. She was thinking that her own position might be less difficult if he had used what he called pressure. He clearly wished her to take the responsibility.

"You have your own future in the back of your mind all the time," Fred began, "and I have it in mine. I'm not going to try to carry you off, as I might another girl. If you wanted to quit me, I couldn't hold you, no matter how many times you had married me. I don't want to overpersuade you. But I'd like mighty well to get you down to that jolly old city, where everything would please you, and give myself a chance. Then, if you thought you could have a better time with me than without me, I'd try to grab you before you changed your mind. You are not a sentimental person."

Thea drew her veil down over her face. "I think I am, a little; about you," she said quietly. Fred's irony somehow hurt her.

"What's at the bottom of your mind, Thea?" he asked hurriedly. "I can't tell. Why do you consider it at all, if you're not sure? Why are you here with me now?"

Her face was half-averted. He was thinking that it looked older and more firm, almost hard, under a veil.

"Isn't it possible to do things without having any very clear reason?" she asked slowly. "I have no plan in the back of my mind. Now that I'm with you, I want to be with you; that's all. I can't settle down to being alone again. I am here to-day because I want to be with you to-day." She paused. "One thing, though; if I gave you my word, I'd keep it. And you could hold me, though you don't seem to think so. Maybe I'm not sentimental, but I'm not very light, either. If I went off with you like this, it wouldn't be to amuse myself."

Ottenburg's eyes fell. His lips worked nervously for a moment. "Do you mean that you really care for me, Thea Kronborg?" he asked unsteadily.

"I guess so. It's like anything else. It takes hold of you and you've got to go through with it, even if you're afraid. I was afraid to leave Moonstone, and afraid to leave Harsanyi. But I had to go through with it."

"And are you afraid now?" Fred asked slowly.

"Yes; more than I've ever been. But I don't think I could go back. The past closes up behind one, somehow. One would rather have a new kind of misery. The old kind seems like death or unconsciousness. You can't force your life back into that mould again. No, one can't go back." She rose and stood by the back grating of the platform, her hand on the brass rail.

Fred went to her side. She pushed up her veil and turned her most glowing face to him. Her eyes were wet and there were tears on her lashes, but she was smiling the rare, whole-hearted smile he had seen once or twice before. He looked at her shining eyes, her parted lips, her chin a little lifted. It was as if they were coloured by a sunrise he could not see. He put his hand over hers and clasped it with a strength she felt. Her eyelashes trembled, her mouth softened, but her eyes were still brilliant.

"Will you always be like you were down there, if I go with you?" she asked under her breath.

His fingers tightened on hers. "By God, I will!" he muttered.

"That's the only promise I'll ask you for. Now go away for a while and let me think about it. Come back at lunch-time and I'll tell you. Will that do?"

"Anything will do, Thea, if you'll only let me keep an eye on you. The rest of the world doesn't interest me much. You've got me in deep."

Fred dropped her hand and turned away. As he glanced back from the front end of the observation car, he saw that she was still standing there, and anyone would have known that she was brooding over something. The earnestness of her head and shoulders had a certain nobility. He stood looking at her for a moment.

When he reached the forward smoking-car, Fred took a seat at the end, where he could shut the other passengers from his sight. He put on his travelling-cap and sat down wearily, keeping his head near the window. "In any case, I shall help her more than I shall hurt her," he kept saying to himself. He admitted that this was not the only motive which impelled him, but it was one of them. "I'll make it my business in life to get her on. There's nothing else I care about so much as seeing her have her chance. She hasn't touched her real force yet. She isn't even aware of it. Lord, don't I know something about them? There isn't one of them that has such a depth to draw from. She'll be one of the great artists of our time. Playing accompaniments for that cheese-faced sneak! I'll get her off to Germany this winter, or take her. She hasn't got any time to waste now. I'll make it up to her, all right."

Ottenburg certainly meant to make it up to her, in so far as he could. His feeling was as generous as strong human feelings are likely to be. The only trouble was, that he was married already, and had been since he was twenty.

His older friends in Chicago, people who had been friends of his family, knew of the unfortunate state of his personal affairs; but they were people whom in the natural course of things Thea Kronborg would scarcely meet. Mrs. Frederick Ottenburg lived in California, at Santa Barbara, where her health was supposed to be better than elsewhere, and her husband lived in Chicago. He visited his wife every winter to re-enforce her position, and his devoted mother, although her hatred for her daughter-in-law was scarcely approachable in words, went to Santa Barbara every year to make things look better and to relieve her son.

When Frederick Ottenburg was beginning his junior year at Harvard, he got a letter from Dick Brisbane, a Kansas City boy he knew, telling him that his fiancée, Miss Edith Beers, was going to New York to buy her trousseau. She would be at the Holland House, with her aunt and a girl from Kansas City who was to be a bridesmaid, for two weeks or more. If Ottenburg happened to be going down to New York, would he call upon Miss Beers and "show her a good time"?

Fred did happen to be going to New York. He was going down from New Haven, after the Thanksgiving game. He called on Miss Beers and found her, as he that night telegraphed Brisbane, a "ripping beauty, no mistake." He took her and her aunt and her uninteresting friend to the theatre and to the opera, and he asked them to lunch with him at the Waldorf. He took no little pains in arranging the luncheon with the head waiter. Miss Beers was the sort of girl with whom a young man liked to seem experienced. She was dark and slender and fiery. She was witty and slangy; said daring things and carried them off with nonchalance. Her childish extravagance and contempt for all the serious facts of life could be charged to her father's generosity and his long packing-house purse. Freaks that would have been vulgar and ostentatious in a more simple-minded girl, in Miss Beers seemed whimsical and picturesque. She darted about in magnificent furs and pumps and close-clinging gowns, though that was the day of full skirts. Her hats were large and floppy. When she wriggled out of her moleskin coat at luncheon, she looked like a slim black weasel. Her satin dress was a mere sheath, so conspicuous by its severity and scantness that everyone in the diningroom stared. She ate nothing but alligator-pear salad and hot-house grapes, drank a little champagne, and took cognac in her coffee. She ridiculed, in the raciest slang, the singers they had heard at the opera the night before, and when her aunt pretended to reprove her, she murmured indifferently, "What's the matter with you, old sport?" She rattled on with a subdued loquaciousness, always keeping her voice low and monotonous, always looking out of the corner of her eye and speaking, as it were, in asides, out of the corner of her mouth. She was scornful of everything—which became her eyebrows. Her face was mobile and discontented, her eyes quick and black. There was a sort of smouldering fire about her, young Ottenburg thought. She entertained him prodigiously.

After luncheon Miss Beers said she was going uptown to be fitted, and that she would go alone because her aunt made her nervous. When Fred held her coat for her, she murmured, "Thank you, Alphonse," as if she were addressing the waiter. As she stepped into a hansom, with a long stretch of thin silk stocking, she said negligently, over her fur collar, "Better let me take you along and drop you somewhere." He sprang in after her, and she told the driver to go to the Park.

It was a bright winter day, and bitterly cold. Miss Beers asked Fred to tell her about the game at New Haven, and when he did so paid no attention to what he said. She sank back into the hansom and held her muff before her face, lowering it occasionally to utter laconic remarks about the people in the carriages they passed, interrupting Fred's narrative in a disconcerting manner. As they entered the Park, he happened to glance under her wide black hat at her black eyes and hair—the muff hid everything else—and discovered that she was crying. To his solicitous inquiry she replied that it "was enough to make you damp, to go and try on dresses to marry a man you weren't keen about."

Further explanations followed. She had thought she was "perfectly cracked" about Brisbane, until she met Fred at the Holland House three days ago. Then she knew she would scratch Brisbane's eyes out if she married him. What was she going to do?

Fred told the driver to keep going. What did she want to do? Well, she didn't know. One had to marry somebody, after all the machinery had been put in motion. Perhaps she might as well scratch Brisbane as anybody else; for scratch she would, if she didn't get what she wanted.

Of course, Fred agreed, one had to marry somebody. And certainly this girl beat anything he had ever been up against before. Again he told the driver to go ahead. Did she mean that she would think of marrying him, by any chance? Of course she did, Alphonse. Hadn't he seen that all over her face three days ago? If he hadn't, he was a snowball.

By this time Fred was beginning to feel sorry for the driver. Miss Beers, however, was compassionless. After a few more turns, Fred suggested tea at the Casino. He was very cold himself, and remembering the shining silk hose and pumps, he wondered that the girl was not frozen. As they got out of the hansom, he slipped the driver a bill and told him to have something hot while he waited.

At the tea-table, in a snug glass enclosure, with the steam sputtering in the pipes beside them and a brilliant winter sunset without, they developed their plan. Miss Beers had with her plenty of money, destined for tradesmen, which she was quite willing to divert into other channels—the first excitement of buying a trousseau had worn off, anyway. It was very much like any other shopping. Fred had his allowance and a few hundred he had won on the game. She would meet him to-morrow morning at the Jersey ferry. They could take one of the west-bound Pennsylvania trains and go—anywhere, some place where the laws weren't too fussy—Fred had not even thought about the laws!—It would be all right with her father; he knew Fred's family.

Now that they were engaged, she thought she would like to drive a little more. They were jerked about in the cab for another hour through the deserted Park. Miss Beers, having removed her hat, reclined upon Fred's shoulder.

The next morning they left Jersey City by the latest fast train out. They had some misadventures, crossed several States before they found a justice obliging enough to marry two persons whose names automatically instigated inquiry. The bride's family were rather pleased with her original-ity; besides, any one of the Ottenburg boys was clearly a better match than young Brisbane. With Otto Ottenburg, however, the affair went down hard, and to his wife, the once proud Katarina Fürst, such a disappointment was almost unbearable. Her sons had always been clay in her hands, and now the *geliebter Sohn* had escaped her.

Beers, the packer, gave his daughter a house in St. Louis, and Fred went into his father's business. At the end of a year, he was mutely appealing to his mother for sympathy. At the end of two, he was drinking and in open rebellion. He had learned to detest his wife. Her wastefulness and cruelty revolted him. The ignorance and the fatuous conceit which lay behind her grimacing mask of slang and ridicule humiliated him so deeply that he became absolutely reckless. Her grace was only an uneasy wriggle, her audacity was the result of insolence and envy, and her wit was restless spite. As her personal mannerisms grew more and more odious to him, he began to dull his perceptions with champagne. He had it for tea, he drank it with dinner, and during the evening he took enough to insure that he would be well insulated when he got home. This behaviour spread alarm among his friends. It was scandalous, and it did not occur among brewers. He was violating the *noblesse oblige* of his guild. His father and his father's partners looked alarmed.

When Fred's mother went to him and with clasped hands entreated an explanation, he told her that the only trouble was that he couldn't hold enough wine to make life endurable, so he was going to get out from under and enlist in the navy. He didn't want anything but the shirt on his back and clean salt air. His mother could look out; he was going to make a scandal.

Mrs. Otto Ottenburg went to Kansas City to see Mr. Beers, and had the satisfaction of telling him that he had brought up his daughter like a savage, *eine Ungebildete*. All the Ottenburgs and all the Beers, and many of their friends, were drawn into the quarrel. It was to public opinion, however, and not to his mother's activities, that Fred owed his partial escape from bondage. The cosmopolitan brewing world of St. Louis had conservative standards. The Ottenburgs' friends were not predisposed in favour of the plunging Kansas City set, and they disliked young Fred's wife from the day that she was brought among them. They found her ignorant and ill-bred and insufferably impertinent. When they became aware of how matters were going between her and Fred, they omitted no opportunity to snub her. Young Fred had always been popular, and St. Louis people took up his cause with warmth. Even the younger men, among whom Mrs. Fred tried to draught a following, at first avoided and then ignored her. Her defeat was so conspicuous, her life became such a desert, that she at last consented to accept the house in Santa Barbara which Mrs. Otto Ottenburg had long owned and cherished. This villa, with its luxuriant gardens, was the price of Fred's furlough. His mother was only too glad to offer it in his behalf.

As soon as his wife was established in California, Fred was transferred from St. Louis to Chicago.

A divorce was the one thing Edith would never, never, give him. She told him so, and she told his family so, and her father stood behind her. She would enter into no arrangement that might eventually lead to divorce. She had insulted her husband before guests and servants, had scratched his face, thrown hand-mirrors and hairbrushes and nail-scissors at him often enough, but she knew that Fred was hardly the fellow who would go into court and offer that sort of evidence. In her behaviour with other men she was discreet.

After Fred went to Chicago, his mother visited him often, and dropped a word to her old friends there, who were already kindly disposed toward the young man. They gossiped as little as was compatible with the interest they felt, undertook to make life agreeable for Fred, and told his story only where they felt it would do good: to girls who seemed to find the young brewer attractive. So far, he had behaved well, and had kept out of entanglements.

Since he was transferred to Chicago, Fred had been abroad several times, and had fallen more and more into the way of going about among young artists, people with whom personal relations were incidental. With women, and even girls, who had careers to follow, a young man might have pleasant friendships without being regarded as a prospective suitor or lover. Among artists his position was not irregular, because with them his marriageableness was not an issue. His tastes, his enthusiasm, and his agreeable personality made him welcome.

With Thea Kronborg he had allowed himself more liberty than he usually did in his friendships or gallantries with young artists, because she seemed to him distinctly not the marrying kind. She impressed him as equipped to be an artist, and to be nothing else; already directed, concentrated, formed as to mental habit. He was generous and sympathetic, and she was lonely and needed friendship; needed cheerfulness. She had not much power of reaching out toward useful people or useful experiences, did not see opportunities. She had no tact about going after good positions or enlisting the interest of influential persons. She antagonized people rather than conciliated them. He discovered at once that she had a merry side, a robust humour that was deep and hearty, like her laugh, but it slept most of the time under her own doubts and the dullness of her life. She had not what is called a "sense of humour." That is, she had no intellectual humour; no power to enjoy the absurdities of people, no relish of their pretentiousness and inconsistencies—which only depressed her. But her joviality, Fred felt, was an asset, and ought to be developed. He discovered that she was more receptive and more effective under a pleasant stimulus than she was under the grey grind which she considered her salvation. She was still Methodist enough to believe that if a thing were hard and irksome, it must be good for her. And yet, whatever she did well was spontaneous. Under the least glow of excitement, as at Mrs. Nathanmeyer's, he had seen the apprehensive, frowning drudge of Bowers's studio flash into a resourceful and consciously beautiful woman.

His interest in Thea was serious, almost from the first, and so sincere that he felt no distrust of himself. He believed that he knew a great deal more about her possibilities than Bowers knew, and he liked to think that he had given her a stronger hold on life. She had never seen herself or known herself as she did at Mrs. Nathanmeyer's musical evenings. She had been a different girl ever since. He had not anticipated that she would grow more fond of him than his immediate usefulness warranted. He thought he knew the ways of artists, and, as he said, she must have been "at it from her cradle." He had imagined, perhaps, but never really believed, that he would find her waiting for him sometime as he found her waiting on the day he reached the Ottenburg ranch. Once he found her so—well, he did not pretend to be anything more or less than a reasonably well-intentioned young man. A lovesick girl or a flirtatious woman he could have handled easily enough. But a personality like that, unconsciously revealing itself for the first time under the exaltation of a personal feeling—what could one do but watch it? As he used to say to himself, in reckless moments back there in the cañon, "You can't put out a sunrise." He had to watch it, and then he had to share it.

Besides, was he really going to do her any harm? The Lord knew he would marry her if he could! Marriage would be an incident, not an end with her; he was sure of that. If it were not he, it would be someone else; someone who would be a weight about her neck, probably; who would hold her back and beat her down and divert her from the first plunge for which he felt she was gathering all her energies. He meant to help her, and he could not think of another man who would. He went over his unmarried friends, East and West, and he could not think of one who would know what she was driving at—or care. The clever ones were selfish, the kindly ones were stupid.

"Damn it, if she's going to fall in love with somebody, it had better be me than any of the others—of the sort she'd find. Get her tied up with some conceited ass who'd try to make her over, train her like a puppy! Give one of 'em a big nature like that, and he'd be horrified. He wouldn't show his face in the clubs until he'd gone after her and combed her down to conform to some fool idea in his own head—put there by some other woman, too, his first sweetheart or his grandmother or a maiden aunt. At least, I understand her. I know what she needs and where she's bound, and I mean to see that she has a fighting chance."

His own conduct looked crooked, he admitted; but he asked himself whether, between men and women, all ways were not more or less crooked. He believed those which are called straight were the most dangerous of all. They seemed to him, for the most part, to lie between windowless stone walls, and their rectitude had been achieved at the expense of light and air. In their unquestioned regularity lurked every sort of human cruelty and meanness, and every kind of humiliation and suffering. He would rather have any woman he cared for wounded than crushed. He would deceive her not once, he told himself fiercely, but a hundred times, to keep her free.

★　★　★

When Fred went back to the observation car at one o'clock, after the luncheon call, it was empty, and he found Thea alone on the platform. She put out her hand, and met his eyes.

"It's as I said. Things have closed behind me. I can't go back, so I am going on—to Mexico?" She lifted her face with an eager, questioning smile.

Fred met it with a sinking heart. Had he really hoped she would give him another answer? He would have given pretty much anything— But there, that did no good. He could give only what he had. Things were never complete in this world; you had to snatch at them as they came or go without. Nobody could look into her face and draw back, nobody who had any courage. She had courage enough for anything—look at her mouth and chin and eyes! Where did it come from, that light? How could a face, a familiar face, become so the picture of hope, be painted with the very colours of youth's exaltation? She was right; she was not one of those who draw back. Some people get on by avoiding dangers, others by riding through them.

They stood by the railing looking back at the sand levels, both feeling that the train was steaming ahead very fast. Fred's mind was a confusion of images and ideas. Only two things were clear to him: the force of her determination, and the belief that, handicapped as he was, he could do better by her than another man would do. He knew he would always remember her, standing there with that expectant, forward-looking smile, enough to turn the future into summer.

Part V

Doctor Archie's
Venture

I

*D*octor Howard Archie had come down to Denver for a meeting of the stockholders in the San Felipe silver mine. It was not absolutely necessary for him to come, but he had no very pressing cases at home. Winter was closing down in Moonstone, and he dreaded the dullness of it. On the tenth day of January, therefore, he was registered at the Brown Palace Hotel. On the morning of the eleventh he came down to breakfast to find the streets white and the air thick with snow. A wild northwester was blowing down from the mountains, one of those beautiful storms that wrap Denver in dry, furry snow, and make the city a loadstone to thousands of men in the mountains and on the plains. The brakemen out on their box-cars, the miners up in their diggings, the lonely homesteaders in the sand hills of Yucca and Kit Carson Counties, begin to think of Denver, muffled in snow, and full of food and drink and good cheer.

Howard Archie was glad he had got in before the storm came. He felt as cheerful as if he had received a legacy that morning, and he greeted the clerk with even greater friendliness than usual when he stopped at the desk for his mail. In the dining-room he found several old friends seated here and there before substantial breakfasts: cattlemen and mining engineers from odd corners of the State, all looking fresh and well pleased with themselves. He had a word with one and another before he sat down at the little table by a window, where the Austrian head waiter stood attentively behind a chair. After his breakfast was put before him, the doctor began to run over his letters. There was one directed in Thea Kronborg's handwriting, forwarded from Moonstone. He saw with astonishment, as he put another lump of sugar into his cup, that this letter bore a New York postmark. He had known that Thea was in Mexico, travelling with some Chicago people, but New York, to a Denver man, seems much farther away than Mexico City. He put the letter behind his plate, upright against the stem of his water goblet, and looked at it thoughtfully while he drank his second cup of coffee. He had been a little anxious about Thea; she had not written to him for a long while.

As he never got good coffee at home, the doctor always drank three cups for breakfast when he was in Denver. Oscar knew just when to bring him a second pot, fresh and smoking. "And more cream, Oscar, please. You know I like lots of cream," the doctor murmured, as he opened the square envelope, marked in the upper right-hand corner, "Everett House, Union Square." The text of the letter was as follows:

DEAR DOCTOR ARCHIE:

I have not written to you for a long time, but it has not been unintentional. I could not write you frankly, and so I would not write at all. I can be frank with you now, but not by letter. It is a great deal to ask, but I wonder if you could come to New York to help me out? I have got into difficulties, and I need your advice. I need your friendship. I am afraid I must even ask you to lend me money, if you can without serious inconvenience. I have to go to Germany to study, and it can't be put off any longer. My voice is ready. Needless to say, I don't want any word of this to reach my family. They are the last people I would turn to, although I love my mother dearly. If you can come, please telegraph me at this hotel. Don't despair of me. I'll make it up to you yet.

Your old friend

THEA KRONBORG

This in a bold, jagged handwriting with a Gothic turn to the letters—something between a highly sophisticated hand and a very unsophisticated one—not in the least smooth or flowing.

The doctor bit off the end of a cigar nervously and read the letter through again, fumbling distractedly in his pockets for matches, while the waiter kept trying to call his attention to the box he had just placed before him. At last Oscar came out, as if the idea had just struck him, "Matches, sir?"

"Yes, thank you." The doctor slipped a coin into his palm and rose, crumpling Thea's letter in his hand and thrusting the others into his pocket unopened. He went back to the desk in the lobby and beckoned the clerk, upon whose kindness he threw himself apologetically.

"Harry, I've got to pull out unexpectedly. Call up the Burlington, will you, and ask them to route me to New York the quickest way, and to let us know. Ask for the hour I'll get in. I have to wire."

"Certainly, Doctor Archie. Have it for you in a minute."

The young man's pallid, clean-scraped face was all sympathetic interest as he reached for the telephone.

Doctor Archie put out his hand and stopped him.

"Wait a minute. Tell me, first, is Captain Harris down yet?"

"No, sir. The captain hasn't come down yet this morning."

"I'll wait here for him. If I don't happen to catch him, nail him and get me. Thank you, Harry."

The doctor spoke gratefully and turned away. He began to pace the lobby, his hands behind him, watching the bronze elevator doors like a hawk. At last Captain Harris issued from one of them, tall and imposing, wearing a Stetson and fierce moustaches, a fur coat on his arm, a solitaire glittering upon his little finger and another in his black satin ascot. He was one of the grand old bluffers of those good old days. As gullible as a schoolboy, he had managed, with his sharp eye and knowing air and twisted blond moustaches, to pass himself off for an astute financier, and the Denver papers respectfully referred to him as the Rothschild of Cripple Creek.

Doctor Archie stopped the captain on his way to breakfast. "Must see you a minute, captain. Can't wait. Want to sell you some shares in the San Felipe. Got to raise money."

The captain grandly bestowed his hat upon an eager porter who had already lifted his fur coat tenderly from his arm and stood nursing it. In removing his hat, the captain exposed a bald, flushed dome, thatched about the ears with yellowish-grey hair.

"Bad time to sell, doctor. You want to hold on to San Felipe, and buy more. What have you got to raise?"

"Oh, not a great sum. Five or six thousand. I've been buying up close and have run short."

"I see, I see. Well, doctor, you'll have to let me get through that door. I was out last night, and I'm going to get my bacon, if you lose your mine." He clapped Archie on the shoulder and pushed him along in front of him. "Come ahead with me, and we'll talk business."

Doctor Archie attended the captain and waited while he gave his order, taking the seat the old promoter indicated.

"Now, sir," the captain turned to him, "you don't want to sell anything. You must be under the impression that I'm one of these damned New England sharks that get their pound of flesh off the widow and orphan. If you're a little short, sign a note and I'll write a cheque. That's the way gentlemen do business. If you want to put up some San Felipe as collateral, let her go, but I shan't touch a share of it. Pens and ink, please, Oscar"—he lifted a large forefinger to the Austrian.

The captain took out his cheque-book and a book of blank notes, and adjusted his nose-nippers. He wrote a few words in one book and Archie wrote a few in the other. Then they each tore across perforations and exchanged slips of paper.

"That's the way. Saves office rent," the captain commented with satisfaction, returning the books to his pocket. "And now, Archie, where are you off to?"

"Got to go East to-night. A deal waiting for me in New York." Doctor Archie rose.

The captain's face brightened as he saw Oscar approaching with a tray, and he began tucking the corner of his napkin inside his collar, over his ascot. "Don't let them unload anything on you back there, doctor," he said genially, "and don't let them relieve you of anything, either. Don't let them get any Cripple stuff off you. We can manage our own silver out here, and we're going to take it out by the ton, sir!"

The doctor left the dining-room, and after another consultation with the clerk, he wrote his first telegram to Thea:

> MISS THEA KRONBORG
> EVERETT HOUSE NEW YORK
> WILL CALL AT YOUR HOTEL ELEVEN O'CLOCK
> FRIDAY MORNING GLAD TO COME THANK YOU
> ARCHIE

He stood and heard the message actually clicked off on the wire, with the feeling that she was hearing the click at the other end. Then he sat down in the lobby and wrote a note to his wife and one to the other doctor in Moonstone. When he at last issued out into the storm, it was with a feeling of elation rather than of anxiety. Whatever was wrong, he could make it right. Her letter had practically said so.

He tramped about the snowy streets, from the bank to the Union Station, where he shoved his money under the grating of the ticket window as if he could not get rid of it fast enough. He had never been in New York, never been farther east than Buffalo. "That's rather a shame," he reflected boyishly as he put the long tickets in his pocket, "for a man nearly forty years old." However, he thought as he walked up toward the club, he was on the whole glad that his first trip had a human interest, that he was going for something, and because he was wanted. "Queer"—he went over it with the snow blowing in his face—"but that sort of thing is more interesting than mines and making your daily bread. It's worth paying out to be in on it- -for a fellow like me. And when it's Thea—oh, I back her!" he laughed aloud as he burst in at the door of the Athletic Club, powdered with snow.

Archie sat down before the New York papers and ran over the advertisements of hotels, but he was too restless to read. Probably he had better get a new overcoat, and he was not sure about the shape of his collars. "I don't want to look different to her from everybody else there," he mused. "I guess I'll go down and have Van look me over. He'll put me right."

So he plunged out into the snow again and started for his tailor's. When he passed a florist's shop, he stopped and looked in at the window, smiling; how naturally pleasant things recalled one another. At the tailor's he kept whistling, "Flow gently, Sweet Afton," while Van Dusen advised him, until that resourceful tailor and haberdasher exclaimed, "You must have a date there, doctor; you behave like a bridegroom," and made him remember that he wasn't one.

Before he let him go, Van put his finger on the Masonic pin in his client's lapel. "Mustn't wear that, doctor. Very bad form back there."

II

*F*red Ottenburg, smartly dressed for the afternoon, with a long black coat and gaiters was sitting in the dusty parlour of the Everett House. His manner was not in accord with his personal freshness, the good lines of his clothes, and the shining smoothness of his hair. His attitude was one of deep dejection, and his face, though it had the cool, unimpeachable fairness possible only to a very blond young man, was by no means happy. A page shuffled into the room and looked about. When he made out the dark figure in a shadowy corner, tracing over the carpet pattern with a cane, he droned, "The lady says you can come up, sir."

Fred picked up his hat and gloves and followed the creature, who seemed an aged boy in uniform, through dark corridors that smelled of old carpets. The page knocked at the door of Thea's sitting-room, and then wandered away. Thea came to the door with a telegram in her hand. She asked Ottenburg to come in and pointed to one of the clumsy, sullen-looking chairs that were as thick as they were high. The room was brown with time, dark in spite of two windows that opened on Union Square, with dull curtains and carpet, and heavy, respectable-looking furniture in sombre colours. The place was saved from utter dismalness by a coal fire under the black marble mantelpiece—brilliantly reflected in a long mirror that hung between the two windows. This was the first time Fred had seen the room, and he took it in quickly, as he put down his hat and gloves.

Thea seated herself at the walnut writing-desk, still holding the slip of yellow paper. "Doctor Archie is coming," she said. "He will be here Friday morning."

"Well, that's good, at any rate," her visitor replied with a determined effort at cheerfulness. Then, turning to the fire, he added blankly, "If you want him."

"Of course I want him. I would never have asked such a thing of him if I hadn't wanted him a great deal. It's a very expensive trip for him." Thea spoke severely. Then she went on, in a milder tone. "He doesn't say anything about the money, but I think his coming means that he can let me have it."

Fred was standing before the mantel, rubbing his hands together nervously. "Probably. You are still determined to call on him?" He sat down tentatively in the chair Thea had indicated. "I don't see why you won't borrow from me, and let him sign with you, for instance. That would constitute a perfectly regular business transaction. I could bring suit against either of you for my money."

Thea turned toward him from the desk. "We won't take that up again, Fred. I should have a different feeling about it if I went on your money. In a way I shall feel freer on Doctor Archie's, and in another way I shall feel more bound. I shall try even harder." She paused. "He is almost like my father," she added irrelevantly.

"Still, he isn't, you know," Fred persisted. "It wouldn't be anything new. I've lent money to students before, and got it back, too."

"Yes; I know you're generous"—Thea hurried over it—"but this will be the best way. He will be here on Friday, did I tell you?"

"I think you mentioned it. That's rather soon. May I smoke?" he took out a small cigarette-case. "I suppose you'll be off next week?" he asked as he struck a match.

"Just as soon as I can," she replied with a restless movement of her arms, as if her dark-blue dress were too tight for her. "It seems as if I'd been here forever."

"And yet," the young man mused, "we got in only four days ago. Facts really don't count for much, do they? It's all in the way people feel: even in little things."

Thea winced, but she did not answer him. She put the telegram back in its envelope and placed it carefully in one of the pigeonholes of the desk.

"I suppose," Fred brought out with effort, "that your friend is in your confidence?"

"He always has been. I shall have to tell him about myself. I wish I could without dragging you in."

Fred shook himself. "Don't bother about where you drag me, please," he put in, flushing. "I don't give—" he subsided suddenly.

"I'm afraid," Thea went on gravely, "that he won't understand. He'll be hard on you."

Fred studied the white ash of his cigarette before he flicked it off. "You mean he'll see me as even worse than I am. Yes, I suppose I shall look very low to him: a fifth-rate scoundrel. But that only matters in so far as it hurts his feelings."

Thea sighed. "We'll both look pretty low. And after all, we must really be just about as we shall look to him."

Ottenburg started up and threw his cigarette into the grate.

"That I deny. Have you ever been really frank with this preceptor of your childhood, even when you *were* a child? Think a minute, have you? Of course not! From your cradle, as I once told you, you've been 'doing it' on the side, living your own life, admitting to yourself things that would horrify him. You've always deceived him to the extent of letting him think you different from what you are. He couldn't understand then, he can't understand now. So why not spare yourself and him?"

She shook her head.

"Of course, I've had my own thoughts. Maybe he has had his, too. But I've never done anything before that he would much mind. I must put myself right with him—as right as I can—to begin over. He'll make allowances for me. He always has. But I'm afraid he won't for you."

"Leave that to him and me. I take it you want me to see him?" Fred sat down again and began absently to trace the carpet pattern with his cane. "At the worst"—he spoke wanderingly—"I thought you'd perhaps let me go in on the business end of it and invest along with you. You'd put in your talent and ambition and hard work, and I'd put in the money and—well, nobody's good wishes are to be scorned, not even mine. Then, when the thing panned out big, we could share together. Your doctor friend hasn't cared half so much about your future as I have."

"He's cared a good deal. He doesn't know as much about such things as you do. Of course you've been a great deal more help to me than anyone else ever has," Thea said quietly. The black clock on the mantel began to strike. She listened to the five strokes and then said, "I'd have liked your helping me eight months ago. But now, you'd simply be keeping me."

"You weren't ready for it eight months ago." Fred leaned back at last in his chair. "You simply weren't ready for it. You were too tired. You were too timid. Your whole tone was too low. You couldn't rise from a chair like that"—she had started up apprehensively and gone toward the window. "You were fumbling and awkward. Since then you've come into your personality. You were always locking horns with it before. You were a sullen little drudge eight months ago, afraid of being caught at either looking or moving like yourself. Nobody could tell anything about you. A voice is not an instrument that's found ready-made. A voice is personality. It can be as big as a circus and as common as dirt.—There's good money in that kind, too, but I don't happen to be interested in them.—Nobody could tell much about what you might be able to do, last winter. I saw more than anybody else."

"Yes, I know you did." Thea walked over to the old-fashioned mantel and held her hands down to the glow of the fire. "I owe so much to you. That's why I have to get away from you altogether. I depend on you for so many things. Oh, I did even last winter in Chicago!" She knelt down by the grate and held her hands closer to the coals. "And one thing leads to another."

Ottenburg watched her as she bent toward the fire. His glance brightened a little. "Anyhow, you couldn't look as you do now, before you knew me. You *were* clumsy. And whatever you do now, you do splendidly. And you can't cry enough to spoil your face for more than ten minutes. It comes right back, in spite of you. It's only since you've known me that you've let yourself be beautiful."

Without rising she turned her face away. Fred went on impetuously. "Oh, you can turn it away from me, Thea: you can take it away from me! All the same—" His spurt died and he fell back. "How can you turn on me so, after all!" he sighed.

"I haven't. But when you arranged with yourself to take me in like that, you couldn't have been thinking very kindly of me. I can't understand how you carried it through, when I was so easy, and all the circumstances were so easy."

Her crouching position by the fire became threatening. Fred got up, and Thea also rose.

"No," he said, "I can't make you see that now. Some time later, perhaps, you will understand better. For one thing, I honestly could not imagine that words, names, meant so much to you." He took a rapid turn about the room and then, as Thea remained standing, he rolled one of the elephantine chairs up to the hearth for her.

"Sit down and listen to me for a moment, Thea." He began pacing from the hearthrug to the window and back again, while she sat down compliantly. "Don't you know most of the people in the world are not individuals at all? They never have an individual idea or experience. A lot of girls go to boarding-school together, come out the same season, dance at the same parties, are married off in groups, have their babies at about the same time, send their children to school together, and so the human crop renews itself. Such women know as much about the reality of the forms they go through as they know about the wars they learned the dates of. They get their most personal experiences out of novels and plays. Everything is second-hand with them. Why, you *couldn't* live like that."

Thea sat looking toward the mantel, her eyes half-closed, her chin level, her head set as if she were enduring something. Her hands, very white, lay passive on her dark gown. From the window corner Fred looked at them and at her. He shook his head and flashed an angry, tormented look out into the blue twilight over the Square, through which muffled cries and calls and the clang of car-bells came up from the street. He turned again and began to pace the floor.

"Say what you will, Thea Kronborg, you are not that sort of person. You will never sit alone with a pacifier and a novel. You won't subsist on what the old ladies have put into the bottle for you. You will always break through into the realities. That was the first thing Harsanyi found out about you; that you couldn't be kept on the outside. If you'd lived in Moonstone all your life and got on with your discreet brakeman, you'd have had just the same nature. Your children would have been the realities then, probably. If they'd been commonplace, you'd have killed them with driving. You'd have managed in some way to live twenty times as much as the people around you."

Fred paused. He sought along the shadowy ceiling and heavy

mouldings for words. "You won't play much. You won't, perhaps, love many times." He paused. "And you did love me, you know. Your railroad friend would have understood me. I *could* have thrown you back. The reverse was there—it stared me in the face—but I couldn't pull it. I let you drive ahead." He threw out his hands. What Thea noticed, oddly enough, was the flash of the firelight on his cuff-link. "And you'll always drive ahead," he muttered. "It's your way."

There was a long silence. Thea put her hand to the back of her neck and pressed it, as if the muscles there were aching.

"Well," she said at last, "I at least overlook more in you than I do in myself. I am always excusing you to myself. I don't do much else."

"Then why, in Heaven's name, won't you let me be your friend? You make a scoundrel of me, borrowing money from another man to get out of my clutches."

"If I borrow from him, it's to study. Anything I took from you would be different. As I said before, you'd be keeping me."

"Keeping! I like your language. It's pure Moonstone, Thea— like your point of view. I wonder how long you'll be a Methodist."

He turned away bitterly.

"Well, I've never said I wasn't Moonstone, have I? I am, and that's why I want Doctor Archie. I can't see anything so funny about Moonstone, you know." She pushed her chair back a little from the hearth and clasped her hands over her knee, still looking thoughtfully into the red coals. "We always come back to the same thing, Fred. The name, as you call it, makes a difference to me how I feel about myself. You would have acted very differently with a girl of your own kind, and that's why I can't take anything from you now. Being married is one thing and not being married is the other thing, and that's all there is to it. You say I was too much alone, and yet what you did was to cut me off more than I ever had been. Now I'm going to try to make good to my friends out there. That's all there is left for me."

"Make good to your friends!" Fred burst out. "What one of them cares as I care, or believes as I believe? I've told you I'll never ask a gracious word from you until I can ask it with all the churches in Christendom at my back."

Thea looked up, and when she saw Fred's face, she thought sadly that he, too, looked as if things were spoiled for him. "If you know me as well as you say you do, Fred," she said slowly, "then you are not being honest with yourself. You know that I can't do things halfway. If you kept me at all—you'd keep me." She dropped her head wearily on her hand and sat with her forehead resting on her fingers.

Fred leaned over her and said just above his breath: "Then, when I get that divorce, you'll take it up with me again? You'll at least let me know, warn me, before there is a serious question of anybody else?"

Without lifting her head, Thea answered him. "Oh, I don't think there will ever be a question of anybody else. Not if I can help it. I suppose I've given you every reason to think there will be—at once, on shipboard, any time!"

Ottenburg drew himself up like a shot. "Stop it, Thea!" he said sharply. "That's one thing you've never done. That's like any common woman." He went to the other side of the room and took up his hat and gloves from the sofa. He came back cheerfully. "I didn't drop in to bully you this afternoon. I came to coax you to go out for tea with me somewhere." He waited, but she did not look up or lift her head, still sunk on her hand.

Her handkerchief had fallen. Fred picked it up and put it on her knee, pressing her fingers over it. "Good night, dear and wonderful," he whispered. He looked down at her bent head, and the curve of her neck that was so sad. He stooped, and with his lips just touched her hair where the firelight made it ruddiest.

From the door he turned back irrelevantly. "As to your old friend, if he's to be here on Friday, why"—he snatched out his watch and held it down to catch the light from the grate—"he's on the train now! That ought to cheer you. Good night." She heard the door close.

III

On Friday afternoon Thea Kronborg was walking excitedly up and down her sitting-room, which at that hour was flooded by thin, clear sunshine. Both windows were open, and the fire in the grate was low, for the day was one of those false springs that sometimes blow into New York from the sea in the middle of winter, soft, warm, with a persuasive salty moisture in the air and a relaxing thaw under foot. Thea was flushed and animated, and she seemed as restless as the sooty sparrows which chirped and cheeped distractingly about the windows. She kept looking at the black clock, and then down into the Square. The room was full of flowers, and she stopped now and then to arrange them or to move them into the sunlight. After the bell-boy came to announce a visitor, she took some Roman hyacinths from a glass and stuck them in the front of her dark-blue dress.

When at last Fred Ottenburg appeared in the doorway, she met him with an exclamation of pleasure. "I am glad you've come, Fred. I was afraid you might not get my note, and I wanted to see you before you see Doctor Archie. He's so nice!" She brought her hands together to emphasize her statement.

"Is he? I'm glad. You see I'm quite out of breath. I didn't wait for the elevator, but ran upstairs. I was so pleased at being sent for." He dropped his hat and overcoat. "I should say he is nice! I don't seem to recognize these," waving his handkerchief about at the flowers.

"Yes, he brought them himself, in a big box. He brought lots with him besides flowers. Oh, lots of things! The old Moonstone feeling"— she moved her hand back and forth in the air, fluttering her fingers—"the feeling of starting out, early in the morning, to take my lesson."

"And you've had everything out with him?"

"No, I haven't."

"Haven't?" He looked up in consternation.

"No, I haven't!" Thea spoke excitedly, moving about over the sunny patches on the grimy carpet. "I've lied to him, just as you said I had always lied to him, and that's why I'm so happy. I've let him think what he likes to think. Oh, I couldn't do anything else, Fred"—she shook her head emphatically. "If you'd seen him when he came in, so pleased and excited! From the moment I began to talk to him, he entreated me not to say too much, not to spoil his notion of me. Not in so many words, of course. But if you'd seen his eyes, his face, his kind hands! Oh, no! I couldn't." She took a deep breath, as if with a renewed sense of her narrow escape.

"Then, what did you tell him?" Fred demanded.

Thea sat down on the edge of the sofa and began shutting and opening her hands nervously. "Well, I told him enough, and not too much. I told him all about how good you were to me last winter, getting me engagements and things, and how you had helped me with my work more than anybody. Then I told him about how you sent me down to the ranch when I had no money or anything." She paused and wrinkled her forehead. "And I told him that I wanted to marry you and ran away to Mexico with you, and that I was awfully happy until you told me that you couldn't marry me because—well, I told him why." She lowered her eyes and moved the toe of her shoe about restlessly on the carpet.

"And he took it from you, like that?" Fred asked, almost with awe.

"Yes, just like that, and asked no questions. He was hurt; he had some wretched moments. I could see him squirming and trying to get past it. He kept shutting his eyes and rubbing his forehead. But when I told him that I absolutely knew you wanted to marry me, that you would whenever you could, that seemed to help him a good deal."

"And that satisfied him?" Fred could not quite imagine what kind of person Doctor Archie might be.

"He took me by the shoulders once and asked, oh, in such a frightened way, 'Thea, was he *good* to you, this young man?' When I told him you were, he looked at me again: 'And you care for him a great deal, you believe in him?' Then he seemed satisfied." Thea paused. "You see, he's just tremendously good, and tremendously afraid of things—of some things. Otherwise he would have got rid of Mrs. Archie." She looked up suddenly: "You were right, though; one can't tell people about things they don't know already."

Fred stood in the window, his back to the sunlight, fingering the jonquils. "Yes, you can, my dear. But you must tell it in such a way that they don't know you're telling it, and that they don't know they're hearing it."

Thea smiled past him, out into the air. "I see. It's a secret. Like the sound in the shell."

"What's that?" Fred was watching her and thinking how moving that far-away expression, in her, happened to be. "What did you say?"

She came back. "Oh, something old and Moonstony! I have almost forgotten it myself. But I feel better now. I can't wait to be off. Oh, Fred," she sprang up, "I want to get at it!" As she broke out with this, she threw up her head and lifted herself a little on her toes. Fred coloured and looked at her fearfully, hesitatingly. Her eyes, which looked out through the window, were bright—they had no memories. No, she did not remember. That momentary elevation had no associations for her. It was unconscious.

He looked her up and down and laughed. "Don't worry, you'll get at it. You are at it. My God! have you ever, for one moment, been at anything else?"

Thea did not answer him, and clearly she had not heard him. She was watching something out in the thin light of the false spring and its treacherously soft air.

Fred waited a moment. "Are you going to dine with your friend to-night?"

"Yes. He has never been in New York before. He wants to go about. Where shall I tell him to go?"

"Wouldn't it be a better plan, since you wish me to meet him, for you both to dine with me? It would seem only natural and friendly. You'll have to live up a little to his notion of us." Thea seemed to consider the suggestion favourably. "If you wish him to be easy in his mind," Fred went on, "that would help. I think, myself, that we are rather nice together. Put on one of the new dresses you got down there, and let him see how lovely you can be. You owe him some pleasure, after all the trouble he has taken."

Thea laughed, and seemed to find the idea exciting and pleasant. "Oh, very well! I'll do my best. Only don't wear a dress coat, please. He hasn't one, and he's nervous about it."

"I'll be here with a cab at eight. I'm anxious to meet him. You've given me the strangest idea of his callow innocence and aged indifference."

She shook her head. "No, he's none of that. He's very good, and he won't admit things. I love him for it. Now, as I look back on it, I see that I've always, even when I was little, shielded him."

As she laughed, Fred caught the bright spark in her eye that he knew so well, and held it for a happy instant. Then he blew her a kiss with his finger-tips and fled.

IV

At nine o'clock that evening our three friends were seated in the balcony of a French restaurant, much gayer and more intimate than any that exists in New York to-day. This old restaurant was built by a lover of pleasure, who knew that to dine gaily human beings must have the reassurance of certain limitations of space and of a certain definite style; that the walls must be near enough to suggest shelter, the ceiling high enough to give the chandeliers a setting. The place was crowded with the kind of people who dine late and well, and Doctor Archie, as he watched the animated groups in the long room below the balcony, said to himself that this evening alone was worth his long journey.

For the first few moments, when he was introduced to young Ottenburg in the parlour of the Everett House, the doctor had been awkward and unbending. But Fred, as his father had often observed, "was not a good mixer for nothing." He had brought Doctor Archie around during the short cab ride, and in an hour they had become friends.

From the moment when the doctor lifted his glass and, looking consciously at Thea, said, "To your success," Fred liked him. He felt his quality; understood his courage in some directions and what Thea called his timidity in others, his unspent and miraculously preserved youthfulness. Men could never impose upon the doctor, he guessed, but women always could. Fred liked, too, the doctor's manner with Thea, his bashful admiration and the little hesitancy by which he betrayed his consciousness of the change in her. It was just this change which, at present, interested Fred more than anything else. That, he felt, was his "created value," and it was his best chance for peace of mind. If that were not real, obvious to an old friend like Archie, then he cut a very poor figure, indeed.

Fred got a good deal, too, out of their talk about Moonstone. From her questions and the doctor's answers he was able to form some conception of the little world that was almost the measure of Thea's experience. As the two ran over the list of their friends, the mere sound of a name seemed to recall volumes to each of them, to indicate mines of knowledge and observation they had in common. At some names they laughed delightedly, at some indulgently and even tenderly.

"You two young people must come out to Moonstone when Thea gets back," the doctor said hospitably.

"Oh, we shall!" Fred caught it up. "I'm keen to know all these people. It is very tantalizing to hear only their names."

"Would they interest an outsider very much, do you think, Doctor Archie?" Thea leaned toward him.

The doctor glanced at her deferentially. "Well, you are practically an outsider yourself, Thea, now," he observed, smiling. "Oh, I know," he went on quickly in response to her gesture of protest—"I know you don't change toward your old friends, but you can see us from a distance now. It's all to your advantage that you can still take your old interest, isn't it, Mr. Ottenburg?"

"That's exactly one of her advantages, Doctor Archie. Nobody can ever take that away from her, and none of us who came later can ever hope to rival Moonstone in the impression we make. Her scale of values will always be the Moonstone scale. And, with an artist, that *is* an advantage." Fred nodded.

Doctor Archie looked at him seriously. "You mean it keeps them from getting affected?"

"Yes; keeps them from getting off the track generally."

While the waiter filled the glasses, Fred pointed out to Thea a big black French baritone who was eating anchovies by their tails at one of the tables below, and the doctor looked about and studied his fellow diners.

"Do you know, Mr. Ottenburg," he said deeply, "these people all look happier to me than our Western people do. Is it simply good manners on their part, or do they get more out of life?"

Fred laughed to Thea above the glass he had just lifted. "Some of them are getting a good deal out of it now, doctor." He leaned forward and touched Thea's wrist. "See that fur coat just coming in, Thea, It's D'Albert. He's just back from his Western tour. Fine head, hasn't he?"

"To go back," said Doctor Archie; "I insist that people do look happier here. I've noticed it even on the street, and especially in the hotels."

Fred turned to him cheerfully. "New York people live a good deal in the fourth dimension, Doctor Archie. It's that you notice in their faces."

The doctor was interested. "The fourth dimension," he repeated slowly; "and is that slang?"

"No"—Fred shook his head—"that's merely a figure. I mean that life is not quite so personal here as it is in your part of the world. People are more taken up by hobbies, interests that are less subject to reverses than their personal affairs. If you're interested in Thea's voice, for instance, or in voices in general, that interest is just the same, even if your mining stocks go down."

The doctor looked at him narrowly. "You think that's about the principal difference between country people and city people, don't you?"

Fred was a little disconcerted at being followed up so resolutely, and he attempted to dismiss it with a pleasantry. "I've never thought much about it, doctor. But I should say, on the spur of the moment, that that is one of the principal differences between people anywhere. It's the consolation of fellows like me who don't accomplish much. The fourth dimension is not good for business, but we think we have a better time."

Doctor Archie leaned back in his chair. His heavy shoulders were contemplative. "And she," he said slowly; "should you say that she is one of the kind you refer to?" He inclined his head toward the shimmer of the pale-green dress beside him. Thea was leaning, just then, over the balcony rail, her head in the light from the chandeliers below.

"Never, never!" Fred protested. "She is as hard-headed as the worst of you—with a difference."

The doctor sighed. "Yes, with a difference; something that makes a good many revolutions to the second. When she was little I used to feel her head to try to locate it."

Fred laughed. "Did you, though? So you were on the track of it? Oh, it's there! We can't get round it, miss," as Thea looked back inquiringly. "Doctor Archie, there's a fellow townsman of yours I feel a real kinship with." He pressed a cigar upon Doctor Archie and struck a match for him. "Tell me about Spanish Johnny."

The doctor smiled benignantly through the first waves of smoke. "Well, Johnny's an old patient of mine, and he's an old admirer of Thea's. She was born a cosmopolitan, and I expect she learned a good deal from Johnny when she used to run away and go to Mexican Town. We thought it a queer freak then." The doctor launched into a long story, in which he was often eagerly interrupted or joyously confirmed by Thea, who was drinking her coffee and forcing open the petals of the roses with an ardent and rather rude hand. It was delightful to see her so radiant and responsive again. She had kept her promise about looking her best; when one could so easily get together the colours of an apple branch in early spring, that was not hard to do. Even Doctor Archie felt, each time he looked at her, a fresh consciousness. He recognized the fine texture of her mother's skin, with the difference that, when she reached across the table to get him a bunch of grapes, her arm was not only white, but a little dazzling. She seemed to him taller, and freer in all her movements. She had now a way of taking a deep breath when she was interested, that made her seem very strong, somehow, and brought her at one quite overpoweringly. If he was shy, it was because her greater positiveness, her whole augmented self, made him feel that his accustomed manner toward her was inadequate.

Fred, on his part, was reflecting that the awkward position in which he had placed her would not confine or chafe her long. She looked about at other people, at other women, curiously. She was not quite sure of herself, but she was not in the least afraid or apologetic. She seemed to sit there on the edge, emerging from one world into another, taking her bearings, but with absolute self-confidence. So far from shrinking, she expanded. The mere kindly effort to please Doctor Archie was enough to bring her out.

V

*T*hea was to sail on Tuesday, at noon, and on Saturday Fred Ottenburg arranged for her passage, while she and Doctor Archie went shopping. With rugs and sea-clothes she was already provided; Fred had got everything of that sort she needed for the voyage up from Vera Cruz. On Sunday afternoon Thea went to see the Harsanyis. When she returned to her hotel, she found a note from Ottenburg, saying that he had called and would come again to-morrow.

On Monday morning, while she was at breakfast, Fred came in. She knew by his hurried, distracted air as he entered the dining-room that something had gone wrong. He had just got a telegram from home. His mother had been thrown from her carriage and hurt; a concussion of some sort, and she was unconscious. He was leaving for St. Louis that night on the eleven-o'clock train. He had a great deal to attend to during the day. He would come that evening, if he might, and stay with her until train time, while she was doing her packing. Scarcely waiting for her consent, he hurried away.

All day Thea was somewhat cast down. She was sorry for Fred, and she missed the feeling that she was the one person in his mind. He had scarcely looked at her. She felt as if she were set aside, and she did not seem so important even to herself as she had yesterday. Certainly, she reflected, it was high time that she began to take care of herself again. Doctor Archie came for dinner, but she sent him away early, telling him that she would be ready to go to the boat with him at half-past ten the next morning. When she went upstairs, she looked gloomily at the open trunk in her sitting-room, and at the trays piled on the sofa. She stood at the window and watched a quiet snowstorm spending itself over the city. More than anything else, falling snow always made her think of Moonstone; of the Kohlers' garden, of Thor's sled, of dressing by lamplight and starting off to school before the paths were broken.

When Fred came, he looked tired, and he took her hand almost without seeing her.

"I'm so sorry, Fred. Have you had any more word?"

"She was still unconscious at four this afternoon. It doesn't look very encouraging." He approached the fire and warmed his hands. He seemed to have contracted, and he had not at all his habitual ease of manner. "Poor mother!" he exclaimed; "nothing like this should have happened to her. She has so much pride of person. She's not at all an old woman, you know. She's never got beyond vigorous and rather dashing middle age." He turned abruptly to Thea and for the first time really looked at her. "How badly things come out! She'd have liked you for a daughter-in-law. Oh, you'd have fought like the devil, but you'd have respected each other." He sank into a chair and thrust his feet out to the fire. "Still," he went on thoughtfully, seeming to address the ceiling, "it might have been bad for you. Our big German houses, our good German cooking—you might have got lost in the upholstery. That substantial comfort might take the temper out of you, dull your edge. Yes," he sighed, "I guess you were meant for the jolt of the breakers."

"I guess I'll get plenty of jolt," Thea murmured, turning to her trunk.

"I'm glad I'm not staying over until to-morrow," Fred went on. "It's easier for me to glide out like this. I feel now as if everything were rather casual, anyhow. A shock like this deadens one's feelings."

Thea, standing by her trunk, made no reply. Presently he shook himself and rose. "Thea, is there nothing—nothing at all you'll let me do for you?"

"Yes, there is one thing, and it's a good deal to ask. If I get knocked out, or never get on, I'd like you to see that Doctor Archie gets his money back. I'm taking three thousand dollars of his."

"Why, of course I shall. You may dismiss that from your mind. How fussy you are about money, Thea. You make such a point of it."

Thea sat down in the chair he had quitted. "It's only poor people who feel that way about money, and who are really honest," she said gravely. "Sometimes I think that to be really honest, you must have been so poor that you've been tempted to steal."

"To what?"

"To steal. I used to be, when I first went to Chicago and saw all the things in the big stores there. Never anything big, but little things, the kind I'd never seen before and could never afford. I did take something once, before I knew it."

Fred came toward her. For the first time she had his whole attention, in the degree to which she was accustomed to having it. "Did you? What was it?" he asked with interest.

"A sachet. A little blue silk bag of orris-root powder. There was a whole counterful of them, marked down to twenty-five cents. I'd never seen any before, and they seemed irresistible. I took one up and wandered about the store with it. Nobody seemed to notice, so I carried it off."

Fred laughed. "Crazy child! Why, your things always smell of orris; is it a penance?"

"No, I love it. But I saw that the firm didn't lose anything by me. I went back and bought some there whenever I had a quarter to spend."

Fred took her hand. "Why didn't I find you that first winter? I'd have loved you just as you came!"

Thea shook her head. "No, you wouldn't, but you might have found me amusing. The Harsanyis said yesterday afternoon that I wore such a funny cape and that my shoes always squeaked."

"Did you sing for Harsanyi?"

"Yes. He thinks I've improved. He said nice things to me. Oh, he was very nice! He agrees with you about my going to Lehmann, if she'll take me."

"If you sang, I wish I had been there. Did you sing well?" Fred turned from her and went back to the window. "I wonder when I shall hear you sing again." He picked up a bunch of violets and smelled them. "You know, your leaving me like this—well, it's almost inhuman to be able to do it so kindly and unconditionally."

"I suppose it is. It was almost inhuman to be able to leave home, too—the last time, when I knew it was for good. But all the same, I cared a great deal more than anybody else did. I lived through it. I'll have to live through this."

Fred bent over her trunk and picked up something which proved to be a score, clumsily bound. "What's this? Did you ever try to sing this?" He opened it and on the engraved title-page read Wunsch's inscription, *"Einst, O Wunder!"* He looked up sharply at Thea.

"Wunsch gave me that when he went away. I've told you about him, my old teacher in Moonstone. He loved that opera."

Fred went toward the fireplace, the book under his arm, singing softly:

> *"Einst, O Wunder, entblüht auf meinem Grabe*
> *Eine Blume der Asche meines Herzens."*

"You have no idea at all where he is, Thea?" He leaned against the mantel and looked down at her.

"No, I wish I had. He may be dead by this time. That was five years ago, and he used himself hard. Mrs. Kohler was always afraid he would die off alone somewhere and be stuck under the prairie. When we last heard of him, he was in Kansas."

"If he were to be found, I'd like to do something for him. I seem to get a good deal of him from this." He opened the book again, where he kept the place with his finger, and scrutinized the purple ink. "How like a German! Had he ever sung the song for you?"

"No. I didn't know where the words were from until once, when Harsanyi sang it for me, I recognized them."

Fred smiled whimsically and dropped the score into the trunk. "You are taking it with you?"

"Surely I am. I haven't so many keepsakes that I can afford to leave that. I haven't got many that I value so highly."

"That you value so highly!" Fred echoed her gravity playfully. "You are delicious when you fall into your vernacular."

"What's the matter with that? Isn't it perfectly good English?"

"It's perfectly good Moonstone, my dear. Like the ready-made clothes that hang in the windows, made to fit everybody and fit nobody, a phrase that can be used on all occasions. Oh"—he started across the room again—"that's one of the fine things about your going! You'll be with the right sort of people and you'll get a new speech. Full of shades and colour like your voice: alive, like your mind. It will be almost like being born again."

She was not offended. Fred had said such things to her before, and she wanted to learn.

He walked about the room smoking nervously. "You'll like the voyage. That first approach to a foreign shore—there's nothing like it. You will let me write to some friends in Berlin? They'll be nice to you."

"Oh, I wish you would! I'll be lonesome." Thea gave a deep sigh. "I wish one could look ahead and see what's coming to one."

"That would never do. It's the uncertainty that makes one try. You've never had any sort of chance, and now you'll make it up to yourself."

Thea went over to the sofa, hunting for something in the trunk trays. When she came back she found Fred sitting in her place. "Here are some handkerchiefs of yours. I've kept one or two. They're larger than mine and useful if one has a headache."

"Thank you." He looked at the white squares for a moment and then put them in his pocket. He kept the low chair, and as she stood beside him he took her hands and sat looking intently at them, as if he were examining them for some special purpose. "There seems to be no limit to how much I can be in love with you. I keep going."

She dropped beside him and slipped into his arms, shutting her eyes and lifting her cheek to his.

"Tell me one thing," Fred whispered. "You said that night on the boat, when I first told you, that if you could you would crush it all up in your hands and throw it into the sea. Would you, all those weeks?"

She shook her head.

"Answer me, would you?"

"No. I was angry then. I'm not now. I'd never give them up. Don't make me pay too much."

In that embrace they lived over again all the others. When Thea drew away from him, she dropped her face in her hands.

Fred looked at his watch and rose. He drew her gently toward the door with him. "Get all you can. Be generous to yourself. I can't help feeling that you'll gain, somehow, by my losing so much. That you'll gain the very thing I lose. Good night." He went out of the door without looking back, just as if he were coming again to-morrow.

Thea went quickly into her bedroom. She brought out an armful of muslin things, knelt down, and began to lay them in the trays. Suddenly she stopped, dropped forward and leaned against the open trunk, her head on her arms. The tears fell down on the dark old carpet. It came over her how many people must have said good-bye and been unhappy in that room. Other people, before her time, had hired this room to cry in. Strange rooms and strange streets and faces, how sick at heart they made one! Why was she going so far, when what she wanted was some familiar place to hide in?—the rock-house in the cañon, her little room in Moonstone, her own bed. Oh, how good it would be to lie down in that little bed, to cut the nerve that kept one struggling, that pulled one on and on: to sink into peace there, with all the family safe and happy downstairs. After all, she was a Moonstone girl, one of the preacher's children. Everything else was in Fred's imagination. Why was she called upon to take such chances? Any safe, humdrum work that did not compromise her would be better. But if she failed now, she would lose her soul. There was nowhere to fall, after one took that step, except into abysses of wretchedness. She knew what abysses, for she could still hear the old man playing in the snowstorm. *"Ach, ich habe sie verloren!"* That melody was released in her like a passion of longing. Every nerve in her body thrilled to it. It brought her to her feet, carried her somehow to bed and into troubled sleep.

That night she taught in Moonstone again: she beat her pupils in hideous rages, she kept on beating them. She sang at funerals, and struggled at the piano with Harsanyi. In one dream she was looking into a hand-glass and thinking that she was getting better-looking, when the glass began to grow smaller and smaller and her own reflection to shrink, until she realized that she was looking into Ray Kennedy's eyes, seeing her face in that look of his which she could never forget. All at once the eyes were Fred Ottenburg's, and not Ray's. All night she heard the shrieking of trains, whistling in and out of Moonstone, as she used to hear them in her sleep when they blew shrill in the winter air.

In the morning she wakened breathless after a struggle with Mrs. Livery Johnson's daughter. She started up with a bound, threw the blankets back and sat on the edge of the bed, her night-dress open, her long braids hanging over her bosom, blinking at the daylight. After all, it was not too late. She was only twenty years old, and the boat sailed at noon. There was still time!

Part VI

Kronborg

I

*I*t is a glorious winter day. Denver, standing on her high plateau under a thrilling green-blue sky, is masked in snow and glittering with sunlight. The Capitol building is actually in armour, and throws off the shafts of the sun until the beholder is dazzled and the outlines of the building are lost in a blaze of reflected light. The stone terrace is a white field over which fiery reflections dance, and the trees and bushes are faithfully repeated in snow—on every black twig a soft, blurred line of white. From the terrace one looks directly over to where the mountains break in their sharp, familiar lines against the sky. Snow fills the gorges, hangs in scarfs on the great slopes, and on the peaks the fiery sunshine is gathered up as by a burning-glass.

Howard Archie is standing at the window of his private room in the offices of the San Felipe Mining Company, on the sixth floor of the Raton Building, looking off at the mountain glories of his State while he gives dictation to his secretary. He is ten years older than when we saw him last, and emphatically ten years more prosperous. A decade of coming into things has not so much aged him as it has fortified, smoothed, and assured him. His sandy hair and imperial conceal whatever grey they harbour. He has not grown heavier, but more flexible, and his massive shoulders carry fifty years and the control of his great mining interests more lightly than they carried forty years and a country practice. In short, he is one of the friends to whom we feel grateful for having got on in the world, for helping to keep up the general temperature and our own confidence in life.

When Archie had finished his morning mail, he turned away from the window and faced his secretary. "Did anything come up yesterday afternoon while I was away, T.B.?"

Thomas Burk turned over the leaf of his calendar. "Governor Alden sent down to say that he wanted to see you before he sends his letter to the Board of Pardons. Asked if you could go over to the State House this morning."

Archie shrugged his shoulders. "I'll think about it."

The young man grinned.

"Anything else?" his chief continued.

T.B. swung round in his chair with a look of interest on his shrewd, clean-shaven face. "Old Jasper Flight was in, Doctor Archie. I never expected to see him alive again. Seems he's tucked away for the winter with a sister who's a housekeeper at the Oxford. He's all crippled up with rheumatism, but as fierce after it as ever. Wants to know if you or the company won't grub-stake him again. Says he's sure of it this time; had located something when the snow shot down on him in December. He wants to crawl out at the first break in the weather, with that same old burro with the split ear. He got somebody to winter the beast for him. He's superstitious about that burro, too; thinks it's divinely guided. You ought to hear the line of talk he put up here yesterday; said when he rode in his carriage, that burro was a-going to ride along with him."

Archie laughed. "Did he leave you his address?"

"He didn't neglect anything," replied the clerk cynically.

"Well, send him a line and tell him to come in again. I like to hear him. Of all the crazy prospectors I've ever known, he's the most interesting, because he's really crazy. It's a religious conviction with him, and with most of 'em it's a gambling fever or pure vagrancy. But Jasper Flight believes that the Almighty keeps the secret of the silver deposits in these hills, and gives it away to the deserving. He's a downright noble figure. Of course I'll stake him! As long as he can crawl out in the spring. He and that burro are a sight together. The beast is nearly as white as Jasper; must be twenty years old."

"If you stake him this time, you won't have to again," said T.B. knowingly. "He'll croak up there, mark my word. Says he never ties the burro at night now, for fear he might be called sudden, and the beast would starve. I guess that animal could eat a lariat rope, all right, and enjoy it."

"I guess if we knew the things those two have eaten, and haven't eaten, in their time, T.B., it would make us vegetarians." The doctor sat down and looked thoughtful. "That's the way for the old man to go. It would be too bad if he had to die in a hospital. I wish he could turn up something before he cashes in. But his kind seldom do; they're bewitched. Still, there was Stratton. I've been meeting Jasper Flight, and his side meat and tin pans, up in the mountains for years, and I'd miss him. I always halfway believe the fairy tales he spins me. Old Jasper Flight," Archie murmured, as if he liked the name or the picture it called up.

A clerk came in from the outer office and handed Archie a card. He sprang up and exclaimed, "Mr. Ottenburg? Bring him in."

Fred Ottenburg entered, clad in a long, fur-lined coat, holding a checked-cloth hat in his hand, his cheeks and eyes bright with the outdoor cold. The two men met before Archie's desk and their handclasp was longer than friendship prompts except in regions where the blood warms and quickens to meet the dry cold. Under the general keying-up of the altitude, manners take on a heartiness, a vivacity, that is one expression of the half-unconscious excitement which Colorado people miss when they drop into lower strata of air. The heart, we are told, wears out early in that high atmosphere, but while it pumps it sends out no sluggish stream. Our two friends stood gripping each other by the hand and smiling.

"When did you get in, Fred? And what have you come for?" Archie gave him a quizzical glance.

"I've come to find out what you think you're doing out here," the younger man declared emphatically. "I want to get next, I do. When can you see me?"

"Anything on to-night? Then suppose you dine with me. Where can I pick you up at five-thirty?"

"Bixby's office, general freight agent of the Burlington." Ottenburg began to button his overcoat and drew on his gloves. "I've got to have one shot at you before I go, Archie. Didn't I tell you Pinky Alden was a cheap squirt?"

Alden's backer laughed and shook his head. "Oh, he's worse than that, Fred. It isn't polite to mention what he is, outside of the Arabian Nights. I guessed you'd come to rub it into me."

That afternoon at five o'clock Doctor Archie emerged from the State House after his talk with Governor Alden, and crossed the terrace under a saffron sky. The snow, beaten hard, was blue in the dusk; a day of blinding sunlight had not even started a thaw. The lights of the city twinkled pale below him in the quivering violet air, and the dome of the State House behind him was still red with the light from the west. Before he got into his car, the doctor paused to look about him at the scene of which he never tired. Archie lived in his own house on Colfax Avenue, where he had roomy grounds and a rose-garden and a conservatory. His housekeeping was done by three Japanese boys, devoted and resourceful, who were able to manage Archie's dinner parties, to see that he kept his engagements, and to make visitors who stayed at the house so comfortable that they were always loath to go away.

Archie had never known what comfort was until he became a widower, though, with characteristic delicacy, or dishonesty, he insisted upon accrediting his peace of mind to the San Felipe, to Time, to anything but his release from Mrs. Archie.

Mrs. Archie died just before her husband left Moonstone and came to live in Denver, six years ago. The poor woman's fight against dust was her undoing at last. One summer day when she was rubbing the parlour upholstery with gasoline—the doctor had often forbidden her to use it on any account, so that was one of the pleasures she seized upon in his absence—an explosion occurred. Nobody ever knew exactly how it happened, for Mrs. Archie was unconscious when the neighbours rushed in to save her from the burning house. She must have inhaled the burning gas and died almost instantly.

Moonstone severity relented toward her somewhat after her death. But even while her old cronies at Mrs. Smiley's millinery store said that it was a terrible thing, they added that nothing but a powerful explosion *could* have killed Mrs. Archie, and that it was only right the doctor should have a chance.

Archie's past was literally destroyed when his wife died. The house burned to the ground, and all those material reminders which have such power over people disappeared in an hour. His mining interests now took him to Denver so often that it seemed better to make his headquarters there. He gave up his practice and left Moonstone for good. Six months afterward, while Doctor Archie was living at the Brown Palace Hotel, the San Felipe mine began to give up that silver hoard which old Captain Harris had always accused it of concealing, and San Felipe headed the list of mining quotations in every daily paper, East and West. In a few years Doctor Archie was a very rich man. His mine was such an important item in the mineral output of the State, and Archie had a hand in so many of the new industries of Colorado and New Mexico, that his political influence was considerable. He had thrown it all, two years ago, to the new reform party, and had brought about the election of a governor of whose conduct he was now heartily ashamed.

II

When Ottenburg and his host reached the house on Colfax Avenue, they went directly to the library, a long double room on the second floor which Archie had arranged exactly to his own taste. It was full of books and mounted specimens of wild game, with a big writing-table at either end, stiff, old-fashioned engravings, heavy hangings and deep upholstery.

When one of the Japanese boys brought the cocktails, Fred turned from the fir e specimen of peccary he had been examining and said: "A man is an owl to live in such a place alone, Archie. Why don't you marry? As for me, just because I can't marry, I find the world full of charming, unattached women, any one of whom I could fit up a house for with alacrity."

"You're more knowing than I." Archie spoke politely. "I'm not very wide awake about women. I'd be likely to pick out one of the uncomfortable ones—and there are a few of them, you know." He drank his cocktail and rubbed his hands together in a friendly way. "My friends here have charming wives, and they don't give me a chance to get lonely. They are very kind to me, and I have a great many pleasant friendships."

Fred put down his glass. "Yes, I've always noticed that women have confidence in you. You have the doctor's way of getting next. And you enjoy that kind of thing?"

"The friendship of attractive women? Oh, dear, yes! I depend upon it a great deal."

The butler announced dinner, and the two men went downstairs to the dining-room. Doctor Archie's dinners were always good and well served, and his wines were excellent.

"I saw the Fuel and Iron people to-day," Ottenburg said, looking up from his soup. "Their heart is in the right place. I can't see why in the mischief you ever got mixed up with that reform gang, Archie. You've got nothing to reform out here. The situation has always been as simple as two and two in Colorado; mostly a matter of a friendly understanding."

"Well"—Archie spoke tolerantly—"some of the young fellows seemed to have red-hot convictions, and I thought it was better to let them try their ideas out."

Ottenburg shrugged his shoulders. "A few dull young men who haven't ability enough to play the old game the old way, so they want to put on a new game which doesn't take so much brains and gives away more advertising: that's what your anti-saloon league and vice commission amount to. How could you fall for a mouse-trap like Pink Alden, Archie?"

Doctor Archie laughed as he began to carve. "Pink seems to get under your skin. He's not worth talking about. He's gone his limit. People won't read about his blameless life any more. I knew those interviews he gave out would cook him."

While Archie and his friend were busy with Colorado politics, the impeccable Japanese attended swiftly and intelligently to his duties, and the dinner, as Ottenburg at last remarked, was worthy of more profitable conversation.

"So it is," the doctor admitted. "Well, we'll go upstairs for our coffee and cut this out. Bring up some cognac and arrack, Tai," he added as he rose from the table.

They stopped to examine a moose's head on the stairway, and when they reached the library the pine logs in the fireplace had been lighted, and the coffee was bubbling before the hearth. Tai placed two chairs before the fire and brought a tray of cigarettes.

"Bring the cigars in my lower desk-drawer, boy," the doctor directed. "Too much light in here, isn't there, Fred? Light the lamp there on my desk, Tai." He turned off the electric glare and settled himself deep into the chair opposite Ottenburg's.

"To go back to our conversation, doctor," Fred began while he waited for the first steam to blow off his coffee; "why don't you make up your mind to go to Washington? There'd be no fight made against you. I needn't say the United Breweries would back you. There'd be some *kudos* coming to us, too; backing a reform candidate."

Doctor Archie measured his length in his chair and thrust his large boots toward the crackling pitch-pine. He drank his coffee and lit a big black cigar while his guest looked over the assortment of cigarettes on the tray.

"You say why don't I"—the doctor spoke with deliberation—"but on the other hand, why should I?" He puffed away and seemed, through his half-closed eyes, to look down several long roads with the intention of luxuriously rejecting all of them and remaining where he was. "I'm sick of politics. I'm disillusioned about serving my crowd, and I don't particularly want to serve yours. Nothing in it that I particularly want; and a man's not effective in politics unless he wants something for himself, and wants it hard."

The doctor poured himself some white cordial and looked over the little glass into the fire with an expression which led Ottenburg to believe that he was getting at something in his own mind. Fred lit a cigarette and let his friend grope for his idea.

"My boys, here," Archie went on, "have got me rather inter-ested in Japan. Think I'll go out there in the spring, and come back the other way, through Siberia. I've always wanted to go to Russia." His eyes still hunted for something in his big fireplace. With a slow turn of his head he brought them back to his guest and fixed them upon him. "Just now, I'm thinking of running on to New York for a few weeks," he ended abruptly.

Ottenb rg lifted his chin. "Ah!" he exclaimed, as if he began to see Archie's drift. "Shall you see Thea?"

"Yes." The doctor refilled his cordial glass. "In fact, I suspect I am going exactly *to* see her."

"You've never heard her at all, have you? Curious, when this is her second season in New York."

"I was going on last March. Had everything arranged. And then old Cap Harris thought he could drive his car and me through a lamp-post and I was laid up with a compound fracture for two months. So I didn't get to see Thea."

Ottenburg studied the red end of his cigarette attentively.

"She might have come out to see you. I remember you covered the distance like a streak when she wanted you."

Archie moved uneasily. "Oh, she couldn't do that. She had to get back to Vienna to work on some new parts for this year. She sailed two days after the New York season closed."

"Well, then she couldn't, of course." Fred smoked his cigarette close and tossed the end into the fire. "I'm tremendously glad you're going now."

"Of course," the doctor apologized, "I want to hear her; but I'm afraid it will be rather wasted on me. I'm no judge of music."

"Never mind that." The younger man pulled himself up in his chair. "She gets it across to people who aren't judges. That's just what she does. If you were stone deaf, it wouldn't all be wasted. It's a great deal to watch her. Incidentally, you know, she is very beautiful. Photographs give you no idea."

Doctor Archie clasped his large hands under his chin. "Oh, I'm counting on that. I don't suppose her voice will sound natural to me. Probably I wouldn't know it."

Ottenburg smiled. "You'll know it, if you ever knew it. It's the same voice, only more so. You'll know it."

"Did you, in Germany that time, when you wrote me? Seven years ago, now. That must have been at the very beginning."

"Yes, somewhere near the beginning. She sang one of the Rhine daughters." Fred paused for a moment. "Sure, I knew it from the first note. I'd heard a good many young voices come up out of the Rhine; but I hadn't heard one like that! Mahler was conducting that night. I met him as he was leaving the house and had a word with him. 'Interesting voice you tried out this evening,' I said. He stopped and smiled. 'Miss Kronborg, you mean? Yes, very. She seems to sing for the idea. Unusual in a young singer.' I'd never heard him admit before that a singer could have an idea."

The doctor looked up at him enviously. "I'm afraid a good deal of it will be lost on me. I suppose college German, gone to seed, wouldn't help me out much? I used to be able to make my German patients understand me."

"Sure it would!" cried Ottenburg heartily. "Her diction is beautiful, and if you know the text you'll get a great deal. You bet in Germany people know their libretto by heart!"

"I'd like to be able to follow her. The papers always say she's such a fine actress." Archie took up the tongs and began to rearrange the logs that had burned through and fallen apart. "I suppose she has changed a great deal?" he asked absently.

"We've all changed, my dear Archie—she more than most of us. I've had only a few words with her in several years. It's better not, when I'm tied up this way. The laws are barbarous, Archie."

"Your wife is—still the same?" the doctor asked sympathetically.

"Absolutely. Hasn't been out of a sanitarium for seven years now. No possibility of her ever being better. Meanwhile, I'm tied hand and foot. What does society get out of such a state of things, I'd like to know, except a tangle of irregularities?"

"It's bad, oh, very bad; I agree with you!" Doctor Archie shook his head. "But there would be complications under another system, too. The whole question of a young man's marrying has looked pretty grave to me for a long while. How have they the courage to keep on doing it?" For some time the doctor watched his guest, who was sunk in bitter reflections. "Such things used to go better than they do now, I believe. Seems to me all the married people I knew when I was a boy were happy enough." He paused again and bit the end off a fresh cigar. "You never saw Thea's mother, did you, Ottenburg? That's a pity. Mrs. Kronborg was a fine woman. I've always felt Thea made a mistake, not coming home when Mrs. Kronborg was ill, no matter what it cost her."

Ottenburg moved about restlessly. "She couldn't, Archie, she positively couldn't. I felt you never understood that, but I was in Dresden at the time, and though I wasn't seeing much of her, I could size up the situation for myself. It was by just a lucky chance that she got to sing *Elisabeth* that time at the Dresden Opera, a complication of circumstances. If she'd run away, for any reason, she might have waited years for such a chance to come ag in. She gave a wonderful performance and made a great impression. They offered her certain terms; she had to take them and follow it up then and there. In that game you can't lose a single trick. She was ill herself, but she sang. No, you mustn't hold that against her, Archie. She did the right thing there." He drew out his watch. "Hello! I must be travelling. You hear from her regularly?"

"More or less regularly. She was never much of a letter-writer. She tells me about her engagements and contracts, but I know so little about that business that it doesn't mean much to me beyond the figures, which seem very impressive. We've had a good deal of business correspondence, about putting up a stone to her father and mother, and, lately, about her youngest brother, Thor. He is with me now; he drives my car. To-day he's up at the mine."

Ottenburg, who had picked up his overcoat, dropped it. "Drives your car?" he asked incredulously.

"Yes. Thea and I have had a good deal of bother about Thor. We tried a business college, and an engineering school, but it was no good. Thor was born a chauffeur before there were cars to drive. He was never good for anything else; lay around home and collected postage stamps and took bicycles to pieces, waiting for the automobile to be invented. I can't find out whether he likes his job with me or not, or whether he feels any curiosity about his sister. You can't find anything out from a Kronborg nowadays. The mother was different."

Doctor Archie saw his guest to the motor which was waiting below, and then went back to his library, where he replenished the fire and sat down for a long smoke. A man of Archie's modest and rather credulous nature develops late, and makes his largest gain between forty and fifty. At thirty, indeed, as we have seen, Archie was a soft-hearted boy under a manly exterior, still whistling to keep up his courage. Prosperity and large responsibilities—above all, getting free of poor Mrs. Archie—had brought out a good deal more than he knew was in him. He was thinking to-night as he sat before the fire, in the comfort he liked so well, that but for lucky chances, and lucky holes in the ground, he would still be a country practitioner, reading his old books by his office lamp. And yet, he was not so fresh and energetic as he ought to be. He was tired of business and of politics.

Worse than that, he was tired of the men with whom he had to do and of the women who, as he said, had been kind to him. He felt as if he were still hunting for something, like old Jasper Flight. He knew that this was an unbecoming and ungrateful state of mind, and he reproached himself for it. But he could not help wondering why it was that life, even when it gave so much, after all gave so little. What was it that he had expected and missed? Why was he, more than he was anything else, disappointed?

He fell to looking back over his life and asking himself which years of it he would like to live over again—just as they had been—and they were not many. His college years he would live again, gladly. After them there was nothing he would care to repeat until he came to Thea Kronborg. There had been something stirring about those years in Moonstone, when he was a restless young man on the verge of breaking into larger enterprises, and when she was a restless child on the verge of growing up into something unknown. He realized now that she had counted for a great deal more to him than he knew at the time. It was a continuous sort of relationship. He was always on the lookout for her as he went about the town, always vaguely expecting her as he sat in his office at night. He had never asked himself then if it was strange that he should find a child of twelve the most interesting and companionable person in Moonstone. It had seemed a pleasant, natural kind of solicitude. He explained it then by the fact that he had no children of his own. Now, as he looked back at those years, the other interests were faded and inanimate. The thought of them was heavy. But wherever his life had touched Thea Kronborg's, there was still a little warmth left, a little sparkle. Their friendship seemed to run over those discontented years like a leafy pattern, still bright and fresh when the other patterns had faded into the dull background. Their walks and drives and confidences, the night they watched the rabbit in the moonlight—why were these things stirring to remember? Whenever he thought of them, they were distinctly different from the other memories of his life; always seemed humorous, gay, with a little thrill of anticipation and mystery about them. They came nearer to being tender secrets than any others he possessed. Nearer than anything else they corresponded to what he had hoped to find in the world, and had not found. It came over him now that the unexpected favours of fortune, no matter how dazzling, do not mean very much to us. They may excite or divert us for a time, but when we look back, the only things we cherish are those which in some way met our original want; the desire which formed in us in early youth, undirected, and of its own accord.

III

*F*or the first four years after Thea went to Germany, things went on as usual with the Kronborg family. Mrs. Kronborg's land in Nebraska increased in value and brought her in a good rental. The family drifted into an easier way of living, half without realizing it, as families will. Then Mr. Kronborg, who had never been ill, died suddenly of cancer of the liver, and after his death Mrs. Kronborg went, as her neighbours said, into a decline. Hearing discouraging reports of her from the physician who had taken over his practice, Doctor Archie went up from Denver to see her. He found her in bed, in the room where he had more than once attended her, a handsome woman of sixty with a body still firm and white, her hair, faded now to a very pale primrose, in two thick braids down her back, her eyes clear and calm. When the doctor arrived, she was sitting up in her bed, knitting. He felt at once how glad she was to see him, but he soon gathered that she had made no determination to get well. She told him, indeed, that she could not very well get along without Mr. Kronborg. The doctor looked at her with astonishment. Was it possible that she could miss the foolish old man so much? He reminded her of her children.

"Yes," she replied; "the children are all very well, but they are not father. We were married young."

The doctor watched her wonderingly as she went on knitting, thinking how much she looked like Thea. The difference was one of degree rather than of kind. The daughter had a compelling enthusiasm, the mother had none. But their framework, their foundation, was very much the same.

In a moment Mrs. Kronborg spoke again. "Have you heard anything from Thea lately?"

During his talk with her, the doctor gathered that what Mrs. Kronborg really wanted was to see her daughter Thea. Lying there day after day, she wanted it calmly and continuously. He told her that, since she felt so, he thought they might ask Thea to come home.

"I've thought a good deal about it," said Mrs. Kronborg slowly. "I hate to interrupt her, now that she's begun to get advancement. I expect she's seen some pretty hard times, though she was never one to complain. Perhaps she'd feel that she would like to come. It would be hard, losing both of us while she's off there."

When Doctor Archie got back to Denver he wrote a long letter to Thea, explaining her mother's condition and how much she wished to see her, and advising Thea to come, if only for a few weeks. Thea had repaid the money she had borrowed from him, and he assured her that if she happened to be short of funds for the journey, she had only to cable him.

A month later, he got a frantic sort of reply from Thea. Complications in the opera at Dresden had given her an unhoped-for opportunity to go on in a big part. Before this letter reached the doctor, she would have made her début as *Elisabeth,* in "Tannhäuser." She wanted to go to her mother more than she wanted anything else in the world, but, unless she failed—which she would not—she absolutely could not leave Dresden for six months. It was not that she chose to stay; she had to stay—or lose everything. The next few months would put her five years ahead, or would put her back so far that it would be of no use to struggle further. As soon as she was free, she would go to Moonstone and take her mother back to Germany with her. Her mother, she was sure, could live for years yet, and she would like German people and German ways, and could be hearing music all the time. Thea said she was writing her mother and begging her to wait for her six months.

Doctor Archie went up to Moonstone at once. He had great confidence in Mrs. Kronborg's power of will, and if Thea's appeal took hold of her enough, he believed she might get better. But when he was shown into the familiar room off the parlour, his heart sank. Mrs. Kronborg was lying serene and fateful on her pillows. On the dresser at the foot of her bed there was a large photograph of Thea in the character in which she was to make her début. Mrs. Kronborg pointed to it.

"Isn't she lovely, doctor? It's nice that she hasn't changed much. I've seen her look like that many a time."

They talked for a while about Thea's good fortune. Mrs. Kronborg had had a cablegram saying: "First performance well received. Great relief."

"Bringing up a family is not all it's cracked up to be," said Mrs. Kronborg with a flicker of irony, as she tucked the letter back under her pillow. "The children you don't especially need, you have always with you, like the poor. But the bright ones get away from you. They have their own way to make in the world. Seems like the brighter they are, the farther they go. I used to feel sorry that you had no family, doctor, but maybe you're as well off."

"Thea's plan seems sound to me, Mrs. Kronborg. There's no reason I can see why you shouldn't live for years yet, under proper care. And it would be nice to live with anybody who looks like that." He nodded at the photograph of the young woman who must have been singing *"Dich, theure Halle, grüss' ich wieder,"* her eyes looking up, her beautiful hands outspread with pleasure.

Mrs. Kronborg laughed quite cheerfully. "Yes, wouldn't it? If father were here, I might rouse myself. . . . It'll be hard for her, losing us both. But when these things happen far away, they don't make such a mark; especially if your hands are full and you've duties of your own to think about. My own father died in Nebraska when Gunner was born—we were living in Iowa then—and I was sorry, but the baby made it up to me. I was father's favourite, too. That's the way it goes, you see."

The doctor took out Thea's letter to him, and read it over to Mrs. Kronborg. She seemed to listen, and not to listen.

When he finished, she said thoughtfully: "I'd counted on hearing her sing again. But I always took my pleasures as they came. I always enjoyed her singing when she was here about the house. While she was practising, I often used to leave my work and sit down in a rocker and give myself up to it, the same as if I'd been at an entertainment. First and last"—she glanced judicially at the photograph—"I guess I got about as much out of Thea's voice as anybody will ever get."

Doctor Archie took her hand, still firm like the hand of a young woman. "You know, I always thought she learned more from you than from any of her teachers."

"Except Wunsch; he was a real musician," said Mrs. Kronborg respectfully. "I gave her what chance I could, in a crowded house. I kept the other children out of the parlour for her. That was about all I could do."

After they had recalled many pleasant memories together, Mrs. Kronborg said suddenly: "I always understood about her going off without coming to see us that time. Oh, I know! You have to keep your own counsel. You were a good friend to her. I've never forgot that." She patted the doctor's sleeve and went on absently. "There was something she didn't want to tell me, and that's why she didn't come. Something happened when she was with those people in Mexico. I worried for a good while, but I guess she's come out of it all right. She'd had a pretty hard time, scratching along alone like that when she was so young, and my farms in Nebraska were down so low that I couldn't help her none. That's no way to send a girl out. But I guess, whatever there was, she wouldn't be afraid to tell me now." Mrs. Kronborg looked up at the photograph with a smile. "She doesn't look like she was beholding to anybody, does she?"

"She isn't, Mrs. Kronborg. She never has been. That was why she borrowed the money from me."

"Oh, I knew she'd never have sent for you if she'd done anything to shame us. She was always proud." Mrs. Kronborg paused and turned a little on her side. "It's been quite a satisfaction to you and me, doctor, having her voice turn out so fine. The things you hope for don't always turn out like that, by a long sight. As long as old Mrs. Kohler lived, she used to translate what it said about Thea in the German papers she sent. I could make some of it out myself—it's not very different from Swedish— but it pleased the old lady. She left Thea her piece-picture of the burning of Moscow. I've got it put away in moth-balls for her, along with the oboe her grandfather brought from Sweden. I want her to take father's oboe back there some day." Mrs. Kronborg paused a moment and compressed her lips. "But I guess she'll take a finer instrument than that with her, back to Sweden!" she added.

Her tone fairly startled the doctor, it was so vibrating with a fierce, defiant kind of pride he had heard often in Thea's voice. He looked down wonderingly at his old friend and patient. After all, one never knew people to the core.

"That last summer at home wasn't very nice for her," Mrs. Kronborg began as placidly as if the fire had never leaped up in her. "The other children were acting-up because they thought I might make a fuss over her and give her the big-head. We gave her the dare, somehow, the lot of us, because we couldn't understand about her changing teachers and all that. That's the trouble about giving the dare to them quiet, unboastful children; you never know how far it'll take 'em. Well, we ought not to complain, doctor; she's given us a good deal to think about."

The next time Doctor Archie came to Moonstone, he came to be a pallbearer at Mrs. Kronborg's funeral. When he last looked at her, she was so serene and queenly that he went back to Denver feeling almost as if he had helped to bury Thea Kronborg herself. The handsome head in the coffin seemed to him much more really Thea than did the radiant young woman in the picture, looking about at the Gothic vaultings and greeting the Hall of Song.

IV

One bright morning late in February, 1909, Doctor Archie was breakfasting comfortably at the Waldorf. He had got into Jersey City on an early train, and a red, windy sunrise over the North River had given him a good appetite. He consulted the morning paper while he drank his coffee and saw that "Lohengrin" was to be sung at the opera that evening. In the list of the artists who would appear was the name "Kronborg." Such abruptness rather startled him. "Kronborg": it was impressive and yet, somehow, disrespectful; somewhat rude and brazen, on the back page of the morning paper. After breakfast he went to the hotel ticket-office and asked the girl if she could give him something for "Lohengrin," "near the front." His manner was a trifle awkward and he wondered whether the girl noticed it. Even if she did, of course, she could scarcely suspect. Before the ticket-stand he saw a bunch of blue posters announcing the opera casts for the week. There was "Lohengrin," and under it he saw:

Elsa von Brabant . . . Thea Kronborg.

That looked better. The girl gave him a ticket for a seat which she said was excellent. He paid for it and went out to the cabstand. He mentioned to the driver a number on Riverside Drive and got into a taxi. It would not, of course, be the right thing to call upon Thea when she was going to sing in the evening. He knew that much, thank goodness! Fred Ottenburg had hinted to him that, more than almost anything else, that would put one in wrong.

When he reached the number to which he directed his letters, he dismissed the cab and got out for a walk. The house in which Thea lived was as impersonal as the Waldorf, and quite as large. It was above 116th Street, where the Drive narrowed, and in front of it the shelving bank dropped to the North River. As Archie strolled about the paths which traversed this slope, below the street level, the fourteen stories of the apartment hotel rose above him like a perpendicular cliff. He had no idea on which floor Thea lived, but he reflected, as his eye ran over the many

windows, that the outlook would be fine from any floor. The forbidding
hugeness of the house made him feel as if he had expected to meet Thea
in a crowd and had missed her. He did not really believe that she was hidden
away behind any of those glittering windows, or that he was to hear her this
evening. His walk was curiously uninspiring and unsuggestive. Presently
remembering that Ottenburg had encouraged him to study his lesson, he
went down to the opera house and bought a libretto. He had even brought
his old *Adler's German and English* in his trunk, and after luncheon he settled
down in his gilded suite at the Waldorf with a big cigar and the text of
"Lohengrin."

The opera was announced for seven-forty-five, but at half-past
seven Archie took his seat in the right front of the orchestra circle. He had
never been inside the Metropolitan Opera House before, and the height of
the audience room, the rich colour, and the sweep of the balconies were
not without their effect upon him. He watched the house fill with a
growing feeling of expectation. When the steel curtain rose and the men of
the orchestra took their places, he felt distinctly nervous. The burst of
applause which greeted the conductor keyed him still higher. He found that
he had taken off his gloves and twisted them to a string. When the lights
went down and the violins began the prelude, the place looked larger than
ever; a great pit, shadowy and solemn. The whole atmosphere, he reflected,
was somehow more serious than he had anticipated.

After the curtains were drawn back upon the scene beside the
Scheldt, he got readily into the swing of the story. He was so much
interested in the bass who sang *King Henry* that he had almost forgotten for
what he was waiting so nervously, when the *Herald* began in stentorian
tones to summon *Elsa von Brabant*. Then he began to realize that he was
rather frightened. There was a flutter of white at the back of the stage, and
women began to come in: two, four, six, eight, but not the right one. It
flashed across him that this was something like buck-fever, the paralyzing
moment that comes upon a man when his first elk looks at him through the
bushes, under its great antlers; the moment when a man's mind is so full of
shooting that he forgets the gun in his hand until the buck is gone.

All at once, she was there. Yes, unquestionably it was she. Her
eyes were downcast, but the head, the cheeks, the chin—there could be no
mistake; she advanced slowly, as if she were walking in her sleep. Someone
spoke to her; she only inclined her head. He spoke again, and she bowed
her head still lower. Archie had forgotten his libretto, and he had not
counted upon these long pauses. He had expected her to appear and sing

and reassure him. They seemed to be waiting for her. Did she ever forget? Why in thunder didn't she—She made a sound, a faint one. The people on the stage whispered together and seemed confounded. His nervousness was absurd. She must have done this often before; she knew her bearings. She made another sound, but he could make nothing of it. Then the King sang to her, and Archie began to remember where they were in the story. She came to the front of the stage, lifted her eyes for the first time, clasped her hands and began, *"Einsam in trüben Tagen."*

Yes, it was exactly like buck-fever. Her face was there, toward the house now, before his eyes, and he positively could not see it. She was singing, at last, and he positively could not hear her. He was conscious of nothing but an uncomfortable dread and a sense of crushing disappointment. He had, after all, missed her. Whatever was there, she was not there—for him.

The King interrupted her. She began again, *"In lichter Waffen Scheine."* Archie did not know when his buck-fever passed, but presently he found that he was sitting quietly in a darkened house, not listening to, but dreaming upon, a river of silver sound. He felt apart from the others, drifting alone on the melody, as if he had been alone with it for a long while and had known it all before. His power of attention was not great just then, but in so far as it went he seemed to be looking through an exalted calmness at a beautiful woman from far away, from another sort of life and feeling and understanding than his own, who had in her face something he had known long ago, much brightened and beautified. As a lad he used to believe that the faces of people who died were like that in the next world; the same faces, but shining with the light of a new understanding.

What he felt was admiration and estrangement. The homely reunion, that he had somehow expected, now seemed foolish. Instead of feeling proud that he knew her better than all these people about him, he felt chagrined at his own ingenuousness. For he did not know her better. This woman he had never known; she had somehow devoured his little friend, as the wolf ate up Red Ridinghood. Beautiful, radiant, tender as she was, she chilled his old affection; that sort of feeling was no longer appropriate. She seemed much, much farther away from him than she had seemed all those years when she was in Germany. The ocean he could cross, but there was something here he could not cross. There was a moment, when she turned to the King and smiled that rare, sunrise smile of her childhood, when he thought she was coming back to him. After the *Herald's* second call for her champion, when she knelt in her impassioned prayer, there was

again something familiar, a kind of wild wonder that she had had the power
to call up long ago.

         After the tenor came on, the doctor ceased trying to make the
woman before him fit into any of his cherished recollections. He took her,
in so far as he could, for what she was then and there. When the knight
raised the kneeling girl and put his mailed hand on her hair, when she lifted
to him a face full of worship and passionate humility, Archie gave up his last
reservation. He knew no more about her than did the hundreds around
him, who sat in the shadow and looked on, as he looked, some with more
understanding, some with less. He knew as much about *Ortrud* or *Lohengrin*
as he knew about *Elsa*—more, because she went farther than they, she
sustained the legendary beauty of her conception more consistently. Even
he could see that. Attitudes, movements, her face, her white arms and
fingers, everything was suffused with a rosy tenderness, a warm humility, a
gracious and yet—to him—wholly estranging beauty.

         During the balcony singing in the second act the doctor's
thoughts were as far away from Moonstone as the singer's doubtless were.
He had begun, indeed, to feel the exhilaration of getting free from personalities, of being released from his own past as well as from Thea Kronborg's.
During the duet with *Ortrud,* and the splendours of the wedding proces-
sional, this new feeling grew and grew. At the end of the act there were
many curtain calls and *Elsa* acknowledged them, brilliant, gracious, spirited,
and with her far-breaking smile; but on the whole she was harder and more
self-contained before the curtain than she was in the scene behind it. Archie
did his part in the applause that greeted her, but it was the new and
wonderful he applauded, not the old and dear. His personal, proprietary
pride in her was frozen out.

         He walked about the house during the *entr'acte,* and here and
there among the people in the foyer he caught the name "Kronborg." On
the staircase, in front of the coffee-room, a long-haired youth with a fat face
was discoursing to a group of women about "die Kronborg." Doctor
Archie gathered that he had crossed on the boat with her.

         After the performance was over, Archie took a taxi and started
for Riverside Drive. He meant to see it through to-night. When he entered
the reception-hall of the hotel before which he had strolled that morning,
the hall porter challenged him. He said he was waiting for Miss Kronborg.
The porter looked at him suspiciously and asked whether he had an appointment. He answered brazenly that he had. He was not used to being
questioned by hall boys. Archie sat first in one tapestry chair and then in

another, keeping a sharp eye on the people who came in and went up in the elevators.

He walked about and looked at his watch. An hour dragged by. No one had come in from the street now for about twenty minutes, when two women entered, carrying a great many flowers and followed by a tall young man in chauffeur's uniform. Archie advanced toward the taller of the two women, who was veiled and carried her head very firmly. He confronted her just as she reached the elevator. Although he did not stand directly in her way, something in his attitude compelled her to stop. She gave him a piercing, defiant glance through the white scarf that covered her face. Then she lifted her hand and brushed the scarf back from her head. There was still black on her eyebrows and lashes. She was very pale and her face was drawn and deeply lined. She looked, the doctor told himself with a sinking heart, forty years old. Her suspicious, mystified stare cleared slowly.

"Pardon me," the doctor murmured, not knowing just how to address her here before the porters, "I came up from the opera. I merely wanted to say good night to you."

Without speaking, still looking incredulous, she pushed him into the elevator. She kept her hand on his arm while the cage shot up, and she looked away from him, frowning, as if she were trying to remember or realize something. When the cage stopped, she pushed him out of the elevator through another door, which a maid opened, into a square hall. There she sank down on a chair and looked up at him.

"Why didn't you let me know?" she asked in a hoarse voice.

Archie heard himself laughing the old, embarrassed laugh that seldom happened to him now. "Oh, I wanted to take my chance with you, like anybody else. It's been so long, now!"

She took his hand through her thick glove and her head dropped forward. "Yes, it has been long," she said in the same husky voice, "and so much has happened."

"And you are so tired, and I am a clumsy old fellow to break in on you to-night," the doctor added sympathetically. "Forgive me, this time." He bent over and put his hand soothingly on her shoulder. He felt a strong shudder run through her from head to foot.

Still bundled in her fur coat as she was, she threw both arms about him and hugged him. "Oh, Doctor Archie, *Doctor Archie*"—she shook him—"don't let me go. Hold on, now you're here," she laughed, breaking away from him at the same moment and sliding out of her fur coat.

She left it for the maid to pick up and pushed the doctor into the sitting-room, where she turned on the lights. "Let me *look* at you. Yes; hands, feet, head, shoulders—just the same. You've grown no older. You can't say as much for me, can you?"

She was standing in the middle of the room, in a white silk shirtwaist and a short black velvet skirt, which somehow suggested that they had "cut off her petticoats all round about." She looked distinctly clipped and plucked. Her hair was parted in the middle and done very close to her head, as she had worn it under the wig. She looked like a fugitive, who had escaped from something in clothes caught up at hazard. It flashed across Doctor Archie that she was running away from the other woman down at the opera house, who had used her hardly.

He took a step toward her. "I can't tell a thing in the world about you, Thea—if I may still call you that."

She took hold of the collar of his overcoat. "Yes, call me that. Do: I like to hear it. You frighten me a little, but I expect I frighten you more. I'm always a scarecrow after I sing a long part like that—so high, too." She absently pulled out the handkerchief that protruded from his breast-pocket and began to wipe the black paint off her eyebrows and lashes. "I can't take you in much to-night, but I must see you for a little while." She pushed him to a chair. "I shall be more recognizable to-morrow. You mustn't think of me as you see me to-night. Come at four to-morrow afternoon and have tea with me. Can you? That's good."

She sat down in a low chair beside him and leaned forward, drawing her shoulders together. She seemed to him inappropriately young and inappropriately old, shorn of her long tresses at one end and of her long robes at the other.

"How do you happen to be here?" she asked abruptly. "How can you leave a silver mine? I couldn't! Sure nobody'll cheat you? But you can explain everything to-morrow." She paused. "You remember how you sewed me up in a poultice, once? I wish you could to-night. I need a poultice, from top to toe. Something very disagreeable happened down there. You said you were out front? Oh, don't say anything about it. I always know exactly how it goes, unfortunately. I was pretty bad in the balcony scene. I never get that. You didn't notice it? Probably not, but I did."

Here the maid appeared at the door and her mistress rose. "My supper? Very well, I'll come. I'd ask you to stay, doctor, but there wouldn't be enough for two. They seldom send up enough for one"—she spoke bitterly. "I haven't got a sense of you yet"—turning directly to Archie again. "You haven't been here. You've only announced yourself, and told me you are coming to-morrow. You haven't seen me, either. This is not I. But I'll be here waiting for you to-morrow, all of me! Good night, till then." She patted him absently on the sleeve and gave him a little shove toward the door.

V

*W*hen Archie got back to his hotel at two o'clock in the morning, he found Fred Ottenburg's card under his door, with a message scribbled across the top: *"When you come in, please call up room 811, this hotel."* A moment later Fred's voice reached him over the telephone.

"That you, Archie? Won't you come up? I'm having some supper and I'd like company. Late? What does that matter? I won't keep you long."

Archie dropped his overcoat and set out for room 811. He found Ottenburg in his sitting-room, in the act of touching a match to a chafing-dish, at a table laid for two. "I'm catering here," he announced cheerfully. "I let the waiter off at midnight, after he'd set me up. You'll have to account for yourself, Archie."

The doctor laughed, pointing to the wine-coolers under the table. "Are you expecting guests?"

"Yes, two"—Ottenburg held up two fingers—"you, and my other self. He's a thirsty boy, and I don't invite him often. He has been known to give me a headache. Now, where have you been, until this shocking hour?"

"Been, Freddy? I expect I've been exactly where you have. Why didn't you tell me you were coming on?"

"I wasn't." Fred lifted the cover of the chafing-dish and stirred the contents. "I had never thought of such a thing. But Landry, a young chap who plays her accompaniments and who keeps an eye out for me, telegraphed me that Madame Rheinecker had gone to Atlantic City with a bad throat, and Thea would sing *Elsa*. She has sung it only twice here before, and I missed it in Dresden. So I came on. I got in at four this afternoon and saw that you were registered, but I thought I wouldn't butt in. How lucky you got here just when she was coming on for this. You couldn't have hit a better time." Ottenburg stirred the contents of the dish faster and put in more sherry. "And where have you been since twelve o'clock, may I ask?"

Archie looked rather self-conscious, as he sat down on a fragile gilt chair that rocked under him, and stretched out his long legs. "Well, if you'll believe me, I had the brutality to go to see her. I wanted to identify her. Couldn't wait."

Ottenburg placed the cover quickly on the chafing-dish and took a step backward. "You did, old sport? My word! None but the brave deserve the fair. Well"—he stooped to turn the wine in the cooler—"and how was she?"

"She seemed rather dazed, and pretty well used-up. She seemed disappointed in herself, and said she hadn't done herself justice in the balcony scene."

"Well, if she didn't, she's not the first. Beastly stuff to sing right in there; lies just on the 'break' in the voice." Fred pulled a bottle out of the ice and drew the cork. Lifting his glass he looked meaningly at his guest. "You know who, doctor!" He drank off his glass with a sigh of satisfaction. "As a backer, you're a winner, Archie. I congratulate you." He bent over the chafing-dish and began to serve the contents. "And now, on the level, how did it strike you?"

Archie turned a frank smile to his friend and shook his head. "It was all miles beyond me, of course, but it gave me a pulse. The general excitement got hold of me, I suppose. She *was* all right, then? You weren't disappointed?"

"Disappointed? My dear Archie, that's the high voice we dream of; so pure and yet so warm and human. That combination hardly ever happens with sopranos." Ottenburg sat down and turned to the doctor, speaking calmly and trying to make himself clear. "There's the voice itself, so beautiful and individual, and then there's something else; the thing in it which responds to every shade of thought and feeling, spontaneously, almost unconsciously. That colour has to be born in a singer, it can't be acquired; lots of beautiful voices haven't a vestige of it. It's almost like another gift—the rarest of all. The voice simply is the mind and is the heart. It can't go wrong in interpretation, because it has in it the thing that makes all interpretation. That's why you feel so sure of her. After you've listened to her for an hour or so, you aren't afraid of anything. All the little dreads you have with other artists vanish."

Archie looked envyingly at Fred's excited, triumphant face. How satisfactory it must be, he thought, to really know what she was doing and not to have to take it on hearsay. He took up his glass with a sigh.

"Yes, Fred, I thought it sounded very beautiful, and I thought she was very beautiful, too."

"Wasn't she? Every attitude a picture, and always the right kind of picture, full of that legendary, supernatural thing she gets into it. I never heard the prayer sung like that before. Of course, you get an *Elsa* who can look through the walls like that, and visions and Grail knights happen naturally. She becomes an abbess, that girl, after *Lohengrin* leaves her. She's made to live with ideas and enthusiasms, not with a husband." Fred folded his arms, leaned back in his chair, and began to sing softly:

> *"In lichter Waffen Scheine*
> *Ein Ritter nahte da."*

"Doesn't she die, then, at the end?" the doctor asked guardedly.

Fred smiled. "Some *Elsas* do; she didn't. She left me with the distinct impression that she was just beginning."

The doctor lit a cigar. "Seriously, Freddy, I wish I knew more about what she's driving at. It makes me jealous, when you are so in it and I'm not."

"In it?" Fred started up. "My God, haven't you seen her this blessed night?—when she'd have kicked any other man down the elevator shaft, if I know her. Leave me something; at least what I can pay my five bucks for."

"Seems to me you get a good deal for your five bucks," said Archie ruefully. "And that, after all, is what she cares about—what people get."

Fred drank off another glass. In his voice there was a longer perspective than usual, a slight remoteness. "You see, Archie, it's all very simple, a natural development. It's exactly what Mahler said back there in the beginning, when she sang *Woglinde*. It's the idea, the basic idea, pulsing behind every bar she sings. She simplifies a character down to the musical idea it's built on, and makes everything conform to that. The people who chatter about her being a great actress don't seem to get the notion of where *she* gets the notion. It all goes back to her original endowment, her tremendous musical talent. Instead of inventing a lot of business and expedients to suggest character, she knows the thing at the root, and lets the musical pattern take care of her. The score pours her into all those lovely postures, makes the light and shadow go over her face, lifts her and drops her. She lies on it, the way she used to lie on the Rhine music."

The doctor frowned dubiously as another bottle made its appearance above the cloth. "Aren't you going in rather strong?"

Fred laughed. "No, I'm becoming too sober. You see, this is breakfast now. Did you notice her to-night when she came down the stairs? I wonder where she gets that bright-and-morning-star look? It carries to the last row of the family circle. I'll tell you a secret: that carrying power was one of the first things that put me wise. I noticed it down there in Arizona, out in the open. That, I said, belongs only to the big ones." Fred got up and began to move rhythmically about the room, his hands in his pockets. "The fact is, *Elsa* isn't a part that's particularly suited to Thea's voice at all, as I see her voice. It's over-lyrical for her. She makes it, but there's nothing in it that fits her like a glove, except, maybe, that long duet in the third act. But wait until they give her a chance at something that lies properly in her voice, and you'll see me rosier than I am to-night."

Archie smoothed the tablecloth with his hand. "I am sure I don't want to see you any rosier, Fred."

Ottenburg threw back his head and laughed. "It's enthusiasm, doctor. It's not the wine. You, too, have your extravagances."

The doctor seemed embarrassed. "I was just thinking how tired she looked, plucked of all her fine feathers, while we get all the fun. Instead of sitting here carousing, we ought to go solemnly to bed."

Ottenburg crossed to the window and threw it open.

"Fine night outside; it begins to smell like morning. After all, Archie, think of the lonely and rather solemn hours we've spent waiting for all this, while she's been—revelling."

Archie lifted his brows. "I somehow didn't get the idea to-night that she revels much."

"I don't mean this sort of thing"—with a nod toward the wine-cooler.—"But take it from me, no matter what she pays, or how much she may see fit to lie about it, the real, the master revel is hers. She has her hour, when she can say, 'There it is, at last, *Wie im Traum ich*—' "

He stood silent a moment, twisting the flower from his coat by the stem and staring at the blank wall.

The doctor rose. Fred followed him to the door. "I say," he asked, "have you a date with anybody?"

The doctor paused, his hand on the knob. "With Thea, you mean? Yes. I'm to go to her at four this afternoon."

"Well, you won't eat me, will you, if I break in and send up my card? She'll probably turn me down, but that won't hurt my feelings. Good night, Archie."

VI

It was late on the morning after the night she sang *Elsa* when Thea Kronborg stirred uneasily in her bed. The room was darkened by two sets of window-shades, and the day outside was thick and cloudy. She turned and tried to recapture unconsciousness, knowing that she would not be able to do so. She dreaded waking stale and disappointed after a great effort. The first thing that came was always the sense of the futility of such endeavour, the absurdity of trying too hard. Up to a certain point, say eighty degrees, artistic endeavour could be fat and comfortable, methodical and prudent. But if you went further than that, if you drew yourself up toward ninety degrees, you parted with your defences and left yourself exposed to mischance. The legend was that in those upper reaches you might be divine; but you were much likelier to be ridiculous. Your public wanted just about eighty degrees; if you gave it more, it blew its nose and put a crimp in you. In the morning, especially, it seemed to her very probable that whatever struggled above the good average was not quite sound. Certainly very little of that superfluous ardour, which cost so dear, ever got across the footlights. These misgivings waited to pounce upon her when she wakened. They hovered about her bed like vultures.

She reached under her pillow for her handkerchief, without opening her eyes. She had a shadowy memory that there was to be something unusual, that this day held more disquieting possibilities than days commonly held. There was something she dreaded; what was it? Oh, yes, Doctor Archie was to come at four.

A reality like Doctor Archie, poking up out of the past, reminded one of disappointments and losses, of a freedom that was no more: reminded her of blue, golden mornings long ago, when she used to waken with a burst of joy at recovering her precious self and her precious world; when she never lay on her pillows at eleven o'clock like something the waves had washed up. After all, why had he come? It had been so long, and so much had happened. The things she had lost, he would miss readily enough. What she had gained, he would scarcely perceive. He, and all that he recalled, lived for her as memories. In sleep, and in hours of illness or exhaustion, she went back to them and held them to her heart. But they were better as memories. They had nothing to do with the struggle that made up her actual life. She felt drearily that she was not flexible enough to be the person her old friend expected her to be, the person she herself wished to be with him.

Thea reached for the bell and rang twice—a signal to her maid to order her breakfast. She rose and ran up the window-shades and turned on the water in her bathroom, glancing into the mirror apprehensively as she passed it. Her bath usually cheered her, even on low mornings like this. Her bathroom, almost as large as her sleeping-room, she regarded as a refuge. When she turned the key behind her, she left care and vexation on the other side of the door. Neither her maid nor the management nor her letters nor her accompanist could get at her now.

When she pinned her braids about her head, dropped her night-gown and stepped out to begin her Swedish movements, she was a natural creature again, and it was so that she liked herself best. She slid into the tub with anticipation and splashed and tumbled about a good deal. Whatever else she hurried, she never hurried her bath. She used her brushes and sponges and soap like toys, fairly playing in the water. Her own body was always a cheering sight to her. When she was careworn, when her mind felt old and tired, the freshness of her physical self, her long, firm lines, the smoothness of her skin, reassured her. This morning, because of awakened memories, she looked at herself more carefully than usual, and was not discouraged. While she was in the tub she began to whistle softly the tenor aria, *"Ah! Fuyez, douce image,"* somehow appropriate to the bath. After a noisy moment under the cold shower, she stepped out upon the rug flushed and glowing, threw her arms above her head, and rose on her toes, keeping the elevation as long as she could. When she dropped back on her heels and began to rub herself with the towels, she took up the aria again, and felt quite in the humour for seeing Doctor Archie. After she had returned to her bed, the maid brought her letters and the morning papers with her breakfast.

"Telephone Mr. Landry and ask him if he can come at half-past three, Thérèse, and order tea to be brought up at five."

When Howard Archie was admitted to Thea's apartment that afternoon, he was shown into the music-room back of the little reception-room. Thea was sitting in a davenport behind the piano, talking to a young man whom she later introduced as her friend Mr. Landry. As she rose, and came to meet him, Archie felt a deep relief, a sudden thankfulness. She no longer looked clipped and plucked, or dazed and fleeing.

Doctor Archie neglected to take account of the young man to whom he was presented. He kept Thea's hands and held her where he met her, taking in the light, lively sweep of her hair, her clear green eyes and her throat which came up strong and dazzlingly white from her green velvet gown. The chin was as lovely as ever, the cheeks were as smooth. All the lines of last night had disappeared. Only at the outer corners of her eyes, between the eye and the temple, were the faintest indications of a future attack—mere kitten scratches which playfully hinted where one day the cat would claw her. He studied her without any embarrassment. Last night everything had been awkward; but now, as he held her hands, a kind of harmony came between them, a re-establishment of confidence.

"After all, Thea—in spite of all, I still know you," he murmured.

She took his arm and led him up to the young man who was standing beside the piano. "Mr. Landry knows all about you, Doctor Archie. He has known about you for many years." While the two men shook hands, she stood between them, drawing them together by her presence and her glances. "When I first went to Germany, Landry was studying there. He used to be good enough to work with me when I could not afford to have an accompanist for more than two hours a day. We got into the way of working together. He is a singer, too, and has his own career to look after, but he still manages to give me some time. I want you to be friends." She smiled from one to the other.

The rooms, Archie noticed, full of last night's flowers, were furnished in light colours, the hotel bleakness of them a little softened by the Steinway piano, white bookshelves full of books and scores, some drawings of ballet dancers, and the very deep sofa behind the piano.

"Of course," Archie asked apologetically, "you have seen the papers?"

"Very cordial, aren't they? They evidently did not expect as much as I did. *Elsa* is not really in my voice. I can sing the music, but I have to go after it."

"That is exactly," the doctor came out boldly, "what Fred Ottenburg said this morning."

They had remained standing, the three of them, by the piano, where the grey afternoon light was strongest. Thea turned to the doctor with interest. "Is Fred in town? They were from him, then—some flowers that came last night without a card." She indicated the white lilacs on the window-sill. "Yes, he would know, certainly," she said thoughtfully. "Why don't we sit down? There will be some tea for you in a minute, Landry. He's very dependent upon it," disapprovingly to Archie. "Now tell me, doctor, did you really have a good time last night, or were you uncomfortable? Did you feel as if I were trying to hold my hat on by my eyebrows?"

He smiled. "I had all kinds of a time. But I had no feeling of that sort. I couldn't be quite sure that it was you at all. That was why I came up here last night. I felt as if I'd lost you."

She leaned toward him and brushed his sleeve reassuringly. "Then I didn't give you an impression of painful struggle? Landry was singing at Weber and Fields' last night. He didn't get in until the performance was half over. But I see the *Tribune* man felt that I was working pretty hard. Did you see that notice, Oliver?"

Doctor Archie looked closely at the red-headed young man for the first time, and met his lively brown eyes, full of a droll, confiding sort of humour. Mr. Landry was not prepossessing. He was undersized and clumsily made, with a red, shiny face and a sharp little nose that looked as if it had been whittled out of wood and was always in the air, on the scent of something. Yet it was this queer little beak, with his eyes, that made his countenance anything of a face at all. From a distance he looked like the groceryman's delivery boy in a small town. His dress seemed an acknowledgement of his grotesqueness: a short coat, like a little boy's roundabout, and a vest fantastically sprigged and dotted, over a lavender shirt.

At the sound of a muffled buzz, Mr. Landry sprang up. "May I answer the telephone for you?" He went to the writing-table and took up the receiver. "Mr. Ottenburg is downstairs," he said, turning to Thea and holding the mouthpiece against his coat.

"Tell him to come up," she replied without hesitation. "How long are you going to be in town, Doctor Archie?"

"Oh, several weeks if you'll let me stay. I won't hang around and be a burden to you, but I want to try to get educated up to you, though I expect it's late to begin."

Thea rose and touched him lightly on the shoulder. "Well, you'll never be any younger, will you?"

"I'm not so sure about that," the doctor replied gallantly.

The maid appeared at the door and announced Mr. Ottenburg. Fred came in, very much got up, the doctor reflected, as he watched him bending over Thea's hand. He was still pale and looked somewhat chastened, and the lock of hair that hung down over his forehead was distinctly moist. But his black afternoon coat, his grey tie and gaiters were of a correctness that Doctor Archie could never attain for all the efforts of his faithful slave, Van Deusen, the Denver haberdasher. To be properly up to those tricks, the doctor supposed, you had to learn them young.

Ottenburg had greeted Thea in German, and as she replied in the same language, Archie joined Mr. Landry at the window. "You know Mr. Ottenburg, he tells me?"

Mr. Landry's eyes twinkled. "Yes, I regularly follow him about, when he's in town. I would, even if he didn't send me such wonderful Christmas presents: Russian vodka by the half-dozen!"

Thea called to them, "Come, Mr. Ottenburg is calling on all of us. Here's the tea."

The maid opened the door and two waiters from downstairs appeared with covered trays. The tea-table was in the parlour. Thea drew Ottenburg with her and went to inspect it. "Where's the rum? Oh, yes, in that thing! Everything seems to be here, but send up some currant preserves and cream cheese for Mr. Ottenburg. And in about fifteen minutes, bring some fresh toast. That's all, thank you."

For the next few minutes there was a clatter of teacups and responses about sugar. "Landry always takes rum. I'm glad the rest of you don't. I'm sure it's bad." Thea poured the tea standing and got through with it as quickly as possible, as if it were a refreshment snatched between trains. The tea-table and the little room in which it stood seemed to be out of scale with her long step, her long reach, and the energy of her movements. Doctor Archie, standing near her, was pleasantly aware of the animation of her figure. Under the clinging velvet, her body seemed independent and unsubdued.

They drifted, with their plates and cups, back to the music-room. When Thea followed them, Ottenburg put down his tea suddenly. "Aren't you taking anything? Please let me." He started back to the table.

"No, thank you, nothing. I'm going to run over that aria for you presently, to convince you that I can do it. How did the duet go, with Schlag?"

She was standing in the doorway and Fred came up to her: "That you'll never do any better. You've worked your voice into it perfectly. Every *nuance*—wonderful!"

"Think so?" She gave him a sidelong glance and spoke with a

certain gruff shyness which did not deceive anybody, and was not meant to deceive. The tone was equivalent to "Keep it up. I like it, but I'm awkward with it."

Fred held her by the door and did keep it up, furiously, for full five minutes. She took it with some confusion, seeming all the while to be hesitating, to be arrested in her course and trying to pass him. But she did not really try to pass, and her colour deepened. Fred spoke in German, and Archie caught from her an occasional *Ja? So?* muttered rather than spoken.

When they rejoined Landry and Doctor Archie, Fred took up his tea again. "I see you're singing *Venus* Saturday night. Will they never let you have a chance at *Elisabeth?*"

She shrugged her shoulders. "Not here. There are so many singers here, and they try us out in such a stingy way. Think of it, last year I came over in October, and it was the first of December before I went on at all! I'm often sorry I left Dresden."

"Still," Fred argued, "Dresden is limited."

"Just so, and I've begun to sigh for those very limitations. In New York everything is impersonal. Your audience never knows its own mind, and its mind is never twice the same. I'd rather sing where the people are pig-headed and throw carrots at you if you don't do it the way they like it. The house here is splendid, and the night audiences are exciting. I hate the matinées; like singing at a *Kaffeeklatsch.*" She rose and turned on the lights.

"Ah!" Fred exclaimed, "why do you do that? That is a signal that tea is over."

"Not at all. Shall you be here Saturday night?" She sat down on the piano-bench and leaned her elbow back on the keyboard. "Necker sings *Elisabeth.* Make Doctor Archie go. Everything she sings is worth hearing."

"But she's failing so. The last time I heard her she had no voice at all. She *is* a poor vocalist!"

Thea cut him off.

"She's a great artist, whether she's in voice or not, and she's the only one here. If you want a big voice, you can take the *Ortrud* of last night; that's big enough, and vulgar enough."

Fred laughed and turned away, this time with decision.

"I don't want her!" he protested energetically. "I only wanted to get a rise out of you. I like Necker's *Elisabeth* well enough. I like your *Venus* well enough, too."

"It's a beautiful part, and it's often dreadfully sung. It's very hard to sing, of course."

Ottenburg bent over the hand she held out to him. "For an uninvited guest, I've fared very well. You were nice to let me come up. I'd have been terribly cut up if you'd sent me away. May I?" He kissed her hand lightly and backed toward the door, still smiling, and promising to keep an eye on Archie. "He can't be trusted at all, Thea. One of the waiters at Martin's worked a Tourainian hare off on him at luncheon yesterday, for seven-twenty-five."

She broke into a laugh, the deep one he recognized. "Did he have a ribbon on, this hare? Did they bring him in a gilt cage?"

"No"—Archie spoke up for himself—"they brought him in a brown sauce, which was very good. He didn't taste very different from any rabbit."

"Probably came from a push-cart on the East Side." Thea looked at her old friend commiseratingly. "Yes, *do* keep an eye on him, Fred. I had no idea"—shaking her head. "Yes, I'll be obliged to you."

"Count on me!" Their eyes met in a gay smile, and Fred bowed himself out.

VII

On Saturday night Doctor Archie went with Fred Ottenburg to hear "Tannhäuser." Thea had a rehearsal on Sunday afternoon, but as she was not on the bill again until Wednesday, she promised to dine with Archie and Ottenburg on Monday, if they could make the dinner early.

At a little after eight on Monday evening, the three friends returned to Thea's apartment and seated themselves for an hour of quiet talk.

"I'm sorry we couldn't have had Landry with us to-night," Thea said, "but he's on at Weber and Fields' every night now. You ought to hear him, Doctor Archie. He often sings the old Scotch airs you used to love."

"Why not go down this evening?" Fred suggested hopefully, glancing at his watch. "That is, if you'd like to go. I can telephone and find what time he comes on."

Thea hesitated. "No, I think not. I took a long walk this after-noon and I'm rather tired. I think I can get to sleep early and be so much ahead. I don't mean at once, however," seeing Doctor Archie's disap-pointed look. "I always like to hear Landry," she added. "He never had much voice, and it's worn, but there's a sweetness about it, and he sings with such taste."

"Yes, doesn't he? May I?" Fred took out his cigarette-case. "It really doesn't bother your throat?"

"A little doesn't. But cigar smoke does. Poor Doctor Archie! Can you do with one of those?"

"I'm learning to like them," the doctor declared, taking one from the case Fred proffered him.

"Landry's the only fellow I know in this country who can do that sort of thing," Fred went on. "Like the best English ballad-singers."

Thea nodded. "Yes; sometimes I make him sing his most foolish things for me. It's restful, as he does it. That's when I'm homesick, Doctor Archie."

"You knew him in Germany, Thea?" Doctor Archie had qui-etly abandoned his cigarette as a comfortless article. "When you first went over?"

"Yes. He was a good friend to a green girl. He helped me with my German and my music and my general discouragement. Seemed to care more about my getting on than about himself. He had no money, either. An old aunt had lent him a little to study on.—Will you answer that, Fred?"

Fred caught up the telephone and stopped the buzz while Thea went on talking to Doctor Archie about Landry. Telling someone to hold the wire, he presently put down the instrument and approached Thea with a startled expression on his face.

"It's the management," he said quietly. "Gloeckler has broken down: fainting fits. Madame Rheinecker is in Atlantic City and Schramm is singing in Philadelphia to-night. They want to know whether you can come down and finish *Sieglinde*."

"What time is it?"

"Eight-fifty-five. The first act is just over. They can hold the curtain twenty-five minutes."

Thea did not move. "Twenty-five and thirty-five makes sixty," she muttered. "Tell them I'll come if they hold the curtain till I am in the dressing-room. Say I'll have to wear her costumes, and the dresser must have everything ready. Then call a taxi, please."

She had not changed her position since he first interrupted her, but she had grown pale and was opening and shutting her hands rapidly. She looked, Fred thought, terrified. He half-turned toward the telephone, but hung on one foot.

"Have you ever sung the part?" he asked.

"No, but I've rehearsed it. That's all right. Get the cab." Still she made no move. She merely turned perfectly blank eyes to Doctor Archie and said absently: "It's curious, but just at this minute I can't remember a bar of 'Walküre' after the first act. And I let my maid go out!" She sprang up and beckoned Archie without so much, he felt sure, as knowing who he was. "Come with me." She went quickly into her sleeping-chamber and threw open a door into a trunk-room. "See that white trunk? It's not locked. It's full of wigs, in boxes. Look until you find one marked 'Ring 2.' Bring it quick!" While she directed him, she threw open a square trunk and began tossing out shoes of every shape and colour.

Ottenburg appeared at the door. "Can I help?"

She threw him some white sandals with long laces and silk stockings pinned to them. "Put those in something, and then go to the piano and give me a few measures in there—you know." She was behaving somewhat like a cyclone now, and while she wrenched open drawers and closet doors, Ottenburg got to the piano as quickly as possible and began to herald the reappearance of the Volsung pair, trusting to memory.

In a few moments Thea came out enveloped in her long fur coat with a scarf over her head and knitted woollen gloves on her hands. Her glassy eye took in the fact that Fred was playing from memory, and even in her distracted state, a faint smile flickered over her colourless lips. She stretched out a woolly hand, "The score, please. Behind you, there."

Doctor Archie followed with a canvas box and a satchel. As they went through the hall, the men caught up their hats and coats. They left the music-room, Fred noticed, just seven minutes after he got the telephone message. In the elevator Thea said in that husky whisper which had so perplexed Doctor Archie when he first heard it, "Tell the driver he must do it in twenty minutes, less if he can. He must leave the light on in the cab. I can do a good deal in twenty minutes. If only you hadn't made me eat—Damn that duck!" she broke out bitterly; "why did you?"

"Wish I had it back! But it won't bother you, to-night. You need strength," he pleaded consolingly.

But she only muttered angrily under her breath, "Idiot, idiot!"

Ottenburg shot ahead and instructed the driver, while the doctor put Thea into the cab and shut the door. She did not speak to either of them again. As the driver scrambled into his seat, she opened the score and fixed her eyes upon it. Her face, in the white light, looked as bleak as a stone quarry.

As her cab slid away, Ottenburg shoved Archie into a second taxi that waited by the curb. "We'd better trail her," he explained. "There might be a hold-up of some kind." As the cab whizzed off, he broke into an eruption of profanity.

"What's the matter, Fred?" the doctor asked. He was a good deal dazed by the rapid evolutions of the last ten minutes.

"Matter enough!" Fred growled, buttoning his overcoat with a shiver. "What a way to sing a part for the first time! The duck really is on my conscience. It will be a wonder if she can do anything but quack! Scrambling on in the middle of a performance like this with no rehearsal! The stuff she has to sing in there is terribly difficult."

"She looked frightened," Doctor Archie said thoughtfully, "but I thought she looked—determined."

Fred sniffed. "Oh, determined! That's the kind of rough deal that makes savages of singers. Here's a part she's worked on for years, and now they give her a chance to go on and butcher it. Goodness knows when she's looked at the score last, or whether she can use the business she's studied, with this cast. Necker's singing *Brünnhilde;* she may help her, if it's not one of her sore nights."

"Is she sore at Thea?" Doctor Archie asked wonderingly.

"My dear man, Necker's sore at everything. She's breaking up; too early; just when she ought to be at her best. There's one story that she is struggling under some serious malady, another that she learned a bad method at the Prague Conservatory and has ruined her organ. She's the sorest thing in the world. If she weathers this winter through, it'll be her last."

The cab stopped and Fred and Doctor Archie hurried to the box-office. The Monday-night house was sold out. They bought standing room and entered the auditorium just as the press representative of the house was thanking the audience for their patience and telling them that, although Madame Gloeckler was too ill to sing, Miss Kronborg had kindly consented to finish her part. This announcement was met with vehement applause from the upper circles of the house.

"She has her—constituents," Doctor Archie murmured.

"Yes, up there, where they're young and hungry. These people down here have dined too well. They won't mind, however. They like fires and accidents and *divertissements*. Two *Sieglindes* are more unusual than one, so they'll be satisfied."

After the final disappearance of the mother of Siegfried, Ottenburg and the doctor slipped out through the crowd and left the house. Near the stage entrance Fred found the driver who had brought Thea down. He dismissed him and got a larger car. He and Archie waited on the sidewalk, and when Kronborg came out alone, they gathered her into the cab and sprang in after her.

Thea sank back into the corner of the seat and yawned. "Well, I got through, eh?" Her tone was reassuring. "On the whole, I think I've given you gentlemen a pretty lively evening, for one who has no social accomplishments."

"Rather! There was something like a popular uprising at the end of the second act. Archie and I couldn't keep it up as long as the rest of them did. A howl like that ought to show the management which way the wind is blowing. You probably know you were magnificent."

"I thought it went pretty well." She spoke impartially. "I was rather smart to catch his tempo there, at the beginning of the first recitative, when he came in too soon, don't you think? It's tricky in there, without a rehearsal. Oh, I was all right! He took that syncopation too fast in the beginning. Some singers take it fast there—think it sounds more impassioned. That's one way!" She sniffed, and Fred shot a mirthful glance at Archie. Her boastfulness would have been childish in a schoolboy. In the light of what she had done, of the strain they had lived through during the last two hours, it made one laugh—almost cry. She went on robustly: "And I didn't feel my dinner, really, Fred. I am hungry again, I'm ashamed to say—and I forgot to order anything at my hotel."

Fred put his hand on the door. "Where to? You must have food."

"Do you know any quiet place, where I won't be stared at? I've still got make-up on."

"I do. Nice English chop-house. Nobody there at night but theatre people after the show, and a few bachelors." He spoke to the driver.

As the car turned, Thea put out her hand and drew Doctor Archie's handkerchief from his breast-pocket. "This comes to me naturally," she said, rubbing her cheeks and eyebrows. "When I was little I always loved your handkerchiefs because they were silk and smelled of

Cologne water. I think they must have been the only really clean handkerchiefs in Moonstone. You were always wiping my face with them when
you met me out in the dust, I remember. Did I never have any?"

"I think you'd nearly always used yours up on your baby
brother."

Thea sighed. "Yes, Thor had such a way of getting messy. You
say he's a good chauffeur?" She closed her eyes for a moment as if they were
tired. Suddenly she looked up. "Isn't it funny, how we travel in circles?
Here you are, still getting me clean, and Fred is still feeding me. I should
have died of starvation at that boarding-house on Indiana Avenue if he
hadn't taken me out to the Buckingham and filled me up once in a while.
What a cavern I was to fill, too! The waiters used to look astonished. I'm
still singing on that food."

Fred alighted and gave Thea his arm as they crossed the icy
sidewalk. They were taken upstairs in an antiquated lift and found the
cheerful chop-room half full of supper parties. An English company playing
at the Empire had just come in. The waiters, in red waist-coats, were
hurrying about. Fred got a table at the back of the room, in a corner, and
urged his waiter to get the oysters on at once.

"Takes a few minutes to open them, sir," the man expostulated.

"Yes, but make it as few as possible, and bring the lady's first.
Then grilled chops with kidneys, and salad."

Thea began eating celery stalks at once, from the base to the
foliage. "Necker said something nice to me to-night. You might have
thought the management would say something, but not they." She looked
at Fred from under her blackened lashes. "It *was* a stunt, to jump in on that
second act without rehearsal. It doesn't sing itself."

Ottenburg was watching her face. She was much handsomer
than she had been early in the evening. Excitement of this sort enriched her.
It was only under such excitement, he reflected, that she was entirely
illuminated, or wholly present. At other times there was something a little
cold and empty, like a big room with no people in it. Even in her most
genial moods there was a shadow of restlessness, as if she were waiting for
something and were exercising the virtue of patience. During dinner she
had been as kind as she knew how to be, to him and to Archie, and had
given them as much of herself as she could. But, clearly, she knew only one
way of being really kind, from the core of her heart out; and there was but
one way in which she could give herself to people largely and gladly,
spontaneously. Even as a girl she had been at her best in vigorous effort, he

remembered; physical effort, when there was no other kind at hand.

Thea turned suddenly from her talk with Archie and peered suspiciously into the corner where Ottenburg sat with folded arms, observing her. "What's the matter with you, Fred? I'm afraid of you when you're quiet—fortunately you almost never are. What are you thinking about?"

"I was wondering how you got right with the orchestra so quickly, there at first. I had a flash of terror," he replied easily.

She bolted her last oyster and ducked her head. "So had I! I don't know how I did catch it. Desperation, I suppose; the same way the Indian babies swim when they're thrown into the river. I *had* to. Now it's over, I'm glad I had to. I learned a whole lot to-night."

Archie, who usually felt that it behooved him to be silent during such discussions, was encouraged by her geniality to venture, "I don't see how you can learn anything in such a turmoil; or how you can keep your mind on it, for that matter."

Thea glanced about the room and suddenly put her hand up to her hair. "With all this paint on my face, I must look like something you picked up on Second Avenue. I hope there are no Colorado reformers about, Doctor Archie." She sniffed the savour of the grill as the waiter uncovered it. "Yes, draught beer, please. No, thank you, Fred, *no* champagne.—To go back to your question, Doctor Archie, you can believe I keep my mind on it! That's the whole trick, in so far as stage experience goes; keeping right there every second. If I think of anything else for a flash, I'm done for. But at the same time, you can take things in—with another part of your brain, maybe. It's different from what you get in study, more practical and conclusive. There are some things you learn best in calm, and some in storm. You learn the delivery of a part only before an audience."

"Heaven help us!" gasped Ottenburg. "Aren't you hungry, though! It's beautiful to see you eat."

"Glad you like it. Of course I'm hungry. Are you staying over for 'Rheingold' Friday afternoon?"

"My dear Thea"—Fred lit a cigarette—"I'm a serious business man now. I have to sell beer. I'm due in Chicago on Wednesday. I'd come back to hear you, but *Fricka* is not an alluring part."

"Then you've never heard it well done." She spoke up hotly. "Fat German woman scolding her husband, eh? That's not my idea. Wait till you hear my *Fricka*. It's a beautiful part." She leaned forward on the table and touched Archie's arm. "You remember, Doctor Archie, how my mother always wore her hair, parted in the middle and done low on her neck behind, so you got the shape of her head, and such a calm, white forehead? I wear mine like that for *Fricka*. A little more coronet effect, built up a little higher at the sides, but the idea's the same. I think you'll notice it."

Fred sighed. "Now I'll have to come back, of course. Archie, you'd better get busy about seats to-morrow."

"I can get you box seats, somewhere. I know nobody here, and I never ask for any." She began hunting among her wraps. "Oh, how funny! I've only these short woollen gloves, and no sleeves. Put on my coat first. Those English people can't make out where you got your lady." She rose laughing and plunged her arms into the coat Doctor Archie held for her. As she settled herself into it and buttoned it under her chin, she gave him an old signal with her eyelid. "I'd like to sing another part to-night. This is the sort of evening I fancy, when there's something to do. Let me see: I have to sing in 'Trovatore' Wednesday night, and there are rehearsals for the 'Ring' every day this week. Consider me dead until Saturday, Doctor Archie. I invite you both to dine with me on Saturday night, the day after 'Rheingold.' And Fred must leave early, for I want to talk to you alone. You've been here nearly a week, and I haven't had a serious word with you."

VIII

*T*he "Ring of the Niebelungs" was to be given at the Metropolitan on four successive Friday afternoons. After the first of these performances, Fred Ottenburg went home with Landry for tea. Landry was one of the few public entertainers who own real estate in New York. He lived in a little three-story brick house in Greenwich Village, which had been left to him by the same aunt who paid for his musical education.

Landry was born, and spent the first fifteen years of his life, on a rocky Connecticut farm not far from Cos Cob. His father was an ignorant, violent man, a bungling farmer and a brutal husband. The farmhouse, dilapidated and damp, stood in a hollow beside a marshy pond. Oliver had worked hard while he lived at home, although he was never clean, or warm in winter, and had wretched food all the year round. His spare, dry figure, his prominent larynx, and the peculiar red of his face and hands belonged to the chore-boy he had never outgrown. It was as if the farm, knowing he would escape from it as early as he could, had ground its mark on him deep. When he was fifteen, Oliver ran away and went to live with his Catholic aunt, whom his mother was never allowed to visit. The priest of Saint Joseph's Parish discovered that he had a voice.

Landry had an affection for the house where he had first learned what cleanliness and order and courtesy were. When his aunt died, he had the place done over, got an Irish housekeeper, and lived there with a great many beautiful things he had collected. His living expenses were never large, but he could not restrain himself from buying graceful and useless objects. He was a collector for much the same reason that he was a Catholic, and he was a Catholic chiefly because his father used to sit in the kitchen and read aloud to his hired men disgusting "exposures" of the Roman Church, enjoying equally the hideous stories and the outrage to his wife's feelings.

Landry had a fine collection of old French and Spanish fans. He kept them in an escritoire he had brought from Spain, but there were always a few of them lying about in his sitting-room. While he and his guest were waiting for the tea to be brought, Fred Ottenburg took up one of these fans from the low marble mantel-shelf and opened it in the firelight. One side was painted with a pearly sky and floating clouds. On the other was a shepherdess and a satin-coated shepherd.

"You ought not to keep these things about, like this, Oliver. The dust from your grate must get at them."

"It does, but I get them to enjoy, not to have. They're pleasant to glance at and to play with at odd times like this, when one is waiting for tea or something."

Fred smiled. The idea of Landry stretched out before his fire playing with his fans amused him. When the tea was brought, he drank his walking about, examining Landry's pictures. Presently he sat down at the piano and began softly to boom forth the shadowy introduction to the opera they had just heard.

He understood now why Thea had wished him to hear her in "Rheingold." It had been clear to him as soon as *Fricka* rose from sleep and looked out over the young world, stretching one white arm toward the new Götterburg gleaming on the heights. *"Wotan! Gemahl! erwache!"* . . . She had wished him to see her because she had a distinct kind of loveliness for this part, a shining beauty like the light of sunset on distant sails. *Fricka* had

been sung as a jealous spouse for so long that he had forgot she meant
wisdom before she meant domestic order, and that, in any event, she was
always a goddess. The *Fricka* of that afternoon was so clear and sunny, so
nobly conceived, that she quite redeemed from shabbiness the helplessness
and unscrupulousness of the gods. Her reproaches to *Wotan* were the
pleadings of a tempered mind, a consistent sense of beauty.

　　　Ottenburg played on, as he happened to remember. In the scene
between *Fricka* and *Wotan,* he stopped. "I can't seem to get the voices, in
there."

　　　Landry chuckled. "Don't try. I know it well enough. I expect
I've been over that with her a thousand times. I was playing for her almost
every day when she was first working on it. When she begins to study a part,
she's hard to work with: so slow you'd think she was stupid if you didn't
know her. Of course she blames it all on her accompanist. It goes on like
that for weeks sometimes. This did. She kept shaking her head and staring
and looking gloomy. All at once, she got her line—it usually comes suddenly, after stretches of not getting anywhere at all—and after that it kept
changing and clearing. As she worked her voice into it, it got more and
more of that 'gold' quality that makes her *Fricka* so different."

　　　Fred began *Fricka's* first aria again. "It's certainly different. Curious how she does it. Such a beautiful idea, out of a part that's always been
so ungrateful."

　　　Landry shook his head. "What she does is interesting because she
does it. Even the things she discards are suggestive. I regret some of them.
Her conceptions are coloured in so many different ways. You've heard her
Elisabeth? Wonderful, isn't it? She was working on that part years ago when
her mother was ill. I could see her anxiety and grief getting more and more
into the part. The last act is heart-breaking. It's as homely as a country
prayer-meeting: might be any lonely woman getting ready to die. It's full
of the thing every plain creature finds out for himself, but that never gets
written down."

　　　Fred looked over his shoulder at Landry, stretched out by the
fire. "You have a great time watching her, don't you?"

　　　"Oh, yes!" replied Landry simply. "I'm not interested in much
that goes on in New York. Now, if you'll excuse me, I'll have to dress."
He rose with a reluctant sigh. "Can I get you anything? Some whiskey?"

　　　"Thank you, no. I'll amuse myself here. I don't often get a
chance at a good piano when I'm away from home. You haven't had this
one long, have you? Action's a bit stiff. I say"—he stopped Landry in the
doorway—"has Thea ever been down here?"

Landry turned back. "Yes. She came several times when I had erysipelas. I was a nice mess, with two nurses. She brought down some inside window-boxes, planted with crocuses and things. Very cheering, only I couldn't see them or her."

"Didn't she like your place?"

"She thought she did, but I fancy it was a good deal cluttered up for her taste. I could hear her pacing about like something in a cage. She pushed the piano back against the wall and the chairs into corners, and she broke my amber elephant." Landry took a yellow object some four inches high from one of his low bookcases. "You can see where his leg is glued on—a souvenir. Yes, he's lemon amber, very fine."

Landry disappeared behind the curtains and in a moment Fred heard the wheeze of an atomizer. He put the amber elephant on the piano beside him and seemed to get a great deal of amusement out of the beast.

IX

*W*hen Archie and Ottenburg dined with Thea on Saturday evening, they were served downstairs in the hotel dining-room, but they were to have their coffee in her own apartment. As they were going up in the elevator after dinner, Fred turned suddenly to Thea. "And why, please, did you break Landry's amber elephant?"

She looked guilty and began to laugh. "Hasn't he got over that yet? I didn't really mean to break it. I was perhaps careless. His things are so overpetted that I was tempted to be careless with a lot of them."

"How can you be so heartless, when they're all he has in the world?"

"He has me. I'm a great deal of diversion for him; all he needs. There," she said as she opened the door into her own hall, "I shouldn't have said that before the elevator boy."

"Even an elevator boy couldn't make a scandal about Oliver."

The waiter arrived with the coffee. Thea poured it impatiently, as if it were a ceremony in which she did not believe. She was wearing a white dress trimmed with crystals which had rattled a good deal during dinner, as all her movements had been abrupt and nervous, and she had twisted the dark velvet rose at her girdle until it looked rumpled and weary.

"I don't see why people go to the opera, anyway," she said

suddenly. "I suppose they get something, or think they do."

Fred approached her. "What's the matter with you to-night? You have something on your mind."

"I've a good deal. Too much to be an agreeable hostess." She turned quickly away from the coffee-table and sat down on the piano-bench, facing the two men. "For one thing, there's a change in the cast for Friday afternoon. They're going to let me sing *Sieglinde*." Her frown did not conceal the pleasure with which she made this announcement.

"Are you going to keep us dangling about here forever, Thea? Archie and I are supposed to have other things to do." Fred looked at her with an excitement quite as apparent as her own.

"Here I've been ready to sing *Sieglinde* for two years, kept in torment, and now it comes off within two weeks, just when I want to be seeing something of Doctor Archie. I don't know what their plans are down there. After Friday they may let me cool for a while, or they may rush me. I suppose it depends somewhat on how things go Friday afternoon."

"Oh, they'll go, fast enough! That's better suited to your voice than anything you've sung here." Ottenburg crossed the room and standing beside her began to play *"Du bist der Lenz."*

With a violent movement Thea caught his wrists and pushed his hands away from the keys.

"Fred, can't you be serious? A thousand things may happen between this and Friday to put me out." She clenched her hands and opened them despairingly. "It's impossible to sing a part like that well the first time, except for the sort who will never sing it any better. Everything hangs on that first performance, and that's bound to be bad. There you are"—she shrugged disdainfully. "For one thing, they change the cast at the eleventh hour and then rehearse the life out of me."

Ottenburg put down his cup with exaggerated care. "Still, you really want to do it, you know."

"Want to?" she repeated indignantly; "of course I want to! If this were only next Thursday night—But between now and Friday I'll do nothing but fret away my strength. Oh, I'm not saying I don't need the rehearsals! But I don't need them strung out through a week. That system's well enough for phlegmatic singers; it only drains me. Every single feature of operatic routine is detrimental to me. I usually go on like a horse that's been fixed to lose a race. I have to work hard to do my worst, let alone my best. I wish you could hear me sing well, just once"—she turned to Fred defiantly; "I have, a few times in my life, when there was nothing to be gained by it."

Fred approached her and held out his hand. "My dear girl, if I could bridge over the agony between now and Friday for you—But you know the rules of the game; why torment yourself? You saw the other night that you had the part under your thumb. Now walk, sleep, play with Archie, keep your tiger hungry, and she'll spring all right on Friday. I'll be there to see her, and there'll be more than I. Harsanyi is on the *Wilhelm der Grosse;* gets in on Thursday."

"Harsanyi?" Thea's eye lighted. "I haven't seen him for years. We always miss each other." She paused, hesitating. "Yes, I should like that. But he'll be busy, maybe?"

"He gives his first concert at Carnegie Hall, week after next. Better send him a box if you can."

"Yes, I'll manage it." Thea took his hand again. "Oh, I should like that, Fred!" she added impulsively. "Even if I were put out, he'd get the idea."

Fred was going toward the door when Thea called him back. She pulled a flower out of a bouquet on the piano and absently drew the stem through the lapel of his coat. "I shall be walking in the Park to-morrow afternoon, on the reservoir path, between four and five, if you care to join me. After Harsanyi I'd rather please you than anyone else. You know a lot, but he knows even more than you."

"Thank you. *Schlafen Sie wohl!*" He kissed her fingers and waved from the door, closing it behind him.

"He's the right sort, Thea." Doctor Archie looked warmly after his disappearing friend. "I've always hoped you'd make it up with Fred."

"Well, haven't I? Oh, marry him, you mean! Just at present he's not in the marriage market any more than I am, is he?"

"No, I suppose not. It's a damned shame that a man should be tied up as he is, wasting all the best years of his life. A woman with general paresis ought to be legally dead."

"Don't let us talk about Fred's wife, please. He had no business to get into such a mess, and he had no business to stay in it. He's always been a softy where women were concerned."

"Most of us are, I'm afraid," Doctor Archie admitted meekly.

"Too much light in here, isn't there? Tires one's eyes. The stage lights are hard on mine." Thea began turning them out. "We'll leave the little one, over the piano." She sank down by Archie on the deep sofa. "We two have so much to talk about that we keep away from it altogether; have you noticed? We don't even nibble the edges. I wish we had Landry here to-night to play for us. He's very comforting."

"I'm afraid you don't have enough personal life, outside your work, Thea." The doctor looked at her anxiously.

She smiled at him with her eyes half-closed. "My dear doctor, I don't have any. Your work becomes your personal life. You are not much good until it does. It's like being woven into a big web. You can't pull away, because all your little tendrils are woven into the picture. It takes you up, and uses you, and spins you out; and that is your life. Not much else can happen to you."

"Didn't you think of marrying, several years ago?"

"You mean Nordquist? Yes; but I changed my mind. We had been singing a good deal together. He's a splendid creature."

"Were you in love with him, Thea?" the doctor asked hopefully.

She smiled again. "I don't think I know just what that expression means. I've never been able to find out. I think I was in love with you when I was little, but not with anyone since then. There are a great many ways of caring for people. It's not, after all, a simple state, like measles or tonsillitis. Nordquist is a taking sort of man. He and I were out in a rowboat once in a terrible storm. The lake was fed by glaciers—ice water—and we couldn't have swum a stroke if the boat had filled. If we hadn't both been strong and kept our heads, we'd have gone down. We pulled for every ounce there was in us, and we just got off with our lives. We were always being thrown together like that, under some kind of pressure. Yes, for a while I thought he would make everything right." She paused and sank back, resting her head on a cushion, pressing her eyelids down with her fingers. "You see," she went on abruptly, "he had a wife and two children. He hadn't lived with her for several years, but when she heard that he wanted to marry again, she began to make trouble. He earned a good deal of money, but he was careless and always wretchedly in debt. He came to me one day and told me he thought his wife would settle for a hundred thousand marks and consent to a divorce. I got very angry and sent him away. Next day he came back and said he thought she'd take fifty thousand."

Doctor Archie drew away from her, to the end of the sofa. "Good God, Thea! What sort of people—" He stopped and shook his head.

Thea rose and stood beside him, her hand on his shoulder. "That's exactly how it struck me," she said quietly. "Oh, we have things in common, things that go away back, under everything. You understand, of course. Nordquist didn't. He thought I wasn't willing to part with the money. I couldn't let myself buy him from Frau Nordquist, and he couldn't see why. He had always thought I was close about money, so he attributed it to that. I am careful"—she ran her arm through Archie's, and when he rose began to walk about the room with him. "I can't be careless with money. I began the world on six hundred dollars, and it was the price of a man's life. Ray Kennedy had worked hard and been sober and denied himself, and when he died he had six hundred dollars to show for it. I always measure things by that six hundred dollars, just as I measure high buildings by the Moonstone standpipe. There are standards we can't get away from."

He took her hand. "I don't believe we should be any happier if we did get away from them. You look"—glancing down at her head and shoulders—"sometimes so like your mother."

"Thank you. You couldn't say anything nicer to me than that. On Friday afternoon, didn't you think?"

"Yes, but at other times, too. I love to see it. Do you know what I thought about, that first night when I heard you sing? I kept remembering the night I took care of you when you had pneumonia, when you were ten years old. You were a terribly sick child, and I was a country doctor without much experience. There were no oxygen tanks about then. You pretty nearly slipped away from me. If you had—"

She dropped her head on his shoulder. "I'd have saved myself and you a lot of trouble, wouldn't I? Dear Doctor Archie!" she murmured.

"As for me, life would have been a pretty bleak stretch, with you left out." The doctor took one of the crystal pendants that hung from her shoulder and looked into it thoughtfully. "I guess I'm a romantic old fellow, underneath. And you've always been my romance. Those years when you were growing up were my happiest. When I dream about you, I always see you as a little girl."

They paused by the open window. "Do you? Nearly all my dreams, except those about breaking down on the stage or missing trains, are about Moonstone. You tell me the old house has been pulled down, but it stands in my mind, every stick and timber. In my sleep I go all about it, and look in the right drawers and cupboards for everything. I often dream that I'm hunting for my rubbers in that pile of overshoes that was always under the hatrack in the hall. I pick up every overshoe and know whose it is, but I can't find my own. Then the school-bell begins to ring and I begin to cry. That's the house I rest in when I'm tired. All the old furniture and the worn spots in the carpet—it rests my mind to go over them."

They were looking out of the window. Thea kept his arm.

Down on the river four battleships were anchored in line, brilliantly lighted, and launches were coming and going, bringing the men ashore. A search-light from one of the ironclads was playing on the great headland up the river, where it makes its first resolute turn. Overhead the night-blue sky was intense and clear.

"There's so much that I want to tell you," she said at last, "and it's hard to explain. My life is full of jealousies and disappointments, you know. You get to hating people who do contemptible work and still get on just as well as you do. There are many disappointments in my profession, and bitter, bitter contempts!" Her face hardened, and looked much older. "If you love the good thing vitally, enough to give up for it all that one must give up, then you must hate the cheap thing just as hard. I tell you, there is such a thing as creative hate! A contempt that drives you through fire, makes you risk everything and lose everything, makes you a long sight better than you ever knew you could be." As she glanced at Doctor Archie's face, Thea stopped short and turned her own face away. Her eyes followed the path of the searchlight up the river and rested upon the illumined headland.

"You see," she went on more calmly, "voices are accidental things. You find plenty of good voices in common women, with common minds and common hearts. Look at that woman who sang *Ortrud* with me last week. She's new here and the people are wild about her. 'Such a beautiful volume of tone!' they say. I give you my word she's as stupid as an owl and as coarse as a pig, and anyone who knows anything about singing would see that in an instant. Yet she's quite as popular as Necker, who's a great artist. How can I get much satisfaction out of the enthusiasm of a house that likes her atrociously bad performance at the same time it pretends to like mine? If they like her, then they ought to hiss me off the stage. We stand for things that are irreconcilable, absolutely. You can't try to do things right and not despise the people who do them wrong. How can I be indifferent? If that doesn't matter, then nothing matters. Well, sometimes I've come home as I did the other night when you first saw me, so full of bitterness that it was as if my mind were full of daggers. And I've gone to sleep and wakened up in the Kohlers' garden, with the pigeons and the white rabbits, so happy! And that saves me." She sat down on the piano-bench. Archie thought she had forgotten all about him, until she called his name. Her voice was soft now, and wonderfully sweet. "You see, Doctor Archie, what one really strives for in art is not the sort of thing you are likely to find when you drop in for a performance at the opera. What one strives for is so far away, so beautiful"—she lifted her shoulders with a long breath, folded her hands in her lap and sat looking at him with a resignation which made her face noble—"that there's nothing one can say about it."

Without understanding her very well, Archie was passionately stirred for her. "I've always believed in you, Thea; always believed," he muttered.

She smiled and closed her eyes. "They save me: the old things, things like the Kohlers' garden. I try all the new things, and then go back to the old. Perhaps my feelings were stronger then. A child's attitude toward everything is an artist's attitude. I am more or less of an artist now, but then I was nothing else. When I went with you to Chicago that first time, I carried with me the essentials of all I shall ever do. The point to which I could go was scratched in me then. I haven't reached it yet, by a long way."

Archie had a swift flash of memory. Pictures passed before him.

"You mean," he asked wonderingly, "that you knew then that you were so gifted?"

Thea looked up at him.

"Oh, I didn't know anything! Not enough to ask you for my trunk when I needed it. But you see, when I set out from Moonstone with you, I had had a rich, romantic past. I had lived a long, eventful life, and an artist's life, every hour of it."

There was a long, warm silence. Thea was looking hard at the floor, as if she were seeing down through years and years, and her old friend stood watching her bent head. His look was one with which he used to watch her long ago, and which, even in thinking about her, had become a habit of his face. It was full of solicitude, and a kind of secret gratitude, as if to thank her for some inexpressible pleasure of the heart. Thea turned presently toward the piano and began softly to waken an old air he loved:

"Ca' the yowes to the knowes,
Ca' them where the heather grows,
Ca' them where the burnie rowes,
        My bonnie dear-ie."

X

*O*ttenburg dismissed his taxicab at the Ninety-First Street entrance of the Park and floundered across the drive through a wild spring snowstorm. When he reached the reservoir path, he saw Thea ahead of him, walking rapidly against the wind. Except for that one figure, the path was deserted. A flock of gulls were hovering over the reservoir, seeming bewildered by the driving currents of snow that whirled above the black water and then disappeared within it. When he had almost overtaken Thea, Fred called to her, and she turned and waited for him with her back to the wind. Her hair and furs were powdered with snowflakes, and she looked like some rich-pelted animal, with warm blood, that had run in out of the woods. Fred laughed as he took her hand.

"No use asking how you do! You surely needn't feel much anxiety about Friday, when you can look like this."

She moved close to the iron fence to make room for him beside her, and faced the wind again. "Oh, I'm *well* enough, in so far as that goes. But I'm not lucky about stage appearances. I'm easily upset, and the most perverse things happen."

"You still get nervous?"

"Of course I do. I don't mind nerves so much as getting numbed," Thea muttered, sheltering her face for a moment with her muff. "It's the thing I *want* to do that I can never do. Any other effects I can get easily enough."

"You get effects—and not only with your voice. You're as much at home on the stage as you were down in Panther Cañon. Didn't you get some of your ideas down there?"

She nodded. "Oh, yes! Out of the rocks, out of the dead people." She put her gloved fingers on Fred's arm. "I don't know how I can ever thank you enough. I don't know if I'd ever have got anywhere without Panther Cañon. How did you know that was the one thing to do for me? It's the sort of thing nobody ever helps one to, in this world. How did you know?"

"I didn't know. Anything else would have done as well. It was your creative hour. I knew you were getting a lot, but I didn't realize how much."

Thea walked on in silence. She seemed to be thinking.

"Do you know what they really taught me?" she came out suddenly. "They taught me the inevitable hardness of human life. No artist gets far who doesn't know that. And you can't know it with your mind. You have to realize it in your body; deep. It's an animal sort of feeling. I sometimes think it's the strongest of all."

She turned her back to the wind, wiping away the snow that clung to her brows and lashes. "Ugh!" she exclaimed; "no matter how long a breath you have, the storm has a longer. I haven't signed for next season, yet, Fred. I'm holding out for a big contract: forty performances. Necker won't be able to do much next winter. It's going to be one of those between seasons; the old singers are too old, and the new ones are too new. They might as well risk me as anybody. So I'm asking good terms. The next five or six years are going to be my best."

"You'll get what you demand, if you are uncompromising. I'm safe in congratulating you now."

Thea laughed. "It's a little early. I may not get it at all. They don't seem to be breaking their necks to meet me. I can go back to Dresden."

As they turned the curve and walked westward, they got the wind from the side, and talking was easier.

Fred lowered his collar and shook the snow from his shoulders. "Oh, I don't mean the contract particularly. I congratulate you on what you can do, and on being able to care so much. That, after all, is the unusual thing."

She looked at him sharply, with a certain apprehension. "Care? Why shouldn't I care? If I didn't, I'd be in a bad way. What else have I got?" She stopped with a challenging interrogation, but Ottenburg did not reply. "You mean," she persisted, "that you don't care as much as you used to?"

"I care about your success, of course." Fred fell into a slower pace. Thea felt at once that he was talking seriously and had dropped the tone of half-ironical exaggeration he had used with her of late years. "And I'm grateful to you for what you demand from yourself, when you might get off so easily. You demand more and more all the time, and you'll do more and more. One is grateful to anybody for that; it makes life in general a little less sordid. But as a matter of fact, I'm not much interested in how anybody sings anything."

"That's too bad of you, when I'm just beginning to see what is worth doing, and how I want to do it!" Thea spoke in an injured tone.

"That's what I congratulate you on. It's how long you're able to keep it up that tells the story. When you needed enthusiasm from the outside, I was able to give it to you. Now you must let me withdraw."

"I'm not tying you, am I?" she flashed out. "But withdraw to what? What do you want?"

He shrugged. "I might ask you, What have I got? I want things that wouldn't interest you; that you probably wouldn't understand. For one thing, I want a son to bring up."

"I can understand that. It seems to me reasonable. Have you also found somebody you want to marry?"

"Not particularly." They turned another curve, which brought the wind to their backs, and they walked on in comparative calm, with the snow blowing past them. "It's not your fault, but, you see, I've had you too much in my mind. I've not given myself a fair chance in other directions. I was in Rome when you and Nordquist were there. If that had kept up, it might have cured me."

"It might have cured a good many things," she remarked grimly.

Fred nodded sympathetically and went on. "I'm nearly forty years old, and I've served my turn. You have done what I hoped for you, what I was honestly willing to lose you for—then. I'm older now, and I think I was an ass. I wouldn't do it again if I had the chance, not much! But I'm not sorry."

Thea stopped by the fence and looked over into the black choppiness on which the snowflakes fell and disappeared with magical rapidity. Her face was both angry and troubled. "So you really feel I've been ungrateful. I thought you sent me out to get something. I didn't know you wanted me to bring in something easy. I thought you wanted something—" She took a deep breath and shrugged her shoulders. "But there! nobody on God's earth wants it, *really!* If one other person wanted it"—she thrust her hand out before him and clenched it—"my God, what I could do!"

Fred laughed dismally. "My girl, can't you see that anybody else who wanted it as you do would be your rival, your deadliest danger?"

But she seemed not to take in his protest at all. She went on vindicating herself. "It's taken me a long while to do anything, of course, and I've only begun to see daylight. But anything good is—expensive. It has not seemed long. I've always felt responsible to you."

Fred looked at her face intently, through the veil of snowflakes, and shook his head. "To me? You are a truthful woman, and you don't mean to lie to me. But after the one responsibility you do feel, I doubt if you've enough left to feel responsible to God! Still, if you've ever in an idle hour fooled yourself with thinking I had anything to do with it, Heaven knows I'm grateful."

"Even if I'd married Nordquist," Thea went on, turning down the path again, "there would have been something left out. There always is. In a way, I've always been married to you. I'm not very flexible; never was and never shall be. You caught me young. I could never have that over again. One can't, after one begins to know anything. But I look back on it. My life hasn't been a gay one, any more than yours. If I shut things out from you, you shut them out from me. We've been a help and a hindrance to each other. I guess it's always that way, the good and the bad all mixed up. There's only one thing that's all beautiful—and always beautiful!"

"Yes, I know." Fred looked sidewise at the outline of her head against the thickening atmosphere. "And you give one the impression that that is enough. I've gradually, gradually given you up."

"See, the lights are coming out." Thea pointed to where they flickered, flashes of violet through the grey tree-tops. Lower down the globes along the drives were becoming a pale lemon colour. "Yes, I don't see why anybody wants to marry an artist, anyhow. I remember Ray Kennedy used to say he didn't see how any woman could marry a gambler, for she would only be marrying what the game left." She shook her shoulders impatiently. "Who marries who is a small matter, after all. But you've cared longer and more than anybody else, and I'd like to have somebody human to make a report to once in a while. If you're not interested, I'll do my best, anyhow. I've only a few friends, but I can lose every one of them, if it has to be. I learned how to lose when my mother died.—We must hurry now. My car must be waiting."

The blue light about them was growing deeper and darker, and the falling snow and the faint trees had become violet. To the south, over Broadway, there was an orange reflection in the clouds. Motor and carriage lights flashed by on the drive below the reservoir path, and the air was strident with horns and shrieks from the whistles of the mounted policemen.

Fred gave Thea his arm as they descended from the embankment. "I guess you'll never manage to lose me or Archie, Thea. But loving you is an heroic discipline. It wears a man out. Tell me one thing: could

I have kept you, once, if I'd put on every screw?"

She hurried him along, talking rapidly, as if to get it over. "You might have kept me in misery for a while, perhaps. I don't know. You could have made it hard. I'm not ungrateful. I was a difficult proposition to deal with. I understand now." She stopped beside a car that waited at the curb and gave him her hand. "There. We part friends?"

Fred looked at her. "You know. Ten years."

"I'm not ungrateful," Thea repeated as she got into her car.

"Yes," she reflected, as the motor cut into the Park carriage road, "we don't get fairy tales in this world, and he has, after all, cared more and longer than anybody else." It was dark outside now, and the light from the lamps along the drive flashed into the car. The snowflakes hovered like swarms of white bees about the globes.

Thea sat motionless in one corner staring out of the window at the car lights that wove in and out among the trees, all seeming to be bent upon joyous courses. Taxicabs were still new in New York, and the theme of popular minstrelsy. Landry had sung her a ditty he heard in some theatre on Third Avenue, about

> "But there passed him a bright-eyed taxi
> With the girl of his heart inside."

Almost inaudibly Thea began to hum the air, though she was thinking of something serious, something that had touched her deeply. At the beginning of the season, when she was not singing often, she had gone one afternoon to hear Paderewski's recital. In front of her sat an old German couple, evidently poor people who had made sacrifices to pay for their excellent seats. Their intelligent enjoyment of the music, and their friendliness with each other, had interested her more than anything on the programme. When the pianist began a lovely melody in the first movement of the Beethoven D minor sonata, the old lady put out her plump hand and touched her husband's sleeve and they looked at each other in recognition. They both wore glasses, but such a look! Like forget-me-nots, and so full of happy recollections. Thea wanted to put her arms around them and ask them how they had been able to keep a feeling like that, like a nosegay in a glass of water.

XI

*D*octor Archie saw nothing of Thea during the following week. After several fruitless efforts, he succeeded in getting a word with her over the telephone, but she sounded so distracted and driven that he was glad to say good night and hang up the instrument. There were, she told him, rehearsals not only for "Walküre," but also for "Götterdämmerung," in which she was to sing *Waltraute* two weeks later.

On Thursday afternoon Thea got home late, after an exhausting rehearsal. She was in no happy frame of mind. Madame Necker, who had been very gracious to her that night when she went on to complete Gloeckler's performance of *Sieglinde,* had, since Thea was cast to sing the part instead of Gloeckler in the production of the "Ring," been chilly and disapproving, distinctly hostile. Thea had always felt that she and Necker stood for the same sort of endeavour, and that Necker recognized it and had a cordial feeling for her. In Germany she had several times sung *Brangane* to Necker's *Isolde,* and the older artist had let her know that she thought she sang it well. It was a bitter disappointment to find that the approval of so honest an artist as Necker could not stand the test of any significant recognition by the management.

Thea had her dinner sent up to her apartment, and it was a very poor one. She tasted the soup and then indignantly put on her wraps to go out and hunt a dinner. As she was going to the elevator, she had to admit that she was behaving foolishly. She took off her hat and coat and ordered another dinner. When it arrived, it was no better than the first. There was even a burnt match under the milk toast. She had a sore throat, which made swallowing painful and boded ill for the morrow. Although she had been speaking in whispers all day to save her throat, she now perversely summoned the housekeeper and demanded an account of some laundry that had been lost. The housekeeper was indifferent and impertinent, and Thea got angry and scolded violently. She knew it was very bad for her to get into a rage just before bedtime, and after the housekeeper left she realized that for ten dollars' worth of underclothing she had been unfitting herself for a performance which might eventually mean many thousands. The best thing now would be to stop reproaching herself for her lack of sense, but she was too tired to control her thoughts.

While she was undressing—Thérèse was brushing out her *Sieglinde* wig in the trunk-room—she went on chiding herself bitterly. "And how am I ever going to get to sleep in this state?" she kept asking herself. "If I don't sleep, I'll be perfectly worthless to-morrow. I'll go down there to-morrow and make a fool of myself. If I'd let that laundry alone with whatever nigger has stolen it—*Why* did I undertake to reform the management of this hotel to-night? After to-morrow I could pack up and leave the place. There's the Philamon—I liked the rooms there better, anyhow—and the Umberto—" She began going over the advantages and disadvantages of different apartment hotels. Suddenly she checked herself. "What *am* I doing this for? I can't move into another hotel to-night. I'll keep this up till morning. I shan't sleep a wink."

Should she take a hot bath, or shouldn't she? Sometimes it relaxed her, and sometimes it roused her and fairly put her beside herself. Between the conviction that she must sleep and the fear that she couldn't, she hung paralyzed. When she looked at her bed, she shrank from it in every nerve. She was much more afraid of it than she had ever been of the stage of any opera house. It yawned before her like the sunken road at Waterloo.

She rushed into her bathroom and locked the door. She would risk the bath, and defer the encounter with the bed a little longer. She lay in the bath half an hour. The warmth of the water penetrated to her bones, induced pleasant reflections and a feeling of well-being. It was very nice to have Doctor Archie in New York, after all, and to see him get so much satisfaction out of the little companionship she was able to give him. She liked people who got on, and who became more interesting as they grew older. There was Fred; he was much more interesting now than he had been at thirty. He was intelligent about music, and he must be very intelligent in his business, or he would not be at the head of the Brewers' Trust. She respected that kind of intelligence and success. Any success was good. She herself had made a good start, at any rate, and now, if she could get to sleep—Yes, they were all more interesting than they used to be. Look at Harsanyi, who had been so long retarded; what a place he had made for himself in Vienna! If she could get to sleep, she would show him something to-morrow that he would understand.

She got quickly into bed and moved about freely between the sheets. Yes, she was warm all over. A cold, dry breeze was coming in from the river, thank goodness! She tried to think about her little rock-house and the Arizona sun and the blue sky. But that led to memories which were still too disturbing. She turned on her side, closed her eyes, and tried an old device.

She entered her father's front door, hung her hat and coat on the rack, and stopped in the parlour to warm her hands at the stove. Then she went out through the dining-room, where the boys were getting their lessons at the long table; through the sitting-room, where Thor was asleep in his cot bed, his dress and stockings hanging on a chair. In the kitchen she stopped for her lantern and her hot brick. She hurried up the back stairs and through the windy loft to her own glacial room. The illusion was marred only by the consciousness that she ought to brush her teeth before she went to bed, and that she never used to do it. Why—? The water was frozen solid in the pitcher, so she got over that. Once between the red blankets there was a short, fierce battle with the cold; then, warmer—warmer. She could hear her father shaking down the hard-coal burner for the night, and the wind rushing and banging down the village street. The boughs of the cottonwood, hard as bone, rattled against her gable. The bed grew softer and warmer. Everybody was warm and well downstairs. The sprawling old house had gathered them all in, like a hen, and had settled down over its brood. They were all warm in her father's house. Softer and softer. She was asleep. She slept ten hours without turning over. From sleep like that, one awakes in shining armour.

On Friday afternoon there was an inspiring audience; not an empty chair in the house. Ottenburg and Doctor Archie had seats in the orchestra circle, got from a ticket broker. Landry had not been able to get a seat, so he roamed about in the back of the house, where he usually stood when he dropped in after his own turn in vaudeville was over. He was there so often and at such irregular hours that the ushers thought he was a singer's husband, or had something to do with the electrical plant.

Harsanyi and his wife were in a box, near the stage, in the second circle. Mrs. Harsanyi's hair was noticeably grey, but her face was fuller and handsomer than in those early years of struggle, and she was beautifully dressed. Harsanyi himself had changed very little. He had put on his best afternoon coat in honour of his pupil, and wore a pearl in his black ascot. His hair was longer and more bushy than he used to wear it, and there was now one grey lock on the right side. He had always been an elegant figure, even when he went about in shabby clothes and was crushed with work. Before the curtain rose, he was restless and nervous, and kept looking at his watch and wishing he had got a few more letters off before he left his hotel. He had not been in New York since the advent of the taxicab, and had allowed himself too much time. His wife knew that he was afraid of being disappointed this afternoon. He did not often go to the opera, because the stupid things that singers did vexed him, and it always put him in a rage if the conductor held the beat or in any way accommodated the score to the singer.

When the lights went out and the violins began to quaver their long D against the rude figure of the basses, Mrs. Harsanyi saw her husband's fingers fluttering on his knee in a rapid tattoo. At the moment when *Sieglinde* entered from the side door, she leaned toward him and whispered in his ear, "Oh, the lovely creature!" But he made no response, either by voice or gesture. Throughout the first scene he sat sunk in his chair, his head forward and his one yellow eye rolling restlessly and shining like a tiger's in the dark. His eye followed *Sieglinde* about the stage like a satellite, and when she sat at the table listening to *Siegmund's* long narrative, it never left her. When she prepared the sleeping draught and disappeared after *Hunding,* Harsanyi bowed his head still lower and put his hand over his eye to rest it. The tenor—a young man who sang with great vigour—went on:

> *"Wälse! Wälse!*
> *Wo ist dein Schwert?"*

Harsanyi smiled, but he did not look forth again until *Sieglinde* reappeared. She went through the story of her shameful bridal feast and into the Walhalla music, which she always sang so nobly, and the entrance of the one-eyed stranger:

> *"Mir allein*
> *Weckte das Auge."*

Mrs. Harsanyi glanced at her husband, wondering whether the singer on the stage could not feel his commanding glance. On came the *crescendo:*

> *"Was je ich verlor,*
> *Was je ich beweint,*
> *Wär' mir gewonnen."*

(All that I have lost,
All that I have mourned,
Would I then have won.)

Harsanyi touched his wife's arm softly.

Seated in the moonlight, the *Volsung* pair began their loving inspection of each other's beauties, and the music born of murmuring sound passed into her face, as the old poet said—and into her body as well. Into one lovely attitude after another the music swept her, love impelled her. And the voice gave out all that was best in it. Like the spring indeed, it blossomed into memories and prophecies, it recounted and it foretold, as she sang the story of her friendless life, and of how the thing which was truly herself, "bright as the day, rose to the surface" when in the hostile world she for the first time beheld her Friend. Fervently she rose into the hardier feeling of action and daring, the pride in hero-strength and hero-blood, until in a splendid burst, tall and shining like a Victory, she christened him:

"Siegmund—
So nenn' ich dich!"

Her impatience for the sword swelled with her anticipation of his act, and throwing her arms above her head, she fairly tore a sword out of the empty air for him, before *Nothung* had left the tree. *In höchster Trunkenheit,* indeed, she burst out with the flaming cry of their kinship: "If you are *Siegmund,* I am *Sieglinde!"* Laughing, singing, exulting—with their passion and their sword—the *Volsungs* ran out into the spring night.

As the curtain fell, Harsanyi turned to his wife. "At last," he sighed, "somebody with *enough!* Enough voice and talent and beauty, enough physical power. And such a noble, noble style!"

"I can scarcely believe it, Andor. I can see her now, that clumsy girl, hunched up over your piano. I can see her shoulders. She always seemed to labour so with her back. And I shall never forget that night when you found her voice."

The audience kept up its clamour until, after many reappearances with the tenor, Kronborg came before the curtain alone. The house met her with a greeting that was almost savage in its fierceness. The singer's eyes, sweeping the house, rested for a moment on Harsanyi, and she waved her long sleeve toward his box.

"She *ought* to be pleased that you are here," said Mrs. Harsanyi.

"I wonder if she knows how much she owes to you."

"She owes me nothing," replied her husband quickly. "She paid her way. She always gave something back, even then."

"I remember you said once that she would do nothing common," said Mrs. Harsanyi thoughtfully.

"Just so. She might fail, die, get lost in the pack. But if she achieved, it would be nothing common. There are people whom one can trust for that. There is one way in which they will never fail." Harsanyi retired into his own reflections.

After the second act, Fred Ottenburg brought Archie to the Harsanyis' box and introduced him as an old friend of Miss Kronborg. The head of a musical publishing house joined them, bringing with him a journalist and the president of a German singing society. The conversation was chiefly about the new *Sieglinde*. Mrs. Harsanyi was gracious and enthusiastic, her husband nervous and uncommunicative. He smiled mechanically, and politely answered questions addressed to him. "Yes, quite so." "Oh, certainly." Everyone, of course, said very usual things with great conviction. Mrs. Harsanyi was used to hearing and uttering the commonplaces which such occasions demanded. When her husband withdrew into the shadow, she covered his retreat by her sympathy and cordiality.

The chorus director said something about "dramatic temperament." The journalist insisted that it was "explosive force," "projecting power."

Ottenburg turned to Harsanyi.

"What is it, Mr. Harsanyi? You know all about her. What's her secret?"

Harsanyi rumpled his hair irritably and shrugged his shoulders. "Her secret? It is every artist's secret"—he waved his hand—"passion. That is all. It is an open secret, and perfectly safe. Like heroism, it is inimitable in cheap materials."

The lights went out. Fred and Archie left the box as the second act came on.

Artistic growth is, more than it is anything else, a refining of the sense of truthfulness. The stupid believe that to be truthful is easy; only the artist, the great artist, knows how difficult it is. That afternoon nothing new came to Thea Kronborg, no enlightenment, no inspiration. She merely came into full possession of things she had been refining and perfecting for so long. Her inhibitions chanced to be fewer than usual, and, within herself, she entered into the inheritance that she herself had laid up, into the fullness of the faith she had kept before she knew its name or its meaning.

Often when she sang, the best she had was unavailable; she could not break through to it, and every sort of distraction and mischance came between it and her. But this afternoon the closed roads opened, the gates dropped. What she had so often tried to reach lay under her hand. She had only to touch an idea to make it live.

While she was on the stage she was conscious that every movement was the right movement, that her body was absolutely the instrument of her idea. Not for nothing had she kept it so severely, kept it filled with such energy and fire. All that deep-rooted vitality flowered in her voice, her face, in her very finger-tips. She felt like a tree bursting into bloom. And her voice was as flexible as her body; equal to any demand, capable of every *nuance*. With the sense of its perfect companionship, its entire trustworthiness, she had been able to throw herself into the dramatic exigencies of the part, everything in her at its best and everything working together.

The third act came on, and the afternoon slipped by. Thea Kronborg's friends, old and new, seated about the house on different floors and levels, enjoyed her triumph according to their natures. There was one man there, whom nobody knew, who perhaps got greater pleasure out of that afternoon than Harsanyi himself. Up in the top gallery a grey-haired little Mexican, withered and bright as a string of peppers beside an adobe door, kept praying and cursing under his breath, beating on the brass railing and shouting "Brava! Brava!" until he was repressed by his neighbours.

He happened to be there because a Mexican band was to be a feature of Barnum and Bailey's circus that year. One of the managers of the show had travelled about the Southwest, signing up a lot of Mexican musicians at low wages, and had brought them to New York. Among them was Spanish Johnny. After Mrs. Tellamantez died, Johnny abandoned his trade and went out with his mandolin to pick up a living. His irregularities had become his regular mode of life.

When Thea Kronborg came out of the stage entrance on Fortieth Street, the sky was still flaming with the last rays of the sun that was sinking off behind the North River. A little crowd was lingering about the door—musicians who were waiting for their comrades in the orchestra, curious young men, and some poorly dressed girls who were hoping to get a glimpse of the singer. She bowed graciously to the group, through her veil, but she did not look to the right or left as she crossed the sidewalk to her car. Had she lifted her eyes an instant and glanced out through her white scarf, she must have seen the only man in the crowd who had removed his hat when she emerged, and who stood with it crushed up in his hand. And she would have known him, changed as he was. His lustrous black hair was full of grey, and his face was a good deal worn by the *extasi,* so that it seemed to have shrunk away from his shining eyes and teeth, and left them too prominent. But she would have known him. She passed so near that he could have touched her, and he did not put on his hat until her car had snorted away. Then he walked down Broadway with his hands in his overcoat pockets, wearing a smile which embraced all the stream of life that passed him and the lighted towers that rose into the limpid blue of the evening sky. If the singer, going home exhausted in her car, was wondering what was the good of it all, that smile, could she have seen it, would have answered her. It is the only commensurate answer.

Epilogue

Moonstone again, nearly twenty years after Thea Kronborg left it for the last time. The Methodists are giving an ice-cream sociable in the grove about the new court-house. It is a warm summer night of full moon. The paper lanterns which hang among the trees are foolish toys, only dimming, in little lurid circles, the great softness of the lunar light which floods the blue heavens and the high plateau. To the east the sand hills shine white as of old.

The people seated about under the cottonwoods are much smarter than the Methodists we used to know. The matrons who attend to serving the refreshments look younger for their years than did the women of Mrs. Kronborg's time, and the children look like city children.

At one of the tables, with her twin boys, sits a fair-haired, dimpled matron who was once Lily Fisher. The twins are well-behaved children; neat about their clothes, and always mindful of the proprieties they have learned at summer hotels. While they are eating their ice cream, a little scream of laughter breaks from an adjacent table. The twins look up. There sits a spry little old spinster whom they know well. She has a long chin, a long nose, and she is dressed like a young girl, with a pink sash and a lace garden hat with pink rosebuds. She is surrounded by a crowd of boys—loose and lanky, short and thick—who are joking with her, roughly but not unkindly.

"Mamma," one of the twins comes out in a shrill treble, "why is Tillie Kronborg always talking about a thousand dollars?"

The boys, hearing this question, break into a roar of laughter, the women titter behind their paper napkins, and even from Tillie there is a

little shriek of appreciation. The observing child's remark had made everyone suddenly realize that Tillie very often mentioned that particular sum of
money. In the spring, when she went to buy early strawberries, and was told
that they were thirty cents a box, she was sure to remind the grocer that,
though her name was Kronborg, she didn't get a thousand dollars a night.
In the autumn, when she bought her coal for the winter, she expressed
amazement at the price quoted her, and told the dealer he must have got
her mixed up with her niece, to think she could pay such a sum.

Tillie is the last Kronborg left in Moonstone. She lives alone in
a little house with a green yard, and keeps a fancy-work and millinery store.
Her business methods are informal, and she would never come out even at
the end of the year, if she did not receive a draft for a good round sum from
her niece at Christmas-time. The arrival of this draft always renews the
discussion as to what Thea would do for her aunt if she really did the right
thing. Most of the Moonstone people think Thea ought to take Tillie to
New York and keep her as a companion. While they are feeling sorry for
Tillie because she does not live at the Plaza, Tillie is trying not to hurt their
feelings by showing too plainly how much she realizes the superiority of her
position. She tries to be modest when she complains to the postmaster that
her New York paper is more than three days late. It means enough, surely,
on the face of it, that she is the only person in Moonstone who takes a New
York paper, or who has any reason for taking one.

When the candles had burned out and the coloured lanterns
were being taken down, a crowd of boys and girls escorted Tillie home. As
she tripped along with them, she was perhaps a shade troubled. The twin's
question rather lingered in her ears. Did she, perhaps, insist too much upon
that thousand dollars? Surely, people didn't for a minute think it was the
money she cared about? As for that, Tillie tossed her head—she didn't care
a rap. They must understand that this money was different.

When the laughing little compnay had left her at her gate and
gone weaving down the sidewalk through the leafy shadows, Tillie brought
out a rocking-chair and sat down on her porch. If you chanced to be passing
down that Moonstone street and saw that alert white figure rocking there
behind the screen of roses and lingering late into the night, you might feel
sorry for her, and how mistaken you would be! Tillie lives in a world full
of secret satisfactions. Thea Kronborg has given much noble pleasure to a
world that needs all it can get, but to no individual has she given more than
to her queer old aunt in Moonstone. What delightful things happen in
Tillie's mind as she sits there rocking! She goes back to those early days of

sand and sun, when Thea was a child and Tillie was herself, so it seems to her, "young." When she used to hurry to church to hear Mr. Kronborg's long sermons, and when Thea used to stand up by the organ and sing. Or she thinks about that wonderful time when the Metropolitan Opera Company sang a week's engagement in Kansas City, and Thea sent for her and had her stay with her at the Coates House and go to every performance at Convention Hall. She let Tillie go through her costume trunks and try on her wigs and jewels. And the kindness of Mr. Ottenburg! When Thea dined in her own room, her husband went down to dinner with Tillie, and never looked bored or absent-minded while she chattered. He took her every night to the performance and left her in a box to go through her raptures unobserved, which was what she had hoped for. Left alone, it seemed to her that she was actually on the stage with *Elsa* or *Elisabeth*. Tillie had lived fifty-odd years for that week, but she got it. Long ago, when she used to be working in the fields on her father's Minnesota farm, she couldn't help believing that she would some day have to do with the "wonderful," though her chances for it had then looked so slender.

On the morning after the sociable, Tillie hurried from her bedroom, threw open the doors and windows, and let the morning breeze blow through her little house. In two minutes a fire was roaring in her kitchen stove, in five she had set the table. At her household work Tillie was always bursting out with shrill snatches of song, and as suddenly stopping, right in the middle of a phrase, as if she had been struck dumb. She emerged upon the back porch with one of these bursts, and bent down to get her butter and cream out of the ice-box. The cat was purring on the bench, and the morning-glories were thrusting their purple trumpets in through the lattice-work in a friendly way. They reminded Tillie that while she was waiting for the coffee to boil she could get some flowers for her breakfast-table. She looked out uncertainly at a bush of sweet-briar that grew at the edge of her yard, off across the long grass and the tomato vines. The front porch, to be sure, was dripping with crimson ramblers: but never the rose in the hand for Tillie! She caught up the kitchen shears and off she dashed through grass and drenching dew. Snip, snip; the short-stemmed sweet-briars, salmon-pink and golden-hearted, with their inimitable woody perfume, fell into her apron.

After she put the eggs and toast on the table, Tillie took last Sunday's New York paper from the rack beside the cupboard and sat down, with it for company. In the Sunday paper there was always a page about singers, even in summer, and that week the musical page began with a

"London Letter," recounting Madame Kronborg's successes at Covent Garden. At the end of the notice, there was a short paragraph about her having sung for the King at Buckingham Palace and having been presented with a jewel by His Majesty.

Singing for the King; but goodness, she was always doing something like that! Tillie tossed her head. All through breakfast she kept sticking her sharp nose down into the glass of sweet-briar, with the old incredible lightness of heart. Once more she has to remind herself that it is all true, and is not something she has "made up." Like other romancers, she is a little terrified at seeing one of her wildest conceits admitted by the hard-headed world.

When her own friends tire of Tillie's stories, she goes over to the east part of town, where her legends are always welcome. The humbler people of Moonstone still live there. The same little houses sit under the cottonwoods; the men smoke their pipes in the front doorways, and the women do their washing in the back yards. The older women remember Thea, and how she used to come kicking her express wagon along the sidewalk, steering by the tongue and holding Thor in her lap. Not much happens in that part of town, and the people have long memories. A boy grew up on one of those streets who went to Omaha and built up a great business, and is now very rich. Moonstone people always speak of him and Thea together, as examples of Moonstone enterprise. They do, however, talk oftener of Thea. A voice has even a wider appeal than a fortune.

However much they may smile at her, the old inhabitants would miss Tillie. Her stories give them something to talk about and to conjecture about, cut off as they are from the restless currents of the world. The many naked little sandbars which lie between Venice and the mainland, in the seemingly stagnant water of the lagoons, are made habitable and wholesome only because, every night, a foot and a half of tide creeps in from the sea and winds its fresh brine up through all that network of shining waterways. So, into all the little settlements of quiet people, tidings of what their boys and girls are doing in the world bring refreshment; bring to the old, memories, and to the young, dreams.

Alexander's
Bridge

I

*L*ate one brilliant April afternoon Professor Lucius Wilson stood at the head of Chestnut Street, looking about him with the pleased air of a man of taste who does not very often get to Boston. He had lived there as a student, but for twenty years and more, since he had been Professor of Philosophy in a Western university, he had seldom come East except to take a steamer for some foreign port. Wilson was standing quite still, contemplating with a whimsical smile the slanting street, with its worn paving, its irregular, gravely colored houses, and the row of naked trees on which the thin sunlight was still shining. The gleam of the river at the foot of the hill made him blink a little, not so much because it was too bright as because he found it so pleasant. The few passers-by glanced at him unconcernedly, and even the children who hurried along with their school-bags under their arms seemed to find it perfectly natural that a tall brown gentleman should be standing there, looking up through his glasses at the gray housetops.

The sun sank rapidly; the silvery light had faded from the bare boughs and the watery twilight was setting in when Wilson at last walked down the hill, descending into cooler and cooler depths of grayish shadow. His nostril, long unused to it, was quick to detect the smell of wood smoke in the air, blended with the odor of moist spring earth and the saltiness that came up the river with the tide. He crossed Charles Street between jangling street cars and shelving lumber drays, and after a moment of uncertainty wound into Brimmer Street. The street was quiet, deserted, and hung with a thin bluish haze. He had already fixed his sharp eye upon the house which he reasoned should be his objective point, when he noticed a woman approaching rapidly from the opposite direction. Always an interested observer of women, Wilson would have slackened his pace anywhere to follow this one with his impersonal, appreciative glance. She was a person of distinction he saw at once, and, moreover, very handsome. She was tall, carried her beautiful head proudly, and moved with ease and certainty. One immediately took for granted the costly privileges and fine spaces that must lie in the background from which such a figure could emerge with this rapid and elegant gait. Wilson noted her dress, too,—for, in his way, he had an eye for such things,—particularly her brown furs and her hat. He got a blurred impression of her fine color, the violets she wore, her white gloves, and, curiously enough, of her veil, as she turned up a flight of steps in front of him and disappeared.

Wilson was able to enjoy lovely things that passed him on the wing as completely and deliberately as if they had been dug-up marvels, long anticipated, and definitely fixed at the end of a railway journey. For a few pleasurable seconds he quite forgot where he was going, and only after the door had closed behind her did he realize that the young woman had entered the house to which he had directed his trunk from the South Station that morning. He hesitated a moment before mounting the steps. "Can that," he murmured in amazement,—"can that possibly have been Mrs. Alexander?"

When the servant admitted him, Mrs. Alexander was still standing in the hallway. She heard him give his name, and came forward holding out her hand.

"Is it you, indeed, Professor Wilson? I was afraid that you might get here before I did. I was detained at a concert, and Bartley telephoned that he would be late. Thomas will show you your room. Had you rather have your tea brought to you there, or will you have it down here with me, while we wait for Bartley?"

Wilson was pleased to find that he had been the cause of her rapid walk, and with her he was even more vastly pleased than before. He followed her through the drawing-room into the library, where the wide back windows looked out upon the garden and the sunset and a fine stretch of silver-colored river. A harp-shaped elm stood stripped against the pale-colored evening sky, with ragged last year's birds' nests in its forks, and through the bare branches the evening star quivered in the misty air. The long brown room breathed the peace of a rich and amply guarded quiet. Tea was brought in immediately and placed in front of the wood fire. Mrs. Alexander sat down in a high-backed chair and began to pour it, while Wilson sank into a low seat opposite her and took his cup with a great sense of ease and harmony and comfort.

"You have had a long journey, have n't you?" Mrs. Alexander asked, after showing gracious concern about his tea. "And I am so sorry Bartley is late. He's often tired when he's late. He flatters himself that it is a little on his account that you have come to this Congress of Psychologists."

"It is," Wilson assented, selecting his muffin carefully; "and I hope he won't be tired to-night. But, on my own account, I'm glad to have a few moments alone with you, before Bartley comes. I was somehow afraid that my knowing him so well would not put me in the way of getting to know you."

"That's very nice of you." She nodded at him above her cup and smiled, but there was a little formal tightness in her tone which had not been there when she greeted him in the hall.

Wilson leaned forward. "Have I said something awkward? I live very far out of the world, you know. But I did n't mean that you would exactly fade dim, even if Bartley *were* here."

Mrs. Alexander laughed relentingly. "Oh, I'm not so vain! How terribly discerning you are."

She looked straight at Wilson, and he felt that this quick, frank glance brought about an understanding between them.

He liked everything about her, he told himself, but he particularly liked her eyes; when she looked at one directly for a moment they were like a glimpse of fine windy sky that may bring all sorts of weather.

"Since you noticed something," Mrs. Alexander went on, "it must have been a flash of the distrust I have come to feel whenever I meet any of the people who knew Bartley when he was a boy. It is always as if they were talking of some one I had never met. Really, Professor Wilson, it would seem that he grew up among the strangest people. They usually say that he has turned out very well, or remark that he always was a fine fellow. I never know what reply to make."

Wilson chuckled and leaned back in his chair, shaking his left foot gently. "I expect the fact is that we none of us knew him very well, Mrs. Alexander. Though I will say for myself that I was always confident he'd do something extraordinary."

Mrs. Alexander's shoulders gave a slight movement, suggestive of impatience. "Oh, I should think that might have been a safe prediction. Another cup, please?"

"Yes, thank you. But predicting, in the case of boys, is not so easy as you might imagine, Mrs. Alexander. Some get a bad hurt early and lose their courage; and some never get a fair wind. Bartley"—he dropped his chin on the back of his long hand and looked at her admiringly— "Bartley caught the wind early, and it has sung in his sails ever since."

Mrs. Alexander sat looking into the fire with intent preoccupation, and Wilson studied her half-averted face. He liked the suggestion of stormy possibilities in the proud curve of her lip and nostril. Without that, he reflected, she would be too cold.

"I should like to know what he was really like when he was a boy. I don't believe he remembers," she said suddenly. "Won't you smoke, Mr. Wilson?"

Wilson lit a cigarette. "No, I don't suppose he does. He was never introspective. He was simply the most tremendous response to stimuli I have ever known. We did n't know exactly what to do with him."

A servant came in and noiselessly removed the tea-tray. Mrs. Alexander screened her face from the firelight, which was beginning to throw wavering bright spots on her dress and hair as the dusk deepened.

"Of course," she said, "I now and again hear stories about things that happened when he was in college."

"But that is n't what you want." Wilson wrinkled his brows and looked at her with the smiling familiarity that had come about so quickly. "What you want is a picture of him, standing back there at the other end of twenty years. You want to look down through my memory."

She dropped her hands in her lap. "Yes, yes; that's exactly what I want."

At this moment they heard the front door shut with a jar, and Wilson laughed as Mrs. Alexander rose quickly. "There he is. Away with perspective! No past, no future for Bartley; just the fiery moment. The only moment that ever was or will be in the world!"

The door from the hall opened, a voice called "Winifred?" hurriedly, and a big man came through the drawing-room with a quick, heavy tread, bringing with him a smell of cigar smoke and chill out-of-doors air. When Alexander reached the library door, he switched on the lights and stood six feet and more in the archway, glowing with strength and cordiality and rugged, blond good looks. There were other bridge-builders in the world, certainly, but it was always Alexander's picture that the Sunday Supplement men wanted, because he looked as a tamer of rivers ought to look. Under his tumbled sandy hair his head seemed as hard and powerful as a catapult, and his shoulders looked strong enough in themselves to support a span of any one of his ten great bridges that cut the air above as many rivers.

After dinner Alexander took Wilson up to his study. It was a large room over the library, and looked out upon the black river and the row of white lights along the Cambridge Embankment. The room was not at all what one might expect of an engineer's study. Wilson felt at once the harmony of beautiful things that have lived long together without obtrusions of ugliness or change. It was none of Alexander's doing, of course; those warm consonances of color had been blending and mellowing before he was born. But t! e wonder was that he was not out of place there,—that it all seemed to glow like the inevitable background for his vigor and vehemence. He sat before the fire, his shoulders deep in the cushions of his chair, his powerful head upright, his hair rumpled above his broad forehead. He sat heavily, a cigar in his large, smooth hand, a flush of after-dinner color in his face, which wind and sun and exposure to all sorts of weather had left fair and clear-skinned.

"You are off for England on Saturday, Bartley, Mrs. Alexander tells me."

"Yes, for a few weeks only. There's a meeting of British engineers, and I'm doing another bridge in Canada, you know."

"Oh, every one knows about that. And it was in Canada that you met your wife, was n't it?"

"Yes, at Allway. She was visiting her great-aunt there. A most remarkable old lady. I was working with MacKeller then, an old Scotch engineer who had picked me up in London and taken me back to Quebec with him. He had the contract for the Allway Bridge, but before he began work on it he found out that he was going to die, and he advised the committee to turn the job over to me. Otherwise I'd never have got anything good so early. MacKeller was an old friend of Mrs. Pemberton, Winifred's aunt. He had mentioned me to her, so when I went to Allway she asked me to come to see her. She was a wonderful old lady."

"Like her niece?" Wilson queried.

Bartley laughed. "She had been very handsome, but not in Winifred's way. When I knew her she was little and fragile, very pink and white, with a splendid head and a face like fine old lace, somehow,—but perhaps I always think of that because she wore a lace scarf on her hair. She had such a flavor of life about her. She had known Gordon and Livingstone and Beaconsfield when she was young,—every one. She was the first woman of that sort I'd ever known. You know how it is in the West,—old people are poked out of the way. Aunt Eleanor fascinated me as few young women have ever done. I used to go up from the works to have tea with her, and sit talking to her for hours. It was very stimulating, for she could n't tolerate stupidity."

"It must have been then that your luck began, Bartley," said

Wilson, flicking his cigar ash with his long finger. "It's curious, watching boys," he went on reflectively. "I'm sure I did you justice in the matter of ability. Yet I always used to feel that there was a weak spot where some day strain would tell. Even after you began to climb, I stood down in the crowd and watched you with—well, not with confidence. The more dazzling the front you presented, the higher your façade rose, the more I expected to see a big crack zigzagging from top to bottom,"—he indicated its course in the air with his forefinger,—"then a crash and clouds of dust. It was curious. I had such a clear picture of it. And another curious thing, Bartley," Wilson spoke with deliberateness and settled deeper into his chair, "is that I don't feel it any longer. I am sure of you."

Alexander laughed. "Nonsense! It's not I you feel sure of; it's Winifred. People often make that mistake."

"No, I'm serious, Alexander. You've changed. You have decided to leave some birds in the bushes. You used to want them all."

Alexander's chair creaked. "I still want a good many," he said rather gloomily. "After all, life does n't offer a man much. You work like the devil and think you're getting on, and suddenly you discover that you've only been getting yourself tied up. A million details drink you dry. Your life keeps going for things you don't want, and all the while you are being built alive into a social structure you don't care a rap about. I sometimes wonder what sort of chap I'd have been if I had n't been this sort; I want to go and live out his potentialities, too. I have n't forgotten that there are birds in the bushes."

Bartley stopped and sat frowning into the fire, his shoulders thrust forward as if he were about to spring at something. Wilson watched him, wondering. His old pupil always stimulated him at first, and then vastly wearied him. The machinery was always pounding away in this man, and Wilson preferred companions of a more reflective habit of mind. He could not help feeling that there were unreasoning and unreasonable activities going on in Alexander all the while; that even after dinner, when most men achieve a decent impersonality, Bartley had merely closed the door of the engine-room and come up for an airing. The machinery itself was still pounding on.

Bartley's abstraction and Wilson's reflections were cut short by a rustle at the door, and almost before they could rise Mrs. Alexander was standing by the hearth. Alexander brought a chair for her, but she shook her head.

"No, dear, thank you. I only came in to see whether you and

Professor Wilson were quite comfortable. I am going down to the music-
room."

"Why not practice here? Wilson and I are growing very dull.
We are tired of talk."

"Yes, I beg you, Mrs. Alexander," Wilson began, but he got no
further.

"Why, certainly, if you won't find me too noisy. I am working
on the Schumann 'Carnival,' and, though I don't practice a great many
hours, I am very methodical," Mrs. Alexander explained, as she crossed to
an upright piano that stood at the back of the room, near the windows.

Wilson followed, and, having seen her seated, dropped into a chair
behind her. She played brilliantly and with great musical feeling. Wilson
could not imagine her permitting herself to do anything badly, but he was
surprised at the cleanness of her execution. He wondered how a woman with
so many duties had managed to keep herself up to a standard really professional. It must take a great deal of time, certainly, and Bartley must take a great
deal of time. Wilson reflected that he had never before known a woman who
had been able, for any considerable while, to support both a personal and an
intellectual passion. Sitting behind her, he watched her with perplexed
admiration, shading his eyes with his hand. In her dinner dress she looked
even younger than in street clothes, and, for all her composure and self-
sufficiency, she seemed to him strangely alert and vibrating, as if in her, too,
there were something never altogether at rest. He felt that he knew pretty
much what she demanded in people and what she demanded from life, and he
wondered how she squared Bartley. After ten years she must know him; and
however one took him, however much one admired him, one had to admit
that he simply wouldn't square. He was a natural force, certainly, but beyond
that, Wilson felt, he was not anything very really or for very long at a time.

Wilson glanced toward the fire, where Bartley's profile was still
wreathed in cigar smoke that curled up more and more slowly. His shoulders were sunk deep in the cushions and one hand hung large and passive
over the arm of his chair. He had slipped on a purple velvet smoking-coat.
His wife, Wilson surmised, had chosen it. She was clearly very proud of his
good looks and his fine color. But, with the glow of an immediate interest
gone out of it, the engineer's face looked tired, even a little haggard. The
three lines in his forehead, directly above the nose, deepened as he sat
thinking, and his powerful head drooped forward heavily. Although Alexander was only forty-three, Wilson thought that beneath his vigorous color
he detected the dulling weariness of on-coming middle age.

★ ★ ★

The next afternoon, at the hour when the river was beginning
to redden under the declining sun, Wilson again found himself facing Mrs.
Alexander at the tea-table in the library.

"Well," he remarked, when he was bidden to give an account
of himself, "there was a long morning with the psychologists, luncheon
with Bartley at his club, more psychologists, and here I am. I've looked
forward to this hour all day."

Mrs. Alexander smiled at him across the vapor from the kettle.
"And do you remember where we stopped yesterday?"

"Perfectly. I was going to show you a picture. But I doubt
whether I have color enough in me. Bartley makes me feel a faded mono-
chrome. You can't get at the young Bartley except by means of color."
Wilson paused and deliberated. Suddenly he broke out: "He was n't a
remarkable student, you know, though he was always strong in higher
mathematics. His work in my own department was quite ordinary. It was
as a powerfully equipped nature that I found him interesting. That is the
most interesting thing a teacher can find. It has the fascination of a scientific
discovery. We come across other pleasing and endearing qualities so much
oftener than we find force."

"And, after all," said Mrs. Alexander, "that is the thing we all
live upon. It is the thing that takes us forward."

Wilson thought she spoke a little wistfully. "Exactly," he assented warmly. "It builds the bridges into the future, over which the feet
of every one of us will go."

"How interested I am to hear you put it in that way. The bridges
into the future—I often say that to myself. Bartley's bridges always seem to
me like that. Have you ever seen his first suspension bridge in Canada, the
one he was doing when I first knew him? I hope you will see it sometime.
We were married as soon as it was finished, and you will laugh when I tell
you that it always has a rather bridal look to me. It is over the wildest river,
with mists and clouds always battling about it, and it is as delicate as a
cobweb hanging in the sky. It really was a bridge into the future. You have
only to look at it to feel that it meant the beginning of a great career. But
I have a photograph of it here." She drew a portfolio from behind a
bookcase. "And there, you see, on the hill, is my aunt's house."

Wilson took up the photograph. "Bartley was telling me something about your aunt last night. She must have been a delightful person."

Winifred laughed. "The bridge, you see, was just at the foot of the hill, and the noise of the engines annoyed her very much at first. But after she met Bartley she pretended to like it, and said it was a good thing to be reminded that there were things going on in the world. She loved life, and Bartley brought a great deal of it in to her when he came to the house. Aunt Eleanor was very worldly in a frank, Early-Victorian manner. She liked men of action, and disliked young men who were careful of themselves and who, as she put it, were always trimming their wick as if they were afraid of their oil's giving out. MacKeller, Bartley's first chief, was an old friend of my aunt, and he told her that Bartley was a wild, ill-governed youth, which really pleased her very much. I remember we were sitting alone in the dusk after Bartley had been there for the first time. I knew that Aunt Eleanor had found him much to her taste, but she had n't said anything. Presently she came out, with a chuckle: 'MacKeller found him sowing wild oats in London, I believe. I hope he did n't stop him too soon. Life coquets with dashing fellows. The coming men are always like that. We must have him to dinner, my dear.' And we did. She grew much fonder of Bartley than she was of me. I had been studying in Vienna, and she thought that absurd. She was interested in the army and in politics, and she had a great contempt for music and art and philosophy. She used to declare that the Prince Consort had brought all that stuff over out of Germany. She always sniffed when Bartley asked me to play for him. She considered that a newfangled way of making a match of it."

When Alexander came in a few moments later, he found Wilson and his wife still confronting the photograph. "Oh, let us get that out of the way," he said, laughing. "Winifred, Thomas can bring my trunk down. I've decided to go over to New York to-morrow night and take a fast boat. I shall save two days."

II

On the night of his arrival in London, Alexander went immediately to the hotel on the Embankment at which he always stopped, and in the lobby he was accosted by an old acquaintance, Maurice Mainhall, who fell upon him with effusive cordiality and indicated a willingness to dine with him. Bartley never dined alone if he could help it, and Mainhall was a good gossip who always knew what had been going on in town; especially, he knew everything that was not printed in the newspapers. The nephew of one of the standard Victorian novelists, Mainhall bobbed about among the various literary cliques of London and its outlying suburbs, careful to lose touch with none of them. He had written a number of books himself; among them a "History of Dancing," a "History of Costume," a "Key to Shakespeare's Sonnets," a study of "The Poetry of Ernest Dowson," etc. Although Mainhall's enthusiasm was often tiresome, and although he was often unable to distinguish between facts and vivid figments of his imagination, his imperturbable good nature overcame even the people whom he bored most, so that they ended by becoming, in a reluctant manner, his friends. In appearance, Mainhall was astonishingly like the conventional stage-Englishman of American drama: tall and thin, with high, hitching shoulders and a small head glistening with closely brushed yellow hair. He spoke with an extreme Oxford accent, and when he was talking well, his face sometimes wore the rapt expression of a very emotional man listening to music. Mainhall liked Alexander because he was an engineer. He had preconceived ideas about everything, and his idea about Americans was that they should be engineers or mechanics. He hated them when they presumed to be anything else.

While they sat at dinner Mainhall acquainted Bartley with the fortunes of his old friends in London, and as they left the table he proposed that they should go to see Hugh MacConnell's new comedy, "Bog Lights."

"It's really quite the best thing MacConnell's done," he explained as they got into a hansom. "It's tremendously well put on, too. Florence Merrill and Cyril Henderson. But Hilda Burgoyne's the hit of the piece. Hugh's written a delightful part for her, and she's quite inexpressible. It's been on only two weeks, and I've been half a dozen times already. I happen to have MacConnell's box for to-night or there'd be no chance of our getting places. There's everything in seeing Hilda while she's fresh in a part. She's apt to grow a bit stale after a time. The ones who have any imagination do."

"Hilda Burgoyne!" Alexander exclaimed mildly. "Why, I have n't heard of her for—years."

Mainhall laughed. "Then you can't have heard much at all, my dear Alexander. It's only lately, since MacConnell and his set have got hold of her, that she's come up. Myself, I always knew she had it in her. If we had one real critic in London—but what can one expect? Do you know, Alexander,"—Mainhall looked with perplexity up into the top of the hansom and rubbed his pink cheek with his gloved finger,—"do you know,

I sometimes think of taking to criticism seriously myself. In a way, it would be a sacrifice; but, dear me, we do need some one."

Just then they drove up to the Duke of York's, so Alexander did not commit himself, but followed Mainhall into the theatre. When they entered the stage-box on the left the first act was well under way, the scene being the interior of a cabin in the south of Ireland. As they sat down, a burst of applause drew Alexander's attention to the stage. Miss Burgoyne and her donkey were thrusting their heads in at the half door. "After all," he reflected, "there's small probability of her recognizing me. She doubtless has n't thought of me for years." He felt the enthusiasm of the house at once, and in a few moments he was caught up by the current of MacConnell's irresistible comedy. The audience had come forewarned, evidently, and whenever the ragged slip of a donkey-girl ran upon the stage there was a deep murmur of approbation, every one smiled and glowed, and Mainhall hitched his heavy chair a little nearer the brass railing.

"You see," he murmured in Alexander's ear, as the curtain fell on the first act, "one almost never sees a part like that done without smartness or mawkishness. Of course, Hilda is Irish,—the Burgoynes have been stage people for generations,—and she has the Irish voice. It's delightful to hear it in a London theatre. That laugh, now, when she doubles over at the hips—who ever heard it out of Galway? She saves her hand, too. She's at her best in the second act. She's really MacConnell's poetic motif, you see; makes the whole thing a fairy tale."

The second act opened before Philly Doyle's underground still, with Peggy and her battered donkey come in to smuggle a load of potheen across the bog, and to bring Philly word of what was doing in the world without, and of what was happening along the roadsides and ditches with the first gleam of fine weather. Alexander, annoyed by Mainhall's sighs and exclamations, watched her with keen, half-skeptical interest. As Mainhall had said, she was the second act; the plot and feeling alike depended upon her lightness of foot, her lightness of touch, upon the shrewdness and deft fancifulness that played alternately, and sometimes together, in her mirthful brown eyes. When she began to dance, by way of showing the gossoons what she had seen in the fairy rings at night, the house broke into a prolonged uproar. After her dance she withdrew from the dialogue and retreated to the ditch wall back of Philly's burrow, where she sat singing "The Rising of the Moon" and making a wreath of primroses for her donkey.

When the act was over Alexander and Mainhall strolled out into the corridor. They met a good many acquaintances; Mainhall, indeed, knew almost every one, and he babbled on incontinently, screwing his small head about over his high collar. Presently he hailed a tall, bearded man, grim-browed and rather battered-looking, who had his opera cloak on his arm and his hat in his hand, and who seemed to be on the point of leaving the theatre.

"MacConnell, let me introduce Mr. Bartley Alexander. I say! It's going famously to-night, Mac. And what an audience! You'll never do anything like this again, mark me. A man writes to the top of his bent only once."

The playwright gave Mainhall a curious look out of his deep-set faded eyes and made a wry face. "And have I done anything so fool as that, now?" he asked.

"That's what I was saying," Mainhall lounged a little nearer and dropped into a tone even more conspicuously confidential. "And you'll never bring Hilda out like this again. Dear me, Mac, the girl could n't possibly be better, you know."

MacConnell grunted. "She'll do well enough if she keeps her pace and does n't go off on us in the middle of the season, as she's more than like to do."

He nodded curtly and made for the door, dodging acquaintances as he went.

"Poor old Hugh," Mainhall murmured. "He's hit terribly hard. He's been wanting to marry Hilda these three years and more. She does n't take up with anybody, you know. Irene Burgoyne, one of her family, told me in confidence that there was a romance somewhere back in the beginning. One of your country-men, Alexander, by the way; an American student whom she met in Paris, I believe. I dare say it's quite true that there's never been any one else." Mainhall vouched for her constancy with a loftiness that made Alexander smile, even while a kind of rapid excitement was tingling through him. Blinking up at the lights, Mainhall added in his luxurious, worldly way: "She's an elegant little person, and quite capable of an extravagant bit of sentiment like that. Here comes Sir Harry Towne. He's another who's awfully keen about her. Let me introduce you. Sir Harry Towne, Mr. Bartley Alexander, the American engineer."

Sir Harry Towne bowed and said that he had met Mr. Alexander and his wife in Tokyo.

Mainhall cut in impatiently.

"I say, Sir Harry, the little girl's going famously to-night, is n't she?"

Sir Harry wrinkled his brows judiciously. "Do you know, I thought the dance a bit conscious to-night, for the first time. The fact is, she's feeling rather seedy, poor child. Westmere and I were back after the first act, and we thought she seemed quite uncertain of herself. A little attack of nerves, possibly."

He bowed as the warning bell rang, and Mainhall whispered: "You know Lord Westmere, of course,—the stooped man with the long gray mustache, talking to Lady Dowle. Lady Westmere is very fond of Hilda."

When they reached their box the house was darkened and the orchestra was playing "The Cloak of Old Gaul." In a moment Peggy was on the stage again, and Alexander applauded vigorously with the rest. He even leaned forward over the rail a little. For some reason he felt pleased and flattered by the enthusiasm of the audience. In the half-light he looked about at the stalls and boxes and smiled a little consciously, recalling with amusement Sir Harry's judicial frown. He was beginning to feel a keen interest in the slender, barefoot donkey-girl who slipped in and out of the play, singing, like some one winding through a hilly field. He leaned forward and beamed felicitations as warmly as Mainhall himself when, at the end of the play, she came again and again before the curtain, panting a little and flushed, her eyes dancing and her eager, nervous little mouth tremulous with excitement.

When Alexander returned to his hotel—he shook Mainhall at the door of the theatre—he had some supper brought up to his room, and it was late before he went to bed. He had not thought of Hilda Burgoyne for years; indeed, he had almost forgotten her. He had last written to her from Canada, after he first met Winifred, telling her that everything was changed with him—that he had met a woman whom he would marry if he could; if he could not, then all the more was everything changed for him. Hilda had never replied to his letter. He felt guilty and unhappy about her for a time, but after Winifred promised to marry him he really forgot Hilda altogether. When he wrote her that everything was changed for him, he was telling the truth. After he met Winifred Pemberton he seemed to himself like a different man. One night when he and Winifred were sitting together on the bridge, he told her that things had happened while he was studying abroad that he was sorry for,—one thing in particular,—and he asked her whether she thought she ought to know about them. She considered a moment and then said: "No, I think not, though I am glad you ask me. You see, one can't be jealous about things in general; but about particular, definite, personal things,"—here she had thrown her hands up to his shoulders with a quick, impulsive gesture—"oh, about those I should be very jealous. I should torture myself—I could n't help it." After that it was easy to forget, actually to forget. He wondered to-night, as he poured his wine, how many times he had thought of Hilda in the last ten years. He had been in London more or less, but he had never happened to hear of her. "All the same," he lifted his glass, "here's to you, little Hilda. You've made things come your way, and I never thought you'd do it.

"Of course," he reflected, "she always had that combination of something homely and sensible, and something utterly wild and daft. But I never thought she'd do anything. She had n't much ambition then, and she was too fond of trifles. She must care about the theatre a great deal more than she used to. Perhaps she has me to thank for something, after all. Sometimes a little jolt like that does one good. She was a daft, generous little thing. I'm glad she's held her own since. After all, we were awfully young. It was youth and poverty and proximity, and everything was young and kindly. I should n't wonder if she could laugh about it with me now. I should n't wonder—But they've probably spoiled her, so that she'd be tiresome if one met her again."

Bartley smiled and yawned and went to bed.

III

The next evening Alexander dined alone at a club, and at about nine o'clock he dropped in at the Duke of York's. The house was sold out and he stood through the second act. When he returned to his hotel he examined the new directory, and found Miss Burgoyne's address still given as off Bedford Square, though at a new number. He remembered that, in so far as she had been brought up at all, she had been brought up in Bloomsbury. Her father and mother played in the provinces most of the year, and she was left a great deal in the care of an old aunt who was crippled by rheumatism and who had had to leave the stage altogether. In the days when Alexander knew her, Hilda always managed to have a lodging of some sort about Bedford Square, because she clung tenaciously to such scraps and shreds of memories as were connected with it. The mummy room of the British Museum had been one of the chief delights of her childhood. That forbidding pile was the goal of her truant fancy, and she was sometimes taken there for a treat, as other children are taken to the theatre. It was long since Alexander had thought of any of these things, but now they came back to him quite fresh, and had a significance they did not have when they were first told him in his restless twenties. So she was still in the old neighborhood, near Bedford Square. The new number probably meant increased prosperity. He hoped so. He would like to know that she was snugly settled. He looked at his watch. It was a quarter past ten; she would not be home for a good two hours yet, and he might as well walk over and have a look at the place. He remembered the shortest way.

It was a warm, smoky evening, and there was a grimy moon. He went through Covent Garden to Oxford Street, and as he turned into Museum Street he walked more slowly, smiling at his own nervousness as he approached the sullen gray mass at the end. He had not been inside the Museum, actually, since he and Hilda used to meet there; sometimes to set out for gay adventures at Twickenham or Richmond, sometimes to linger about the place for a while and to ponder by Lord Elgin's marbles upon the lastingness of some things, or, in the mummy room, upon the awful brevity of others. Since then Bartley had always thought of the British Museum as the ultimate repository of mortality, where all the dead things in the world were assembled to make one's hour of youth the more precious. One trembled lest before he got out it might somehow escape him, lest he might drop the glass from over-eagerness and see it shivered on the stone floor at his feet. How one hid his youth under his coat and hugged it! And how good it was to turn one's back upon all that vaulted cold, to take Hilda's arm and hurry out of the great door and down the steps into the sunlight among the pigeons—to know that the warm and vital thing within him was still there and had not been snatched away to flush Caesar's lean cheek or to feed the veins of some bearded Assyrian king. They in their day had carried the flaming liquor, but to-day was his! So the song used to run in his head those summer mornings a dozen years ago. Alexander walked by the place very quietly, as if he were afraid of waking some one.

He crossed Bedford Square and found the number he was looking for. The house, a comfortable, well-kept place enough, was dark except for the four front windows on the second floor, where a low, even light was burning behind the white muslin sash curtains. Outside there were window boxes, painted white and full of flowers. Bartley was making a third round of the Square when he heard the far-flung hoof-beats of a hansom-cab horse, driven rapidly. He looked at his watch, and was astonished to find that it was a few minutes after twelve. He turned and walked back along the iron railing as the cab came up to Hilda's number and stopped. The hansom must have been one that she employed regularly, for she did not stop to pay the driver. She stepped out quickly and lightly. He heard her cheerful "Good-night, cabby," as she ran up the steps and opened the door with a latchkey. In a few moments the lights flared up brightly behind the white curtains, and as he walked away he heard a window raised. But he had gone too far to look up without turning round. He went back to his hotel, feeling that he had had a good evening, and he slept well.

For the next few days Alexander was very busy. He took a desk in the office of a Scotch engineering firm on Henrietta Street, and was at work almost constantly. He avoided the clubs and usually dined alone at his hotel. One afternoon, after he had tea, he started for a walk down the Embankment toward Westminster, intending to end his stroll at Bedford Square and to ask whether Miss Burgoyne would let him take her to the theatre. But he did not go so far. When he reached the Abbey, he turned back and crossed Westminster Bridge and sat down to watch the trails of smoke behind the Houses of Parliament catch fire with the sunset. The slender towers were washed by a rain of golden light and licked by little flickering flames; Somerset House and the bleached gray pinnacles about Whitehall were floated in a luminous haze. The yellow light poured through the trees and the leaves seemed to burn with soft fires. There was a smell of acacias in the air everywhere, and the laburnums were dripping gold over the walls of the gardens. It was a sweet, lonely kind of summer evening. Remembering Hilda as she used to be, was doubtless more satis-factory than seeing her as she must be now—and, after all, Alexander asked himself, what was it but his own young years that he was remembering?

He crossed back to Westminster, went up to the Temple, and sat down to smoke in the Middle Temple gardens, listening to the thin voice of the fountain and smelling the spice of the sycamores that came out heavily in the damp evening air. He thought, as he sat there, about a great many things: about his own youth and Hilda's; above all, he thought of how glorious it had been, and how quickly it had passed; and, when it had passed; how little worth while anything was. None of the things he had gained in the least compensated. In the last six years his reputation had become, as the saying is, popular. Four years ago he had been called to Japan to deliver, at the Emperor's request, a course of lectures at the Imperial University, and had instituted reforms throughout the islands, not only in the practice of bridge-building but in drainage and road-making. On his return he had undertaken the bridge at Moorlock, in Canada, the most important piece of bridge-building going on in the world,—a test, indeed, of how far the latest practice in bridge structure could be carried. It was a spectacular undertaking by reason of its very size, and Bartley realized that, whatever else he might do, he would probably always be known as the engineer who designed the great Moorlock Bridge, the longest cantilever in existence. Yet it was to him the least satisfactory thing he had ever done. He was cramped in every way by a niggardly commission, and was using lighter structural material than he thought proper. He had vexations enough, too, with his work at home. He had several bridges under way in the United States, and they were always being held up by strikes and delays resulting from a general industrial unrest.

Though Alexander often told himself he had never put more into his work than he had done in the last few years, he had to admit that he had never got so little out of it. He was paying for success, too, in the demands made on his time by boards of civic enterprise and committees of public welfare. The obligations imposed by his wife's fortune and position were sometimes distracting to a man who followed his profession, and he was expected to be interested in a great many worthy endeavors on her account as well as on his own. His existence was becoming a network of great and little details. He had expected that success would bring him freedom and power; but it had brought only power that was in itself another kind of restraint. He had always meant to keep his personal liberty at all costs, as old MacKeller, his first chief, had done, and not, like so many American engineers, to become a part of a professional movement, a cautious board member, a Nestor *de pontibus*. He happened to be engaged in work of public utility, but he was not willing to become what is called a public man. He found himself living exactly the kind of life he had determined to escape. What, he asked himself, did he want with these genial honors and substantial comforts? Hardships and difficulties he had carried lightly; overwork had not exhausted him; but this dead calm of middle life which confronted him,—of that he was afraid. He was not ready for it. It was like being buried alive. In his youth he would not have believed such a thing possible. The one thing he had really wanted all his life was to be free; and there was still something unconquered in him, something besides the strong work-horse that his profession had made of him. He felt rich to-night in the possession of that unstultified survival; in the light of his experience, it was more precious than honors or achievement. In all those busy, successful years there had been nothing so good as this hour of wild light-heartedness. This feeling was the only happiness that was real to him, and such hours were the only ones in which he could feel his own continuous identity—feel the boy he had been in the rough days of the old West, feel the youth who had worked his way across the ocean on a cattle-ship and gone to study in Paris without a dollar in his pocket. The man who sat in his offices in Boston was only a powerful machine. Under the activities of that machine the person who, at such moments as this, he felt to be himself, was fading and dying. He remembered how, when he was a little boy and his father called him in the morning, he used to leap from his bed into the full consciousness of himself. That consciousness was Life itself. Whatever took its place, action, reflection, the power of concentrated thought, were only functions of a mechanism useful to society; things that could be bought in the market. There was only one thing that had an absolute value for each individual, and it was just that original impulse, that internal heat, that feeling of one's self in one's own breast.

When Alexander walked back to his hotel, the red and green lights were blinking along the docks on the farther shore, and the soft white stars were shining in the wide sky above the river.

The next night, and the next, Alexander repeated this same foolish performance. It was always Miss Burgoyne whom he started out to find, and he got no farther than the Temple gardens and the Embankment. It was a pleasant kind of loneliness. To a man who was so little given to reflection, whose dreams always took the form of definite ideas, reaching into the future, there was a seductive excitement in renewing old experiences in imagination. He started out upon these walks half guiltily, with a curious longing and expectancy which were wholly gratified by solitude. Solitude, but not solitariness; for he walked shoulder to shoulder with a shadowy companion—not little Hilda Burgoyne, by any means, but some one vastly dearer to him than she had ever been—his own young self, the youth who had waited for him upon the steps of the British Museum that night, and who, though he had tried to pass so quietly, had known him and come down and linked an arm in his.

It was not until long afterward that Alexander learned that for him this youth was the most dangerous of companions.

One Sunday evening, at Lady Walford's, Alexander did at last meet Hilda Burgoyne. Mainhall had told him that she would probably be there. He looked about for her rather nervously, and finally found her at the farther end of the large drawing-room, the centre of a circle of men, young and old. She was apparently telling them a story. They were all laughing and bending toward her. When she saw Alexander, she rose quickly and put out her hand. The other men drew back a little to let him approach.

"Mr. Alexander! I am delighted. Have you been in London long?"

Bartley bowed, somewhat laboriously, over her hand. "Long enough to have seen you more than once. How fine it all is!"

She laughed as if she were pleased. "I'm glad you think so. I like it. Won't you join us here?"

"Miss Burgoyne was just telling us about a donkey-boy she had in Galway last summer," Sir Harry Towne explained as the circle closed up again. Lord Westmere stroked his long white mustache with his bloodless hand and looked at Alexander blankly. Hilda was a good story-teller. She was sitting on the edge of her chair, as if she had alighted there for a moment only. Her primrose satin gown seemed like a soft sheath for her slender, supple figure, and its delicate color suited her white Irish skin and brown hair. Whatever she wore, people felt the charm of her active, girlish body with its slender hips and quick, eager shoulders. Alexander heard little of the story, but he watched Hilda intently. She must certainly, he reflected, be thirty, and he was honestly delighted to see that the years had treated her so indulgently. If her face had changed at all, it was in a slight hardening of the mouth—still eager enough to be very disconcerting at times, he felt—and in an added air of self-possession and self-reliance. She carried her head, too, a little more resolutely.

When the story was finished, Miss Burgoyne turned pointedly to Alexander, and the other men drifted away.

"I thought I saw you in MacConnell's box with Mainhall one evening, but I supposed you had left town before this."

She looked at him frankly and cordially, as if he were indeed merely an old friend whom she was glad to meet again.

"No, I've been mooning about here."

Hilda laughed gayly. "Mooning! I see you mooning! You must be the busiest man in the world. Time and success have done well by you, you know. You're handsomer than ever and you've gained a grand manner."

Alexander blushed and bowed. "Time and success have been good friends to both of us. Are n't you tremendously pleased with yourself?"

She laughed again and shrugged her shoulders. "Oh, so-so. But

I want to hear about you. Several years ago I read such a lot in the papers
about the wonderful things you did in Japan, and how the Emperor decorated you. What was it, Commander of the Order of the Rising Sun? That
sounds like 'The Mikado.' And what about your new bridge—in Canada,
is n't it, and it's to be the longest one in the world and has some queer name
I can't remember."

Bartley shook his head and smiled drolly. "Since when have you
been interested in bridges? Or have you learned to be interested in everything? And is that a part of success?"

"Why, how absurd! As if I were not always interested!" Hilda
exclaimed.

"Well, I think we won't talk about bridges here, at any rate."
Bartley looked down at the toe of her yellow slipper which was tapping the
rug impatiently under the hem of her gown. "But I wonder whether you'd
think me impertinent if I asked you to let me come to see you sometime
and tell you about them?"

"Why should I? Ever so many people come on Sunday afternoons."

"I know. Mainhall offered to take me. But you must know that
I've been in London several times within the last few years, and you might
very well think that just now is a rather inopportune time—"

She cut him short. "Nonsense. One of the pleasantest things
about success is that it makes people want to look one up, if that's what you
mean. I'm like every one else—more agreeable to meet when things are
going well with me. Don't you suppose it gives me any pleasure to do
something that people like?"

"Does it? Oh, how fine it all is, your coming on like this! But
I did n't want you to think it was because of that I wanted to see you." He
spoke very seriously and looked down at the floor.

Hilda studied him in wide-eyed astonishment for a moment, and
then broke into a low, amused laugh. "My dear Mr. Alexander, you have
strange delicacies. If you please, that is exactly why you wish to see me. We
understand that, do we not?"

Bartley looked ruffled and turned the seal ring on his little finger
about awkwardly.

Hilda leaned back in her chair, watching him indulgently out of
her shrewd eyes. "Come, don't be angry, but don't try to pose for me, or
to be anything but what you are. If you care to come, it's yourself I'll be
glad to see, and you thinking well of yourself. Don't try to wear a cloak of

humility; it does n't become you. Stalk in as you are and don't make excuses. I'm not accustomed to inquiring into the motives of my guests. That would hardly be safe, even for Lady Walford, in a great house like this."

"Sunday afternoon, then," said Alexander, as she rose to join her hostess. "How early may I come?"

"I'm at home after four, and I'll be glad to see you, Bartley."

She gave him her hand and flushed and laughed. He bent over it a little stiffly. She went away on Lady Walford's arm, and as he stood watching her yellow train glide down the long floor he looked rather sullen. He felt that he had not come out of it very brilliantly.

IV

On Sunday afternoon Alexander remembered Miss Burgoyne's invitation and called at her apartment. He found it a delightful little place and he met charming people there. Hilda lived alone, attended by a very pretty and competent French servant who answered the door and brought in the tea. Alexander arrived early, and some twenty-odd people dropped in during the course of the afternoon. Hugh MacConnell came with his sister, and stood about, managing his tea-cup awkwardly and watching every one out of his deep-set, faded eyes. He seemed to have made a resolute effort at tidiness of attire, and his sister, a robust, florid woman with a splendid joviality about her, kept eyeing his freshly creased clothes apprehensively. It was not very long, indeed, before his coat hung with a discouraged sag from his gaunt shoulders and his hair and beard were rumpled as if he had been out in a gale. His dry humor went under a cloud of absent-minded kindliness which, Mainhall explained, always overtook him here. He was never so witty or so sharp here as elsewhere, and Alexander thought he behaved as if he were an elderly relative come in to a young girl's party.

The editor of a monthly review came with his wife, and Lady Kildare, the Irish philanthropist, brought her young nephew, Robert Owen, who had come up from Oxford, and who was visibly excited and gratified by his first introduction to Miss Burgoyne. Hilda was very nice to him, and he sat on the edge of his chair, flushed with his conversational

efforts and moving his chin about nervously over his high collar. Sarah
Frost, the novelist, came with her husband, a very genial and placid old
scholar who had become slightly deranged upon the subject of the fourth
dimension. On other matters he was perfectly rational and he was easy and
pleasing in conversation. He looked very much like Agassiz, and his wife,
in her old-fashioned black silk dress, overskirted and tight-sleeved, reminded Alexander of the early pictures of Mrs. Browning. Hilda seemed
particularly fond of this quaint couple, and Bartley himself was so pleased
with their mild and thoughtful converse that he took his leave when they
did, and walked with them over to Oxford Street, where they waited for
their 'bus. They asked him to come to see them in Chelsea, and they spoke
very tenderly of Hilda. "She's a dear, unworldly little thing," said the
philosopher absently; "more like the stage people of my young days—folk
of simple manners. There are n't many such left. American tours have
spoiled them, I'm afraid. They have all grown very smart. Lamb would n't
care a great deal about many of them, I fancy."

Alexander went back to Bedford Square a second Sunday afternoon. He had a long talk with MacConnell, but he got no word with Hilda
alone, and he left in a discontented state of mind. For the rest of the week
he was nervous and unsettled, and kept rushing his work as if he were
preparing for immediate departure. On Thursday afternoon he cut short a
committee meeting, jumped into a hansom, and drove to Bedford Square.
He sent up his card, but it came back to him with a message scribbled across
the front.

> *So sorry I can't see you. Will you come and dine with me*
> *Sunday evening at half-past seven?*
>
> H. B.

When Bartley arrived at Bedford Square on Sunday evening,
Marie, the pretty little French girl, met him at the door and conducted him
upstairs. Hilda was writing in her living-room, under the light of a tall desk
lamp. Bartley recognized the primrose satin gown she had worn that first
evening at Lady Walford's.

"I'm so pleased that you think me worth that yellow dress, you
know," he said, taking her hand and looking her over admiringly from the
toes of her canary slippers to her smoothly parted brown hair. "Yes, it's
very, very pretty. Every one at Lady Walford's was looking at it."

Hilda curtsied. "Is that why you think it pretty? I've no need for fine clothes in Mac's play this time, so I can afford a few duddies for myself. It's owing to that same chance, by the way, that I am able to ask you to dinner. I don't need Marie to dress me this season, so she keeps house for me, and my little Galway girl has gone home for a visit. I should never have asked you if Molly had been here, for I remember you don't like English cookery."

Alexander walked about the room, looking at everything.

"I have n't had a chance yet to tell you what a jolly little place I think this is. Where did you get those etchings? They're quite unusual, are n't they?"

"Lady Westmere sent them to me from Rome last Christmas. She is very much interested in the American artist who did them. They are all sketches made about the Villa d'Este, you see. He painted that group of cypresses for the Salon, and it was bought for the Luxembourg."

Alexander walked over to the bookcases. "It's the air of the whole place here that I like. You have n't got anything that does n't belong. Seems to me it looks particularly well to-night. And you have so many flowers. I like these little yellow irises."

"Rooms always look better by lamplight—in London, at least. Though Marie is clean—really clean, as the French are. Why do you look at the flowers so critically? Marie got them all fresh in Covent Garden market yesterday morning."

"I'm glad," said Alexander simply. "I can't tell you how glad I am to have you so pretty and comfortable here, and to hear every one saying such nice things about you. You've got awfully nice friends," he added humbly, picking up a little jade elephant from her desk. "Those fellows are all very loyal, even Mainhall. They don't talk of any one else as they do of you."

Hilda sat down on the couch and said seriously: "I've a neat little sum in the bank, too, now, and I own a mite of a hut in Galway. It's not worth much, but I love it. I've managed to save something every year, and that with helping my three sisters now and then, and tiding poor Cousin Mike over bad seasons. He's that gifted, you know, but he will drink and loses more good engagements than other fellows ever get. And I've traveled a bit, too."

Marie opened the door and smilingly announced that dinner was served.

"My dining-room," Hilda explained, as she led the way, "is the tiniest place you have ever seen."

It was a tiny room, hung all round with French prints, above which ran a shelf full of china. Hilda saw Alexander look up at it.

"It's not particularly rare," she said, "but some of it was my mother's. Heaven knows how she managed to keep it whole, through all our wanderings, or in what baskets and bundles and theatre trunks it has n't been stowed away. We always had our tea out of those blue cups when I was a little girl, sometimes in the queerest lodgings, and sometimes on a trunk at the theatre—queer theatres, for that matter."

It was a wonderful little dinner. There was watercress soup, and sole, and a delightful omelette stuffed with mushrooms and truffles, and two small rare ducklings, and artichokes, and a dry yellow Rhone wine of which Bartley had always been very fond. He drank it appreciatively and remarked that there was still no other he liked so well.

"I have some champagne for you, too. I don't drink it myself, but I like to see it behave when it's poured. There is nothing else that looks so jolly."

"Thank you. But I don't like it so well as this." Bartley held the yellow wine against the light and squinted into it as he turned the glass slowly about. "You have traveled, you say. Have you been in Paris much these late years?"

Hilda lowered one of the candle-shades carefully. "Oh, yes, I go over to Paris often. There are few changes in the old Quarter. Dear old Madame Anger is dead—but perhaps you don't remember her?"

"Don't I, though! I'm so sorry to hear it. How did her son turn out? I remember how she saved and scraped for him, and how he always lay abed till ten o'clock. He was the laziest fellow at the Beaux Arts; and that's saying a good deal."

"Well, he is still clever and lazy. They say he is a good architect when he will work. He's a big, handsome creature, and he hates Americans as much as ever. But Angel—do you remember Angel?"

"Perfectly. Did she ever get back to Brittany and her *bains de mer?*"

"Ah, no. Poor Angel! She got tired of cooking and scouring the coppers in Madame Anger's little kitchen, so she ran away with a soldier, and then with another soldier. Too bad! She still lives about the Quarter, and, though there is always a *soldat,* she has become a *blanchisseuse de fin.* She did my blouses beautifully the last time I was there, and was so delighted to see me again. I gave her all my old clothes, even my old hats, though she always wears her Breton head-dress. Her hair is still like flax, and her blue eyes are just like a baby's, and she has the same three freckles on her little nose, and talks about going back to her *bains de mer.*"

Bartley looked at Hilda across the yellow light of the candles and broke into a low, happy laugh. "How jolly it was being young, Hilda! Do you remember that first walk we took together in Paris? We walked down to the Place Saint-Michel to buy some lilacs. Do you remember how sweet they smelled?"

"Indeed I do. Come, we'll have our coffee in the other room, and you can smoke."

Hilda rose quickly, as if she wished to change the drift of their talk, but Bartley found it pleasant to continue it.

"What a warm, soft spring evening that was," he went on, as they sat down in the study with the coffee on a little table between them; "and the sky, over the bridges, was just the color of the lilacs. We walked on down by the river, did n't we?"

Hilda laughed and looked at him questioningly. He saw a gleam in her eyes that he remembered even better than the episode he was recalling.

"I think we did," she answered demurely. "It was on the Quai we met that woman who was crying so bitterly. I gave her a spray of lilac, I remember, and you gave her a franc. I was frightened at your prodigality."

"I expect it was the last franc I had. What a strong brown face she had, and very tragic. She looked at us with such despair and longing, out from under her black shawl. What she wanted from us was neither our flowers nor our francs, but just our youth. I remember it touched me so. I would have given her some of mine off my back, if I could. I had enough and to spare then," Bartley mused, and looked thoughtfully at his cigar.

They were both remembering what the woman had said when she took the money: "God give you a happy love!" It was not in the ingratiating tone of the habitual beggar: it had come out of the depths of the poor creature's sorrow, vibrating with pity for their youth and despair at the terribleness of human life; it had the anguish of a voice of prophecy. Until she spoke, Bartley had not realized that he was in love. The strange woman, and her passionate sentence that rang out so sharply, had frightened them both. They went home sadly with the lilacs, back to the Rue Saint-Jacques, walking very slowly, arm in arm. When they reached the house where Hilda lodged, Bartley went across the court with her, and up the dark old stairs to the third landing; and there he had kissed her for the first time. He had shut his eyes to give him the courage, he remembered, and she had trembled so—

Bartley started when Hilda rang the little bell beside her. "Dear me, why did you do that? I had quite forgotten—I was back there. It was very jolly," he murmured lazily, as Marie came in to take away the coffee.

Hilda laughed and went over to the piano. "Well, we are neither of us twenty now, you know. Have I told you about my new play? Mac is writing one, really for me this time. You see, I'm coming on."

"I've seen nothing else. What kind of a part is it? Shall you wear yellow gowns? I hope so."

He was looking at her round, slender figure, as she stood by the piano, turning over a pile of music, and he felt the energy in every line of it.

"No, it is n't a dress-up part. He does n't seem to fancy me in fine feathers. He says I ought to be minding the pigs at home, and I suppose I ought. But he's given me some good Irish songs. Listen."

She sat down at the piano and sang. When she finished, Alexander shook himself out of a reverie.

"Sing 'The Harp that Once,' Hilda. You used to sing it so well."

"Nonsense. Of course I can't really sing, except the way my mother and grandmother did before me. Most actresses nowadays learn to sing properly, so I tried a master; but he confused me, just!"

Alexander laughed. "All the same, sing it, Hilda."

Hilda started up from the stool and moved restlessly toward the window. "It's really too warm in this room to sing. Don't you feel it?"

Alexander went over and opened the window for her. "Are n't you afraid to let the wind blow like that on your neck? Can't I get a scarf or something?"

"Ask a theatre lydy if she's afraid of drafts!" Hilda laughed. "But perhaps, as I'm so warm—give me your handkerchief. There, just in front." He slipped the corners carefully under her shoulder-straps. "There, that will do. It looks like a bib." She pushed his hand away quickly and stood looking out into the deserted square. "Is n't London a tomb on Sunday night?"

Alexander caught the agitation in her voice. He stood a little behind her, and tried to steady himself as he said: "It's soft and misty. See how white the stars are."

For a long time neither Hilda nor Bartley spoke. They stood close together, looking out into the wan, watery sky, breathing always more quickly and lightly, and it seemed as if all the clocks in the world had stopped. Suddenly he moved the clenched hand he held behind him and dropped it violently at his side. He felt a tremor run through the slender yellow figure in front of him.

She caught his handkerchief from her throat and thrust it at him without turning round. "Here, take it. You must go now, Bartley. Good-night."

Bartley leaned over her shoulder, without touching her, and whispered in her ear: "You are giving me a chance?"

"Yes. Take it and go. This is n't fair, you know. Good-night."

Alexander unclenched the two hands at his sides. With one he threw down the window and with the other—still standing behind her—he drew her back against him.

She uttered a little cry, threw her arms over her head, and drew his face down to hers. "Are you going to let me love you a little, Bartley?" she whispered.

V

*I*t was the afternoon of the day before Christmas. Mrs Alexander had been driving about all the morning, leaving presents at the houses of her friends. She lunched alone, and as she rose from the table she spoke to the butler: "Thomas, I am going down to the kitchen now to see Norah. In half an hour you are to bring the greens up from the cellar and put them in the library. Mr. Alexander will be home at three to hang them himself. Don't forget the step-ladder, and plenty of tacks and string. You may bring the azaleas upstairs. Take the white one to Mr. Alexander's study. Put the two pink ones in this room, and the red one in the drawing-room."

A little before three o'clock Mrs. Alexander went into the library to see that everything was ready. She pulled the window shades high, for the weather was dark and stormy, and there was little light, even in the streets. A foot of snow had fallen during the morning, and the wide space over the river was thick with flying flakes that fell and wreathed the masses of floating ice. Winifred was standing by the window when she heard the front door open. She hurried to the hall as Alexander came stamping in, covered with snow. He kissed her joyfully and brushed away the snow that fell on her hair.

"I wish I had asked you to meet me at the office and walk home with me, Winifred. The Common is beautiful. The boys have swept the snow off the pond and are skating furiously. Did the cyclamens come?"

"An hour ago. What splendid ones! But are n't you frightfully extravagant?"

"Not for Christmas-time. I'll go upstairs and change my coat. I shall· be down in a moment. Tell Thomas to get everything ready."

When Alexander reappeared, he took his wife's arm and went with her into the library. "When did the azaleas get here? Thomas has got the white one in my room."

"I told him to put it there."

"But, I say, it's much the finest of the lot!"

"That's why I had it put there. There is too much color in that room for a red one, you know."

Bartley began to sort the greens. "It looks very splendid there, but I feel piggish to have it. However, we really spend more time there than anywhere else in the house. Will you hand me the holly?"

He climbed up the stepladder, which creaked under his weight, and began to twist the tough stems of the holly into the framework of the chandelier.

"I forgot to tell you that I had a letter from Wilson, this morning, explaining his telegram. He is coming on because an old uncle up in Vermont has conveniently died and left Wilson a little money—something like ten thousand. He's coming on to settle up the estate. Won't it be jolly to have him?"

"And how fine that he's come into a little money. I can see him posting down State Street to the steamship offices. He will get a good many trips out of that ten thousand. What can have detained him? I expected him here for luncheon."

"Those trains from Albany are always late. He'll be along sometime this afternoon. And now, don't you want to go upstairs and lie down for an hour? You've had a busy morning and I don't want you to be tired to-night."

After his wife went upstairs Alexander worked energetically at the greens for a few moments. Then, as he was cutting off a length of string, he sighed suddenly and sat down, staring out of the window at the snow. The animation died out of his face, but in his eyes there was a restless light, a look of apprehension and suspense. He kept clasping and unclasping his big hands as if he were trying to realize something. The clock ticked through the minutes of a half-hour and the afternoon outside began to thicken and darken turbidly. Alexander, since he first sat down, had not changed his position. He leaned forward, his hands between his knees, scarcely breathing, as if he were holding himself away from his surroundings, from the room, and from the very chair in which he sat, from everything except the wild eddies of snow above the river on which his eyes were fixed with feverish intentness, as if he were trying to project himself thither. When at last Lucius Wilson was announced, Alexander sprang eagerly to his feet and hurried to meet his old instructor.

"Hello, Wilson. What luck! Come into the library. We are to have a lot of people to dinner to-night, and Winifred's lying down. You will excuse her, won't you? And now what about yourself? Sit down and tell me everything."

"I think I'd rather move about, if you don't mind. I've been sitting in the train for a week, it seems to me." Wilson stood before the fire with his hands behind him and looked about the room. "You *have* been busy. Bartley, if I'd had my choice of all possible places in which to spend Christmas, your house would certainly be the place I'd have chosen. Happy people do a great deal for their friends. A house like this throws its warmth out. I felt it distinctly as I was coming through the Berkshires. I could scarcely believe that I was to see Mrs. Bartley again so soon."

"Thank you, Wilson. She'll be as glad to see you. Shall we have tea now? I'll ring for Thomas to clear away this litter. Winifred says I always wreck the house when I try to do anything. Do you know, I am quite tired. Looks as if I were not used to work, does n't it?" Alexander laughed and dropped into a chair. "You know, I'm sailing the day after New Year's."

"Again? Why, you've been over twice since I was here in the spring, have n't you?"

"Oh, I was in London about ten days in the summer. Went to escape the hot weather more than anything else. I shan't be gone more than a month this time. Winifred and I have been up in Canada for most of the autumn. That Moorlock Bridge is on my back all the time. I never had so much trouble with a job before." Alexander moved about restlessly and fell to poking the fire.

"Have n't I seen in the papers that there is some trouble about a tidewater bridge of yours in New Jersey?"

"Oh, that does n't amount to anything. It's held up by a steel strike. A bother, of course, but the sort of thing one is always having to put up with. But the Moorlock Bridge is a continual anxiety. You see, the truth is, we are having to build pretty well to the strain limit up there. They've crowded me too much on the cost. It's all very well if everything goes well, but these estimates have never been used for anything of such length before. However, there's nothing to be done. They hold me to the scale I've used in shorter bridges. The last thing a bridge commission cares about is the kind of bridge you build."

When Bartley had finished dressing for dinner he went into his study, where he found his wife arranging flowers on his writing-table.

"These pink roses just came from Mrs. Hastings," she said, smiling, "and I am sure she meant them for you."

Bartley looked about with an air of satisfaction at the greens and the wreaths in the windows. "Have you a moment, Winifred? I have just now been thinking that this is our twelfth Christmas. Can you realize it?" He went up to the table and took her hands away from the flowers, drying them with his pocket handkerchief. "They've been awfully happy ones, all of them, have n't they?" He took her in his arms and bent back, lifting her a little and giving her a long kiss. "You are happy, are n't you, Winifred? More than anything else in the world, I want you to be happy. Sometimes, of late, I've thought you looked as if you were troubled."

"No; it's only when you are troubled and harassed that I feel worried, Bartley. I wish you always seemed as you do to-night. But you don't, always." She looked earnestly and inquiringly into his eyes.

Alexander took her two hands from his shoulders and swung them back and forth in his own, laughing his big blond laugh.

"I'm growing older, my dear; that's what you feel. Now, may I show you something? I meant to save them until to-morrow, but I want you to wear them to-night." He took a little leather box out of his pocket and opened it. On the white velvet lay two long pendants of curiously worked gold, set with pearls. Winifred looked from the box to Bartley and exclaimed:—

"Where did you ever find such gold work, Bartley?"

"It's old Flemish. Is n't it fine?"

"They are the most beautiful things, dear. But, you know, I never wear earrings."

"Yes, yes, I know. But I want you to wear them. I have always wanted you to. So few women can. There must be a good ear, to begin with, and a nose"—he waved his hand—"above reproach. Most women look silly in them. They go only with faces like yours—very, very proud, and just a little hard."

Winifred laughed as she went over to the mirror and fitted the delicate springs to the lobes of her ears. "Oh, Bartley, that old foolishness about my being hard. It really hurts my feelings. But I must go down now. People are beginning to come."

Bartley drew her arm about his neck and went to the door with her. "Not hard to me, Winifred," he whispered. "Never, never hard to me."

Left alone, he paced up and down his study. He was at home again, among all the dear familiar things that spoke to him of so many happy years. His house to-night would be full of charming people, who liked and admired him. Yet all the time, underneath his pleasure and hopefulness and satisfaction, he was conscious of the vibration of an unnatural excitement. Amid this light and warmth and friendliness, he sometimes started and shuddered, as if some one had stepped on his grave. Something had broken loose in him of which he knew nothing except that it was sullen and powerful, and that it wrung and tortured him. Sometimes it came upon him softly, in enervating reveries. Sometimes it battered him like the cannon rolling in the hold of the vessel. Always, now, it brought with it a sense of quickened life, of stimulating danger. To-night it came upon him suddenly, as he was walking the floor, after his wife left him. It seemed impossible; he could not believe it. He glanced entreatingly at the door, as if to call her back. He heard voices in the hall below, and knew that he must go down. Going over to the window, he looked out at the lights across the river. How could this happen here, in his own house, among the things he loved? What was it that reached in out of the darkness and thrilled him? As he stood there he had a feeling that he would never escape. He shut his eyes and pressed his forehead against the cold window glass, breathing in the chill that came through it. "That this," he groaned, "that this should have happened to *me!*"

On New Year's day a thaw set in, and during the night torrents of rain fell. In the morning, the morning of Alexander's departure for England, the river was streaked with fog and the rain drove hard against the windows of the breakfast-room. Alexander had finished his coffee and was pacing up and down. His wife sat at the table, watching him. She was pale and unnaturally calm. When Thomas brought the letters, Bartley sank into his chair and ran them over rapidly.

"Here's a note from old Wilson. He's safe back at his grind, and says he had a bully time. 'The memory of Mrs. Bartley will make my whole winter fragrant.' Just like him. He will go on getting measureless satisfaction out of you by his study fire. What a man he is for looking on at life!" Bartley sighed, pushed the letters back impatiently, and went over to the window. "This is a nasty sort of day to sail. I've a notion to call it off. Next week would be time enough."

"That would only mean starting twice. It would n't really help you out at all," Mrs. Alexander spoke soothingly. "And you'd come back late for all your engagements."

Bartley began jingling some loose coins in his pocket. "I wish things would let me rest. I'm tired of work, tired of people, tired of trailing about." He looked out at the storm-beaten river.

Winifred came up behind him and put a hand on his shoulder. "That's what you always say, poor Bartley! At bottom you really like all these things. Can't you remember that?"

He put his arm about her. "All the same, life runs smoothly enough with some people, and with me it's always a messy sort of patch-work. It's like the song; peace is where I am not. How can you face it all with so much fortitude?"

She looked at him with that clear gaze which Wilson had so much admired, which he had felt implied such high confidence and fearless pride. "Oh, I faced that long ago, when you were on your first bridge, up at old Allway. I knew then that your paths were not to be paths of peace, but I decided that I wanted to follow them."

Bartley and his wife stood silent for a long time; the fire crackled in the grate, the rain beat insistently upon the windows, and the sleepy Angora looked up at them curiously.

Presently Thomas made a discreet sound at the door. "Shall Edward bring down your trunks, sir?"

"Yes; they are ready. Tell him not to forget the big portfolio on the study table."

Thomas withdrew, closing the door softly. Bartley turned away from his wife, still holding her hand. "It never gets any easier, Winifred."

They both started at the sound of the carriage on the pavement outside. Alexander sat down and leaned his head on his hand. His wife bent over him. "Courage," she said gayly. Bartley rose and rang the bell. Thomas brought him his hat and stick and ulster. At the sight of these, the supercilious Angora moved restlessly, quitted her red cushion by the fire, and came up, waving her tail in vexation at these ominous indications of change. Alexander stooped to stroke her, and then plunged into his coat and drew on his gloves. His wife held his stick, smiling. Bartley smiled too, and his eyes cleared. "I'll work like the devil, Winifred, and be home again before you realize I've gone." He kissed her quickly several times, hurried out of the front door into the rain, and waved to her from the carriage window as the driver was starting his melancholy, dripping black horses. Alexander sat with his hands clenched on his knees. As the carriage turned up the hill, he lifted one hand and brought it down violently. "This time"—he spoke aloud and through his set teeth—"this time I'm going to end it!"

On the afternoon of the third day out, Alexander was sitting well to the stern, on the windward side where the chairs were few, his rugs over him and the collar of his fur-lined coat turned up about his ears. The weather had so far been dark and raw. For two hours he had been watching the low, dirty sky and the beating of the heavy rain upon the iron-colored sea. There was a long, oily swell that made exercise laborious. The decks smelled of damp woolens, and the air was so humid that drops of moisture kept gathering upon his hair and mustache. He seldom moved except to brush them away. The great open spaces made him passive and the restlessness of the water quieted him. He intended during the voyage to decide upon a course of action, but he held all this away from him for the present and lay in a blessed gray oblivion. Deep down in him somewhere his resolution was weakening and strengthening, ebbing and flowing. The thing that perturbed him went on as steadily as his pulse, but he was almost unconscious of it. He was submerged in the vast impersonal grayness about him, and at intervals the sidelong roll of the boat measured off time like the ticking of a clock. He felt released from everything that troubled and perplexed him. It was as if he had tricked and outwitted torturing memories, had actually managed to get on board without them. He thought of nothing at all. If his mind now and again picked a face out of the grayness, it was Lucius Wilson's, or the face of an old schoolmate, forgotten for years; or it was the slim outline of a favorite greyhound he used to hunt jack-rabbits with when he was a boy.

Toward six o'clock the wind rose and tugged at the tarpaulin and brought the swell higher. After dinner Alexander came back to the wet deck, piled his damp rugs over him again, and sat smoking, losing himself in the obliterating blackness and drowsing in the rush of the gale. Before he went below a few bright stars were pricked off between heavily moving masses of cloud.

The next morning was bright and mild, with a fresh breeze. Alexander felt the need of exercise even before he came out of his cabin.

When he went on deck the sky was blue and blinding, with heavy whiffs of white cloud, smoke-colored at the edges, moving rapidly across it. The water was roughish, a cold, clear indigo breaking into whitecaps. Bartley walked for two hours, and then stretched himself in the sun until lunchtime.

In the afternoon he wrote a long letter to Winifred. Later, as he walked the deck through a splendid golden sunset, his spirits rose continually. It was agreeable to come to himself again after several days of numbness and torpor. He stayed out until the last tinge of violet had faded from the water. There was literally a taste of life on his lips as he sat down to dinner and ordered a bottle of champagne. He was late in finishing his dinner, and drank rather more wine than he had meant to. When he went above, the wind had risen and the deck was almost deserted. As he stepped out of the door a gale lifted his heavy fur coat about his shoulders. He fought his way up the deck with keen exhilaration. The moment he stepped, almost out of breath, behind the shelter of the stern, the wind was cut off, and he felt, like a rush of warm air, a sense of close and intimate companionship. He started back and tore his coat open as if something warm were actually clinging to him beneath it. He hurried up the deck and went into the saloon parlor, full of women who had retreated thither from the sharp wind. He threw himself upon them. He talked delightfully to the older ones and played accompaniments for the younger ones until the last sleepy girl had followed her mother below. Then he went into the smoking-room. He played bridge until two o'clock in the morning, and managed to lose a considerable sum of money without really noticing that he was doing so.

After the break of one fine day the weather was pretty consistently dull. When the low sky thinned a trifle, the pale white spot of a sun did no more than throw a bluish lustre on the water, giving it the dark brightness of newly cut lead. Through one after another of those gray days Alexander drowsed and mused, drinking in the grateful moisture. But the complete peace of the first part of the voyage was over. Sometimes he rose suddenly from his chair as if driven out, and paced the deck for hours. People noticed his propensity for walking in rough weather, and watched him curiously as he did his rounds. From his abstraction and the determined set of his jaw, they fancied he must be thinking about his bridge. Every one had heard of the new cantilever bridge in Canada.

But Alexander was not thinking about his work. After the fourth night out, when his will suddenly softened under his hands, he had been continually hammering away at himself. More and more often, when he first wakened in the morning or when he stepped into a warm place after being chilled on the deck, he felt a sudden painful delight at being nearer another shore. Sometimes when he was most despondent, when he thought himself worn out with this struggle, in a flash he was free of it and leaped into an overwhelming consciousness of himself. On the instant he felt that marvelous return of the impetuousness, the intense excitement, the increasing expectancy of youth.

VI

The last two days of the voyage Bartley found almost intolerable. The stop at Queenstown, the tedious passage up the Mersey, were things that he noted dimly through his growing impatience. He had planned to stop in Liverpool; but, instead, he took the boat train for London.

Emerging at Euston at half-past three o'clock in the afternoon, Alexander had his luggage sent to the Savoy and drove at once to Bedford Square. When Marie met him at the door, even her strong sense of the proprieties could not restrain her surprise and delight. She blushed and smiled and fumbled his card in her confusion before she ran upstairs. Alexander paced up and down the hallway, buttoning and unbuttoning his overcoat, until she returned and took him up to Hilda's living-room. The room was empty when he entered. A coal fire was crackling in the grate and the lamps were lit, for it was already beginning to grow dark outside. Alexander did not sit down. He stood his ground over by the windows until Hilda came in. She called his name on the threshold, but in her swift flight across the room she felt a change in him and caught herself up so deftly that he could not tell just when she did it. She merely brushed his cheek with her lips and put a hand lightly and joyously on either shoulder.

"Oh, what a grand thing to happen on a raw day! I felt it in my bones when I woke this morning that something splendid was going to turn up. I thought it might be Sister Kate or Cousin Mike would be happening along. I never dreamed it would be you, Bartley. But why do you let me chatter on like this? Come over to the fire; you're chilled through."

She pushed him toward the big chair by the fire, and sat down on a stool at the opposite side of the hearth, her knees drawn up to her chin, laughing like a happy little girl.

"When did you come, Bartley, and how did it happen? You have n't spoken a word."

"I got in about ten minutes ago. I landed at Liverpool this morning and came down on the boat train."

Alexander leaned forward and warmed his hands before the blaze. Hilda watched him with perplexity.

"There's something troubling you, Bartley. What is it?"

Bartley bent lower over the fire. "It's the whole thing that troubles me, Hilda. You and I."

Hilda took a quick, soft breath. She looked at his heavy shoulders and big, determined head, thrust forward like a catapult in leash.

"What about us, Bartley?" she asked in a thin voice.

He locked and unlocked his hands over the grate and spread his fingers close to the bluish flame, while the coals crackled and the clock ticked and a street vendor began to call under the window. At last Alexander brought out one word:—

"Everything!"

Hilda was pale by this time, and her eyes were wide with fright. She looked about desperately from Bartley to the door, then to the windows, and back again to Bartley. She rose uncertainly, touched his hair with her hand, then sank back upon her stool.

"I'll do anything you wish me to, Bartley," she said tremulously. "I can't stand seeing you miserable."

"I can't live with myself any longer," he answered roughly.

He rose and pushed the chair behind him and began to walk miserably about the room, seeming to find it too small for him. He pulled up a window as if the air were heavy.

Hilda watched him from her corner, trembling and scarcely breathing, dark shadows growing about her eyes.

"It . . . it has n't always made you miserable, has it?" Her eyelids fell and her lips quivered.

"Always. But it's worse now. It's unbearable. It tortures me every minute."

"But why *now?*" she asked piteously, wringing her hands.

He ignored her question. "I am not a man who can live two lives," he went on feverishly. "Each life spoils the other. I get nothing but misery out of either. The world is all there, just as it used to be, but I can't get at it any more. There is this deception between me and everything."

At that word "deception," spoken with such self-contempt, the color flashed back into Hilda's face as suddenly as if she had been struck by a whiplash. She bit her lip and looked down at her hands, which were clasped tightly in front of her.

"Could you—could you sit down and talk about it quietly, Bartley, as if I wer : a friend, and not some one who had to be defied?"

He dropped back heavily into his chair by the fire. "It was myself I was defying, Hilda. I have thought about it until I am worn out."

He looked at her and his haggard face softened. He put out his hand toward her as he looked away again into the fire.

She crept across to him, drawing her stool after her. "When did you first begin to feel like this, Bartley?"

"After the very first. The first was—sort of in play, was n't it?"

Hilda's face quivered, but she whispered: "Yes, I think it must have been. But why did n't you tell me when you were here in the summer?"

Alexander groaned. "I meant to, but somehow I could n't. We had only a few days, and your new play was just on, and you were so happy."

"Yes, I was happy, was n't I?" She pressed his hand gently in gratitude. "Were n't you happy then, at all?"

She closed her eyes and took a deep breath, as if to draw in again the fragrance of those days. Something of their troubling sweetness came back to Alexander, too. He moved uneasily and his chair creaked.

"Yes, I was then. You know. But afterward . . ."

"Yes, yes," she hurried, pulling her hand gently away from him. Presently it stole back to his coat sleeve. "Please tell me one thing, Bartley. At least, tell me that you believe I thought I was making you happy."

His hand shut down quickly over the questioning fingers on his sleeves. "Yes, Hilda; I know that," he said simply.

She leaned her head against his arm and spoke softly:—

"You see, my mistake was in wanting you to have everything. I wanted you to eat all the cakes and have them, too. I somehow believed that I could take all the bad consequences for you. I wanted you always to be happy and handsome and successful—to have all the things that a great man ought to have, and, once in a way, the careless holidays that great men are not permitted."

Bartley gave a bitter little laugh, and Hilda looked up and read in the deepening lines of his face that youth and Bartley would not much longer struggle together.

"I understand, Bartley. I was wrong. But I did n't know. You've only to tell me now. What must I do that I've not done, or what must I not do?" She listened intently, but she heard nothing but the creaking of his chair. "You want me to say it?" she whispered. "You want to tell me that you can only see me like this, as old friends do, or out in the world among people? I can do that."

"I can't," he said heavily.

Hilda shivered and sat still. Bartley leaned his head in his hands and spoke through his teeth. "It's got to be a clean break, Hilda. I can't see you at all, anywhere. What I mean is that I want you to promise never to see me again, no matter how often I come, no matter how hard I beg."

Hilda sprang up like a flame. She stood over him with her hands clenched at her side, her body rigid.

"No!" she gasped. "It's too late to ask that. Do you hear me, Bartley? It's too late. I won't promise. It's abominable of you to ask me. Keep away if you wish; when have I ever followed you? But, if you come to me, I'll do as I see fit. The shamefulness of your asking me to do that! If you come to me, I'll do as I see fit. Do you understand? Bartley, you're cowardly!"

Alexander rose and shook himself angrily. "Yes, I know I'm cowardly. I'm afraid of myself. I don't trust myself any more. I carried it all lightly enough at first, but now I don't dare trifle with it. It's getting the better of me. It's different now. I'm growing older, and you've got my young self here with you. It's through him that I've come to wish for you all and all the time." He took her roughly in his arms. "Do you know what I mean?"

Hilda held her face back from him and began to cry bitterly. "Oh, Bartley, what am I to do? Why did n't you let me be angry with you? You ask me to stay away from you because you want me! And I've got nobody but you. I will do anything you say—but that! I will ask the least imaginable, but I must have *something!*"

Bartley turned away and sank down in his chair again. Hilda sat on the arm of it and put her hands lightly on his shoulders.

"Just something, Bartley. I must have you to think of through the months and months of loneliness. I must see you. I must know about you. The sight of you, Bartley, to see you living and happy and successful— can I never make you understand what that means to me?" She pressed his shoulders gently. "You see, loving some one as I love you makes the whole world different. If I'd met you later, if I had n't loved you so well—but

that's all over, long ago. Then came all those years without you, lonely and
hurt and discouraged; those decent young fellows and poor Mac, and me
never heeding—hard as a steel spring. And then you came back, not caring
very much, but it made no difference."

She slid to the floor beside him, as if she were too tired to sit up
any longer. Bartley bent over and took her in his arms, kissing her mouth
and her wet, tired eyes.

"Don't cry, don't cry," he whispered. "We've tortured each
other enough for to-night. Forget everything except that I am here."

"I think I have forgotten everything but that already," she
murmured. "Ah, your dear arms!"

VII

During the fortnight that Alexander
was in London he drove himself hard. He got through a great deal of
personal business and saw a great many men who were doing interesting
things in his own profession. He disliked to think of his visits to London as
holidays, and when he was there he worked even harder than he did at
home.

The day before his departure for Liverpool was a singularly fine
one. The thick air had cleared overnight in a strong wind which brought
in a golden dawn and then fell off to a fresh breeze. When Bartley looked
out of his windows from the Savoy, the river was flashing silver and the gray
stone along the Embankment was bathed in bright, clear sunshine. London
had wakened to life after three weeks of cold and sodden rain. Bartley
breakfasted hurriedly and went over his mail while the hotel valet packed
his trunks. Then he paid his account and walked rapidly down the Strand
past Charing Cross Station. His spirits rose with every step, and when he
reached Trafalgar Square, blazing in the sun, with its fountains playing and
its column reaching up into the bright air, he signaled to a hansom, and,
before he knew what he was about, told the driver to go to Bedford Square
by way of the British Museum.

When he reached Hilda's apartment she met him, fresh as the
morning itself. Her rooms were flooded with sunshine and full of the
flowers he had been sending her. She would never let him give her anything
else.

"Are you busy this morning, Hilda?" he asked as he sat down, his hat and gloves in his hand.

"Very. I've been up and about three hours, working at my part. We open in February, you know."

"Well, then you've worked enough. And so have I. I've seen all my men, my packing is done, and I go up to Liverpool this evening. But this morning we are going to have a holiday. What do you say to a drive out to Kew and Richmond? You may not get another day like this all winter. It's like a fine April day at home. May I use your telephone? I want to order the carriage."

"Oh, how jolly! There, sit down at the desk. And while you are telephoning I'll change my dress. I shan't be long. All the morning papers are on the table."

Hilda was back in a few moments wearing a long gray squirrel coat and a broad fur hat.

Bartley rose and inspected her. "Why don't you wear some of those pink roses?" he asked.

"But they came only this morning, and they have not even begun to open. I was saving them. I am so unconsciously thrifty!" She laughed as she looked about the room. "You've been sending me far too many flowers, Bartley. New ones every day. That's too often; though I do love to open the boxes, and I take good care of them."

"Why won't you let me send you any of those jade or ivory things you are so fond of? Or pictures? I know a good deal about pictures."

Hilda shook her large hat as she drew the roses out of the tall glass. "No, there are some things you can't do. There's the carriage. Will you button my gloves for me?"

Bartley took her wrist and began to button the long gray suede glove. "How gay your eyes are this morning, Hilda."

"That's because I've been studying. It always stirs me up a little."

He pushed the top of the glove up slowly. "When did you learn to take hold of your parts like that?"

"When I had nothing else to think of. Come, the carriage is waiting. What a shocking while you take."

"I'm in no hurry. We've plenty of time."

They found all London abroad. Piccadilly was a stream of rapidly moving carriages, from which flashed furs and flowers and bright winter costumes. The metal trappings of the harnesses shone dazzlingly, and the wheels were revolving disks that threw off rays of light. The parks were full of children and nursemaids and joyful dogs that leaped and yelped and scratched up the b.own earth with their paws.

"I'm not going until to-morrow, you know," Bartley announced suddenly. "I'll cut off a day in Liverpool. I have n't felt so jolly this long while."

Hilda looked up with a smile which she tried not to make too glad. "I think people were meant to be happy, a little," she said.

They had lunch at Richmond and then walked to Twickenham, where they had sent the carriage. They drove back, with a glorious sunset behind them, toward the distant gold-washed city. It was one of those rare afternoons when all the thickness and shadow of London are changed to a kind of shining, pulsing, special atmosphere; when the smoky vapors become fluttering golden clouds, nacreous veils of pink and amber; when all that bleakness of gray stone and dullness of dirty brick trembles in aureate light, and all the roofs and spires, and one great dome, are floated in golden haze. On such rare afternoons the ugliest of cities becomes the most beautiful, the most prosaic becomes the most poetic, and months of sodden days are offset by a moment of miracle.

"It's like that with us Londoners, too," Hilda was saying. "Everything is awfully grim and cheerless, our weather and our houses and our ways of amusing ourselves. But we can be happier than anybody. We can go mad with joy, as the people do out in the fields on a fine Whitsunday. We make the most of our moment."

She thrust her little chin out defiantly over her gray fur collar, and Bartley looked down at her and laughed.

"You are a plucky one, you." He patted her glove with his hand. "Yes, you are a plucky one."

Hilda sighed. "No, I'm not. Not about some things, at any rate. It does n't take pluck to fight for one's moment, but it takes pluck to go without—a lot. More than I have. I can't help it," she added fiercely.

After miles of outlying streets and little gloomy houses, they reached London itself, red and roaring and murky, with a thick dampness coming up from the river, that betokened fog again to-morrow. The streets were full of people who had worked indoors all through the priceless day and had now come hungrily out to drink the muddy lees of it. They stood in long black lines, waiting before the pit entrances of the theatres—short-coated boys, and girls in sailor hats, all shivering and chatting gayly. There was a blurred rhythm in all the dull city noises—in the clatter of the cab horses and the rumbling of the busses, in the street calls, and in the undulating tramp, tramp of the crowd. It was like the deep vibration of some vast underground machinery, and like the muffled pulsations of millions of human hearts.

"Seems good to get back, does n't it?" Bartley whispered, as they drove from Bayswater Road into Oxford Street. "London always makes me want to live more than any other city in the world. You remember our priestess mummy over in the mummy-room, and how we used to long to go and bring her out on nights like this? Three thousand years! Ugh!"

"All the same, I believe she used to feel it when we stood there and watched her and wished her well. I believe she used to remember," Hilda said thoughtfully.

"I hope so. Now let's go to some awfully jolly place for dinner before we go home. I could eat all the dinners there are in London to-night. Where shall I tell the driver? The Piccadilly Restaurant? The music's good there."

"There are too many people there whom one knows. Why not that little French place in Soho, where we went so often when you were here in the summer? I love it, and I've never been there with any one but you. Sometimes I go by myself, when I am particularly lonely."

"Very well, the sole's good there. How many street pianos there are about to-night! The fine weather must have thawed them out. We've had five miles of 'Il Trovatore' now. They always make me feel jaunty. Are you comfy, and not too tired?"

"I'm not tired at all. I was just wondering how people can ever die. Why did you remind me of the mummy? Life seems the strongest and most indestructible thing in the world. Do you really believe that all those people rushing about down there, going to good dinners and clubs and theatres, will be dead some day, and not care about anything? I don't believe it, and I know I shan't die, ever! You see, I feel too—too powerful!"

The carriage stopped. Bartley sprang out and swung her quickly to the pavement. As he lifted her in his two hands he whispered: "You are—powerful!"

VIII

*T*he last rehearsal was over, a tedious dress rehearsal which had lasted all day and exhausted the patience of every one who had to do with it. When Hilda had dressed for the street and came out of her dressing-room, she found Hugh MacConnell waiting for her in the corridor.

"The fog's thicker than ever, Hilda. There have been a great many accidents to-day. It's positively unsafe for you to be out alone. Will you let me take you home?"

"How good of you, Mac. If you are going with me, I think I'd rather walk. I've had no exercise to-day, and all this has made me nervous."

"I should n't wonder," said MacConnell dryly. Hilda pulled down her veil and they stepped out into the thick brown wash that submerged St. Martin's Lane. MacConnell took her hand and tucked it snugly under his arm. "I'm sorry I was such a savage. I hope you did n't think I made an ass of myself."

"Not a bit of it. I don't wonder you were peppery. Those things are awfully trying. How do you think it's going?"

"Magnificently. That's why I got so stirred up. We are going to hear from this, both of us. And that reminds me; I've got news for you. They are going to begin repairs on the theatre about the middle of March, and we are to run over to New York for six weeks. Bennett told me yesterday that it was decided."

Hilda looked up delightedly at the tall gray figure beside her. He was the only thing she could see, for they were moving through a dense opaqueness, as if they were walking at the bottom of the ocean.

"Oh, Mac, how glad I am! And they love your things over there, don't they?"

"Shall you be glad for—any other reason, Hilda?"

MacConnell put his hand in front of her to ward off some dark object. It proved to be only a lamp-post, and they beat in farther from the edge of the pavement.

"What do you mean, Mac?" Hilda asked nervously.

"I was just thinking there might be people over there you'd be glad to see," he brought out awkwardly. Hilda said nothing, and as they walked on MacConnell spoke again, apologetically: "I hope you don't mind my knowing about it, Hilda. Don't stiffen up like that. No one else knows, and I did n't try to find out anything. I felt it, even before I knew who he was. I knew there was somebody, and that it was n't I."

They crossed Oxford Street in silence, feeling their way. The busses had stopped running and the cab-drivers were leading their horses. When they reached the other side, MacConnell said suddenly, "I hope you are happy."

"Terribly, dangerously happy, Mac,"—Hilda spoke quietly, pressing the rough sleeve of his greatcoat with her gloved hand.

"You've always thought me too old for you, Hilda,—oh, of course you've never said just that,—and here this fellow is not more than eight years younger than I. I've always felt that if I could get out of my old case I might win you yet. It's a fine, brave youth I carry inside me, only he'll never be seen."

"Nonsense, Mac. That has nothing to do with it. It's because you seem too close to me, too much my own kind. It would be like marrying Cousin Mike, almost. I really tried to care as you wanted me to, away back in the beginning."

"Well, here we are, turning out of the Square. You are not angry with me, Hilda? Thank you for this walk, my dear. Go in and get dry things on at once. You'll be having a great night to-morrow."

She put out her hand. "Thank you, Mac, for everything. Goodnight."

MacConnell trudged off through the fog, and she went slowly upstairs. Her slippers and dressing gown were waiting for her before the fire. "I shall certainly see him in New York. He will see by the papers that we are coming. Perhaps he knows it already," Hilda kept thinking as she undressed. "Perhaps he will be at the dock. No, scarcely that; but I may meet him in the street even before he comes to see me." Marie placed the tea-table by the fire and brought Hilda her letters. She looked them over, and started as she came to one in a handwriting that she did not often see; Alexander had written to her only twice before, and he did not allow her to write to him at all. "Thank you, Marie. You may go now."

Hilda sat down by the table with the letter in her hand, still unopened. She looked at it intently, turned it over, and felt its thickness with her fingers. She believed that she sometimes had a kind of second-sight about letters, and could tell before she read them whether they brought good or evil tidings. She put this one down on the table in front of her while she poured her tea. At last, with a little shiver of expectancy, she tore open the envelope and read:—

BOSTON, February——

MY DEAR HILDA:—

It is after twelve o'clock. Every one else is in bed and I am sitting alone in my study. I have been happier in this room than anywhere else in the world. Happiness like that makes one insolent. I used to think these four walls could stand against anything. And now I scarcely know myself here. Now I know that no one can build his security upon the nobleness of another person. Two people, when they love each other, grow alike in their tastes and habits and pride, but their moral natures (whatever we may mean by that canting expression) are never welded. The base one goes on being base, and the noble one noble, to the end.

The last week has been a bad one; I have been realizing how things used to be with me. Sometimes I get used to being dead inside, but lately it has been as if a window beside me had suddenly opened, and as if all the smells of spring blew in to me. There is a garden out there, with stars overhead, where I used to walk at night when I had a single purpose and a single heart. I can remember how I used to feel there, how beautiful everything about me was, and what life and power and freedom I felt in myself. When the window opens I know exactly how it would feel to be out there. But that garden is closed to me. How is it, I ask myself, that everything can be so different with me when nothing here has changed? I am in my own house, in my own study, in the midst of all these quiet streets where my friends live. They are all safe and at peace with themselves. But I am never at peace. I feel always on the edge of danger and change.

I keep remembering locoed horses I used to see on the range when I was a boy. They changed like that. We used to catch them and put them up in the corral, and they developed great cunning. They would pretend to eat their

oats like the other horses, but we knew they were always
scheming to get back at the loco.

It seems that a man is meant to live only one life in this
world. When he tries to live a second, he develops another
nature. I feel as if a second man had been grafted into me.
At first he seemed only a pleasure-loving simpleton, of
whose company I was rather ashamed, and whom I used
to hide under my coat when I walked the Embankment,
in London. But now he is strong and sullen, and he is
fighting for his life at the cost of mine. That is his one
activity: to grow strong. No creature ever wanted so much
to live. Eventually, I suppose, he will absorb me altogether.
Believe me, you will hate me then.

And what have you to do, Hilda, with this ugly story?
Nothing at all. The little boy drank of the prettiest brook
in the forest and he became a stag. I write all this because
I can never tell it to you, and because it seems as if I could
not keep silent any longer. And because I suffer, Hilda. If
any one I loved suffered like this, I'd want to know it. Help
me, Hilda!

B. A.

IX

On the last Saturday in April, the
New York "Times" published an account of the strike complications
which were delaying Alexander's New Jersey bridge, and stated that the
engineer himself was in town and at his office on West Tenth Street.

On Sunday, the day after this notice appeared, Alexander
worked all day at his Tenth Street rooms. His business often called him to
New York, and he had kept an apartment there for years, subletting it when
he went abroad for any length of time. Besides his sleeping-room and bath,
there was a large room, formerly a painter's studio, which he used as a study
and office. It was furnished with the cast-off possessions of his bachelor days
and with odd things which he sheltered for friends of his who followed
itinerant and more or less artistic callings. Over the fireplace there was a

large old-fashioned gilt mirror. Alexander's big work-table stood in front of one of the three windows, and above the couch hung the one picture in the room, a big canvas of charming color and spirit, a study of the Luxembourg Gardens in early spring, painted in his youth by a man who had since become a portrait-painter of international renown. He had done it for Alexander when they were students together in Paris.

Sunday was a cold, raw day and a fine rain fell continuously. When Alexander came back from dinner he put more wood on his fire, made himself comfortable, and settled down at his desk, where he began checking over estimate sheets. It was after nine o'clock and he was lighting a second pipe, when he thought he heard a sound at his door. He started and listened, holding the burning match in his hand; again he heard the same sound, like a firm, light tap. He rose and crossed the room quickly. When he threw open the door he recognized the figure that shrank back into the bare, dimly lit hallway. He stood for a moment in awkward constraint, his pipe in his hand.

"Come in," he said to Hilda at last, and closed the door behind her. He pointed to a chair by the fire and went back to his work-table. "Won't you sit down?"

He was standing behind the table, turning over a pile of blue-prints nervously. The yellow light from the student's lamp fell on his hands and the purple sleeves of his velvet smoking-jacket, but his flushed face and big, hard head were in the shadow. There was something about him that made Hilda wish herself at her hotel again, in the street below, anywhere but where she was.

"Of course I know, Bartley," she said at last, "that after this you won't owe me the least consideration. But we sail on Tuesday. I saw that interview in the paper yesterday, telling where you were, and I thought I had to see you. That's all. Good-night; I'm going now." She turned and her hand closed on the door-knob.

Alexander hurried toward her and took her gently by the arm. "Sit down, Hilda; you're wet through. Let me take off your coat—and your boots; they're oozing water." He knelt down and began to unlace her shoes, while Hilda shrank into the chair. "Here, put your feet on this stool. You don't mean to say you walked down—and without overshoes!"

Hilda hid her face in her hands. "I was afraid to take a cab. Can't you see, Bartley, that I'm terribly frightened? I've been through this a hundred times to-day. Don't be any more angry than you can help. I was all right until I knew you were in town. If you'd sent me a note, or telephoned me, or anything! But you won't let me write to you, and I had to see you after that letter, that terrible letter you wrote me when you got home.''

Alexander faced her, resting his arm on the mantel behind him, and began to brush the sleeve of his jacket. "Is this the way you mean to answer it, Hilda?'' he asked unsteadily.

She was afraid to look up at him. "Did n't—did n't you mean even to say good-by to me, Bartley? Did you mean just to—quit me?'' she asked. "I came to tell you that I'm willing to do as you asked me. But it's no use talking about that now. Give me my things, please.'' She put her hand out toward the fender.

Alexander sat down on the arm of her chair. "Did you think I had forgotten you were in town, Hilda? Do you think I kept away by accident? Did you suppose I did n't know you were sailing on Tuesday? There is a letter for you there, in my desk drawer. It was to have reached you on the steamer. I was all the morning writing it. I told myself that if I were really thinking of you, and not of myself, a letter would be better than nothing. Marks on paper mean something to you.'' He paused. "They never did to me.''

Hilda smiled up at him beautifully and put her hand on his sleeve. "Oh, Bartley! Did you write to me? Why did n't you telephone me to let me know that you had? Then I would n't have come.''

Alexander slipped his arm about her. "I did n't know it before, Hilda, on my honor I did n't, but I believe it was because, deep down in me somewhere, I was hoping I might drive you to do just this. I've watched that door all day. I've jumped up if the fire crackled. I think I have felt that you were coming.'' He bent his face over her hair.

"And I,'' she whispered,—"I felt that you were feeling that. But when I came, I thought I had been mistaken.''

Alexander started up and began to walk up and down the room.

"No, you were n't mistaken. I've been up in Canada with my bridge, and I arranged not to come to New York until after you had gone. Then, when your manager added two more weeks, I was already committed.'' He dropped upon the stool in front of her and sat with his hands hanging between his knees. "What am I to do, Hilda?''

"That's what I wanted to see you about, Bartley. I'm going to do what you asked me to do, when you were in London. Only I'll do it more completely. I'm going to marry.''

"Who?''

"Oh, it does n't matter much! One of them. Only not Mac. I'm too fond of him."

Alexander moved restlessly. "Are you joking, Hilda?"

"Indeed I'm not."

"Then you don't know what you're talking about."

"Yes, I know very well. I've thought about it a great deal, and I've quite decided. I never used to understand how women did things like that, but I know now. It's because they can't be at the mercy of the man they love any longer."

Alexander flushed angrily. "So it's better to be at the mercy of a man you don't love?"

"Under such circumstances, infinitely!"

There was a flash in her eyes that made Alexander's fall. He got up and went over to the window, threw it open, and leaned out. He heard Hilda moving about behind him. When he looked over his shoulder she was lacing her boots. He went back and stood over her.

"Hilda, you'd better think a while longer before you do that. I don't know what I ought to say, but I don't believe you'd be happy; truly I don't. Are n't you trying to frighten me?"

She tied the knot of the last lacing and put her boot-heel down firmly. "No; I'm telling you what I've made up my mind to do. I suppose I would better do it without telling you. But afterward I shan't have an opportunity to explain, for I shan't be seeing you again."

Alexander started to speak, but caught himself. When Hilda rose he sat down on the arm of her chair and drew her back into it.

"I would n't be so much alarmed if I did n't know how utterly reckless you *can* be. Don't do anything like that rashly." His face grew troubled. "You would n't be happy. You are not that kind of woman. I'd never have another hour's peace if I helped to make you do a thing like that." He took her face between his hands and looked down into it. "You see, you are different, Hilda. Don't you know you are?" His voice grew softer, his touch more and more tender. "Some women can do that sort of thing, but you—you can love as queens did, in the old time."

Hilda had heard that soft, deep tone in his voice only once before. She closed her eyes; her lips and eyelids trembled. "Only one, Bartley. Only one. And he threw it back at me a second time."

She felt the strength leap in the arms that held her so lightly.

"Try him again, Hilda. Try him once again."

She looked up into his eyes, and hid her face in her hands.

X

On Tuesday afternoon a Boston lawyer, who had been trying a case in Vermont, was standing on the siding at White River Junction when the Canadian Express pulled by on its northward journey. As the day-coaches at the rear end of the long train swept by him, the lawyer noticed at one of the windows a man's head, with thick rumpled hair. "Curious," he thought; "that looked like Alexander, but what would he be doing back there in the day-coaches?"

It was, indeed, Alexander.

That morning a telegram from Moorlock had reached him, telling him that there was serious trouble with the bridge and that he was needed there at once, so he had caught the first train out of New York. He had taken a seat in a day-coach to avoid the risk of meeting any one he knew, and because he did not wish to be comfortable. When the telegram arrived, Alexander was at his rooms on Tenth Street, packing his bag to go to Boston. On Monday night he had written a long letter to his wife, but when morning came he was afraid to send it, and the letter was still in his pocket. Winifred was not a woman who could bear disappointment. She demanded a great deal of herself and of the people she loved; and she never failed herself. If he told her now, he knew, it would be irretrievable. There would be no going back. He would lose the thing he valued most in the world; he would be destroying himself and his own happiness. There would be nothing for him afterward. He seemed to see himself dragging out a restless existence on the Continent—Cannes, Hyères, Algiers, Cairo—among smartly dressed, disabled men of every nationality; forever going on journeys that led nowhere; hurrying to catch trains that he might just as well miss; getting up in the morning with a great bustle and splashing of water, to begin a day that had no purpose and no meaning; dining late to shorten the night, sleeping late to shorten the day.

And for what? For a mere folly, a masquerade, a little thing that he could not let go. *And he could even let it go,* he told himself. But he had promised to be in London at midsummer, and he knew that he would go. . . . It was impossible to live like this any longer.

And this, then, was to be the disaster that his old professor had foreseen for him: the crack in the wall, the crash, the cloud of dust. And he could not understand how it had come about. He felt that he himself was unchanged, that he was still there, the same man he had been five years ago, and that he was sitting stupidly by and letting some resolute offshoot of himself spoil his life for him. This new force was not he, it was but a part of him. He would not even admit that it was stronger than he; but it was more active. It was by its energy that this new feeling got the better of him. His wife was the woman who had made his life, gratified his pride, given direction to his tastes and habits. The life they led together seemed to him beautiful. Winifred still was, as she had always been, Romance for him, and whenever he was deeply stirred he turned to her. When the grandeur and beauty of the world challenged him—as it challenges even the most self-absorbed people—he always answered with her name. That was his reply to the question put by the mountains and the stars; to all the spiritual aspects of life. In his feeling for his wife there was all the tenderness, all the pride, all the devotion of which he was capable. There was everything but energy; the energy of youth which must register itself and cut its name before it passes. This new feeling was so fresh, so unsatisfied and light of foot. It ran and was not wearied, anticipated him everywhere. It put a girdle round the earth while he was going from New York to Moorlock. At this moment, it was tingling through him, exultant, and live as quicksilver, whispering, "In July you will be in England."

Already he dreaded the long, empty days at sea, the monotonous Irish coast, the sluggish passage up the Mersey, the flash of the boat train through the summer country. He closed his eyes and gave himself up to the feeling of rapid motion and to swift, terrifying thoughts. He was sitting so, his face shaded by his hand, when the Boston lawyer saw him from the siding at White River Junction.

When at last Alexander roused himself, the afternoon had wanted to sunset. The train was passing through a gray country and the sky overhead was flushed with a wide flood of clear color. There was a rose-colored light over the gray rocks and hills and meadows. Off to the left, under the approach of a weather-stained wooden bridge, a group of boys were sitting around a little fire. The smell of the wood smoke blew in at the window. Except for an old farmer, jogging along the highroad in his box-wagon, there was not another living creature to be seen. Alexander looked back wistfully at the boys, camped on the edge of a little marsh, crouching under their shelter and looking gravely at their fire. They took his mind back a long way, to a campfire on a sandbar in a Western river, and he wished he could go back and sit down with them. He could remember exactly how the world had looked then.

It was quite dark and Alexander was still thinking of the boys, when it occurred to him that the train must be nearing Allway. In going to his new bridge at Moorlock he had always to pass through Allway. The train stopped at Allway Mills, then wound two miles up the river, and then the hollow sound under his feet told Bartley that he was on his first bridge again. The bridge seemed longer than it had ever seemed before, and he was glad when he felt the beat of the wheels on the solid roadbed again. He did not like coming and going across that bridge, or remembering the man who built it. And was he, indeed, the same man who used to walk that bridge at night, promising such things to himself and to the stars? And yet, he could remember it all so well: the quiet hills sleeping in the moonlight, the slender skeleton of the bridge reaching out into the river, and up yonder, alone on the hill, the big white house; upstairs, in Winifred's window, the light that told him she was still awake and still thinking of him. And after the light went out he walked alone, taking the heavens into his confidence, unable to tear himself away from the white magic of the night, unwilling to sleep because longing was so sweet to him, and because, for the first time since first the hills were hung with moonlight, there was a lover in the world. And always there was the sound of the rushing water underneath, the sound which, more than anything else, meant death; the wearing away of things under the impact of physical forces which men could direct but never circumvent or diminish. Then, in the exaltation of love, more than ever it seemed to him to mean death, the only other thing as strong as love. Under the moon, under the cold, splendid stars, there were only those two things awake and sleepless; death and love, the rushing river and his burning heart.

Alexander sat up and looked about him. The train was tearing on through the darkness. All his companions in the day-coach were either dozing or sleeping heavily, and the murky lamps were turned low. How came he here among all these dirty people? Why was he going to London? What did it mean—what was the answer? How could this happen to a man who had lived through that magical spring and summer, and who had felt that the stars themselves were but flaming particles in the far-away infinitudes of his love?

What had he done to lose it? How could he endure the baseness of life without it? And with every revolution of the wheels beneath him, the unquiet quicksilver in his breast told him that at midsummer he would be in London. He remembered his last night there: the red foggy darkness, the hungry crowds before the theatres, the hand-organs, the feverish rhythm of the blurred, crowded streets, and the feeling of letting himself go with the crowd. He shuddered and looked about him at the poor unconscious companions of his journey, unkempt and travel-stained, now doubled in unlovely attitudes, who had come to stand to him for the ugliness he had brought into the world.

And those boys back there, beginning it all just as he had begun it; he wished he could promise them better luck. Ah, if one could promise any one better luck, if one could assure a single human being of happiness! He had thought he could do so, once; and it was thinking of that that he at last fell asleep. In his sleep, as if it had nothing fresher to work upon, his mind went back and tortured itself with something years and years away, an old, long-forgotten sorrow of his childhood.

When Alexander awoke in the morning, the sun was just rising through pale golden ripples of cloud, and the fresh yellow light was vibrating through the pine woods. The white birches, with their little unfolding leaves, gleamed in the lowlands, and the marsh meadows were already coming to life with their first green, a thin, bright color which had run over them like fire. As the train rushed along the trestles, thousands of wild birds rose screaming into the light. The sky was already a pale blue and of the clearness of crystal. Bartley caught up his bag and hurried through the Pullman coaches until he found the conductor. There was a stateroom unoccupied, and he took it and set about changing his clothes. Last night he would not have believed that anything could be so pleasant as the cold water he dashed over his head and shoulders and the freshness of clean linen on his body.

After he had dressed, Alexander sat down at the window and drew into his lungs deep breaths of the pine-scented air. He had awakened with all his old sense of power. He could not believe that things were as bad with him as they had seemed last night, that there was no way to set them entirely right. Even if he went to London at midsummer, what would that mean except that he was a fool? And he had been a fool before. That was not the reality of his life. Yet he knew that he would go to London.

Half an hour later the train stopped at Moorlock. Alexander sprang to the platform and hurried up the siding, waving to Philip Horton, one of his assistants, who was anxiously looking up at the windows of the coaches. Bartley took his arm and they went together into the station buffet.

"I'll have my coffee first, Philip. Have you had yours? And now, what seems to be the matter up here?"

The young man, in a hurried, nervous way, began his explanation.

But Alexander cut him short. "When did you stop work?" he asked sharply.

The young engineer looked confused. "I have n't stopped work yet, Mr. Alexander. I did n't feel that I could go so far without definite authorization from you."

"Then why did n't you say in your telegram exactly what you thought, and ask for your authorization? You'd have got it quick enough."

"Well, really, Mr. Alexander, I could n't be absolutely sure, you know, and I did n't like to take the responsibility of making it public."

Alexander pushed back his chair and rose. "Anything I do can be made public, Phil. You say that you believe the lower chords are showing strain, and that even the workmen have been talking about it, and yet you've gone on adding weight."

"I'm sorry, Mr. Alexander, but I had counted on your getting here yesterday. My first telegram missed you somehow. I sent one Sunday evening, to the same address, but it was returned to me."

"Have you a carriage out there? I must stop to send a wire."

Alexander went up to the telegraph-desk and penciled the following message to his wife:—

> *I may have to be here for some time. Can you come up at once?*
> *Urgent.*
>
> BARTLEY.

The Moorlock Bridge lay three miles above the town. When they were seated in the carriage, Alexander began to question his assistant further. If it were true that the compression members showed strain, with the bridge only two thirds done, then there was nothing to do but pull the whole structure down and begin over again. Horton kept repeating that he was sure there could be nothing wrong with the estimates.

Alexander grew impatient. "That's all true, Phil, but we never were justified in assuming that a scale that was perfectly safe for an ordinary bridge would work with anything of such length. It's all very well on paper, but it remains to be seen whether it can be done in practice. I should have thrown up the job when they crowded me. It's all nonsense to try to do what other engineers are doing when you know they're not sound."

"But just now, when there is such competition," the younger man demurred. "And certainly that's the new line of development."

Alexander shrugged his shoulders and made no reply.

When they reached the bridge works, Alexander began his examination immediately. An hour later he sent for the superintendent. "I think you had better stop work out there at once, Dan. I should say that the lower chord here might buckle at any moment. I told the Commission that we were using higher unit stresses than any practice has established, and we've put the dead load at a low estimate. Theoretically it worked out well enough, but it had never actually been tried." Alexander put on his overcoat and took the superintendent by the arm. "Don't look so chopfallen, Dan. It's a jolt, but we've got to face it. It is n't the end of the world, you know. Now we'll go out and call the men off quietly. They're already nervous, Horton tells me, and there's no use alarming them. I'll go with you, and we'll send the end riveters in first."

Alexander and the superintendent picked their way out slowly over the long span. They went deliberately, stopping to see what each gang was doing, as if they were on an ordinary round of inspection. When they reached the end of the river span, Alexander nodded to the superintendent, who quietly gave an order to the foreman. The men in the end gang picked up their tools and, glancing curiously at each other, started back across the bridge toward the river-bank. Alexander himself remained standing where they had been working, looking about him. It was hard to believe, as he looked back over it, that the whole great span was incurably disabled, was already as good as condemned, because something was out of line in the lower chord of the cantilever arm.

The end riveters had reached the bank and were dispersing among the tool-houses, and the second gang had picked up their tools and were starting toward the shore. Alexander, still standing at the end of the river span, saw the lower chord of the cantilever arm give a little, like an elbow bending. He shouted and ran after the second gang, but by this time every one knew that the big river span was slowly settling. There was a burst of shouting that was immediately drowned by the scream and cracking of tearing iron, as all the tension work began to pull asunder. Once the chords began to buckle, there were thousands of tons of ironwork, all riveted together and lying in midair without support. It tore itself to pieces with roaring and grinding and noises that were like the shrieks of a steam whistle. There was no shock of any kind; the bridge had no impetus except from its own weight. It lurched neither to right nor left, but sank almost in a vertical line, snapping and breaking and tearing as it went, because no integral part could bear for an instant the enormous strain loosed upon it. Some of the men jumped and some ran, trying to make the shore.

At the first shriek of the tearing iron, Alexander jumped from the downstream side of the bridge. He struck the water without injury and disappeared. He was under the river a long time and had great difficulty in holding his breath. When it seemed impossible, and his chest was about to heave, he thought he heard his wife telling him that he could hold out a little longer. An instant later his face cleared the water. For a moment, in the depths of the river, he had realized what it would mean to die a hypocrite, and to lie dead under the last abandonment of her tenderness. But once in the light and air, he knew he should live to tell her and to recover all he had lost. Now, at last, he felt sure of himself. He was not startled. It seemed to him that he had been through something of this sort before. There was nothing horrible about it. This, too, was life, and life was activity, just as it was in Boston or in London. He was himself, and there was something to be done; everything seemed perfectly natural. Alexander was a strong swimmer, but he had gone scarcely a dozen strokes when the bridge itself, which had been settling faster and faster, crashed into the water behind him. Immediately the river was full of drowning men. A gang of French Canadians fell almost on top of him. He thought he had cleared them, when they began coming up all around him, clutching at him and at each other. Some of them could swim, but they were either hurt or crazed with fright. Alexander tried to beat them off, but there were too many of them. One caught him about the neck, another gripped him about the middle, and they went down together. When he sank, his wife seemed to be there in the water beside him, telling him to keep his head, that if he could hold out the men would drown and release him. There was something he wanted to tell his wife, but he could not think clearly for the roaring in his ears. Suddenly he remembered what it was. He caught his breath, and then she let him go.

The work of recovering the dead went on all day and all the following night. By the next morning forty-eight bodies had been taken out of the river, but there were still twenty missing. Many of the men had fallen with the bridge and were held down under the débris. Early on the morning of the second day a closed carriage was driven slowly along the river-bank and stopped a little below the works, where the river boiled and churned about the great iron carcass which lay in a straight line two thirds across it.

The carriage stood there hour after hour, and word soon spread among the crowds on the shore that its occupant was the wife of the Chief Engineer; his body had not yet been found. The widows of the lost workmen, moving up and down the bank with shawls over their heads, some of them carrying babies, looked at the rusty hired hack many times that morning. They drew near it and walked about it, but none of them ventured to peer within. Even half-indifferent sight-seers dropped their voices as they told a newcomer: "You see that carriage over there? That's Mrs. Alexander. They have n't found him yet. She got off the train this morning. Horton met her. She heard it in Boston yesterday—heard the newsboys crying it in the street."

At noon Philip Horton made his way through the crowd with a tray and a tin coffee-pot from the camp kitchen. When he reached the carriage he found Mrs. Alexander just as he had left her in the early morning, leaning forward a little, with her hand on the lowered window, looking at the river. Hour after hour she had been watching the water, the lonely, useless stone towers, and the convulsed mass of iron wreckage over which the angry river continually spat up its yellow foam.

"Those poor women out there, do they blame him very much?" she asked, as she handed the coffee-cup back to Horton.

"Nobody blames him, Mrs. Alexander. If any one is to blame, I'm afraid it's I. I should have stopped work before he came. He said so as soon as I met him. I tried to get him here a day earlier, but my telegram missed him, somehow. He did n't have time really to explain to me. If he'd got here Monday, he'd have had all the men off at once. But, you see, Mrs. Alexander, such a thing never happened before. According to all human calculations, it simply could n't happen."

Horton leaned wearily against the front wheel of the cab. He had not had his clothes off for thirty hours, and the stimulus of violent excitement was beginning to wear off.

"Don't be afraid to tell me the worst, Mr. Horton. Don't leave me to the dread of finding out things that people may be saying. If he is blamed, if he needs any one to speak for him,"—for the first time her voice broke and a flush of life, tearful, painful, and confused, swept over her rigid pallor,—"if he needs any one, tell me, show me what to do." She began to sob, and Horton hurried away.

When he came back at four o'clock in the afternoon he was carrying his hat in his hand, and Winifred knew as soon as she saw him that they had found Bartley. She opened the carriage door before he reached her and stepped to the ground.

Horton put out his hand as if to hold her back and spoke

pleadingly: "Won't you drive up to my house, Mrs. Alexander? They will take him up there."

"Take me to him now, please. I shall not make any trouble."

The group of men down under the river-bank fell back when they saw a woman coming, and one of them threw a tarpaulin over the stretcher. They took off their hats and caps as Winifred approached, and although she had pulled her veil down over her face they did not look up at her. She was taller than Horton, and some of the men thought she was the tallest woman they had ever seen. "As tall as himself," some one whispered. Horton motioned to the men, and six of them lifted the stretcher and began to carry it up the embankment. Winifred followed them the half-mile to Horton's house. She walked quietly, without once breaking or stumbling. When the bearers put the stretcher down in Horton's spare bedroom, she thanked them and gave her hand to each in turn. The men went out of the house and through the yard with their caps in their hands. They were too much confused to say anything as they went down the hill.

Horton himself was almost as deeply perplexed. "Mamie," he said to his wife, when he came out of the spare room half an hour later, "will you take Mrs. Alexander the things she needs? She is going to do everything herself. Just stay about where you can hear her and go in if she wants you."

Everything happened as Alexander had foreseen in that moment of prescience under the river. With her own hands she washed him clean of every mark of disaster. All night he was alone with her in the still house, his great head lying deep in the pillow. In the pocket of his coat Winifred found the letter that he had written her the night before he left New York, water-soaked and illegible, but because of its length, she knew it had been meant for her.

For Alexander death was an easy creditor. Fortune, which had smiled upon him consistently all his life, did not desert him in the end. His harshest critics did not doubt that, had he lived, he would have retrieved himself. Even Lucius Wilson did not see in this accident the disaster he had once foretold.

When a great man dies in his prime there is no surgeon who can say whether he did well; whether or not the future was his, as it seemed to be. The mind that society had come to regard as a powerful and reliable machine, dedicated to its service, may for a long time have been sick within itself and bent upon its own destruction.

Epilogue

*P*rofessor Wilson had been living in London for six years and he was just back from a visit to America. One afternoon, soon after his return, he put on his frock-coat and drove in a hansom to pay a call upon Hilda Burgoyne, who still lived at her old number, off Bedford Square. He and Miss Burgoyne had been fast friends for a long time. He had first noticed her about the corridors of the British Museum, where he read constantly. Her being there so often had made him feel that he would like to know her, and as she was not an inaccessible person, an introduction was not difficult. The preliminaries once over, they came to depend a great deal upon each other, and Wilson, after his day's reading, often went round to Bedford Square for his tea. They had much more in common than their memories of a common friend. Indeed, they seldom spoke of him. They saved that for the deep moments which do not come often, and then their talk of him was mostly silence. Wilson knew that Hilda had loved him; more than this he had not tried to know.

It was late when Wilson reached Hilda's apartment on this particular December afternoon, and he found her alone. She sent for fresh tea and made him comfortable, as she had such a knack of making people comfortable.

"How good you were to come back before Christmas! I quite dreaded the Holidays without you. You've helped me over a good many Christmases." She smiled at him gayly.

"As if you needed me for that! But, at any rate, I needed *you*. How well you are looking, my dear, and how rested."

He peered up at her from his low chair, balancing the tips of his long fingers together in a judicial manner which had grown on him with years.

Hilda laughed as she carefully poured his cream. "That means that I was looking very seedy at the end of the season, does n't it? Well, we must show wear at last, you know."

Wilson took the cup gratefully. "Ah, no need to remind a man of seventy, who has just been home to find that he has survived all his contemporaries. I was most gently treated—as a sort of precious relic. But, do you know, it made me feel awkward to be hanging about still."

"Seventy? Never mention it to me." Hilda looked appreciatively at the Professor's alert face, with so many kindly lines about the mouth and so many quizzical ones about the eyes. "You've got to hang about for me, you know. I can't even let you go home again. You must stay put, now that I have you back. You're the realest thing I have."

Wilson chuckled. "Dear me, am I? Out of so many conquests and the spoils of conquered cities! You've really missed me? Well, then, I shall hang. Even if you have at last to put *me* in the mummy-room with the others. You'll visit me often, won't you?"

"Every day in the calendar. Here, your cigarettes are in this drawer, where you left them." She struck a match and lit one for him. "But you did, after all, enjoy being at home again?"

"Oh, yes. I found the long railway journeys trying. People live a thousand miles apart. But I did it thoroughly; I was all over the place. It was in Boston I lingered longest."

"Ah, you saw Mrs. Alexander?"

"Often. I dined with her, and had tea there a dozen different times, I should think. Indeed, it was to see her that I lingered on and on. I found that I still loved to go to the house. It always seemed as if Bartley were there, somehow, and that at any moment one might hear his heavy tramp on the stairs. Do you know, I kept feeling that he must be up in his study." The Professor looked reflectively into the grate. "I should really have liked to go up there. That was where I had my last long talk with him. But Mrs. Alexander never suggested it."

"Why?"

Wilson was a little startled by her tone, and he turned his head so quickly that his cufflink caught the string of his nose-glasses and pulled them awry. "Why? Why, dear me, I don't know. She probably never thought of it."

Hilda bit her lip. "I don't know what made me say that. I did n't mean to interrupt. Go on, please, and tell me how it was."

"Well, it was like that. Almost as if he were there. In a way, he really is there. She never lets him go. It's the most beautiful and dignified sorrow I've ever known. It's so beautiful that it has its compensations, I should think. Its very completeness is a compensation. It gives her a fixed star to steer by. She does n't drift. We sat there evening after evening in the quiet of that magically haunted room, and watched the sunset burn on the river, and felt him. Felt him with a difference, of course."

Hilda leaned forward, her elbow on her knee, her chin on her hand. "With a difference? Because of her, you mean?"

Wilson's brow wrinkled. "Something like that, yes. Of course, as time goes on, to her he becomes more and more their simple personal relation."

Hilda studied the droop of the Professor's head intently. "You did n't altogether like that? You felt it was n't wholly fair to him?"

Wilson shook himself and readjusted his glasses. "Oh, fair enough. More than fair. Of course, I always felt that my image of him was just a little different from hers. No relation is so complete that it can hold absolutely all of a person. And I liked him just as he was; his deviations, too; the places where he did n't square."

Hilda considered vaguely. "Has she grown much older?" she asked at last.

"Yes, and no. In a tragic way she is even handsomer. But colder. Cold for everything but him. 'Forget thyself to marble'; I kept thinking of that. Her happiness was a happiness à deux, not apart from the world, but actually against it. And now her grief is like that. She saves herself for it and does n't even go through the form of seeing people much. I'm sorry. It would be better for her, and might be so good for them, if she could let other people in."

"Perhaps she's afraid of letting him out a little, of sharing him with somebody."

Wilson put down his cup and looked up with vague alarm. "Dear me, it takes a woman to think of that, now! I don't, you know, think we ought to be hard on her. More, even, than the rest of us she did n't choose her destiny. She underwent it. And it has left her chilled. As to her not wishing to take the world into her confidence—well, it is a pretty brutal and stupid world, after all, you know."

Hilda leaned forward. "Yes, I know, I know. Only I can't help being glad that there was something for him even in stupid and vulgar people. My little Marie worshiped him. When she is dusting I always know when she has come to his picture."

Wilson nodded. "Oh, yes! He left an echo. The ripples go on in all of us. He belonged to the people who make the play, and most of us are only onlookers at the best. We should n't wonder too much at Mrs. Alexander. She must feel how useless it would be to stir about, that she may as well sit still; that nothing can happen to her after Bartley."

"Yes," said Hilda softly, "nothing can happen to one after Bartley."

They both sat looking into the fire.

Selected
Stories

The Profile

The subject of discussion at the Impressionists' Club was a picture, *Circe's Swine,* by a young German painter; a grotesque study showing the enchantress among a herd of bestial things, variously diverging from the human type—furry-eared fauns, shaggy-hipped satyrs, apes with pink palms, snuffing jackals, and thick-jowled swine, all with more or less of human intelligence protesting mutely from their hideous lineaments.

"They are all errors, these freakish excesses," declared an old painter of the Second Empire. "Triboulet, Quasimodo, Gwynplaine, have no proper place in art. Such art belongs to the Huns and Iroquois, who could only be stirred by laceration and dismemberment. The only effects of horror properly within the province of the artist are psychological. Everything else is a mere matter of the abattoir. The body, as Nature has evolved it, is sanctified by her purpose; in any natural function or attitude decent and comely. But lop away so much as a finger, and you have wounded the creature beyond reparation."

Once launched upon this subject, there was no stopping the old lion, and several of his confrères were relieved when Aaron Dunlap quietly rose and left the room. They felt that this was a subject which might well be distasteful to him.

I

*D*unlap was a portrait painter—preferably a painter of women. He had the faculty of transferring personalities to his canvas, rather than of putting conceptions there. He was finely sensitive to the merest prettiness, was tender and indulgent of it, careful never to deflower a pretty woman of her little charm, however commonplace.

Nicer critics always discerned, even in his most radiant portraits, a certain quiet element of sympathy, almost of pity, in the treatment. The sharp, flexible profile of Madame R—— of the Française; the worn, but subtle and all-capricious physiognomy of her great Semitic rival; the plump contours of a shopkeeper's pretty wife—Dunlap treated them with equal respect and fidelity. He accepted each as she was, and could touch even obvious prettiness with dignity. Behind the delicate pleasure manifested in his treatment of a beautiful face, one could divine the sadness of knowledge, and one felt that the painter had yearned to arrest what was so fleeting and to hold it back from the cruelty of the years. At an exhibition of Dunlap's pictures, the old painter of the Second Empire had said, with a sigh, that he ought to get together all his portraits of young women and call them "Les Fiançées," so abloom were they with the confidence of their beautiful secret. Then, with that sensitiveness to style, which comes from long and passionate study of form, the old painter had added reflectively, "And, after all, how sad a thing it is to be young."

Dunlap had come from a country where women are hardly used. He had grown up on a farm in the remote mountains of West Virginia, and his mother had died of pneumonia contracted from taking her place at the washtub too soon after the birth of a child. When a boy, he had been apprenticed to his grandfather, a country cobbler, who, in his drunken rages, used to beat his wife with odd strips of shoe leather. The painter's hands still bore the mark of that apprenticeship, and the suffering of the mountain women he had seen about him in his childhood had left him almost morbidly sensitive.

Just how or why Dunlap had come to Paris, none of his fellowpainters had ever learned. When he ran away from his grandfather, he had been sent by a missionary fund to some sectarian college in his own state, after which he had taught a country school for three winters and saved money enough for his passage. He arrived in Paris with something less than a hundred dollars, wholly ignorant of the language, without friends, and, apparently, without especial qualifications for study there.

Perhaps the real reason that he never succumbed to want was, that he was never afraid of it. He felt that he could never be really hungry so long as the poplars flickered along the gray quay behind the Louvre; never friendless while the gay busses rolled home across the bridges through the violet twilight, and the barge lights winked above the water.

Little by little his stripes were healed, his agony of ignorance alleviated. The city herself taught him whatever was needful for him to know. She repeated with him that fanciful romance which she has played at with youth for centuries, in which her spontaneity is ever young. She gave him of her best, quickened in him a sense of the more slight and feminine fairness in things; trained his hand and eye to the subtleties of the thousand types of subtle beauty in which she abounds; made him, after a delicate and chivalrous fashion, the expiator of his mountain race. He lived in a bright atmosphere of clear vision and happy associations, delighted at having to do with what was fair and exquisitely brief.

Life went on so during the first ten years of his residence in Paris—a happiness which, despite its almost timorous modesty, tempted fate. It was after Dunlap's name had become somewhat the fashion, that he chanced one day, in a café on the Boulevard St. Michel, to be of some service to an American who was having trouble about his order. After assisting him, Dunlap had some conversation with the man, a Californian, whose wheatlands comprised acres enough for a principality, and whose enthusiasm was as fresh as a boy's. Several days later, at the Luxembourg, he met him again, standing in a state of abject bewilderment before Manet's *Olympe*. Dunlap again came to his rescue and took him off to lunch, after which they went to the painter's studio. The acquaintance warmed on both sides, and, before they separated, Dunlap was engaged to paint the old gentleman's daughter, agreeing that the sittings should be at the house on the Boulevard de Courcelles, which the family had taken for the winter.

When Dunlap called at the house, he went through one of the most excruciating experiences of his life. He found Mrs. Gilbert and her daughter waiting to receive him. The shock of the introduction over, the strain of desultory conversation began. The only thing that made conversation tolerable—though it added a new element of perplexity—was the girl's seeming unconsciousness, her utter openness and unabashedness. She laughed and spoke, almost with coquetry, of the honor of sitting to him, of having heard that he was fastidious as to his subjects. Dunlap felt that he wanted to rush from the house and escape the situation which confronted him. The conviction kept recurring that it had just happened, had come upon her since last she had passed a mirror; that she would suddenly become conscious of it, and be suffocated with shame. He felt as if some one ought to tell her and lead her away.

"Shall we get to work?" she asked presently, apparently curious and eager to begin. "How do you wish me to sit to you?"

Dunlap murmured something about usually asking his sitters to decide that for themselves.

"Suppose we try a profile, then?" she suggested carelessly, sitting down in a carved wooden chair.

For the first time since he had entered the room, Dunlap felt the pressure about his throat relax. For the first time it was entirely turned from him, and he could not see it at all. What he did see was a girlish profile, unusually firm for a thing so softly colored; oval, flower-tinted, and shadowed by soft, blonde hair that wound about her head and curled and clung about her brow and neck and ears.

Dunlap began setting up his easel, recovering from his first discomfort and grateful to the girl for having solved his difficulty so gracefully. But no sooner was it turned from him than he felt a strong desire to see it again. Perhaps it had been only a delusion, after all; the clear profile before him so absolutely contradicted it. He went behind her chair to experiment with the window shades, and there, as he drew them up and down, he could look unseen. He gazed long and hard, to blunt his curiosity once and for all, and prevent a further temptation to covert glances. It had evidently been caused by a deep burn, as if from a splash of molten metal. It drew the left eye and the corner of the mouth; made of her smile a grinning distortion, like the shameful conception of some despairing medieval imagination. It was as if some grotesque mask, worn for disport, were just slipping sidewise from her face.

When Dunlap crossed to the right again, he found the same clear profile awaiting him, the same curves of twining, silken hair. "What courage," he thought, "what magnificent courage!" His heart ached at the injustice of it; that her very beauty, the alert, girlish figure, the firm, smooth throat and chin, even her delicate hands, should, through an inch or two of seared flesh, seem tainted and false. He felt that in a plain woman it would have been so much less horrible.

Dunlap left the house overcast by a haunting sense of tragedy, and for the rest of the day he was a prey to distressing memories. All that he had tried to forget seemed no longer dim and faraway—like the cruelties of vanished civilizations—but present and painfully near. He thought of his mother and grandmother, of his little sister, who had died from the bite of a copperhead snake, as if they were creatures yet unreleased from suffering.

II

*F*rom the first, Virginia's interest in the portrait never wavered; yet, as the sittings progressed, it became evident to Dunlap that her enthusiasm for the picture was but accessory to her interest in him. By her every look and action she asserted her feeling, as a woman, young and handsome and independent may sometimes do.

As time went on, he was drawn to her by what had once repelled him. Her courageous candor appealed to his chivalry, and he came to love her, not despite the scar, but, in a manner, for its very sake. He had some indefinite feeling that love might heal her; that in time her hurt might disappear, like the deformities imposed by enchantment to test the hardihood of lovers.

He gathered from her attitude, as well as from that of her family, that the thing had never been mentioned to her, never alluded to by word or look. Both her father and mother had made it their first care to shield her. Had she ever, in the streets of some foreign city, heard a brutal allusion to it? He shuddered to think of such a possibility. Was she not living for the moment when she could throw down the mask and point to it and weep, to be comforted for all time? He looked forward to the hour when there would be no lie of unconsciousness between them. The moment must come when she would give him her confidence; perhaps it would be only a whisper, a gesture, a guiding of his hand in the dark; but, however it might come, it was the pledge he awaited.

During the last few weeks before his marriage, the scar, through the mere strength of his anticipation, had ceased to exist for him. He had already entered to the perfect creature which he felt must dwell behind it;

the soul of tragic serenity and twofold loveliness.

They went to the South for their honeymoon, through the Midi and along the coast to Italy. Never, by word or sign, did Virginia reveal any consciousness of what he felt must be said once, and only once, between them. She was spirited, adventurous, impassioned; she exacted much, but she gave magnificently. Her interests in the material world were absorbing, and she demanded continual excitement and continual novelty. Granted these, her good spirits were unfailing.

It was during their wedding journey that he discovered her two all-absorbing interests, which were to become intensified as years went on: her passion for dress and her feverish admiration of physical beauty, whether in men or women or children. This touched Dunlap deeply, as it seemed in a manner an admission of a thing she could not speak.

Before their return to Paris Dunlap had, for the time, quite renounced his hope of completely winning her confidence. He tried to believe his exclusion just; he told himself that it was only a part of her splendid self-respect. He thought of how, from her very childhood, she had been fashioning, day by day, that armor of unconsciousness in which she sheathed her scar. After all, so deep a hurt could, perhaps, be bared to any one rather than the man she loved.

Yet, he felt that their life was enmeshed in falsehood; that he could not live year after year with a woman who shut so deep a part of her nature from him; that since he had married a woman outwardly different from others, he must have that within her which other women did not possess. Until this was granted him, he felt there would be a sacredness lacking in their relation which it peculiarly ought to have. He counted upon the birth of her child to bring this about. It would touch deeper than he could hope to do, and with fingers that could not wound. That would be a tenderness more penetrating, more softening than passion; without pride or caprice; a feeling that would dwell most in the one part of her he had failed to reach. The child, certainly, she could not shut out; whatever hardness or defiant shame it was that held him away from her, her maternity would bring enlightenment; would bring that sad wisdom, that admission of the necessity and destiny to suffer, which is, somehow, so essential in a woman.

Virginia's child was a girl, a sickly baby which cried miserably from the day it was born. The listless, wailing, almost unwilling battle for life that daily went on before his eyes saddened Dunlap profoundly. All his painter's sophistries fell away from him, and more than ever his early destiny seemed closing about him. There was, then, no escaping from the cruelty of physical things—no matter how high and bright the sunshine, how gray and poplar-clad the ways of one's life. The more willing the child seemed to relinquish its feeble hold, the more tenderly he loved it, and the more determinedly he fought to save it.

Virginia, on the contrary, had almost from the first exhibited a marked indifference toward her daughter. She showed plainly that the sight of its wan, aged little face was unpleasant to her; she disliked being clutched by its skeleton fingers, and said its wailing made her head ache. She was always taking Madame de Montebello and her handsome children to drive in the Bois, but she was never to be seen with little Eleanor. If her friends asked to see the child, she usually put them off, saying that she was asleep or in her bath.

When Dunlap once impatiently asked her whether she never intended to permit any one to see her daughter, she replied coldly: "Certainly, when she has filled out and begins to look like something."

Little Eleanor grew into a shy, awkward child, who slipped about the house like an unwelcome dependent. She was four years old when a cousin of Virginia's came from California to spend a winter in Paris. Virginia had known her only slightly at home, but, as she proved to be a charming girl, and as she was ill-equipped to bear the hardships of a winter in a *pension,* the Dunlaps insisted upon her staying with them. The cousin's name was also Eleanor—she had been called so after Virginia's mother—and, from the first, the two Eleanors seemed drawn to each other. Miss Vane was studying, and went out to her lectures every day, but whenever she was at home, little Eleanor was with her. The child would sit quietly in her room while she wrote, playing with anything her cousin happened to give her; or would lie for hours on the hearth rug, whispering to her woolly dog. Dunlap felt a weight lifted from his mind. Whenever Eleanor was at home, he knew that the child was happy.

He had long ceased to expect any solicitude for her from Virginia. That had gone with everything else. It was one of so many disappointments that he took it rather as a matter of course, and it seldom occurred to him that it might have been otherwise. For two years he had been living like a man who knows that some reptile has housed itself and hatched its young in his cellar, and who never cautiously puts his foot out of his bed without the dread of touching its coils. The change in his feeling toward his wife kept him in perpetual apprehension; it seemed to threaten everything he held dear, even his self-respect. His life was a continual effort of self-control, and he found it necessary to make frequent trips to London or sketching tours into Brittany to escape from the strain of the repression he put upon himself. Under this state of things, Dunlap aged perceptibly, and his friends made various and usual conjectures. Whether Virginia was conscious of the change in him, he never knew. Her feeling for him had, in its very nature, been as temporary as it was violent; it had abated naturally, and she probably took for granted that the same readjustment had taken place in him. Perhaps she was too much engrossed in other things to notice it at all.

In Dunlap the change seemed never to be finally established, but forever painfully working. Whereas he had once seen the scar on his wife's face not at all, he now saw it continually. Inch by inch it had crept over her whole countenance. Yet the scar itself seemed now a trivial thing; he had known for a long time that the burn had gone deeper than the flesh.

Virginia's extravagant fondness for gaiety seemed to increase, and her mania for lavish display, doubtless common enough in the Californian wheat empire, was a discordant note in Paris. Dunlap found himself condemned to an existence which daily did violence to his sense of propriety. His wife gave fêtes, the cost of which was noised abroad by the Associated Press and flaunted in American newspapers. Her vanity, the pageantries of her toilet, made them both ridiculous, he felt. She was a woman now, with a husband and child; she had no longer a pretext for keeping up the pitiful bravado under which she had hidden the smarting pride of her girlhood.

He became more and more convinced that she had been shielded from a realization of her disfigurement only to the end of a shocking perversity. Her costumes, her very jewels, blazed defiance. Her confidence became almost insolent, and her laugh was nothing but a frantic denial of a thing so cruelly obvious. The unconsciousness he had once reverenced now continually tempted his brutality, and when he felt himself reduced to the point of actual vituperation, he fled to Normandy or Languedoc to save himself. He had begun, indeed, to feel strangely out of place in Paris. The ancient comfort of the city, never lacking in the days when he had known cold and hunger, failed him now. A certain sordidness had spread itself over ways and places once singularly perfect and pure.

III

One evening when Virginia refused to allow little Eleanor to go down to the music room to see some pantomime performers who were to entertain their guests, Dunlap, to conceal his displeasure, stepped quickly out upon the balcony and closed the window behind him. He stood for some moments in the cold, clear night air.

"God help me," he groaned. "Some day I shall tell her. I shall hold her and tell her."

When he entered the house again, it was by another window, and his anger had cooled. As he stepped into the hallway, he met Eleanor the elder, going upstairs with the little girl in her arms. For the life of him he could not refrain from appealing for sympathy to her kind, grave eyes. He was so hurt, so sick, that he could have put his face down beside the child's and wept.

"Give her to me, little cousin. She is too heavy for you," he said gently, as they went upstairs together.

He remembered with resentment his wife's perfectly candid and careless jests about his fondness for her cousin. After he had put the little girl down in Eleanor's room, as they leaned together above the child's head in the firelight, he became, for the first time, really aware. A sudden tenderness weakened him. He put out his hand and took hers, which was holding the child's, and murmured: "Thank you, thank you, little cousin."

She started violently and caught her hand away from him, trembling all over. Dunlap left the room, thrice more miserable than he had entered it.

After that evening he noticed that Eleanor avoided meeting him alone. Virginia also noticed it, but upon this point she was consistently silent. One morning, as Dunlap was leaving his wife's dressing room, having been to consult her as to whether she intended going to the ball at the Russian Embassy, she called him back. She was carefully arranging her beautiful hair, which she always dressed herself, and said carelessly, without looking up at him:

"Eleanor has a foolish notion of returning home in March. I

wish you would speak to her about it. Her family expect her to stay until June, and her going now would be commented upon."

"I scarcely see how I can interfere," he replied coolly. "She doubtless has her reasons."

"Her reasons are not far to seek, I should say," remarked Virginia, carefully slipping the pins into the yellow coils of her hair. "She is pathetically ingenuous about it. I should think you might improve upon the present state of affairs if you were to treat it—well, say a trifle more lightly. That would put her more at ease, at least."

"What nonsense, Virginia," he exclaimed, laughing unnaturally and closing the door behind him with guarded gentleness.

That evening Dunlap joined his wife in her dressing room, his coat on his arm and his hat in his hand. The maid had gone upstairs to hunt for Virginia's last year's fur shoes, as the pair warming before the grate would not fit over her new dancing slippers. Virginia was standing before the mirror, carefully surveying the effect of a new gown, which struck her husband as more than usually conspicuous and defiant. He watched her arranging a pink-and-gold butterfly in her hair and held his peace, but when she put on a pink chiffon collar, with a flaring bow which came directly under her left cheek, in spite of himself he shuddered.

"For heaven's sake, Virginia, take that thing off," he cried. "You ought really to be more careful about such extremes. They only emphasize the scar." He was frightened at the brittleness of his own voice; it seemed to whistle dryly in the air like his grandfather's thong.

She caught her breath and wheeled suddenly about, her face crimson and then gray. She opened her lips twice, but no sound escaped them. He saw the muscles of her throat stiffen, and she began to shudder convulsively, like one who has been plunged into icy water. He started toward her, sick with pity; at last, perhaps—but she pointed him steadily to the door, her eyes as hard as shell, and bright and small, like the sleepless eyes of reptiles.

He went to bed with the sick feeling of a man who has tortured an animal, yet with a certain sense of relief and finality which he had not known in years.

When he came down to breakfast in the morning, the butler told him that Madame and her maid had left for Nice by the early train. Mademoiselle Vane had gone out to her lectures. Madame requested that Monsieur take Mademoiselle to the opera in the evening, where the widowed sister of Madame de Montebello would join them; she would come home with them to remain until Madame's return. Dunlap accepted these instructions as a matter of course, and announced that he would not dine at home.

When he entered the hall upon his return that evening, he heard little Eleanor sobbing, and she flew to meet him, with her dress burned, and her hands black. Dunlap smelled the sickening odor of ointments. The nurse followed with explanations. The doctor was upstairs. Mademoiselle Vane always used a little alcohol lamp in making her toilet; tonight, when she touched a match to it, it exploded. Little Eleanor was leaning against her dressing table at the time, and her dress caught fire; Mademoiselle Vane had wrapped the rug about her and extinguished it. When the nurse arrived, Mademoiselle Vane was standing in the middle of the floor, plucking at her scorched hair, her face and arms badly burned. She had bent over the lamp in lighting it, and had received the full force of the explosion in her face. The doctor was unable to discover what the explosive had been, as it was entirely consumed. Mademoiselle always filled the little lamp herself; all the servants knew about it, for Madame had sent the nurse to borrow it on several occasions, when little Eleanor had the earache.

The next morning Dunlap received a telegram from his wife, stating that she would go to St. Petersburg for the remainder of the winter. In May he heard that she had sailed for America, and a year later her attorneys wrote that she had begun action for divorce. Immediately after the decree was granted, Dunlap married Eleanor Vane. He never met or directly heard from Virginia again, though when she returned to Russia and took up her residence in St. Petersburg, the fame of her toilets spread even to Paris.

Society, always prone to crude antitheses, knew of Dunlap only that he had painted many of the most beautiful women of his time, that he had been twice married, and that each of his wives had been disfigured by a scar on the face.

The Willing Muse

Various opinions were held among Kenneth Gray's friends regarding his approaching marriage, but on the whole it was considered a hopeful venture, and, what was with some of us much more to the point, a hopeful indication. From the hour his engagement was an assured relation, he had seemed to gain. There was now a certain intention in his step, an eager, almost confident flash behind his thick glasses, which cheered his friends like indications of recovery after long illness. Even his shoulders seemed to droop less despondently and his head to sit upon them more securely. Those of us who knew him best drew a long sigh of relief that Kenneth had at last managed to get right with the current.

If, on the insecurity of a meager income and a career at its belated dawn, he was to marry at all, we felt that a special indulgence of destiny had allowed him to fix his choice upon Bertha Torrence. If there was anywhere a woman who seemed able to give him what he needed, to play upon him a continual stream of inspiriting confidence, to order the very simple affairs which he had so besottedly bungled, surely Bertha was the woman.

There were certain of his friends in Olympia who held out that it was a mistake for him to marry a woman who followed his own profession; who was, indeed, already much more within the public consciousness than Kenneth himself. To refute such arguments, one had only to ask what was possible between that and a housekeeper. Could any one conceive of Kenneth's living in daily intercourse with a woman who had no immediate and personal interest in letters, bitten to the bone as he was by his slow, consuming passion?

Perhaps, in so far as I was concerned, my personal satisfaction at Kenneth's projected marriage was not without its alloy of selfishness, and I think more than one of us counted upon carrying lighter hearts to his wedding than we had known in his company for some time. It was not that we did not believe in him. Hadn't it become a fixed habit to believe? But we, perhaps, felt slightly aggrieved that our faith had not wrought for him the miracles we could have hoped. We were, we found, willing enough to place the direct administration, the first responsibility, upon Bertha's firm young shoulders.

With Harrison, the musical critic, and me, Kenneth was an old issue. We had been college classmates of his, out in Olympia, Ohio, and even then no one had questioned his calling and election, unless it was Kenneth himself. But he had taxed us all sorely, the town and the college, and he had continued to tax us long afterward. As Harrison put it, he had kept us all holding our breath for years. There was never such a man for getting people into a fever of interest and determination for him, for making people (even people who had very vague surmises as to the particular eminence toward which he might be headed) fervidly desire to push him and for refusing, on any terms, to be pushed. There was nothing more individual about Kenneth than his inability to be exploited. Coercion and encouragement spent themselves upon him like summer rain.

He was thirty-five when his first book, *Charles de Montpensier,* was published, and the work was, to those who knew its author intimately, a kind of record of his inverse development. It was first conceived and written as a prose drama, then amplified into an historical novel, and had finally been compressed into a psychological study of two hundred pages, in which the action was hushed to a whisper and the teeming pageantry of his background, which he had spent years in developing and which had cost him several laborious summers in France and Italy, was reduced to a shadowy atmosphere, suggestive enough, doubtless, but presenting very little that was appreciable to the eyes of the flesh. The majority of Kenneth's readers, even those baptized into his faith, must have recalled the fable of the mouse and the mountain. As for those of us who had travailed with him, confident as we were of the high order of the ultimate production, we had a baffled feeling that there had been a distressing leakage of power. However, when this study of the High Constable of Bourbon was followed by an exquisite prose idyl, *The Wood of Ronsard,* we began to take heart, and when we learned that a stimulus so reassuring as a determination to marry had hurried this charming bit of romance into the world, we felt that

Kenneth had at last entered upon the future that had seemed for so long only a step before him.

Since Gray's arrival in New York, Harrison and I had had more than ever the feeling of having him on our hands. He had been so long accustomed to the respectful calm of Olympia that he was unable to find his way about in a new environment. He was incapable of falling in with any of the prevailing attitudes, and even of civilly tolerating them in other people. Commercialism wounded him, flippancy put him out of countenance, and he clung stubbornly to certain fond, Olympian superstitions regarding his profession. One by one his new acquaintances chilled, offended by his arrogant reception of their genial efforts to put him in the way of things. Even those of us who had known him at his best, and who remembered the summer evenings in his garden at Olympia, found his seriousness and punctilious reservations tedious in the broad glare of short, noisy working days.

Some weeks before the day set for Kenneth's marriage, I learned that it might be necessary for me to go to Paris for a time to take the place of our correspondent there, who had fallen into precarious health, and I called at Bertha's apartment for a serious talk with her. I found her in the high tide of work; but she made a point of accepting interruptions agreeably, just as she made a point of looking astonishingly well, of being indispensable in an appalling number of "circles," and of generally nullifying the traditional reproach attaching to clever women.

"In all loyalty to you both," I remarked, "I feel that I ought to remind you that you are accepting a responsibility."

"His uncertainty, you mean?"

"Oh, I mean all of them—the barriers which are so intangible he cannot climb them and so terrifying he can't jump them, which lie between him and everything."

Bertha looked at me thoughtfully out of her candid blue eyes. "But what he needs is, after all, so little compared with what he has."

"What he has," I admitted, "is inestimably precious; but the problem is to keep it from going back into the ground with him."

She shot a glance of alarm at me from under her blond lashes. "But certainly he is endlessly more capable of doing than any of us. With such depth to draw from, how can he possibly fail?"

"Perhaps it's his succeeding that I fear more than anything. I think the fair way to measure Kenneth is by what he simply can't do."

"The cheap, you mean?" she asked reflectively. "Oh, that he

will never do. We may just eliminate that from our discussion. The problem is simply to make him mine his vein, even if, from his fanciful angle of vision, it's at first a losing business."

"Ah, my dear young lady, but it's just his fanciful angle, as you so happily term it, that puts a stop to everything, and I've never quite dared to urge him past his scruples, though I'm not saying I could if I would. If there is anything at all in the whole business, any element of chosenness, of a special call, any such value in individual tone as he fancies, then, the question is, dare one urge him?"

"Nonsense!" snapped Bertha, drawing up her slender shoulders with decision—I had purposely set out to exhaust her patience—"you have all put a halo about him until he daren't move for fear of putting it out. What he needs is simply to keep at it. How much satisfaction do you suppose he gets out of hanging back?"

"The point, it seems to me, my dear Bertha, is not that, but the remarkableness of any one's having the conviction, the moral force, just now and under the circumstances, to hang back at all. There must be either very much or very little in a man when he refuses to make the most of his vogue and sell out on a rising market. If he would rather bring up a little water out of the well than turn the river across his lands, has one a right to coerce him?" I put my shaft home steadily, and Bertha caught fire with proper spirit.

"All I can say is, that it's a miracle he's as adaptable as he is. I simply can't understand what you meant, you and Harrison, by keeping him out there in Ohio so long."

"But we didn't," I expostulated. "We didn't keep him there. We only did not succeed in getting him away. We, too, had our scruples. He had his old house there, and his garden, his friends, and the peace of God. And then, Olympia isn't a bad sort of place. It kept his feeling fresh, at least, and in fifteen years or so you'll begin to know the value of that. There everything centers about the college, and every one reads, just as every one goes to church. It's a part of the decent, comely life of the place. In Olympia there is a deep-seated, old-fashioned respect for the printed page, and Kenneth naturally found himself in the place of official sanctity. The townswomen reverently attended his college lectures, along with their sons and daughters, and, had he been corruptible, he might have established a walled supremacy of personal devotion behind which he could have sheltered himself to the end of his days."

"But he didn't, you see," said Bertha, triumphantly; "which is proof that he was meant for the open waters. Oh, we shall do fine things, I promise you! I can just fancy the hushed breath of the place for wonder at him. And his rose garden! Will people never have done with his rose garden! I remember you and Harrison told me of it, with an air, before I had met Kenneth at all. I wonder that you didn't keep him down there forever from a pure sense of the picturesque. What sort of days and nights do you imagine he passed in his garden, in his miserably uncertain state? I suppose we should all like well enough to grow roses, if we had nothing else to do."

I felt that Bertha was considerately keeping her eyes from the clock, and I rose to go.

"Well, Bertha, I suppose the only reason we haven't brought him to a worse pass than we have, is just the fact that he happens to have been born an anachronism, and such a stubborn one that we leave him pretty much where we found him."

II

After Kenneth's wedding, I left immediately for Paris, and during the next four years I knew of the Grays only what I could sense from Kenneth's labored letters, ever more astonishing in their aridity, and from the parcels I received twice a year by book-post, containing Bertha's latest work. I never picked up an American periodical that Bertha's name was not the first to greet my eye on the advertising pages. She surpassed all legendary accounts of phenomenal productiveness, and I could feel no anxiety for the fortunes of the pair while Bertha's publishers thought her worth such a display of heavy type. There was scarcely a phase of colonial life left untouched by her, and her last, *The Maid of Domremy,* showed that she had fairly crowded herself out of her own field.

The real wonder was, that, making so many, she could make them so well—should make them, indeed, rather better and better. Even were one so unreasonable as to consider her gain a loss, there was no denying it. I read her latest, one after another, as they arrived, with growing interest and amazement, wholly unable to justify my first suspicion. There was every evidence that she had absorbed from Kenneth like a water plant, but none that she had used him more violently than a clever woman may properly use her husband. Knowing him as I did, I could never accredit him with having any hand in Bertha's intrepid, wholehearted, unimpeachable conventionality. One could not exactly call her unscrupulous; one could observe only that no predicament embarrassed her; that she went ahead and pulled it off.

When I returned to New York, I found a curious state of feeling prevalent concerning the Grays. Bertha was *la fille du régiment* more than ever. Every one championed her, every one went to her teas, every one was smilingly and conspicuously present in her triumph. Even those who had formerly stood somewhat aloof, now found no courage to dissent. With Bertha herself so gracious, so eager to please, the charge of pettiness, of jealousy, even, could be too easily incurred. She quite floated the sourest and heaviest upon her rising tide.

There was, however, the undertow. I felt it even before I had actually made sure of it—in the peculiar warmth with which people spoke of Kenneth. In him they saw their own grievances magnified until he became symbolic. Publicly every one talked of Bertha; but behind closed doors it was of Kenneth they spoke—*sotto voce* and with a shake of the head. As he had published nothing since his marriage, this smothered feeling had resulted in a new and sumptuous edition of *Montpensier* and *The Wood of Ronsard;* one of those final, votive editions, suggestive of the bust and the catafalque.

I called upon the Grays at the first opportunity. They had moved from their downtown flat into a new apartment house on Eighty-fifth street. The servant who took my card did not return, but Kenneth himself stumbled into the reception hall, overturning a gilt chair in his haste, and gripped my hands as if he would never let them go. He held on to my arm as he took me to his study, telling me again and again that I couldn't possibly know what pleasure it gave him to see me. When he dropped limply into his desk chair, he seemed really quite overcome with excitement. It was not until I asked him about his wife that he collected himself and began to talk coherently.

"I'm sorry I can't speak to her now," he explained, rapidly twirling a paper cutter between his long fingers. "She won't be free until four o'clock. She will be so pleased that I'm almost tempted to call her at once. But she's so overworked, poor girl, and she will go out so much."

"My dear Kenneth, how does she ever manage it all? She must have nerves of iron."

"Oh, she's wonderful, wonderful!" he exclaimed, brushing his limp hair back from his forehead with a perplexed gesture. "As to how she does it, I really don't know much more than you. It all gets done, somehow." He glanced quickly toward the partition, through which we heard the steady clicking of a typewriter. "I scarcely know what she is up to until her proofs come in. I usually go at those with her." He darted a piercing look at me, and I wondered whether he had got a hint of the malicious stories which found their way about concerning his varied usefulness to Bertha.

"If you'll excuse me for a moment, Philip," he went on, "I'll finish a letter that must go out this afternoon, and then I shall be quite free."

He turned in his revolving chair to a desk littered deep with papers, and began writing hurriedly. I could see that the simplest kind of composition still perplexed and disconcerted him. He stopped, hesitated, bit his nails, then scratched desperately ahead, darting an annoyed glance at the partition as if the sharp, regular click of the machine bewildered him.

He had grown older, I noticed, but it was good to see him again—his limp, straight hair, which always hung down in a triangle over his high forehead; his lean cheek, loose under lip, and long whimsical chin; his faded, serious eyes, which were always peering inquiringly from behind his thick glasses; his long, tremulous fingers, which handled a pen as uncertainly as ever. There was a general looseness of articulation about his gaunt frame that made his every movement seem more or less haphazard.

On the desk lay a heap of letters, the envelopes marked "answered" in Kenneth's small, irregular hand, and all of them, I noticed, addressed to Bertha. In the open drawer at his left were half a dozen manuscript envelopes, addressed to her in as many different hands.

"What on earth!" I gasped. "Does Bertha conduct a literary agency as well?"

Kenneth swung round in his chair, and made a wry face as he glanced at the contents of the drawer. "It's almost as bad as that. Really, it's the most abominable nuisance. But we're the victims of success, as Bertha says. Sometimes a dozen manuscripts come in to her for criticism in one week. She dislikes to hurt any one's feelings, so one of us usually takes a look at them."

"Bertha's correspondence must be something of a responsibility in itself," I ventured.

"Oh, it is, I assure you. People are most inconsiderate. I'm rather glad, though, when it piles up like this and I can take a hand at it. It gives me an excuse for putting off my own work, and you know how I welcome any pretext," he added, with a flushed, embarrassed smile.

"What are you doing, anyhow? I don't know where you'll ever learn industry if Bertha can't teach you."

"I'm working, I'm working," he insisted, hurriedly crossing out the last sentence of his letter and blotting it carefully. "You know how reprehensibly slow I am. It seems to grow on me. I'm finishing up some studies in the French Renaissance. They'll be ready by next fall, I think." As he spoke, he again glanced hurriedly over the closely written page before him; then, stopping abruptly, he tore the sheet across the middle. "Really, you've quite upset me. Tell me about yourself, Philip. Are you going out to Olympia?"

"That depends upon whether I remain here or decamp immediately for China, which prospect is in the cards. Olympia is greatly changed, Harrison tells me."

Kenneth sighed and sank deeper into his chair, reaching again for the paper cutter. "Ruined completely. Capital and enterprise have broken in even there. They've all sorts of new industries, and the place is black with smoke and thick with noise from sunrise to sunset. I still own my house there, but I seldom go back. I don't know where we're bound for, I'm sure. There must be places, somewhere in the world, where a man can take a book or two and drop behind the procession for an hour; but they seem impossibly far from here."

I could not help smiling at the deeply despondent gaze which he fixed upon the paper cutter. "But the procession itself is the thing we've got to enjoy," I suggested, "the mere sense of speed."

"I suppose so, I suppose so," he reiterated, wiping his forehead with his handkerchief. "The six-day bicycle race seems to be what we've all come to, and doubtless one form of it's as much worth while as another. We don't get anywhere, but we go. We certainly go; and that's what we're after. You'll be lucky if you are sent to China. There must be calm there as yet, I imagine."

Our conversation went on fitfully, with interruptions, irrelevant remarks, and much laughter, as talk goes between two persons who have once been frank with each other, and who find that frankness has become impossible. My coming had clearly upset him, and his agitation of manner visibly increased when he spoke of his wife. He wiped his forehead and hands repeatedly, and finally opened a window. He fairly wrested the conversation out of my hands and was continually interrupting and forestalling me, as if he were apprehensive that I might say something he did not wish to hear. He started and leaned forward in his chair whenever I approached a question.

At last we were aware of a sudden slack in the tension; the typewriter had stopped. Kenneth looked at his watch, and disappeared through a door into his wife's study. When he returned, Bertha was beside him, her hand on his shoulder, taller, straighter, younger than I had left her—positively childlike in her freshness and candor.

"Didn't I tell you," she cried, "that we should do fine things?"

III

A few weeks later I was sent to Hong Kong, where I remained for two years. Before my return to America, I was ordered into the interior for eight months, during which time my mail was to be held for me at the consul's office in Canton, the port where I was to take ship for home. Once in the Sze Chuen province, floods and bad roads delayed me to such an extent that I barely reached Canton on the day my vessel sailed. I hurried on board with all my letters unread, having had barely time to examine the instructions from my paper.

We were well out at sea when I opened a letter from Harrison in which he gave an account of Kenneth Gray's disappearance. He had, Harrison stated, gone out to Olympia to dispose of his property there which, since the development of the town, had greatly increased in value. He completed his business after a week's stay, and left for New York by the night train, several of his friends accompanying him to the station. Since that night he had not been seen or heard of. Detectives had been at work; hospitals and morgues had been searched without result.

The date of this communication put me beside myself. It had awaited me in Canton for nearly seven months, and Gray had last been seen on the tenth of November, four months before the date of Harrison's letter, which was written as soon as the matter was made public. It was eleven months, then, since Kenneth Gray had been seen in America. During my long voyage I went through an accumulated bulk of American newspapers, but found nothing more reassuring than occasional items to the effect that the mystery surrounding Gray's disappearance remained unsolved. In a "literary supplement" of comparatively recent date, I came upon a notice to the effect that the new novel by Bertha Torrence Gray, announced for spring publication, would, owing to the excruciating experience through which the young authoress had lately passed, be delayed until the autumn.

I bore my suspense as best I could across ocean and continent. When I arrived in New York, I went from the ferry to the *Messenger* office, and, once there, directly to Harrison's room.

"What's all this," I cried, "about Kenneth Gray? I tell you I saw Gray in Canton ten months ago."

Harrison sprang to his feet and put his finger to his lip.

"Hush! Don't say another word! There are leaky walls about here. Go and attend to your business, and then come back and go to lunch with me. In the meantime, be careful not to discuss Gray with any one."

Four hours later, when we were sitting in a quiet corner of a café, Harrison dismissed the waiter and turned to me. "Now," he said, leaning across the table, "if you can be sufficiently guarded, you may tell me what you know about our friend."

"Well," I replied, "it would have been, under ordinary circumstances, a commonplace thing enough. On the day before I started for the interior, I was in Canton, making some last purchases to complete my outfit. I stepped out of a shop on one of the crooked streets in the old part of the city, and I saw him as plainly as I see you, being trundled by in a jinrikisha, got up in a helmet and white duck, a fat white umbrella across his knees, peering hopefully out through his glasses. He was so like himself, his look and attitude, his curious chin poked forward, that I simply stood and stared until he had passed me and turned a corner, vanishing like a stereopticon picture traveling across the screen. I hurried to the banks, the big hotels, to the consul's, getting no word of him, but leaving letters for him everywhere. My party started the next day, and I was compelled to leave for an eight-months' nightmare in the interior. I got back to Canton barely in time to catch my steamer, and did not open your letter until we were down the river and losing sight of land. Either I saw Kenneth, or I am a subject for the Society for Psychical Research."

"Just so," said Harrison, peering mysteriously above his coffee cup. "And now forget it. Simply disabuse yourself of any notion that you've seen him since we crossed the ferry with you three years ago. It's your last service to him, probably."

"Speak up," I cried, exasperated. "I've had about all of this I can stand. I came near wiring the story in from San Francisco. I don't know why I didn't."

"Well, here's to whatever withheld you! When a man comes to the pass where he wants to wipe himself off the face of the earth, when it's the last play he can make for his self-respect, the only decent thing is to let him do it. You know the yielding stuff he's made of well enough to appreciate the amount of pressure it must have taken to harden him to such an exit. I'm sure I never supposed he had it in him."

"But what, short of insanity—"

"Insanity? Nonsense! I wonder that people don't do it oftener. The pressure simply got past the bearing-point. His life was going, and going for nothing—worse than nothing. His future was chalked out for him, and whichever way he turned he was confronted by his unescapable destiny. In the light of Bertha's splendid success, he couldn't be churlish or ungracious; he had to play his little part along with the rest of us. And Bertha, you know, has passed all the limits of nature, not to speak of decorum. They come as certainly as the seasons, her new ones, each cleverer and more damnable than the last. And yet there is nothing that one can actually put one's finger on—not, at least, without saying the word that would lay us open to a charge which as her friends we are none of us willing to incur, and which no one would listen to if it were said.

"I tell you," Harrison continued, "the whole thing sickened him. He had dried up like a stockfish. His brain was beaten into torpidity by the mere hammer of her machine, as by so many tiny mallets. He had lived to help lessen the value of all that he held precious, to disprove all that he wanted to believe. Having ridden to victory under the banners of what he most despised, there was nothing for him but to live in the blaze of her conquest, and that was the very measure of his fall. His usefulness to the world was over when he had done what he did for Bertha. I don't believe he even knew where he stood; the thing had gone so, seemed to answer the purpose so wonderfully well, and there was never anything that one could really put one's finger on—except all of it. It was a trial of faith, and Bertha had won out so beautifully. He had proved the fallacy of his own position. There was nothing left for him to say. I'm sure I don't know whether he had anything left to think."

"Do you remember," I said slowly, "I used to hold that, in the end, Kenneth would be measured by what he didn't do, by what he couldn't do? What a wonder he was at not being able to do it. Surely, if Bertha couldn't convince him, fire and faggots couldn't."

"For, after all," sighed Harrison, as we rose to go, "Bertha is a wonderful woman—a woman of her time and people; and she has managed, in spite of her fatal facility, to be enough sight better than most of us."

Eleanor's House

Shall you, then," Harriet ventured, "go to Fortuney?" The girl threw a startled glance toward the corner of the garden where Westfield and Harold were examining a leak in the basin of the little fountain, and Harriet was sorry that she had put the question so directly. Ethel's reply, when it came, seemed a mere emission of breath rather than articulation.

"I think we shall go later. It's very trying for him there, of course. He hasn't been there since." She relapsed into silence—indeed, she had never come very far out of it—and Harriet called to Westfield. She found that she couldn't help resenting Ethel's singular inadeptness at keeping herself in hand.

"Come, Robert. Harold is tired after his journey, and he and Ethel must have much to say to each other."

Both Harold and his wife, however, broke into hurried random remarks with an eagerness which seemed like a protest.

"It is delightful to be near you here at Arques, with only a wall between our gardens," Ethel spurred herself to say. "It will mean so much to Harold. He has so many old associations with you, Mrs. Westfield."

The two men had come back to the tea table, and as the younger one overheard his wife's last remark, his handsome brown face took on the blackness of disapproval.

Ethel glanced at him furtively, but Harriet was unable to detect whether she realized just why or to what extent her remark had been unfortunate. She certainly looked as if she might not be particularly acute, drooping about in her big garden hat and her limp white frock, which had not been very well put on. However, some sense of maladroitness certainly penetrated her vagueness, for she shrank behind the tea table, gathering her scarf about her shoulders as if she were mysteriously blown upon by a chilling current.

The Westfields drew together to take their leave. Harold stepped to his wife's side as they went toward the gate with their guests, and put his hand lightly on her shoulder, at which she waveringly emerged from her eclipse and smiled.

Harriet could not help looking back at them from under her sunshade as they stood there in the gateway; the man with his tense brown face and abstracted smile, the girl drooping, positively swaying in her softness and uncertainty.

When they reached the sunny square of their own garden, Harriet sank into a wicker chair in the deep shadow of the stucco wall and addressed her husband with conviction:

"I know now, my dear, why he wished so much to come. I sensed it yesterday, when I first met her. But now that I've seen them together, it's perfectly clear. He brought her here to keep her away from Fortuney, and he's counting on us to help him."

Westfield, who was carefully examining his rose trees, looked at his wife with interest and frank bewilderment, a form of interrogation with which she was perfectly familiar.

"If there is one thing that's plainer even than his misery," Harriet continued, "it is that she is headed toward Fortuney. They've been married over two years, and he couldn't, I suppose, keep her across the Channel any longer. So he has simply deflected her course, and we are the pretext."

"Certainly," Westfield admitted, as he looked up from his pruning, "one feels something not altogether comfortable with them, but why should it be Fortuney any more than a hundred other things? There are opportunities enough for people who wish to play at cross-purposes."

"Ah! But Fortuney," sighed his wife, "Fortuney's the summing up of all his past. It's Eleanor herself. How could he, Robert, take this poor girl there? It would be cruelty. The figure she'd cut in a place of such distinction!"

"I should think that if he could marry her, he could take her to Fortuney," Westfield maintained bluntly.

"Oh, as to his marrying her! But I suppose we are all to blame for that—all his and Eleanor's old friends. We certainly failed him. We fled at the poor fellow's approach. We simply couldn't face the extent of his bereavement. He seemed a mere fragment of a man dragged out from under the wreckage. They had so grown together that when she died there was nothing in him left whole. We dreaded him, and were glad enough to get him off to India. I even hoped he would marry out there. When the news came that he had, I supposed that would end it; that he would become merely a chapter in natural history. But, you see, he hasn't; he's more widowed than before. He can't do anything well without her. You see, he couldn't even do this."

"This?" repeated Westfield, quitting his gardening abruptly. "Am I to understand that she would have been of assistance in selecting another wife for him?"

Harriet preferred to ignore that his tone implied an enormity. "She would certainly have kept him from getting into such a box as he's in now. She could at least have found him some one who wouldn't lacerate him by her every movement. Oh, that poor, limp, tactless, terrified girl! Have you noticed the exasperating way in which she walks, even? It's as if she were treading pain, forbearing and forgiving, when she but steps to the tea table. There was never a person so haunted by the notion of her own untidy picturesqueness. It wears her thin and consumes her, like her unhappy passion. I know how he feels; he hates the way she likes what she likes, and he hates the way she dislikes what she doesn't like. And, mark my words, she is bent upon Fortuney. That, at least, Robert, he certainly can't permit. At Fortuney, Eleanor is living still. The place is so intensely, so rarely personal. The girl has fixed her eye, made up her mind. It's symbolic to her, too, and she's circling about it; she can't endure to be kept out. Yesterday, when I went to see her, she couldn't wait to begin explaining her husband to me. She seemed to be afraid I might think she hadn't poked into everything."

While his wife grew more and more vehement, Westfield lay back in a garden chair, half succumbing to the drowsy warmth of the afternoon.

"It seems to me," he remarked, with a discreet yawn, "that the poor child is only putting up a good fight against the tormenting suspicion that she hasn't got into anything. She may be just decently trying to conceal her uncertainty."

Harriet looked at him intently for a moment, watching the shadows of the sycamore leaves play across his face, and then laughed indulgently. "The idea of her decently trying to conceal anything amuses me. So that's how much you know of her!" she sighed. "She's taken you in just as she took him. He doubtless thought she wouldn't poke; that she would go on keeping the door of the chamber, breathing faint benedictions and smiling her moonbeam smile as he came and went. But, under all her meekness and air of poetically foregoing, she has a forthcomingness and an outputtingness which all the brutality he's driven to can't discourage. I've known her kind before! You may clip their tendrils every day of your life only to find them renewed and sweetly taking hold the next morning. She'd find the crevices in polished alabaster. Can't you see what she wants?" Mrs. Westfield sat up with flashing eyes. "She wants to be to him what Eleanor was; she sees no reason why she shouldn't be!"

Westfield rubbed the stiff blond hair above his ear in perplexity. "Well, why, in Heaven's name, shouldn't she be? He married her. What less can she expect?"

"Oh, Robert!" cried Harriet, as if he had uttered something impious. "But then, you never knew them. Why, Eleanor made him. He is the work of her hands. She saved him from being something terrible."

Westfield smiled ironically.

"Was he, then, in his natural state, so—so very much worse?"

"Oh, he was better than he is now, even then. But he was somehow terribly off the key. He was the most immature thing ever born into the world. Youth was a disease with him; he almost died of it. He was so absorbed in his own waking up, and he so overestimated its importance. He made such a clamor about it and so thrust it upon one that I used to wonder whether he would ever get past the stage of opening packages under the Christmas tree and shouting. I suppose he did know that his experiences were not unique, but I'm sure he felt that the degree of them was peculiarly his.

"When he met Eleanor he lost himself, and that was what he needed. She happened to be born tempered and poised. There never was a time when she wasn't discriminating. She could enjoy all kinds of things and people, but she was never, never mistaken in the kind. The beauty of it was that her distinctions had nothing to do with reason; they were purely shades of feeling.

"Well, you can conjecture what followed. She gave him the one thing which made everything else he had pertinent and dignified. He simply had better fiber than any of us realized, and she saw it. She was infallible in detecting quality.

"Two years after their marriage, I spent six weeks with them at

Fortuney, and even then I saw their possibilities, what they would do for each other. And they went on and on. They had all there is—except children. I suppose they were selfish. As Eleanor once said to me, they needed only eternity and each other. But, whatever it was, it was Olympian."

II

*H*arriet was walking one morning on the green hill that rises, topped by its sprawling feudal ruin, behind Arques-la-Bataille. The sunlight still had the magical golden hue of early day, and the dew shone on the smooth, grassy folds and clefts that mark the outlines of the old fortifications. Below lay the delicately colored town—seen through a grove of glistening white birches—the shining, sinuous curves of the little river, and the green, open stretches of the pleasant Norman country.

As she skirted the base of one of the thick towers on the inner edge of the moat, her sunshade over her shoulder and her white shoes gray with dew, she all but stepped upon a man who lay in a shaded corner within the elbow of the wall and the tower, his straw hat tilted over his eyes.

"Why, Harold Forscythe!" she exclaimed breathlessly.

He sprang to his feet, baring his head in the sun.

"Sit down, do," he urged. "It's quite dry there—the masonry crops out—and the view's delightful."

"You didn't seem to be doing much with the view as I came up." Harriet put down her sunshade and stood looking at him, taking in his careless morning dress, his gray, unshaven face and heavy eyes. "But I shall sit down," she affectionately assured him, "to look at you, since I have so few opportunities. Why haven't you been to see me?"

Forscythe gazed attentively at her canvas shoes, hesitating and thrusting out his lower lip, an impetuous mannerism she had liked in him as a boy. "Perhaps—perhaps I haven't quite dared," he suggested.

"Which means," commented Harriet reproachfully, "that you accredit me with a very disagreeable kind of stupidity."

"You? Oh, dear, no! I didn't—I don't. How could you suppose it?" He helped her to her seat on the slant of gray rock, moving about her solicitously, but avoiding her eyes.

"Then why do you stand there, hesitating?"

"I was just thinking"—he shot her a nervous glance from under a frown—"whether I ought not to cut away now, on your account. I'm in the devil of a way in the early morning sometimes."

Mrs. Westfield looked at him compassionately as he stood poking the turf with his stick. She wondered how he could have reached eight-and-thirty without growing at all older than he had been in his twenties. And yet, that was just what their happiness had done for them. If it had kept them young, gloriously and resplendently young, it had also kept them from arriving anywhere. It had prolonged his flowering time, but it hadn't mellowed him. Growing older would have meant making concessions. He had never made any; had not even learned how, and was still striking back like a boy.

Harriet pointed to the turf beside her, and he dropped down suddenly.

"I'm really not fit to see any one this morning. These first hours—" He shrugged his shoulders and began to pull the grass blades swiftly, one at a time.

"Are hard for you?"

He nodded.

"Because they used to be your happiest?" Harriet continued, feeling her way.

"It's queer," he said quietly, "but in the morning I often feel such an absurd certainty of finding her. I suppose one has more vitality at this time of day, a keener sense of things."

"My poor boy! Is it still as hard as that?"

"Did you for a moment suppose that it would ever be any—easier?" he asked, with a short laugh.

"I hoped so. Oh, I hoped so."

Forscythe shook his head. "You know why I haven't been to see you," he brought out abruptly.

Harriet touched his arm. "You ought not to be afraid with me. If I didn't love her as much as you did, at least I never loved anything else so well."

"I know. That's one reason I came here. You were always together when I first knew her, and it's easy to see her beside you. Sometimes I think the image of her—coming down the stairs, crossing the garden, holding out her hand—is growing dimmer, and that terrifies me. Some people and some places give me the feeling of her." He stopped with

a jerk, and threw a pebble across the moat, where the sloping bank, softened
and made shallower by the slow centuries, was yellow with buttercups.

"But that feeling, Harold, must be more in you than anywhere.
There's where she willed it and breathed it and stored it for years."

Harold was looking fixedly at the bare spot under his hand and
pulling the grass blades out delicately. When he spoke, his voice fairly
startled her with its sound of water working underground.

"It was like that once, but now I lose it sometimes—for weeks
together. It's like trying to hold some delicate scent in your nostrils, and
heavier odors come in and blur it."

"My poor boy, what can I say to you?" Harriet's eyes were so
dim that she could only put out a hand to be sure that he was there. He
pressed it and held it a moment.

"You don't have to say anything. Your thinking reaches me. It's
extraordinary how we can be trained down, how little we can do with. If
she could only have written to me—if there could have been a sign, a
shadow on the grass or in the sky, to show that she went on with me, it
would have been enough. And now—I wouldn't ask anything but to be left
alone with my hurt. It's all that's left me. It's the most precious thing in the
world."

"Oh, but that, my dear Harold, is too terrible! She couldn't have
endured your doing it," murmured Harriet, overcome.

"Yes, she could. She'd have done it. She'd have kept me alive
in her anguish, in her incompleteness."

Mrs. Westfield put out her hand entreatingly to stop him. He
had lain beside her on the grass so often in the days of his courtship, of his
first tempestuous happiness. It was incredible that he should have changed
so little. He hadn't grown older, or wiser, or, in himself, better. He had
simply grown more and more to be Eleanor. The misery of his entanglement touched her afresh, and she put her hands to her eyes and murmured,
"Oh, that poor little Ethel! How could you do it?"

She heard him bound up, and when she lifted her face he was
half the length of the wall away. She called to him, but he waved his hat
meaninglessly, and she watched him hurry across the smooth green swell of
the hill. Harriet leaned back into the warm angle of masonry and tried to
settle into the deep peace of the place, where so many follies and passions
had spent themselves and ebbed back into the stillness of the grass. But a
sense of pain kept throbbing about her. It seemed to come from the spot
where poor Forscythe had lain, and to rise like a miasma between her and

the farms and orchards and the gray-green windings of the river. When at
last she rose with a sigh, she murmured to herself, "Oh, my poor Eleanor!
If you know, I pity you. Wherever you are, I pity you."

III

*T*he silence once broken, Forscythe
came often to Mrs. Westfield's garden. He spent whole mornings there,
watching her embroider, or walked with her about the ruins on the hilltop,
or along the streams that wound through the fertile farm country. Though
he said little himself, he made it supremely easy for her to talk. He followed
her about in grateful silence while she told him, freely and almost lightly,
of her girlhood with Eleanor Sanford; of their life at a convent-school in
Paris; of the copy of *Manon Lescaut* which they kept sewed up in the little
pine pillow they had brought from Schenectady; of the adroit machinations
by which, on her fête-day, under the guardianship of an innocent aunt from
Albany, Eleanor had managed to convey all her birthday roses out to
Père-la-Chaise and arrange them under de Musset's willow.

Harriet even found a quiet happiness in being with him. She felt
that he was making amends; that she could trust him not to renew the
terrible experience which had crushed her at their first meeting on the hill.
When he spoke of Eleanor at all, it was only to recall the beauty of their
companionship, a thing she loved to reflect upon. For if they had been
selfish, at least their selfishness had never taken the form of comfortable
indolence. They had kept the edge of their zest for action; their affection
had never grown stocky and middle-aged. How, Harriet often asked herself, could two people have crowded so much into ten circumscribed mortal
years? And, of course, the best of it was that all the things they did and the
places they went to and the people they knew didn't in the least matter,
were only the incidental music of their drama.

The end, when it came, had, by the mercy of Heaven, come
suddenly. An illness of three days at Fortuney, their own place on the Oise,
and it was over. He was flung out into space to find his way alone; to keep
fighting about in his circle, forever yearning toward the center.

One morning, when Harold asked her to go for a long walk into
the country, Harriet felt from the moment they left the town behind them

that he had something serious to say to her. They were having their déjeuner in the garden of a little auberge, sitting at a table beside a yellow clay wall overgrown with wall peaches, when he told her that he was going away.

"I don't know for just how long. Perhaps a week; perhaps two. I'd hate to have you misunderstand. I don't want you to underestimate the good you've done me these last weeks. But, you see, this is a sort of—a sort of tryst," he explained, smiling faintly. "We got stranded once in an absurd little town down on the Mediterranean, not far from Hyères. We liked it and stayed for days, and when we left, Eleanor said we'd go back every year when the grapes were ripe. We never did go back, for that was the last year. But I've been there that same week every autumn. The people there all remember her. It's a little bit of a place."

Harriet looked at him, holding her breath. The black kitten came up and brushed against him, tapping his arm with its paw and mewing to be fed.

"Is that why you go away so much? Ethel has told me. She said there was some business, but I doubted that."

"I'm sorry it has to be so. Of course, I feel despicable—do all the time, for that matter." He wiped his face and hands miserably with his napkin and pushed back his chair. "You see," he went on, beginning to make geometrical figures in the sand with his walking stick, "you see, I can't settle down to anything, and I'm so driven. There are times when places pull me—places where things happened, you know. Not big things, but just our own things." He stopped, and then added thoughtfully, "Going to miss her is almost what going to meet her used to be. I get in such a state of impatience."

Harriet couldn't, she simply couldn't, altogether despise him, and it was because, as he said, she did know. They sat in the quiet, sunny little garden, full of dahlias and sunflowers and the hum of bees, and she remembered what Eleanor had told her about this fishing village where they had lived on figs and goat's milk and watched the meager vintage being gathered; how, when they had to leave it, got into their compartment and flashed away along the panoramic Mediterranean shore, she had cried—she who never wept for pain or weariness, Harriet put in fondly. It was not the blue bay and the lavender and the pine hills they were leaving, but some peculiar shade of being together. Yet they were always leaving that. Every day brought colors in the sky, on the sea, in the heart, which could not possibly come just so again. That tomorrow's would be just as beautiful never quite satisfied them. They wanted it all. Yes, whatever they were, those two, they were Olympian.

As they were nearing home in the late afternoon, Forscythe turned suddenly to Harriet. "I shall have to count on you for something while I am away, you know."

"About the business? Oh, yes, I'll understand."

"And you'll do what you can for her, won't you?" he asked shakily. "It's such a hellish existence for her. I'd do anything if I could undo what I've done—anything."

Harriet paused a moment. "It simply can't, you know, go on like this."

"Yes, yes, I know that," he replied abstractedly. "But that's not the worst of it. The worst is that sometimes I feel as if Eleanor wants me to give her up; that she can't stand it any longer and is begging me to let her rest."

Harriet tried to look at him, but he had turned away his face.

IV

*F*orscythe's absence stretched beyond a fortnight, and no one seemed very definitely informed as to when he might return. Meanwhile, Mrs. Westfield had his wife considerably upon her hands. She could not, indeed, account for the degree to which she seemed responsible. It was always there, groping for her and pulling at her, as she told Westfield. The garden wall was not high enough to shut out entirely the other side; the girl pacing the gravel paths with the meek, bent step which poor Harriet found so exasperating, her wistful eyes peering from under her garden hat, her preposterous skirts trailing behind her like the brier-torn gown of some wandering Griselda.

During the long, dull hours in which they had their tea together, Harriet realized more and more the justice of the girl's position—of her claim, since she apparently had no position that one could well define. The reasonableness of it was all the more trying since Harriet felt so compelled to deny it. They read and walked and talked, and the subject to which they never alluded was always in the air. It was in the girl's long, silent, entreating looks; in her thin hands, nervously clasping and unclasping; in her ceaseless pacing about. Harriet distinctly felt that she was working herself up to something, and she declared to Westfield every morning that, whatever it was, she wouldn't be a party to it.

"I can understand perfectly," she insisted to her husband, "how he did it. He married her to talk to her about Eleanor. Eleanor had been the theme of their courtship. The rest of the world went on attending to its own business and shaking him off, and she stopped and sympathized and let him pour himself out. He didn't see, I suppose, why he shouldn't have just a wife like other men, for it didn't occur to him that he couldn't be just a husband. He thought she'd be content to console; he never dreamed she'd try to heal."

As for Ethel, Harriet had to admit that she, too, could be perfectly accounted for. She had gone into it, doubtless, in the spirit of self-sacrifice, a mood she was romantically fond of permitting herself and humanly unable to live up to. She had married him in one stage of feeling, and had inevitably arrived at another—had come, indeed, to the place where she must be just one thing to him. What she was, or was not, hung on the throw of the dice in a way that savored of trembling captives and barbarous manners, and Harriet had to acknowledge that almost anything might be expected of a woman who had let herself go to such lengths and had yet got nowhere worth mentioning.

"She is certainly going to do something," Harriet declared. "But whatever can she hope to do now? What weapon has she left? How is she, after she's poured herself out so, ever to gather herself up again? What she'll do is the horror. It's sure to be ineffectual, and it's equally sure to have distinctly dramatic aspects."

Harriet was not, however, quite prepared for the issue which confronted her one morning. She sat down shaken and aghast when Ethel, pale and wraith-like, glided somnambulantly into her garden and asked whether Mrs. Westfield would accompany her to Fortuney on the following day.

"But, my dear girl, ought you to go there alone?"

"Without Harold, you mean?" the other inaudibly suggested. "Yes, I think I ought. He has such a dread of going back there, and yet I feel that he'll never be satisfied until he gets among his own things. He would be happier if he took the shock and had done with it. And my going there first might make it easier for him."

Harriet stared. "Don't you think he should be left to decide that for himself?" she reasoned mildly. "He may wish to forget the place in so far as he can."

"He doesn't forget," Ethel replied simply. "He thinks about it all the time. He ought to live there; it's his home. He ought not," she brought out, with a fierce little burst, "to be kept away."

"I don't know that he or any one else can do much in regard to that," commented Harriet dryly.

"He ought to live there," Ethel repeated automatically; "and it might make it easier for him if I went first."

"How?" gasped Mrs. Westfield.

"It might," she insisted childishly, twisting her handkerchief around her fingers. "We can take an early train and get there in the afternoon. It's but a short drive from the station. I am sure"—she looked pleadingly at Harriet—"I'm sure he'd like it better if you went with me."

Harriet made a clutch at herself and looked pointedly at the ground. "I really don't see how I could, Ethel. It doesn't seem to me a proper thing to do."

Ethel sat straight and still. Her liquid eyes brimmed over and the tears rolled mildly down her cheeks. "I'm sorry it seems wrong to you. Of course you can't go if it does. I shall go alone, then, tomorrow." She rose and stood poised in uncertainty, her hand on the back of the chair.

Harriet moved quickly toward her. The girl's infatuate obstinacy carried a power with it.

"But why, dear child, do you wish me to go with you? What good could that possibly do?"

There was a long silence, trembling and gentle tears. At last Ethel murmured: "I thought, because you were her friend, that would make it better. If you were with me, it couldn't seem quite so—indelicate." Her shoulders shook with a sudden wrench of feeling and she pressed her hands over her face. "You see," she faltered, "I'm so at a loss. I haven't—any one."

Harriet put an arm firmly about her drooping slenderness. "Well, for this venture, at least, you shall have me. I can't see it, but I'm willing to go; more willing than I am that you should go alone. I must tell Robert and ask him to look up the trains for us."

The girl drew gently away from her and stood in an attitude of deep dejection. "It's difficult for you, too, our being here. We ought never to have come. And I must not take advantage of you. Before letting you go with me, I must tell you the real reason why I am going to Fortuney."

"The real reason?" echoed Harriet.

"Yes. I think he's there now."

"Harold? At Fortuney?"

"Yes. I haven't heard from him for five days. Then it was only a telegram, dated from Pontoise. That's very near Fortuney. Since then I haven't had a word."

"You poor child, how dreadful! Come here and tell me about it." Harriet drew 'ier to a chair, into which she sank limply.

"There's nothing to tell, except what one fears. I've lost sleep until I imagine all sorts of horrible things. If he has been alone there for days, shut up with all those memories, who knows what may have happened to him? I shouldn't, you know, feel like this if he were with—any one. But this—oh, you are all against me! You none of you understand. You think I am trying to make him—inconstant" (for the first time her voice broke into passionate scorn). "But there's no other way to save him. It's simply killing him. He's been frightfully ill twice, once in London and once before we left India. The London doctors told me that unless he was got out of this state he might do almost anything. They even wanted me to leave him. So, you see, I must do something."

Harriet sat down on the stool beside her and took her hand.

"Why don't you, then, my dear, do it—leave him?"

The girl looked wildly toward the garden wall. "I can't—not now. I might have once, perhaps. Oh!" with a burst of trembling, "don't, please don't talk about it. Just help me to save him if you can."

"Had you rather, Ethel, that I went to Fortuney alone?" Harriet suggested hopefully.

The girl shook her head. "No; he'd know I sent you, and he'd think I was afraid. I am, of course, but not in the way he thinks. I've never crossed him in anything, but we can't go on like this any longer. I'll go, and he'll just have to—choose."

Having seen Ethel safely to her own door, Harriet went to her husband, who was at work in the library, and told him to what she had committed herself. Westfield received the intelligence with marked discouragement. He disliked her being drawn more and more into the Forscythes' affairs, which he found very depressing and disconcerting, and he flatly declared that he wanted nothing so much as to get away from all that hysteria next door and finish the summer in Switzerland.

"It's an obsession with her to get to Fortuney," Harriet explained. "To her it somehow means getting into everything she's out of. I really can't have her thinking I'm against her in that definite, petty sort of way. So I've promised to go. Besides, if she is going down there, where all Eleanor's things are—"

"Ah, so it's to keep her out, and not to help her in, that you're going," Westfield deduced.

"I declare to you, I don't know which it is. I'm going for both of them—for her and for Eleanor."

V

*F*ortuney stood in its cluster of cool green, halfway up the hillside and overlooking the green loop of the river. Harriet remembered, as she approached it, how Eleanor used to say that after the South, it was good to come back and rest her eyes there. Nowhere were skies so gray, streams so clear, or fields so pleasantly interspersed with woodland. The hill on which the house stood overlooked an island where the haymakers were busy cutting a second crop, swinging their bright scythes in the long grass and stopping to hail the heavy lumber barges as they passed slowly up the glassy river.

Ethel insisted upon leaving the carriage by the roadside, so the two women alighted and walked up the long driveway that wound under the linden trees. An old man who was clipping the hedge looked curiously at them as they passed. Except for the snipping of his big shears and occasional halloos from the island, a pale, sunny quiet lay over the place, and their approach, Harriet reflected, certainly savored all too much of a reluctance to break it. She looked at Ethel with all the exasperation of fatigue, and felt that there was something positively stealthy about her soft, driven tread.

The front door was open, but, as they approached, a bent old woman ran out from the garden behind the house, her apron full of gourds, calling to them as she ran. Ethel addressed her without embarrassment: "I am Madame Forscythe. Monsieur is awaiting me. Yes, I know that he is ill. You need not announce me."

The old woman tried to detain her by salutations and questions, tried to explain that she would immediately get rooms ready for Madame and her friend. Why had she not been told?

But Ethel brushed past her, seeming to float over the threshold and up the staircase, while Harriet followed her, protesting. They went through the salon, the library, into Harold's study, straight toward the room which had been Eleanor's.

"Let us wait for him here in his study, please, Ethel," Harriet whispered. "We've no right to steal upon any one like this."

But Ethel seemed drawn like the victim of mesmerism. The door opening from the study into Eleanor's room was hung with a heavy curtain. She lifted i, and there they paused, noiselessly. It was just as Harriet remembered it; the tapestries, the prie-Dieu, the Louis Seize furniture— absolutely unchanged, except that her own portrait, by Constant, hung where Harold's used to be. Across the foot of the bed, in a tennis shirt and trousers, lay Harold himself, asleep. He was lying on his side, his face turned toward the door and one arm thrown over his head. The habit of being on his guard must have sharpened his senses, for as they looked at him he awoke and sprang up, flushed and disordered.

"Ethel, what on earth—?" he cried hotly.

She was frightened enough now. She trembled from head to foot and pressed her hands tightly over her breast. "You never told me not to come," she panted. "You only said," with a wild burst of reproach, "that you couldn't."

Harold gripped the foot of the bed with both hands and his voice shook with anger. "Please go downstairs and wait in the reception room, while I ask Mrs. Westfield to enlighten me."

Something leaped into Ethel's eyes as she took another step forward into the room and let the curtain fall behind her. "I won't go, Harold, until you go with me," she cried. Drawing up her frail shoulders, she glanced desperately about her—at the room, at her husband, at Harriet, and finally at her, the handsome, disdainful face which glowed out of the canvas. "You have no right to come here secretly," she broke out. "It's shameful to her as well as to me. I'm not afraid of her. She couldn't but loathe you for what you do to me. She couldn't have been so contemptible as you all make her—so jealous!"

Forscythe swung round on his heel, his clenched hands hanging at his side, and, throwing back his head, faced the picture.

"Jealous? Of whom—my God!"

"Harold!" cried Mrs. Westfield entreatingly.

But she was too late. The girl had slipped to the floor as if she had been cut down.

VI

One rainy night, four weeks after her visit to Fortuney, Forscythe stood at Mrs. Westfield's door, his hat in his hand, bidding her good night. Harriet looked worn and troubled, but Forscythe himself was calm.

"I'm so glad you gave me a chance at Fortuney, Harold. I couldn't bear to see it go to strangers. I'll keep it just as it is—as it was; you may be sure of that, and if ever you wish to come back—"

Forscythe spoke up quickly: "I don't think I shall be coming back again, Mrs. Westfield. And please don't hesitate to make any changes. As I've tried to tell you, I don't feel the need of it any longer. She has come back to me as much as she ever can."

"In another person?"

Harold smiled a little and shook his head. "In another way. She lived and died, dear Harriet, and I'm all there is to show for it. That's pitiful enough, but I must do what I can. I shall die very far short of the mark—but she was always generous."

He held out his hand to Mrs. Westfield and took hers resolutely, though she hesitated as if to detain him.

"Tell Ethel I shall go over to see her in the morning before you leave, and thank her for her message," Harriet murmured.

"Please come. She has been seeing to the packing in spite of me, and is quite worn out. She'll be herself again, once I get her back to Surrey, and she's very keen about going to America. Good night, dear lady," he called after him as he crossed the veranda.

Harriet heard him splash down the gravel walk to the gate and then closed the door. She went slowly through the hall and into her husband's study, where she sat quietly down by the wood fire.

Westfield rose from his work and looked at her with concern.

"Why didn't you send that madman home long ago, Harriet? It's past midnight, and you're completely done out. You look like a ghost." He opened a cabinet and poured her a glass of wine.

"I feel like one, dear. I'm beginning to feel my age. I've no spirit to hold it off any longer. I'm going to buy Fortuney and give up to it. It will be pleasant to grow old there in that atmosphere of lovely things past and forgotten."

Westfield sat down on the arm of her chair and drew her head to him. "He is real'y going to sell it, then? He has come round sure enough, hasn't he?"

"Oh, he melts the heart in me, Robert. He makes me feel so old and lonely; that he and I are left over from another age—a lovely time that's gone. He's giving up everything. He's going to take her home to America after her child is born."

"Her child?"

"Yes. He didn't know until after that dreadful day at Fortuney. She had never told any one. He says he's so glad—that it will make up to her for everything. Oh, Robert! if only Eleanor had left him children all this wouldn't have been."

"Do you think," Westfield asked after a long silence, "that he is glad?"

"I know it. He's been so gentle and comprehending with her." Harriet stopped to dry the tears on her cheek, and put her head down on her husband's shoulder. "And oh, Robert, I never would have believed that he could be so splendid about it. It's as if he had come up to his possibilities for the first time, through this silly, infatuated girl, while Eleanor, who gave him kingdoms—"

She cried softly on his shoulder for a long while, and then he felt that she was thinking. When at last she looked up, she smiled gratefully into his eyes.

"Well, we'll have Fortuney, dearest. We'll have all that's left of them. He'll never turn back; I feel such a strength in him now. He'll go on doing it and being finer and finer. And do you know, Robert," her lips trembled again, but she still smiled from her misty eyes, "if Eleanor knows, I believe she'll be glad; for—oh, my Eleanor!—she loved him beyond anything, beyond even his love."

On the Gulls' Road

The Ambassador's Story

*I*t often happens that one or another of my friends stops before a red chalk drawing in my study and asks me where I ever found so lovely a creature. I have never told the story of that picture to any one, and the beautiful woman on the wall, until yesterday, in all these twenty years has spoken to no one but me. Yesterday a young painter, a countryman of mine, came to consult me on a matter of business, and upon seeing my drawing of Alexandra Ebbling, straightway forgot his errand. He examined the date upon the sketch and asked me, very earnestly, if I could tell him whether the lady were still living. When I answered him, he stepped back from the picture and said slowly:

"So long ago? She must have been very young. She was happy?"

"As to that, who can say—about any one of us?" I replied. "Out of all that is supposed to make for happiness, she had very little."

He shrugged his shoulders and turned away to the window, saying as he did so: "Well, there is very little use in troubling about anything, when we can stand here and look at her, and you can tell me that she has been dead all these years, and that she had very little."

We returned to the object of his visit, but when he bade me goodbye at the door his troubled gaze again went back to the drawing, and it was only by turning sharply about that he took his eyes away from her.

I went back to my study fire, and as the rain kept away less impetuous visitors, I had a long time in which to think of Mrs. Ebbling. I even got out the little box she gave me, which I had not opened for years, and when Mrs. Hemway brought my tea I had barely time to close the lid and defeat her disapproving gaze.

My young countryman's perplexity, as he looked at Mrs. Ebbling, had recalled to me the delight and pain she gave me when I was of his years. I sat looking at her face and trying to see it through his eyes—freshly, as I saw it first upon the deck of the *Germania,* twenty years ago. Was it her loveline s, I often ask myself, or her loneliness, or her simplicity, or was it merely my own youth? Was her mystery only that of the mysterious North out of which she came? I still feel that she was very different from all the beautiful and brilliant women I have known; as the night is different from the day, or as the sea is different from the land. But this is our story, as it comes back to me.

For two years I had been studying Italian and working in the capacity of clerk to the American legation at Rome, and I was going home to secure my first consular appointment. Upon boarding my steamer at Genoa, I saw my luggage into my cabin and then started for a rapid circuit of the deck. Everything promised well. The boat was thinly peopled, even for a July crossing; the decks were roomy; the day was fine; the sea was blue; I was sure of my appointment, and, best of all, I was coming back to Italy. All these things were in my mind when I stopped sharply before a *chaise longue* placed sidewise near the stern. Its occupant was a woman, apparently ill, who lay with her eyes closed, and in her open arm was a chubby little red-haired girl, asleep. I can still remember that first glance at Mrs. Ebbling, and how I stopped as a wheel does when the band slips. Her splendid, vigorous body lay still and relaxed under the loose folds of her clothing, her white throat and arms and red-gold hair were drenched with sunlight. Such hair as it was: wayward as some kind of gleaming seaweed that curls and undulates with the tide. A moment gave me her face; the high cheekbones, the thin cheeks, the gentle chin, arching back to a girlish throat, and singular loveliness of the mouth. Even then it flashed through me that the mouth gave the whole face its peculiar beauty and distinction. It was proud and sad and tender, and strangely calm. The curve of the lips could not have been cut more cleanly with the most delicate instrument, and whatever shade of feeling passed over them seemed to partake of their exquisiteness.

But I am anticipating. While I stood stupidly staring (as if, at twenty-five, I had never before beheld a beautiful woman) the whistles broke into a hoarse scream, and the deck under us began to vibrate. The woman opened her eyes, and the little girl struggled into a sitting position, rolled out of her mother's arm, and ran to the deck rail. After putting my chair near the stern, I went forward to see the gangplank up and did not return until we were dragging out to sea at the end of a long towline.

The woman in the *chaise longue* was still alone. She lay there all day, looking at the sea. The little girl, Carin, played noisily about the deck. Occasionally she returned and struggled up into the chair, plunged her head, round and red as a little pumpkin, against her mother's shoulder in an impetuous embrace, and then struggled down again with a lively flourishing of arms and legs. Her mother took such opportunities to pull up the child's socks or to smooth the fiery little braids; her beautiful hands, rather large and very white, played about the riotous little girl with a quieting tenderness. Carin chattered away in Italian and kept asking for her father, only to be told that he was busy.

When any of the ship's officers passed, they stopped for a word with my neighbor, and I heard the first mate address her as Mrs. Ebbling. When they spoke to her, she smiled appreciatively and answered in low, faltering Italian, but I fancied that she was glad when they passed on and left her to her fixed contemplation of the sea. Her eyes seemed to drink the color of it all day long, and after every interruption they went back to it. There was a kind of pleasure in watching her satisfaction, a kind of excitement in wondering what the water made her remember or forget. She seemed not to wish to talk to any one, but I knew I should like to hear whatever she might be thinking. One could catch some hint of her thoughts, I imagined, from the shadows that came and went across her lips, like the reflection of light clouds. She had a pile of books beside her, but she did not read, and neither could I. I gave up trying at last, and watched the sea, very conscious of her presence, almost of her thoughts. When the sun dropped low and shone in her face, I rose and asked if she would like me to move her chair. She smiled and thanked me, but said the sun was good for her. Her yellow-hazel eyes followed me for a moment and then went back to the sea.

After the first bugle sounded for dinner, a heavy man in uniform came up the deck and stood beside the *chaise longue,* looking down at its two occupants with a smile of satisfied possession. The breast of his trim coat was hidden by waves of soft blond beard, as long and heavy as a woman's hair, which blew about his face in glittering profusion. He wore a large turquoise ring upon the thick hand that he rubbed good-humoredly over the little girl's head. To her he spoke Italian, but he and his wife conversed in some Scandinavian tongue. He stood stroking his fine beard until the second bugle blew, then bent stiffly from his hips, like a soldier, and patted his wife's hand as it lay on the arm of her chair. He hurried down the deck, taking stock of the passengers as he went, and stopped before a thin girl with frizzed hair and a lace coat, asking her a facetious question in thick English. They began to talk about Chicago and went below. Later I saw him at the head of his table in the dining room, the befrizzed Chicago lady on his left. They must have got a famous start at luncheon, for by the end of the dinner Ebbling was peeling figs for her and presenting them on the end of a fork.

The Doctor confided to me that Ebbling was the chief engineer and the dandy of the boat; but this time he would have to behave himself, for he had brought his sick wife along for the voyage. She had a bad heart valve, he added, and was in a serious way.

After dinner Ebbling disappeared, presumably to his engines, and at ten o'clock, when the stewardess came to put Mrs. Ebbling to bed, I helped her to rise from her chair, and the second mate ran up and supported her down to her cabin. About midnight I found the engineer in the card room, playing with the Doctor, an Italian naval officer, and the commodore of a Long Island yacht club. His face was even pinker than it had been at dinner, and his fine beard was full of smoke. I thought a long while about Ebbling and his wife before I went to sleep.

The next morning we tied up at Naples to take on our cargo, and I went on shore for the day. I did not, however, entirely escape the ubiquitous engineer, whom I saw lunching with the Long Island commodore at a hotel in the Santa Lucia. When I returned to the boat in the early evening, the passengers had gone down to dinner, and I found Mrs. Ebbling quite alone upon the deserted deck. I approached her and asked whether she had had a dull day. She looked up smiling and shook her head, as if her Italian had quite failed her. I saw that she was flushed with excitement, and her yellow eyes were shining like two clear topazes.

"Dull? Oh, no! I love to watch Naples from the sea, in this white heat. She has just lain there on her hillside among the vines and laughed for me all day long. I have been able to pick out many of the places I like best."

I felt that she was really going to talk to me at last. She had turned to me frankly, as to an old acquaintance, and seemed not to be hiding from me anything of what she felt. I sat down in a glow of pleasure and excitement and asked her if she knew Naples well.

"Oh, yes! I lived there for a year after I was first married. My husband has a great many friends in Naples. But he was at sea most of the time, so I went about alone. Nothing helps one to know a city like that. I came first by sea, like this. Directly to Naples from Finmark, and I had never been south before." Mrs. Ebbling stopped and looked over my shoulder. Then, with a quick, eager glance at me, she said abruptly: "It was like a baptism of fire. Nothing has ever been quite the same since. Imagine how this bay looked to a Finmark girl. It seemed like the overture to Italy."

I laughed. "And then one goes up the country—song by song and wine by wine."

Mrs. Ebbling sighed. "Ah, yes. It must be fine to follow it. I have never been away from the seaports myself. We live now in Genoa."

The deck steward brought her tray, and I moved forward a little and stood by the rail. When I looked back, she smiled and nodded to let me know that she was not missing anything. I could feel her intentness as keenly as if she were standing beside me.

The sun had disappeared over the high ridge behind the city, and the stone pines stood black and flat against the fires of the afterglow. The lilac haze that hung over the long, lazy slopes of Vesuvius warmed with golden light, and films of blue vapor began to float down toward Baiæ. The sky, the sea, and the city between them turned a shimmering violet, fading grayer as the lights began to glow like luminous pearls along the water-front—the necklace of an irreclaimable queen. Behind me I heard a low exclamation; a slight, stifled sound, but it seemed the perfect vocalization of that weariness with which we at last let go of beauty, after we have held it until the senses are darkened. When I turned to her again, she seemed to have fallen asleep.

That night, as we were moving out to sea and the tail lights of Naples were winking across the widening stretch of black water, I helped Mrs. Ebbling to the foot of the stairway. She drew herself up from her chair with effort and leaned on me wearily. I could have carried her all night without fatigue.

"May I come and talk to you tomorrow?" I asked. She did not reply at once. "Like an old friend?" I added. She gave me her languid hand, and her mouth, set with the exertion of walking, softened altogether. *"Grazia,"* she murmured.

I returned to the deck and joined a group of my countrywomen, who, primed with inexhaustible information, were discussing the baseness of Renaissance art. They were intelligent and alert, and as they leaned forward in their deck chairs under the circle of light, their faces recalled to me Rembrandt's picture of a clinical lecture. I heard them through, against my will, and then went to the stern to smoke and to see the last of the island lights. The sky had clouded over, and a soft, melancholy wind was rushing over the sea. I could not help thinking how disappointed I would be if rain should keep Mrs. Ebbling in her cabin tomorrow. My mind played constantly with her image. At one moment she was very clear and directly in front of me; the next she was far away. Whatever else I thought about, some part of my consciousness was busy with Mrs. Ebbling; hunting for her, finding her, losing her, then groping again. How was it that I was so conscious of whatever she might be feeling? That when she sat still behind me and watched the evening sky, I had had a sense of speed and change, almost of danger; and when she was tired and sighed, I had wished for night and loneliness.

II

*T*hough when we are young we sel-dom think much about it, there is now and again a golden day when we feel a sudden, arrogant pride in our youth; in the lightness of our feet and the strength of our arms, in the warm fluid that courses so surely within us; when we are conscious of something powerful and mercurial in our breasts, which comes up wave after wave and leaves us irresponsible and free. All the next morning I felt this flow of life, which continually impelled me toward Mrs. Ebbling. After the merest greeting, however, I kept away. I found it pleasant to thwart myself, to measure myself against a current that was sure to carry me with it in the end. I was content to let her watch the sea the sea that seemed now to have come into me, warm and soft, still and strong. I played shuffleboard with the Commodore, who was anxious to keep down his figure, and ran about the deck with the stout legs of the little pumpkin-colored Carin about my neck. It was not until the child was having her afternoon nap below that I at last came up and stood beside her mother.

"You are better today," I exclaimed, looking down at her white gown. She colored unreasonably, and I laughed with a familiarity which she must have accepted as the mere foolish noise of happiness, or it would have seemed impertinent.

We talked at first of a hundred trivial things, and we watched the sea. The coast of Sardinia had lain to our port for some hours and would lie there for hours to come, now advancing in rocky promontories, now retreating behind blue bays. It was the naked south coast of the island, and though our course held very near the shore, not a village or habitation was visible; there was not even a goatherd's hut hidden away among the low pinkish sand hills. Pinkish sand hills and yellow headlands; with dull-colored scrubby bushes massed about their bases and following the dried water-courses. A narrow strip of beach glistened like white paint between the purple sea and the umber rocks, and the whole island lay gleaming in the yellow sunshine and translucent air. Not a wave broke on that fringe of white sand, not the shadow of a cloud played across the bare hills. In the air about us there was no sound but that of a vessel moving rapidly through absolutely still water. She seemed like some great sea-animal, swimming silently, her head well up. The sea before us was so rich and heavy and opaque that it might have been lapis lazuli. It was the blue of legend, simply; the color that satisfies the soul like sleep.

And it was of the sea we talked, for it was the substance of Mrs. Ebbling's story. She seemed always to have been swept along by ocean streams, warm or cold, and to have hovered about the edge of great waters. She was born and had grown up in a little fishing town on the Arctic Ocean. Her father was a doctor, a widower, who lived with his daughter and who divided his time between his books and his fishing rod. Her uncle was skipper on a coasting vessel, and with him she had made many trips along the Norwegian coast. But she was always reading and thinking about the blue seas of the South.

"There was a curious old woman in our village, Dame Ericson, who had been in Italy in her youth. She had gone to Rome to study art, and had copied a great many pictures there. She was well connected, but had little money, and as she grew older and poorer she sold her pictures one by one, until there was scarcely a well-to-do family in our district that did not own one of Dame Ericson's paintings. But she brought home many other strange things; a little orange tree which she cherished until the day of her death, and bits of colored marble, and sea shells and pieces of coral, and a thin flask full of water from the Mediterranean. When I was a little girl she used to show me her things and tell me about the South; about the coral fishers, and the pink islands, and the smoking mountains, and the old, underground Naples. I suppose the water in her flask was like any other, but it never seemed so to me. It looked so elastic and alive, that I used to think if one unsealed the bottle something penetrating and fruitful might leap out and work an enchantment over Finmark."

Lars Ebbling, I learned, was one of her father's friends. She could remember him from the time when she was a little girl and he a dashing young man who used to come home from the sea and make a stir in the village. After he got his promotion to an Atlantic liner and went South, she did not see him until the summer she was twenty, when he came home to marry her. That was five years ago. The little girl, Carin, was three. From her talk, one might have supposed that Ebbling was proprietor of the Mediterranean and its adjacent lands, and could have kept her away at his pleasure. Her own rights in him she seemed not to consider.

But we wasted very little time on Lars Ebbling. We talked, like two very young persons, of arms and men, of the sea beneath us and the shores it washed. We were carried a little beyond ourselves, for we were in the presence of the things of youth that never change; fleeing past them. Tomorrow they would be gone, and no effort of will or memory could bring them back again. All about us was the sea of great adventure, and below us, caught somewhere in its gleaming meshes, were the bones of nations and navies . . . nations and navies that gave youth its hope and made life something more than a hunger of the bowels. The unpeopled Sardinian coast unfolded gently before us, like something left over out of a world that was gone; a place that might well have had no later news since the corn ships brought the tidings of Actium.

"I shall never go to Sardinia," said Mrs. Ebbling. "It could not possibly be as beautiful as this."

"Neither shall I," I replied.

As I was going down to dinner that evening, I was stopped by Lars Ebbling, freshly brushed and scented, wearing a white uniform, and polished and glistening as one of his own engines. He smiled at me with his own kind of geniality. "You have been very kind of talk to my wife," he explained. "It is very bad for her this trip that she speaks no English. I am indebted to you."

I told him curtly that he was mistaken, but my acrimony made no impression upon his blandness. I felt that I should certainly strike the fellow if he stood there much longer, running his blue ring up and down his beard. I should probably have hated any man who was Mrs. Ebbling's husband, but Ebbling made me sick.

III

*T*he next day I began my drawing of Mrs. Ebbling. She seemed pleased and a little puzzled when I asked her to sit for me. It occurred to me that she had always been among dull people who took her looks as a matter of course, and that she was not at all sure that she was really beautiful. I can see now her quick, confused look of pleasure. I thought very little about the drawing then, except that the making of it gave me an opportunity to study her face; to look as long as I pleased into her yellow eyes, at the noble lines of her mouth, at her splendid, vigorous hair.

"We have a yellow vine at home," I told her, "that is very like your hair. It seems to be growing while one looks at it, and it twines and tangles about itself and throws out little tendrils in the wind."

"Has it any name?"

"We call it love vine."

How little a thing could disconcert her!

As for me, nothing disconcerted me. I awoke every morning with a sense of speed and joy. At night I loved to hear the swish of the water rushing by. As fast as the pistons could carry us, as fast as the water could bear us, we were going forward to something delightful; to something together. When Mrs. Ebbling told me that she and her husband would be five days in the docks in New York and then return to Genoa, I was not disturbed, for I did not believe her. I came and went, and she sat still all day, watching the water. I heard an American lady say that she watched it like one who is going to die, but even that did not frighten me: I somehow felt that she had promised me to live.

All those long blue days when I sat beside her talking about Finmark and the sea, she must have known that I loved her. I sat with my hands idle on my knees and let the tide come up in me. It carried me so swiftly that, across the narrow space of deck between us, it must have swayed her, too, a little. I had no wish to disturb or distress her. If a little, a very little of it reached her, I was satisfied. If it drew her softly, but drew her, I wanted no more. Sometimes I could see that even the light pressure of my thoughts made her paler. One still evening, after a long talk, she whispered to me, "You must go and walk now, and—don't think about me." She had been held too long and too closely in my thoughts, and she begged me to release her for a little while. I went out into the bow and put her far away, at the skyline, with the faintest star, and thought of her gently across the water. When I went back to her, she was asleep.

But even in those first days I had my hours of misery. Why, for instance, should she have been born in Finmark, and why should Lars Ebbling have been her only door of escape? Why should she be silently taking leave of the world at the age when I was just beginning it, having had nothing, nothing of whatever is worth while?

She never talked about taking leave of things and yet I sometimes felt that she was counting the sunsets. One yellow afternoon, when we were gliding between the shores of Spain and Africa, she spoke of her illness for the first time. I had got some magnolias at Gibraltar, and she wore a bunch of them in her girdle and the rest lay on her lap. She held the cool leaves against her cheek and fingered the white petals. "I can never," she remarked, "get enough of the flowers of the South. They make me breathless, just as they did at first. Because of them I should like to live a long while—almost forever."

I leaned forward and looked at her. "We could live almost forever if we had enough courage. It's of our lives that we die. If we had the courage to change it all, to run away to some blue coast like that over there, we could live on and on, until we were tired."

She smiled tolerantly and looked southward through half-shut eyes. "I am afraid I should never have courage enough to go behind that mountain, at least. Look at it, it looks as if it hid horrible things."

A sea mist, blown in from the Atlantic, began to mask the impassive African coast, and above the fog, the gray mountain peak took on the angry red of the sunset. It burned sullen and threatening until the dark land drew the night about her and settled back into the sea. We watched it sink, while under us, slowly but ever increasing, we felt the throb of the Atlantic come and go, the thrill of the vast, untamed waters of that lugubrious and passionate sea. I drew Mrs. Ebbling's wraps about her and shut the magnolias under her cloak. When I left her, she slipped me one warm, white flower.

IV

*F*rom the Straits of Gibraltar we dropped into the abyss, and by morning we were rolling in the trough of a sea that drew us down and held us deep, shaking us gently back and forth until the timbers creaked, and then shooting us out on the crest of a swelling mountain. The water was bright and blue, but so cold that the breath of it penetrated one's bones, as if the chill of the deep underfathoms of the sea were being loosed upon us. There were not more than a dozen people upon the deck that morning, and Mrs. Ebbling was sheltered behind the stern, muffled in a sea jacket, with drops of moisture upon her long lashes and on her hair. When a shower of icy spray beat back over the deck rail, she took it gleefully.

"After all," she insisted, "this is my own kind of water; the kind I was born in. This is first cousin to the Pole waters, and the sea we have left is only a kind of fairy tale. It's like the burnt-out volcanoes; its day is over. This is the real sea now, where the doings of the world go on."

"It is not our reality, at any rate," I answered.

"Oh, yes, it is! These are the waters that carry men to their work, and they will carry you to yours."

I sat down and watched her hair grow more alive and iridescent in the moisture. "You are pleased to take an attitude," I complained.

"No, I don't love realities any more than another, but I admit them, all the same."

"And who are you and I to define the realities?"

"Our minds define them clearly enough, yours and mine, everybody's. Those are the lines we never cross, though we flee from the equator to the Pole. I have never really got out of Finmark, of course. I shall live and die in a fishing town on the Arctic Ocean, and the blue seas and the pink islands are as much a dream as they ever were. All the same, I shall continue to dream them."

The Gulf Stream gave us warm blue days again, but pale, like sad memories. The water had faded, and the thin, tepid sunshine made something tighten about one's heart. The stars watched us coldly, and seemed always to be asking me what I was going to do. The advancing line on the chart, which at first had been mere foolishness, began to mean something, and the wind from the west brought disturbing fears and forebodings. I slept lightly, and all day I was restless and uncertain except when I was with Mrs. Ebbling. She quieted me as she did little Carin, and soothed me without saying anything, as she had done that evening at Naples when we watched the sunset. It seemed to me that every day her eyes grew more tender and her lips more calm. A kind of fortitude seemed to be gathering about her mouth, and I dreaded it. Yet when, in an involuntary glance, I put to her the question that tortured me, her eyes always met mine steadily, deep and gentle and full of reassurance. That I had my word at last, happened almost by accident.

On the second night out from shore there was the concert for the Sailors' Orphanage, and Mrs. Ebbling dressed and went down to dinner for the first time, and sat on her husband's right. I was not the only one who was glad to see her. Even the women were pleased. She wore a pale green gown, and she came up out of it regally white and gold. I was so proud that I blushed when any one spoke of her. After dinner she was standing by her deck chair talking to her husband when people began to go below for the concert. She took up a long cloak and attempted to put it on. The wind blew the light thing about, and Ebbling chatted and smiled his public smile while she struggled with it. Suddenly his roving eye caught sight of the Chicago girl, who was having a similar difficulty with her draperies, and he pranced half the length of the deck to assist her. I had been watching from the rail, and when she was left alone I threw my cigar away and wrapped Mrs. Ebbling up roughly.

"Don't go down," I begged. "Stay up here. I want to talk to you."

She hesitated a moment and looked at me thoughtfully. Then, with a sigh, she sat down. Every one hurried down to the saloon, and we were absolutely alone at last, behind the shelter of the stern, with the thick darkness all about us and a warm east wind rushing over the sea. I was too sore and angry to think. I leaned toward her, holding the arm of her chair with both hands, and began anywhere.

"You remember those two blue coasts out of Gibraltar? It shall be either one you choose, if you will come with me. I have not much money, but we shall get on somehow. There has got to be an end of this. We are neither one of us cowards, and this is humiliating, intolerable."

She sat looking down at her hands, and I pulled her chair impatiently toward me.

"I felt," she said at last, "that you were going to say something like this. You are sorry for me, and I don't wish to be pitied. You think Ebbling neglects me, but you are mistaken. He has had his disappointments, too. He wants children and a gay, hospitable house, and he is tied to a sick woman who cannot get on with people. He has more to complain of than I have, and yet he bears with me. I am grateful to him, and there is no more to be said."

"Oh, isn't there?" I cried, "and I?"

She laid her hand entreatingly upon my arm. "Ah, you! you! Don't ask me to talk about that. *You——*" Her fingers slipped down my coat sleeve to my hand and pressed it. I caught her two hands and held them, telling her I would never let them go.

"And you meant to leave me day after tomorrow, to say good-bye to me as you will to the other people on this boat? You meant to cut me adrift like this, with my heart on fire and all my life unspent in me?"

She sighed despondently. "I am willing to suffer—whatever I must suffer—to have had you," she answered simply. "I was ill—and so lonely—and it came so quickly and quietly. Ah, don't begrudge it to me! Do not leave me in bitterness. If I have been wrong, forgive me." She bowed her head and pressed my fingers entreatingly. A warm tear splashed on my hand. It occurred to me that she bore my anger as she bore little Carin's importunities, as she bore Ebbling. What a circle of pettiness she had about her! I fell back in my chair and my hands dropped at my side. I felt like a creature with its back broken. I asked her what she wished me to do.

"Don't ask me," she whispered. "There is nothing that we can do. I thought you knew that. You forget that—that I am too ill to begin my life over. Even if there were nothing else in the way, that would be enough. And that is what has made it all possible, our loving each other, I mean. If I were well, we couldn't have had even this much. Don't reproach me. Hasn't it been at all pleasant to you to find me waiting for you every morning, to feel me thinking of you when you went to sleep? Every night I have watched the sea for you, as if it were mine and I had made it, and I have listened to the water rushing by you, full of sleep and youth and hope. And everything you had done or said during the day came back to me, and when I went to sleep it was only to feel you more. You see there was never any one else; I have never thought of any one in the dark but you." She spoke pleadingly, and her voice had sunk so low that I could scarcely hear her.

"And yet you will do nothing," I groaned. "You will dare nothing. You will give me nothing."

"Don't say that. When I leave you day after tomorrow, I shall have given you all my life. I can't tell you how, but it is true. There is something in each of us that does not belong to the family or to society, not even to ourselves. Sometimes it is given in marriage, and sometimes it is given in love, but oftener it is never given at all. We have nothing to do with giving or withholding it. It is a wild thing that sings in us once and flies away and never comes back, and mine has flown to you. When one loves like that, it is enough, somehow. The other things can go if they must. That is why I can live without you, and die without you."

I caught her hands and looked into her eyes that shone warm in the darkness. She shivered and whispered in a tone so different from any I ever heard from her before or afterward: "Do you grudge it to me? You are so young and strong, and you have everything before you. I shall have only a little while to want you in—and I could want you forever and not weary." I kissed her hair, her cheeks, her lips, until her head fell forward on my shoulder and she put my face away with her soft, trembling fingers. She took my hand and held it close to her, in both her own. We sat silent, and the moments came and went, bringing us closer and closer, and the wind and water rushed by us, obliterating our tomorrows and all our yesterdays.

The next day Mrs. Ebbling kept her cabin, and I sat stupidly by her chair until dark, with the rugged little girl to keep me company, and an occasional nod from the engineer.

I saw Mrs. Ebbling again only for a few moments, when we were coming into the New York harbor. She wore a street dress and a hat, and these alone would have made her seem far away from me. She was very pale and looked down when she spoke to me, as if she had been guilty of a wrong toward me. I have never been able to remember that interview without heartache and shame, but then I was too desperate to care about anything. I stood like a wooden post and let her approach me, let her speak to me, let her leave me. She came up to me as if it were a hard thing to do, and held out a little package, timidly, and her gloved hand shook as if she were afraid of me.

"I want to give you something," she said. "You will not want it now, so I shall ask you to keep it until you hear from me. You gave me your address a long time ago, when you were making that drawing. Some day I shall write to you and ask you to open this. You must not come to tell me goodbye this morning, but I shall be watching you when you go ashore. Please don't forget that."

I took the little box mechanically and thanked her. I think my eyes must have filled, for she uttered an exclamation of pity, touched my sleeve quickly, and left me. It was one of those strange, low, musical exclamations which meant everything and nothing, like the one that had thrilled me that night at Naples, and it was the last sound I ever heard from her lips.

An hour later I went on shore, one of those who crowded over the gangplank the moment it was lowered. But the next afternoon I wandered back to the docks and went on board the *Germania*. I asked for the engineer, and he came up in his shirt sleeves from the engine room. He was red and dishevelled, angry and voluble; his bright eye had a hard glint, and I did not once see his masterful smile. When he heard my inquiry he became profane. Mrs. Ebbling had sailed for Bremen on the *Hohenstauffen* that morning at eleven o'clock. She had decided to return by the northern route and pay a visit to her father in Finmark. She was in no condition to travel alone, he said. He evidently smarted under her extravagance. But who, he asked, with a blow of his fist on the rail, could stand between a woman and her whim? She had always been a wilful girl, and she had a doting father behind her. When she set her head with the wind, there was no holding her; she ought to have married the Arctic Ocean. I think Ebbling was still talking when I walked away.

I spent that winter in New York. My consular appointment hung fire (indeed, I did not pursue it with much enthusiasm), and I had a good many idle hours in which to think of Mrs. Ebbling. She had never mentioned the name of her father's village, and somehow I could never quite bring myself to go to the docks when Ebbling's boat was in and ask for news of her. More than once I made up my mind definitely to go to Finmark and take my chance at finding her; the shipping people would know where Ebbling came from. But I never went. I have often wondered why. When my resolve was made and my courage high, when I could almost feel myself approaching her, suddenly everything crumbled under me, and I fell back as I had done that night when I dropped her hands, after telling her, only a moment before, that I would never let them go.

In the twilight of a wet March day, when the gutters were running black outside and the Square was liquefying under crusts of dirty snow, the housekeeper brought me a damp letter which bore a blurred foreign postmark. It was from Niels Nannestad, who wrote that it was his sad duty to inform me that his daughter, Alexandra Ebbling, had died on the second day of February, in the twenty-sixth year of her age. Complying with her request, he inclosed a letter which she had written some days before her death.

I at last brought myself to break the seal of the second letter. It read thus:

My Friend:—You may open now the little package I gave you. May I ask you to keep it? I gave it to you because there is no one else who would care about it in just that way. Ever since I left you I have been thinking what it would be like to live a lifetime caring and being cared for like that. It was not the life I was meant to live, and yet, in a way, I have been living it ever since I first knew you.

Of course you understand now why I could not go with you. I would have spoiled your life for you. Besides that, I was ill—and I was too proud to give you the shadow of myself. I had much to give you, if you had come earlier. As it was, I was ashamed. Vanity sometimes saves us when nothing else will, and mine saved you. Thank you for everything. I hold this to my heart, where I once held your hand.

Alexandra

The dusk had thickened into night long before I got up from my chair and took the little box from its place in my desk drawer. I opened it and lifted out a thick coil, cut from where her hair grew thickest and brightest. It was tied firmly at one end, and when it fell over my arm it curled and clung about my sleeve like a living thing set free. How it gleamed, how it still gleams in the firelight! It was warm and softly scented under my lips, and stirred under my breath like seaweed in the tide. This, and a withered magnolia flower, and two pink sea shells; nothing more. And it was all twenty years ago!

Flavia and Her Artists

As the train neared Tarrytown, Imo-
gen Willard began to wonder why she had consented to be one of Flavia's
house party at all. She had not felt enthusiastic about it since leaving the city,
and was experiencing a prolonged ebb of purpose, a current of chilling
indecision, under which she vainly sought for the motive which had induced her to accept Flavia's invitation.

Perhaps it was a vague curiosity to see Flavia's husband, who had
been the magician of her childhood and the hero of innumerable Arabian
fairy tales. Perhaps it was a desire to see M. Roux, whom Flavia had
announced as the especial attraction of the occasion. Perhaps it was a wish
to study that remarkable woman in her own setting.

Imogen admitted a mild curiosity concerning Flavia. She was in
the habit of taking people rather seriously, but somehow found it impossible
to take Flavia so, because of the very vehemence and insistence with which
Flavia demanded it. Submerged in her studies, Imogen had, of late years,
seen very little of Flavia; but Flavia, in her hurried visits to New York,
between her excursions from studio to studio—her luncheons with this lady
who had to play at a matinée, and her dinners with that singer who had an
evening concert—had seen enough of her friend's handsome daughter to
conceive for her an inclination of such violence and assurance as only Flavia
could afford. The fact that Imogen had shown rather marked capacity in
certain esoteric lines of scholarship, and had decided to specialize in a
well-sounding branch of philology at the Ecole des Chartes, had fairly
placed her in that category of "interesting people" whom Flavia considered
her natural affinities, and lawful prey.

When Imogen stepped upon the station platform she was immediately appropriated by her hostess, whose commanding figure and assurance of attire she had recognized from a distance. She was hurried into a high tilbury and Flavia, taking the driver's cushion beside her, gathered up the reins with an experienced hand.

"My dear girl," she remarked, as she turned the horses up the street, "I was afraid the train might be late. M. Roux insisted upon coming up by boat and did not arrive until after seven."

"To think of M. Roux's being in this part of the world at all, and subject to the vicissitudes of river boats! Why in the world did he come over?" queried Imogen with lively interest. "He is the sort of man who must dissolve and become a shadow outside of Paris."

"Oh, we have a houseful of the most interesting people," said Flavia, professionally. "We have actually managed to get Ivan Schemetzkin. He was ill in California at the close of his concert tour, you know, and he is recuperating with us, after his wearing journey from the coast. Then there is Jules Martel, the painter; Signor Donati, the tenor; Professor Schotte, who has dug up Assyria, you know; Restzhoff, the Russian chemist; Alcée Buisson, the philologist; Frank Wellington, the novelist; and Will Maidenwood, the editor of *Woman*. Then there is my second cousin, Jemima Broadwood, who made such a hit in Pinero's comedy last winter, and Frau Lichtenfeld. *Have* you read her?"

Imogen confessed her utter ignorance of Frau Lichtenfeld, and Flavia went on.

"Well, she is a most remarkable person; one of those advanced German women, a militant iconoclast, and this drive will not be long enough to permit of my telling you her history. Such a story! Her novels were the talk of all Germany when I was there last, and several of them have been suppressed—an honour in Germany, I understand. 'At Whose Door' has been translated. I am so unfortunate as not to read German."

"I'm all excitement at the prospect of meeting Miss Broadwood," said Imogen. "I've seen her in nearly everything she does. Her stage personality is delightful. She always reminds me of a nice, clean, pink-and-white boy who has just had his cold bath, and come down all aglow for a run before breakfast."

"Yes, but isn't it unfortunate that she will limit herself to those minor comedy parts that are so little appreciated in this country? One ought to be satisfied with nothing less than the best, ought one?" The peculiar, breathy tone in which Flavia always uttered that word "best," the most worn in her vocabulary, always jarred on Imogen and always made her obdurate.

"I don't at all agree with you," she said reservedly. "I thought every one admitted that the most remarkable thing about Miss Broadwood is her admirable sense of fitness, which is rare enough in her profession."

Flavia could not endure being contradicted; she always seemed to regard it in the light of a defeat, and usually coloured unbecomingly. Now she changed the subject.

"Look, my dear," she cried, "there is Frau Lichtenfeld now, coming to meet us. Doesn't she look as if she had just escaped out of Walhalla? She is actually over six feet."

Imogen saw a woman of immense stature, in a very short skirt and a broad, flapping sun hat, striding down the hillside at a long, swinging gait. The refugee from Walhalla approached, panting. Her heavy, Teutonic features were scarlet from the rigour of her exercise, and her hair, under her flapping sun hat, was tightly befrizzled about her brow. She fixed her sharp little eyes upon Imogen and extended both her hands.

"So this is the little friend?" she cried, in a rolling baritone.

Imogen was quite as tall as her hostess; but everything, she reflected, is comparative. After the introduction Flavia apologized.

"I wish I could ask you to drive up with us, Frau Lichtenfeld."

"Ah, no!" cried the giantess, drooping her head in humorous caricature of a time-honoured pose of the heroines of sentimental romances. "It has never been my fate to be fitted into corners. I have never known the sweet privileges of the tiny."

Laughing, Flavia started the ponies, and the colossal woman, standing in the middle of the dusty road, took off her wide hat and waved them a farewell which, in scope of gesture, recalled the salute of a plumed cavalier.

When they arrived at the house, Imogen looked about her with keen curiosity, for this was veritably the work of Flavia's hands, the materialization of hopes long deferred. They passed directly into a large, square hall with a gallery on three sides, studio fashion. This opened at one end into a Dutch breakfast-room, beyond which was the large dining-room. At the other end of the hall was the music-room. There was a smoking-room, which one entered through the library behind the staircase. On the second floor there was the same general arrangement; a square hall, and, opening from it, the guest chambers, or, as Miss Broadwood termed them, the "cages."

When Imogen went to her room, the guests had begun to return from their various afternoon excursions. Boys were gliding through the halls with ice-water, covered trays, and flowers, colliding with maids and valets who carried shoes and other articles of wearing apparel. Yet, all this was done in response to inaudible bells, on felt soles, and in hushed voices, so that there was very little confusion about it.

Flavia had at last builded her house and hewn out her seven pillars; there could be no doubt, now, that the asylum for talent, the sanatorium of the arts, so long projected, was an accomplished fact. Her ambition had long ago outgrown the dimensions of her house on Prairie Avenue; besides, she had bitterly complained that in Chicago traditions were against her. Her project had been delayed by Arthur's doggedly standing out for the Michigan woods, but Flavia knew well enough that certain of the *aves rares*—"the best"—could not be lured so far away from the seaport, so she declared herself for the historic Hudson and knew no retreat. The establishing of a New York office had at length overthrown Arthur's last valid objection to quitting the lake country for three months of the year; and Arthur could be wearied into anything, as those who knew him knew.

Flavia's house was the mirror of her exultation; it was a temple to the gods of Victory, a sort of triumphal arch. In her earlier days she had swallowed experiences that would have unmanned one of less torrential enthusiasm or blind pertinacity. But, of late years, her determination had told; she saw less and less of those mysterious persons with mysterious obstacles in their path and mysterious grievances against the world, who had once frequented her house on Prairie Avenue. In the stead of this multitude of the unarrived, she had now the few, the select, "the best." Of all that band of indigent retainers who had once fed at her board like the suitors in the halls of Penelope, only Alcée Buisson still retained his right of entrée. He alone had remembered that ambition hath a knapsack at his back, wherein he puts alms to oblivion, and he alone had been considerate enough to do what Flavia had expected of him, and give his name a current value in the world. Then, as Miss Broadwood put it, "he was her first real one,"—and Flavia, like Mahomet, could remember her first believer.

The "House of Song," as Miss Broadwood had called it, was the outcome of Flavia's more exalted strategies. A woman who made less a point of sympathizing with their delicate organisms, might have sought to plunge these phosphorescent pieces into the tepid bath of domestic life; but Flavia's discernment was deeper. This must be a refuge where the shrinking soul, the sensitive brain, should be unconstrained; where the caprice of fancy should outweigh the civil code, if necessary. She considered that this much Arthur owed her; for she, in her turn, had made concessions. Flavia, had, indeed, quite an equipment of epigrams to the effect that our century creates the iron genii which evolve its fairy tales: but the fact that her husband's name was annually painted upon some ten thousand threshing machines, in reality contributed very little to her happiness.

Arthur Hamilton was born, and had spent his boyhood in the West Indies, and physically he had never lost the brand of the tropics. His father, after inventing the machine which bore his name, had returned to the States to patent and manufacture it. After leaving college, Arthur had spent five years ranching in the West and travelling abroad. Upon his father's death he had returned to Chicago and, to the astonishment of all his friends, had taken up the business,—without any demonstration of enthusiasm, but with quiet perseverance, marked ability, and amazing industry. Why or how a self-sufficient, rather ascetic man of thirty, indifferent in manner, wholly negative in all other personal relations, should have doggedly wooed and finally married Flavia Malcolm, was a problem that had vexed older heads than Imogen's.

While Imogen was dressing she heard a knock at her door, and a young woman entered whom she at once recognized as Jemima Broadwood—"Jimmy" Broadwood, she was called by people in her own profession. While there was something unmistakably professional in her frank *savoir-faire,* "Jimmy's" was one of those faces to which the rouge never seems to stick. Her eyes were keen and grey as a windy April sky, and so far from having been seared by calcium lights, you might have fancied they had never looked on anything less bucolic than growing fields and country fairs. She wore her thick, brown hair short and parted at the side; and, rather than hinting at freakishness, this seemed admirably in keeping with her fresh, boyish countenance. She extended to Imogen a large, well-shaped hand which it was a pleasure to clasp.

"Ah! you are Miss Willard, and I see I need not introduce myself. Flavia said you were kind enough to express a wish to meet me, and I preferred to meet you alone. Do you mind if I smoke?"

"Why, certainly not," said Imogen, somewhat disconcerted and looking hurriedly about for matches.

"There, be calm, I'm always prepared," said Miss Broadwood, checking Imogen's flurry with a soothing gesture, and producing an oddly-fashioned silver match-case from some mysterious recess in her dinner-gown. She sat down in a deep chair, crossed her patent-leather Oxfords, and lit her cigarette. "This match-box," she went on meditatively, "once belonged to a Prussian officer. He shot himself in his bath-tub, and I bought it at the sale of his effects."

Imogen had not yet found any suitable reply to make to this rather irrelevant confidence, when Miss Broadwood turned to her cordially: "I'm awfully glad you've come, Miss Willard, though I've not quite decided why you did it. I wanted very much to meet you. Flavia gave me your thesis to read."

"Why, how funny!" ejaculated Imogen.

"On the contrary," remarked Miss Broadwood. "I thought it decidedly lacked humour."

"I meant," stammered Imogen, beginning to feel very much like Alice in Wonderland, "I meant that I thought it rather strange Mrs. Hamilton should fancy you would be interested."

Miss Broadwood laughed heartily. "Now, don't let my rudeness frighten you. Really, I found it very interesting, and no end impressive. You see, most people in my profession are good for absolutely nothing else, and, therefore, they have a deep and abiding conviction that in some other line they might have shone. Strange to say, scholarship is the object of our envious and particular admiration. Anything in type impresses us greatly; that's why so many of us marry authors or newspaper men and lead miserable lives." Miss Broadwood saw that she had rather disconcerted Imogen, and blithely tacked in another direction. "You see," she went on, tossing aside her half-consumed cigarette, "some years ago Flavia would not have deemed me worthy to open the pages of your thesis—nor to be one of her house party of the chosen, for that matter. I've Pinero to thank for both pleasures. It all depends on the class of business I'm playing whether I'm in favour or not. Flavia is my second cousin, you know, so I can say whatever disagreeable things I choose with perfect good grace. I'm quite desperate for some one to laugh with, so I'm going to fasten myself upon you—for, of course, one can't expect any of these gypsy-dago people to see anything funny. I don't intend you shall lose the humour of the situation. What do you think of Flavia's infirmary for the arts, anyway?"

"Well, it's rather too soon for me to have any opinion at all," said Imogen, as she again turned to her dressing. "So far, you are the only one of the artists I've met."

"One of them?" echoed Miss Broadwood. "One of the *artists?* My offence may be rank, my dear, but I really don't deserve that. Come, now, whatever badges of my tribe I may bear upon me, just let me divest you of any notion that I take myself seriously."

Imogen turned from the mirror in blank astonishment, and sat down on the arm of a chair, facing her visitor. "I can't fathom you at all, Miss Broadwood," she said frankly. "Why shouldn't you take yourself seriously? What's the use of beating about the bush? Surely you know that you are one of the few players on this side of the water who have at all the spirit of natural or ingenuous comedy?"

"Thank you, my dear. Now we are quite even about the thesis, aren't we? Oh! did you mean it? Well, you *are* a clever girl. But you see it doesn't do to permit oneself to look at it in that light. If we do, we always go to pieces, and waste our substance a-starring as the unhappy daughter of the Capulets. But there, I hear Flavia coming to take you down; and just remember I'm not one of them; the artists, I mean."

Flavia conducted Imogen and Miss Broadwood downstairs. As they reached the lower hall they heard voices from the music-room, and dim figures were lurking in the shadows under the gallery, but their hostess led straight to the smoking-room. The June evening was chilly, and a fire had been lighted in the fireplace. Through the deepening dusk the firelight flickered upon the pipes and curious weapons on the wall, and threw an orange glow over the Turkish hangings. One side of the smoking-room was entirely of glass, separating it from the conservatory, which was flooded with white light from the electric bulbs. There was about the darkened room some suggestion of certain chambers in the Arabian Nights, opening on a court of palms. Perhaps it was partially this memory-evoking suggestion that caused Imogen to start so violently when she saw dimly, in a blur of shadow, the figure of a man, who sat smoking in a low, deep chair before the fire. He was long, and thin, and brown. His long, nerveless hands drooped from the arms of his chair. A brown moustache shaded his mouth, and his eyes were sleepy and apathetic. When Imogen entered, he rose indolently and gave her his hand, his manner barely courteous.

"I am glad you arrived promptly, Miss Willard," he said with an indifferent drawl. "Flavia was afraid you might be late. You had a pleasant ride up, I hope?"

"O, very, thank you, Mr. Hamilton," she replied, feeling that he did not particularly care whether she replied at all.

Flavia explained that she had not yet had time to dress for dinner, as she had been attending to Mr. Will Maidenwood, who had become faint after hurting his finger in an obdurate window, and immediately excused herself. As she left, Hamilton turned to Miss Broadwood with a rather spiritless smile.

"Well, Jimmy," he remarked, "I brought up a piano box full of fireworks for the boys. How do you suppose we'll manage to keep them until the Fourth?"

"We can't, unless we steel ourselves to deny there are any on the premises," said Miss Broadwood, seating herself on a low stool by Hamilton's chair, and leaning back against the mantel. "Have you seen Helen, and has she told you the tragedy of the tooth?"

"She met me at the station, with her tooth wrapped up in tissue paper. I had tea with her an hour ago. Better sit down, Miss Willard;" he rose and pushed a chair toward Imogen, who was standing peering into the conservatory. "We are scheduled to dine at seven, but they seldom get around before eight."

By this time Imogen had made out that here the plural pronoun, third person, always referred to the artists. As Hamilton's manner did not spur one to cordial intercourse, and as his attention seemed directed to Miss Broadwood, in so far as it could be said to be directed to any one, she sat down facing the conservatory and watched him, unable to decide in how far he was identical with the man who had first met Flavia Malcolm in her mother's house, twelve years ago. Did he at all remember having known her as a little girl, and why did his indifference hurt her so, after all these years? Had some remnant of her childish affection for him gone on living, somewhere down in the sealed caves of her consciousness, and had she really expected to find it possible to be fond of him again? Suddenly she saw a light in the man's sleepy eyes, an unmistakable expression of interest and pleasure that fairly startled her. She turned quickly in the direction of his glance, and saw Flavia, just entering, dressed for dinner and lit by the effulgence of her most radiant manner. Most people considered Flavia handsome, and there was no gainsaying that she carried her five-and-thirty years splendidly. Her figure had never grown matronly, and her face was of the sort that does not show wear. Its blond tints were as fresh and enduring as enamel,—and quite as hard. Its usual expression was one of tense, often strained, animation, which compressed her lips nervously. A perfect scream of animation, Miss Broadwood had called it—created and maintained by sheer, indomitable force of will. Flavia's appearance on any scene whatever made a ripple, caused a certain agitation and recognition, and, among impressionable people, a certain uneasiness. For all her sparkling assurance of manner, Flavia was certainly always ill at ease, and even more certainly anxious. She seemed not convinced of the established order of material things, seemed always trying to conceal her feeling that walls might crumble, chasms open, or the fabric of her life fly to the winds in irretrievable entanglement. At least this was the impression Imogen got from that note in Flavia which was so manifestly false.

Hamilton's keen, quick, satisfied glance at his wife had recalled to Imogen all her inventory of speculations about them. She looked at him with compassionate surprise. As a child she had never permitted herself to believe that Hamilton cared at all for the woman who had taken him away from her; and since she had begun to think about them again, it had never occurred to her that any one could become attached to Flavia in that deeply personal and exclusive sense. It seemed quite as irrational as trying to possess oneself of Broadway at noon.

When they went out to dinner, Imogen realized the completeness of Flavia's triumph. They were people of one name, mostly, like kings; people whose names stirred the imagination like a romance or a melody. With the notable exception of M. Roux, Imogen had seen most of them before, either in concert halls or lecture rooms; but they looked noticeably older and dimmer than she remembered them.

Opposite her sat Schemetzkin, the Russian pianist, a short, corpulent man, with an apoplectic face and purpleish skin, his thick, iron-grey hair tossed back from his forehead. Next the German giantess sat the Italian tenor—the tiniest of men—pale, with soft, light hair, much in disorder, very red lips and fingers yellowed by cigarettes. Frau Lichtenfeld shone in a gown of emerald green, fitting so closely as to enhance her natural floridness. However, to do the good lady justice, let her attire be never so modest, it gave an effect of barbaric splendour. At her left sat Herr Schotte, the Assyriologist, whose features were effectually concealed by the convergence of his hair and beard, and whose glasses were continually falling into his plate. This gentleman had removed more tons of earth in the course of his explorations than had any of his confrères, and his vigorous attack upon his food seemed to suggest the strenuous nature of his accustomed toil. His eyes were small and deeply set, and his forehead bulged fiercely above his eyes in a bony ridge. His heavy brows completed the leonine suggestion of his face. Even to Imogen, who knew something of his work and greatly respected it, he was entirely too reminiscent of the stone age to be altogether an agreeable dinner companion. He seemed, indeed, to have absorbed something of the savagery of those early types of life which he continually studied.

Frank Wellington, the young Kansas man who had been two years out of Harvard and had published three historical novels, sat next Mr. Will Maidenwood, who was still pale from his recent sufferings, and carried his hand bandaged. They took little part in the general conversation, but, like the lion and the unicorn, were always at it; discussing, every time they met, whether there were or were not passages in Mr. Wellington's works which should be eliminated, out of consideration for the Young Person. Wellington had fallen into the hands of a great American syndicate which most effectually befriended struggling authors whose struggles were in the right direction, and which had guaranteed to make him famous before he was thirty. Feeling the security of his position, he stoutly defended those passages which jarred upon the sensitive nerves of the young editor of *Woman*. Maidenwood, in the smoothest of voices, urged the necessity of the author's recognizing certain restrictions at the outset, and Miss Broadwood, who joined the argument quite without invitation or encouragement, seconded him with pointed and malicious remarks which caused the young editor manifest discomfort. Restzhoff, the chemist, demanded the attention of the entire company for his exposition of his devices for manufacturing ice-cream from vegetable oils, and for administering drugs in bonbons.

Flavia, always noticeably restless at dinner, was somewhat apathetic toward the advocate of peptonized chocolate, and was plainly concerned about the sudden departure of M. Roux, who had announced that it would be necessary for him to leave to-morrow. M. Emile Roux, who sat at Flavia's right, was a man in middle life and quite bald, clearly without personal vanity, though his publishers preferred to circulate only those of his portraits taken in his ambrosial youth. Imogen was considerably shocked at his unlikeness to the slender, black-stocked Rolla he had looked at twenty. He had declined into the florid, settled heaviness of indifference and approaching age. There was, however, a certain look of durability and solidity about him; the look of a man who has earned the right to be fat and bald, and even silent at dinner if he chooses.

Throughout the discussion between Wellington and Will Maidenwood, though they invited his participation, he remained silent, betraying no sign either of interest or contempt. Since his arrival he had directed most of his conversation to Hamilton, who had never read one of his twelve great novels. This perplexed and troubled Flavia. On the night of his arrival, Jules Martel had enthusiastically declared, "There are schools and schools, manners and manners; but Roux is Roux, and Paris sets its watches by his clock." Flavia had already repeated this remark to Imogen.

It haunted her, and each time she quoted it she was impressed anew.

Flavia shifted the conversation uneasily, evidently exasperated and excited by her repeated failures to draw the novelist out. "Monsieur Roux," she began abruptly, with her most animated smile, "I remember so well a statement I read some years ago in your 'Mes Etudes des Femmes,' to the effect that you had never met a really intellectual woman. May I ask, without being impertinent, whether that assertion still represents your experience?"

"I meant, madam," said the novelist conservatively, "intellectual in a sense very special, as we say of men in whom the purely intellectual functions seem almost independent."

"And you still think a woman so constituted a mythical personage?" persisted Flavia, nodding her head encouragingly.

"*Une Méduse,* madam, who, if she were discovered, would transmute us all into stone," said the novelist, bowing gravely. "If she existed at all," he added deliberately, "it was my business to find her, and she has cost me many a vain pilgrimage. Like Rudel of Tripoli, I have crossed seas and penetrated deserts to seek her out. I have, indeed, encountered women of learning whose industry I have been compelled to respect; many who have possessed beauty and charm and perplexing cleverness; a few with remarkable information, and a sort of fatal facility."

"And Mrs. Browning, George Eliot, and your own Mme. Dudevant?" queried Flavia with that fervid enthusiasm with which she could, on occasion, utter things simply incomprehensible for their banality—at her feats of this sort Miss Broadwood was wont to sit breathless with admiration.

"Madam, while the intellect was undeniably present in the performances of those women, it was only the stick of the rocket. Although this woman has eluded me, I have studied her conditions and perturbations as astronomers conjecture the orbits of planets they have never seen. If she exists, she is probably neither an artist nor a woman with a mission, but an obscure personage, with imperative intellectual needs, who absorbs rather than produces."

Flavia, still nodding nervously, fixed a strained glance of interrogation upon M. Roux. "Then you think she would be a woman whose first necessity would be to know, whose instincts would be satisfied only with the best, who could draw from others; appreciative, merely?"

The novelist lifted his dull eyes to his interlocutress with an untranslatable smile, and a slight inclination of his shoulders. "Exactly so;

you are really remarkable, madame," he added, in a tone of cold astonishment.

After dinner the guests took their coffee in the music-room, where Schemetzkin sat down at the piano to drum rag-time, and give his celebrated imitatic 1 of the boarding-school girl's execution of Chopin. He flatly refused to play anything more serious, and would practise only in the morning, when he had the music-room to himself. Hamilton and M. Roux repaired to the smoking-room to discuss the necessity of extending the tax on manufactured articles in France,—one of those conversations which particularly exasperated Flavia.

After Schemetzkin had grimaced and tortured the keyboard with malicious vulgarities for half an hour, Signor Donati, to put an end to his torture, consented to sing, and Flavia and Imogen went to fetch Arthur to play his accompaniments. Hamilton rose with an annoyed look, and placed his cigarette on the mantel. "Why yes, Flavia, I'll accompany him, provided he sings something with a melody, Italian arias or ballads, and provided the recital is not interminable."

"You will join us, M. Roux?"

"Thank you, but I have some letters to write," replied the novelist bowing.

As Flavia had remarked to Imogen, "Arthur really played accompaniments remarkably well." To hear him recalled vividly the days of her childhood, when he always used to spend his business vacations at her mother's home in Maine. He had possessed for her that almost hypnotic influence which young men sometimes exert upon little girls. It was a sort of phantom love affair, subjective and fanciful, a precocity of instinct, like that tender and maternal concern which some little girls feel for their dolls. Yet this childish infatuation is capable of all the depressions and exaltations of love itself; it has its bitter jealousies, cruel disappointments, its exacting caprices.

Summer after summer she had awaited his coming and wept at his departure, indifferent to the gayer young men who had called her their sweetheart, and laughed at everything she said. Although Hamilton never said so, she had been always quite sure that he was fond of her. When he pulled her up the river to hunt for fairy knolls shut about by low, hanging willows, he was often silent for an hour at a time, yet she never felt that he was bored or was neglecting her. He would lie in the sand smoking, his eyes half closed, watching her play and she was always conscious that she was entertaining him. Sometimes he would take a copy of "Alice in Wonderland" in his pocket, and no one could read it as he could, laughing at her with his dark eyes, when anything amused him. No one else could laugh so, with just their eyes, and without moving a muscle of their face. Though he usually smiled at passages that seemed not at all funny to the child, she always laughed gleefully, because he was so seldom moved to mirth that any such demonstration delighted her and she took the credit of it entirely to herself. Her own inclination had been for serious stories, with sad endings, like the Little Mermaid, which he had once told her in an unguarded moment when she had a cold, and was put to bed early on her birthday night and cried because she could not have her party. But he highly disapproved of this preference, and had called it a morbid taste, and always shook his finger at her when she asked for the story. When she had been particularly good, or particularly neglected by other people, then he would sometimes melt and tell her the story, and never laugh at her if she enjoyed the "sad ending" even to tears. When Flavia had taken him away and he came no more, she wept inconsolably for the space of two weeks, and refused to learn her lessons. Then she found the story of the Little Mermaid herself, and forgot him.

Imogen had discovered at dinner that he could still smile at one secretly, out of his eyes, and that he had the old manner of outwardly seeming bored, but letting you know that he was not. She was intensely curious about his exact state of feeling toward his wife, and more curious still to catch a sense of his final adjustment to the conditions of life in general. This, she could not help feeling, she might get again—if she could have him alone for an hour, in some place where there was a little river and a sandy cove bordered by drooping willows, and a blue sky seen through white sycamore boughs.

That evening, before retiring, Flavia entered her husband's room, where he sat in his smoking-jacket, in one of his favourite low chairs.

"I suppose it's a grave responsibility to bring an ardent, serious young thing like Imogen here among all these fascinating personages," she remarked reflectively. "But, after all, one can never tell. These grave, silent girls have their own charm, even for facile people."

"O, so that is your plan?" queried her husband dryly. "I was wondering why you got her up here. She doesn't seem to mix well with the faciles. At least, so it struck me."

Flavia paid no heed to this jeering remark, but repeated, "No, after all, it may not be a bad thing."

"Then do consign her to that shaken reed, the tenor," said her husband yawning. "I remember she used to have a taste for the pathetic."

"And then," remarked Flavia coquettishly, "after all, I owe her mother a return in kind. She was not afraid to trifle with destiny."

But Hamilton was asleep in his chair.

Next morning Imogen found only Miss Broadwood in the breakfast-room.

"Good-morning, my dear girl, whatever are you doing up so early? They never breakfast before eleven. Most of them take their coffee in their room. Take this place by me."

Miss Broadwood looked particularly fresh and encouraging in her blue serge walking-skirt, her open jacket displaying an expanse of stiff, white, shirt bosom, dotted with some almost imperceptible figure, and a dark blue-and-white necktie, neatly knotted under her wide, rolling collar. She wore a white rosebud in the lapel of her coat, and decidedly she seemed more than ever like a nice, clean boy on his holiday. Imogen was just hoping that they would breakfast alone when Miss Broadwood exclaimed, "Ah, there comes Arthur with the children. That's the reward of early rising in this house; you never get to see the youngsters at any other time."

Hamilton entered, followed by two dark, handsome little boys. The girl, who was very tiny, blonde like her mother, and exceedingly frail, he carried in his arms. The boys came up and said good-morning with an ease and cheerfulness uncommon, even in well-bred children, but the little girl hid her face on her father's shoulder.

"She's a shy little lady," he explained, as he put her gently down in her chair. "I'm afraid she's like her father; she can't seem to get used to meeting people. And you, Miss Willard, did you dream of the white rabbit or the little mermaid?"

"O, I dreamed of them all! All the personages of that buried civilization," cried Imogen, delighted that his estranged manner of the night before had entirely vanished, and feeling that, somehow, the old confidential relations had been restored during the night.

"Come, William," said Miss Broadwood, turning to the younger of the two boys, "and what did you dream about?"

"We dreamed," said William gravely—he was the more assertive of the two and always spoke for both—"we dreamed that there were fireworks hidden in the basement of the carriage-house; lots and lots of fireworks."

His elder brother looked up at him with apprehensive astonishment, while Miss Broadwood hastily put her napkin to her lips, and Hamilton dropped his eyes. "If little boys dream things, they are so apt not to come true," he reflected sadly. This shook even the redoubtable William, and he glanced nervously at his brother. "But do things vanish just because they have been dreamed?" he objected.

"Generally that is the very best reason for their vanishing," said Arthur gravely.

"But, father, people can't help what they dream," remonstrated Edward gently.

"Oh, come! You're making these children talk like a Maeterlinck dialogue," laughed Miss Broadwood.

Flavia presently entered, a book in her hand, and bade them all good-morning. "Come, little people, which story shall it be this morning?" she asked winningly. Greatly excited, the children followed her into the garden. "She does then, sometimes," murmured Imogen as they left the breakfast-room.

"Oh, yes, to be sure," said Miss Broadwood cheerfully. "She reads a story to them every morning in the most picturesque part of the garden. The mother of the Gracchi, you know. She does so long, she says, for the time when they will be intellectual companions for her. What do you say to a walk over the hills?"

As they left the house they met Frau Lichtenfeld and the bushy Herr Schotte—the professor cut an astonishing figure in golf stockings—returning from a walk and engaged in an animated conversation on the tendencies of German fiction.

"Aren't they the most attractive little children," exclaimed Imogen as they wound down the road toward the river.

"Yes, and you must not fail to tell Flavia that you think so. She will look at you in a sort of startled way and say, 'Yes, aren't they?' and maybe she will go off and hunt them up and have tea with them, to fully appreciate them. She is awfully afraid of missing anything good, is Flavia. The way those youngsters manage to conceal their guilty presence in the House of Song is a wonder."

"But don't any of the artist-folk fancy children?" asked Imogen.

"Yes, they just fancy them and no more. The chemist remarked the other day that children are like certain salts which need not be actualized because the formulæ are quite sufficient for practical purposes. I don't see how even Flavia can endure to have that man about."

"I have always been rather curious to know what Arthur thinks of it all," remarked Imogen cautiously.

"Thinks of it!" ejaculated Miss Broadwood. "Why, my dear,

what would any man think of having his house turned into an hotel, habited by freaks who discharge his servants, borrow his money, and insult his neighbours? This place is shunned like a lazaretto!"

"Well, then, why does he—why does he—" persisted Imogen.

"Bah!" interrupted Miss Broadwood impatiently, "why did he in the first place? That's the question."

"Marry her, you mean?" said Imogen colouring.

"Exactly so," said Miss Broadwood sharply, as she snapped the lid of her match-box.

"I suppose that is a question rather beyond us, and certainly one which we cannot discuss," said Imogen. "But his toleration on this one point puzzles me, quite apart from other complications."

"Toleration? Why this point, as you call it, simply *is* Flavia. Who could conceive of her without it? I don't know where it's all going to end, I'm sure, and I'm equally sure that, if it were not for Arthur, I shouldn't care," declared Miss Broadwood, drawing her shoulders together.

"But will it end at all, now?"

"Such an absurd state of things can't go on indefinitely. A man isn't going to see his wife make a guy of herself forever, is he? Chaos has already begun in the servants' quarters. There are six different languages spoken there now. You see, it's all on an entirely false basis. Flavia hasn't the slightest notion of what these people are really like, their good and their bad alike escape her. They, on the other hand, can't imagine what she is driving at. Now, Arthur is worse off than either faction; he is not in the fairy story in that he sees these people exactly as they are, *but* he is utterly unable to see Flavia as they see her. There you have the situation. Why can't he see her as we do? My dear, that has kept me awake o' nights. This man who has thought so much and lived so much, who is naturally a critic, really takes Flavia at very nearly her own estimate. But now I am entering upon a wilderness. From a brief acquaintance with her, you can know nothing of the icy fastnesses of Flavia's self-esteem. It's like St. Peter's; you can't realize its magnitude at once. You have to grow into a sense of it by living under its shadow. It has perplexed even Emile Roux, that merciless dissector of egoism. She has puzzled him the more because he saw at a glance what some of them do not perceive at once, and what will be mercifully concealed from Arthur until the trump sounds; namely, that all Flavia's artists have done or ever will do means exactly as much to her as a symphony means to an oyster; that there is no bridge by which the significance of any work of art could be conveyed to her."

"Then, in the name of goodness, why does she bother?" gasped

Imogen. "She is pretty, wealthy, well-established; why should she bother?"

"That's what M. Roux has kept asking himself. I can't pretend to analyse it. She reads papers on the Literary Landmarks of Paris, and the Loves of the Poets, and that sort of thing, to clubs out in Chicago. To Flavia it is more necessary to be called clever than to breathe. I would give a good deal to know that glum Frenchman's diagnosis. He has been watching her out of those fishy eyes of his as a biologist watches a hemisphereless frog."

For several days after M. Roux's departure, Flavia gave an embarrassing share of her attention to Imogen. Embarrassing, because Imogen had the feeling of being energetically and futilely explored, she knew not for what. She felt herself under the globe of an air pump, expected to yield up something. When she confined the conversation to matters of general interest, Flavia conveyed to her with some pique that her one endeavour in life had been to fit herself to converse with her friends upon those things which vitally interested them. "One has no right to accept their best from people unless one gives, isn't it so? I want to be able to give—!" she declared vaguely. Yet whenever Imogen strove to pay her tithes and plunged bravely into her plans for study next winter, Flavia grew absent-minded and interrupted her by amazing generalizations or by such embarrassing questions as, "And these grim studies really have charm for you; you are quite buried in them; they make other things seem light and ephemeral?"

"I rather feel as though I had got in here under false pretences," Imogen confided to Miss Broadwood, "I'm sure I don't know what it is that she wants of me."

"Ah," chuckled Jemima, "you are not equal to these heart to heart talks with Flavia. You utterly fail to communicate to her the atmosphere of that untroubled joy in which you dwell. You must remember that she gets no feeling out of things herself, and she demands that you impart yours to her by some process of psychic transmission. I once met a blind girl, blind from birth, who could discuss the peculiarities of the Barbizon school with just Flavia's glibness and enthusiasm. Ordinarily Flavia knows how to get what she wants from people, and her memory is wonderful. One evening I heard her giving Frau Lichtenfeld some random impressions about Hedda Gabler which she extracted from me five years ago; giving them with an impassioned conviction of which I was never guilty. But I have known other people who could appropriate your stories and opinions; Flavia is infinitely more subtle than that; she can soak up the very thrash and drift of your day dreams, and take the very thrills off your back, as it were."

After some days of unsuccessful effort, Flavia withdrew herself, and Imogen found Hamilton ready to catch her when she was tossed a-field. He seemed only to have been awaiting this crisis, and at once their old intimacy re-established itself as a thing inevitable and beautifully prepared for. She convinced herself that she had not been mistaken in him, despite all the doubts that had come up in later years, and this renewal of faith set more than one question thumping in her brain. "How did he, how can he?" she kept repeating with a tinge of her childish resentment, "what right had he to waste anything so fine?"

When Imogen and Arthur were returning from a walk before luncheon one morning about a week after M. Roux's departure, they noticed an absorbed group before one of the hall windows. Herr Schotte and Restzhoff sat on the window seat with a newspaper between them, while Wellington, Schemetzkin and Will Maidenwood looked over their shoulders. They seemed intensely interested, Herr Schotte occasionally pounding his knees with his fists in ebullitions of barbaric glee. When Imogen entered the hall, however, the men were all sauntering toward the breakfast-room and the paper was lying innocently on the divan. During luncheon the personnel of that window group were unwontedly animated and agreeable,—all save Schemetzkin, whose stare was blanker than ever, as though Roux's mantle of insulting indifference had fallen upon him, in addition to his own oblivious self absorption. Will Maidenwood seemed embarrassed and annoyed; the chemist employed himself with making polite speeches to Hamilton—Flavia did not come down to lunch—and there was a malicious gleam under Herr Schotte's eyebrows. Frank Wellington announced nervously that an imperative letter from his protecting syndicate summoned him to the city.

After luncheon the men went to the golf links, and Imogen, at the first opportunity, possessed herself of the newspaper which had been left on the divan. One of the first things that caught her eye was an article headed "Roux on Tuft Hunters; The Advanced American Woman As He Sees Her; Aggressive, Superficial and Insincere." The entire interview was nothing more nor less than a satiric characterization of Flavia, a-quiver with irritation and vitriolic malice. No one could mistake it; it was done with all his deftness of portraiture. Imogen had not finished the article when she heard a footstep, and clutching the paper she started precipitately toward the stairway as Arthur entered. He put out his hand, looking critically at her distressed face.

"Wait a moment, Miss Willard," he said preemptorily, "I want to see whether we can find what it was that so interested our friends this morning. Give me the paper, please."

Imogen grew quite white as he opened the journal. She reached forward and crumpled it with her hands. "Please don't, please don't," she pleaded, "it's something I don't want you to see. Oh! why will you? It's just something low and despicable that you can't notice."

Arthur had gently loosed her hands and he pointed her to a chair. He lit a cigar and read the article through without comment. When he had finished it, he walked to the fireplace, struck a match, and tossed the flaming journal between the brass andirons.

"You are right," he remarked as he came back, dusting his hands with his handkerchief. "It's quite impossible to comment. There are extremes of blackguardism for which we have no name. The only thing necessary is to see that Flavia gets no wind of this. This seems to be my cue to act; poor girl."

Imogen looked at him tearfully; she could only murmur, "Oh, why did you read it!"

Hamilton laughed spiritlessly. "Come, don't you worry about it. You always took other people's troubles too seriously. When you were little and all the world was gay and everybody happy, you must needs get the Little Mermaid's troubles to grieve over. Come with me into the music-room. You remember the musical setting I once made you for the Lay of the Jabberwock? I was trying it over the other night, long after you were in bed, and I decided it was quite as fine as the Erl-King music. How I wish I could give you some of the cake that Alice ate and make you a little girl again. Then, when you had got through the glass door into the little garden, you could call to me, perhaps, and tell me all the fine things that were going on there. What a pity it is that you ever grew up!" he added, laughing, and Imogen, too, was thinking just that.

At dinner that evening, Flavia, with fatal persistence, insisted upon turning the conversation to M. Roux. She had been reading one of his novels and had remembered anew that Paris set its watches by his clock. Imogen surmised that she was tortured by a feeling that she had not sufficiently appreciated him while she had had him. When she first mentioned his name, she was answered only by the pall of silence that fell over the company. Then every one began to talk at once, as though to correct a false position. They spoke of him with a fervid, defiant admiration, with the sort of hot praise that covers a double purpose. Imogen fancied she could see that they felt a kind of relief at what the man had done, even those who despised him for doing it; that they felt a spiteful heat against Flavia, as though she had tricked them, and a certain contempt for themselves that they had been beguiled. She was reminded of the fury of the crowd in the fairy tale, when once the child had called out that the king was in his night-clothes. Surely these people knew no more about Flavia than they had known before, but the mere fact that the thing had been said, altered the situation. Flavia, meanwhile, sat chattering amiably, pathetically unconscious of her nakedness.

Hamilton lounged, fingering the stem of his wine glass, gazing down the table at one face after another and studying the various degrees of self-consciousness they exhibited. Imogen's eyes followed his, fearfully. When a lull came in the spasmodic flow of conversation, Arthur, leaning back in his chair, remarked deliberately, "As for M. Roux, his very profession places him in that class of men whom society has never been able to accept unconditionally because it has never been able to assume that they have any ordered notion of taste. He and his ilk remain, with the mountebanks and snake charmers, people indispensable to our civilization, but wholly unreclaimed by it; people whom we receive, but whose invitations we do not accept."

Fortunately for Flavia, this mine was not exploded until just before the coffee was brought. Her laughter was pitiful to hear; it echoed through the silent room as in a vault, while she made some tremulously light remark about her husband's drollery, grim as a jest from the dying. No one responded and she sat nodding her head like a mechanical toy and smiling her white, set smile through her teeth, until Alcée Buisson and Frau Lichtenfeld came to her support.

After dinner the guests retired immediately to their rooms, and Imogen went upstairs on tiptoe, feeling the echo of breakage and the dust of crumbling in the air. She wondered whether Flavia's habitual note of uneasiness were not, in a manner, prophetic, and a sort of unconscious premonition, after all. She sat down to write a letter, but she found herself so nervous, her head so hot and her hands so cold, that she soon abandoned the effort. Just as she was about to seek Miss Broadwood, Flavia entered and embraced her hysterically.

"My dearest girl," she began, "was there ever such an unfortunate and incomprehensible speech made before? Of course it is scarcely necessary to explain to you poor Arthur's lack of tact, and that he meant nothing. But they! Can they be expected to understand? He will feel wretchedly about it when he realizes what he has done, but in the mean-time? And M. Roux, of all men! When we were so fortunate as to get him, and he made himself so unreservedly agreeable, and I fancied that, in his way, Arthur quite admired him. My dear, you have no idea what that speech has done. Schemetzkin and Herr Schotte have already sent me word that they must leave us to-morrow. Such a thing from a host!" Flavia paused, choked by tears of vexation and despair.

Imogen was thoroughly disconcerted; this was the first time she had ever seen Flavia betray any personal emotion which was indubitably genuine. She replied with what consolation she could. "Need they take it personally at all? It was a mere observation upon a class of people—"

"Which he knows nothing whatever about, and with whom he has no sympathy," interrupted Flavia. "Ah, my dear, you could not be *expected* to understand. You can't realize, knowing Arthur as you do, his entire lack of any æsthetic sense whatever. He is absolutely *nil,* stone deaf and stark blind, on that side. He doesn't mean to be brutal, it is just the brutality of utter ignorance. They always feel it—they are so sensitive to unsympathetic influences, you know; they know it the moment they come into the house. I have spent my life apologizing for him and struggling to conceal it; but in spite of me, he wounds them; his very attitude, even in silence, offends them. Heavens! do I not know, is it not perpetually and forever wounding me? But there has never been anything so dreadful as this, never! If I could conceive of any possible motive, even!"

"But, surely, Mrs. Hamilton, it was, after all, a mere expression of opinion, such as we are any of us likely to venture upon any subject whatever. It was neither more personal nor more extravagant than many of M. Roux's remarks."

"But, Imogen, certainly M. Roux has the right. It is a part of his art, and that is altogether another matter. Oh, this is not the only instance!" continued Flavia passionately, "I've always had that narrow, bigoted preju-dice to contend with. It has always held me back. But this—!"

"I think you mistake his attitude," replied Imogen, feeling a flush that made her ears tingle, "that is, I fancy he is more appreciative than he seems. A man can't be very demonstrative about those things—not if he is a real man. I should not think you would care much about saving the feelings of people who are too narrow to admit of any other point of view than their own." She stopped, finding herself in the impossible position of attempting to explain Hamilton to his wife; a task which, if once begun, would necessitate an entire course of enlightenment which she doubted

Flavia's ability to receive, and which she could offer only with very poor grace.

"That's just where it stings most," here Flavia began pacing the floor, "it is just because they have all shown such tolerance, and have treated Arthur with such unfailing consideration, that I can find no reasonable pretext for his rancour. How can he fail to see the value of such friendships on the children's account, if for nothing else! What an advantage for them to grow up among such associations! Even though he cares nothing about these things himself he might realize that. Is there nothing I could say by way of explanation? To them, I mean? If some one were to explain to them how unfortunately limited he is in these things—"

"I'm afraid I cannot advise you," said Imogen decidedly, "but that, at least, seems to me impossible."

Flavia took her hand and glanced at her affectionately, nodding nervously. "Of course, dear girl, I can't ask you to be quite frank with me. Poor child, you are trembling and your hands are icy. Poor Arthur! But you must not judge him by this altogether; think how much he misses in life. What a cruel shock you've had. I'll send you some sherry. Goodnight, my dear."

When Flavia shut the door, Imogen burst into a fit of nervous weeping.

Next morning she awoke after a troubled and restless night. At eight o'clock Miss Broadwood entered in a red and white striped bath-robe.

"Up, up, and see the great doom's image!" she cried, her eyes sparkling with excitement. "The hall is full of trunks, they are packing. What bolt has fallen? It's you, *ma chérie*, you've brought Ulysses home again and the slaughter has begun!" she blew a cloud of smoke triumphantly from her lips and threw herself into a chair beside the bed.

Imogen, rising on her elbow, plunged excitedly into the story of the Roux interview, which Miss Broadwood heard with the keenest interest, frequently interrupting her by exclamations of delight. When Imogen reached the dramatic scene which terminated in the destruction of the newspaper, Miss Broadwood rose and took a turn about the room, violently switching the tasselled cords of her bath-robe.

"Stop a moment," she cried, "you mean to tell me that he had such a heaven-sent means to bring her to her senses and didn't use it, that he held such a weapon and threw it away?"

"Use it?" cried Imogen unsteadily, "of course he didn't! He bared his back to the tormentor, signed himself over to punishment in that speech he made at dinner, which every one understands but Flavia. She was here for an hour last night and disregarded every limit of taste in her maledictions."

"My dear!" cried Miss Broadwood, catching her hand in inordinate delight at the situation, "do you see what he has done? There'll be no end to it. Why he has sacrificed himself to spare the very vanity that devours him, put rancours in the vessels of his peace, and his eternal jewel given to the common enemy of man, to make them kings, the seed of Banquo kings! He is magnificent!"

"Isn't he always that?" cried Imogen hotly. "He's like a pillar of sanity and law in this house of shams and swollen vanities, where people stalk about with a sort of mad-house dignity, each one fancying himself a king or a pope. If you could have heard that woman talk of him! Why she thinks him stupid, bigoted, blinded by middle-class prejudices. She talked about his having no æsthetic sense, and insisted that her artists had always shown him tolerance. I don't know why it should get on my nerves so, I'm sure, but her stupidity and assurance are enough to drive one to the brink of collapse."

"Yes, as opposed to his singular fineness, they are calculated to do just that," said Miss Broadwood gravely, wisely ignoring Imogen's tears. "But what has been is nothing to what will be. Just wait until Flavia's black swans have flown! You ought not to try to stick it out; that would only make it harder for every one. Suppose you let me telephone your mother to wire you to come home by the evening train?"

"Anything, rather than have her come at me like that again. It puts me in a perfectly impossible position, and he *is* so fine!"

"Of course it does," said Miss Broadwood sympathetically, "and there is no good to be got from facing it. I will stay, because such things interest me, and Frau Lichtenfeld will stay because she has no money to get away, and Buisson will stay because he feels somewhat responsible. These complications are interesting enough to cold-blooded folk like myself who have an eye for the dramatic element, but they are distracting and demoralizing to young people with any serious purpose in life."

Miss Broadwood's counsel was all the more generous seeing that, for her, the most interesting element of this dénouement would be eliminated by Imogen's departure. "If she goes now, she'll get over it," soliloquized Miss Broadwood, "if she stays she'll be wrung for him, and the hurt may go deep enough to last. I haven't the heart to see her spoiling things for herself." She telephoned Mrs. Willard, and helped Imogen to pack. She even took it upon herself to break the news of Imogen's going to Arthur, who remarked, as he rolled a cigarette in his nerveless fingers:

"Right enough, too. What should she do here with old cynics like you and me, Jimmy? Seeing that she is brim full of dates and formulæ and other positivisms, and is so girt about with illusions that she still casts a shadow in the sun. You've been very tender of her, haven't you? I've watched you. And to think it may all be gone when we see her next. 'The common fate of all things rare,' you know. What a good fellow you are, anyway, Jimmy," he added, putting his hands affectionately on her shoulders.

Arthur went with them to the station. Flavia was so prostrated by the concerted action of her guests that she was able to see Imogen only for a moment in her darkened sleeping chamber, where she kissed her hysterically, without lifting her head, bandaged in aromatic vinegar. On the way to the station both Arthur and Imogen threw the burden of keeping up appearances entirely upon Miss Broadwood, who blithely rose to the occasion. When Hamilton carried Imogen's bag into the car, Miss Broadwood detained her for a moment, whispering as she gave her a large, warm handclasp, "I'll come to see you when I get back to town; and, in the meantime, if you meet any of our artists, tell them you have left Caius Marius among the ruins of Carthage."

The Marriage of Phædra

The sequence of events was such that MacMaster did not make his pilgrimage to Hugh Treffinger's studio until three years after that painter's death. MacMaster was himself a painter, an American of the Gallicized type, who spent his winters in New York, his summers in Paris, and no inconsiderable amount of time on the broad waters between. He had often contemplated stopping in London on one of his return trips in the late autumn, but he had always deferred leaving Paris until the prick of necessity drove him home by the quickest and shortest route.

Treffinger was a comparatively young man at the time of his death, and there had seemed no occasion for haste until haste was of no avail. Then, possibly, though there had been some correspondence between them, MacMaster felt certain qualms about meeting in the flesh a man who in the flesh was so diversely reported. His intercourse with Treffinger's work had been so deep and satisfying, so apart from other appreciations, that he rather dreaded a critical juncture of any sort. He had always felt himself singularly inadept in personal relations, and in this case he had avoided the issue until it was no longer to be feared or hoped for. There still remained, however, Treffinger's great unfinished picture, the *Marriage of Phædra,* which had never left his studio, and of which MacMaster's friends had now and again brought report that it was the painter's most characteristic production.

The young man arrived in London in the evening, and the next morning went out to Kensington to find Treffinger's studio. It lay in one of the perplexing by-streets off Holland Road, and the number he found on a door set in a high garden wall, the top of which was covered with broken green glass and over which a budding lilac-bush nodded. Treffinger's plate was still there, and a card requesting visitors to ring for the attendant. In response to MacMaster's ring, the door was opened by a cleanly built little man, clad in a shooting jacket and trousers that had been made for an ampler figure. He had a fresh complexion, eyes of that common uncertain shade of grey, and was closely shaven except for the incipient mutton-chops on his ruddy cheeks. He bore himself in a manner strikingly capable, and there was a sort of trimness and alertness about him, despite the too-generous shoulders of his coat. In one hand he held a bulldog pipe, and in the other a copy of *Sporting Life*. While MacMaster was explaining the purpose of his call, he noticed that the man surveyed him critically, though not impertinently. He was admitted into a little tank of a lodge made of white-washed stone, the back door and windows opening upon a garden. A visitor's book and a pile of catalogues lay on a deal table, together with a bottle of ink and some rusty pens. The wall was ornamented with photographs and coloured prints of racing favourites.

"The studio is h'only open to the public on Saturdays and Sundays," explained the man—he referred to himself as "Jymes"—"but of course we make exceptions in the case of pynters. Lydy Elling Treffinger 'erself is on the Continent, but Sir 'Ugh's orders was that pynters was to 'ave the run of the place." He selected a key from his pocket and threw open the door into the studio which, like the lodge, was built against the wall of the garden.

MacMaster entered a long, narrow room, built of smoothed planks, painted a light green; cold and damp even on that fine May morning. The room was utterly bare of furniture—unless a step-ladder, a model throne, and a rack laden with large leather portfolios could be accounted such—and was windowless, without other openings than the door and the skylight, under which hung the unfinished picture itself. MacMaster had never seen so many of Treffinger's paintings together. He knew the painter had married a woman with money and had been able to keep such of his pictures as he wished. These, with all of his replicas and studies, he had left as a sort of common legacy to the younger men of the school he had originated.

As soon as he was left alone, MacMaster sat down on the edge of the model throne before the unfinished picture. Here indeed was what he had come for; it rather paralysed his receptivity for the moment, but gradually the thing found its way to him.

At one o'clock he was standing before the collection of studies done for *Boccaccio's Garden* when he heard a voice at his elbow.

"Pardon, sir, but I was just about to lock up and go to lunch. Are you lookin' for the figure study of Boccaccio 'imself?" James queried respectfully, "Lydy Elling Treffinger give it to Mr. Rossiter to take down to Oxford for some lectures he's been a-giving there."

"Did he never paint out his studies, then?" asked MacMaster with perplexity. "Here are two completed ones for this picture. Why did he keep them?"

"I don't know as I could say as to that, sir," replied James, smiling indulgently, "but that was 'is way. That is to say, 'e pynted out very frequent, but 'e always made two studies to stand; one in water colours and one in oils, before 'e went at the final picture,—to say nothink of all the pose studies 'e made in pencil before he begun on the composition proper at all. He was that particular. You see 'e wasn't so keen for the final effect as for the proper pyntin' of 'is pictures. 'E used to say they ought to be well made, the same as any other h'article of trade. I can lay my 'and on the pose studies for you, sir." He rummaged in one of the portfolios and produced half a dozen drawings. "These three," he continued, "was discarded: these two was the pose he finally accepted; this one without alteration, as it were."

"That's in Paris, as I remember," James continued reflectively. "It went with the *Saint Cecilia* into the Baron H—'s collection. Could you tell me, sir, 'as 'e it still? I don't like to lose account of them, but some 'as changed 'ands since Sir 'Ugh's death."

"H—'s collection is still intact, I believe," replied MacMaster. "You were with Treffinger long?"

"From my boyhood, sir," replied James with gravity. "I was a stable boy when 'e took me."

"You were his man, then?"

"That's it, sir. Nobody else ever done anything around the studio. I always mixed 'is colours and 'e taught me to do a share of the varnishin'; 'e said as 'ow there wasn't a 'ouse in England as could do it proper. You aynt looked at the *Marriage* yet, sir?" he asked abruptly, glancing doubtfully at MacMaster, and indicating with his thumb the picture under the north light.

"Not very closely. I prefer to begin with something simpler; that's rather appalling, at first glance," replied MacMaster.

"Well may you say that, sir," said James warmly. "That one

regular killed Sir 'Ugh; it regular broke 'im up, and nothink will ever convince me as 'ow it didn't bring on 'is second stroke."

When MacMaster walked back to High Street to take his buss, his mind was divided between two exultant convictions. He felt that he had not only found Treffinger's greatest picture, but that, in James, he had discovered a kind of cryptic index to the painter's personality—a clue which, if tactfully followed, might lead to much.

Several days after his first visit to the studio, MacMaster wrote to Lady Mary Percy, telling her that he would be in London for some time and asking her if he might call. Lady Mary was an only sister of Lady Ellen Treffinger, the painter's widow, and MacMaster had known her during one winter he spent at Nice. He had known her, indeed, very well, and Lady Mary, who was astonishingly frank and communicative upon all subjects, had been no less so upon the matter of her sister's unfortunate marriage.

In her reply to his note, Lady Mary named an afternoon when she would be alone. She was as good as her word, and when MacMaster arrived he found the drawing-room empty. Lady Mary entered shortly after he was announced. She was a tall woman, thin and stiffly jointed; and her body stood out under the folds of her gown with the rigour of cast-iron. This rather metallic suggestion was further carried out in her heavily knuckled hands, her stiff grey hair and long, bold-featured face, which was saved from freakishness only by her alert eyes.

"Really," said Lady Mary, taking a seat beside him and giving him a sort of military inspection through her nose-glasses, "Really, I had begun to fear that I had lost you altogether. It's four years since I saw you at Nice, isn't it? I was in Paris last winter, but I heard nothing from you."

"I was in New York then."

"It occurred to me that you might be. And why are you in London?"

"Can you ask?" replied MacMaster gallantly.

Lady Mary smiled ironically. "But for what else, incidentally?"

"Well, incidentally, I came to see Treffinger's studio and his unfinished picture. Since I've been here, I've decided to stay the summer. I'm even thinking of attempting to do a biography of him."

"So that is what brought you to London?"

"Not exactly. I had really no intention of anything so serious when I came. It's his last picture, I fancy, that has rather thrust it upon me. The notion has settled down on me like a thing destined."

"You'll not be offended if I question the clemency of such a destiny," remarked Lady Mary dryly. "Isn't there rather a surplus of books on that subject already?"

"Such as they are. Oh, I've read them all," here MacMaster faced Lady Mary triumphantly. "He has quite escaped your amiable critics," he added, smiling.

"I know well enough what you think, and I dare say we are not much on art," said Lady Mary with tolerant good humour. "We leave that to peoples who have no physique. Treffinger made a stir for a time, but it seems that we are not capable of a sustained appreciation of such extraordinary methods. In the end we go back to the pictures we find agreeable and unperplexing. He was regarded as an experiment, I fancy; and now it seems that he was rather an unsuccessful one. If you've come to us in a missionary spirit, we'll tolerate you politely, but we'll laugh in our sleeve, I warn you."

"That really doesn't daunt me, Lady Mary," declared MacMaster blandly, "As I told you, I'm a man with a mission."

Lady Mary laughed her hoarse baritone laugh. "Bravo! and you've come to me for inspiration for your panegyric?"

MacMaster smiled with some embarrassment. "Not altogether for that purpose. But I want to consult you, Lady Mary, about the advisability of troubling Lady Ellen Treffinger in the matter. It seems scarcely legitimate to go on without asking her to give some sort of grace to my proceedings, yet I feared the whole subject might be painful to her. I shall rely wholly upon your discretion."

"I think she would prefer to be consulted," replied Lady Mary judicially. "I can't understand how she endures to have the wretched affair continually raked up, but she does. She seems to feel a sort of moral responsibility. Ellen has always been singularly conscientious about this matter, in so far as her light goes,—which rather puzzles me, as hers is not exactly a magnanimous nature. She is certainly trying to do what she believes to be the right thing. I shall write to her, and you can see her when she returns from Italy."

"I want very much to meet her. She is, I hope, quite recovered in every way," queried MacMaster, hesitatingly.

"No, I can't say that she is. She has remained in much the same condition she sank to before his death. He trampled over pretty much whatever there was in her, I fancy. Women don't recover from wounds of that sort; at least, not women of Ellen's grain. They go on bleeding inwardly."

"You, at any rate have not grown more reconciled," MacMaster ventured.

"Oh, I give him his dues. He was a colourist, I grant you; but that is a vague and unsatisfactory quality to marry to; Lady Ellen Treffinger found it so."

"But, my dear Lady Mary," expostulated MacMaster, "and just repress me if I'm becoming too personal—but it must, in the first place, have been a marriage of choice on her part as well as on his."

Lady Mary poised her glasses on her large forefinger and assumed an attitude suggestive of the clinical lecture room as she replied. "Ellen, my dear boy, is an essentially romantic person. She is quiet about it, but she runs deep. I never knew how deep until I came against her on the issue of that marriage. She was always discontented as a girl; she found things dull and prosaic, and the ardour of his courtship was agreeable to her. He met her during her first season in town. She is handsome, and there were plenty of other men, but I grant you your scowling brigand was the most picturesque of the lot. In his courtship, as in everything else, he was theatrical to the point of being ridiculous, but Ellen's sense of humour is not her strongest quality. He had the charm of celebrity, the air of a man who could storm his way through anything to get what he wanted. That sort of vehemence is particularly effective with women like Ellen, who can be warmed only by reflected heat, and she couldn't at all stand out against it. He convinced her of his necessity; and that done, all's done."

"I can't help thinking that, even on such a basis, the marriage should have turned out better," MacMaster remarked reflectively.

"The marriage," Lady Mary continued with a shrug, "was made on the basis of a mutual misunderstanding. Ellen, in the nature of the case, believed that she was doing something quite out of the ordinary in accepting him, and expected concessions which, apparently, it never occurred to him to make. After his marriage he relapsed into his old habits of incessant work, broken by violent and often brutal relaxations. He insulted her friends and foisted his own upon her—many of them well calculated to arouse aversion in any well-bred girl. He had Ghillini constantly at the house—a homeless vagabond, whose conversation was impossible. I don't say, mind you, that he had not grievances on his side. He had probably over-rated the girl's possibilities, and he let her see that he was disappointed in her. Only a large and generous nature could have borne with him, and Ellen's is not that. She could not at all understand that odious strain of plebeian pride which plumes itself upon not having risen above its sources."

As MacMaster drove back to his hotel, he reflected that Lady Mary Percy had probably had good cause for dissatisfaction with her brother-in-law. Treffinger was, indeed, the last man who should have married into the Percy family. The son of a small tobacconist, he had grown up a sign painter's apprentice; idle, lawless, and practically letterless until he had drifted into the night classes of the Albert League, where Ghillini sometimes lectured. From the moment he came under the eye and influence of that erratic Italian, then a political exile, his life had swerved sharply from its old channel. This man had been at once incentive and guide, friend and master, to his pupil. He had taken the raw clay out of the London streets and moulded it anew. Seemingly he had divined at once where the boy's possibilities lay, and had thrown aside every canon of orthodox instruction in the training of him. Under him Treffinger acquired his superficial, yet facile, knowledge of the classics; had steeped himself in the monkish Latin and mediæval romances which later gave his work so naive and remote a quality. That was the beginning of the wattle fences, the cobble pave, the brown roof beams, the cunningly wrought fabrics that gave to his pictures such a richness of decorative effect.

As he had told Lady Mary Percy, MacMaster had found the imperative inspiration of his purpose in Treffinger's unfinished picture, the *Marriage of Phædra*. He had always believed that the key to Treffinger's individuality lay in his singular education; in the *Roman de la Rose,* in Boccaccio, and Amadis, those works which had literally transcribed themselves upon the blank soul of the London street boy, and through which he had been born into the world of spiritual things. Treffinger had been a man who lived after his imagination; and his mind, his ideals and, as MacMaster believed, even his personal ethics, had to the last been coloured by the trend of his early training. There was in him alike the freshness and spontaneity, the frank brutality and the religious mysticism which lay well back of the fifteenth century. In the *Marriage of Phædra* MacMaster found the ultimate expression of this spirit, the final word as to Treffinger's point of view.

As in all Treffinger's classical subjects, the conception was wholly mediæval. This Phædra, just turning from her husband and maidens to greet her husband's son, giving him her first fearsome glance from under her half lifted veil, was no daughter of Minos. The daughter of *heathenesse* and the early church she was; doomed to torturing visions and scourgings, and the wrangling of soul with flesh. The venerable Theseus might have been victorious Charlemagne, and Phædra's maidens belonged rather in the train of Blanche of Castile than at the Cretan court. In the earlier studies Hippolytus had been done with a more pagan suggestion, but in each successive drawing the glorious figure had been deflowered of something of its serene unconsciousness; until, in the canvas under the skylight, he appeared a very Christian knight. This male figure, and the face of Phædra, painted with such magical preservation of tone under the heavy shadow of the veil, were plainly Treffinger's highest achievements of craftsmanship. By what labour he had reached the seemingly inevitable composition of the picture—with its twenty figures, its plenitude of light and air, its restful distances seen through white porticoes—countless studies bore witness.

From James's attitude toward the picture, MacMaster could well conjecture what the painter's had been. This picture was always uppermost in James's mind; its custodianship formed, in his eyes, his occupation. He was manifestly apprehensive when visitors—not many came now-a-days— lingered near it. "It was the *Marriage* as killed 'im," he would often say, "and for the matter 'o that, it did like to 'av been the death of all of us."

By the end of his second week in London, MacMaster had begun the notes for his study of Hugh Treffinger and his work. When his researches led him occasionally to visit the studios of Treffinger's friends and erstwhile disciples, he found their Treffinger manner fading as the ring of Treffinger's personality died out in them. One by one they were stealing back into the fold of national British art; the hand that had wound them up was still. MacMaster despaired of them and confined himself more and more exclusively to the studio, to such of Treffinger's letters as were available—they were for the most part singularly negative and colourless— and to his interrogation of Treffinger's man.

He could not himself have traced the successive steps by which he was gradually admitted into James's confidence. Certainly most of his adroit strategies to that end failed humiliatingly, and whatever it was that built up an understanding between them, must have been instinctive and intuitive on both sides. When at last James became anecdotal, personal, there was that in every word he let fall which put breath and blood into MacMaster's book. James had so long been steeped in that penetrating personality that he fairly exuded it. Many of his very phrases, mannerisms and opinions were impressions that he had taken on like wet plaster in his daily contact with Treffinger. Inwardly he was lined with cast off epithelia, as outwardly he was clad in the painter's discarded coats. If the painter's letters were formal and perfunctory, if his expressions to his friends had been extravagant, contradictory and often apparently insincere—still, MacMaster felt himself not entirely without authentic sources. It was James who possessed Treffinger's legend; it was with James that he had laid aside his pose. Only in his studio, alone, and face to face with his work, as it seemed, had the man invariably been himself. James had known him in the one attitude in which he was entirely honest; their relation had fallen well within the painter's only indubitable integrity. James's report of Treffinger was distorted by no hallucination of artistic insight, coloured by no interpretation of his own. He merely held what he had heard and seen; his mind was a sort of camera obscura. His very limitations made him the more literal and minutely accurate.

One morning when MacMaster was seated before the *Marriage of Phædra,* James entered on his usual round of dusting.

"I've 'eard from Lydy Elling by the post, sir," he remarked, "an' she's give h'orders to 'ave the 'ouse put in readiness. I doubt she'll be 'ere by Thursday or Friday next."

"She spends most of her time abroad?" queried MacMaster; on the subject of Lady Treffinger James consistently maintained a very delicate reserve.

"Well, you could 'ardly say she does that, sir. She finds the 'ouse a bit dull, I daresay, so durin' the season she stops mostly with Lydy Mary Percy, at Grosvenor Square. Lydy Mary's a h'only sister." After a few moments he continued, speaking in jerks governed by the rigour of his dusting: "Honly this morning I come upon this scarf-pin," exhibiting a very striking instance of that article, "an' I recalled as 'ow Sir 'Ugh give it me when 'e was a-courting of Lydy Elling. Blowed if I ever see a man go in for a 'oman like 'im! 'E was that gone, sir. 'E never went in on anythink so 'ard before nor since, till 'e went in on the *Marriage* there—though 'e mostly went in on things pretty keen; 'ad the measles when 'e was thirty, strong as cholera, an' come close to dyin' of 'em. 'E wasn't strong for Lydy Elling's set; they was a bit too stiff for 'im. A free an' easy gentleman, 'e was; 'e liked 'is dinner with a few friends an' them jolly, but 'e wasn't much on what you might call big affairs. But once 'e went in for Lydy Elling, 'e broke 'imself to new paces. He give away 'is rings an' pins, an' the tylor's man an' the 'abberdasher's man was at 'is rooms continual. 'E got 'imself put up for a club in Piccadilly; 'e starved 'imself thin, an' worrited 'imself white, an' ironed 'imself out, an' drawed 'imself tight as a bow string. It was a good job 'e come a winner, or I don't know w'at'd 'a been to pay."

The next week, in consequence of an invitation from Lady Ellen Treffinger, MacMaster went one afternoon to take tea with her. He was shown into the garden that lay between the residence and the studio, where the tea-table was set under a gnarled pear tree. Lady Ellen rose as he approached—he was astonished to note how tall she was—and greeted him graciously, saying that she already knew him through her sister. MacMaster felt a certain satisfaction in her; in her reassuring poise and repose, in the charming modulations of her voice and the indolent reserve of her full, almond eyes. He was even delighted to find her face so inscrutable, though it chilled his own warmth and made the open frankness he had wished to permit himself impossible. It was a long face, narrow at the chin, very delicately featured, yet steeled by an impassive mask of self-control. It was behind just such finely cut, close-sealed faces, MacMaster reflected, that nature sometimes hid astonishing secrets. But in spite of this suggestion of hardness, he felt that the unerring taste that Treffinger had always shown in larger matters had not deserted him when he came to the choosing of a wife, and he admitted that he could not himself have selected a woman who looked more as Treffinger's wife should look.

While he was explaining the purpose of his frequent visits to the studio, she heard him with courteous interest. "I have read, I think, everything that has been published on Sir Hugh Treffinger's work, and it seems to me that there is much left to be said," he concluded.

"I believe they are rather inadequate," she remarked vaguely. She hesitated a moment, absently fingering the ribbons of her gown, then continued, without raising her eyes; "I hope you will not think me too exacting if I ask to see the proofs of such chapters of your work as have to do with Sir Hugh's personal life. I have always asked that privilege."

MacMaster hastily assured her as to this, adding, "I mean to touch on only such facts in his personal life as have to do directly with his work—such as his monkish education under Ghillini."

"I see your meaning, I think," said Lady Ellen, looking at him with wide, uncomprehending eyes.

When MacMaster stopped at the studio on leaving the house, he stood for some time before Treffinger's one portrait of himself; that brigand of a picture, with its full throat and square head; the short upper lip blackened by the close-clipped moustache, the wiry hair tossed down over the forehead, the strong white teeth set hard on a short pipe stem. He could well understand what manifold tortures the mere grain of the man's strong red and brown flesh might have inflicted upon a woman like Lady Ellen. He could conjecture, too, Treffinger's impotent revolt against that very repose which had so dazzled him when it first defied his daring; and how once possessed of it, his first instinct had been to crush it, since he could not melt it.

Toward the close of the season, Lady Ellen Treffinger left town. MacMaster's work was progressing rapidly, and he and James wore away the days in their peculiar relation, which by this time had much of friendliness. Excepting for the regular visits of a Jewish picture dealer, there were few intrusions upon their solitude. Occasionally a party of Americans rang at the little door in the garden wall, but usually they departed speedily for the Moorish hall and tinkling fountain of the great show studio of London, not far away.

This Jew, an Austrian by birth, who had a large business in Melbourne, Australia, was a man of considerable discrimination, and at once selected the *Marriage of Phædra* as the object of his especial interest. When, upon his first visit, Lichtenstein had declared the picture one of the things done for time, MacMaster had rather warmed toward him and had talked to him very freely. Later, however, the man's repulsive personality and innate vulgarity so wore upon him that, the more genuine the Jew's appreciation, the more he resented it and the more base he somehow felt it to be. It annoyed him to see Lichtenstein walking up and down before the picture, shaking his head and blinking his watery eyes over his nose-glasses, ejaculating: "Dot is a chem, a chem! It is wordt to gome den dousant miles for such a bainting, eh? To make Eurobe abbreciate such a work of ardt it is necessary to take it away while she is napping. She has never abbreciated until she has lost, but," knowingly, "She will buy back."

James had, from the first, felt such a distrust of the man that he would never leave him alone in the studio for a moment. When Lichtenstein insisted upon having Lady Ellen Treffinger's address, James rose to the point of insolence. "It ay'nt no use to give it, noway. Lydy Treffinger never has nothink to do with dealers." MacMaster quietly repented his rash confidences, fearing that he might indirectly cause Lady Ellen annoyance from this merciless speculator, and he recalled with chagrin that Lichtenstein had extorted from him, little by little, pretty much the entire plan of his book, and especially the place in it which the *Marriage of Phædra* was to occupy.

By this time the first chapters of MacMaster's book were in the hands of his publisher, and his visits to the studio were necessarily less frequent. The greater part of his time was now employed with the engravers who were to reproduce such of Treffinger's pictures as he intended to use as illustrations.

He returned to his hotel late one evening after a long and vexing day at the engravers, to find James in his room, seated on his steamer trunk by the window, with the outline of a great square draped in sheets resting against his knee.

"Why, James, what's up?" he cried in astonishment, glancing enquiringly at the sheeted object.

"Ay'nt you seen the pypers, sir?" jerked out the man.

"No, now I think of it, I haven't even looked at a paper. I've been at the engravers' plant all day. I haven't seen anything."

James drew a copy of the *Times* from his pocket and handed it to him, pointing with a tragic finger to a paragraph in the social column. It was merely the announcement of Lady Ellen Treffinger's engagement to Captain Alexander Gresham.

"Well, what of it, my man? That surely is her privilege."

James took the paper, turned to another page, and silently pointed to a paragraph in the art notes which stated that Lady Treffinger had presented to the X—gallery the entire collection of paintings and sketches now in her late husband's studio, with the exception of his unfinished picture, the *Marriage of Phædra,* which she had sold for a large sum to an Australian dealer who had come to London purposely to secure some of Treffinger's paintings.

MacMaster pursed up his lips and sat down, his overcoat still on. "Well, James, this is something of a—something of a jolt, eh? It never occurred to me she'd really do it."

"Lord, you don't know 'er, sir," said James bitterly, still staring at the floor in an attitude of abandoned dejection.

MacMaster started up in a flash of enlightenment, "What on earth have you got there, James? It's not—surely it's not—"

"Yes, it is, sir," broke in the man excitedly. "It's the *Marriage* itself. It aynt a-going to H'australia, no'ow!"

"But man, what are you going to do with it? It's Lichtenstein's property now, as it seems."

"It aynt, sir, that it aynt. No, by Gawd it aynt!" shouted James, breaking into a choking fury. He controlled himself with an effort and added supplicatingly: "Oh, sir, you aynt a-going to see it go to H'australia, w'ere they send convic's?" He unpinned and flung aside the sheets as though to let *Phædra* plead for herself.

MacMaster sat down again and looked sadly at the doomed masterpiece. The notion of James having carried it across London that night rather appealed to his fancy. There was certainly a flavour about such a high-handed proceeding. "However did you get it here?" he queried.

"I got a four-wheeler and come over direct, sir. Good job I 'appened to 'ave the chaynge about me."

"You came up High Street, up Piccadilly, through the Haymarket and Trafalgar Square, and into the Strand?" queried MacMaster with a relish.

"Yes, sir. Of course, sir," assented James with surprise.

MacMaster laughed delightedly. "It was a beautiful idea, James, but I'm afraid we can't carry it any further."

"I was thinkin' as 'ow it would be a rare chance to get you to take the *Marriage* over to Paris for a year or two, sir, until the thing blows over?" suggested James blandly.

"I'm afraid that's out of the question, James. I haven't the right stuff in me for a pirate, or even a vulgar smuggler, I'm afraid." MacMaster found it surprisingly difficult to say this, and he busied himself with the lamp as he said it. He heard James's hand fall heavily on the trunk top, and he discovered that he very much disliked sinking in the man's estimation.

"Well, sir," remarked James in a more formal tone, after a protracted silence; "then there's nothink for it but as 'ow I'll 'ave to make way with it myself."

"And how about your character, James? The evidence would be heavy against you, and even if Lady Treffinger didn't prosecute, you'd be done for."

"Blow my character!—your pardon, sir," cried James, starting to his feet. "W'at do I want of a character? I'll chuck the 'ole thing, and damned lively, too. The shop's to be sold out, an' my place is gone any'ow. I'm a-going to enlist, or try the gold-fields. I've lived too long with h'artists; I'd never give satisfaction in livery now. You know 'ow it is yourself, sir; there aynt no life like it, no'ow."

For a moment MacMaster was almost equal to abetting James in his theft. He reflected that pictures had been whitewashed, or hidden in the crypts of churches, or under the floors of palaces from meaner motives, and to save them from a fate less ignominious. But presently, with a sigh, he shook his head.

"No, James, it won't do at all. It has been tried over and over again, ever since the world has been a-going and pictures a-making. It was tried in Florence and in Venice, but the pictures were always carried away in the end. You see the difficulty is that, although Treffinger told you what was not to be done with the picture, he did not say definitely what was to be done with it. Do you think Lady Treffinger really understands that he did not want it to be sold?"

"Well, sir, it was like this, sir," said James resuming his seat on the trunk and again resting the picture against his knee. "My memory is as clear as glass about it. After Sir 'Ugh got up from 'is first stroke, 'e took a fresh start at the *Marriage*. Before that 'e 'ad been working at it only at night for awhile back; the *Legend* was the big picture then, an' was under the north light w'ere 'e worked of a morning. But one day 'e bid me take the *Legend* down an' put the *Marriage* in its place, an' 'e says, dashin' on 'is jacket, 'Jymes, this is a start for the finish, this time.'

"From that on 'e worked at the night picture in the mornin'—a thing contrary to 'is custom. The *Marriage* went wrong, and wrong—an' Sir 'Ugh a-gettin' seedier an' seedier every day. 'E tried models an' models, an' smudged an' pynted out on account of 'er face goin' wrong in the shadow. Sometimes 'e layed it on the colours, an' swore at me an' things general. He got that discouraged about 'imself that on 'is low days 'e used to say to me: 'Jymes, remember one thing; if anythink 'appens to me, the *Marriage* is not to go out of 'ere unfinished. It's worth the lot of 'em, my boy, an' it's not a-going to go shabby for lack of pains.' 'E said things to that effect repeated.

"He was workin' at the picture the last day, before 'e went to 'is club. 'E kept the carriage waitin' near an hour while 'e put on a stroke an' then drawed back for to look at it, an' then put on another, careful like. After 'e 'ad 'is gloves on, 'e come back an' took away the brushes I was startin' to clean, an' put in another touch or two. 'It's a-comin', Jymes,' 'e says, 'by gad if it aynt.' An' with that 'e goes out. It was cruel sudden, w'at come after.

"That night I was lookin' to 'is clothes at the 'ouse when they brought 'im 'ome. He was conscious, but w'en I ran down stairs for to 'elp lift 'im up, I knowed 'e was a finished man. After we got 'im into bed, 'e kept lookin' restless at me and then at Lydy Elling and a-jerkin' of 'is 'and. Finally 'e quite raised it an' shot 'is thumb out towards the wall. 'He wants water; ring Jymes,' says Lydy Elling, placid. But I knowed 'e was pointin' to the shop.

" 'Lydy Treffinger,' says I, bold, 'he's pointin' to the studio. He means about the *Marriage;* 'e told me to-day as 'ow 'e never wanted it sold unfinished. Is that it, Sir 'Ugh?'

"He smiled an' nodded slight an' closed 'is eyes. 'Thank you, Jymes,' says Lydy Elling, placid. Then 'e opened 'is eyes an' looked long and 'ard at Lydy Elling.

" 'Of course I'll try to do as you'd wish about the pictures, 'Ugh, if that's w'at's troublin' you,' she says quiet. With that 'e closed 'is eyes and 'e never opened 'em. He died unconscious at four that mornin'.

"You see, sir, Lydy Elling was always cruel 'ard on the *Marriage*. From the first it went wrong, an' Sir 'Ugh was out of temper pretty constant. She came into the studio one day and looked at the picture an' asked 'im why 'e didn't throw it up an' quit a-worriting 'imself. He answered sharp, an' with that she said as 'ow she didn't see w'at there was to make such a row about, no'ow. She spoke 'er mind about that picture, free; an' Sir 'Ugh swore 'ot an' let a 'andful of brushes fly at 'is study, an' Lydy Elling picked up 'er skirts careful an' chill, an' drifted out of the studio with 'er eyes calm and 'er chin 'igh. If there was one thing Lydy Elling 'ad no comprehension of, it was the usefulness of swearin'. So the *Marriage* was a sore thing between 'em. She is uncommon calm, but uncommon bitter, is Lydy Elling. She's never come a-near the studio since that day she went out 'oldin' up of 'er skirts. W'en 'er friends goes over she excuses 'erself along o' the strain. Strain—Gawd!" James ground his wrath short in his teeth.

"I'll tell you what I'll do, James, and it's our only hope. I'll see Lady Ellen to-morrow. The *Times* says she returned today. You take the picture back to its place, and I'll do what I can for it. If anything is done to save it, it must be done through Lady Ellen Treffinger herself; that much is clear. I can't think that she fully understands the situation. If she did, you know, she really couldn't have any motive—" He stopped suddenly. Somehow, in the dusky lamplight her small, close-sealed face came ominously back to him. He rubbed his forehead and knitted his brows thoughtfully. After a moment he shook his head and went on: "I am positive that nothing can be gained by high-handed methods, James. Captain Gresham is one of the most popular men in London, and his friends would tear up Treffinger's bones if he were annoyed by any scandal of our making—and this scheme you propose would inevitably result in scandal. Lady Ellen has, of course, every legal right to sell the picture. Treffinger made considerable inroads upon her estate, and, as she is about to marry a man without income, she doubtless feels that she has a right to replenish her patrimony."

He found James amenable, though doggedly sceptical. He went down into the street, called a carriage, and saw James and his burden into it. Standing in the doorway, he watched the carriage roll away through the drizzling mist, weave in and out among the wet, black vehicles and darting cab lights, until it was swallowed up in the glare and confusion of the Strand. "It is rather a fine touch of irony," he reflected, "that he, who is so out of it, should be the one to really care. Poor Treffinger," he murmured as, with a rather spiritless smile, he turned back into his hotel, "Poor Treffinger; *sic transit gloria.*"

The next afternoon MacMaster kept his promise. When he arrived at Lady Mary Percy's house he saw preparations for a function of some sort, but he went resolutely up the steps, telling the footman that his business was urgent. Lady Ellen came down alone, excusing her sister. She was dressed for receiving, and MacMaster had never seen her so beautiful. The colour in her cheeks sent a softening glow over her small, delicately cut features.

MacMaster apologized for his intrusion and came unflinchingly to the object of his call. He had come, he said, not only to offer her his warmest congratulations, but to express his regret that a great work of art was to leave England.

Lady Treffinger looked at him in wide-eyed astonishment. Surely, she said, she had been careful to select the best of the pictures for the X— gallery, in accordance with Sir Hugh Treffinger's wishes.

"And did he—pardon me, Lady Treffinger, but in mercy set my mind at rest—did he or did he not express any definite wish concerning this one picture, which to me seems worth all the others, unfinished as it is?"

Lady Treffinger paled perceptibly, but it was not the pallor of confusion. When she spoke there was a sharp tremor in her smooth voice, the edge of a resentment that tore her like pain. "I think his man has some such impression, but I believe it to be utterly unfounded. I cannot find that he ever expressed any wish concerning the disposition of the picture to any of his friends. Unfortunately, Sir Hugh was not always discreet in his remarks to his servants."

"Captain Gresham, Lady Ellingham and Miss Ellingham," announced a servant, appearing at the door.

There was a murmur in the hall, and MacMaster greeted the smiling Captain and his aunt as he bowed himself out.

To all intents and purposes the *Marriage of Phædra* was already entombed in a vague continent in the Pacific, somewhere on the other side of the world.

The Garden Lodge

When Caroline Noble's friends
learned that Raymond d'Esquerré was to spend a month at her place on the
Sound before he sailed to fill his engagement for the London opera season,
they considered it another striking instance of the perversity of things. That
the month was May, and the most mild and florescent of all the blue-and-
white Mays the middle coast had known in years, but added to their sense
of wrong. D'Esquerré, they learned, was ensconced in the lodge in the
apple orchard, just beyond Caroline's glorious garden, and report went that
at almost any hour the sound of the tenor's voice and of Caroline's crashing
accompaniment could be heard floating through the open windows, out
among the snowy apple boughs. The Sound, steel-blue and dotted with
white sails, was splendidly seen from the windows of the lodge. The garden
to the left and the orchard to the right had never been so riotous with
spring, and had burst into impassioned bloom, as if to accommodate Caroline, though she was certainly the last woman to whom the witchery of
Freya could be attributed; the last woman, as her friends affirmed, to at all
adequately appreciate and make the most of such a setting for the great
tenor.

Of course, they admitted, Caroline was musical—well, she
ought to be!—but in that as in everything she was paramountly cool-
headed, slow of impulse, and disgustingly practical; in that, as in everything
else, she had herself so provokingly well in hand. Of course it would be she,
always mistress of herself in any situation, she who would never be lifted
one inch from the ground by it, and who would go on superintending her
gardeners and workmen as usual, it would be she who got him. Perhaps

some of them suspected that this was exactly why she did get him, and it but nettled them the more.

Caroline's coolness, her capableness, her general success, especially exasperated people because they felt that, for the most part, she had made herself what she was; that she had cold-bloodedly set about complying with the demands of life and making her position comfortable and masterful. That was why, every one said, she had married Howard Noble. Women who did not get through life so well as Caroline, who could not make such good terms either with fortune or their husbands, who did not find their health so unfailingly good, or hold their looks so well, or manage their children so easily, or give such distinction to all they did, were fond of stamping Caroline as a materialist and called her hard.

The impression of cold calculation, of having a definite policy, which Caroline gave, was far from a false one; but there was this to be said for her, that there were extenuating circumstances which her friends could not know.

If Caroline held determinedly to the middle course, if she was apt to regard with distrust everything which inclined toward extravagance, it was not because she was unacquainted with other standards than her own, or had never seen another side of life. She had grown up in Brooklyn, in a shabby little house under the vacillating administration of her father, a music teacher who usually neglected his duties to write orchestral compositions for which the world seemed to have no especial need. His spirit was warped by bitter vindictiveness and puerile self-commiseration, and he spent his days in scorn of the labour that brought him bread and in pitiful devotion to the labour that brought him only disappointment, writing interminable scores which demanded of the orchestra everything under heaven except melody.

It was not a cheerful home for a girl to grow up in. The mother, who idolized her husband as the music lord of the future, was left to a life-long battle with broom and dust-pan, to never ending conciliatory overtures to the butcher and grocer, to the making of her own gowns and of Caroline's, and to the delicate task of mollifying Auguste's neglected pupils.

The son, Heinrich, a painter, Caroline's only brother, had inherited all his father's vindictive sensitiveness without his capacity for slavish application. His little studio on the third floor had been much frequented by young men as unsuccessful as himself, who met there to give themselves over to contemptuous derision of this or that artist whose industry and stupidity had won him recognition. Heinrich, when he worked at all, did newspaper sketches at twenty-five dollars a week. He was too indolent and vacillating to set himself seriously to his art, too irascible and poignantly self-conscious to make a living, too much addicted to lying late in bed, to the incontinent reading of poetry and to the use of chloral, to be anything very positive except painful. At twenty-six he shot himself in a frenzy, and the whole wretched affair had effectually shattered his mother's health and brought on the decline of which she died. Caroline had been fond of him, but she felt a certain relief when he no longer wandered about the little house, commenting ironically upon its shabbiness, a Turkish cap on his head and a cigarette hanging from between his long, tremulous fingers.

After her mother's death Caroline assumed the management of that bankrupt establishment. The funeral expenses were unpaid, and Auguste's pupils had been frightened away by the shock of successive disasters and the general atmosphere of wretchedness that pervaded the house. Auguste himself was writing a symphonic poem, Icarus, dedicated to the memory of his son. Caroline was barely twenty when she was called upon to face this tangle of difficulties, but she reviewed the situation candidly. The house had served its time at the shrine of idealism; vague, distressing, unsatisfied yearnings had brought it low enough. Her mother, thirty years before, had eloped and left Germany with her music teacher, to give herself over to life-long, drudging bondage at the kitchen range. Ever since Caroline could remember, the law in the house had been a sort of mystic worship of things distant, intangible and unattainable. The family had lived in successive ebullitions of generous enthusiasm, in talk of masters and master-pieces, only to come down to the cold facts in the case; to boiled mutton and to the necessity of turning the dining-room carpet. All these emotional pyrotechnics had ended in petty jealousies, in neglected duties and in cowardly fear of the little grocer on the corner.

From her childhood she had hated it, that humiliating and un-certain existence, with its glib tongue and empty pockets, its poetic ideals and sordid realities, its indolence and poverty tricked out in paper roses. Even as a little girl, when vague dreams beset her, when she wanted to lie late in bed and commune with visions, or to leap and sing because the sooty little trees along the street were putting out their first pale leaves in the sunshine, she would clench her hands and go to help her mother sponge the spots from her father's waistcoat or press Heinrich's trousers. Her mother never permitted the slightest question concerning anything Auguste or Heinrich saw fit to do, but from the time Caroline could reason at all she could not help thinking that many things went wrong at home. She knew, for example, that her father's pupils ought not to be kept waiting half an hour while he discussed Schopenhauer with some bearded socialist over a dish of herrings and a spotted table cloth. She knew that Heinrich ought not to give a dinner on Heine's birthday, when the laundress had not been paid for a month and when he frequently had to ask his mother for car fare. Certainly Caroline had served her apprenticeship to idealism and to all the embarrassing inconsistencies which it sometimes entails, and she decided to deny herself this diffuse, ineffectual answer to the sharp questions of life.

When she came into the control of herself and the house, she refused to proceed any further with her musical education. Her father, who had intended to make a concert pianist of her, set this down as another item in his long list of disappointments and his grievances against the world. She was young and pretty, and she had worn turned gowns and soiled gloves and improvised hats all her life. She wanted the luxury of being like other people, of being honest from her hat to her boots, of having nothing to hide, not even in the matter of stockings, and she was willing to work for it. She rented a little studio away from that house of misfortune, and began to give lessons. She managed well and was the sort of girl people liked to help. The bills were paid and Auguste went on composing, growing indignant only when she refused to insist that her pupils should study his compositions for the piano. She began to get engagements in New York to play accompaniments at song recitals. She dressed well, made herself agreeable, and gave herself a chance. She never permitted herself to look further than a step ahead, and set herself with all the strength of her will to see things as they are and meet them squarely in the broad day. There were two things she feared even more than poverty; the part of one that sets up an idol and the part of one that bows down and worships it.

When Caroline was twenty-four she married Howard Noble, then a widower of forty, who had been for ten years a power in Wall street. Then, for the first time, she had paused to take breath. It took a substantialness as unquestionable as his; his money, his position, his energy, the big vigour of his robust person, to satisfy her that she was entirely safe. Then she relaxed a little, feeling that there was a barrier to be counted upon between her and that world of visions and quagmires and failure.

Caroline had been married for six years when Raymond d'Esquerré came to stay with them. He came chiefly because Caroline was what she was; because he, too, felt occasionally the need of getting out of Klingsor's garden, of dropping down somewhere for a time near a quiet nature, a cool head, a strong hand. The hours he had spent in the garden lodge were hours of such concentrated study as, in his fevered life, he seldom got in anywhere. She had, as he told Noble, a fine appreciation of the seriousness of work.

One evening two weeks after d'Esquerré had sailed, Caroline was in the library giving her husband an account of the work she had laid out for the gardeners. She superintended the care of the grounds herself. Her garden, indeed, had become quite a part of her; a sort of beautiful adjunct, like gowns or jewels. It was a famous spot, and Noble was very proud of it.

"What do you think, Caroline, of having the garden lodge torn down and putting a new summer house there at the end of the arbour; a big rustic affair where you could have tea served in mid-summer?" he asked.

"The lodge?" repeated Caroline looking at him quickly. "Why, that seems almost a shame, doesn't it, after d'Esquerré has used it?"

Noble put down his book with a smile of amusement.

"Are you going to be sentimental about it? Why, I'd sacrifice the whole place to see that come to pass. But I don't believe you could do it for an hour together."

"I don't believe so, either," said his wife, smiling.

Noble took up his book again and Caroline went into the music-room to practise. She was not ready to have the lodge torn down. She had gone there for a quiet hour every day during the two weeks since d'Esquerré had left them. It was the sheerest sentiment she had ever permitted herself. She was ashamed of it, but she was childishly unwilling to let it go.

Caroline went to bed soon after her husband, but she was not able to sleep. The night was close and warm, presaging storm. The wind had fallen and the water slept, fixed and motionless as the sand. She rose and thrust her feet into slippers and putting a dressing-gown over her shoulders opened the door of her husband's room; he was sleeping soundly. She went into the hall and down the stairs; then, leaving the house through a side door, stepped into the vine covered arbour that led to the garden lodge. The scent of the June roses was heavy in the still air, and the stones that paved the path felt pleasantly cool through the thin soles of her slippers. Heat-lightning flashed continuously from the bank of clouds that had gathered over the sea, but the shore was flooded with moonlight and, beyond, the rim of the Sound lay smooth and shining. Caroline had the key of the lodge, and the door creaked as she opened it. She stepped into the long, low room radiant with the moonlight which streamed through the bow window and lay in a silvery pool along the waxed floor. Even that part of the room which lay in the shadow was vaguely illuminated; the piano, the tall candlesticks, the picture frames and white casts standing out as clearly in the half-light as did the sycamores and black poplars of the garden against the still, expectant night sky. Caroline sat down to think it all over. She had come here to do just that every day of the two weeks since d'Esquerré's departure, but, far from ever having reached a conclusion, she had succeeded only in losing her way in a maze of memories—sometimes bewilderingly confused, sometimes too acutely distinct—where there was neither path, nor clue, nor any hope of finality. She had, she realized, defeated a life-long regimen; completely confounded herself by falling unaware and incontinently into that luxury of revery which, even as a little girl, she had so determinedly denied herself; she had been developing with alarming celerity that part of one which sets up an idol and that part of one which bows down and worships it.

It was a mistake, she felt, ever to have asked d'Esquerré to come at all. She had an angry feeling that she had done it rather in self-defiance, to rid herself finally of that instinctive fear of him which had always troubled and perplexed her. She knew that she had reckoned with herself before he came; but she had been equal to so much that she had never really doubted she would be equal to this. She had come to believe, indeed, almost arrogantly in her own malleability and endurance; she had done so much with herself that she had come to think that there was nothing which she could not do; like swimmers, overbold, who reckon upon their strength and their power to hoard it, forgetting the ever changing moods of their adversary, the sea.

And d'Esquerré was a man to reckon with. Caroline did not deceive herself now upon that score. She admitted it humbly enough, and since she had said good-bye to him she had not been free for a moment from the sense of his formidable power. It formed the undercurrent of her consciousness; whatever she might be doing or thinking, it went on, involuntarily, like her breathing; sometimes welling up until suddenly she found herself suffocating. There was a moment of this to-night, and Caroline rose and stood shuddering, looking about her in the blue duskiness of the silent room. She had not been here at night before, and the spirit of the place seemed more troubled and insistent than ever it had been in the quiet of the afternoons. Caroline brushed her hair back from her damp forehead

and went over to the bow window. After raising it she sat down upon the
low seat. Leaning her head against the sill, and loosening her night-gown
at the throat, she half closed her eyes and looked off into the troubled night,
watching the play of the sheet-lightning upon the massing clouds between
the pointed tops of the poplars.

Yes, she knew, she knew well enough, of what absurdities this
spell was woven; she mocked, even while she winced. His power she knew,
lay not so much in anything that he actually had—though he had so
much—or in anything that he actually was; but in what he suggested, in
what he seemed picturesque enough to have or be—and that was just
anything that one chose to believe or to desire. His appeal was all the more
persuasive and alluring that it was to the imagination alone, that it was as
indefinite and impersonal as those cults of idealism which so have their way
with women. What he had was that, in his mere personality, he quickened
and in a measure gratified that something without which—to women—life
is no better than sawdust, and to the desire for which most of their mistakes
and tragedies and astonishingly poor bargains are due.

D'Esquerré had become the centre of a movement, and the
Metropolitan had become the temple of a cult. When he could be induced
to cross the Atlantic, the opera season in New York was successful; when
he could not, the management lost money; so much every one knew. It was
understood, too, that his superb art had disproportionately little to do with
his peculiar position. Women swayed the balance this way or that; the
opera, the orchestra, even his own glorious art, achieved at such a cost, were
but the accessories of himself; like the scenery and costumes and even the
soprano, they all went to produce atmosphere, were the mere mechanics of
the beautiful illusion.

Caroline understood all this; to-night was not the first time that
she had put it to herself so. She had seen the same feeling in other people;
watched for it in her friends, studied it in the house night after night when
he sang, candidly putting herself among a thousand others.

D'Esquerré's arrival in the early winter was the signal for a
feminine hegira toward New York. On the nights when he sang, women
flocked to the Metropolitan from mansions and hotels, from typewriter
desks, school-rooms, shops and fitting-rooms. They were of all conditions
and complexions. Women of the world who accepted him knowingly, as
they sometimes took champagne for its agreeable effect; sisters of charity
and overworked shop-girls, who received him devoutly; withered women
who had taken doctorate degrees and who worshipped furtively through

prism spectacles; business women and women of affairs, the Amazons who dwelt afar from men in the stony fastnesses of apartment houses. They all entered into the same romance; dreamed, in terms as various as the hues of phantasy, the same dream; drew the same quick breath when he stepped upon the stage, an :, at his exit, felt the same dull pain of shouldering the pack again.

There were the maimed, even; those who came on crutches, who were pitted by smallpox or grotesquely painted by cruel birth stains. These, too, entered with him into enchantment. Stout matrons became slender girls again; worn spinsters felt their cheeks flush with the tenderness of their lost youth. Young and old, however hideous, however fair, they yielded up their heat—whether quick or latent—sat hungering for the mystic bread wherewith he fed them at this eucharist of sentiment.

Sometimes when the house was crowded from the orchestra to the last row of the gallery, when the air was charged with this ecstasy of fancy, he himself was the victim of the burning reflection of his power. They acted upon him in turn; he felt their fervent and despairing appeal to him; it stirred him as the spring drives the sap up into an old tree; he, too, burst into bloom. For the moment he, too, believed again, desired again, he knew not what, but something.

But it was not in these exalted moments that Caroline had learned to fear him most. It was in the quiet, tired reserve, the dullness, even, that kept him company between these outbursts that she found that exhausting drain upon her sympathies which was the very pith and substance of their alliance. It was the tacit admission of disappointment under all this glamour of success—the helplessness of the enchanter to at all enchant himself—that awoke in her an illogical, womanish desire to in some way compensate, to make it up to him.

She had observed drastically to herself that it was her eighteenth year he awoke in her—those hard years she had spent in turning gowns and placating tradesmen, and which she had never had time to live. After all, she reflected, it was better to allow one's self a little youth; to dance a little at the carnival and to live these things when they are natural and lovely, not to have them coming back on one and demanding arrears when they are humiliating and impossible. She went over tonight all the catalogue of her self-deprivations; recalled how, in the light of her father's example, she had even refused to humour her innocent taste for improvising at the piano; how, when she began to teach, after her mother's death, she had struck out one little indulgence after another, reducing her life to a relentless routine, unvarying as clockwork. It seemed to her that ever since d'Esquerré first came into the house she had been haunted by an imploring little girlish ghost that followed her about, wringing its hands and entreating for an hour of life.

The storm had held off unconscionably long; the air within the lodge was stifling, and without the garden waited, breathless. Everything seemed pervaded by a poignant distress; the hush of feverish, intolerable expectation. The still earth, the heavy flowers, even the growing darkness, breathed the exhaustion of protracted waiting. Caroline felt that she ought to go; that it was wrong to stay; that the hour and the place were as treacherous as her own reflections. She rose and began to pace the floor, stepping softly, as though in fear of awakening some one, her figure, in its thin drapery, diaphanously vague and white. Still unable to shake off the obsession of the intense stillness, she sat down at the piano and began to run over the first act of the *Walküre,* the last of his rôles they had practised together; playing listlessly and absently at first, but with gradually increasing seriousness. Perhaps it was the still heat of the summer night, perhaps it was the heavy odours from the garden that came in through the open windows; but as she played there grew and grew the feeling that he was there, beside her, standing in his accustomed place. In the duett at the end of the first act she heard him clearly: *"Thou art the Spring for which I sighed in Winter's cold embraces."* Once as he sang it, he had put his arm about her, his one hand under her heart, while with the other he took her right from the keyboard, holding her as he always held *Sieglinde* when he drew her toward the window. She had been wonderfully the mistress of herself at the time; neither repellant nor acquiescent. She remembered that she had rather exulted, then, in her self-control—which he had seemed to take for granted, though there was perhaps the whisper of a question from the hand under her heart. *"Thou art the Spring for which I sighed in Winter's cold embraces."* Caroline lifted her hands quickly from the keyboard, and she bowed her head in them, sobbing.

The storm broke and the rain beat in, spattering her night-dress until she rose and lowered the windows. She dropped upon the couch and began fighting over again the battles of other days, while the ghosts of the slain rose as from a sowing of dragon's teeth. The shadows of things, always so scorned and flouted, bore down upon her merciless and triumphant. It was not enough; this happy, useful, well-ordered life was not enough. It did not satisfy, it was not even real. No, the other things, the shadows—they were the realities. Her father, poor Heinrich, even her mother, who had been able to sustain her poor romance and keep her little illusions amid the tasks of a scullion, were nearer happiness than she. Her sure foundation was but made ground, after all, and the people in Klingsor's garden were more fortunate, however barren the sands from which they conjured their paradise.

The lodge was still and silent; her fit of weeping over, Caroline made no sound, and within the room, as without in the garden, was the blackness of storm. Only now and then a flash of lightning showed a woman's slender figure rigid on the couch, her face buried in her hands.

Toward morning, when the occasional rumbling of thunder was heard no more and the beat of the rain drops upon the orchard leaves was steadier, she fell asleep and did not waken until the first red streaks of dawn shone through the twisted boughs of the apple trees. There was a moment between world and world, when, neither asleep nor awake, she felt her dream grow thin, melting away from her, felt the warmth under her heart growing cold. Something seemed to slip from the clinging hold of her arms, and she groaned protestingly through her parted lips, following it a little way with fluttering hands. Then her eyes opened wide and she sprang up and sat holding dizzily to the cushions of the couch, staring down at her bare, cold feet, at her labouring breast, rising and falling under her open night-dress.

The dream was gone, but the feverish reality of it still pervaded her and she held it as the vibrating string holds a tone. In the last hour the shadows had had their way with Caroline. They had shown her the nothingness of time and space, of system and discipline, of closed doors and broad waters. Shuddering, she thought of the Arabian fairy tale in which the Genii brought the princess of China to the sleeping prince of Damascus, and carried her through the air back to her palace at dawn. Caroline closed her eyes and dropped her elbows weakly upon her knees, her shoulders sinking together. The horror was that it had not come from without, but from within. The dream was no blind chance; it was the expression of something she had kept so close a prisoner that she had never seen it herself; it was the wail from the donjon deeps when the watch slept. Only as the outcome of such a night of sorcery could the thing have been loosed to straighten its limbs and measure itself with her; so heavy were the chains upon it, so many a fathom deep it was crushed down into darkness. The fact that d'Esquerré happened to be on the other side of the world meant nothing; had he been here, beside her, it could scarcely have hurt her self-respect so much. As it was, she was without even the extenuation of an outer impulse, and she